Critical acclaim for David Baldacci's novels

'Baldacci inhabits the skin of his creations – tripping us up with unexpected empathy and subtle identification'
Sunday Express

'Compelling . . . finely drawn . . . a page-turner worth losing sleep over'
USA Today

'As expertly plotted as all Baldacci's work'
Sunday Times

'Baldacci cuts everyone's grass – Grisham's, Ludlum's, even Patricia Cornwell's – and more than gets away with it'
People

'A plot strong enough to make the bath go cold around you'
Independent on Sunday

'Yet another winner . . . The excitement builds . . . The plot's many planted bombs explode unpredictably'
New York Times

'As usual, Baldacci
with thr
Inde

stone cold & divine justice

David Baldacci is the internationally acclaimed author of 18 bestselling novels. With his books published in at least 45 different languages, and with over 90 million copies in print, he is one of the world's favourite storytellers. His family foundation, the Wish You Well Foundation, a non-profit organization, works to eliminate illiteracy across America. Still a resident of his native Virginia, he invites you to visit him at www.DavidBaldacci.com, and his foundation at www.WishYouWellFoundation.org, and to look into its programme to spread books across America at www.FeedingBodyandMind.com.

By David Baldacci

The Camel Club series

The Camel Club

The Collectors

Stone Cold

Divine Justice

Hell's Corner

Sean King and Michelle Maxwell series

Split Second

Hour Game

Simple Genius

First Family

Shaw series

The Whole Truth

Deliver Us From Evil

Other novels

Absolute Power

Total Control

The Winner

The Simple Truth

Saving Faith

Wish You Well

Last Man Standing

The Christmas Train

True Blue

DAVID BALDACCI

stone cold
&
divine justice

PAN BOOKS

Stone Cold first published 2007 by Hachette Book Group USA
First published in Great Britain 2007 by Macmillan
First published in paperback 2008 by Pan Books

Divine Justice first published 2008 by Warner Books USA
First published in Great Britain 2008 by Macmillan
First published in paperback 2009 by Pan Books

This omnibus first published 2011 by Pan Books
an imprint of Pan Macmillan, a division of Macmillan Publishers Limited
Pan Macmillan, 20 New Wharf Road, London N1 9RR
Basingstoke and Oxford
Associated companies throughout the world
www.panmacmillan.com

ISBN 978-0-330-54538-9

1 3 5 7 9 8 6 4 2

A CIP catalogue record for this book is available from
the British Library.

Printed in the Uk by CPI Mackays, Chatham ME5 8TD

stone cold

To Bernard Mason,
steel true, blade straight

and

To the memory of Frank L. Jennings,
who meant so much to so many.

1

Harry Finn rose as usual at six-thirty, made coffee, let the dog out into the fenced backyard for its morning constitutional, showered, shaved, woke the kids for school and oversaw that complicated operation for the next half hour as breakfasts were gulped, backpacks and shoes grabbed and arguments started and settled. His wife joined him, looking sleepy but nonetheless game for another day as a mother/chauffeur of three, including a precocious, independent-minded teenage boy.

Harry Finn was in his thirties with still boyish features and a pair of clear blue eyes that missed nothing. He'd married young and loved his wife and three children and even held sincere affection toward the family dog, a floppy-eared golden Labradoodle named George. Finn was an inch over six feet tall, with a long-limbed, wiry build ideally suited for speed and endurance. He was dressed in his usual faded jeans and shirttail-out clothing. And with round eyeglasses on and his intelligent, introspective expression, he looked like an accountant who enjoyed listening to Aerosmith after a day of crunching numbers. Although he was amazingly athletic, living by his wits was actually how he put bread on the table and iPods in his kids' ears, and he was very good at his work. Indeed, there were very few people who could do what Harry Finn could. And live.

He kissed his wife good-bye, hugged his kids, even the teenager, grabbed a duffel bag that he'd placed near the front door the night before, slid into his Toyota Prius and drove to National Airport on the Potomac River right outside of Washington, D.C. Its official name had been changed to Ronald Reagan Washington National Airport, but to the locals it would be forever simply National. Finn parked in one of the lots near the main terminal building, whose chief architectural feature was a series of connected domes copied from Thomas Jefferson's beloved Monticello. Bag in hand, he trudged across a skywalk into the sleek interior of the airport. Inside a restroom stall he opened his duffel, pulled on a heavy blue jacket with reflective stripes on the sleeves and a pair of blue workpants, slid a pair of orange noise mufflers around his neck and clipped the official-looking ID badge onto his jacket.

Employing a standard turnstile crash maneuver, he inserted himself into a herd of airport employees trekking through a "special" security line. Ironically, this line lacked even the cursory level of scrutiny forced on ordinary passengers. Once on the other side of the barrier he bought a cup of coffee and casually followed another airport worker through a secure door to the tarmac area. The man actually held the door open for him.

"What shift you working?" Finn asked the man, who told him.

"I'm just coming on," Finn said. "Which would be okay if I hadn't stayed up for the damn football game."

"Tell me about it," the man agreed.

Finn skittered down the metal steps and walked over to a 737 that was being prepped for a short-haul flight to Detroit with continuing service to Seattle. He passed several people along the way, including a fuel man, two baggage loaders and a mechanic inspecting the wheels of the Michigan-bound plane. No one confronted him because he looked and acted as though he had every right to be there. He made his way around the aircraft as he finished his coffee.

He next walked over to an Airbus A320 that would be on its way to Florida in about an hour. A baggage train was parked next to it. In one practiced motion, Finn pulled the small package from his jacket and slipped it into a side pocket of one of the bags stacked on the train. Then he knelt next to the plane's rear wheels and pretended to check out its tire tread. Again, people around him took no notice because Harry Finn exuded an air of a man perfectly at home in his surroundings. A minute later he was chatting up one of the ground crew, analyzing the prospects of the Washington Redskins and the deplorable state of employment for those toiling in the aviation industry.

"Everyone except the head honchos," Finn said. "Those bastards are printing money."

"You got that right," the other man said, and the two did a little knuckle smack to seal their solemn agreement on the disgusting greed of the rich and the ruthless who ruled the not-so-friendly skies.

Finn noted that the rear cargo hatch of the Detroit flight was now open. He waited until the handlers left with their train of luggage carts to fetch the bags and then climbed up on the lift parked there. He slipped into the cargo hold and inserted himself into his hiding place. He'd already picked it by studying interior cargo schematics of the 737 series, which were readily available if one knew where to look, and Finn clearly did. He'd also learned from open source research on the Internet that this plane was only going to be half full so his added weight in the rear would not be an issue.

While he lay curled in his hiding place the plane was loaded with fat bags and stressed passengers, and then it was wheels up to Detroit. Finn rode comfortably in the pressurized cargo hold, although it *was* a bit cooler here than in the main cabin and he was glad of the thick jacket he wore. About an hour after takeoff the plane landed and taxied to the gate. The cargo door was opened a few minutes later and the baggage offloaded. Finn patiently waited for a bit after the last bag was removed before he came out of concealment and peered through the open aft door. There were people around, but none looking his way. He climbed off the plane and dropped to the tarmac. A minute later he noticed a pair of security officers heading in his direction, sipping coffee and gabbing. He reached in his pocket, pulled out a lunch bag, took out a ham sandwich and began eating it as he walked away from the plane.

When the two guards passed him he nodded. "You regular coffee drinkers or is that half-caf caramel latte with a twist and four shots of who the hell knows what?" He grinned with his mouth full of ham sandwich. The two cops chuckled at his remark as he walked off.

He entered the terminal, went to a restroom, took off his jacket, ear mufflers and ID badge, made a quick phone call and marched to the airport security office.

"I put a bomb in a bag that was loaded onto an A320 at National Airport this morning," he explained to the officer on duty. "And I just rode in the cargo hold of a 737 from D.C. I could've downed the plane anytime I wanted."

The stunned officer was not wearing his weapon, so he leaped over the desk to tackle him. Finn neatly sidestepped this attack, and the fellow sprawled on the floor screaming for help. Other officers poured out of the back room and advanced on Finn, guns drawn. Yet Finn had pulled out his credentialing letter before the pistols had even appeared.

At that instant the door to the office flew open and three men strode in, their federal badges held high like the scepters of kings.

"Homeland Security," one of the men barked at the guards. He pointed at Harry Finn. "This man works for us. And somebody's in a shitload of trouble."

2

"Great job, Harry, as usual," the head of the Homeland Security team said later, clapping Finn on the back. People had been screamed at and reports filed, e-mails fired off and cell phone batteries sucked dry as the clear lapses in airport security revealed by Harry Finn had been broadcast to all appropriate parties. Ordinarily, Finn would not have been tasked by the Department of Homeland Security, or DHS as it is commonly known, to execute an airport security breach because the FAA kept a stranglehold on that field. Finn suspected it was because the FAA boys were well aware of how many flaws there were in the system and didn't want anyone outside their domain to realize it as well. However, folks at DHS had managed to get authorization to do this one, and picked him to pull the trigger.

Finn wasn't an employee of DHS. The firm he worked for had been retained by the agency to test the security strength of both government and sensitive private facilities around the country. They did this using a hands-on, head-on approach: They tried to breach the places any way they could. DHS did a lot of this type of outsourcing. They had roughly a $40 billion annual budget and had to throw the money somewhere. Finn's firm got a little out of this business, but then even a little slice of billions was a nice revenue stream.

Normally Finn would have left the airport without revealing what he'd done and let the chips fall. However, DHS, obviously fed up with the state of airport security and no doubt wanting to make a robust statement, had instructed him to go in and confess so they could dramatically storm in after him and make a big splash. The media would be salivating and the airline industry reeling, and Homeland Security would look very efficient and heroic. Finn never got in the middle of that. He did not give interviews and his name was never in the newspapers. He just quietly did his job.

He *would* conduct a follow-up briefing for the airport security personnel he'd just run rings around, trying to be both encouraging and diplomatic in assessing their performance or lack thereof and recommending changes in the future. Sometimes the briefing sessions were the most dangerous things he did. People could get very ticked off after finding out they'd been both snookered *and* embarrassed. In the past Finn literally had had to fight his way out of a room.

The DHS man added, "We'll get these people in shape somehow, some way."

"I'm not sure it'll be in my lifetime, sir," Finn said.

"You can wing it back to D.C. with us," the man said. "We have an agency Falcon standing by."

"Thanks, but I have someone here I've been meaning to visit. I'm going back tomorrow."

"Right. Until next time."

Until next time, Finn thought.

The men left and Finn rented a car and drove into the Detroit suburbs, stopping at a strip mall. From his knapsack he pulled out a map and a file with a photo in it. The man in the picture was sixty-three years of age, bald with several distinguishing tattoos, and went by the name Dan Ross.

It wasn't his real name, but then neither was Harry Finn's.

3

Arthritis. And on top of that the damn lupus. They were a lovely duo, perfectly synchronized to make his life a painfully throbbing hell. Every bone creaked, every solitary tendon shrieked. Each movement sent a mule kick right to his gut and yet he kept going, because if you stopped, you stopped for good. He downed a couple of potent pills he wasn't supposed to have and plunked a ball cap on his hairless, pale-skinned head, pulling the brim low over his eyes and then donning sunglasses. He never liked people seeing what he was looking at. And he never wanted people to get a good look at him.

He eased himself into his car and drove to the store. Along the way the meds kicked in and he felt okay, or at least he would for a couple hours.

"Thank you, Mr. Ross," the sales clerk said, glancing at the name on the credit card before handing it back along with his purchases. "You have a good day."

"I don't have good days anymore," Dan Ross replied. "I only have days *left*."

The clerk glanced at the hat covering the hairless head.

"Not cancer," Ross said, reading the man's thoughts. "Might be better if it was. Quicker, you know what I mean?"

The clerk, who was in his early twenties and of course still immortal, didn't look like he knew what Ross meant at all. He gave an awkward nod and turned to help another customer.

Ross left the store and debated what to do next. He had no money worries. Uncle Sam had taken care of him in his old, busted-up age. Pension was first-rate, health care coverage gold-plated; that was one thing the feds did well. One of a *short* list was his opinion. Now he just had time. That was his chief concern. What now? Home to do nothing? Or lunch at the local deli where he could fill his belly, watch ESPN and flirt with the pretty waitresses who wouldn't give him the time of day? Yet he could still dream, couldn't he? Dream of the days when the ladies gave him far more than simply time.

Not much of a life, he had to admit. He thought this as his gaze discreetly eased in all directions. Even to this day he could not overcome the impulse to check whether he was being followed. You got that way when people were always trying to kill you. God, he had loved it, though. Beat the hell out of the deli-or-home bullshit debate every miserable day of this screwed-up dilemma playing out as his "golden" years.

Over three decades ago he'd been in a different country every month. Every month during the busy season anyway. Seen the world on a wing, a prayer and a weapon of choice, he'd always said. He allowed himself a nostalgia-fueled smile. That's all he had now, memories. And the damn lupus. *I guess there is a God after all.* Pretty damn shitty to find out now.

Unfortunately for Ross, while his observation skills were good, they were no longer infallible. Down the block in his rental car Harry Finn sat and studied the inimitable Mr. Ross. *Where to, Danny? Home or the deli? Deli or home? What a long fall it's been for you.*

During the times Finn had observed this internal debate, Dan Ross had picked the deli over home about three-quarters of the time. This ratio held true today as he turned and walked down the street and into the Edsel Deli, going strong since 1954, the sign over the door said, making it far more popular than the dismal car after which it was named.

Ross would be in there eating and watching every move of the cute waitresses for at least an hour. Then it was twenty minutes by car back to his house. After that he would sit out in his backyard, read the newspaper, and then it was time to go in, take a nap, fix a modest dinner, watch TV, play Solitaire by the small table near the front window with the lamp illuminating the cards, and then the man would call it a night. By nine o'clock the lights in the small bungalow would go out, and Dan Ross would fall asleep and wake up the next day to do it all over again. Finn methodically counted off in his head these ticks of the older man's threadbare life.

After Finn had tracked Ross to this town, he'd made several trips here to learn the man's routine. This surveillance had enabled him to concoct the perfect plan to complete his task.

About five minutes before Ross would appear from the Edsel, Finn got out of his car, strode across the street, glanced in the window of the deli, and located Ross at his usual table in the rear, studying the bill he'd just been handed. Finn walked unhurriedly down the street to where Ross' car was parked. In two minutes he was back in his rental. Three minutes after that Ross emerged from the restaurant, slowly edged down the street, climbed in his car and drove off.

Finn left in the opposite direction.

Ross went through his usual litany of triviality that evening, finishing it off with three fingers of Johnnie Walker Black and, ignoring all label warnings, combining it with a potent pop of meds for the pain. He barely made it to his bed before the paralysis set in. At first he assumed it was the drugs, and he actually welcomed the numbing feeling. Yet as he lay on the bed it occurred to him with slight panic that it might be the lupus moving to a higher, more aggressive stage. When he suddenly found it difficult to breathe he knew it was something else altogether. Heart attack? But where was the elephant on the chest, the shooting pain down the left arm? Stroke? He could still think, still talk. He said a few words and none of them constituted a mumble. His face didn't seem lopsided. He had felt no pain beforehand, other than his usual. That was the problem; he could feel nothing in his limbs now, nothing at all. His gaze ran down his arm until it reached his left hand. He tried to rub the fingers together but his mind's command apparently was not reaching the digits.

Yet earlier there *had* been something on his fingers. It had felt slick, like Vaseline. You could rub and rub and never get it to feel dry. He had washed his hands when he got home, and that seemed to do the trick. The fingers didn't feel slick anymore. He didn't know if it was due to the soap and water or to whatever it was having evaporated.

Then the truth hit him like a .50 caliber round. *Or absorbed. As in absorbed into my body.*

Where had his fingers become wet? He strained his mind to think. Not this morning. Not at the store, or the deli. After that? Perhaps. Getting in the car. The car handle! If he could have managed it, Ross would've sat up in a Eureka! moment. But he couldn't manage it. He could now barely breathe. All that emitted from his mouth was a sort of shortened wheeze. The door handle of his car had been slicked with something that was now killing him. He eyed the phone on the nightstand. Two feet away and it might as well have been in China for all the good it would do him now.

In the darkness the figure appeared beside his bed. The man wore no disguise; Ross could make out his features even in the weak light. He was young and normal-looking. Ross had seen thousands of faces just like that and had paid little attention to any of them. His job had not involved normal; it had encompassed extraordinary. He couldn't imagine how someone like this man had managed to kill him.

As Ross' breathing became more labored, the fellow pulled something from his pocket and held it up to him. It was a photo, but Ross couldn't make out who was in the picture. Realizing this, Harry Finn flicked on a small penlight and shone it on the photo. Ross' gaze ran up and down the image. Still recognition didn't come until Finn said the name.

"Now you know," Finn said quietly. "Now you know."

He put the photo away and stood silently looking down at Ross as the paralysis continued to wend its way through. He kept his gaze on the other man until the chest gave one last erratic heave and the pupils turned glassy.

Two minutes later Harry Finn was walking through the woods at the back of Ross' house. The next morning he was on a plane, this time in the main cabin. He landed, drove home, kissed his wife, played with his dog and picked the kids up from school. That night they all went out to dinner to celebrate his youngest child, eight-year-old Susie, being named to portray a talking tree in a school play.

Around midnight, Harry Finn ventured downstairs to the kitchen, where George the faithful Labradoodle rose from his soft bed and greeted him. As he sat at the kitchen table and stroked the dog, Finn mentally crossed Dan Ross off his list.

Now he focused on the next name: *Carter Gray*, the former chief of America's intelligence empire.

4

Annabelle Conroy stretched out her long legs and watched the landscape drift by outside the window of the Amtrak Acela train car. She almost never took the train anywhere; her ride was typically at 39,000 feet where she popped peanuts, sipped watered-down seven-dollar cocktails, and dreamt up the next con. Today she was on the train because her companion, Milton Farb, would not set foot on anything that had the capacity and intent to leave the ground.

"Flying is the safest way to travel, Milton," she'd informed him.

"Not if you're on a plane that's in a death spiral. Then your chances of dying are roughly one hundred percent. And I don't like those odds."

It was hard to argue with geniuses, Annabelle had discovered. Still, Milton, the man with the photographic memory and a budding talent for brilliantly lying to people, had done good work. They had left Boston after a successful job. The item was back where it needed to be and no one had thought to call the cops. In Annabelle's world of high-stakes cons that was equal to perfection.

Thirty minutes later, as Amtrak's only bullet train service wound its way down the East Coast and pulled into a station, Annabelle glanced out the window and involuntarily shuddered when the conductor announced they were arriving in Newark, New Jersey. Jersey was Jerry Bagger land, although thankfully the Acela train didn't stop at Atlantic City where the maniacal casino boss had his empire. If it did Annabelle wouldn't have been on it.

Yet she was smart enough to realize that Jerry Bagger had every motivation to leave Atlantic City and come looking for her wherever she might be. When you ripped a guy like that off for $40 million, assuming that Bagger would do his best to tear thousands of pieces of your flesh off one at a time was hardly irrational thinking.

She glanced over at Milton, who looked about eighteen with his boyish face and longish hair. In reality the man was pushing fifty. He was on his computer, doing something that neither Annabelle nor anyone else below the level of genius would be able to understand.

Bored, Annabelle rose, went to the café car and purchased a beer and a bag of chips. On the way back she spied a *New York Times* lying discarded on one of the café tables. She sat down on a stool, drank her beer and munched her chips as she idly turned the pages looking for that one bit of information that might spark her next adventure. Once she got back to Washington, D.C., she had some decisions to make, chiefly whether to stay put or flee the country. She knew what her answer *should* be. A no-name island in the South Pacific was the safest place for her right now, where she could just wait out the tsunami named Jerry. Bagger was in his mid-sixties and her long con against him had without a doubt considerably raised the man's blood pressure. With a little luck he'd soon croak from a heart attack and she would be scot-free. However, she couldn't count on that. With Jerry you just had to figure that all your luck would turn out to be bad.

It shouldn't have been a difficult decision and yet it was. She had grown close, or as close as someone like her could get, to an oddball collection of men who called themselves the Camel Club. She smiled to herself as she thought about the foursome, one of whom was named Caleb Shaw and worked at the Library of Congress. He reminded her remarkably of the cowardly lion from *The Wizard of Oz*. Then her smile faded. Oliver Stone, the head of this little band of miscreants, was something altogether more. He must've had one hell of a past, Annabelle thought—a history that might even surpass hers in the unusual and extraordinary department, and that was saying something. She didn't know if she could say good-bye to Oliver Stone. She doubted she would ever run across another one like him.

Her gaze flicked up at a young man passing by who did not attempt to hide his admiration for her tall, curvy figure, long blonde hair, and thirty-six-year-old face that, if it didn't actually hit the "wow" level, came awfully close. This was so despite a small, fishhook-shaped scar under her eye; a present from her father, Paddy Conroy, the best short con artist of his generation, and the world's worst father, at least in his only child's estimation.

"Hey," the young man said. With his lean physique, tousled hair and expensive clothes that were designed to appear cheap and grungy, he looked like an Abercrombie & Fitch ad. She quickly sized him up as a privileged college kid with far more money than was healthy and the insufferably cocky attitude to match.

"Hey back at you," she said and returned to her newspaper.

"Where you headed to?" he asked, sitting down next to her.

"Not where you're headed."

"But you don't know where I'm going," he said in a playful tone.

"That's sort of the point, right?"

He either didn't get her point or didn't care. "I go to Harvard."

"Wow, I never would've guessed that."

"But I'm from Philly. The Main Line. My parents have an estate there."

"Wow again. It's nice to have parents who have estates," she said in a clearly uninterested tone.

"It's also nice to have parents who are out of the country half the time. I'm having a little party there tonight. It's going to be a wild ride. You interested?"

Annabelle could feel the guy's gaze running down her. *Okay, here we go again.* She knew she shouldn't, but with guys like this she just couldn't seem to help herself.

She closed the newspaper. "I don't know. When you say wild, how wild do you mean?"

"How wild do you want it to be?" She could see him forming the word "baby," but he apparently thought better of using it, at least so soon in the conversation.

"I hate being disappointed."

He touched her arm. "I don't think you'll be disappointed."

She smiled and patted his hand. "So what are we talking about here? Booze and sex?"

"A given." He squeezed her arm. "Hey, I'm up in first class, why don't you join me?"

"You have anything other than booze and sex going on?"

"You like to get into the details?"

"It's all in the details, uh . . ."

"Steve. Steve Brinkman." He gave a practiced little chuckle. "You know, one of *those* Brinkmans. My father's the vice chairman of one of the biggest banks in the country."

"FYI, Steve, if you've just got coke at this party, and I'm not talking the soft drink, that would definitely disappoint me."

"What are you looking for? I'm sure I can get it. I've got connections."

"Goofballs, Dollies, Hog, with artillery to do it right, and no lemonade, lemonade always pisses me off," she added, referring to crap-quality drugs.

"Wow, you know your stuff," Steve said, nervously looking around at the other people in the café car.

"You ever chased the dragon, Steve?" she asked.

"Uh, no."

"It's a funky way to inhale heroin. It'll give you the greatest pop in the world, if it doesn't kill you."

He removed his hand from her arm. "Doesn't sound very smart."

"How old are you?"

"Twenty. Why?"

"I like my men a little younger than that. I find that when a guy reaches eighteen he's left his best ball-banging behind. So you gonna have any minors at this party?"

He rose. "Maybe this wasn't such a good idea."

"Oh, I'm not picky. It can be guys or girls. I mean, when you're shit-faced on meth, who cares?"

"Okay, I'm leaving now," Steve said hurriedly.

"One more thing." Annabelle took out her wallet and flashed a fake badge at him. She said in a low voice, "You recognize the DEA insignia, Steve? For Drug Enforcement Agency?"

"Omigod!"

"And now that you've told me about mommy and daddy Brinkman's estate on the Main Line, I'm sure my strike team will have no problem finding the place. That is if you're still intending on having a *wild* party."

"Please, I swear to God, I was just . . ." He put a hand out to steady himself. Annabelle seized it and gave his fingers a hard squeeze.

"Go back to Harvard, Stevie, and when you graduate, you can screw up your life however you want to. But in the future just be careful what you say to strange women on trains."

She watched him hurry down the aisle and disappear safely back into first class.

Annabelle finished her beer and idly read the last couple pages of the newspaper. Now it was her turn to have the blood drain from her face.

An American tentatively identified as Anthony Wallace had been found nearly beaten to death at a Portugal seaside estate. Three other people had been found murdered at the home on a remote stretch of shoreline. Robbery was thought to be the motive. Although Wallace was still alive, he was in a coma after suffering extensive brain injuries and doctors were not hopeful for a recovery.

Annabelle tore out the story and walked unsteadily back to her seat.

Jerry Bagger had gotten to Tony, one of her partners in the con. An estate? She'd expressly told Tony to lay low and not flash the cash. He hadn't listened and now he was brain dead. Jerry typically didn't leave any witnesses behind.

But what had Jerry managed to beat out of Tony? She knew the answer to that question. *Everything.*

Milton stopped typing on his computer and gazed up at her. "You okay?"

Annabelle didn't answer. As the train sailed back to D.C. she looked out the window but didn't see the Jersey countryside. Her confidence evaporated, she now only saw graphic details of her coming death, courtesy of Jerry Bagger.

5

Oliver Stone managed to lift the old, mossy tombstone to an upright position and packed dirt around it to keep it there. He sat back on his haunches and wiped his brow. He had a portable radio beside him on the ground turned to the local all-news station. Stone craved information like others needed oxygen. As he listened to the radio he got an unexpected jolt. There would be an awards ceremony at the White House that very afternoon where none other than Carter Gray, recently retired chief of the nation's intelligence agencies, was scheduled to receive the Presidential Medal of Freedom, the nation's highest civilian honor. Gray had served his country with distinction for nearly four decades, the announcer read, and quoted the president as saying that Carter Gray was a man that all of America should be proud of; a true patriot and public servant.

Stone didn't exactly agree with this assessment. In fact, he'd been the reason Carter Gray had abruptly resigned from his post as the nation's intelligence czar.

Stone thought to himself, *If only the president knew*

that the man he's going to be presenting that medal to is the same man who was prepared to put a bullet through his head. The country would never be ready for *that* truth.

He looked at his watch. The dead could certainly exist without him for a little while. An hour later, showered and dressed in his best clothes, which consisted of secondhand issue from Goodwill, he walked out of his cottage, where he was caretaker of Mt. Zion Cemetery, a stop on the Underground Railroad and the final resting place of notable African Americans from the nineteenth century. The trip from the outskirts of Georgetown to the White House was eaten up quickly by the long strides of Stone's lean six-foot-two-inch frame.

At age sixty-one, he had lost very little of his energy and vigor. With his close-cropped white hair, he looked like a retired Marine drill sergeant. He was still a commander of sorts, though his ragtag regiment called the Camel Club was completely unofficial. It consisted of himself and three others: Caleb Shaw, Reuben Rhodes and Milton Farb.

And yet Stone might have to add another name to the roster, Annabelle Conroy. She had nearly died along with the rest of them in their last adventure. The truth was, Annabelle was as nimble, capable and nervy a person as Stone had ever met. Yet his gut told him the woman, who was attending to a piece of unfinished business with Milton Farb's help, would be leaving them soon. Someone was after her, Stone knew, someone Annabelle actually feared. And under those circumstances sometimes the smartest move was to run. Stone understood that concept very well.

The White House was dead ahead. He would never be allowed to enter the hallowed front gates and lacked even the right to stand on that coveted side of Pennsylvania Avenue. What he could do was wait in Lafayette Park across the street. He used to have a tent there until the Secret Service recently made him take it down. Yet freedom of speech was still alive and well in America and thus his banner had remained. Unfurled between two pieces of rebar stuck in the ground, it read, "I want the truth." So did a *few* other people in this town, it was rumored. To date, Stone had never heard of anyone actually finding it within the confines of the world capital of spin and deceit.

He passed the time chatting with a couple of uniformed Secret Service agents he knew. When the White House gates started to open, he broke off his conversation and watched the black sedan coming out. He couldn't see through the tinted glass, but for some reason he knew that Carter Gray was inside the Town Car. Perhaps it was the man's smell.

His hunch proved right when the window came down and he found himself eye to eye with the ex–intelligence chief, new Medal of Freedom winner and major Oliver Stone hater.

As the car slowed to make the turn onto the street, Gray's wide, bespectacled face stared impassively at him. Then, smiling, Gray held up his big, shiny medal so Stone could see it.

Not having a medal of his own, Stone opted for giving Gray the finger. The man's smile turned to a snarl and the window zipped back up.

Stone turned and walked back to his cemetery feeling the trip had been damn well worth it.

When Carter Gray's car turned onto 17th Street, another vehicle followed it. Harry Finn had driven into D.C. that morning. He too had heard of Gray's big day at the White House and like Oliver Stone had come down to see the man. While Stone had ventured here to show defiance to a man he loathed, Finn had come to continue devising a suitable way to kill Gray.

The drive took them out of D.C. and into Maryland, up to the waterfront city of Annapolis situated on the Chesapeake Bay. It was famous for, among other things, its crab cakes and for being home to the U.S. Naval Academy. Gray had recently traded his remote Virginia farm for an isolated place on a cliff overlooking the bay. Since he was no longer with the government his security detail was much smaller than it had been. Yet because he was a former director of Central Intelligence he still received daily briefings. And he had two guards assigned to him because his past work had angered a number of America's enemies, who would love nothing better than to put a slug right between Gray's close-set eyes.

Finn knew killing Gray would be far more difficult than bagging someone like Dan Ross. Because of the complexities, this was one of countless trips he had made reconnoitering Gray. Each time he had used a different vehicle rented under fake names and worn disguises to avoid any profiling. And even if he lost the Town Car in traffic he knew where it was going. He only broke off the tail when the car pulled onto a private gravel road and headed toward Gray's house and the cliffs, where thirty feet down the waters of the bay boomed against solid rock.

Later, using long-range binoculars while perched in a tree, Finn saw the thing in the rear of Gray's house that would enable him to kill the man. He actually smiled as the plan swiftly came together in his mind.

That night he took his daughter, Susie, to swim practice. As he sat in the bleachers and proudly watched her small body glide in perfect form across the pool, he imagined the last few seconds of Carter Gray's life. It all would be worth it.

He drove his daughter home, helped put her and her ten-year-old brother Patrick to bed, had an argument with his teenager and then shot hoops with the boy in the driveway of their home until both were sweating and laughing. Later, he made love to his wife, Amanda, whom everyone called Mandy, and, restless, got up around midnight and packed school lunches for the next day. He also signed a permission slip for his oldest, David, to go on an upcoming field trip to the U.S. Capitol and other downtown sights. David would be attending high school next year and Finn and Mandy had taken him to several school open houses. David liked math and science. He would probably end up being an engineer, Finn thought. Mechanically inclined too, Finn had almost gone that route before his life had taken a bit of a detour. He'd joined the navy, and quickly worked himself to an elite status.

Finn was a former Navy SEAL with special ops experience and combat duty on his résumé. And he possessed unique foreign-language skills from immersion school in California, where he'd spent a chunk of his life learning Arabic, and later acquired the dialects the school hadn't taught him when on the ground in that part of the world. With his current job he traveled a good deal but he was also home a lot. He almost never missed a sporting or major school event. He was there for his children in the hope that they would be there for him later. That's the best a parent could shoot for, he felt.

He finished the lunches, went to his small den, closed the door and began drawing up firm plans for Carter Gray. Out of practicality it would not mirror his confrontation with Dan Ross. Yet Finn had never been one to pound a round peg into a square hole.

Even killers had to be flexible; in fact, perhaps the most flexible of all.

Finn's gaze settled on the pictures of his three kids that sat on his desk front and center. Birth and death. It was the same for everyone. You started breathing on one end and stopped on the other. What you did in between defined who and what you were. Yet Harry Finn realized he would be awfully difficult to categorize. Some days even he didn't truly understand it.

6

The rental car pulled up to the gates of the cemetery as Oliver Stone was finishing some work. As he brushed off his pants and glanced that way, he had a feeling of déjà vu. She had done this to him before, but had eventually come back. Somehow Stone didn't think the lady would let that happen again. He would have to see what he could do about that, because he didn't want to lose her.

Annabelle Conroy got out of the car and walked through the open gates. Her long black coat flapped open in the wind, revealing a brown knee-length skirt and boots; her hair was hidden underneath a wide-brimmed floppy hat. Stone closed the door on the small storage shed near his cottage and padlocked it.

He said, "Milton told me your trip to Boston was a great success. I don't believe I've heard the words 'brilliant,' 'amazing' and 'unflappable' used that many times in describing a person. I hope you recognize yourself."

"Milton would make a great con. Not that I'd recommend that life to anyone I actually cared about."

"He also said you looked troubled on the way back. Did something happen?"

She glanced at his cottage. "Can we talk inside?"

Describing the interior of Stone's cottage as spartan would have been generous indeed. A few chairs, a number of odd tables, sagging shelves of books in multiple languages and an old worm-eaten partner's desk, together with a small kitchen area, bedroom and tiny bath all outlined in roughly six hundred square feet constituted the man's entire domicile footprint.

They sat near the empty fireplace on the two most comfortable chairs, meaning the only ones with padding.

"I came here to tell you I'm leaving. And after everything that's happened, I feel like I owe you an explanation," she said.

"You don't owe me anything, Annabelle."

"Don't say that!" she snapped. "This is hard enough as it is. So hear me out, Oliver."

He sat back, crossed his arms and waited.

She pulled the newspaper article from her jacket pocket and passed it across to him. "Read this first."

"Who is this Anthony Wallace?" he asked after he'd finished.

"Someone I worked with," she said vaguely.

"Someone you worked a *con* with?"

She nodded absently.

"Three people killed?"

Annabelle rose and started pacing. "That's the thing

that's driving me crazy. I told Tony to lay low and not flash the cash. But what did he do? He did the exact opposite and now three innocent people are dead who shouldn't be."

Stone tapped the paper. "Well, from the looks of it your Mr. Wallace will soon be making it a quartet."

"But Tony wasn't innocent. He knew exactly what he was getting into."

"And what exactly was that?"

She stopped pacing. "Oliver, I like you and I respect you, but this is a little . . ."

"Illegal? I hope you realize that comes as no great shock to me."

"And that doesn't bother you?"

"I doubt anything you could have possibly done would surpass what I've seen in life."

She cocked her head. "Seen, or done?"

"Who's after you and why?"

"That's no concern of yours."

"It is if you want me to help you."

"I'm not looking for help. I just wanted you to understand why I have to leave."

"Do you really think you'll be safer on your own?"

"I think you and the others will be a lot safer without me around."

"That's not what I asked you."

"I've been in plenty of jams before and I've always managed to get myself out of them."

"Out of a jam this tight?" He glanced at the paper. "This person doesn't seem to fool around."

"Tony made a mistake, a big one. I don't intend on doing that. I lay low, for as long as it takes, and as far away from here as I can get."

"But you don't know what Tony might have told them. Did he have any information that could be used to track you down?"

Annabelle perched on the edge of the fireplace's raised hearth. "Maybe," she said tersely. "Probably," she corrected.

"Then all the more reason for you not to go this alone. We can help protect you."

"Oliver, I appreciate the sentiment but you have no idea what you're getting into. Not only is this guy the scum of the earth with a lot of money and muscle behind him, but on top of that, what I did was illegal. You'd be harboring a criminal on top of risking your life."

"Not the first time on either count," he replied.

"Who *are* you?" she asked pointedly.

"You know all you need to know about me."

"And I thought *I* was a world-class liar."

"We're wasting time, tell me about him."

She rubbed her long, thin fingers together, drew a deep breath and said, "His name's Jerry Bagger. He owns the Pompeii Casino, the biggest in Atlantic City. He was run out of Vegas years ago because he was a whack job. He would literally rip out your intestines if you tried to steal a five-dollar casino chip."

"And how much did you, um, *relieve* him of?"

"Why do you need to know?"

"It's important to know how much motivation the man has to come after you."

"Forty million dollars. Think that'll motivate him?"

"I'm impressed. It doesn't sound like Bagger is a man easily conned."

Annabelle allowed herself a brief smile. "It was one of my better scams, I have to admit. But Jerry is also very dangerous, and not entirely sane. If he even thinks someone is helping me, that person might as well be me. He'll get the same treatment: death by pain, great pain."

"You have no reason to believe that he's aware you're in D.C.?"

"No. Tony had no idea I'd be coming here. Neither did the others."

"So there are others on the con team? Bagger might get to them."

"He might. But like I said, they don't know I'm here either."

Stone slowly nodded. "Of course, we can't be sure of what Bagger really knows or doesn't know at this point. I'm sure that the public details of our little adventure involving the Library of Congress didn't include your name or picture. However, we can't be absolutely certain there isn't something out there that would help him track you down."

"My original plan was to head to the South Pacific."

Stone shook his head. "Fugitives always head to the South Pacific. That's probably the first place Bagger will check."

"You're kidding me, right?"

"Partly, yes. But only partly."

"So you really think I should stay here?"

"I do. I'm assuming you've covered your tracks well. No trails leading here, names, travel arrangements, phones, friends?"

She shook her head. "Coming here was pretty much a spur-of-the-moment thing. And all under an alias."

"The smart thing to do would be to find out, as quietly as possible, what Bagger knows."

"Oliver, you can't possibly get anywhere near that guy. It would be suicide."

"I know how to look, so let me start looking."

"I've never asked anyone to help me before."

"It took me decades before I could ask anyone to help me."

She looked puzzled. "But you're glad you did?"

"It's the only reason I'm alive right now. Move out of your hotel and into another one. I'm assuming you have money."

"Cash is not a problem." She rose and started to the door but turned back. "Oliver, I appreciate this."

"Let's hope you can say that when it's all over."

7

"Do you think I'm stupid?" screamed Jerry Bagger. The casino chief wedged his arm against the other man's windpipe as he mashed him against the wall in Bagger's luxurious office on the twenty-third floor of the Pompeii Casino. The drapes were closed. Bagger always closed the drapes when he was either going to bang a willing lady on his couch or kick the shit out of somebody who deserved it. These matters should always be kept private, he felt. It was a point of honor with him.

The man didn't answer Bagger's question chiefly because he couldn't breathe. However, Bagger wasn't waiting for a reply. His first blow caught the guy flush on the nose and broke it. The second one knocked a front tooth out. The man fell to the floor weeping. For good measure Bagger kicked him in the gut. That made the beaten fellow vomit on the carpet. As the puke spread across the expensive inlaid wool Bagger's own security force had to pull their furious boss off the fallen man before real damage was done.

The guy was carted away, crying and bleeding and

mumbling that he was sorry. Bagger sat down behind his desk and rubbed his cracked knuckles. Glaring at his security chief, he growled, "Bobby, you bring me any more pissants like that one who say they know something about Annabelle Conroy and end up trying to shake me down while feeding me a sack of shit, I swear to God I will kill your mother. And I like your mother but I will kill her. Do you *hear* me!"

The burly black security chief took a step back and swallowed nervously. "Never again, Mr. Bagger. I'm sorry, sir. Really, really sorry."

"Everybody's sorry but nobody's doing a damn thing to get me the bitch, are they?" Bagger roared.

"We thought we had a lead on her. A good one."

"You thought? You thought? Well, maybe you should stop thinking, then."

Bagger hit a button on his desk and the drapes opened. He jumped up and looked out the window. "Forty million bucks she took from me. This could screw up my whole business, you know that? I don't have enough reserves to meet the state regs. You get a government bean counter in here right now looking at my books he could shut me down. Me! You used to be able to pay those assholes off, but now with all this anticorruption and ethical bullshit going around, you can't do that no more. You mark my word, that full disclosure crap is gonna destroy a great country."

"We'll find her, boss, and get the money back," his security chief assured him.

Bagger didn't appear to be listening. Staring down at the street far below, he said, "I see the bitch everywhere. In my dreams, in my food, when I'm shaving there she is in my mirror. Hell, even when I'm taking a leak, her face is in the toilet bowl staring at me. It's driving me nuts!"

He sat on the couch and calmed down. "What's the latest on our boy Tony Wallace?"

"We got somebody on the inside at the hospital in Portugal. Jerk's still in a coma. But even if he comes out of it, there's nothing there. Our source says the guy's a permanent retard."

"If you ask me he was a retard long before we got to him."

"You know, boss, we probably should've just killed him like we did everybody else."

"I gave him my word. He told me what he knew, he got to live; that was the deal. But in my book brain dead means you're still alive. Lots of people live forty, fifty years like that. It's like being a baby until you're eighty. Get fed through a tube, get your ass wiped every day and you play with blocks. Granted, it's not much of a life, but I didn't go back on my word. People can say I'm violent and I got a bad temper and all that crap but they can never point to one time where I ever went back on my word. You know why?"

The security chief shook his head warily, obviously unsure whether his boss wanted an answer or not.

"Because I got standards, that's why. Now get outta here."

Alone, Bagger sat down behind his desk and put his head in his hands. He would never admit this to anyone, but mixed in with all the hatred he had for Annabelle Conroy was a sincere, if grudging, admiration. "Annabelle," he said aloud. "You are without a doubt the greatest con artist in the world. It would've been a pleasure working with you. And you were probably the best piece of ass I've ever put my hand on. So it's too bad you were so stupid as to take me on because now I gotta kill you. I gotta make an example of you. And it's a waste, but that's just the way it's gotta be."

It wasn't just the loss of the forty million that had enraged Bagger. Ever since word of the successful con had leaked out, cheaters had become far more brazen in his casino. Losses had quickly risen. And his competitors and business associates were also not quite as respectful as they had once been, sensing that Bagger was no longer at the top of his game, that he was vulnerable. Calls weren't immediately returned. Action that he could always count on getting didn't always come through now.

"An example," Bagger said again. "To show these assholes that not only am I still at the top, I'm getting stronger every day. And I will find you, lady. I will find you."

8

The contact Oliver Stone proposed using was an honorary member of the Camel Club named Alex Ford, a Secret Service agent. The two men trusted each other fully and Stone knew it was the one place he could turn to for discreet intelligence.

"Does this have something to do with that woman you were working with? Her name was Susan, right?" Alex asked when Stone called and relayed his request.

"It has nothing to do with her," Stone lied. "She's actually leaving town soon. This has to do with something else I'm involved in."

"For a cemetery worker you get around a lot."

"It keeps me young."

"The Bureau can help out too. After what you did for them last time they owe you. When do you need to know?"

"As soon as you can get something."

"Just so you know, I've heard of this Jerry Bagger guy. The Justice Department has been trying to get something on him for a long time."

"I'm sure the attention is well-deserved. Thanks, Alex."

Later that night, Reuben Rhodes and Caleb Shaw visited Stone at his cottage. Caleb was in a high state of indecision.

"They asked me, but I don't know if I should accept or not. I just don't know," he wailed.

"So the Library of Congress wants you to become the director of the Rare Books Division," Stone said. "That sounds like a great promotion, Caleb. What's to decide?"

Caleb said stiffly, "Well, considering the fact that the position became available *only* because the former director was horribly murdered on the premises and the acting director after him suffered a nervous breakdown from what happened there, it *does* give one pause."

Reuben growled, "Hell, Caleb, go for it. I mean, who's going to mess with a fine young buck like you?"

Caleb, who was in his fifties, of medium height and a bit pudgy, with not a trace of athleticism or personal courage, was not amused by this comment.

"You said it *is* more money," Stone reminded him. "In fact a good deal more."

"Yes, but if that only means I can afford a much nicer funeral, I'm not sure I'm interested."

Reuben added gruffly, "But when you die, you die knowing that you have more to leave to your friends.

Now if that's not true comfort, I don't know what is."

"Why I even bother to ask for your opinion I don't know," Caleb said hotly.

Reuben turned his attention to Stone. "You seen Susan lately?"

Only Stone knew Annabelle's real name.

"She came by the other day, but only for a few minutes. She successfully completed her task with Milton. The item is back where it belongs."

"I have to admit," Caleb said. "She did what she said she was going to do."

Reuben said, "Now if I could just get her to go out with me. She keeps having other plans. I'm not sure if she's trying to brush me off or not. But I don't get it. Look at me. What's not to love?"

Reuben was nearly sixty, with a full beard and dark curly hair mixed with gray down to his shoulders. He was six-five with the build of an NFL left tackle. A highly decorated Vietnam War vet and former military intelligence officer, he had burned many professional bridges and nearly succumbed to pills and the bottle before Oliver Stone had brought him back from the edge. He now worked on a loading dock.

"I saw where your 'friend' Carter Gray received the Medal of Freedom," Caleb said after giving Reuben an incredulous look. "Talk about your ironies. If that man had his way you two would be dead and the rest of us would be getting water-dunked in some CIA-run torture chamber."

Reuben roared, "For the hundredth time it's water-*boarding*, not water-dunking."

"Well, whatever it is, he's a nasty man."

"He's actually a man who believes his way is the right way, and he's certainly not alone in that belief," Stone said. "I went down to the White House and saw him off after he received his award."

"You went down to the White House?" Caleb exclaimed.

"Well, he showed me his medal and I sort of *waved* at him."

"What, you two are now best buds?" Reuben added with a snort. "From a man who tried to kill you a few times?"

"He also saved someone for me," Stone said quietly.

"Care to explain that?" Reuben asked curiously.

"No."

Someone banged on his door. Stone rose to answer it, thinking it might be Milton or perhaps Annabelle.

The man at the door was dressed in a dark suit and had a pistol under his jacket, Stone observed. He handed Stone a piece of paper and walked off. Stone opened the note.

Carter Gray wanted Stone to visit him at his house two days from today. A car would pick him up. There did not seem to be an opportunity to decline the command. When he told the others Caleb said, "Oliver, you're not going."

"Of course I am," Stone said.

9

Harry Finn was currently sucking on oxygen and peering out of his specially designed headgear. They were going so fast there wasn't a lot to see. A storm was raging and those on the deck of the boat were no doubt getting wet and jostled. It wasn't any better where Finn was. Demonstrating once more his affinity for unusual choices in transportation, he was attached to the side of a ship in a very tight ball near the stern using a support device not available to the public. He had discovered a seam in the exterior video and human surveillance perimeters and was now an invisible bump against the gunmetal gray side of the naval ship. The ride was far less comfortable than the plane cargo hold had been. In fact, despite his special device, Finn was nearly jolted off his perch twice. Had he been, his life probably would have ended on impact with the twin screws that were thrusting the ship through the water. His ride had started at what should have been a highly secure military dock at the Norfolk Naval Station. However, the "highly secure" component had broken down completely when confronted by Harry Finn wearing one of his vast array of disguises and his air of belonging perfectly in whatever situation he found himself.

The boat slowed and swung around to the port side of the larger vessel. Finn let it drift to a stop before he slipped underneath the water, kicking away from the boat as he did so. He had a waterproof knapsack slung over his back and an electronic jammer around his waist making him invisible to any tracking gear on board either boat. He dove down farther and headed underneath the other ship, which rode quite low in the water, and for good reason. It weighed over 80,000 tons, carried nearly a hundred aircraft and 6,000 sea and air personnel, housed not one but two nuclear powered generators, and had set the American taxpayer back over $3 billion.

Once he reached the spot, it took him only two minutes to attach the device to the bottom of the ship's hull, and then, keeping well away from the massive screws, he made his way back to the other boat, reattached himself, and rode it back in. He had accepted this mission largely because it would give him some practice for another upcoming task of a more personal nature. He actually thought about the details of that job as the boat he was piggybacking on made its jog back to land. After it docked, he slipped out from his hiding place, swam to a remote part of the pier, clambered out and stripped off his gear. He made his phone call and later reported to the duty officer's chambers with a high-level military escort, the members of which had privately bet there was no way anyone could do what Finn had just done: place a bomb on the hull bottom of the navy's prized Nimitz-class *George Washington* aircraft carrier as it sat off the coast of Virginia. It was a bomb powerful enough to sink the carrier and all hands on board along with a couple billion dollars' worth of aircraft.

This time the admiral of the Atlantic fleet and everyone down his chain of command was given a ten-megaton blast by the chairman of the Joint Chiefs, who happened to be a four-star army general. The man could barely hide his delight at delivering this meltdown to his naval colleague, a dressing-down so loud, it was said the four-star could be heard all the way back at the Pentagon nearly two hundred miles away. This very public whipping was reinforced by the presence of the secretary of defense, who had been standing by in his chopper waiting to see if Harry Finn could actually pull it off. The fact that the man had scored an improbable triumph against massively high odds prompted the secdef immediately to offer Harry Finn a position on his staff.

The secretary of Homeland Security was not amenable to this co-opting of a prized contractor. The two cabinet members went at it like schoolboys on a playground until the president himself interceded by secure video conference call and decreed that Harry Finn would stay right where he was, as an independent contractor to DHS. The defeated and miffed secdef climbed on his private chopper and flew back to Washington.

Harry Finn stayed down in Norfolk to give a briefing to a group of chagrined naval security personnel. While he was always courteous and unfailingly respectful, his comments were not watered down. Failures had happened, here is how I did it, and here is what you need to do to prevent a bona fide terrorist from doing it for real.

What Finn did for a living was often referred to in the field as "red cells." The term had been coined by a former Navy SEAL who'd helped start the program. The red cell project had commenced after the Vietnam War at the request of a vice admiral to test the security of military installations. After 9/11, it had been expanded to test the security of nonmilitary facilities to penetration by terrorists and other criminal organizations.

People with Finn's special skills, almost all of whom were formerly in the military, were tasked to impersonate terrorist cells and attempt to overcome a facility's security. Often the penetrations were conducted in a nontraditional way, something also referred to as humanizing the task. That meant that Finn and his team members would emulate the skill levels of the terrorists they were attacking. Presently, Muslim terrorists were not deemed to have sophisticated skill levels. Even after 9/11 there was disbelief in American intelligence circles that such terror cells could take over a major facility or do what Finn had done that night with the aircraft carrier. They were good at blowing themselves and others up in public or driving planes into skyscrapers, but attacking a nuclear power plant or military installation was a whole different ball game.

However, it had finally occurred to both politicians and higher-ups in the military that Muslims were not the only potential terrorists in the world. China, Russia and other former Soviet bloc countries, as well as several nations in America's own hemisphere, might well want to do harm to the United States. And these countries *did* have the infrastructure, personnel and access to intelligence to make determined and possibly successful attacks on secure American installations. Thus, Finn had been instructed to pull out the stops, use all his skills and cutting-edge equipment to break through the navy's defenses. And he had.

Other men, including several on red cell teams Finn had worked with, might have stayed out all night celebrating this dramatic triumph. However, Finn was not like most people. He had stayed down in the Norfolk area an extra day for one very important reason. His oldest son, David, was on a soccer travel team that had a match in the area. The day after his briefing Finn attended his son's match and then drove the victorious—and in high spirits—David back home that night. Along the way they talked about school, girls, sports. And then David, who at thirteen was nearly as tall as his dad, asked his father, "So what were you doing down there? Was it work-related?"

Finn nodded. "Some people were having problems with a security issue and asked me to come down and help them with it."

"Did you get it figured out?"

"Oh, yeah. Everyone's on the same page now. It actually wasn't that complicated once the problems were identified."

"Security with what?"

"A wide range of things. Nothing too exciting."

"So can you tell me about it?"

"I doubt you'd find it interesting. It's the same stuff lots of people do across the country. The only good thing is I don't have to sit behind a desk every day."

"I asked Mom about it once. She said she wasn't sure what you did."

"I think your mother was just kidding you."

"You're not a spy, are you?"

Finn smiled. "Well, if I were I couldn't tell you."

"Or if you did you'd have to kill me, right?" David said, laughing.

"All I do is help people run things better by pointing out flaws in their systems."

"Like a computer guy does with bugs? So you're like a debugger."

"Exactly. Like I said, pretty boring stuff, but it pays well and keeps food on the table, which, by the way, you seem to be eating about a hundred pounds of a day."

"I'm a growing boy, Pop. Hey, did you know that Barry Waller's dad chased a guy in his police car down an alleyway and wrestled a gun out of his hand after the dude robbed a bank? Barry said the guy almost shot his dad."

"Police work can be very dangerous. Barry's dad is a brave man."

"I'm glad you don't do stuff like that."

"Me too."

"So just keep doing your boring debugging stuff, Pop." David gave his father a playful punch in the arm. "And stay out of trouble, will ya?"

"I will, son. I will," said Harry Finn.

10

Stone and Alex Ford met at a familiar place for both men, Lafayette Park across from the White House. Here the six-foot-three-inch Alex had guarded the occupant of the Oval Office for years and Stone had respectfully protested against this same inhabitant, as he had against the man's predecessors, from across the street. The two men sat on a bench near the statue of a Polish general whom history remembered as a sound ally of the Americans in their war for independence. He was also a man, it was probably safe to say, hardly any American alive today would either know or care about.

"What do you have for me?" Stone said, eyeing the manila folder Alex pulled from a trim black leather briefcase.

"I wasn't sure what you were looking for, so I thought I'd cast a broad net."

"That's perfect, Alex, thanks."

As Stone looked over the file, Alex studied his friend. "Like I told you on the phone, the Justice Department has been interested in Bagger for a long time but can't make anything stick. I talked to Kate about it. She said Justice hasn't given up but if they can't pin something on him soon, they're going to have to move on. Even Uncle Sam has limited resources."

"How is Kate?" Stone asked, referring to Kate Adams, the Justice lawyer Alex had been dating.

"Things didn't work out. She's seeing someone else."

"I'm sorry to hear that. She's a wonderful woman," Stone replied.

"Yes she is, but just not the woman for me or me the man for her. Speaking of women, where's Adelphia?"

Adelphia, a strange woman of undetermined origin and interesting accent, had been the only other protester left in Lafayette Park besides Stone. Alex had long suspected that she had a crush on his friend.

"I haven't seen her for some time," Stone replied. "She even took her sign down."

"She was a strange bird."

"We're all strange birds." He closed the folder and stood. "I appreciate this. It will be a big help."

"Jerry Bagger, Jersey casino operator. So you thinking about doing some gambling?"

"Maybe, just not the way you probably imagine it."

"From what I've heard, Bagger is a real psycho with a mean streak. Not a guy to mess around with."

"I have no intention of doing anything like that."

Alex rose too. "Even so, should I be expecting another eleventh-hour phone call for the cavalry?"

"Let's hope it doesn't come to that."

"Saw our favorite buddy Carter Gray got the Medal of Freedom. It took all my willpower not to call the prick up and tell him to go to hell."

"My willpower's obviously not as strong as yours." Stone then explained what he'd done.

Alex's expression brightened. "You didn't!"

"Yes, I did. And on top of that Gray's asked me to visit him at his house tonight."

"And you're going?"

"I wouldn't miss it."

"Why? What could he possibly have to say that you'd want to hear?"

"I have some questions to ask him about . . . my daughter."

Alex's expression softened and he patted Stone's shoulder. "I'm sorry. I'm really sorry."

"Life is what it is, Alex. You just have to accept it, because you have no other choice."

11

The boat Harry Finn was currently riding on the side of was not quite as fast as the naval vessel he'd piggybacked on previously, but it was more than adequate. Like the military folks, the people he had hitched the ride from tonight had no idea of his presence. He had chosen it because they were heading in the direction he wanted to go. He would have to get home another way, a way he'd already figured out. He had timed out the ride and kept glancing at his illuminated watch in anticipation of when to peel away and swim for shore. A storm was percolating, which was both good and bad for his plan. He'd come prepared; he always did.

As the boat neared where he would be leaving it, Finn reflected on the last conversation he'd had with his wife, Mandy. He'd just finished cutting the grass and gone inside to shower. She stopped him in the bedroom.

"David said he'd talked to you about your work."

"That's right. He said you'd told him you weren't sure what I did for a living."

"I'm not."

"You know once I left the military I started doing contract work for Homeland Security."

"But David can't know that? And I can't know more?"

"It's just better that way. I'm sorry. But you have to trust me on that."

"At least when you were in the navy I knew what I was getting into. What do they ask you to do now?"

He slipped an arm around her waist. "Like I've told you before, I help make us safer. There are lots of holes out there. My job is to patch them up, make us stronger. It's not even remotely dangerous."

The tension was clear on her face. "If it's not even remotely dangerous why can't you tell me?"

"I just can't."

"You never have been much of a talker, have you?'

"I always assumed it was one of the things you loved most about me."

And they had left it at that. Mandy would never know that he illegally flew in the cargo holds of commercial aircraft, and rode without a shred of authorization on the hulls of military ships, because what spouse needed to know such things? And she would never know of the Dan Rosses of the world and the fates that had befallen them. Or of the Carter Grays who once held all the cards, but no longer did.

Yet it was still troubling for Harry Finn; he was a scrupulously honest man, who did not enjoy keeping anything from the woman he'd loved ever since seeing her walk across a college campus nearly fifteen years ago. He'd been on leave then and visiting a friend after rotating back from deployment overseas. He had always been shy and something of an introvert, an attribute that had graded out well for him in his military career. His line of work called for weeks or even months of thoughtful, meticulous preparation followed by seconds of adrenaline-fueled chaos in the midst of which he had to function with a maddening and lethal calm. He had excelled at both ends of that demanding spectrum.

Yet that day seeing the former Amanda Graham walk across that lawn in her jean short-shorts and open-toed sandals, with waist-length blonde hair and a face more lovely than he'd ever seen before, he had walked right up to the young woman and asked her out for that very night. She had declined at first, perhaps offended that he believed she would be free on such short notice. But Finn was nothing if not persistent. He got his date, and his wife. Finn wrangled from the navy a stint stateside and he and Mandy had married right after her graduation. Less than a year later David had arrived, followed by Patrick and Susie. They were a very happy couple. They had raised good kids, children who would make a difference in their world, perhaps only in small ways, but *positive* differences nonetheless.

Finn had no idea why he had some of his deepest

reflections while doing impossibly crazy things, like riding on the sides of boats at high speeds, but he did.

He checked his watch, tightened the strap on the waterproof bag he carried over his shoulder and prepared himself for the next step. This was the tricky part, letting go of his ride at speed and avoiding the screws at the stern. Because when he let go, there was a distinct possibility that if he didn't kick hard enough away from the direction the boat was going and didn't go down deep enough in the water his last memory would be the props savagely cleaving his torso in two.

He coiled his legs and positioned them against the side of the boat. Counting to three, he kicked as hard as he could against the boat's hull and plunged out and then downward even as he felt the force of the screws pulling him toward the stern. He came up to the surface and watched the running lights of the craft disappear. He looked around, quickly gained his bearings and swam hard toward the cliffs.

12

Jerry Bagger never ventured much out of Atlantic City anymore. He had his own Learjet but seldom used it. The last trip on it had been the deadly visit to the unfortunate Tony Wallace in Portugal. He once had a yacht but sold it when he discovered he easily became seasick, an embarrassment for a man who prided himself on toughness. Indeed, he rarely left his casino anymore. It was really the only place he felt comfortable these days.

Ironically, Bagger hadn't been born in Vegas or Jersey. The ballsy, streetwise urban boy had seen his first light in, of all places, Wyoming, on a ranch where his father labored for something less than minimum wage. His mother had lost her life on Bagger's first day from pregnancy complications, complications any hospital could have easily taken care of. But there had been no hospital within three hundred miles, so she'd died. Bagger's father had joined her eighteen months later after an accident involving whiskey and a cantankerous horse.

The Wyoming ranch owner had no interest in

raising a bastard child—Bagger's mother and father had not bothered to marry—and he was shipped off to his mother's family in Brooklyn. It was in the close confines of this New York melting pot, not in the wide-open spaces of Wyoming, that Bagger was meant to be and had thrived.

He had eventually gone back west. After fifteen years of twenty-hour workdays, nonstop hustling and risking and then nearly losing everything he had about a dozen times, he had his own casino. And soon business was so good he started printing money. Then his temper got the best of him and he was eventually run out of Vegas and ordered never to return. He had honored that request, although every time he flew over it he looked out the plane window and ceremoniously flipped off the entire state of Nevada.

Bagger left his penthouse and took the private elevator down to the casino floor. There he walked through a sea of slots, gaming tables and sport betting rooms where gamblers from the novice to the experienced dropped far more money than they would ever get back. Whenever he spotted a kid sitting bored on the floor, with their parents hovering nearby feeding buckets of nickels into the slots—their hands blackened from the process—Bagger would order that food, books and video games be brought to the child, and he would slip a twenty-dollar bill in the kid's hand. Then he would make a call and someone from the Pompeii would immediately confront the parents and remind them that while children were allowed in the casino, they could not be in the playing areas.

Bagger would crush any adult who crossed him, but kids were not to be screwed with. That would change when they hit eighteen—then everyone was fair game—but until then kids were off-limits. It was shitty enough being adults, was his opinion, so let the little punks enjoy the time they had not being grown up. Underlying this philosophy might have been the fact that Jerry Bagger had never had a childhood. Dirt poor, he had run his first racket out of a Brooklyn tenement house at age nine and never looked back. That hard life was a major reason for his success, but the scars ran deep. So deep he didn't even think about them anymore. They were simply what made him what he was.

On his walk Bagger made three such calls for kids left in the playing area by their parents, shaking his head each time. "Losers," he muttered. Jerry Bagger had never bet one dime on anything. That was for suckers. He was many things, but a fool wasn't one of them. These idiots would scream and jump around after winning a hundred bucks, forgetting that they'd thrown away *two* hundred bucks for the privilege. And yet this weird psychological quirk humans possessed had made Bagger rich, so he wasn't complaining.

He stopped at one of the bars and raised an eyebrow at a waitress, who rushed to bring him his usual club soda with a lime. He never drank alcohol on the casino floor, nor did any of his employees. He perched on a bar stool and watched the Pompeii operate at maximum efficiency. All age ranges were represented here. And the whack jobs were aplenty, he knew from decades of experience. There wasn't a single category of nutcase that hadn't at one point strolled into his casino. Truth was, Bagger related to them better than he did the "normal" folks.

He eyed a newlywed couple still in their wedding clothes. The Pompeii offered a cut-rate, tips-not-included deal for those wanting to get hitched, which provided a standard room with a sturdy new mattress, a cheap bouquet of flowers, the services of a properly licensed minister, dinner, drinks and twin massages to work out the kinks from all that screwing. And, most importantly, the deal provided fifty dollars' worth of casino chips. Bagger had no interest in promoting love; he knew from experience that those fifty bucks of free chips typically turned into a two-thousand-dollar profit for the house by the end of a long weekend, even taking into account the freebies.

The couple he was watching seemed to be trying their best to swallow each other's tongues. Bagger grimaced at this public display. "Get a room," he muttered. "It's the cheapest thing you'll find in this town other than the booze. And the sex."

Bagger had never married, chiefly because he had never met a woman who could hold his interest.

Annabelle Conroy *had* captured and held his interest. She was beyond mesmerizing. He'd wanted to spend all his time with her. In fact, before he found out she'd conned him, he had wondered if after all these years he'd finally found a lady he could escort down the aisle. It seemed crazy now, considering what had happened, how she'd screwed him over. And yet with all that Bagger just had to grin. What a picture that would've made. He and Annabelle as husband and wife? What a hoot.

And then, as was often the case, Jerry Bagger had a brilliant idea while he wasn't even trying to.

He finished his club soda and headed back to his office to make some phone calls to find out one thing. When she'd been conning him Annabelle had told him she'd never been married or had children. But what if in reality Annabelle Conroy had been married? Because if she ever had said "I do" it was a golden way to track the lady down.

13

Stone refused Gray's offer of a drink. The two men settled down in Gray's comfortable study, which held as many books in as many languages as there were in Stone's cottage, although here they were kept in much finer style.

Stone looked out the long window that faced the cliffs overlooking the water.

"Tired of Virginia farm country?" he said.

"My ambition as a young man was to be a sailor, see the world from the deck of a ship," Gray said, cradling his Scotch, his wide face strangely offset by a pair of narrowly placed eyes. There was a lot in that head, Stone well knew. Gray was not a man that one could ever reasonably *over*estimate.

"A young man's ambition, can there be a more fleeting prospect?" Stone said idly. The darkness outside the window was complete. No moon, no stars; an approaching storm had hidden the sky.

"I never thought John Carr would be given to lapses into philosophizing."

"Goes to show how little you really knew me. And

I don't go by John Carr anymore. He's dead. I'm sure you were briefed on it years ago."

Unperturbed, Gray continued. "This place used to belong to another former director of CIA, who went on to become vice president. It has everything I need to be comfortable and secure in my old age."

"I'm so happy for you," Stone said.

"I'm actually surprised you came. After your little gesture outside the White House?"

"How is the president, by the way?"

"Fine."

"Did you feel any homicidal impulses when he plunked that medal on you? Or are you over wanting to kill the man?"

"Without directly answering your ridiculous question, circumstances change. It's never personal. You should know that as well as any man alive."

"The point is, I *wouldn't* have been alive if you'd had your way." Before Gray could respond, Stone said, "I have some questions I want to ask you and I'd appreciate answers, truthful ones."

Gray put down his Scotch. "All right."

Stone turned from the window to look at him. "That easy?"

"Why waste what time we have left playing games that don't matter anymore? I take it you want to know about Elizabeth."

"I want to know about *Beth*, my daughter."

"I'll answer what I can."

Stone sat down opposite him and asked question after question for about twenty minutes. His final one was articulated with some trepidation. "Did she ever ask about me, about her father?"

"As you know, Senator Simpson and his wife raised her after they adopted her."

"But you told me you brought them Beth when Simpson was still at CIA. If she had said something, surely—"

Gray put up a hand. "She did. It was actually after Simpson had left CIA and begun his political career. Understand she may have mentioned something about it before, but this was the first I'd heard of such a query. They had told her years before of her adoption. It's not something Beth seemed to dwell on. In fact, I'm not sure she told many people about it."

Stone leaned forward. "What did she say about her real parents?"

"In all fairness, you should know that she asked about her mother first. Girls, you understand, they want to know."

"Of course she should know about her mother."

"They had to be delicate, considering the . . . uh . . . the circumstances of her mother's death."

"Of her *murder*, you mean. By people who were looking to kill me."

"As I told you, I had nothing to do with that. I sincerely liked your wife. And if truth be known, she'd be alive today if you had—"

Stone rose and stared down at him with a look that chilled even Gray, who well knew how many ways John Carr could kill another human being. And no man he'd ever employed had been better at it. "I'm sorry, John—I mean, Oliver. I admit that was not your fault." He paused while Stone slowly sat back down. "They told her a little about her mother, all positive I can assure you, and that she had died in an accident."

"And me?"

"She was told her father was a soldier who was killed in the line of duty. I believe they even took her to your 'grave' at Arlington. To your daughter you died a hero." Gray paused and added, "Does that satisfy you?"

The way he said it made Stone wonder something. "Is this the real truth or the truth Carter Gray style, meaning a load of bullshit to appease me?"

"What possible reason would I have to lie to you now? It doesn't matter anymore, does it? You and me, we don't matter anymore."

"Why did you ask me here tonight?"

In answer Gray went behind his desk and picked up a file. He opened it and held up three color photos of men in their sixties. He placed them one by one in front of Stone. "This first man is Joel Walker, the second Douglas Bennett and the last Dan Ross."

"Those names mean nothing to me, and neither do these pictures."

Gray pulled three more photos from the file, all much older and in black and white. "I think these will look far more familiar to you. And the names as well: Judd Bingham, Bob Cole and Lou Cincetti."

Stone barely heard the names. He was staring at photos of men he'd lived, worked and nearly died beside for over a decade. He looked up at Gray.

"Why are you showing me this?"

"Because in the last two months all three of these former comrades of yours have died."

"Died how?"

"Bingham was found in his bed. He had lupus. The autopsy found nothing unusual. Cole hanged himself. At least it appeared that way, and the police have officially closed that case. Cincetti apparently got drunk, stumbled into his pool and drowned."

"So natural causes for Bingham, suicide for Cole and an accident with Cincetti."

"And you don't believe that any more than I do; three men from the same unit dying within two months of each other?"

"It's a dangerous world out there."

"Something we both know all too well."

"You think they were killed?"

"Of course."

"And you invited me here to what, warn me?"

"It seemed like the most prudent thing to do."

"But like you said, John Carr is dead. Who looks to kill a dead man?"

"These three fellows had excellent cover. Cincetti was particularly deeply buried. If someone could find him, they could find out John Carr isn't really in that box at Arlington. That he's actually a man very much alive who calls himself Oliver Stone."

"And what about you? Carter Gray was the master strategist for our little group. And you've had no cover all these years."

"I have protection. You don't."

"Then you've given me fair warning." Stone rose.

"I'm sorry things ended up as they did. You deserved better."

"You were prepared to sacrifice me and my friends not too long ago, for the good of the country."

"Everything I ever did was for the good of this country."

"At least how *you* defined it, anyway. Not me."

"We can agree to disagree on that."

Stone turned and walked out the door.

14

Carter Gray's mail was screened at an off-site center run by the FBI and then delivered to him in the evening. The courier duly drove up and the mail was given to one of the men assigned to protect Gray. These men lived in a cottage about a hundred yards from the main house. Gray would not agree to anyone living with him in the house, which was protected by a latest-generation security system.

Gray opened the letters and packages, not really focusing on any of them until he reached one item. The envelope was red and had been postmarked from Washington, D.C. There was only one thing in it, a photo. He looked at the picture and then over at the file on his desk. His time had come, it seemed.

He turned out the lights in his study and went to his bedroom. He kissed the pictures of his wife and daughter that had places of honor on the fireplace mantel. In a grotesque twist of fate, both women had perished at the Pentagon on 9/11. He knelt, said his customary prayers and then turned off the light.

Outside, about five hundred yards away from the

house, Harry Finn lowered his long-range nightscope. He'd seen Gray open the red envelope. He'd gotten a good look at the man's face as he stared at the photo. Gray knew. The climb up the sheer rock cliff had been a challenge, even for Finn. But it had allowed him to get this far. And he only had a little farther to go.

Finn waited another hour to allow Gray to fall asleep and then slid over to the gas regulator post. A natural gas line had been placed here specifically because Carter Gray preferred gas heat and cooking. Ten minutes later the gas pressure going into Gray's home blew out all the pilot lights and overwhelmed the built-in safety systems. In seconds the house was full of the deadly gas. If he were still awake Gray would be able to smell it, because the utility company added an odor to the naturally odorless gas as a warning. Yes, Gray could smell it if he were awake, but that would be all he could do.

Finn loaded one bullet into his rifle. It looked rather ordinary except its nose was green-colored. He took aim and fired at the long window in the back of the house. It was not a difficult shot. The slug cracked the glass and the small amount of flame-creating powder in the incendiary bullet he'd chambered ignited. The roof was blown ten feet into the air while the walls were knocked outward a dozen feet on all sides. What was left of the roof came back down, landing squarely on a raging fire. Within seconds it was hard to believe a house had actually been there at all.

Finn had turned to flee on his planned escape route when he heard a scream and looked back. One of the guards had come out of the guesthouse, been hit with a chunk of flaming debris and was on fire. There was no sign of the other guard. Without really thinking about it, Finn ran forward, tackled the man, who was flailing around, and rolled him on the ground, putting out the flames. Then he leapt up and ran full tilt back to his gear near the gas regulator post. He'd already turned the pressure setting back to normal and relocked the access door. He grabbed his bag and gun, sprinted to the cliffs and flung his rifle and other equipment over the edge. The tide would soon carry them far out to sea.

Finn took a few steps back and sprinted toward the cliff. He flew out into space and plummeted down, his body unfolding into classic high-dive form. He hit the water cleanly, went under, and then resurfaced. He struck out with a strong, practiced stroke and made it to shore about a half mile down. In a small wooded area here he had covered under a layer of leaves a small motorcycle. He cut through myriad back trails to a main road, then finally pulled off on a small side street where a van was parked. He rolled the bike into the rear of the van, hopped into the driver's seat and sped off. The van and motorcycle were left at a private garage Finn maintained about ten miles from his house. He drove home in his Prius, and changed in the garage before coming into the house, putting his dirty clothes into the washer and turning on the machine.

A few minutes later he headed quietly upstairs, looking in on his kids. Mandy was asleep; a book she'd been reading was still lying across her chest. He closed the book, put it away and turned off the lamp on her nightstand before slipping into bed. Finn mentally crossed Carter Gray off his list and moved on to the next name.

He looked down at his hands. Even though he'd worn gloves they were slightly singed from putting out the fire on the man. He'd put ice on them and then some salve in the kitchen before coming upstairs. "Don't do that again, Harry," he whispered to himself, but still causing his wife to moan and roll a bit in her sleep. He put a hand on her head and started rubbing her hair. His reddened hand and his wife's beautiful blonde hair; the odd pairing suddenly made Finn want to run as fast as he could, as if he could outrun any of it. His lovely wife and their three wonderful children. A nice house, a job he enjoyed and was very good at. His life was filled with things he had always wanted to have. And with one thing he had never wanted to face. It didn't seem fair really. Yet how in the world could he stop? It had been beaten into his head ever since he could remember. It had become more a part of him than anything else, even more than his role as husband and father. And that was the only thing in all of this that truly scared him.

Finn hid his hands under the covers and tried to sleep.

15

“Bagger got to Tony,” Annabelle said. She hadn’t slept all night and had called her former partner Leo Richter at the crack of dawn. She had no idea what time zone he was even in and didn’t really care.

On the other end of the phone Leo sat up straight and felt his last meal start to come up on him. “What the hell are you talking about?”

“Tony screwed up. Flashed the cash and Bagger tracked him down. Bagger killed three people and left Tony for dead after turning his brains to mush.”

“Well you can bet the little weasel ratted us out, then. Why can’t somebody just kill Bagger? Is it that hard?”

Annabelle said, “What if Tony found out my last name? You told Freddy, maybe Freddy told Tony. Or the kid might’ve overheard.”

“I don’t know what to tell you, Annabelle. We both might be screwed regardless. There are only so many Annabelles and Leos in the con world who operate at that level.”

“If you know where Freddy is you might want to warn him.”

"I'll do my best. Look, you want me to hook up with you? Try to get us out of this mess?"

"And make it easier for Jerry to bag two for the price of one? Just stay where you are, Leo, and dig as deep as you can." She clicked off the phone and sat back on her bed. Maybe she should put her millions to work for her right now. Just use it to run like hell. Private plane, private island, plenty of guards. It sounded tempting, but her gut told her this would be like waving a flag in front of a bull. She was still pondering what to do when her phone rang. It was Oliver Stone.

"I hope I didn't wake you," he said.

"I'm an early riser," she lied.

"I have news. We can meet at my cottage later," he said.

"Why don't you come my way, Oliver," she said. "We can have some breakfast. There's a place around the corner from where I'm staying." She gave him the address. Thirty minutes later they took a corner table in the back away from the other customers. After they ordered, he told Annabelle what he'd found out.

"I'm not sure how that helps," she said, spooning sugar into her coffee.

"The best defense is a good offense. The government would love to nail him to a wall. If we can help them do that, I doubt he'd have time for you. Actually, if we can simply distract Bagger with a government investigation, that may be enough to keep you safe."

Annabelle looked uncertain. "You don't know Jerry. He has forty million reasons to devote every second of the remainder of his life to killing me."

Stone nodded knowingly. "I do know Jerry, at least men like him. It's not just about the money, of course. It's about loss of face, of respect. He has to seem invincible to everyone. Otherwise he's not Jerry Bagger."

"You sized him up right away."

"As I said, I've known many men like Bagger, even worked for some."

She said cautiously, "So if we *were* going to go after Jerry how would we do it?"

"We have to find where he's vulnerable. There's the point of least resistance, of course. He killed three people in Portugal and put a fourth in a coma. If we can pin that on him he goes away forever."

"I know he did it, but I have no proof. And if I go to the cops, I'll have to explain everything, and then I don't think they'll be waiting to hand me a medal."

"Or you could give your share of the money back to Bagger and hope that's enough."

"I earned that money, every last cent of it. And like you said, it's not about the money. He'd still want to kill me."

"But if we can tie Bagger to these crimes without

you having to give testimony or being involved at all?"

"Well, that would just solve all my problems, wouldn't it? Only I don't quite see how that can work."

"That's for us to figure out." Stone was about to say something else when his cell phone rang. It was Alex Ford and his voice was strained.

"Oliver, did you see Carter Gray last night?"

"Yes, I did."

"What time did you get there and what time did you leave?"

Stone told him. "I'm sure the driver can verify that. What's this all about?"

"I can't believe you haven't heard."

"Heard what?"

"Somebody blew up Carter Gray's house last night, with him in it. I know this is going to be awkward, but I think the FBI will want to talk to you about your meeting with Gray."

Stone clicked off. *The FBI will want to talk to me. About Gray.*

Annabelle said sharply, "Trouble?"

"A little," he said slowly as his thoughts raced ahead. "Maybe more than a little, actually."

She tapped her coffee cup against his. "Welcome to the club."

16

Oliver Stone stared at the wall opposite him while the two thirty-something men in shirtsleeves with their guns and badges hanging on their black belts hovered around like vultures over roadkill. His voluntary appearance at the FBI's Washington Field Office had not earned him any brownie points, even with Alex Ford of the Secret Service accompanying him to the interview. Alex had told the agents in charge of Carter Gray's homicide investigation about Stone's recent heroics in foiling an espionage ring. However, the agents had brushed that off.

One of them said to Alex, "I deal with murder and I got a big one hanging around my neck and a lot of pressure from upstairs to get results." He plopped down in front of Stone at the small table.

"Now let's try the name thing one more time. What's yours?"

"Oliver Stone, like I told you the last four times you asked."

"Let me see some ID."

"And as I told you four times before, I don't have any."

The other agent said incredulously, "How does anybody in the twenty-first century not have ID?"

Stone looked at him, bemused. "I know who I am. And I don't really care if no one else does."

"So you came all the way down here to tell us what—nothing other than the fact that you're apparently a famous film director who dresses like a bum?"

"Actually, I came down here to tell you that I visited Carter Gray at his home last night at *his* request. I arrived around nine and left about forty-five minutes later. He sent his driver for me. The man can certainly vouch for the fact that when I left, the house was still standing and the man inside that house was still alive."

Alex interjected, "Have you talked to the driver?"

The two agents glanced at each other. One said to Stone, "What'd you two talk about?"

"It was private. I'm certain it had nothing to do with what happened to Mr. Gray." Stone of course had every reason to believe that what Gray had told him about the other three men dying was very much tied to Gray's death.

"I sense uncooperative behavior," the same agent said.

His partner added, "And I sense an obstruction charge coming. You like to sit in a jail cell, Mr. Stone, while we run down who you really are?"

Stone said calmly, "If you believe you have enough to charge me then charge me. If you don't I'm late for another appointment."

"You're a busy man are you, *Mr.* Stone?" one of the agents remarked sarcastically.

"I try to stay productive. But I'll make a deal with you."

"We don't do deals."

"I'll go with you to the crime scene. If I see anything that strikes me funny, I'll let you know."

"Strikes you funny? What the hell is that supposed to mean?" the first agent said.

"Just what it sounds like."

"No way in hell are we taking you to the crime scene."

"If you killed the guy you might be looking to screw up some evidence," the other agent said.

Stone sighed. "Call the director of the FBI, please."

"Excuse me?" one agent snapped, looking incredulously at him.

"Call the head of the FBI. He sent me a commendation letter recently. By coincidence I brought a copy of it with me. I called his office before coming down here. I told him if I had any trouble, I'd give him a call."

Stone handed the letter across to the agent. With his partner looking over his shoulder they read it word for word, then glanced at Alex, who merely shrugged.

Stone said, "Do you call or do we choose not to bother the director and just go to the crime scene? I don't have all day."

"No reason to bother the director," one of the agents said finally.

Stone rose. "Delighted to hear it."

17

Stone walked near the wreckage of Carter Gray's house with one of the FBI agents and Alex Ford.

"Gas explosion?" Alex asked the agent.

"That's what it looks like, although I'm not sure how it was possible. The place wasn't that old. And it had all the latest safety features."

Stone was staring at what was left of the house he'd been sitting in only last night. "Where was his body found?"

"Sorry, can't say. The *remains* of a body were found in the bedroom."

"Positive ID?"

"Suffice it to say that we consider this a homicide investigation regarding the owner of the property."

"Did you find the driver to confirm Oliver's story?"

The agent shook his head. "The man's gone missing. He was with the CIA. Not sure what the story was there. Of course, that means we just have your word for it that he drove you home," he added, eyeballing Stone.

"If I were going to blow up the man I wouldn't have told anyone I was meeting with him, especially a United States Secret Service agent. And I certainly wouldn't have done the deed on the very night I did meet with him."

"The fact that the house blew up right after he met with you *is* the reason you're a suspect," the agent countered.

"And it's also the reason I'm out here," Stone said. "Because the faster you find the real killer, the sooner I'm off that list."

"Anyone else around?" Alex asked.

The agent nodded, his gaze still on Stone. "A guard. He came out of the guesthouse over there and got hit by some debris and was actually on fire. He says he remembers somebody knocking him down and putting out the flames. He passed out and the next thing he remembers is being put in the back of an ambulance. He's in the burn unit at a hospital in Annapolis. He'll be okay."

Alex said, "So there *was* somebody else out here last night."

The agent was still staring at Stone, who raised his hands and said, "You can check me for burns, if you'd like."

"It wasn't the other guy, the driver?" Alex said quickly while giving Stone a "knock it off" look.

"The guard was in so much pain he could only see

it was a guy," the agent admitted. "But if it *was* the driver why should he have run off?"

"He would if he had something to do with the explosion," Stone noted. "And the fact that he's gone missing now? Not to tell you how to run your investigation, but it is something to think about."

"We have thought about it," the agent said gruffly.

"Find anything useful in the house?" Stone asked.

"If we did, you would not be on the list of people we would inform."

Stone smiled, turned away and saw it. He said slowly, "Well, since I'm not in the loop you won't mind if I just take a walk along the cliffs. Be sure to keep me in your line of sight in case I make a run for it."

As he walked away the agent said to Alex, "Okay, fed to fed, who the hell is that guy?"

"Someone I'd trust my life with. Someone I *have* trusted my life with."

"Care to share?"

"No, it's national security stuff and you'd never believe me anyway."

The agent stared at the rumpled Stone. "National security! The guy looks borderline homeless."

"Actually, he works in a cemetery," Alex said helpfully.

The agent just shook his head and then followed Stone, who was over near the cliffs.

What had caught Stone's eye was the gas regulator post. As he headed toward it the same agent called out, "We've checked that out already. Obvious point."

"And?"

"And it was working fine and no forced entry."

"There wouldn't be any sign of forced entry if the person knew what he was doing. But the gas pressure can be manipulated from here?"

"Presumably. But we checked the box and the pressure hadn't been changed."

Stone recalled the long window of Gray's house looking out onto the cliffs. There was something gnawing at his memory. He turned back to the agent.

"Well, if you can change the pressure, you can change it back."

"Okay, anything else strike you funny?" the man asked.

"Let's say you greatly increase the gas pressure going into the house, which blows out the safety overrides. In seconds the place is filled with gas."

"But you need something to ignite that gas."

"Turning on a light would create enough of a spark to do it."

"True. We've got some bomb-sniffing dogs coming out. Unless they turn up some dynamite or C4, we might have to look at the gas angle more closely."

Stone suddenly remembered what he needed to. He left the agent and rejoined Alex.

"Anything occur to you?" Alex asked.

"You fill the house with gas by manipulating the pressure. A light spark will ignite the gas, but if Gray is asleep you can't count on that. And you don't want him to smell the gas and escape. So you have a man standing about two hundred yards from the back of the house, near the cliffs over there. He fires an incendiary bullet through the window. The bullet passes through the glass, igniting on impact and triggering the gas explosion. If they find a colored bit of metal in there it may be from the bullet's nose. Incendiary rounds are typically colored so people don't mix them up."

Alex nodded thoughtfully. "But how would he get away? The front was blocked. Unless the guard who got burned passed out and didn't see the guy get by him."

Stone and Alex walked back over to the agent. "Any evidence of the person leaving through the woods over there?" Stone asked the FBI man.

The agent shook his head. "We've been all over it. No trace, and there would have been. And there's no easy way to get back to the main road from there."

"But the person could have left directly by the main road, then?"

"Don't think so. I forgot to mention that the guard who got burned said the guy who helped him ran back this way, not toward the road."

Stone walked over to the cliffs with the agent tagging along. "Then he went out this way. Probably came in the same way."

The agent looked down. "That's sheer rock, a good thirty feet."

"It's not sheer. There're plenty of handholds if you know where to look."

"Okay, you climb up. But what about the going down part?"

"Well, since I don't see anything around here you could attach a rope to, I'm assuming he jumped."

The agent gazed at the swirling water far below. "That's impossible."

"Not really." Stone thought, *Actually, I did the same thing thirty years ago. Only it was fifty feet up and there were people shooting at me.*

Stone drove back to D.C. with Alex.

"Not a bad morning's work," Alex said appreciatively.

"Knowing how it was done and finding out who did it are two very different things. Carter Gray had a lot of enemies."

"Granted, but don't you have any guesses? I mean he had to have some reason to want to meet with you."

Stone hesitated. He didn't like keeping things back from Alex, but sometimes honest disclosure, even for good reasons, turned out to be a bad decision. "I don't believe it's connected."

He could tell Alex didn't buy this statement, but he chose not to add to it.

As they drove on Stone stared out the window. Three men he'd worked with decades ago were suddenly all dead. Carter Gray had met to warn him about this strange chain of events. The very night of that warning he had been blown up. Whoever had done this had found three deeply covered, highly skilled former assassins and murdered them. And then he had succeeded in killing Carter Gray, a man who had few peers when it came to outwitting the competition.

A person smart enough to do all that could conceivably discover who Oliver Stone really was. And come and kill him too.

And maybe I would deserve it, Stone thought. Because the only thing he had in common with the dead men was that they were all former killers themselves.

18

Annabelle stood outside the gates of the cemetery where Stone was caretaker. After her talk with Leo and her conversation with Stone, she had made up her mind. This was not Oliver Stone's fight. Friend or not, she could not allow him to get involved. If Bagger somehow killed him, Annabelle knew she could not live with that guilt.

The gates were locked, but with a tension tool and lock pick two minutes later they were open and she was on the front porch of the cottage. She slipped the note she had taken nearly an hour to compose, despite its brevity, under the door. A minute later she was back in her car. Three hours later she was riding into the sky inside a United Airlines jet. As the plane tracked the Potomac River on the climb out, Annabelle glanced out the window. Georgetown was directly below them. She thought she could see the little well-tended cemetery, *his* cemetery. Perhaps he was down there amid the hallowed ground working away at his tombstones, attending to the dead and buried, atoning for past sins.

"So long, Oliver Stone," she said to herself. *Goodbye, John Carr.*

"I love this Internet crap," Bagger bellowed as he stared at the papers one of his IT guys had just handed to him.

"It is quite amazing, Mr. Bagger," the young bespectacled man began in an immodest tone. "And frankly—"

"Get the hell outta here," Bagger roared and the terrified man fled.

Bagger sat down behind his desk and studied the papers again. He'd retained an Internet search organization. He didn't know what their sources were and he didn't really care. They had delivered, that's all that mattered. Annabelle Conroy had walked down the aisle, over fifteen years ago, with a guy named Jonathan DeHaven. They had been married, ironically Bagger thought, in Vegas. The downside was there were no pictures of the happy couple, only the names. It had to be the same Annabelle Conroy, how many people getting married in Sin City would have that name? But he had to be sure. So Bagger picked up his phone and called a PI firm he had used in the past. These folks worked right on the edge of the envelope and occasionally skirted past that barrier. He loved them for it, and also because they got results. He would have put them onto Annabelle before now, but he wanted a piece of information for them to start with, and now he had it. When people got married they signed lots of documents. And they had to live somewhere and get things like insurance, and utilities and maybe wills and cars in both the names.

He chuckled. Annabelle had posed as a CIA operative when running her scam on him. Well, he would show the lady what real intelligence was.

He said into the phone, "Hey, Joe, it's Jerry Bagger, got a job for you. A really, really important job. I need to find an old friend. And I need to do it fast because I want to wrap my arms around her and give the lady a nice big squeeze."

19

When Stone arrived back home he saw the note. Instinctively knowing what it was before he even opened it, he still took his time reading through it. When he was done he sat back and sighed deeply. Then he got angry. He called Reuben, Milton and Caleb. He told them there would be a meeting of the Camel Club that night at his cottage. Though Caleb whined about having to work late to finish a project, Stone insisted that he be there. "It's important, Caleb. It has to do with our friend."

"Which friend?" he'd said suspiciously.

"Susan."

"Is she in trouble?"

"Yes."

"Then I'll be there," Caleb said without hesitation.

Stone spent the next few hours working in the cemetery, shoring up old tombstones that always seemed to lose their grip on the earth after a rainstorm no matter how many times he straightened and reinforced them. He was not merely doing busy work. He wanted to get something that had been buried for a long time, both in the ground and also in his mind.

The old tombstone had a statue of an eagle perched on top. Pretending to be trying to straighten the headstone in case anyone was watching, Stone let it fall to the ground as though by accident. Revealed underneath was a small hole in the dirt. In this hole was a rectangular-shaped airtight metal box. Stone lifted the box out and placed it in the trash bag he was using to collect weeds. He left the tombstone on its side, dusted off his hands and went inside the cottage with the bag.

At his desk he opened the box with a key he kept taped behind the light switch panel in his tiny bathroom. He spread the box's contents out in front of him. This was his insurance policy, in case anyone ever came looking to do him harm. Stone had been smart enough to know that what he was being asked to do for his country could be seen, from another perspective, as simply crimes done under the flimsy banner of counterintelligence. He had been told on countless occasions that if he or his team members were ever caught during one of their missions, they couldn't rely on Uncle Sam to bail them out. They were on their own. To young men possessing special skills and insane levels of confidence that had seemed like a challenge they couldn't refuse.

He and men like Lou Cincetti and Bob Cole had often joked, in sessions of gallows humor, that if their capture seemed imminent they would each simply shoot the other, fittingly leaving the world together, as a team. Yet as the years passed and the killings went on, Stone had started collecting information and documentation from these "tasks." Uncle Sam could say he wouldn't be there for him, but it was another thing altogether if Stone could hold his agency accountable. In the end none of it had mattered, though. His wife had died, his daughter was lost to him and the people who'd ordered his destruction, simply because he didn't want to kill anymore, had never suffered a single minute for it.

Stone stared at one photo for a long time. It was from Vietnam when he'd still been a soldier, albeit one with highly specialized skills. He had been given the assignment of assassinating a North Vietnamese politician, a man the enemy had been rallying around. Normally, long-range sniping was done by a team. You had lookouts and spotters and people to check the wind and other weather conditions. However, Stone had been sent in alone, charged with a task that even for him seemed impossible. He would be dropped by chopper into a jungle crawling with Viet Cong. He was to travel five miles by foot over dangerous terrain and kill the man at a rally that would be attended by over ten thousand people, with massive military security. He was then to reverse his tracks and travel miles back to an assigned spot that would be difficult to find in the daylight, much less at night.

The chopper would be there precisely four hours after dropping him off. It would make one pass. If he wasn't back in time, Stone was target practice for the Viet Cong.

Ostensibly he'd been chosen for what amounted to a suicide mission because he was the best they had; the finest shooter and the most tireless in the field, it was generally acknowledged. Back then Stone was a machine. He could run all day and night. He had been dropped into the South China Sea from a chopper once, and swam miles through rough water to kill someone deemed hostile to the United States. From half a mile away he'd placed a shot through the man's head while he sat at his kitchen table reading the newspaper and smoking a cigarette. Then he'd swum back out and been picked up by a sub.

Yet with the assignment in Vietnam Stone had suspected his superiors were making a statement about his increasingly reluctant attitude about the war. Some of them were no doubt praying he would fail. And die. He hadn't accommodated them that night. He had killed the politician from a challenging distance even for a top sniper using a scope that expert marksmen today would have laughed at. Stone had made it back to the clearing to find the chopper about to turn off after its single pass. He knew the pilots had seen him but apparently couldn't be bothered to come back to get him. He put a heavy-caliber round right through the open cargo doors to show them the error of their ways.

They had landed, only momentarily, but enough to allow him to jump on the skids. As the chopper flew off, shots poured at them from the jungle below. Stone had run that night like never before in his life. Yet, still, he hadn't been that far ahead of a battalion of angry North Vietnamese. It had been that successful assignment that had garnered the attention of the CIA, and resulted in his induction into the "esteemed group" of government assassins known as the Triple Six Division.

The Triple Six was a component that even most people at the Agency didn't realize existed. They probably slept better for not knowing. Yet every "civilized" country had its assassins who did things to protect their national interests, and America was certainly entitled to hers. At least that was the company line.

Stone turned to another piece of paper with some names on it and a photo attached. They were Stone, Bob Cole, Lou Cincetti, Roger Simpson, Judd Bingham and Carter Gray. This was the only photo he knew of that had all six men in it. And it had only been possible because, after a particularly difficult mission, they had all gone out and gotten drunk as soon as the plane touched back down on American soil. As Stone looked into his mostly unlined face from decades ago, a killer's confident face that had no idea of the personal hardship and loss to come, he felt a heaviness in his chest.

He squinted at the picture of the tall, elegant man that Roger Simpson had been back then. Simpson had never been a field agent; instead, like Carter Gray, he'd orchestrated the activities of Stone and the others from a relatively safe distance. He had gone on to the political arena where he was still tall, still handsome. However, the ambitious streak he possessed that had seemed a very positive attribute when he was younger had turned him over three decades later into a devious plotter and a man who never forgot a slight no matter how trivial. Not content merely to be one of a hundred senators, he desperately wanted the presidency, and had worked long and hard to win it. And when the term of the current president ended, it seemed that Simpson was indeed a front-runner to take his place. His wife, a former Miss Alabama, gave him a glamour quotient that the somewhat stiff Simpson could never have inspired himself. It was discreetly and anonymously bandied about that Mrs. Simpson didn't really enjoy her husband's company all that much. Yet apparently she wanted to be First Lady badly enough to play along.

Stone had always considered Simpson a weak-willed, backstabbing prick. That such a man was in position to capture the top office in the land in a few short years merely reinforced Stone's already low opinion of American politics.

He put the items back in the box and returned it to the hole, setting the monument back in place. While he waited for someone to possibly come and kill him, he would focus on ensuring that Annabelle Conroy stayed among the living, even if she said she didn't want his help.

He had lost his daughter. He was not going to lose Annabelle.

20

The Camel Club met that night at eight o'clock at Stone's cottage. As usual, Milton brought his laptop and pecked on the keys, while Caleb sat anxiously in a rickety chair and Reuben leaned against a wall.

Stone told them about Susan's dilemma and also that she had left town.

"Well, damn," Reuben said. "We never even got to go out for a drink."

Stone explained, "Jerry Bagger probably killed those people in Portugal and left her partner for dead. She needs our help, but feels it would put us in too much danger."

Caleb squared his shoulders. "She obviously doesn't know that this group absolutely *revels* in danger."

Stone cleared his throat. "Yes, well, my original plan had been to investigate this Jerry Bagger and see if we could work to have him put in prison."

"A good plan in *theory*, but how do we do it for real?" Reuben said.

"I thought it might be worthwhile to go up to Atlantic City and check him out."

Milton said, "Here's a picture of him. The Pompeii Casino has its own Web site."

Caleb looked at Bagger smiling up from the computer screen and moaned fearfully. "Good God, look at that face; those eyes. He's clearly a mobster, Oliver. You don't go and *check out* mobsters."

Reuben eyed Stone. "It might be a little dicey going to his home turf."

"It's only for information gathering," Stone said. "No confrontations at all. Just observing and perhaps talking to a few people who might be helpful."

"But if this Bagger person finds out? He might come after us!" Caleb said.

"What happened to you *reveling* in danger, Caleb?" Reuben reminded him.

Caleb retorted, "This man kills people, probably for jollies."

"The good news is you don't have to go, Caleb," Stone said. He turned to the other two. "I thought Milton and Reuben could do the first recon; that is if Reuben can get some time off from the dock."

"I can always find an excuse not to go lug big shit off big trucks for not-so-big bucks."

Milton said simply, "Sounds good."

"Sounds good?" Caleb exclaimed. "Milton, this man is dangerous. He's a *casino* operator, for God sakes," he added in a hiss. "He makes money off people's addictions. I bet he's involved in drugs too. And prostitution!" He ended with a dramatic flourish.

"You need to be careful," Stone warned. "No unnecessary risks."

"Understood," Reuben said. "I can pick Milton up in the truck tomorrow morning."

"And while you're doing that, I'm going to track down Susan. She's checked out of her hotel, but I have some ideas."

"So what am I supposed to do while the three of you are out gallivanting around?" Caleb asked.

"Just the usual stuff, Superman," Reuben said. "Keeping the nation's capital safe for truth, justice and the American way."

Stone said, "Oh, Caleb, I need to borrow your car. I doubt Susan's still in the city so I'll have to travel."

Caleb stared at him in alarm. "You want to borrow my car? My car! That's impossible." Caleb's ride was an ancient pewter gray Nova with an eternally rattling tailpipe. It had more rust than metal, more springs than upholstery, no working heat or AC, and the man treated it as though the wreck were a vintage Bentley.

"Just give him the keys," Reuben growled.

"Then how will I get home tonight?"

"I'll drive you on my motorcycle."

"I refuse to ride in that death trap."

Reuben gave him such a ferocious look that Caleb hastily pulled out his car keys and handed them to Stone. "Then again, there's nothing wrong with trying new things."

Caleb said suddenly, "Oliver, do you even have a driver's license?"

"Yes, but unfortunately it's been expired for over twenty years."

Caleb paled. "But that means you can't drive legally."

"That's right. But given the seriousness of what we're doing I knew you'd understand."

Stone left Caleb standing there openmouthed and moved over to Reuben, who was motioning to him from the front door.

Reuben spoke in a low voice. "Carter Gray's house was blown up with him in it."

"I was aware of it."

"I hope not *too* aware."

"The FBI has already spent time with me. I went out to Gray's house or what's left of it with a pair of agents and Alex Ford and gave them the benefit of my thoughts."

"Murder?"

"Undoubtedly."

Reuben said, "This doesn't have anything to do with, you know, your past?" He was the only member of the Camel Club who remotely had any knowledge of what Stone had done decades ago.

"I hope not. I'll see you when you get back from Atlantic City. Remember, keep a low profile."

"While I'm there, you want me to lay down a bet for you at the craps table?"

"I never gamble, Reuben."

"How come?"

"One, I don't have any money, and two, I hate to lose."

21

The next morning Bagger met with Joe, from the PI firm. The man was trim, with calm gray eyes. Though soft-spoken, Joe was not intimidated in the least by the casino king. It was one of the things Bagger loved about him. He sat down across from Bagger and opened a file.

"We got some quick results on this one, Mr. Bagger." He scanned the pages and then looked up. "I've got a written report for you, but let me just give you the essentials." He handed a photo across. "We had an associate of ours in Vegas check out the wedding chapel where Conroy and DeHaven were married. It's a typical mom-and-pop; the same couple run it today, in fact. After a little financial encouragement they let us take a peek at their records, and that's where we got a copy of that photo. Apparently they take pictures of all the people they marry and put them up on the wall. I'm assuming from the look on your face, Mr. Bagger, that that's our girl."

Bagger was smiling and nodding as he stared down at a photo of a much younger Annabelle Conroy and her brand-new husband, Jonathan DeHaven. "That's my little friend. Good work, Joe. What else you got?"

"Well, this has the potential to make our job easier. I'm just not sure yet."

Bagger looked up from the photo. "What has the potential?"

In answer, Joe handed Bagger a newspaper clipping. "The name DeHaven rang a bell for me, but I didn't know why at the time. Then I did some digging. And bingo!"

"He was murdered!" Bagger exclaimed, reading the headline.

"Very recently. Found in some vault at the Library of Congress in D.C. It was all tied into some spy ring going down in Washington."

"Are we sure it's the same DeHaven?"

Joe handed Bagger another photo of DeHaven from a newspaper article detailing his death. "You can see it's the same guy, only older."

"So Annabelle's hubby was a spy and got whacked?"

"Her ex-husband. We also found out that the marriage was annulled a year later."

"Annulled? Doesn't that mean they didn't have sex or something? For a whole freaking year?" Bagger stared down at Annabelle's wedding picture. The lady was a stunner. Bagger of course hated the woman for ripping him off, but how in God's name did her husband keep from jumping her the minute the "I do's" were said? "Was this DeHaven guy secretly gay or something?"

"I don't know the details of why the annulment took place, but it did and was made a matter of record in Washington, D.C., where the couple presumably came back to live. And DeHaven wasn't part of the spy ring. Details are still coming out and some of it's being buried because of national security interests, but it looks like he was an innocent guy who got killed because he stumbled onto something he shouldn't have."

A pensive Bagger sat back. Annabelle had conned him into thinking she was with CIA and that the money he had given her was a way for the government to launder cash overseas. But what if she really was with CIA? What if it had been the government that had screwed him? You couldn't sue the government. You couldn't kill Uncle Sam.

He stared across at Joe. "Good work, Joe. Keep digging and see what you come up with."

Joe rose. "Already on it, Mr. Bagger."

After Joe left, Bagger stared down at the picture of the youthful Annabelle. She looked happy although her new hubby looked like, well, like a librarian.

Bagger rose and looked out the window, onto his empire that occupied nearly an entire block on the Boardwalk. Making up his mind, he picked up his phone and called his chief of security. "Warm up the jet, we're heading out."

"Where to, Mr. Bagger?"

"My favorite city. Washington, D.C."

22

The next morning, while Reuben and Milton drove to Atlantic City, Harry Finn was also busy. He and two team members were surveying a parcel of land near the United States Capitol. Their uniforms were perfect, their equipment spot-on. Most importantly, they exuded the confident air of people who had every right to be where they were. When two Capitol police officers approached them, Finn calmly pulled a piece of paper from his pocket and showed the pair his official-looking orders.

"I just go where they send me, guys," he said apologetically. "We won't be here much longer. It's the damn visitor center project."

"You mean that taxpayer hell pit?" one of the cops growled. The project had become D.C.'s version of the Big Dig fiasco in Boston.

Finn nodded. "You know in this town everybody thinks somebody else has jurisdiction. So we have to do the same thing ten times because somebody's panties got in a wad."

"Tell me about it," the other cop said. "Just make it quick."

"Roger that," Finn said, turning back to his work.

The surveyor's apparatus they were using was actually a video camera currently filming two entrances to the Capitol building and detailing the rotation of security guards and other essential elements for a successful penetration later. Ever since a man had broken through the Capitol security perimeter with comparative ease, several high-ranking pols had been livid. They had secretly retained Finn's company to test whether the "enhanced" security measures put in place were the real fix or not. From what Finn had seen so far, they clearly weren't.

Back at the office, Finn spent the next two hours "phone freaking." This was a complex exercise involving phoning one person after another and building on the intelligence with each call to elicit more specific information from each new person called. Finn had used this technique to learn the central location in the United States of the vaccine for a nasty bioterrorism bug by pretending to be a marketing student doing a term paper on commercial distribution techniques. He talked to eight different people, finishing with a vice president of the company that manufactured the vaccine, who unknowingly confirmed the location while answering what he obviously thought was a totally unrelated series of questions.

Today Finn was gathering info on two upcoming

projects: the hit on the Capitol and a far more involved crashing of the Pentagon. While it had been unfortunately proved beyond doubt that one could fly a large plane into the headquarters of the U.S. military and damage it, there were far subtler ways of breaching the facility's security and perhaps doing more harm than the doomed jumbo jet had. Among other possible scenarios, one could booby-trap the military's command and control system, or sabotage its air filtration system, killing or sickening tens of thousands of key government personnel, or even blow up the building from the inside out.

As Finn went about his work, he kept an eye on the Internet for news of Carter Gray's death. As expected, the authorities were keeping a tight lid on all of it. There had been no leaks and most stories were confined to telling and retelling the glorious career and public service of the dead man, Carter Robert Gray. Finally, Finn couldn't take it anymore. He went for a walk.

And then he decided, on impulse, to visit his mother. He would catch a flight that very night, after the kids were in bed. He could see her the next day and be back home that same night. After the navy gig, he had some downtime coming anyway. His was not a nine-to-five occupation. And with several jobs percolating in the prep stage before the field operations would begin, now was actually a good time to go.

He both loved and hated to see his mother. The

routine never varied; it couldn't, actually. Yet since it had all begun with her, Finn had to return to that touchstone from time to time. It wasn't like he was reporting in, but in a way that's exactly what he was doing.

He booked the flight online and called Mandy and told her. He left work early, drove his two youngest to swimming and baseball practice respectively, and then picked them up later. After they were asleep he left for the airport, for the short ride to one of the longest days of his life.

23

Stone punched in Annabelle's phone number. Four rings went by and he assumed she wasn't going to answer when her voice said, "Hello?"

"Where are you?" he said.

"Oliver, I left a note."

"The note is bullshit. Where are you?"

"I don't want you involved in this, so just forget me."

"I've sent Milton and Reuben up to Atlantic City to do a recon on Bagger."

"You did what?" she screamed into the phone. "Are you insane!"

"Now there's the Annabelle I've come to know and admire."

"That's suicide, sending them to Bagger's turf."

"They know how to take care of themselves."

"Oliver, I left town so you *wouldn't* get involved."

"Then come back, because we *are* involved."

"I can't come back. I won't come back."

"Then just answer one question for me."

"What?" she said warily.

"What did Jerry Bagger do to you to make you rip him off for millions?"

"I ripped him off because that's what I do. I'm a con."

"If you keep lying to me I'm going to get really upset."

"Why do you care?"

"You helped us, now it's our turn to help you."

"I helped myself. You guys were just in the way."

"So be it, but you still need us. And we're wasting time. If Bagger's as good as you say he is, you may not have much time left."

"Thanks for your vote of confidence."

"I'm just being practical. Where are you?"

"Forget it."

"Then let me guess. But if I guess correctly you have to tell me where you are. Deal?"

"Whatever makes you happy."

"I said deal?"

"Fine. Deal."

"Okay, you've taken my advice and you're trying to pin something on Bagger. And what you're trying to pin on him is the reason you ripped him off. And that's where you are right now, at a place where he did something so bad to you or yours that you had to come back at him. And do it damn hard. Am I right?"

Annabelle was dead silent.

He said, "Now, since I won the bet you have to tell me where you are."

"You didn't give me a specific location."

"I didn't say I'd give you a specific location. In fact, what I told you was far more than just naming a town. But if you want to welch on a bet."

"I never go back on a bet."

"Then tell me."

There was a very long pause. "I'm in Maine."

"Where in Maine?"

"A little south of Kennebunk on the coast."

"Is that where it happened?"

Stone waited through another long pause.

"Yes."

"And what was it that did happen?"

"It's my business," she snapped.

"I think I've proved that you can trust me."

"I'm not sure anyone can prove that to me."

"Okay, have it your way. I'll head up to Atlantic City and have a go at old Jerry myself."

"Oliver, you can't do that. He will kill you. Don't you understand that?"

"Then my blood will be on your hands," he said in a joking tone.

"Don't screw with me. I don't need this shit right now."

"Exactly," Stone said in a tight voice. "You don't need stupid wisecracks from me; you need a plan to get you out of Bagger's gunsights. And then you need to execute on that plan."

"And you think you can do that?"

"I used to do it for a living. And I'm sure Jerry Bagger is one bad SOB, but my old playground wasn't exactly Disneyland." There was silence on the phone. Stone thought she had hung up.

"Annabelle?"

"He killed my mother. There, now you know."

"What'd your mother do to Bagger?"

"Nothing. It was my father, Paddy. He ripped Jerry off for ten thousand bucks and it cost my mother her life."

"Did he kill your father too?"

"No, somehow my old man slipped away and forgot to tell my mother that homicidal Bagger was coming to town."

Stone let out a long breath. "That's a lot of baggage to have to carry around. I'm sorry, Annabelle."

"I don't need sympathy, Oliver. I just need a way to take this animal down once and for all, because, to tell the truth, stealing forty million bucks from him didn't even come close to squaring things with that bastard."

"Tell me exactly where you are. I can be there tonight."

"How are you going to get here? Fly?"

"I don't have the money to fly."

"I can get you the plane ticket."

"Unfortunately, I don't have any ID, and without that I can't get on an aircraft."

"I wish you'd told me, I could get you stuff so

good the FBI couldn't spot it as fake, much less TSA grunts."

"I may take you up on that one day. For now, I'm driving."

She told him where she was. "You're sure about this? You can still walk, no questions asked. I'm used to going it alone."

"No friend of the Camel Club goes it alone. I'll see you in Maine, Annabelle."

24

Milton was standing behind some players at a blackjack table watching the action, his gaze roving like a laser beam over the cards coming out of the chute.

Reuben appeared beside him. "How's it going?"

Milton smiled. "This looks like fun."

"Well, it's our job to blend in, so play a few hands. Just don't lose your shirt. We need gas money to get back home."

Reuben strolled along, his gaze wandering here and there, looking for anything or anyone that might be useful. After being in combat in Vietnam he had toiled for years with the Defense Intelligence Agency, or DIA, the military equivalent of CIA. Though he'd been out of the game for a long time now, it wasn't hard to remember how to do it well. And for Reuben, that meant heading to a bar for a drink.

He parked his butt on a stool and ordered a gin and tonic, checked his watch and ran his gaze over the bartender, an attractive middle-aged woman but with the pasty, beaten-down look of someone who'd spent too many years on the casino clock and under casino lights.

"So what action looks good these days?" he asked her as he munched on peanuts and idly sipped his cocktail.

She wiped the bar with a rag and said, "Depends on what you're looking for."

"Something besides slots and dice and other things that cost money."

"Then you came to the wrong place."

He laughed. "Story of my life. I'm Roy." He put out a hand.

She shook it. "Angie. Where you from?"

"Someplace a little south of here. You a native?"

"I started life in Minnesota, if you can believe that. Been here long enough I guess I qualify for native status. Once the casinos moved in how many people can say they're from Atlantic City? I mean, it's a place you go to, not come from, at least not anymore."

Reuben raised his glass. "I toast your eloquence." He stared around at the expensively decorated interior. "Must be some big-ass corporation that owns this place. It makes the Bellagio or Mandalay Bay look cheap."

Angie shook her head. "No corporation. One man."

"Get out of here, Angie. I thought all casinos were run by fat-cat companies."

"Not this one. It's owned by Jerry Bagger."

"Bagger? Name sounds familiar."

"He's pretty memorable. You meet him once, you don't forget it."

"From the way you say it I take it he's not your basic, loving humanitarian."

"You don't build a place like this being a human anything." She suddenly eyed Reuben with suspicion. "This isn't some trick, is it? You don't work for Mr. Bagger, do you? I'm not saying anything against him. He's a good boss."

"Angie, relax. I am what I look like, a poor sucker from out of town who blew his wad early at craps and decided to spend his last evening here having some real fun before hitting the road with my tail tucked between my legs." He looked behind him. "But thanks for the info. I don't want to run into this guy and say something I shouldn't. He sounds pretty tough."

"Not to worry, he's out of town. Saw him leave with his boys yesterday."

"Oh, he travels a lot?"

"Not really, even though he has his own jet."

"Then he's probably going to Vegas to check out the competition."

"He was run out of Vegas a long time ago. I actually know where he went, because my best girlfriend is dating Mr. Bagger's pilot."

"So where's the big honcho off to, then?" Reuben said in a bored tone as he swallowed a handful of nuts.

"Washington, D.C."

Reuben gagged so badly Angie had to pound him on the back.

Recovered, he said, "Damn reflux. It's closed my throat down to almost nothing."

"Jeez, you gave me a scare. Never had anyone die on me yet, though." She looked around and lowered her voice. "Can't say the same about everybody else in this place."

Reuben said slowly, "You have somebody kick the bucket here recently?"

"Let's just say we had a couple top-level employees in the hospital. We were told they had the flu. I got a friend who works over at the hospital they were taken to. Since when does the flu cause cuts and bruises? Tell me that."

"But they're still alive."

"They are, but we had another guy here, a computer whiz type. He disappeared. They said he left to take another job. Well, he didn't tell his family and he forgot to clean out his apartment."

"Damn, what could have happened to him?"

Angie eyed Reuben's big frame appreciatively. "I get off work at nine, Roy. You buy me dinner and I'll tell you some more. Okay?"

After he left the bar Reuben called Stone on his cell phone and told him about Bagger being in D.C.

"Good work, Reuben," Stone said. "I'm on my way to see Susan now."

"I thought you said she was gone."

"Let's just say I convinced her to give us another chance. You didn't find out why Bagger's in Washington?"

"Figured I'd try and get that out of her tonight. Didn't want to push too hard. You know what I mean?"

"Absolutely. Keep me informed."

"And tell Susan I still want a date."

25

Reuben continued walking around the casino, trying to memorize as many key details as he could. He didn't know exactly what sort of intelligence Stone wanted so he decided to be over- rather than under-inclusive. In any event it beat the hell out of working on the loading dock.

He finally decided to hook back up with Milton at the blackjack table. When he got there his jaw dropped. Milton had huge columns of chips stacked neatly in front of him.

Reuben said, "Milton, what the hell happened?"

"What happened," the bettor next to Milton said, "is that your buddy's up about four thousand bucks."

Reuben stared at the man and then at the beefy pit boss glaring at Milton and his winnings.

"Holy hell, Batman," Reuben exclaimed. "Four grand!"

The pit boss leaned down into Milton's face. "You're cheating."

"No I'm not," Milton said indignantly.

"You're counting cards, you little slimeball. Is that

how you get your kicks? What, the ladies a problem for you? You have to come here and cheat? And then you go home and jack off. Is that it?"

Milton flushed red. "This is the first time I've ever been in a casino."

The pit boss roared, "Do you really think I'm buying that bullshit?"

Reuben said politely, "Look, I'm sure it's nothing really—"

Milton cut in. "And so what if I am counting cards? Is that illegal in New Jersey? I don't think so, because I looked it up. And you can employ countermeasures against me, but only if I'm a 'skilled player,' which I'm not, and by law the countermeasures you can use are limited. Now, in Vegas you can claim I'm trespassing, read me the Trespass Act and ban me from the casinos for a year, but this isn't Vegas, now is it?"

"You know all this stuff and you say this is the first time you've been in a casino," the pit boss scoffed.

"I looked all that up last night online. Gee, what a concept. So back off and let me play my cards."

The thick-necked boss looked like he was going to come over the table at Milton, but Reuben stepped between them. "I think my friend will cash out now."

"But Reuben," Milton protested. "I'm on a roll."

"He'll cash out now," Reuben said very firmly.

Later, Milton said to Reuben, "Why wouldn't you let me keep playing?"

"How about that whole living thing, Milton, you still interested in that?"

"Oh come on, this is the twenty-first century. They don't do that stuff anymore."

"You think so? Forget the laws, a casino can pretty much kick you out for any reason they want. You're lucky the pit boss was probably slow to get to the table. Dollars to donuts we gotta couple goons tailing us right now."

Milton whipped his head around. "Where?"

"You can't see them!" Reuben paused. "So how'd you win all that money?"

Milton said in a low voice, "I started out employing a multilevel Hi-Lo scheme with a side count add-on based on the Zen Count system. Of course I was utilizing an overall true count methodology to take into account the multiple decks being played. Later, I took it up a peg to the Uston Advanced Point Count method and paid particular attention to strategically optimizing my bets using the three-color chip scenario to disguise my wager."

Reuben gaped. "Milton, how the hell do you know all this stuff?"

"I read twelve Internet articles on the subject last night. It was very interesting. And once I read something—"

"You never forget it, I know, I know." Reuben sighed. There seemed no limit to his friend's intellectual gifts. "So the pit boss was right, you were counting cards. Luckily you were doing it without a computer, that's a big no-no."

"I've got a computer, it's called my brain."

"Okay, Mr. Brain, just so you know, it's a rule on recon missions that the team splits everything right down the middle."

"Down the middle?"

"Yep. So I'm two grand ahead. Now fork it over."

Milton handed over the cash. "Remember, you have to pay taxes on that."

"I don't pay taxes."

"Reuben, you have to pay your taxes."

"Uncle Sam can get his pound of flesh off somebody else. And while you were cleaning out the casino I was doing some real intelligence gathering." He told Milton about Angie.

"That's sounds really promising, Reuben, good work."

"The way Angie was eyeballing me, the price might be pretty damn steep."

"Well, that shouldn't be a problem, you've got two thousand dollars."

Reuben gazed at his friend and just shook his head.

26

Carter Gray walked slowly down the long corridor that was for some reason painted a salmon color, perhaps to induce calmness, he thought. However, this was not a building that inspired calm, only crisis. At the end of the underground hall was a solitary room housed behind a bank-vault-class door. He entered his security codes and let the biometric readers sweep over him. The door noiselessly swung open. This James Bond style of security had set the taxpayers back millions. Yet what else were taxpayers good for, he thought. They consumed far too much, paid too much in taxes and their government spent far more than it should, usually on stupid things. If that wasn't balance, he didn't know what was.

Gray walked over to the wall of locked miniature vaults and slid his electronic key in one while he simultaneously rubbed his thumb across a fingerprint reader. The door slid open and he took the file out, sat down in a chair and began to read.

A half hour later Gray had finished perusing the file. Next, he took out the photo he'd received in the mail, comparing it with the one in the file. It was the same man, of course. He'd known him very well. In many ways he'd been Gray's closest confidant. For decades he'd feared that the unfortunate matter of Rayfield Solomon would come back to haunt him. Now it had.

Cole, Cincetti, Bingham, all dead. And Carter Gray had almost joined them. And he would have except for the safe room built underneath the house by the former CIA director and VP who had lived there before him; an underground room that was both fire- and bombproof. When Gray had explained to Oliver Stone that he was both comfortable and *secure* in his new home, he was being quite literal. And his home included a fortified tunnel that had carried him safely off the property and to the other side of the main road, where a car driven by one of his guards had picked him up. Gray had been gone from the house for over an hour when it exploded. He'd left minutes after receiving the photo. Still, it had been a relatively close call. The FBI had initiated a homicide investigation, publicly acknowledging that a body had been found in the wreckage. Gray had put this in motion behind the scenes. He *wanted* people to think he was dead.

He would've been dead except for the fact that his would-be killer had sent him this photo. What a risk that had been. What a tactical error. And yet it must have been important for the person that Gray clearly understood why he was being killed; that fortunately revealed much about his potential murderer. It was undoubtedly someone who cared very much about Rayfield Solomon. And for Gray, that evidenced a familial relationship or something close to it.

The other targets were now obvious, Gray mused as he sat in his chair a hundred feet underneath the headquarters of the CIA in Langley, Virginia, a juggernaut he had once commanded. Only the current and former directors of the CIA were allowed in this room. Here there were files that contained secrets the American public would never know. Indeed, there were stories here of which American presidents were ignorant. When one said "files," of course, one meant more than mere paper. It included flesh and blood. Certainly that had been the case with Ray Solomon. Gray hadn't known about the order to kill Solomon. If he had he would've prevented it from being executed. He had regretted his friend's death all these years. Yet in this case regret was a very cheap emotion to have. You felt bad, but the other person was dead.

Gray put the files back and locked the vault. There were many important folks who would not want the matter of Ray Solomon ever to resurface. They would use all their resources to hunt down whoever tried to kill Gray before the person struck again. And now Gray was fully on their side. His friend had been dead for decades. No good could come from rekindling those fires.

And he had played fair by warning John Carr. The man would get no more help from him. And if he died, he died.

27

As Jerry Bagger was being driven through Washington he passed by the Justice Department building. On noticing this, he immediately gave the finger to the entire federal agency.

"Talk about a great place for a nuclear strike. And maybe they could take out the FBI at the same time. I mean lawyers and cops, who needs 'em? Not me." He looked at one of his men. "Mike, you need 'em?"

"No, sir, Mr. Bagger."

"Good thinking."

Bagger had received a more detailed report from his PI after arriving in D.C.; that's why he was now climbing out of the car and walking into a library. It wasn't any library; it was, for many erudite folks, *the* library: the Library of Congress.

His men made some inquiries, and two minutes later Bagger and his entourage walked into the rare book reading room where the late Jonathan DeHaven, who was also Annabelle's ex-husband, had once been director. It was also where Caleb Shaw currently worked. The man himself came out of the vaults as Bagger walked in.

To his credit Caleb did not start vomiting on recognizing Bagger from the picture Milton had shown him, although his gurgling stomach made that a clear possibility. Instead, he simply stood there as a smile spread across his face. He had no idea why he was smiling. With a sudden pang of horror he thought it might actually be a first step in his becoming hysterical. He had to do something and fast.

"Can I help you?" he said, walking over to the group of big young men in dark suits surrounding the very fit, sixty-six-year-old, broad-shouldered, white-haired and deeply tanned Bagger, with his broken nose and hideous scar running down one cheek.

He looked like a pirate, Caleb thought.

"I hope so," Bagger began politely. "This is the rare book thing here?" He looked around.

"The rare book reading room, yes."

"So how rare are the books in this place?"

"Very, and it's not just books, we have codex manuscripts, incunabula, broadsheets, a Gutenberg Bible, a copy of the Declaration of Independence, Jefferson's personal library and many other fine works. Some of them the only one of their kind in the world. Literally one of one."

"Yeah?" Bagger said, clearly not impressed. "Well, I got something even rarer than that."

"Really, what is it?" Caleb inquired.

"The book that *I* read," Bagger said. "Because that's zero of zero." He laughed and so did his men. Caleb chuckled politely even as he clutched the back of a chair to steady himself.

Bagger put an arm around Caleb's shoulders. "You look like a guy who can help me. What's your name?"

Caleb desperately tried to think of an alias, but all that came out was, "Caleb Shaw."

"Caleb? Whoa, you don't hear that one every day. You Amish or something?"

"No, I'm a Republican," Caleb said in a small voice as Bagger's muscular arm cinched tighter around him. *Is this the same arm that killed all those people?*

"Okay, Mr. Republican, is there someplace we can talk in private? I mean, this is a big building. Must be someplace we can do a little mano a mano."

Caleb had feared something like this. At least in the reading room there were potential witnesses around, if only to see him being hacked to death by the mobster.

"I, uh, I'm quite busy right now." Bagger's arm instantly tightened even more around him. "But I can certainly spare you a few minutes."

Caleb led them to a small office down the hall from the reading room.

"Sit," Bagger ordered Caleb, and he quickly sat in the only chair in the room. "Okay, now, I understand that the guy who used to run this place got whacked."

"The director of the Rare Book and Special Collections Division was killed, that's correct."

"Jonathan DeHaven?"

"That's right." Caleb added in a low voice, "He was murdered. Right in this very building."

"Wow," Bagger said as he eyed his men. "In a freaking library. I mean, is this world we live in violent or what?" He turned back to Caleb. "Thing is, I got a friend who knew this DeHaven character. She was actually married to him at some point."

"Really? I never knew Jonathan was married." Caleb managed to tell this lie quite capably.

"Well he was. Kind of short-lived, though. I mean he was a book geek. No offense. And the woman, well, the woman wasn't. She was sort of like a, how do you say—"

"A tornado and a hurricane all wrapped into one?" Caleb offered.

Bagger shot him a suspicious glance. "Yeah, what makes you say that?"

Realizing he had come dangerously close to giving Bagger adequate reason to torture him for further information, Caleb said smoothly, "I was married once too, and my wife left me after only four months. She was a hurricane and a tornado and, like you said, I'm a book geek." It was stunning how easily lying came to him.

"Right, right, you get the picture. Anyway, I haven't seen the woman in a long time and wanted to catch up with her. So it occurred to me that she might have heard about her ex's death and come for the funeral." He looked expectantly at Caleb.

"Well, I went to the service but I didn't notice anyone I didn't know. What does this woman look like and what's her name?"

"Tall, nice curves, a real looker. Little scar under her right eye. Hair color and style depends on the day of the week, you know what I mean? Her name is Annabelle Conroy, but that also depends on the day of the week."

"Doesn't ring a bell at all." The name clearly didn't, since Caleb only knew Annabelle by the name Susan Hunter, but the physical description was certainly dead-on. "I'm sure I would have noticed someone like that. Most of the people at the funeral were pretty average-looking. You know, like me."

"Yeah, I bet," Bagger grumbled. He snapped his fingers and one of his men produced a card that Bagger handed to Caleb. "You remember something useful, call me. I pay well. I mean really well. Five figures."

Caleb's eyes widened as he clutched the card. "You must really want to find her."

"Oh, you got no idea how bad, Mr. Republican."

28

Harry Finn quietly entered the room, sat down in the chair and stared at her. The woman looked back at him, or through him, Finn was never sure. She had once spoken fluent English without a trace of any accent. But the multilingual lady had, perhaps out of growing paranoia, decided to mash four languages into one, creating a confusing amalgam of chaotic communication. He didn't quite know how, but Finn managed to understand it. She would have accepted nothing less from him.

She muttered in his direction and he answered her blunt greeting in a few words. This seemed to please her, because she nodded appreciatively, a smile edging across her fallen cheeks. Actually she had known that he was here before Finn had even entered the room. She had explained this before as having felt his *presence*. He had a particular aura, she'd told him; a pleasant one, but distinctive. As a man who did not like to leave any trace of himself anywhere, this bothered Finn greatly. Yet how did one wipe away his aura?

As a child he remembered his mother's tall, strong

body with the hands of a pianist. Now she was shrunken, withered. He studied her face. It had once held a rare, fragile beauty, a loveliness that growing up he had always associated with the most beautiful of daylilies. This was because when he was a child, at night, the beauty receded and she became moody and sometimes violent; never against him, but against herself. And then Finn would have to step in and take charge. As early as age seven he had done this. The experience had made him grow up quickly, faster than he should have. Now the beauty was gone from her face, the body collapsed, the once lovely hands scarred and wrinkled in her lap. She was only in her early seventies and yet looked more than ready for the grave.

But she still could dominate him with her indignation, with her demand that a wrong be righted. Despite her physical disintegration her words had retained the power to make him feel the grief, the injustice she'd endured.

"I have heard the news," she said in her strange talk. "It is done and it is good. You are good."

He stood and looked out the window at the grounds of this place that he thought they still called a sanatorium. Stacked neatly on the windowsill were the four newspapers that she read every day, cover to cover, word for word. When the papers were done she listened to the radio, or watched the TV, until she fell asleep late at night. The morning would bring more news that she would devour. There was nothing in the world that she seemed to miss.

"And now you move on to the next," she said, in a higher voice as though she feared her words might not reach him from across the room.

He nodded and said, "Yes."

"You are a good *son*."

Harry resumed his seat. "How's your health?"

"What health?" she said, smiling and swaying her head. She had always done that, he remembered. Always, as though she heard a song no one else did. As a child he had loved that about her, that mysterious quality all children sought out in their parents. Now he didn't like it as much.

"I have no health. You know what they did to me. You cannot believe this is natural. I am not that old. I sit here and I rot a little more each day."

They had poisoned her, years ago, she had told him. They had gotten to her somehow, she wasn't quite sure how. The poison was meant to kill, but she had survived it. Yet it was eating away at her, from the inside out, laying claim to organs one by one until there would be none left. She probably believed that one day she would simply vanish from the earth.

"You can leave. You're not like the others here."

"And where would I go, tell me that? Where would I go? I am safe here. So here I will stay until they take me away in the bag and burn me. Those are my wishes."

Finn held up his hands in mock surrender. They had this same discussion during each of his visits, with the same result. She was rotting and afraid and here she would die. He could have articulated both parts of this conversation, so well did he know them.

"And how is your wife, and those beautiful children?"

"They're fine. I'm sure they miss seeing you."

"There's not much left to see. Your little one, Susie. She still has the bear I gave her?"

"It's her favorite. She's never without it."

"You tell her never to let it go. It represents my love for her. She must never let it go. I have not been a proper grandmother to them. I know this. But it would kill me if she ever let go of the bear. Kill me."

"I know. And she knows. Like I said, she loves it."

She rose on shaky legs, went to a drawer and pulled out a photo. In twisted fingers she clutched the item before handing it across to him. "Take it," she said. "You've earned it."

He slipped the photograph out of her hands and held it up. It was the same picture that Judd Bingham, Bob Cole and Lou Cincetti had seen before they died. Carter Gray, too, had gazed on this image before he was blown to the next world.

Finn traced the delicate line of Rayfield Solomon's cheek with his index finger. In a flash the past came racing back to him: the separation, the news of his father's death, the erasing of the past and meticulous creation of a new one, and over the years the devastating revelations of a wife and mother telling her son what had happened.

"And now Roger Simpson," she said.

"Yes. The last one," Finn replied, a hint of relief in his voice.

It had taken him years to track down Bingham, Cincetti and Cole. Yet he had finally located all of them, and that's when the killing had started a few months ago. He had known the whereabouts of Gray and Senator Roger Simpson since they were public figures. But they were also harder targets. He had gone for the points of least resistance first. It made it more likely that Gray and Simpson would be forewarned, but he had built that into his equation. And when Gray had left the government, he had also left most of his protection behind. And even forewarned, Finn had managed to kill him. Simpson was next in line. Senators had protection too, but Finn was confident he would eventually get to the man.

When Finn looked on the life he had now as part of a family of five in a quite ordinary Virginia suburb complete with a lovable dog, music lessons, soccer matches, baseball games and swim meets, and compared it to the life he had as a child, the juxtaposition was close to apocalyptic in its effect on him. That's why he rarely thought of these things together. That's why he was Harry Finn, King of Compartmentalization. He could build walls in his mind nothing could pierce.

Then his mother said, "Let me tell you a story, Harry."

He sat back in his chair and listened, though he had heard it all before—in fact, could have told it as well as she could now. And yet he listened as she spoke in her fractured, discordant collage of words that still managed to radiate a visceral power; her memories carved out an eloquent factual case that only truth could arouse. It was both wonderful and terrifying—her ability to conjure a world from decades ago with such force that it appeared to be occupying the room they were in with the agonized heartbreak surrounding a flaming pyre. And when she was finished and her energy spent, he would kiss her goodbye and continue his journey, a journey he carried on for her. And maybe for him too.

29

"Calm down, Caleb," Stone said. "And tell me exactly what happened." Stone had pulled off the road on the way to Maine when he'd received Caleb's frantic call. He listened for ten minutes to his friend's breathless recounting of his face-to-face with Jerry Bagger.

"Caleb, are you sure he didn't know you were lying? Really sure?"

"I was good, Oliver, you would've been proud of me. He gave me his card. Said to call if I had any other information. He offered to pay five figures." Caleb paused. "And I found out her real name is Annabelle Conroy."

"Don't tell that to anyone!"

"What do you want me to do now?"

"Nothing. Do not contact Bagger. I'll give you a call later."

Stone clicked off and then phoned Reuben in Atlantic City, relaying what Caleb had told him. "Well, your information was correct, Reuben, Bagger *is* in D.C."

"Hopefully this Angie gal will be even more

informative tonight. By the way, where are you, Oliver?"

"I'm on my way to Maine."

"Maine? Is that where she is?"

"Yes."

"Why Maine?"

"Let's just say our friend has some unfinished business up there."

"Having to do with this Bagger dude?"

"Yes."

Stone put his phone down and continued driving. Caleb's car, though old and rotting, had performed well enough, though on no occasion had he been able to coax it past sixty. Hours later, the night well established, Stone crossed from New Hampshire into Maine. Checking his map, he exited off the interstate and headed east, toward the Atlantic Ocean. Twenty minutes later he slowed and drove through the downtown area of the place Annabelle was staying. It was quaint and filled with shops offering everything from touristy items to nautical gear, as many coastal New England towns did. This was the off-season though, and most of the visitors were long gone, having no desire to expose themselves to the coming Maine winter.

Stone found the B&B where Annabelle was staying, parked in the small lot, grabbed his duffel bag and went in.

She was waiting in the parlor for him, standing in

front of the fire that flickered pleasantly behind her. The floors and doors here creaked; the smell was of a recently served dinner mixed with the aroma of centuries-old wood and the heavy bite of the ocean's salt air.

"I got the owner to save us some supper," Annabelle said. They ate in the small dining room, and a hungry Stone wolfed down the chowder, thick buttered bread and crispy cod while Annabelle merely picked at hers.

Finished, he said, "Where can we talk?"

"I got you a room next to mine."

"Um, I'm a bit short of funds right now."

"Oliver, don't even go there. Come on."

She got a carafe of coffee and two cups from the kitchen and led him upstairs, first to his room to drop off his small bag and then to hers, which had a tiny sitting room off the bedroom. There was also a fire crackling in the fireplace. They sat and drank the hot coffee.

Annabelle reached in her bag, pulled out an ID, a credit card and a wad of cash and tossed them to Stone. The ID had his picture on it and other pertinent information making him a citizen of the District of Columbia.

"Quick job from a guy I found. I used a picture of you I had with me. The credit card's legit."

"Thank you. But why'd you do it?"

"Again, don't go there."

Annabelle just stared into the flames while Stone studied her, debating whether to tell her or not.

"Annabelle, put your cup down."

"What?"

"I have something to tell you and I don't want you to spill hot coffee."

A rare look of fear crossed her features as she slowly put down the cup. "Reuben? Milton? Dammit, I told you not to send them to Atlantic City!"

"They're fine. This has to do with Caleb and he's fine too. But he had an unexpected visitor today at the library."

Annabelle seemed to stare right through him as she said, "Jerry?"

Stone nodded. "Caleb apparently played his part well. Bagger offered a lot of money for information on you."

"How did he know to come to the library?"

"He found out you were married to DeHaven. It was a public record and these days that information is easily available on the Internet if you know where to look."

Annabelle slumped back against the small sofa. "I should have just followed my damn exit plan. God, I'm so stupid."

"No, you're human. You came to pay your respects to a man you were married to and cared for. It's normal."

"Not when you've ripped off a homicidal nutcase

like Jerry Bagger for forty million bucks it's not. Then it's just stupid," she added bitterly.

"Okay, but you didn't go to your island, your partner screwed up and Bagger is on your tail and he's narrowed the gap decisively. Those are the facts we have to deal with. You can't run now, because no matter how well you run, you will leave some sort of trail. And he's too close to miss it. If you go to your island, all that guarantees is that when Bagger shows up at your door, you'll be all alone when he kills you."

"Thanks, Oliver. That really makes me feel better."

"It should. Because here you have people willing to risk their lives to help you!"

Her expression softened. "I know that. I didn't mean what it sounded like."

Stone looked toward the window. "This is quite the sleepy town. It's hard to believe someone could be murdered here. Where did it happen?"

"Right on the outskirts. I was planning to go there tomorrow morning."

"Do you want to talk about it tonight?"

"You had a long drive and you must be tired. And, no, I don't want to talk about it tonight. If I'm going to face this tomorrow I need to get some sleep. Good night."

Stone watched her bedroom door close, then he rose and headed to his room, unsure of what the morning would bring.

30

Reuben dropped over a hundred bucks for drinks and dinner with Angie, but he figured it was a good return on his investment for he learned some interesting things. The two guys who'd ended up in the hospital and the one who'd disappeared completely had evidently displeased their boss, Jerry Bagger. How, Angie was not quite sure, but it seemed to come down to money. Unfortunately, Angie didn't know why Bagger had gone to Washington, only that it had happened all of a sudden.

I bet, thought Reuben.

Over her third "Dark and Stormy," a rum and ginger beer concoction that Reuben tried a sip of and almost retched as a result, Angie said, "Funny stuff going on around here lately. Got a buddy in finance for the casino. He told me he was under strict instructions to do everything he could to delay a routine Control Commission inspection of the casino's books."

"This Bagger guy in money trouble?"

She shook her head. "Don't see how. The Pompeii

Casino is like the Bureau of Engraving and Printing. It's a gold mine, and Mr. Bagger is the smartest operator in town. Tough with a nickel, and he knows how to make a buck."

"Something must have happened, then," Reuben said. "Maybe the guys who got hurt and the one who disappeared screwed up somehow with some of the casino's cash. Maybe they were ripping him off, and Bagger found out and brought the hammer down."

"Mr. Bagger ain't dumb. You don't break knees anymore; you just sic the cops or lawyers on cheaters. So this must've been something really big, and he took it personally."

"Cops looking into it?"

She looked incredulous. "Mr. Bagger knows what palms to grease. And do you know how much tax revenue the Pompeii generates for New Jersey?"

Reuben nodded thoughtfully. "He probably paid off the pair in the hospital. And the other guy's not gonna be squealing to the police."

"Dead men don't talk, you're right." Angie had scooted closer to Reuben in the booth they were sharing. She patted his thigh with her hand and then kept it there. "So enough shop talk, tell me about yourself. Did you use to play pro football? You look big enough." She squeezed his leg and leaned into him.

"Played some in college. Did a couple tours in Nam. Won some medals, collected some shrapnel."

"Really? Where? Here?" She playfully poked a finger into his chest.

"Let's just say I won't be having any more children." Reuben couldn't believe he was telling this lie to a woman who obviously wanted to go to bed with him, but he had other things on his mind.

Angie's jaw fell so far, it was in jeopardy of smacking the table.

"Check, please," Reuben called out to the waiter as he passed by.

31

While Reuben was disappointing Angie, Milton was trying out a system he'd read about for the craps table. So far he wasn't doing as well as he'd hoped. Granted, he had gone up eight thousand dollars fairly early on in his run; however, he had higher standards than most people. Still, fellow gamblers were lined up around the rail, telling him he was hot, he was on fire. Over two dozen players were riding bets on his coattails desperately hoping he would lead them all to riches, or at least allow them to recoup some of the cash they'd lost thus far to Jerry Bagger.

Women with their boobs falling out of their halter tops and sipping cocktails crowded around him, pushing their bosoms into his shoulders and splashing liquor on his shirt. They also pestered him with silly questions as to his technique. Milton didn't know they were casino ringers whose job it was to break the concentration and hopefully the streak of any hot roller. Yet it didn't matter. It would take far more than multiple pairs of inflatable breasts and inane queries to interfere with Milton Farb's focus.

The two croupiers and the stickman running the table scrutinized the action, accounting for bets and keeping an eye on all that was going on, including those hovering around the rails and players looking to get in on the action. At this point there was little room at the rail, but if someone caught the eye of one of the croupiers and flashed enough chips, he might get in. And this was a table everyone wanted to join.

The stone-faced pit boss hovered in the back taking this all in too. He was the court of last resort in case there were any problems, and it was his job to see to the casino's well-being at all times while putting on a front of being fair to players. The casino world was not a touchy-feely one; there was only one god here and his name was money. And at the end of the day the casino had to keep more of it than it paid out. Yet this pit boss was worried, because he'd been doing this long enough to know a truly hot shooter when he saw one. The Pompeii was going to take one on the chin; he just had a bad feeling.

The table had a $50 minimum bet and a ten grand maximum, and Milton was laying his bets with surgical precision. He'd long since figured out all the statistical probabilities and was putting that knowledge to good use. He'd rolled a seven on his very first throw, the only time that number could be a winner. He'd won $500 on that fling of the dice with an aggressive initial bet and never looked back. He was leveraging his behind-the-pass-line bets, maxing out the fives, sixes and eights up top, then the nines and fives and the most lucrative, but least likely odds-wise, tens and fours, with the finesse of a decades-long craps impresario. He'd nailed a hard four twice and hit a hard eight and ten once each. He'd rolled his points six times now and the heat just kept building.

Finally, the nervous pit boss ordered a change in the table crew. The croupiers and the stickman were more than a little upset about this and their sour expressions showed it. Tips were laid on the house at the end of a shooter's run, so these folks wouldn't be seeing a dime of Milton's winnings. Yet the pit boss's command was law. He'd done it to cool down Milton and the table. But such a move, while allowable under the gaming rules, was always unpopular, and howls of protest erupted from around the rail.

Two security gents drifted over to the table after receiving a call from the pit boss over his headset. After seeing the hulking figures approach, the crowd quickly calmed down.

The pit boss' ploy didn't work because Milton hit his points three more times over an array of intricate bets. He was now up over twenty-five grand. Unless he rolled the dice off the table, the croupier couldn't change them on him, so the nervous pit boss really had few tricks left to pull. He just stood and watched as Milton continued to mow down the Pompeii Casino.

A stunned quiet hit the table when Milton laid

$500 down on a one-time horn bet that he would roll a three. When the one-two combo flashed up the bet paid off with fifteen-to-one odds, turning his $500 into $7,500. He was now up $35,000.

The sweating pit boss was forced to play his final card, subtly nodding his head at a ringer stationed at the table. The man immediately laid down a bet on number seven. This, in effect, was betting against Milton, for if he rolled a seven now, or craps, he was done as shooter and all bets on the table lost. In the gambling world it was generally believed that betting against the shooter generated bad karma, siphoning the energy off the table and causing the shooter to lose his steam. The crowd immediately started growling at the ringer betting craps. One man at the rail even bumped him, but the security stepped in and quelled this mini-riot.

Milton was unfazed by the casino's obvious move to derail him. With the stunned crowd looking on, he calmly laid a thousand dollars' worth of chips on boxcars, or the combination of six and six. This, along with betting snake eyes, was the most aggressive move one could make on a craps table, for it paid off thirty-to-one. However, because it was a one-time bet only, if he didn't roll double sixes on the next throw, Milton lost the cash. Thus, betting a thousand bucks on boxcars was considered insane.

Absolute silence prevailed at the table. There wasn't one square inch of free space at the rail and the onlookers were packed six deep behind the players, straining to see the action. Nothing spread faster through a casino than word of a craps shooter on absolute fire.

Milton glanced over at the pit boss and said, "Do you feel lucky? Because I do."

Before the stunned man could reply Milton let the dice fly. The two cubes rolled down the felt, neatly missing all stacked chips on the table and bouncing off the far rail.

There was a moment of intense calm and then a collective scream audible around the casino erupted as the double sixes came to rest face up. Milton Farb had just won thirty grand and nearly doubled his take to $65,000. The guy beside him was whooping and pounding him on the back. The next words out of Milton's mouth caused the cheers to be replaced with groans of disbelief.

"I'm cashing out," he said to his croupier.

The sea of faces around the rail would have looked far more appropriate at a funeral or plane crash site.

"Let it ride," one man screamed. "You are smoking hot. Let it ride."

"This is paying off my kids' college tuition," yelled another.

Milton said, "I'm smarter than I am lucky. I know when to stop."

This bit of truth never goes over well in a casino.

"Screw you," a big man exclaimed as he strode up

to Milton and put a meaty paw on his shoulder. “You keep rolling that dice, you hear me, you little prick? I’ve been losing all night until you came along. Keep rolling, you hear me!”

“He heard you,” a voice said as a far bigger hand was placed on the man’s shoulder, jerking him backward.

“What the hell,” the man spat out, whirling around with fists balled. He stared up into the face of the towering Reuben Rhodes, who snatched the stick off the table and held it up.

Reuben said, “The man’s done playing, so I suggest you let him collect his chips and go on his way, before I take this stick and ram it right up your fat ass.”

32

Later, over a drink in a bar, Reuben scolded Milton. "Dammit, first blackjack and now craps. I told you to blend in, Milton, not stick out. You're making our job a lot harder by turning into a casino shark."

Milton looked chastened. "I'm sorry, Reuben, you're right, of course. I guess I got carried away. It won't happen again."

"And exactly how are you going to get your cash without revealing who you are? When you win big in a casino you have to fill out tax paperwork with your name, address and Social Security number. You want Bagger to have that info?"

"I read about that requirement, Reuben. I'm going to use a fake ID. They won't know the difference."

"What if they run the ID from here on some database?"

"My ID shows me to be a citizen of Great Britain; the U.S. has no taxing authority over me. And I highly doubt the casino is linked to any database in England."

Sufficiently mollified, Reuben explained to Milton what he had learned from Angie.

"So if we can pin those crimes on Bagger, Susan will be home free," Milton said.

"Easier said than done. A guy like Bagger knows how to cover his tracks."

"Well, maybe I can start uncovering them."

"How?"

"Oliver told us about this Anthony Wallace. Bagger found out about him and nearly killed him. Well, *how* did he find out about him?"

"I don't know."

"I know it's late but call Oliver and Susan. Ask her for any information about Wallace that she can think of. Where he was staying, doing, that sort of thing."

Reuben made the call and then turned back to his friend.

"Oliver woke her up and asked her. Wallace was staying in the hotel right across the street from the Pompeii. He was using an alias, Robby Thomas, from Michigan. Five-eight, slender, dark hair, a real cute-boy type. He was staying in a room with a direct sight line onto Bagger's office."

"That's what I needed to know." Milton rose.

"Where are you going?" Reuben asked.

"Across the street. Because the probabilities are that Bagger figured out Wallace was spying on him. If so, he'd want to check it out. So that's what I'm going to do."

"How?"

"I haven't been hanging around Susan for nothing. Sit tight."

Milton's nimble mind worked out the details on the way across the street.

At the front desk of the hotel he said, "I'm looking for a Mr. Robert Thomas. He goes by Robby. He's supposed to be staying at this hotel. Could you ring his room for me?"

After a quick check on the computer the clerk shook his head. "We don't have a guest by that name."

Milton displayed a confused look. "That's very odd. He and my son went to Michigan together. We were supposed to have dinner together."

"I'm sorry, sir."

"Could I have gotten the date wrong? My secretary made the arrangements and she's been known to mess up in the past. I'd feel just terrible if I stood him up."

The clerk clicked a few keys. "We did have a Robert Thomas from Michigan staying with us, but that was some time back."

"Oh my God, I am going to fire my secretary the minute I get back home. I wonder why Robby didn't call me."

"Who gave him your contact information?"

Milton let out a gasp. "My secretary! That idiot!

Wrong date, probably wrong phone number if she bothered to give him one at all."

The clerk gave him a sympathetic look.

"Well, I hope Robby had a good time while he was here."

The clerk glanced at the screen. "Records show he had a massage. So if you missed dinner with him, at least he was relaxed."

Milton laughed. "God, a massage, I haven't had one of those in years."

"We have a great staff."

"Do you have to be a guest here?"

"Oh no, I can make an appointment for you right now if you'd like."

"I tell you what, let me have the same masseuse Robby did. She and I can swap Robby stories. He's quite a character and I'm sure the masseuse will remember him."

The clerk smiled. "Right you are, sir. Let me make the call."

The clerk dialed the spa, spoke for a couple minutes and then his face clouded. "Oh, right, I didn't realize it was her. Okay, I'll get back to you." He hung up and turned to Milton.

"I'm afraid you can't have the same masseuse, sir."

"Oh, she no longer works here?"

"It's not that." The clerk dropped his voice. "She, well, she died."

"Oh my God. Accident?"

"I really can't say, sir."

"I completely understand. So sad. Was she young?"

"Yes. And Cindy was a really nice person."

"Well, that's just awful."

"Would you still like a massage with someone else? We actually have an opening for you now."

"Yes, yes, I believe I will. Cindy, you said her name was?"

"That's right. Cindy Johnson."

"I'll have to let Robby know."

An hour later Milton had received a vigorous massage by a very enthusiastic woman named Helen. However, when he casually raised the issue of Cindy's death, Helen became somber.

"It was awful. Here today, gone tomorrow sort of thing."

"Accident, I heard," Milton said as he sat in the lounge wrapped in a robe and sipping a cup of spring water.

Helen snorted. "Accident?"

"You don't think it was?"

"I'm not saying one way or another. None of my business really. But her poor mom's busted up over it, I can tell you that."

"Her mother? Poor woman? Did she have to come to town to ID the body?"

"What? No, Dolores lives right here. Works a craps table at the Pompeii."

"Well, goodness gracious, I was just there."

"Small world," Helen said.

"Poor Mrs. Johnson," Milton said. "To lose one's daughter like that."

"I know. And it's Mrs. Radnor now, she remarried. Cin liked her stepdad all right, so she said."

Milton finished his water. "Well, thank you for a great massage. I feel like a new man."

"Anytime, sir, anytime."

33

Once back at the Pompeii, Milton filled Reuben in on what he'd discovered.

His friend looked impressed. "Damn, Milton, Susan *has* rubbed off on you."

A few well-placed twenties later, the two men were directed to Dolores Radnor's craps table. Milton bet on a hot shooter while he sized up the woman. She was thin and wrinkle-faced with a perpetually sad air about her. An hour later she took a break and Milton followed her to a table outside the bar area where she sipped on a cup of coffee, an unlit cigarette dangling in her free hand.

Milton said, "Mrs. Radnor?"

Startled, the woman looked at him warily. "How do you know my name? Is there a problem?"

"This is very awkward," Milton began as Dolores looked at him expectantly. "I was in town a few months ago and your daughter gave me the best massage I ever had."

The woman's lips began to quiver. "My Cindy was

damn good at giving massages. She went to school for it, had a certificate and everything."

"I know, I know. She was great. And I promised her the next time I was in town I'd look her up. I was just over there and they told me what happened. And they were kind enough to give me your name and where you worked."

"Why did you want to know that?" she asked, though her look was now more sad than suspicious.

"She was so nice to me that I told Cindy that the next time I was in town I was going to place a bet for her on the craps table."

Dolores looked at him more closely. "Hey, aren't you the shooter who burned up Table No. 7? I popped over there on a break because people were all talking about it."

"I am the very one." He took out his wallet. "And I wanted to deliver Cindy's share to you."

"Sir, you don't have to do that."

"A promise is a promise." Milton handed her twenty one-hundred-dollar bills.

"Oh my God," Dolores said. She tried to give it back but Milton insisted until she put it away in her pocket.

"You coming over and giving me this money is the only good thing that's happened to me in a long time." She suddenly broke down in tears.

Milton handed her some napkins from the holder

on the table. She wiped her eyes and blew her nose. "Thank you," she said.

"Is there anything I can do to help, Mrs. Radnor?"

"You can just call me Dolores. And you just did something wonderful."

"Helen over at the spa told me she died in an accident. Was it a car accident?"

The woman's face hardened. "*Accidental* overdose, they said. That's crap. Cindy never took drugs in her life. And I'd know, because I did drugs, in my time. A druggie knows another druggie, and she wasn't one."

"So why did they think that's what killed her?"

"Stuff in her body. And a container of stuff by her bed, and bam, she's a crackhead. But I know my Cindy. She saw what the stuff did to me. I finally got myself straightened out, got a good job, and now this. Now my baby's gone." She started snuffling again.

"Again, I'm very sorry." Milton left and rejoined Reuben.

Milton said, "Okay, Cindy gives Tony Wallace a.k.a. Robby Thomas a massage. Wallace gets nearly beaten to death by Bagger. And Cindy dies of an accidental drug overdose even though it appears she didn't use drugs."

"Can't be a coincidence," Reuben said.

"The probabilities are Bagger had her killed. I can do some poking around on the Pompeii Web site. There might be a back door there I can exploit."

They walked off without noticing the man in the suit who'd been watching Milton talk to Dolores. He spoke into a walkie-talkie. "We might have a big problem. Get hold of Mr. Bagger."

34

It was a late-stage probe and penetration mission, which was the only reason Harry Finn was standing in a queue early in the morning after having flown in the night before from visiting his mother. While he listened to the man in the front of the group drone on, Finn's thoughts kept going back to his frail mother with the resolute spirit. The story she had told him, as she had hundreds of times before, concerned Rayfield Solomon, who was Harry Finn's father. Solomon had been a man of inexhaustible intellectual curiosity and possessed an unassailable integrity. He had labored on behalf of his country for decades, building a reputation as not only a true patriot but a man who could fix things with his ideas, who could see the answer when no one else could. Then, later in life, he'd fallen in love with Harry Finn's mother and married her. Finn was born and then things began to change, or, more accurately, implode.

And then his father was dead, by his own hand it was claimed, in a fit of guilt. Yet Finn's mother knew better.

"It was all lies," she had told him over and over. "None of it was true. Not about me or him. They killed him for their own reasons."

Finn knew what these reasons were because his mother had drilled them into him. Rayfield Solomon's career as a servant of his country had been forgotten, his good name besmirched. It wasn't the unjust shame that hurt Finn's mother so much. It was the fact that she had lost the man she loved far sooner than she should have.

"He deserved none of this," she had told Finn. "And now there must be retribution."

Finn remembered hearing this story for the first time when he was just seven years old, soon after his father's death. It had astounded him then, assaulting his still developing sense of justice. Today it still stunned him, how one man could be destroyed so unfairly, so completely.

He broke free from these thoughts and concentrated on the task ahead. In the crowd with him were three other members of his team. Two were college students pulled out of his office for a little adventure in the field. The third was a woman who was nearly as accomplished at her work as him.

With some wrangling and sleight of hand they had garnered tickets for a VIP tour of the almost completed U.S. Capitol Visitor Center. The nearly 600,000-square-foot three-level complex was located beneath the east Capitol grounds. This was because its footprint was larger than the Capitol building and the planners didn't want it to detract from the historic structure. The visitor center included orientation theaters, gift shops, food services, a great hall, exhibition space, an auditorium and other attributes both functional and ceremonial, including much-needed space for the operations of the House and Senate. Once open, it would host millions of visitors a year from all around the world. And in keeping with Washington's stellar reputation for efficiency and integrity, the project was only years behind schedule and only several hundred million dollars over budget.

Finn was most intrigued by two elements: first, the connecting tunnel from the visitor center to the Capitol itself, and second, a service tunnel for truck deliveries. The delivery he had in mind was one that no member of Congress ever would have wanted.

Each member of the team carried a buttonhole digital camera and surreptitiously snapped byte after byte of the underground site. Unfinished tunnels and hallways veered off in interesting directions that would come in very handy to Finn and his people later.

Finn asked several questions of the guide, innocent enough on the surface. Yet just as he did with phone freaking, these queries were subtly designed to elicit information that the guide would never have knowingly revealed. On cue, other members of Finn's team asked tagalong questions that revealed even more. Once all was put together, the unsuspecting tour guide had given them nearly enough information to take down the Capitol and everyone in it.

You're a terrorist's best friend and you don't even know it, Finn thought to himself about the affable guide.

Outside, Finn studied the bronze Statue of Freedom that crowned the dome of the Capitol. It was a nice image, he thought. Yet he didn't know if the people who worked inside the building deserved such a nice topper to their digs. It seemed to him that concepts like freedom, truth and honor were the last things on people's minds here.

He and his team strolled through the Capitol's nearly sixty acres of grounds, compiling still more useful data. They congregated at an empty deli off Independence Avenue to go over their results and form new additions to their planned assault on the Capitol.

"I guess congressmen like to keep safe," said one of the team. "Because the operation we're putting together is costing Uncle Sam a bundle."

"Just another drop in the federal budget," the woman said. "We're heading back to the office now, Harry. I've got some phone freaking to do on the Pentagon assignment."

"You can go back," Finn said. "I've got something else to do."

He left them at the deli and headed to the Hart Senate Office Building, the newest and biggest of the three complexes devoted to taking care of America's one hundred senators and their enormous staffs. It amazed Finn sometimes that a hundred people couldn't manage to fit their operations inside something less than the over *two million* square feet the Hart, Russell and Dirksen Senate office buildings collectively provided. After all, this equaled over twenty thousand square feet per senator. And still the politicians were clamoring for ever more expansive digs and more tax dollars with which to build them.

The Hart Senate Building was located at Second and Constitution and was named after Philip Aloysius Hart, a Michigan senator who died in 1976. The deceased Hart, as the inscription above the main entrance to the building said, "Was a man of incorruptible integrity."

The gent would feel quite alone in the Capitol these days, Finn thought.

He strolled around the interior of the building admiring the ninety-foot-high central atrium and its major feature, a mobile-stabile entitled *Mountains and Clouds*, sculpted by the renowned Alexander Calder. The sculptor had come to D.C. in 1976 to make the final adjustments to the piece, which was enormous—the tallest peak in the mountain rose fifty-one feet high—and then had promptly died that same night back in New York. This was a stark testament to the old saying that "Washington can be downright deadly to your health."

While there were over fifty senators in the Hart

Building, Finn was only interested in one: Roger Simpson of the great state of Alabama.

The security in the building, even post-9/11, was a joke. Once you passed through a metal detector, you could pretty much go wherever you wanted. Finn took the elevator up to the floor where Simpson's office was located. It was hard to miss. The Alabama state flag was standing at attention next to the man's portal. As Finn waited near the glass door he took several shots of the office's interior with his buttonhole camera, focusing on the young female receptionist. He noted all other details on this floor and was about to leave when the door opened again and the man himself came out, accompanied by a considerable entourage.

Roger Simpson was tall, nearly six-five and fit, with blondish hair that had white infringing all over, and the calm, aloof air of a man used to having his personal boundaries respected and his commands followed.

The elevator door down the hall opened and a tall blonde woman stepped out. When he saw her Simpson smiled and stepped forward, giving her a quick embrace. She in turn favored him with a peck on the cheek that to Finn's eye was all show and no substance. This was Mrs. Simpson, a former Miss Alabama, with an MBA from an Ivy League school. It was an unusual résumé for a potential First Lady.

Finn noted the two men next to Simpson. They

had earpieces and were armed, maybe Secret Service. Simpson had no doubt taken extra precautions, particularly since the three former Triple Sixes and Carter Gray had died. Finn's plan did not involve a direct attack on Simpson. The only problematic piece might be the picture of Rayfield Solomon. Simpson needed to know why his life was ending. Yet Finn would think of a way; he always did.

He quietly left the building.

35

Stone rose early but Annabelle was already downstairs having hot tea in front of the fireplace. He nodded to her as he came into the room, and then looked for others about.

"We're it," she said bluntly. "You want some breakfast?"

They ate in a chilly room off the small kitchen. Annabelle barely looked at her food while Stone chewed his eggs and toast and shot her glances.

"Did you hear back from Milton and Reuben after they called you?" she asked. "Did they find out anything else?"

"Not yet but I'm sure they'll let us know."

As soon as he finished his cup of coffee she rose. "You ready?"

"Are we going to see the house?"

"We can't. They knocked it down and put up a monster in its place. But we can still check out the area."

Her cheeks were flushed and her eyes looked unfocused. Stone wondered if she was ill.

As though in answer to his thoughts she said, "I'm fine. I just didn't sleep much."

A half hour later they were standing in front of the plot of land where Annabelle's mother had been murdered.

Annabelle said, "That's it. Or at least where it was. My mom's place was just a little cottage."

The current house wasn't a little anything. It was a ten-thousand-square-foot shingled and turreted *Architectural Digest* cover home wannabe right on the ocean.

"How long ago was the cottage knocked down?" Stone asked.

"Six years. Not too long after she was killed. Ocean views trump brutal murder every time."

"Okay, how do you want to do this?" he asked.

"I suggest we're a father and daughter, no offense, looking for someplace for you to retire. We grab a local Realtor and start asking questions."

Later that afternoon Annabelle and Stone followed a short dark-haired woman built like a keg of beer around the exterior of a large house for sale. It was four lots down from where Annabelle's mother had gotten a bullet fired into her brain courtesy of Jerry Bagger.

"It's adorable, Dad," Annabelle cooed as they surveyed the tumbledown place. "I can't understand why no one has snatched it up."

"First of all, it's not little. And second, it obviously needs some work," Stone said firmly.

"Come on, Dad," Annabelle said. "It's oceanfront. You've been looking a long time and never found anything worth writing home about. Can't you see yourself retiring here? Just look at those views."

He turned to the Realtor. "The place at the end of the street on the right is a real beaut and in great condition. Know whether they're interested in selling?"

"The MacIntoshes? No, I don't think they want to sell."

Annabelle said, "MacIntoshes? That doesn't sound familiar. But I did know some folks that used to live up here. Well, I didn't really know them, friend of a friend thing. Visited them once; that's why we're up here looking, actually. I remember it being so pretty."

"I've been here a long time, do you remember their names?"

Annabelle pretended to think. "Connor, or Conway. No, Conroy, that's right, Conroy."

"Not Tammy Conroy?" the Realtor said sharply.

"I think so, yes. Now I remember. A tall, thin woman with red hair."

The Realtor looked flustered. "Tammy Conroy, oh dear. You're sure?"

"Why, is something wrong?" Annabelle said.

"How well did you know her?"

"Like I said, friend of a friend. Why?"

"Well, I guess you'll find out sooner or later. Some

years ago Tammy Conroy was killed in a little cottage that used to be on the site of the MacIntosh house."

"Killed!" Annabelle clutched Stone's arm.

Stone said, "When you say killed, do you mean by accident?"

"Actually no, she was, well, she was murdered." The woman added quickly, "But we've never had another murder since. This is really a very safe place."

"Did they catch whoever did it?" Annabelle asked.

The Realtor looked even more uncomfortable. "Actually, no, they never caught the person."

Stone said, "Hell, he could still be out there waiting to kill again. Maybe he has a fixation on this neighborhood. Stranger things have happened."

"I don't think that was the case," the Realtor said. "Before the woman who was killed owned it, an elderly widow lived there. She died of old age and her son sold the place to Mrs. Conroy. In fact, I represented the seller in the transaction."

"Maybe her husband did it," Annabelle suggested. "I mean, if she was married. So many murders are domestic in nature. It's awful!"

"There *was* a husband, can't recall his name offhand. But he was gone by the time she was killed, I believe. Leastways, the police never named him a suspect. I always thought some stranger did it. Tammy kept to herself. I don't even think she had any children. But that was years ago, and, like I said, this is actually a very safe area. Now, would you like to see the inside of this house?"

After a quick tour of the house they took the woman's card and said they would get back to her.

As they drove off Annabelle pulled out a brown scarf from her pocket and rubbed it gently.

"What's that?"

"A scarf my mother gave to me. It was for my birthday. It's the last thing she ever had a chance to give me."

"I'm sorry, Annabelle."

She sat back against the car seat and closed her eyes. "I couldn't even attend the funeral. I'd heard rumors in the con world that Bagger was involved and that my father had gotten off scot-free as usual. I knew Bagger would be watching. I've never even been to her grave."

"And you think your father is dead?"

"Let's put it this way, if my dream came true he is."

As they were driving down the street, the light changed and Stone stopped. Annabelle idly glanced at a tall, thin man coming out of a bar and her face froze.

Stone noted her look and said, "What is it?"

"The man coming out of that bar across the street," she whispered as she stared.

Stone glanced over. "What about him?"

"He's my father, Paddy Conroy."

36

"Pull over, Oliver," Annabelle barked.

"What are you going to do?"

"Right now, I'm trying hard not to throw up." She rested her chin on the dashboard, but kept her gaze on her father. "God, it's like I'm seeing a damn ghost."

She slowly sat back up and wiped clammy sweat from her forehead.

"What do you want to do?" he asked.

"I don't know. My mind pretty much just shut down on me."

"Okay, I'll make the call. We follow him. It might lead to something useful."

"That bastard let my mother die." Stone could see that Annabelle was clenching the armrest so tightly her fingers were turning white. He put a calming hand on her shoulder.

"I understand, Annabelle. I understand completely about how and why people get to live and die all for the wrong reasons. And I know it's been a shock finding out that your father is, one, alive, and, two, right here. But we need to keep our wits about us. I can't believe it's a coincidence he's here. Can you?"

She shook her head.

"So we're going to follow him," he said again. "You up for that? Or do you want me to drop you off? I can do it alone."

"No, I want in on this," she said sharply. Then she added more calmly, "I'm good now, Oliver. Thanks." She gave his hand a grateful squeeze.

They both looked out the window where Paddy Conroy was climbing into a beat-up pickup truck parked on the street.

The drive only took ten minutes. By that time they were well away from the small downtown area and out in the country. When the truck turned in through the wrought-iron gates, Annabelle snatched a breath.

Stone waited a few moments and then pulled through the gates into Mt. Holy Cemetery. A few minutes later they were out of the car and slipping stealthily toward a stand of trees. They watched from this concealment while Paddy shuffled along until he came to a flat grave marker on the ground. He produced a few flowers from inside his shabby overcoat, knelt down and placed them on the sunken earth.

He took off his hat, revealing thick white hair, put his hands together and seemed to be praying. Once they heard a long, loud moan come from the man. He reached in his pocket, pulled out a handkerchief and wiped his face.

"Your mother's grave?" Stone asked.

She nodded curtly. "Like I said, I've never been to see it, but I looked up the location."

"He seems to be grieving."

"He's only doing it to make him feel better about what he did, the asshole. He's never changed."

"People do change," Stone said.

"Not him, not ever." She grabbed him as he stepped past her. "Oliver, what are you doing?"

"Putting your theory to the test."

Before she could stop him he walked out into the open and headed toward Paddy. Stone slowed and seemed to be reading the grave markers before stopping at one two down from where Paddy was kneeling and crying.

Stone said softly, "I don't mean to intrude on your privacy. I haven't been by to see my aunt's grave in a few years. I wanted to pay my respects."

Paddy looked up, rubbed his wide face with the cloth. "It's a public cemetery, friend."

Stone knelt down in front of the grave marker he'd picked out, though he was also keeping Paddy in his peripheral vision. "Graveyards just seem to take all the energy out of you, don't they?" he said quietly.

Paddy nodded. "It's penance, you know, for the living. And a warning to us all."

"A warning?" Stone turned to look at him. And now he knew. Paddy Conroy was terminal. He could see it in the gray tinges around the white sunken face, the emaciated body and the trembling hands.

Paddy nodded. “Look at all these graves.” He held up a shaky arm. “All these dead people waiting for the Almighty to come down and tell them where they’re headed. Waiting in the dirt or in Purgatory if you believe that way. Waiting for the Man to come down and tell them. For all eternity.”

“Heaven or hell,” Stone said, nodding.

“You a betting man?”

Stone shook his head.

“I spent all my life betting on one thing or another. But if you were a betting man, how many of ’em you reckon are going up and how many going down?”

“Hopefully far more going up than down,” Stone said.

“You’d lose your money, you would.”

“More people evil than not, is that it?”

“Take me. I might as well pick out a nice sunny spot in the pit of hell right now. Ain’t no question where this old boy’s headed.”

“You have things you regret?”

“Regrets? Mister, if regrets were dollars, I’d be Mr. Bill Gates himself.”

Paddy bent forward and kissed the grave marker. “Good-bye, me darling Tammy. You rest easy now, girl.” He rose to his feet on rubbery legs and put his hat back on.

He turned to Stone. "Now this one here, she'll be getting into heaven. You know why?" Stone shook his head. "Because she's a saint. She's a saint because she put up with the likes of me. And for that reason alone, come Judgment Day, old Saint Peter will welcome her with open arms. Only wish I could be there to see it."

37

It was early morning. Jerry Bagger was sitting in his suite at his posh hotel seriously thinking that he should up the room rate at the Pompeii. For him a view of the White House was not worth a grand a night. As he was gazing out the window at the president's house one member of his security team, Mike, came into the room. "We just got a call from the casino late last night but we didn't want to wake you. There was a guy talking to Dolores."

Bagger turned around. "Talking to Dolores about *what?*"

"From the little he overheard, the daughter's name came up a couple times."

"Old Cindy," Bagger said slowly. "I guess Dolores is still pining away for her kid. Who's the guy? Cop? Fed?"

"We're running that down right now. And he's got a big guy with him. We've got a tail on them. They're staying at a dump outside the Boardwalk area."

"Well, run it down fast."

"And if it is a cop?"

"You let me know. Then we'll see. Killing a cop is a whole other ball of wax. You kill one, a bunch pop up, same with feds. Keep on top of it. Check around to see where else this guy's been." Bagger sat down as Mike headed out. "Wait a minute, Mike, did that Republican Amish jerk-off call?"

"No sir."

"You know, his story sounded legit, so why do I think he was lying his ass off?"

"You got the best instincts of anybody I know, Mr. Bagger."

Not good enough, Bagger thought. *Annabelle Conroy took me right by the balls and squeezed me dry.*

"You want us to have a chat with the guy?"

Bagger shook his head. "Not right now. But follow him. I wanta see where rare book boy goes at night."

"So we gonna be in town for a while?"

Bagger looked through the window. "Why not? Place is starting to grow on me." He pointed at the White House. "Look there, Mike. That's the home of the president, the most powerful son of a bitch in the world. One nod of his head an entire country gets nuked. He farts funny, the stock market drops a thousand points. He's got a freaking army surrounding him. Anything he wants, he gets it." Bagger snapped his fingers. "Like that. Blow job in the Oval Office, tax breaks for the rich, invading other countries, pinching some queen's ass, anything. Cause he's the man. I respect that. The guy only makes four hundred thousand bucks a year, but the perks are sweet and he gets a free ride on a jet a lot bigger than mine. But with all that, you know what, Mike?"

"What, Mr. Bagger?"

"Once he's out of office, he's nothing. But I'm still Jerry Bagger."

38

Harry Finn watched his youngest son, Patrick, swing and miss on a ball that was at eye level. Parents in the stands next to Finn groaned, the third strike was called and the game was over. Patrick had left the tying run on second and the winning run was standing in the boy's cleats at home plate. The ten-year-old walked dejectedly back to his dugout, bat dragging, while the other team started celebrating. Patrick's coach gave them all a little pep talk, the boys had their after-game snack, which for many was the highlight of the entire evening, and parents started rounding up their future all-stars for the ride home.

Patrick was still sitting in the dugout, his helmet and batting gloves on as though he were just waiting for another shot to put the ball over the fence. Finn grabbed a snack for him and sat down next to him in the dugout.

"You played a great game, Pat," he said, handing the boy a bag of Doritos and an orange Gatorade. "I'm proud of you."

"I struck out, Dad. I *lost* the game for my team."

"You also got on base twice, scored both times and drove in three more. And playing center field you caught a ball that was actually over the fence with two men on and two outs. That saved three runs right there." He rubbed his son's shoulder. "You played a good game. But you can't win them all."

"Is this where you tell me losing builds character?"

"Yeah, it is. Just don't make a habit out of it. Everybody really hates a loser." He playfully slapped his son's helmet. "And if you're not going to eat those chips I'll take 'em." He grabbed the bag.

"Hey, those are mine. I earned them."

"I thought you lost the game for your team."

"The game wouldn't have been close except for me."

"Finally figured that out, did you? I knew you had the Finns' brains in there somewhere." He rapped his knuckles on the helmet. "And take this thing off, you're hardheaded enough already."

"Gee, Dad, thanks for all your support."

"How about we grab some dinner on the way home?"

Patrick looked pleasantly surprised. "Just you and me?"

"Just you and me."

"Won't David be mad?"

"Your brother is thirteen. He doesn't really like having his old man around all that much right now. I'm just not that cool or smart. That'll change in about ten years when he's in debt from college, can't find a job and I'm suddenly brilliant again."

"I think you're smart. And cool."

"That's what I love about you." As they walked back to the car, Finn lifted Patrick on his shoulders and took off running. As they arrived at the parking lot, a breathless Finn put his son down.

Laughing, Patrick said, "Dad, why do you keep carrying me around on your shoulders?"

Finn's smile eased off his face and his eyes grew a little moist. "Because pretty soon I won't be able to do it anymore, son. You'll be too big. And even if you weren't you wouldn't want me to anyway."

"Is it that big of a deal?" Patrick said as he munched on his chips.

Finn unlocked the car and threw his son's bag inside. "Yeah, it is. You'll understand really well when you're a dad."

They ate at a local burger place about a mile from their house.

Patrick said, "I love this food; nothing but grease."

"Enjoy it while you can. When you get to be my age, it's not that easy on the body."

Patrick stuffed a french fry in his mouth and said, "How's Grandma?" Finn stiffened just a bit. "Mom said you went to visit her. How's she doing?"

"Okay. Well, actually not too great."

"How come we never visit her anymore?"

"I'm not sure she'd want you to see her like she is now."

"I don't care about stuff like that. She was fun even if she talked a little funny."

"Yeah, she was," Finn said, staring down at his half-eaten cheeseburger, his appetite suddenly gone. "Maybe we'll go see her soon."

"You know, Dad, she doesn't look very Irish."

Finn thought of the tall, broad-shouldered woman with the sharply chiseled, near-gaunt features so many Eastern Europeans from that generation possessed. He could barely reconcile that image with the shrunken mass his mother had become. His son was right, she didn't look very Irish, because she wasn't. Still, Finn looked far more like his mother than his father. He said quickly, "She's not. Your grandfather was Irish." He didn't enjoy lying to his son, but he knew the truth was not possible on this subject. Yes, his father, the Irish Jew.

"You said he was a cool guy."

"Very cool."

"I wish I could've known him."

Me too, thought Finn. *For a lot longer than I did*.

"So where's Grandma from, then?"

"Your grandmother was really from all over," he answered vaguely.

★

When they got home Mandy met them at the door. After sending Patrick to get changed for bed she said, "Harry, you're supposed to go into Susie's class tomorrow. It's parents' career day."

"Mandy, I told you I really don't feel comfortable doing that."

"All the other kids' parents are doing it. We can't leave Susie out. I'd go but I'm not sure cooking, cleaning and driving qualifies as a career."

He gave her a kiss. "It does with me. You work harder than anybody I know."

"You have to go, Harry. Susie will be so disappointed if you don't."

"Honey, come on. Give me a break."

"Fine, but if you're copping out, you go and tell her. She's waiting up in bed."

Mandy walked off, leaving Finn standing by the door. Groaning, he trudged up the stairs.

Susie was sitting up in bed, surrounded by her stuffed animals. She had eleven of them she kept on her bed; she couldn't go to sleep without them. She called them her guardian angels. Around the foot of the bed were ten more stuffed animals. These were her "Knights of the Round Table."

Her big blue eyes looked up at him as she got right to the point. "Are you coming tomorrow, Daddy?"

"I was just talking to Mom about that."

"Jimmy Potts' mom came in today. She's a marine biologist." Susie formed the words slowly while she scratched her cheek. "I don't know what that is, but, Daddy, she brought live fish."

"That sounds really cool."

"I know you'll be cool too. I've been telling everybody about you."

"What have you been telling them?" Susie had no idea what he did for a living.

"That you were a soldier."

"Oh, that's right, I was."

"I've been telling everybody that you were in the navy. And that you were a *walrus*," she added importantly.

Finn tried hard not to laugh as he patiently explained that he had been a Navy *SEAL*, not a walrus. "Remember, sweetie, up in this area there are a lot of people who used to be in the military. It's not that special."

"But you'll be the best, Daddy, I know you will. Please come, please." She tugged on his sleeve and then wrapped her arms around him.

In the face of this, what father could say no? "Okay, honey, I'll be there."

As he turned out the light and was leaving, Susie said, "Daddy, can I ask you something?"

"Sure, what is it?"

"When you were a soldier, did you ever kill anybody?"

Finn leaned back against the door. This was not the question he'd been expecting.

Susie added, "'Cause Joey Menkel said his dad killed lots of bad people in Iraq. And he's a soldier too. So did you?"

Finn sat back down next to her, took his daughter's hand and said slowly, "When people fight, people get hurt, sweetie. It's never a good thing to hurt someone else. And soldiers only do it to protect themselves and their country, where their families live."

"So did you?" she persisted.

"I'll see you at school tomorrow, baby. Hope you sleep well." He kissed her on the forehead and nearly sprinted from the room.

A minute later he was in the garage. He kept his gun safe here. It weighed nearly a thousand pounds and had a key, combo and biometric lock system that only he could open. He unlocked the heavy door and took out another, smaller box that also was key and combo protected. Opening that, he carried the file over to his workbench and started looking through it. The photos, the reports, were both now faded, yet they never failed to incite in him a nearly uncontrollable rage. He read the words aloud to himself: "Rayfield Solomon, Alleged Traitor, Commits Suicide in South America." He looked at the photo of Rayfield Solomon, his father, a dead man with a hole in his right temple, and the legacy of having betrayed his country.

Finn still felt rage tonight, but it was not the same as all the other times he had looked at the final wreckage of his father's past, and that was due to a little girl's question: *Did you ever kill anybody, Daddy?*

Yes, honey, Daddy *has.*

He locked the items back up and turned out the garage light. He didn't return to the house. He went for a walk. He walked until it was midnight. When he got back to the house, everyone was long since asleep. His wife was used to his late-night ramblings around the neighborhood. He slipped into Susie's room, sat on her bed and watched her chest rise and fall as she clutched one of her precious guardian angels.

When dawn came, Finn left his daughter, showered, dressed and got ready to go to school, to talk about being a soldier. Of course, he would not talk to them about being a killer. Though a killer he was.

As he walked through the hall to his daughter's third grade class, a tiny crack appeared in the wall of his mind that separated Harry Finn from the other man he had to be. It was doubtful he even knew it had happened. He opened the door to the class and was nearly knocked down by his daughter, who flew across the room to give him a hug.

"This is my daddy," she announced proudly to her classmates. "And he's a seal, not a walrus. And he's a good guy."

Am I? thought Harry Finn.

39

Stone filled Annabelle in on his conversation with her father at the grave site. "He looks like he's dying."

"I'm delighted to hear it."

"And he seems sincerely guilty about what happened to your mother."

"I highly doubt that."

"Do you want to follow him?"

"No, I want to kill him."

"Okay, what now? More sleuthing around town?"

"No. Let's just go back to the inn. I need to drink and I want to do it in the privacy of my own room."

Stone dropped her off at the inn and headed back out. He drove through the town's few streets until he saw Paddy's truck parked at the curb. Father and daughter had had the same idea. He parked and went inside.

The bar was dirty and dark. At this time of the afternoon there was only one man at the bar, a pitcher in front of him. Stone sat down next to Paddy, who barely looked up.

"I guess cemeteries make people thirsty," Stone said.

Paddy gave him a sideways glance and took a sip of his beer. His eyelids were droopy, his skin grayer inside the bar than it had been in the sunshine.

"Never needed a reason to have a pint or two," Paddy replied, his speech a little slurred.

"My name's Oliver," Stone said, extending his hand.

Paddy didn't take it; he studied Stone warily.

"You run into a man once, no problem. You run into a man twice in the span of an hour, it makes a body wonder."

"Town's not that big."

"Big enough to let a man have his space."

"I can move."

Paddy's gaze burned into him for another second or two. "Forget it. What are you having? I'm buying."

"No need to do that."

"There's never a need to buy another man a drink. It's a privilege. And don't turn it down. I'm Irish. I'd have to slit your bloody throat for refusing."

Two hours later, Stone and Paddy left the bar, Stone holding Paddy up.

"You're a good bloke, you are," Paddy blubbered. "A good frien'."

"Glad you feel that way. I don't think you're in any shape to drive. Tell me where you live and I'll drop you off."

Paddy fell asleep in Stone's car. It was for the best because Stone was taking father to see daughter.

Annabelle had stared at the bottle of gin for at least an hour without touching a drop. She only drank when a con demanded that she do so. She had enough memories of her drunken father saying and doing incredibly stupid things to swear her off the stuff forever. The knock on the door barely made her look up.

"Yeah?"

"It's Oliver."

"Door's unlocked."

It opened. Annabelle didn't glance over until she realized she was hearing the sounds of four feet instead of two.

"What the hell are you doing?" she screamed.

Stone half carried Paddy over to a sofa and let him drop onto it.

However, the sounds of his daughter's voice had managed to pierce right through the wall of booze. Paddy half sat up. "Annabelle?"

Annabelle moved so fast that Stone had no chance to stop her. She lunged at Paddy, hit him right in the gut with her shoulder and they both toppled to the floor. She pinned the old man to the floor and started slapping his face.

Stone wrenched her away, holding her off the floor as she tried to kick and punch her father.

Stone pushed Annabelle up against the wall, holding her there. When she wouldn't stop thrashing he slapped her. She froze, stunned. Then she looked over at her father lying there on the floor in time to see his face turn white, and he threw up.

In the next instant she had ripped free from Stone and had fled the room.

Two hours later Paddy opened his eyes and stared around. Then he sat up and immediately felt Stone's hand on his shoulder.

"Just take it easy," Stone said. "You had a nasty shock."

"Annie? Annie?" Paddy scanned the room.

"She'll be back," Stone said. "She had to, uh, step out for a minute." He'd already cleaned up Paddy's sick and had waited for the man to awaken.

"Was it really Annie?" Paddy asked, a shaky hand gripping Stone's arm.

"Yeah, it was really Annie."

When Stone heard Annabelle's footsteps on the stairs he put himself between Paddy and his daughter. The door opened and she stood there, her face white, her expression, well, expressionless. For a terrifying moment Stone wondered if she'd gone out and bought a gun.

She closed the door behind her, pulled a chair out from the small dinette set in one corner and sat down facing the two men.

She stared between Stone and her father before settling her gaze on Paddy. "You done puking?"

He nodded dumbly. "Annie?"

She held up a hand. "Just shut up. I didn't say you could talk, did I?"

He shook his head and sat back against the sofa, a hand over his flat stomach.

She turned her attention to Stone. "Why the hell did you bring him here?"

"I figured it was time the two of you talked."

"You figured wrong."

"I didn't get a chance to tell you before you stormed out. When your mother was killed, your father was in a federal holding cell in Boston on a counterfeit check kiting charge."

Stone sat back next to Paddy and studied Annabelle. The woman *was* the greatest con of her generation, he felt, because her face didn't betray the slightest hint of emotion at the stunning news.

"How do you know that?" she finally said, her gaze never leaving his.

"I checked with my friend Alex on the way over here. The stuff's all computerized now."

"How did you even know to check?" she asked dully.

"Because the bloke asked me about your mother's death when we were sitting at the bar," Paddy broke in. "I told him. I was in that damn cell for nearly a month. They didn't have enough to convict me, but

I couldn't afford a lawyer. By the time I got out your mother was long since buried."

"That doesn't change the fact that you're the reason she died in the first place."

"I never said it did. Not a minute goes by that I don't wish it was me in the ground instead of her."

Annabelle stared over at Stone. "And you bought that sob story? That's Con 101."

"No, it's the truth, and I don't give a damn if you believe it or not," Paddy exclaimed, rising unsteadily to his feet.

"He comes all the time to see her grave," Stone added.

"Who cares?" Annabelle snapped. "But for a lousy ten thousand bucks that this scum ripped off Bagger, she'd be alive today."

"I never thought he'd come after your mum. I don't know who tipped Bagger off where she was. If I did know, I'd have killed the bastard."

"Save it for someone who cares."

"And not a day goes by that I don't think about having my hands around Jerry Bagger's neck."

"Really? So why haven't you? It's not like you don't know where the guy lives."

"He's got a damn army around him."

"Tell me something I don't know."

Paddy stared at her curiously. "I heard Bagger ran into some trouble recently. Scuttlebutt around the con world. Was that you?"

Annabelle rose and opened the door. "Get out."

"Annie—"

"Get out!"

Paddy left, stumbling against the wall as he did so. Annabelle looked at Stone. "I'll never forgive you for this."

"I'm not looking for forgiveness." He stood.

"So why did you really bring him here?"

"Why don't you think about it and see if you can come up with the answer on your own. It might mean more to you that way."

Stone walked out the door and Annabelle kicked it shut.

40

Two of Bagger's men discovered that Milton had been to the hotel across the street from the Pompeii. They talked to the clerk on duty and also to Helen, the masseuse who'd worked on Milton. Confronted with Bagger's grim foot soldiers, neither held back anything. And Milton clearly was not a cop or a fed. The call was made later that morning to Bagger with this information.

"Pick him and his friend up, find out what they're up to and then kill them," was Bagger's response. "Then make sure Dolores knows about it. If that doesn't shut her up for good, I know something else that will."

The men drove to Milton and Reuben's motel on the outskirts of the casino strip, where Bagger's surveillance team had told them the men were staying.

They pulled to a stop in front of the motel and got out. Milton and Reuben were on the second floor, room 214.

They went in hard and fast. Milton was on the bed packing his bag.

One of Bagger's men said, "Okay, you sorry sack of—" That was all he could manage because his jaw was cracked by Reuben's hammer fist. He dropped to the carpet, out cold. Reuben grabbed the other fellow, lifted him up and slammed him against the wall, laid a massive elbow into the back of his head and then let him fall limp to the floor.

Reuben quickly rifled through their pockets, taking the ammo from their pistols and their car keys. He flipped through their IDs. Pompeii Casino. They were Bagger's goons. He had watched them drive up in the Hummer, slipped into the bathroom and pounced when they'd burst in.

"How'd you know they were coming here?" Milton asked as he gazed at the two unconscious men.

"I figured if they killed that Cindy chick, they'd probably be keeping a close eye on the mother. They must've spotted you last night talking to her, spent the time in between retracing your steps, found out you were interested in this Robby Thomas guy and Bagger ordered a little visit."

"Pretty good deduction."

"Ten years in military intelligence wasn't entirely wasted on me. Let's go."

They loaded their bags in Reuben's truck. Five minutes later they were heading south as fast as Reuben's decade-old ride could carry them.

"Reuben, I'm scared," Milton said as they hit the interstate.

"You should be scared, because *I'm* shitting in my pants."

41

Carter Gray was briefing the current CIA director on the matter of Rayfield Solomon. "I think it's someone close to Solomon," Gray told the director. "The picture that was sent, they wanted me to know why I was being killed."

"Did Solomon have any family?" the director asked. "I know about the case, of course, but it was before my time here."

"Solomon was involved with a Russian. That's what started the whole thing. We only knew her first name, Lesya."

"And after Solomon died, what happened?"

"She disappeared. Actually, she disappeared *before* he died. We believed it was prearranged. They knew we were closing in. We got him, but not her."

"And this was how long ago?"

Gray said, "Over thirty years."

"Well, that means if she's still alive I doubt it's her running around killing people."

"I don't believe that it is. But that doesn't mean

she's not involved. She was always very good at manipulation."

"You know that much about her, but not her surname?"

"Actually, since she's Russian, she would have *three* names: her given name or *imia*, a patronymic name or *otchestvo*, and a surname or *familia*." By Gray's condescending expression, he could've finished this mini-lecture off with the words "you idiot," but he wisely refrained.

"Cold War baggage," the director replied. "Not really our focus anymore."

"You might want to rethink your priorities. While you're placing all your bets on Muhammad, Putin, Chávez and Hu are eating this country's lunch. And they make Al Qaeda look like kindergarteners as far as their potential for destruction on a large scale."

The director cleared his throat. "Yes, well, how come you didn't try to find this Lesya back then?"

"We had other priorities. Solomon had been eliminated. Lesya had gone deep underground. We made a tactical decision that using additional assets to pursue her was not worth the cost. We did believe that we had for all intents and purposes put her out of commission. And for over three decades she has been."

"Until now, at least you believe. So any associates of this Lesya we have to account for?"

"We have to find that out."

"What specifically *do* you know about the woman?"

"She was one of the best counterintelligence agents the Soviet Union ever produced. I've never seen her in person, only photo images. Tall and beautiful, she hardly fit the model of a spy because she tended to stick out. But she proved that stereotype wrong. She had more sheer nerve than just about anyone in the field. Indeed, she was aptly named, as Lesya means 'bravery' in Russian. She didn't work directly for the KGB. She was a cut above that. We always believed that her chain of command went right to the Soviet leadership. She worked in this country for a time, then England, France, Japan, China and all the other typical high-level assignments. She did her best turning others. She recruited Solomon, secretly married him and turned him against his country. His treachery cost America dearly."

"How do you know they were married?"

"Let me correct that. We *believe* that they were married. It was based on facts uncovered at the time. Largely circumstantial, but taken together, it looks like they walked down the aisle."

"And he killed himself?"

"That's what the file says, yes. I believe it was both from guilt at what he'd done to hurt his homeland and also the fact that we were closing in on him."

"But you said before that 'we' got him. So did we

kill him and the suicide was window dressing? Or did he really commit suicide?"

"Whether we did it or he killed himself, it doesn't really matter; he would have been executed for treason in any event." From Gray's tone it was clear he was not going to say any more on that particular subject, even to the director of CIA.

"I looked at the file. There seem to be some gaps in it."

"We didn't have reliable computers back then. And paper files are notoriously incomplete from that era," Gray replied smoothly.

The director apparently gave up on this line of inquiry. He had actually worked under Gray years ago and wasn't nearly as smart as the man, and he knew it. "Fine, Carter. And you've alerted Senator Simpson?"

"Of course. He's well-prepared."

"Anyone else?"

"There was another man who was part of the team, a John Carr, but he's long dead."

The meeting ended there. It was obvious that Gray hadn't told the entire truth. He had astutely gauged that that was for the best because no one wanted to hear the entire truth anyway. The country had too many current problems than to bother with what really occurred over thirty years ago to a man remembered only as a traitor.

Gray personally loathed what had happened to

Solomon, but he could do nothing to change it. He had to look ahead, not to the past. And that meant finding a killer before he struck again. And Lesya, too, finally had to be run to ground.

The result of Gray's meeting with the director was that a regiment of agents in the field were officially now "looking into the matter." Though innocent-sounding, it actually meant that they were doing their best to find whoever was killing ex–CIA agents. And their orders were to terminate the person or persons responsible. No one wanted a trial on this. They simply wanted a body.

42

Harry Finn escaped the third graders relatively unscathed. They'd asked a lot of questions, though, and once or twice Finn actually wished he *had* been a walrus instead of a SEAL.

When he'd finished Susie had given him a hug and said, "You have a really great rest of the day, Daddy."

She sounded so grown-up, for a moment he felt like his heart would burst. His former SEAL team members would have been astonished to learn that beneath Finn's stainless steel skin was a heart as vulnerable and susceptible to emotion as one could find. His only defense, his only way of keeping going, was to block it out. He led two lives and never let either of them mix. What he did for his mother would never wash over into his own family. And what he did with his family would never become part of his other life. At least he prayed to God it wouldn't.

He drove to the office and met with his team to go over the hit on the Capitol. The session lasted for several hours as they carefully mapped out their strategy and then did more prep work. Toward the end of this meeting, Finn, whose mind worked best when multi-tasking, had reason to smile. He had just thought of a way to kill Simpson.

He grabbed some lunch and headed to his storage unit. He had a bomb to build.

Jerry Bagger screamed into the phone, "Nice going! That's just great. Why don't I come back to town and kick your asses too." He calmed down when he heard the next bit of news. With a little more digging they'd ascertained that the little guy had won a ton of cash. And in a casino that meant one thing that was as certain as death: In order to get your money you had to fill out what amounted to a 1099 so Uncle Sam would know you'd won the money in case you forgot to pay tax on it.

Bagger took down this information and said, "Wait a minute, the guy's from England?"

"That's what it says."

"Did he sound British?"

"I don't know."

"You don't know! Does anybody know?"

"I'll have to check," the man said nervously.

"Yeah, well after you *check* and then find out the ID's total bullshit, why don't you *check* back with me so I can strangle you." Bagger slammed down the phone.

43

When Stone walked outside the next day, a bleary-eyed Annabelle was sitting on the front steps of the B&B.

"What do you want from me?" she said bitterly.

"Nothing. What do you want from yourself?"

"Don't play shrink with me."

"Your father was in jail when your mother was murdered."

"He was still the reason she was killed."

"All right. But what's wrong with giving him the benefit of the doubt and believing that he never intended your mother to be hurt by Bagger?"

"What's wrong with that? What's wrong with that is that my father is a liar who has never cared about anyone except himself."

"So he was really bad to your mother? Beat her, starved her?"

"Don't make this into a joke!"

"I'm just trying to understand the situation."

"No, he never abused her."

"So he might have loved her."

"Why are you doing this to me? Why are you taking his side?"

"I'm not taking sides, Annabelle. The man is dying. He was at your mother's grave paying his respects. You thought he'd set your mom up but he didn't." Stone spread his hands. "All I'm saying is you might want to reconsider the situation. Life is short. Family is not forever. I know that as well as anyone."

Annabelle slouched against the car, hands tucked into her armpits.

"It took me two years to plan my hit on Bagger. Two shorts and then the long. I put nearly every dime I had into it. Took more risks than I ever had before. One little mistake in front of Jerry and I'd be dead. And I loved every minute of it. Do you know why?"

Stone shook his head. "Tell me."

"Because I was finally getting back at the son of a bitch who killed my mother. After all those years he was finally going to pay. And I did it, I won. I conned more money from him than anybody ever had. Enough to really hurt him."

"And?"

"And after I did it I realized it was all for nothing. Jerry was just being Jerry when he killed my mother. Jerry took his pound of flesh; that's the law of the street we all live on. Don't get me wrong, I'll always hate the bastard for what he did. But the man I hated most of all was my father."

"And today you found out he was innocent, at least of that."

She pointed to the scar under her eye. "Some innocent. He gave me this when I was just a teenager, for blowing a claim in a casino. He said it was the only way to learn. And he's the reason my mother's dead. And what's happened to him? Not a damn thing. Everything just bounces off the son of a bitch. He just goes along like the bullet in her brain never even happened."

"I'm not seeing it that way, Annabelle. It doesn't look like life has been kind to him. And he was here grieving over your mother. Doesn't sound like a guy who got off scot-free."

"I can never forget it, Oliver. I can never forget what he did."

"I'm not asking you to forget. I'm just asking you to maybe think about forgiving. People do bad things all the time. It doesn't necessarily make them bad people."

"So what do you want me to do? Run and give him a hug?"

"This is something you need to deal with inside yourself. Before it destroys you. Because if we manage to nail Bagger you still won't be satisfied because you have all this hate inside for Paddy. If you really want to get on with your life, you need to deal with that."

Annabelle pulled her car keys out of her pocket. "Well, you know what? I don't want to."

She drove off in a spit of gravel.

As soon as she was out of sight Stone's phone buzzed. It was Reuben recounting everything that had happened to them when they were in Atlantic City, including Milton's big winnings and them being attacked by Bagger's men. Stone told Reuben to not take Milton home, but to go to Reuben's house instead.

"He didn't use his real ID there when he collected his winnings, Oliver," Reuben pointed out.

"It doesn't matter. I don't want to take a chance. You recently moved. Your house doesn't even have an address. It'd be very hard for Bagger to track you down."

"How's it going with Susan?"

"Couldn't be better." Stone clicked off and stared after the fleeing Annabelle.

Family. It just doesn't get any more complicated than that.

44

Gray was on a secure phone in a bunker the CIA had arranged for him to use. The president had been briefed on the matter and had used his executive powers to give Gray, even in an unofficial capacity, any and all resources of the United States government that he required to set the situation right. Gray of course had only communicated his version of the truth to the president and his top people, but it had been enough to allow him the carte blanche he needed to carry out the required mission.

Though set fifty feet in the dirt, the bunker had all the amenities of a five-star hotel in downtown Manhattan, including its own valet and a chef. Gray had always been treated like a rock star by the intelligence community.

Into the phone he said, "If Lesya and Rayfield Solomon were married there has to be a record of it somewhere. I know we couldn't find it back then, but times have changed. The Russians are, at least in public, our ally. Run down every lead you can on that angle. There are some old codgers still running around the reincarnation of the KGB that may be able to help us. Bring euros, they prefer them to dollars, at least these days." He nodded as the man on the other end said something. "The former Russian ambassador to this country, Gregori Tupikov, is an old friend of mine. It might just be worth a phone call to him. Tell him you're doing it in connection with the investigation of my murder. Vodka by the barrel, two-pound lobsters and a natural redhead, that's all you ever needed to corrupt old Gregori."

Gray clicked off and continued to study the file while his four-course dinner was being finalized. Though computers and servers dominated his business these days, the old Cold Warrior loved the feel of paper between his fingers. He ate his sumptuous meal alone in front of a gas fire that gave the room an enchanting glow even this far underground. Gray never did things like others. Even dead he was fifty feet under the earth instead of the normal six and his "coffin" was far more luxurious than the rank and file got.

Taking a snifter of brandy into a wood-paneled library, he sat behind an ornate desk and continued to ponder the matter. He loved this part of the game. It was a battle of the minds, a perpetual chess match; one side trying to outmaneuver, outthink the other. And the United States had never had a man who could perform those tasks better than Carter Gray. His actions had saved so many Americans that he had long since lost count. The Medal of Freedom was the least his country could do. If he was a Brit he'd already have been knighted. And yet he'd been forced to resign, long before he was ready. Because John Carr had forced his hand.

The more Gray thought about this, the angrier he became. Yet from within that anger a cold-blooded idea took form. Whoever was killing Gray's old assassination team one by one probably believed John Carr to be dead. Yet why should Carr be spared the thrill of being a target? And the man had given him the finger!

Gray picked up his secure phone and hit a button. "I want to get some information out using the normal channels. It has to do with the alleged death of a man named John Carr. I think the time has come to set the record straight."

45

Finn held up the device. Barely the size of his palm, combined with a few seemingly innocuous elements it could easily kill anyone within thirty feet. But it would only kill one man; Finn would make sure of that.

He tried on his disguise and thought through all the steps he would take to enter the Hart Building and penetrate where he needed to go.

Once Finn had gotten on Roger Simpson's trail and dug deeply, he'd learned that the distinguished senior senator from Alabama had been a hellion early in life, with little regard for anyone or anything other than himself. Though the man was still like that, this flaw had been buried under layers of PR once his political career had begun. This was done with the full though invisible support of the CIA, where he had worked in a very special though undisclosed capacity. His c.v. was filled with accolades from the Agency and very little in the way of hard facts. Yet to his country he was a hero. And he was poised to make a run for the White House, Finn had heard.

I don't think so.

Simpson had never forgotten his former employer's support. As head of the powerful Senate Select Committee on Intelligence he'd let the CIA get away with whatever it wanted. There did not seem to be any action too extreme that Simpson did not find necessary for national security reasons. He had been Carter Gray's champion or lapdog, depending on how one looked at it, for years. Finn considered it perfect justice to send them to the same place, and in the same manner.

He drove home late that night, but Mandy was still up waiting for him. Over a couple slices of pumpkin pie and some hot tea she said, "You were a big hit today at school. Susie waited up to tell you but she couldn't stay awake."

"I'm sorry I'm late, but something came up."

"Are you sure everything's okay? You haven't really seemed yourself lately."

"Just work. Lot to think about."

"How's Lily?"

Lily was Finn's mother. Like Finn it wasn't her real name. Harry Finn wouldn't have known what it was like to use a real name for anything.

"The same. Actually, a little worse." Finn didn't use his mother's word, "rotting."

"I know we have a lot going on, but if you want your mother to come and live with us, I'm okay with that. We'll make it work somehow."

"Not a good idea, Mandy. She's fine right where she is."

"Okay, Harry, but there might come a time when we need to make that decision."

"Maybe, but that time isn't now. So let's not worry about it. We have enough on our plates."

"You're sure there's nothing bothering you?"

He shook his head, but didn't look at his wife.

She touched his hand. "Harry, you seem to be drifting away from us."

His response was delivered with a harshness that surprised even him. "I went to Susie's school. I almost never miss a ball game or soccer match. The yard doesn't have a weed in it. I help with all the homework and housework. I play chauffeur as much as you do. What more do you want from me, Mandy?"

She withdrew her hand slowly. "Nothing, I guess."

They finished their pie in silence. Mandy slowly headed upstairs but Finn remained sitting in the kitchen staring at nothing.

"Not coming?" she said.

"Got a few things to do."

"Don't go out, Harry, not tonight."

"Maybe just a walk. You know."

"Yes, I know," Mandy said to herself as she climbed the stairs.

"Mandy?"

She turned back around.

"Things will get better. I promise. They'll get better soon." *I'm almost there.*

"Sure, Harry, sure."

46

There was really only one place for Annabelle to go: the graveyard. She had never had the opportunity to pay her respects to her mother. She was going to take care of that tonight.

She parked her rental, slipped through the gate and walked along the darkened pathways. The location of her mother's grave was seared into her head. However, when she arrived there, she found that her mother already had a visitor. She ducked behind an evergreen and watched.

He was stretched out on the ground next to the grave. As Annabelle listened she could hear the words floating to her from the prone figure. He was singing an Irish ditty to the dead woman. It was a song that Annabelle had heard him sing to her mother when Annabelle was a little girl. The lyrics had to do with dreams and a green, lush land and a man and a woman very much in love. As she continued to listen tears started sliding down her cheeks, though she didn't want them to. The sounds grew fainter and she finally realized her father had fallen asleep next to the grave of his wife—her mother.

Annabelle stepped out from behind the tree, strode quietly over to the burial plot and knelt down on the other side of the grave from where her father lay quietly snoring. Then she did something she hadn't done since attending mass as a little girl. She crossed herself and prayed over her mother. More tears poured down her face as she spoke to God and tried to talk to her mother, telling her how much she missed her, how much she wanted her to be alive.

She prayed and spoke until her heart was nearly bursting. Then she rose, crossed herself again and, staring down at her slumbering father, made up her mind.

He was painfully light as she gripped him under the armpits, lifting him to his feet. He awakened slightly. She half carried him to her car, put him in, drove back to the inn and got him to bed in her room. She sat outside on the couch until she heard a tap on her door.

It was Stone. He looked worried. He filled her in on what had happened with Milton and Reuben. Then he glanced toward her bedroom door, from which loud snores were now pouring forth.

Stone didn't say anything about that because the look on Annabelle's face told him quite clearly that any questions would not be welcome.

"Do you want to go back home tomorrow?" he asked instead.

"I don't have a home," she replied. "But we can go back to *your* home tomorrow."

The next morning Annabelle had breakfast sent up to the room. When her father came out of the bedroom hot coffee was poured and eggs and bacon were on the plate.

"You look like you could use some food," she said.

He looked around. "How the hell did I get here?"

"You were at the grave last night. So was I."

He nodded slowly, rubbing his tangled hair down with one hand. "I see."

"Come and eat."

"You don't have to do this, Annie."

"I know that. Eat."

He sat and managed to down a few bites and drink a bit of the coffee.

"How bad is it?" she asked, studying his gaunt, gray face.

"Bad enough. Six months without treatment. A year with. But who wants to go out sick all the time?"

"Do you need anything? Money? A place to live?"

He sat back and wiped the napkin across his lips. "You owe me nothing, Annie. And I ain't taking nothing from you."

"There's no reason you have to be in pain or sleeping in the back of a truck. I have money."

"I've got whiskey for the pain and that old truck of mine is what they call a low-end recreational vehicle. I'm fine."

"You're obviously not fine."

His expression darkened as he pushed away from the table. "I don't want your pity, Annie, okay? I can deal with your hatred a lot easier."

"Is that why you never found me and told me you were in jail when Bagger killed Mom?"

"Would it have made a difference to you?"

"Probably not," she admitted.

"So there you go. Would've been a bloody waste of time."

He rose and fumbled in his pocket, fishing out a cigarette pack and a lighter. "Do you mind, seeing as how it's already killed me?" She shook her head and he stepped to the window, opened it and blew the smoke out that way.

"So did you hit Jerry up in Atlantic City?"

"I did."

"Did you hit the bastard hard?"

"Millions."

"Well, then you're a lock for heaven, 'cause there ain't no man what deserves it more than that bloke."

"But it wasn't enough," Annabelle said in a low voice.

Paddy stared moodily out the window. "Course it wasn't. One thing Jerry has is lots of money. You can take all you want and he'll make it all back off the sorry types tramping through his casino every bloody minute."

"So how do I hurt him enough?"

He swung around to look at her. "You take away one of two things: either his life or his freedom. Only way."

"There's no statute of limitations on killing someone."

"You got proof he murdered your mum?"

"Nothing that will stand up in court. But I know he did it."

"I do too."

Father and daughter stared at each other for a long time.

He finally said, "There're only two people in the whole world who've conned that bastard and lived to tell about it. And they're both in this room."

"So you want to con Jerry, together?"

"I want him to pay for what he did to your mum."

"You think I don't?"

"I know you do. You went after the bastard. I never had the balls to do it. Sure, I'm a good con, maybe one of the best. I've got nerve, more than most."

"And things have changed?"

"I'm dying already. So what the hell does it matter to me? Better to get a bullet in the brain courtesy of Jerry than watch my insides dissolve on me."

"And how exactly do you propose doing that?"

"I've been thinking about it a lot actually. Probably the only thing I've been thinking about. But your conning Jerry gives us a way to nail him."

"Because he's coming after me?"

"Right. You had a crew of course."

"Two people you know, or know of, one you don't."

Paddy flicked his cigarette out the window and sat back down at the table. "Jerry hit any of them?"

"One. He's a veg."

"And maybe ratted you out?"

"No maybe about it, he did. In fact, Jerry is in D.C. trying to find me right now."

"That tall, older bloke with you, can you trust him?"

"He's never let me down."

"Good friend to have." Paddy fell silent, staring down at his unfinished breakfast.

"You think you're in shape to run a con on Jerry? I got away from him last time because I worked it to perfection. I'm not looking to walk in and get my head blown off because you fall on your face."

"Always admired your bluntness."

"Guess who taught me?" she shot back.

"I *am* ready for this. In fact, it's the only thing keeping me alive. And I've got the plan."

"What is it?"

"Basically to get Jerry to confess to killing your mum."

"Oh, really, is that all? Hell, I wish I would've thought of that one."

"You have a problem with the concept?"

"No, with the execution, as in yours and mine. Because correct me if I'm wrong, but getting someone to confess to a murder, wouldn't that involve getting up close and personal?"

"Absolutely. The closest possible proximity."

"Well why don't we stop right there then. I've done my face time with Jerry. I have no desire to do it again."

"With my plan the risk will be minimal to you."

"Define minimal."

"Just trust me, Annie."

"You must be insane."

"No, I'm just a dying man who's got to make peace with his God. And to do that, I have to make this right. I have to."

This remark came so out of left field that Annabelle could only stare at him.

"But there is a small problem with the plan," he said.

"How small?'

"We need access to the good guys, the cops. Not exactly my specialty." He glanced at her. "Any ideas on that score?"

Annabelle sat back, not looking very confident. "You know this is suicide, don't you?"

"I will never let you come to harm at the hands of Jerry. But I have to do this. I swear that to you on your mother's grave."

This last remark did something to Annabelle she never thought any words could ever do. She actually started feeling something for her father. She wasn't sure if it was sympathy, pity, or maybe even something more.

"Then maybe I can find the good guys to help us," she said quietly.

47

Annabelle left her father and walked to Stone's room.

"He wants to team with me to con Jerry into confessing to my mother's murder," she said bluntly and then collapsed on the small couch next to Stone's bed.

"You think you can trust him?"

"Damn it, Oliver, you just spent all that time telling me to forgive the man."

"Forgive him, yes, not trust him."

"I have no reason to trust him at all."

Stone looked at her warily. "I sense a but coming."

"But with all that I *do* trust him. I don't know why, just call it my gut."

"But you need the cavalry?"

"That's what he says."

"I might be able to help."

"I thought so. I mean, they owe you after the last time."

"They never owe you, Annabelle. Or at least they never think they do. But let me see what I can work.

So what do you do with your father in the meantime?"

"I was sort of hoping he could come back to D.C. with us."

"And stay with you? That might be a little dicey with Bagger in the same town."

"Any help there would be appreciated."

"Tell your father to get his things together."

Paddy didn't have anything *to* get together. Everything he owned was already in his battered truck. He insisted on following them down. "Truck's all I've got left. I ain't letting it go."

With Paddy behind them, Stone and Annabelle drove south to Reuben's house in one of the few remaining rural areas of northern Virginia. It was very late when they arrived there, but Stone had called ahead.

They pulled down a gravel drive that was more path than road and bracketed by thick woods. They passed leaning shacks and rotting cars as the wilderness and poverty grew with each click of the odometer. A few minutes later the Nova's headlights flicked across a weed-filled yard and spotlighted a garage with its single overhead door open. The interior was bursting with tools and car parts. Parked beside the garage were six cars, two trucks, three motorcycles and what looked to be a dune buggy, all in various states of being rebuilt. Next to the garage was a mobile trailer that was no longer mobile, being set firmly on cinder blocks.

"Reuben just moved here recently," Stone remarked.

Annabelle gazed back at the garage. "Does he run a chop shop on the side?"

"No, the man's a mechanical genius. I think he's closer to his machines than he is to most people. That's why he loves his motorcycle so much. He says it's far more reliable than any of his three wives ever were."

"Oliver, do you have any *normal* friends?"

"Well, there's you."

"Oh, God, are you in serious trouble."

Stone noted Reuben's truck in the yard and a light on in the trailer.

"They're waiting for us," he said.

Reuben met them at the door and then stared over at the pickup truck, Paddy at the wheel.

"Who's that?"

"A friend," Annabelle answered quickly.

"I thought he might be able to stay here, at least for tonight," Stone said.

"What the hell's one more? He can have the presidential suite. It's right next to the bathroom."

"Where's Milton?" Stone asked.

"Crashed. Apparently winning a shitload of money at a casino and then nearly getting whacked is really exhausting."

"We're going to return Caleb's car now," Stone said. "And then tomorrow I want to meet at my cottage, put all our facts together and see where we go from there. And I'm going to call in Alex to help us." He shot a glance at Annabelle. "With a new angle."

Reuben looked from one to the other. "Okay," he said slowly.

"Thanks, Reuben."

An hour later Stone and Annabelle pulled into the parking lot of Caleb's condo building in D.C. and rode the elevator to the man's apartment. Stone knocked and they heard footsteps approaching the door. It opened. Unfortunately, it wasn't Caleb standing there.

48

"This really is intolerable, Carter," Senator Roger Simpson said.

The two men were in the CIA bunker, seated in leather armchairs and nursing glasses of cabernet.

Simpson continued, "For something like this to raise its ugly head now. When in a few years I'll be sitting in the White House if things go according to plan."

"Roger, if this comes out, you won't be in the running. You might actually be in prison."

Simpson flushed at Gray's stinger but only stared moodily into his wineglass before saying, "Ray Solomon. Who would've thought that would come back to haunt us?"

"It was always a possibility. It was a calculated risk. Sometimes they work, sometimes they don't. I'm sure you did what you thought was right at the time."

"You sound like you weren't involved at all. You were up to your neck in it, same as me."

Gray snapped, "*I* didn't order Ray's death. He was my friend. *You* are the reason he's dead."

"The man committed suicide, in Brazil."

"No, you sent John Carr and his team to kill the man because you were afraid if he found out the truth, he'd expose you."

Simpson stared at Gray over the lip of his glass. "Expose *us*, Carter. Don't ever forget that."

"Ray Solomon was a good man, and a top agent. And now he's called a traitor. His memory has been besmirched."

"Sacrifices are necessary all the time, for the greater good."

"Funny, why do I think you'd never be willing to sacrifice your life for the greater good?"

"Fate has a way of preserving those who can truly make a difference, Carter. The great men always persevere."

"Well, you should call upon the fates now, because someone clearly wants you dead."

"And you too. Don't forget that."

"The fact that the killer thinks I'm already dead gives me a certain latitude with which to operate. Yet in one sense you can't blame the person. Indeed, what you did was inexcusable."

Simpson flushed angrily. "I did what I did for the right reasons. And it was a long time ago. The world was very different. I was very different."

"None of us are *that* different. And it wasn't really that long ago. In fact, it's not past, it's now the present.

It's a lesson in never burning bridges or doing stupid things."

Simpson said nervously, "Donna will go ballistic if any of this comes out."

"And can you blame your wife? Your action could be seen as abominable."

"My action! You had people killed, Carter. Killed."

"We were running the Triple Six Division, Roger, not a preschool for wannabe spies. Every target we were given was duly authorized, often right from 1600 Pennsylvania Avenue. It was our duty to execute on those orders, because the other side was playing the game for all it was worth. Anything less on our part would have been akin to treason."

"Not every killing was authorized, Carter, you know that."

Gray stared pointedly at the senator. "Sometimes it's better that the politicians don't know everything. But Ray Solomon should not have been one of those times, Roger. You shouldn't have done it."

"Easy to say in hindsight. And it was the only time I did such a thing."

"Really? What about John Carr?"

"He was the worst of the lot. Tried to resign from Triple Six. I mean, come on."

"As usual your judgment is simply *stellar.* Carr was actually the *best* of them all."

"That's your opinion."

"And that's why you ordered his death? Because he wanted to stop being an assassin?"

Simpson stiffened. "I don't know what you're talking about. Kill one of our own men? Preposterous."

"You're a very bad liar, Roger. If you really want to make a run for the White House you're going to have to improve your poker face."

"I did not have the man killed."

"About four years ago I had a long chat with Judd Bingham. He told me. It was he, Cole and Cincetti that did it. Carr's own team went after him on *your* orders."

"That is an outrageous comment. I didn't have the authority to order that."

"Authority? Back then? We ran a group of killers. Most of them, except for Carr, enjoyed their work immensely. Bingham said he and the other two were glad to do it for you. They were very upset that Carr wanted to quit the club. They took it as a personal affront."

"Well, since Bingham and the other two are dead there's really no proof of that, is there?"

"And Carr too. He's currently residing at Arlington National Cemetery."

Simpson took a sip of his wine. "I know that."

"At least that's what the official record says."

Simpson glanced at him sharply. "What are you talking about?"

"Carr isn't dead."

Simpson sputtered, "But Bingham said—" He caught himself a second too late.

"Thank you for confirming what I already knew to be true. Bingham was always a liar. He didn't want to admit that Carr got away that night. And Carr managed to kill three of our operatives in the process. Bingham, Cole and Cincetti barely got out alive, though apparently Carr didn't know it was them. Carr was in a class by himself when it came to killing. It was a costly mission, Roger. And one that you should have been taken to task for. You're lucky that Bingham and the other two kept their mouths shut all these years. But they would've been in just as much trouble as you if the truth had come out."

"Again, I don't know what you're talking about."

Gray waited until Simpson had swallowed a mouthful of wine before saying, "Jackie was Carr's daughter; did I ever tell you that? You adopted his daughter."

Simpson slowly set down his glass. Gray noted that the man's hand was trembling.

"No, you failed to mention that," Simpson said in a strained voice. "You said she'd been orphaned but you didn't say who the parents were. I didn't even know Carr had a daughter."

"You'd think when you tried to kill a man that you'd know those details."

"If you suspected my involvement, why did you give the child to us?"

"Something had to be done with the little girl. And you and Donna couldn't have any children. Despite what some people think, I do have a conscience, Roger. It wasn't her fault what happened. And it wasn't mine. It was yours, Bingham's, Cincetti's and Cole's. Do you sense a pattern?"

Simpson jerked straight up. "You think Carr killed them?"

"And tried to kill me. He must've thought, understandably, that I had something to do with his family's death."

"But why would he wait all this time to do it?"

"There, I can only speculate. But he must be considered a suspect."

"If he's still alive."

"Men like Carr are awfully difficult to kill, as you must surely admit now. A team of Triple Sixes couldn't get the job done."

"But I don't understand, how does this tie into Solomon?"

"It may not. Carr may be operating alone and using the Solomon angle as a cover. That's for us to find out. But if Carr is working with someone connected to Solomon's past then we need to track those people down. I have the resources to do so. The current director certainly sees things my way. He should; I trained him."

"And you'll get whoever's doing this?"

"Yes, hopefully before he gets *you.* Since you are most assuredly on the hit list—and quite the easy target actually."

"That's not funny."

"I didn't mean it as a joke. Three men who were far more skilled and far more deeply buried than you are dead. Practically speaking, you're a much softer target."

"I'm getting out of the country for a while, starting tomorrow morning," Simpson snapped. "I'm not going to wait around here to be murdered by some psychopath."

"I'm sure the American taxpayers will understand your shirking your duties in the Congress."

"I don't like your tone, Carter."

In response Gray picked up his Medal of Freedom off the table next to his chair and held it up. "They gave me a lump of metal in return for nearly forty years of service to my country. I was surprised to get it, actually. After all, I had resigned my post as director of National Intelligence, leaving the administration in the lurch."

"I often wondered why you did that."

"You can keep wondering, Roger. That bit of intelligence is mine alone."

Simpson gazed contemptuously around the bunker's interior. "Feels a bit like a rat in a hole down here."

"A person that can kill three former Triple Sixes and nearly me as well is not someone to underestimate. I'll take being in my cozy bunker, for now."

"Wonderful, while I'm exposed on the surface," Simpson said angrily.

"Don't worry, Roger, I understand that they award the Freedom Medal posthumously."

49

Harry Finn had worked hard the next day and, that night, visited an apartment complex in Arlington. The parking spaces were all numbered so it was simple for him to locate the right one. He pulled his van into an empty space, walked over to the jet black Lincoln Navigator and pressed a device against the left rear fender. The blinking red alarm light on the SUV's dashboard instantly died. Finn slid the lock buster out of his jacket pocket and in seconds the truck's door lock cylinder was in his hand. He slid the special ID badge off the rearview mirror where the moron who owned the Lincoln always kept it, replacing it with an identical one, although it wouldn't work like it was supposed to. It didn't have the encryption codes burned into it—codes that were impossible for Finn to duplicate, hence the theft tonight. The owner would just believe it to be defective and have a new one issued. Yet this particular federal agency was notorious for failing to cancel old ID badges. Old badge, new badge, it didn't seem to matter to many bloated bureaucracies. Yet it mattered very much to Finn.

He put the cylinder back, relocked the door, pressed his device against the fender and the alarm system came back to life. There was no sign he'd ever been there. If only the public knew what was out there to rip them off. Yet better they remain oblivious in the belief that they were actually secure.

On the way home Finn glanced at the stolen badge. Good thing he wasn't really a bad guy, because with a little doctoring of the plastic he could topple the entire legislative branch of government single-handed, all 535 members. But there was only one he wanted. Just one.

Stone, Annabelle and Caleb were in the back of a van. Mike Manson, one of Bagger's men, sat next to them. Mike had been the one to open Caleb's door, gun pointed straight at them. Stone hadn't thought they would be following Caleb; it was a miscalculation that apparently was going to lead to their deaths.

"So how's Jerry?" Annabelle asked casually. "Run into any good scams lately?"

Mike said, "Don't know what you're talking about."

"I doubt we're going to the hotel where he's staying," Stone said. "A little too public."

To this Mike said nothing.

An anguished Caleb had his face pressed to the window and seemed focused on not passing out.

"I guess a bribe wouldn't do any good, would it?" Annabelle asked.

Caleb wrenched his face away from the window. "Are you aware that you could go to prison for this!"

Mike pointed his pistol at Caleb's head. "Shut the hell up!"

The van swerved to the side as another vehicle suddenly cut it off. As the driver fought the wheel, Mike took his gaze off Stone for only an instant, but that was enough.

"What the–" Mike began before he slumped hard against the door. His gun clattered to the floorboard. Stone snagged the weapon and leveled it at his head.

Mike's left side was in spasms after Stone had pressed his finger against a spot near the man's rib cage. "Come on, *old man*, give me the pistol before you hurt yourself," Mike said, grimacing in pain.

Stone cranked off a round, blowing away a tip of Mike's ear before the bullet shattered the window. Then he pointed the gun at the driver's head. "Pull it over *now*, before I put the next one in your brain."

The van jerked to a stop on the dirt shoulder.

Stone stared at the stunned and bleeding Mike. "Next time you kidnap someone, *sonny*, tie them up. That way, you won't look like an idiot again."

"Who the hell are you?" Mike cried out.

"Just hope you never really find out."

They bound Mike and the driver using straps and rope they found in the van, and then laid them in a ditch next to the road. They searched them for ID but found none.

Stone climbed in the driver's seat and the three drove off.

Annabelle looked over at Caleb. "Are you all right?"

He turned to her, his face a delicate shade of rage. "I'm fine. Why shouldn't I be? In less than an hour's time I've had my home broken into, been kidnapped and then nearly killed. And now this Bagger monster knows that I lied to him. And he also knows where I live and where I work. Oh joy, joy for me."

"Well, we're not dead, that's something," Stone pointed out.

"Not dead *yet*!" Caleb shot back.

Stone handed Caleb his phone. "Call Alex Ford at home. His number's on my speed dial. Tell him what happened and where he can pick up Bagger's men." He looked at Annabelle. "Jerry made a big mistake. And now we have something to hang him with that doesn't require you and Paddy going after him."

Caleb made the call and they continued on down the road. When they passed a curve a truck shot out from a side road and blocked their way. Stone tried to swerve around it but Annabelle cried out, "It's my father. And Reuben."

It was indeed Paddy Conroy driving and Reuben in the passenger seat. Paddy pulled the truck up next to the van and rolled his window down.

Annabelle leaned across Stone. "What the hell are you two doing here?"

Reuben said, "Got to thinking after you two left that Bagger had visited Caleb at work and maybe he had his guys follow him home. So me and Paddy decided to play a little backup."

Paddy added, "We drove to your friend's place in time to see them come out with you. From what Reuben told me, you"—he pointed at Stone—"just needed a bit of a distraction to take over the situation. And I guess he was right, as it turns out." He glanced over at Annabelle. "I can see why my daughter trusts you so much."

Stone shot a look at Reuben.

"Paddy and me had a nice chat on the way over." He clapped the Irishman on the back. "And let me tell you, the dude can drive."

"Started my career as a wheelman." Paddy added hastily, "For the army, of course."

Stone drove off in the van with Paddy and Reuben following. All were in high spirits at having nailed Bagger and his men. Yet it was not to be.

After Alex sent agents to get Bagger's men, they reported back that the pair had disappeared. After that the news didn't get any better. The pistol Stone had taken from Mike was sterilized; the van stolen. Their kidnappers had not mentioned Bagger's name, so there was nothing to connect any of it to the casino chief. They didn't even have enough to bring him in for questioning. The authorities were not happy about coming up empty. In the future it was made very clear that the cavalry would not come running when called.

It seemed to put them back at square one in their war with Bagger.

Yet it was Oliver Stone who was the most worried. Sterilized weapon, stolen van, no IDs, bound people disappearing in the night with no trace? What if it hadn't been Bagger's men who'd kidnapped them? What if instead of being after Annabelle they were after him?

50

When Mike and his prisoners didn't show up at the pre-arranged spot, Bagger didn't shout or throw objects. He was far more introspective than most people realized. You didn't get to his level without thinking things through from every angle.

The casino boss knew that losing Mike was not a good thing. Worse than that, he didn't know who he'd lost Mike to, or what Mike might be saying to them. The town was crawling with feds. You could spit on any street corner and hit five of them, easy. Bagger's instincts had allowed him to survive many dangerous moments. He could sense this was one of them. He could hop on his jet and make a run for it. Yet that cut against everything he'd built his career on. Jerry Bagger never ran from trouble.

He made some calls. The first one was to bring down some reinforcements from Atlantic City. Bagger then called Joe, his PI guy, and instructed him to dig up some more information that Bagger felt he would need as this whole thing unfolded. The last call was to his lawyer, who knew more of Bagger's secrets than anyone. The man immediately began constructing alibis and legal strategies in case the feds knocked on his client's door.

With that business finished, Bagger decided to take a stroll alone. Unlike Atlantic City, D.C. closed shop early. On a weeknight there were few restaurants, bars or clubs open this late. Yet after about a ten-block jaunt, Jerry found a neon-lighted dive, went inside, grabbed a stool at the bar and ordered a whiskey sour with a chaser from a bartender whose features clearly showed that life had come down on him like a sledgehammer. The fat guy seated next to him gazed droopily into his beer while an Elvis Costello song drifted from the dented jukebox that was coated with decades' worth of beers and tears.

Bagger had grown up in places just like this, hustling for scraps. Nearly sixty years later he was still hustling, only the scraps were now valued in the millions. Yet sometimes he wished he were again that dirty-faced kid with the infectious smile and mile-a-minute mouth ripping people off for dollars with tried-and-true scams, the marks never knowing what had hit them until he was long gone and on to the next scheme.

"So what do people do for fun in this town?" he asked the bartender.

The man started mopping the bar and said, "It's not a town built for fun, least that's my opinion."

"Serious business here, you mean?"

The man grinned. "Only place that can nuke you *and* tax you."

"Some people think we'd all be a lot better off if somebody nuked *this* place."

"Hey, just give me twenty-four hours' warning."

"I'm from Atlantic City."

"Cool place. Afraid I dropped enough of my retirement dollars there, though."

"Ever been to the Pompeii?"

"Oh yeah. Neat casino. Guy who runs it is bad news, so I've heard. Real hardass. But I guess you gotta be to make money in that racket. So more power to the man."

"You been tending bar long?"

"Too long. I wanted to be a Major League pitcher, but my stuff wasn't quite good enough. By the time I realized it, pouring drinks was all I knew how to do. But with three kids to feed, you do what you gotta do."

"What about your wife?"

"Cancer, three years ago. Just when things were looking good, life kicks you right in the gut. Know what I mean?"

"Yeah, I do." Bagger laid ten Franklins down for a tip and rose to leave.

The stunned bartender said, "Mister, what the hell's this for?"

"Just a reminder that even assholes aren't all bad."

Bagger walked back to his hotel. His cell phone

was buzzing, no doubt his security detail checking up on him. He had a lot of enemies and his boys didn't like him being out alone. It wasn't because they loved him, Bagger knew. If he went down, their jobs went away. In Bagger's world you got loyalty either at the end of a gun barrel or by waving enough dollars in front of someone. He didn't bother to answer the call.

He passed by the Washington Monument and stopped. The 555-foot-tall obelisk wasn't capturing his attention, it was the man and woman walking hand in hand along the path near the monument.

Bagger had never had a serious relationship with any woman; he'd been too busy hustling for his fortune. All the women he'd been involved with had either been paid for or looking to get some action from old Jerry in return for giving in. He knew they didn't really care for him and so he never cared about them.

That was his life until Annabelle Conroy had come along and turned him upside down. There had been something about her right from the get-go that had hit him in a place he didn't think he even had anymore. He'd allowed himself to believe that she actually cared for him and not because he could do anything for her.

And then the bottom had dropped out and here he was in the city he hated almost as much as Vegas, looking to kill a woman he could've loved forever. The loss of the forty million hadn't destroyed him. He could always make more money when it came down to it. Yet Annabelle Conroy had stolen the unthinkable from him: his heart.

So enraged was Bagger by this sense of betrayal that if he'd had a gun, he would have shot the couple passing just a few feet away from him. It was all he could do to keep himself from running over and pounding both of them into the dirt.

He turned and walked quickly back to his hotel. When he got there he was in for another surprise. Mike Manson and his sidekick had just returned looking bloody and disheveled.

Before Bagger said anything to them he motioned to one of his other men and mouthed the word, "Clean?"

"We searched 'em," the man said. "No surveillance devices."

Bagger looked at Mike. "What the hell happened?"

"We blew it, Mr. Bagger," Mike admitted. "We had 'em in the van, then the old guy got the gun away from me and tied us up. Took us all this time to get free and back here."

"We had to walk five miles," the other man said.

"I don't give a shit if you had to crawl using your tongues," Bagger roared. "You let a woman and a damn librarian get the drop on you?"

"It wasn't the librarian," Mike said. "He was an older guy, but he was one serious dude. He stuck a finger against my ribs and my whole body went numb." He pointed to his wounded ear. "Then he took a chunk of my ear off with a round from my gun like it was nothing. He was a pro, Mr. Bagger. We weren't expecting that kind of trouble."

"Mike, if I didn't know you're not a screw-up, I'd put a round right through your head."

Mike said nervously, "Yes sir, Mr. Bagger. I know. We crawled behind some trees, and Joe found a chunk of glass we used to cut the ropes off. Right as we were taking off the cops showed up. They must've called them. They didn't see us, though."

"You're sure?"

"Yes sir."

"The guy who nicked you was a pro, huh? What'd he look like?"

Mike told him.

"Maybe a fed?"

"He wasn't dressed like a fed. And he was a little old for that. But the guy was still a pro. And he and Conroy were tight."

Bagger slowly sat down in a chair. Who the hell was Annabelle hooked up with?

51

The senator was not in today, having departed on a sudden fact-finding trip, taking many of his staff with him and leaving only a skeleton crew behind. Finn had found this helpful information out on Simpson's Web site, where the senator touted the trip as one that would benefit all Alabamans and Americans. How a first-class trek to the Grand Cayman Islands was going to accomplish that, Finn didn't know. What he did think was that Simpson had been warned about the other killings and had decided to get out of town. That was all right, he had to come back to D.C. at some point. After all, he was a U.S. senator. They couldn't avoid their duties forever, though some had made valiant efforts to do so over the years.

Finn was dressed in government-standard work clothes, his badge dangling from his neck, his case of tools swinging in one hand. His assured demeanor, dead-on photo ID and polished story of work to be done here resulted in his being quickly allowed on his way.

Getting off the elevator, Finn eyed the glass door

of Roger Simpson's office, the Alabama state flag next to it. The banner was a crimson Saint Andrew's Cross on a white field patterned after the Confederate battle flag. As it had over 150 years ago for the Union Blue, the flag represented a perfect target for Harry Finn. He walked up to the door and through the glass saw the young receptionist sitting at the front desk.

He'd enlarged the photos he'd taken of the office and the woman on his previous visit here. They had clearly shown her nameplate on the desk.

He poked his head in the door and held up his phony work order. "Hey, Cheryl, Bobby from building maintenance. I was called about your front door lock a few days ago. Sorry I'm just getting to it, but we've had a backlog. Do you know what's wrong with the darn thing? We've had complaints from other offices about theirs too."

The harried young woman, who was fielding phone calls in rapid succession, cupped her hand over the phone receiver. "No idea."

"I'll just take a quick look at it, then. Just sit tight," Finn said. The receptionist smiled gratefully before turning back to her work.

Finn knelt down, examined the lock and slid a tiny piece of metal into the keyhole. He spent a couple more minutes pretending to fuss with the door and said, "You're good to go now, Cheryl."

She gave him a wave. As Finn packed up his tools he glanced inside the office. He had already learned there was no alarm panel and no motion sensors, but it never hurt to check again.

Out in the hall there was a surveillance camera set up on the ceiling at the juncture of two halls. Finn had already timed it. It changed positions every two minutes so it could sweep both corridors. He walked down the hall and watched the camera while checking his watch. It was still on the two-minute sweeps. That would be all he needed. Guards patrolled the halls at night, but he had learned that they did the even floors on odd hours and the odd floors on even hours. He waited until the hall was clear of people and the camera pointed away from him. Then he quickly jimmied the lock of a room he knew was used to store holiday decorations, and slipped inside. He wedged himself in the back, lay on the floor and went to sleep.

At two minutes after midnight, Finn slipped a video wire under the door of the storage room and did a quick look-see up and down the hall. It was clear. The camera was sweeping the other corridor.

He hustled to Simpson's office door. The piece of metal he'd inserted in the lock earlier performed only one function, but did it flawlessly. It made the door seem to be locked when it actually wasn't if you had one special piece of equipment, which Finn did. He inserted the magnetized end of his tool in the lock, pulled out the metal piece and the door clicked open.

Finn immediately went to work. He jogged

through the anterooms and into Simpson's spacious office. He knelt down by the desk's kneehole and flipped the computer CPU around, revealing the back. He unscrewed the cover, slipped his device inside and connected it to other components inside the computer.

Finn had been able to get his device past security because it didn't have any explosive materials in it. Instead, the device had been designed to ignite a chemical reaction inside the components in the CPU. It was a reaction that would make the otherwise harmless CPU a bomb, a possibility no one in the computer industry would want you to know. The device had attached to it a wireless receiver with a range of about fifteen hundred yards, more than enough, Finn had calculated. He replaced the CPU's cover and put the unit back under the desk.

Next, he sat down at the computer and turned it on. The screen powered up but a password was needed. Busy senators didn't have time to recall elaborate or obscure passwords, so Finn started simply typing in names. The third one did the trick: "Montgomery," the capital of Alabama.

He typed in the commands he needed and then shut the computer down. The last thing he did was place a miniature battery-powered surveillance device near a flowerpot on a high shelf by the senator's couch. The vines of the plant provided an ideal cover for the tiny camera. Now Finn had a direct video and audio link to Simpson's office. He would put it to good use.

He went back to the glass door and checked his watch, waiting for the surveillance camera to click to the other hall. As soon as it did, he was out the door and back into the storage room. He retrieved from his tool bag and powered up a small receiving unit that looked like a BlackBerry, and stared at the picture on the screen. He had chosen the location of his miniature camera well; he could see all of Simpson's office clearly. He turned off the unit, lay on the floor and went back to sleep.

The next morning he slipped out of the storage room and spent some time going up and down elevators, pretending to be heading to assignments. Then he walked out of the building with a group of other people, caught the Metro out to Virginia, picked up his car and drove to the office.

Now all he had to do was wait for Roger Simpson to return. And what a homecoming it would be for the man who'd helped kill his father.

Yet even more than that, Simpson's death would mean the end of Harry Finn's journey. No more killing, no more hearing the story from his mother. Something told him that his mother was only alive because she was waiting for that to happen. As soon as Simpson was dead, Finn suspected that his mother's life would also end. Revenge was a powerful force, and could keep even death at bay. And when his mother passed, Finn would mourn her, grieve for her, but also be immensely relieved at finally being free.

After doing some work at the office and going over still more details on the plan of attack against the Capitol, he left and picked the kids up from school. He spent an hour of batting-cage time with Patrick, helped Susie with her homework and went over high school choices with David. When Mandy got back from the grocery store, he helped her make dinner.

"You seem to be in a good mood," she commented as he scraped potatoes in the kitchen sink.

"I had a great day yesterday," he said.

"I wish you hadn't had to pull an all-nighter. You must be exhausted."

"No, I'm actually pretty full of energy." He finished with the last potato, wiped off his hands and slipped his arms around her. "I was thinking we all could take a trip somewhere, maybe out of the country. The kids have never been to Europe."

"That would be great, Harry, but it's expensive."

"We've had a good year. I've got some money socked away. Next summer might be a good time to do it. I've sort of got things mapped out."

"How come I'm always the last to know about these things?"

"Just wanted to have my ducks in a row before I presented it to the commander in chief for approval, ma'am. That's how the navy trains you." He gave her a kiss.

"You really do have mood swings, mister," she said.

"Like I said before, I see light at the end of the tunnel."

She laughed. "Let's just hope the light isn't a train heading your way."

As she turned back to the stove, Finn's jovial manner disappeared.

A train heading my way, he thought. He hoped his wife didn't turn out to be prophetic.

52

After the spoiled kidnapping attempt Caleb and Paddy had stayed at Stone's cottage, while Annabelle had gone back to her hotel, checked out and moved into another one in a different part of the city. She called Stone with the new address.

Early in the morning Stone received a call from an upset Reuben.

"Milton's driving me nuts, Oliver," Reuben complained. "He's cleaned up my whole house. I can't find a damn thing. And Delta Dawn's afraid to even come inside because the damn vacuum's been running nonstop for hours." Delta Dawn was Reuben's hound of no pedigree whatsoever.

His voice dropped to a near whisper. "And you're not going to believe what he's done in the bathroom. It looks like something out of a women's magazine. I'm too damn embarrassed to even take a crap in there."

Stone said wearily, "I don't have room for him here, I'm pretty full at the moment, Reuben."

"I know, that's why I called. I thought Paddy could

come and stay with me while Milton bunked with you. I mean, Paddy's more my kind of roommate."

"Finding you the ideal companion is not a priority right now; staying alive is," Stone said bluntly. "And the less Paddy's out in public the better."

Reuben let out a deep sigh. "Okay, I guess I can hang with Mr. OCD for a little while longer. But we better nail this Bagger creep soon. Milton's already started to talk about taking me clothes shopping. And I draw the line at that shit."

Several hours later Stone watched as a very irritable and wrinkled-looking Caleb came out of the bathroom dressed in his clothes from the night before.

"Caleb, when the men grabbed you last night, did they say anything?"

Caleb scowled. "Oh, yes. They said if I made a sound they'd kill me! And to think that when I was putting the key in my door, all I was contemplating was having a nice glass of sherry and rereading the opening to *Don Quixote*."

"I meant did they mention that they were working for Jerry Bagger?"

"No, they didn't. Actually, they didn't really say anything. They didn't have to, they had guns."

"Did they mention Annabelle?"

"No, nothing like that. Why?"

"Did they mention someone named John Carr?"

"Who's he?"

"Never mind. Did they say that name?"

"No."

Stone really had no way of knowing if the kidnappers were after Annabelle or John Carr. They could have tracked him down through Caleb, Stone reasoned. He had been to the library before to visit his friend. They had all just assumed that the men were with Bagger. But what if they were part of the team that had been killing Triple Sixes? That had killed Carter Gray? Yet if they were after him, surely they could have discovered his alter ego and also where he lived.

"So what do I do now?" Caleb asked, breaking in on Stone's musings. "I should've left for work ten minutes ago. I've got no clothes, no toiletries, nothing."

Stone, annoyed at being interrupted, said curtly, "Call in sick."

"That takes care of today. What about tomorrow and the day after that?"

"Do you have vacation time?"

"Yes, but I work for the federal government. You can't just up and take vacation time. You have to plan, you have to give notice."

"We'll worry about that tomorrow. For now, just stay here and relax."

"Relax! After being kidnapped and almost being killed? After being shut out of my home and job because some maniac is after me? You expect me to relax?"

"Well, it's either that or slit your wrists. I'll let you make the decision," Stone snapped as he headed out the door.

"Where are you going?"

"To see our friend."

"Great. You can tell *Annabelle* that I need more friends like her like I need a colonoscopy without anesthesia."

Paddy emerged from the bathroom, his hair wet from the shower. "What's going on?"

Stone said, "Caleb here was just about to make you some breakfast, right, Caleb?"

"What?"

Paddy looked from Stone to Caleb and smiled. "Well, that's damn nice of you."

For an instant Caleb looked like he might start screaming, but he calmed just as quickly. While Paddy had been sleeping, Stone had told Caleb all about the man, including the fact that he was dying.

Caleb said graciously, "I am a *public* servant after all."

"I'll leave you to it then," Stone replied.

As Stone walked quickly out of the graveyard part of him was afraid that Annabelle would have fled again, after the close call the night before. Yet half an hour later he found her in her room at the new hotel. She'd just finished breakfast. She poured him a cup of coffee and perched on the edge of the bed in her hotel robe, looking tired and anxious.

"How's Paddy?"

"He actually seems better this morning. More of a spring in his step."

"It's because of the action last night. He thrives on that. Always has."

"We're lucky he was there last night. He saved our lives."

"I know," Annabelle said in a not-so-pleased tone. "It pisses me off. Now I sort of owe him."

Choosing his words carefully, Stone said, "Did you recognize the men last night? I mean as definitely being with Bagger?"

"No, but who else could it be?"

"You remember that little problem of mine I mentioned?"

"Yes."

"Well, it might be possible that the men last night were after *me*, not you."

"What? Who would be after you?"

"Get dressed. We're going to take a little ride. There's something you need to know about me."

"Where are we going?"

"Arlington National Cemetery. There's something I have to show you."

53

"Oliver, don't you get tired of graveyards? I mean, it seems a little obsessive," Annabelle commented as they trudged along the asphalt at Arlington, the nation's most exalted burial ground for its military dead. Most of the graves were represented by a simple white marker, although some of the statuary over the tombs of the famous, or else the very rich, were extraordinarily ostentatious, and often in rather poor taste. To Stone it seemed the less grandiose the grave marker the more the departed had actually done for his country.

He said, "Come on. It's not much farther."

He led her down the familiar path, counting off the rows in his head. This was a quiet section of the cemetery, one that he had often visited just to have some peace.

An instant later, he felt himself stagger, his balance suddenly gone. The area was not so quiet and peaceful today. At the thirty-ninth grave marker in the fourth row of this section of dead there was a great deal of activity in fact. Men were digging. As Stone and

Annabelle watched, the coffin was raised out of the earth and carried past them to a waiting van that had been driven onto the path.

"Oliver?" Annabelle said. "What is it? What's wrong?" She put a hand on his shoulder as he steadied himself against a tree.

Stone finally found his voice. "Do not follow me out of here. I'll meet you back at the cottage."

"But—"

"Just go." He set off in the direction of the departing van.

As the cemetery workers started to fill the hole back in, Annabelle strolled casually by the grave.

"I thought they were supposed to put coffins *in* the graves, not take them *out*," she said.

One worker glanced up at her, but said nothing. He went back to his shoveling.

She moved a bit closer, squinting to read the name on the marker.

"Uh, can you tell me where they do the changing of the guard here?" she asked as she edged closer.

As the worker told her she glanced over his shoulder and finally made out the name chiseled on the marker.

"John Carr," she said to herself.

On foot, Stone followed the van until it hit the main road and then shot out of sight, after passing around the traffic circle leading away from the cemetery. It didn't cross over Memorial Bridge into Washington. Instead the van headed west, farther into Virginia. Stone had a good idea where it and the coffin were going: Langley, home of the CIA.

He called Reuben on his cell phone.

"I want you to contact every friend you have at DIA and find out why a grave was exhumed at Arlington National Cemetery today."

"Whose grave?" Reuben asked.

"A man by the name of John Carr."

"Did you know the guy?"

"As well as I know myself. Hurry, Reuben, it's important."

Stone clicked off and made another phone call, this time to Alex Ford, the only living person other than Annabelle Conroy who knew that Stone's real name was John Carr.

"You saw them dig it up?" Alex said.

"Yes. Please find out what you can."

Stone walked back to his cottage, certain that Annabelle, who'd driven them both over to Arlington National, would beat him there.

She was standing by his desk when he walked in. "You look good for a dead man."

He said, "Where are Paddy and Caleb?"

"They went to the grocery store. You apparently don't keep much food here. Caleb told me to tell you he was appalled." She motioned to the papers on

Stone's desk. "You've got quite a file going on Jerry here."

"Jerry and you," he said, startling her.

"You dug up stuff on me?"

"No, my friend only pulled Bagger's file. The stuff on you is just conjecture."

He sat down behind his desk.

"So the cemetery piece is bad, I take it."

Stone said, "Let's put it this way—when they open that coffin, they'll be surprised what they don't find in it, namely me."

"Is there another body in the coffin?"

He shrugged. "I didn't have any input in the decision. I was too busy avoiding *being* the body in the coffin."

"Why would they be digging it up now?"

"I don't know."

"So what was the problem you mentioned earlier?"

"It's not something I can really talk about."

Her face flushed angrily. "You're telling *me* that? After I spilled my guts to you? And I've never done that with anybody. Ever! Now I want the truth."

Inwardly, Stone winced. For years he'd kept a sign in Lafayette Park that had read, "I want the truth."

"Annabelle, it's not something I can talk—"

"Don't. Don't try to make bullshit excuses. I took bullshit to an art form."

Stone simply sat there, while Annabelle tapped the heel of her shoe on the plank flooring. "Look,

Oliver, or John, or whatever the hell your real name is."

"I told you my real name before. It's John Carr."

"Good, that's a start. Keep going."

He rose. "No. I won't. And I can't help you now with Jerry Bagger. In fact, the faster you can get away from me the better. Take your father and use all your money to run as far and as fast as you can. I'm sorry, Annabelle. I'm sorry. If you're anywhere near me, you'll die. I can't have that on my conscience too."

He gripped her arm, walked her to the front door and closed it behind her.

54

Harry Finn's mother rose early. The pain, the gnawing at her bones, always made her rise before dawn.

She used the bathroom, shuffled back to her bed and read through her newspapers with the discipline of a lifetime. The radio and TV news shows followed in her ritual of endless fact-finding. And that's when she found herself staring at his face up there on the screen. She clawed at the remote control, and his grinning, smug countenance disappeared.

Her breaths coming in gasps, she looked down at the cell phone her son had given her. She had never called him on it; it was only reserved for emergencies, he'd told her. She kept it tied to a string that she wore around her neck. She only took it off to bathe. She needed to call him. She needed to know about the man. The face on the TV. Was it true? Could it be true?

She heard someone coming and quickly slipped back on the bed. The door opened and the attendant came in, whistling.

"How are we today, Miss Queenie?" the attendant

said. The nickname had come from her patient's imperious manner.

The old woman's face had assumed a vacant expression. She muttered a few words in the odd language she spoke. To anyone else it would sound like mindless ramblings, which was exactly what she intended. The attendant was very familiar with this speech.

"Okay, you just go right on jabbering while I get your dirty clothes and clean up the bathroom. Whatever makes you happy, Miss Queenie." The attendant glanced over at the well-thumbed newspapers and smiled. Miss Queenie wasn't nearly as out of it as she wanted people to think.

The woman performed her duties and left. Only then did she sit up and look at the phone again. It was odd that when one grew old decisions that were made quickly when young now required extensive internal deliberation. To call or not to call?

Before she had actually made up her mind her fingers punched in the numbers.

It was answered before the first ring was even finished. He had obviously recognized the number on the caller ID.

Finn's voice was low but clear. "What's happened? Are you hurt?' he asked firmly.

"No. I am fine."

"Then why did you call?"

"I saw on the news that he left the country. The

man is going on vacation. This man can take a holiday? Is this true? Tell me!"

"I'll take care of it. Hang up, now."

"But he must—"

"Don't say it. Hang up. Now."

"No one can understand what we're saying."

"Now!"

She clicked off and put the phone back around her neck. Harry was angry with her. She should not have called. But she could not help herself. All day and all night she sat here, in this place, in this hell, rotting, and thinking only of it. And then to see the man on the TV.

She scuttled over to the window and looked out. It was a beautiful day and it didn't matter to her. She did not belong to this world anymore. She belonged to the past and that was nearly gone as well. Her family, her friends, her husband, all dead. Only Harry was left. And now he was angry at her. Yet he would get over it. He always got over it. He was a good son; a mother could have no better son than she did. She opened the drawer and pulled out the single remaining photo she had of her husband.

She lay back on her bed, the photo over her heart, and dreamed of the death of Roger Simpson.

Harry Finn slowly put the phone back in his pocket and returned to the kitchen, where Mandy and the children stared anxiously at him. When his phone had rung and he saw the number come up, he'd forgotten that he even had a family. He had raced from the room, certain that his mother was calling to tell him they had found her. That she was about to die.

Susie had a bit of oatmeal dangling from her mouth. Patrick had dropped his fork on the floor, where George the Labradoodle was licking the egg off it. David had stopped stuffing his backpack with schoolbooks and was staring worriedly at his dad. Mandy was standing by the stove, spatula in hand, the pancake in the pan turning black.

She said anxiously, "Harry, is everything okay?"

He tried to smile, but his mouth couldn't manage it. "False alarm. Thought something weird was happening, my mistake."

Susie, perhaps because of the look on her dad's face, or the unnatural tremor in his voice, started to cry. He picked her up and pressed her face against his. "Hey, baby, it's okay. Daddy just made a mistake. That's all."

She cupped his face with her soft hands and gave him the kind of penetrating stare that only little kids seemed able to muster. "You promise?" she said in a tiny voice. The undercurrents of fear in her question cut right through Finn's soul.

He kissed her on the cheek, partly so he wouldn't have to look into those pleading, piercing eyes. "I promise. Even daddies make mistakes." He looked over at his wife, who had recovered a bit from her own terror. "But mommies don't, right?" He gave Susie a tickle and with his other hand squeezed Patrick's slender shoulder. "Right?"

"Right, Daddy," Susie said.

"Right," Patrick agreed.

Finn drove the kids to school and dropped them off. David was the last out of the car. He leaned back in, pretending to fiddle with his shoelaces while his siblings headed into the building.

"Hey, Pop, you sure everything's cool?"

"Absolutely, buddy, no worries."

"You can talk to me, you know, about anything."

Finn smiled. "I thought that was my line."

"I'm serious, Pop. I know sometimes it's hard to talk to Mom about stuff. Sometimes you need another guy to kick stuff around."

Finn reached out and shook his son's hand. "I appreciate that, Dave. More than you'll ever know." *I wish I could tell you everything, son, but I can't. I will never be able to. I'm sorry.* He thought this even as his immensely strong fingers tightened around his son's. He didn't want to let go.

"Have a good one, Pop." David closed the door and followed Susie and Patrick inside.

Finn slowly drove off, passing the cars of other parents, who, he was reasonably certain, would never knowingly trade their lives for his.

He looked in the rearview mirror as David disappeared into the school building.

If I fail, son, just remember me for the father I was, not the man I had to become.

Down the hall from Finn's mother's room a man named Herb Daschle yawned and stretched as he sat in front of a bed where another man lay unconscious. Daschle had been here since midnight and his shift did not end for another four hours. He nodded to an attendant as she came in to check the patient. It was at that instant that the man in the bed started moaning and a few words rolled from his mouth. Daschle jumped up, grabbed the attendant by the arm and pushed her out the door, slamming it shut behind her. He bent down to the man's face and listened intently. When he fell silent, Daschle whipped out a telephone and made a call, repeating exactly what he had said. Then he went to the door and called out. The attendant came back in, looking a little flustered. But this had happened before.

"Sorry about that," Daschle said politely as he resumed his seat.

"You people are going to give me a heart attack," the woman said under her breath. She didn't dare say it out loud. No, she didn't dare. Not with people like that.

55

"I'm grateful that Gregori was so helpful," Carter Gray said to the CIA director.

The men were sitting in the study in the bunker. Gray was actually growing quite fond of his current billet. There was something to be said for living underground. The weather was never a problem, no traffic jams, and he rarely enjoyed anyone's company as much as his own.

The former Soviet ambassador to the U.S. during the final years of the Cold War, Gregori Tupikov, was no longer serving the Russian people; he was doing quite well serving himself. He was now a fat and happy capitalist and a recent export from his homeland. He had joined an investment group that had taken over the formerly state-controlled coal industry and then sold it to another group of fellow Russians. Gregori had been wise enough to flee the country before the government hammer came down on the country's newly minted rich. He lived most of the year in Switzerland but owned apartments in Paris and New York, his millions carefully managed by Goldman Sachs.

Gray finished reading over the file report obtained from the meeting with Tupikov. "So Lesya and Rayfield Solomon *were* married in Volgograd; then the newlyweds managed to get out of the Soviet Union."

The director nodded. "According to what Gregori remembered and found out from old colleagues, they apparently made their way first to Poland, then to France and from there to Greenland. Was Lesya Jewish, by the way?"

"I don't know. Solomon was, although he wasn't a practicing Jew. The spy business oftentimes put a cramp in one's religious obligations."

"I make it to the Presbyterian church every Sunday," the director said.

"Congratulations. If Gregori knew that much back then, why didn't he do something about it?" Gray answered his own question. "He assumed she was still working for the Soviets."

"Well, wasn't she?" the director said in a puzzled tone.

"Of course," Gray said casually. "And after Greenland?"

"Unfortunately, there the trail turns cold. And it might well remain cold. It was a long time ago, after all."

"It *can't* remain cold," Gray snapped.

"Where exactly was Solomon found dead? That part of the file is missing too."

Gray looked up from the documents he was studying, pretending to recall the details. They were actually seared into his mind. "Brazil. São Paulo."

"What was he doing in São Paulo?"

"Not sure. He wasn't working for us then, of course. Lesya had turned him."

"And he died there?"

Gray nodded. "We were alerted by our contacts in South America. We did an investigation. But it was clear he'd killed himself."

The director looked at Gray and Gray looked at the director.

"Of course," the director said. "And Lesya was left on her own?"

"Looks that way. Anything else?"

"Perhaps."

Gray glanced up to see the director smiling smugly. He recalled that as a young case agent the current CIA director had possessed the worst poker face of any man he'd ever trained, and also a vastly annoying air of superiority, most of it undeserved. Gray believed he had shamed these weaknesses out of the man. Yet as head of the CIA it was clear his insufferable qualities had risen once more.

"Tell me."

"Gregori must've been in a good mood. As you suggested when our man met him in Paris, he fed him lobsters by the ton."

"And Moskovskaya vodka? That's his favorite."

"By the gallon. And we scrounged up a redhead or two."

"And?"

"And he said that he recalled a rumor that Lesya *had* to get married."

"*Had* to get married?" Gray said, looking puzzled.

The director made a motion with his hand in front of his stomach.

"She was pregnant?" Gray said immediately.

"That's evidently what Gregori believes."

Gray sat back. *It's the son out there murdering people.* "So based on the rough timeline we're working with, the child would be in his or her mid-thirties today?"

The director nodded. "But I highly doubt that the kid's last name is Solomon."

"But if Lesya and Solomon married in Russia while she was pregnant, and showing, where was the child born? If they left Russia immediately after the wedding the birth could have been in Poland, France, Greenland, or of course Canada."

"Canada? The last known stop of theirs was in Greenland. Where does Canada come in?"

Gray studied the man who headed up the nation's premier intelligence agency. He had started out at the CIA, then gone into politics, and there he had stayed until a president of dubious judgment had tossed his friend a political bone and made him CIA director. *God help this country.*

"Why does one go westward to Greenland except on the way to Canada? Even back then there were numerous direct flights to the U.S. And it was a favorite stopping place for spies. When I was in the field I often stopped in Greenland before coming home. You could always spot someone following you in Greenland. Humanity damn well stuck out in the frozen tundra!"

"Okay, but maybe they came to *this* country to have the child? That would make him a U.S. citizen. It'd be easier."

"I don't think so, not for the birth. And less complicated for her to sneak into Canada and have the baby there than in the U.S. The records could always be falsified later."

"Even with all that, it doesn't leave us much to go on."

"I disagree. From Greenland to Canada the ports of entry are limited, and were even more so back then. Montreal? Toronto? Ottawa? Perhaps Nova Scotia and Newfoundland? We can start there."

"Start there doing what exactly?"

"We'll limit it to a single twelve-month period." Gray named the year. "And we will search the records of births in those places. Just boys for now."

"Why not girls too?"

"Just boys for now," Gray repeated.

"That's still an enormous search. And we have that disaster readiness drill on Capitol Hill coming up that

DHS demanded and left us to do the lion's share of the work. It's requiring an inordinate amount of our time."

"The birth records should be computerized now. That should simplify things greatly."

"Yes, but still. The resources required to—"

Gray leaned forward and silenced the man with one of his most intimidating stares. "The consequences of *not* doing so are potentially catastrophic to this country."

56

Annabelle waited outside until her father returned from the nearby grocery store with Caleb. Without a word of explanation she told Paddy to follow her back to her hotel in his truck. When they got there she led her father up to her room.

Annabelle's mind was racing. She'd been counting on Stone to help her. And now the man had simply abandoned her, literally closing the door in her face. She should never have trusted him. She should've learned by now that you could only count on yourself.

"Annie?" Paddy finally said. "Talk to me, girl, what the hell's going on?"

She looked over at her father as though she'd forgotten he was even there. "What's going on is we just got screwed. The help I thought we were going to get with Bagger isn't coming."

"No cavalry?"

"No cavalry."

"The guy named Oliver. Reuben told me a bit about him. Is he the guy who was going to help us do it?"

"Yes, but he's not going to anymore. He apparently has more pressing business."

He slapped the arm of his chair. "Now what?"

"Now we run. Bagger will have the airports and train station watched, but he doesn't have enough manpower to cover the roads. We'll need to dump your truck. Then we'll be on our way."

"On our way where?"

"Does it matter? So long as it's not here?"

"And we just let Jerry walk away?"

"Better than him *carrying* us away, don't you think? We live to fight another day." As soon as she said the words she glanced at her father. "I'm sorry, I didn't mean . . ."

"I don't have another day. I either do it now, or I don't do it at all."

"I told you, we don't have the cavalry."

"Then I'll think of something else."

"You can't take on Jerry by yourself."

"I've got you, don't I?"

She looked out the window, shaking her head. "Do you know how long it took me to plan my hit on Jerry?"

"Probably longer than I've got left. But I'm not walking away from this. I *can't* walk away from this."

"Yesterday you weren't doing anything to go after Jerry. What's changed?"

He rose and gripped her arm. "What's changed is *you*. Now you know I was in jail when your mum got killed. I'm still a son of a bitch, but not as big of a one as you thought."

"What are you saying, that you're doing this for me?"

"No, I mean, not just you. I'm doing it for Tammy, because she didn't deserve to die like that. And I'm doing it for me, because Bagger took the only person I ever really loved from me."

Annabelle pulled her arm free and looked away.

"I didn't mean it that way, Annabelle."

She pointed to the scar on her face. "Let's just say I never had any delusions that you actually loved me."

Paddy reached his hand out to touch her face but she jerked back.

"I had no right to do that," he said. "But I was teaching you a lesson I never wanted you to forget. You blew that claim at the casino. Sure, you were young, and the young make mistakes. But I'll wager you never made that mistake again, did you?"

"No."

"I never gave a shit about any of the crews I worked with. Hell, I never bothered giving any of 'em a scar. If they made a mistake I let 'em know it, sure. But I didn't give a damn if they screwed up down the road with somebody else and got their knees broken for the trouble."

"So, my scar was what, tough love?"

"Your mum never wanted you to get into the con.

But we were shorthanded that summer and it was my idea to use you. You caught on fast, faster than I did at your age. Ten years later you were better than I ever was. Moved on to the long cons while I was still doing my three-card monte on street corners. For chump change."

"That was your choice."

"No, not really. Plain fact was I wasn't good enough to do the long. They say you're either born to it or not. I wasn't."

"Okay, where does that leave things? You can't do the long and the long is what it'll take to get to Jerry."

"I can't do it without you, Annabelle. But if you won't help me, I'm going to try anyway."

"If you do, he'll kill you."

"I'm dead anyway. And I doubt even Jerry could come up with a more painful way to die than what I've got ahead of me."

"You are really complicating my life."

"Will you help me?"

Annabelle didn't answer him.

"Look, can't you talk to your friend again? Maybe he'll reconsider."

Annabelle was about to say no, but hesitated. What she was thinking was she might go back to Stone's cottage. If he was there she could make another pitch for help. But if he wasn't there, which she suspected was the case, Annabelle would just take all of the "files" that Stone had compiled on her and her problems with Jerry. She didn't want any of that just lying around for someone, cops or bad guys, to find.

"I'll give it another shot."

As she walked down to her car she realized she couldn't just leave her father to deal with Jerry alone. Which meant they would both end up dying.

Some choice.

57

After Annabelle and Paddy had left, Stone put Caleb in a taxi with some old clothes of his and gave the driver the address of a hotel nearby.

"Oliver, why can't I stay here?" Caleb said, obviously frightened.

"That would not be smart. I'll call you later."

It was only when the cab had driven away and he was finally alone that Stone started thinking about what he'd done to Annabelle.

"I abandoned her," he said. "After I promised to help. After I told her to stay." Yet what could he do? And anyway, she'd probably be on a flight within a few hours, on her way to that South Pacific island. She'd be safe there.

But what if she didn't run? What if she stubbornly decided to go after Bagger anyway? With no support? She'd said she needed the cavalry. Could he still deliver that to her?

The next instant the phone rang. It was Reuben. He said, "Nothing from my contacts at DIA, Oliver. They didn't know about the cemetery thing. But

Milton did find something on the Net. Here, I'll put him on."

Milton's voice came over the phone. "It wasn't much, Oliver, but there was breaking news about a grave being dug up at Arlington. No one from the government would comment."

"Did it mention the name on the grave marker?"

"Someone named John Carr," Milton said. "Is that a problem?"

Stone didn't bother to answer. He clicked off.

After all these years John Carr had suddenly come back to life. Ironically, Stone had never felt more dead than he did right now.

Why now? What had happened? The truth struck him as he slowly walked back through the cemetery gates and sat down on his front porch.

He'd been set up.

If John Carr was no longer dead, then the person killing old members of Triple Six would now add him back onto his list of targets.

I'm bait, Stone said to himself. *They're going to use me to flush the killer. And if he murders me before they catch him, who cares. And even if I do manage to survive? It won't be for very long.* All John Carr would be now was an embarrassment to the government. His own country would have many reasons to want him dead and not a single one that Stone could think of to keep him alive. It was absolutely brilliant in its simplicity. His death warrant had been signed.

And there was only one man who would've been capable of thinking it all up, Stone knew.

Carter Gray! He is alive.

He packed a small bag, locked up the cottage and fled through the woods behind the cemetery.

Harry Finn was carefully balancing a butter knife on a table where he was sitting so the knife was standing up on edge. It was harder than it looked, yet Finn could accomplish it every time and within a few seconds. He did this whenever he was unsure of something. He was seeking balance. If he could do it with the knife, he could do it with his life. At least that was his thinking. It was never that easy in reality.

"Harry?"

He looked up into the face of one of his team members. They had been discussing the Capitol building project over lunch at their office.

"Did you get a chance to review the ventilation plans?" the woman asked.

He nodded. They'd gotten the documentation through an ingenious tactical combination that involved breaking into the van of the architect hired to work on the Capitol Visitor Center. From that they copied necessary information and then used that to phone freak their way to many details of the new construction.

"The plans indicated that it will hook into the

Capitol building, but I need to confirm that. We're going tonight, in fact, to do it. And it should be accessible from the delivery tunnel, but I'm going to verify that too." He looked at the man sitting next to him, who was going over a set of drawings and specs. "How about the transport?"

"All done." The man laid out the details to Finn.

Finn glanced down at the ID badge he'd earlier stolen from the SUV. This one badge had gotten him a lot of mileage. With the embedded encryption he could simply change out the surface information—photo, name, etcetera—and the badge would get him into myriad places, none of which he should have access to. He'd heard the government was beginning to discover this flaw in their security system, but Congress moved with glacial speed when it came to things like that. Finn figured they'd have the problem worked out by the time he was drawing Social Security. And even that might be optimistic.

The meeting adjourned and he went to his office and worked for the rest of the day. Later, he changed into a Capitol police uniform, doctored his badge and headed to D.C. that night, where he met up with a buddy, similarly dressed. There were sixteen hundred officers on the Capitol police force to guard roughly one square mile of land. It was a ratio any other city would have killed for. Congress liked to feel safe, and it did control the purse strings.

And yet all that money had not made the folks

much safer, thought Finn as he and his colleague strolled around the grounds of the Capitol that night. In fact, he was going to prove the truth of that statement tonight.

They made their way to the construction site of the visitor center and went in, pretending to make rounds. Work here went on 24/7, so he and his buddy jawed with some of the construction workers and then moved along. They passed a fellow officer, whom they exchanged both pleasantries and gripes with. Finn informed the cop that he'd just transferred over from the U.S. Park Police, where he'd been assigned to the San Francisco area.

"Housing is cheaper here," Finn said. "San Fran is off the charts. I actually bought a town house for what I paid for a condo out there."

"You're lucky," said the other cop. "I was a postal cop down in *Arkansas* before I moved here about five years ago. I'm still living in a three-bedroom apartment in Manassas that I can barely afford, and I've got four kids."

Finn and his friend headed on and finally arrived at the spot that was the only reason they'd come here tonight.

It was right where the plans indicated it would be. Ready access from the tunnel, and by the look of things it was already operational. That would make their task easier. Finn picked the lock of one door and they slipped inside it. He studied the instrument boxes on the wall and then snapped several pictures of the flow schematic. Next he drew a diagram of the area on a notepad, listing all access doors, halls and checkpoints they'd passed. Then they made their way through a series of hallways and into a small HVAC room. The ventilation return was in the ceiling. The opening was too narrow for Finn to get through, but his partner was smaller. Finn gave him a boost and the fellow disappeared into the ductwork. Thirty minutes later he was back.

"Like we thought, Harry, goes right into the Capitol." The man gave Finn a detailed description of the route he'd just taken, and Finn drew it out on paper.

They slipped back outside, walked away from the Capitol and turned down a street toward the Hart Senate Building. His partner went to the right and Finn to the left. He passed alongside the building, where nine stories up sat Roger Simpson's office. As Finn counted across the windows to the one he knew was the Alabama senator's digs, he pointed his finger at the window and said, "Boom."

He couldn't wait.

He reached his car and drove off. Turning on the radio to the local news station, he heard the announcer talking about a grave being dug up at Arlington National Cemetery that morning. As yet no one knew why.

"John Carr," the radio said. "That's the name of the soldier whose grave was dug up."

"John Carr," Finn repeated in a voice brimming with disbelief. Surely his omniscient mother would have heard this news by now.

And he started to wonder if his nightmare would ever end.

58

Alex Ford sat at home worrying. He had been trying to reach Stone but the man wasn't answering his phone. The story about the grave being dug up at Arlington was not front-page news but it had people talking. Alex didn't know what had been found in that coffin. He knew, however, that it wasn't the body of John Carr. He had learned much about Stone's past when they both had nearly died at a place called Murder Mountain not too far from Washington. And yet Alex felt that there was a part of Oliver Stone/John Carr that neither he nor anyone else would ever know.

He tried to reach Stone by phone one more time, and then his own phone started ringing. He answered. It was the man himself.

"Oliver, what the hell is going on?"

"Not a lot of time to talk, Alex. You heard about the grave?"

"Yes."

"It was Carter Gray's doing."

"But he's—"

"No, he's not. He's alive and trying to set me up for a series of murders related to my past."

"Oliver, what the—"

"Just listen! I can take care of myself. Reuben and Milton are laying low. So is Caleb. But I need you to do me a favor."

"What is it?"

"My friend, Susan Hunter. You remember her?"

"Tall, leggy, with a fast mouth."

"She's in trouble and I offered to help her, but I can't now. Will you step in for me?"

"Is she the reason we got called out last night?"

"That was my fault, not hers. But if you do help her you have to promise me something."

"What?" Alex said warily.

"Her past is not exactly perfect. But she's a good person with good motives. Don't dig too deep there."

"Oliver, if she's a criminal—"

"Alex, you and I have been through a lot together. I would trust this woman with my life. I hope that means something to you."

Alex sat back and let out a deep breath. "What do you want me to do?"

"Go to my cottage. On the desk are some notes. They will help you to understand the situation better. I'll give you Susan's phone number. You can contact her and tell her that I asked you to help."

"This is really important to you, isn't it?"

"I wouldn't be asking this big of a favor if it weren't."

"Okay, Oliver, I'll do it."

"I appreciate it, Alex, more than you'll ever know."

"Are you sure I can't help *you*?"

"No. This is something I have to handle on my own."

Alex drove to Stone's cottage. It looked empty, yet he still pulled his gun before unlocking the door, using a key Stone had once given him. It didn't take long for him to see that no one was there. Following Stone's instructions, he sat down at the desk and started going over the papers there, all in Stone's precise handwriting.

There were names: Jerry Bagger, Annabelle Conroy with a circle around it, Paddy Conroy, Tammy Conroy and someone named Anthony Wallace. There were notes about Stone's recent trip to Maine, along with some lines detailing conversations with Reuben, Milton and Caleb. And apparently Milton and Reuben had been to Atlantic City, to the Pompeii Casino.

Bagger's place.

Alex stuffed the notes in his pocket, rose and stretched out his lean six-foot-three-inch frame, massaging the muscles in his neck with his hand. He'd broken his neck in an accident years ago while on presidential protection detail and the surgically installed metal there sometimes gave him fits. Next step was to contact this Susan Hunter, if that was really her name, which, after seeing these notes, he was pretty certain wasn't the case.

The next instant he froze. Someone was coming. He slid over next to the bathroom door and waited.

The intruder came in, went immediately over to the desk and seemed to be very upset that nothing was there.

Alex stepped out and put his gun against the person's head.

True to her unflappable nature, Annabelle Conroy didn't scream, but she did say, "I hope to hell you have the safety on."

He lowered his gun and stepped back. Annabelle was dressed in a short skirt, sandals and a jean jacket; her long blonde hair was tied back in a ponytail and partially covered under a ball cap. She took off her sunglasses and stared up at the tall federal agent.

"You're Secret Service, right?"

He nodded. "Alex Ford. And I know you, you're—"

"Unemployed." She looked around. "He's not here?"

Alex was staring at the small hook-shaped scar under Annabelle's right eye. He caught himself and said, "No, he's not."

"Any idea where he might be?"

"Not really."

"Good-bye then."

As she headed to the door, Alex said sharply, "Annabelle!"

She jerked around.

Alex smiled. "Annabelle Conroy, pleased to meet you. Let me guess, father is Paddy, mother or maybe sister's name is Tammy?" He pulled out the notes from his pocket. "And it seemed you might have been looking for these."

She eyed the papers and said, "I thought Oliver was more discreet than that."

"He is. I figured it out on my own."

"Good for you. Well, I guess I'll be leaving."

"You want me to tell Oliver anything in case I see him?" Alex asked.

"No. I don't think I have anything to say to him. Not anymore, anyway."

"But you came to see him?"

"So? Why are *you* here?" she said.

"Because I'm his friend and I'm worried about him."

"He can take care of himself."

"Any idea why he disappeared?" Alex asked, though he knew the answer.

"It's because they dug up a grave at Arlington Cemetery. *His* grave, apparently." She watched Alex closely, presumably to see how he would react to this. "Did I pass your little test?"

He nodded. "Oliver must really trust you if he told you about that."

"Let's put it this way: I thought he did trust me, but it turns out he didn't."

"I heard Bagger can be pretty ruthless."

If she was startled by this Annabelle didn't show it. "What's a Bagger? You mean like at a grocery store?"

He handed her one of his cards. "Oliver called me and told me to help you while he was otherwise engaged."

This news did startle her. "He asked you to help me?"

"He insisted on it, in fact."

"And you do what he tells you to?" she said.

"He said he'd trust you with his life. There aren't many people he says that about. I happen to be one of them. We tend to look out for each other."

She hesitated, before slipping the card in her purse. "Thanks."

Alex watched in silence as she walked back to her car.

59

Camp David, though it was often used as a working retreat, was also a place that allowed the president of the United States to get away from the stresses of the most impossible job on earth. The White House Press Office had issued a notice to journalists covering the president that this weekend was only for the president and his family. That was a lie, or at least a subterfuge, as statements issued by the press office sometimes were. The president was receiving a visitor, a very special visitor, and complete secrecy was necessary.

"Thank you, Mr. President, for seeing me so swiftly," Carter Gray said as he sat down across from the man in his private office at the camp. As much as Gray had come to enjoy his bunker life, there was something to be said for venturing aboveground every once in a while.

"I'm just glad you're all right," the president said. "A very narrow escape for you."

"Well, I can't say it was the first time, but I hope it is the last. And I appreciate the latitude you've given me, on an unofficial basis of course, to pursue this matter."

"I could sense its urgency when we spoke by phone. But I'd like a fuller understanding."

"Of course." Gray gave the president a thumbnail history of Lesya, the treachery of Rayfield Solomon and the recent murders of the Triple Sixes. "And now we come to the last member of that unit, John Carr."

"The fellow who they dug up at Arlington? I've been briefed on that."

"Yes, well, that coffin did not hold the remains of John Carr."

"Who was it, then?"

"Not important, sir. What is critical is that John Carr escaped thirty years ago."

"Escaped? Was he a prisoner?"

"No, a traitor. He worked for us, but we had cause to terminate his association with CIA because of his actions."

"Terminate? Why not just prosecute him?"

"There were extenuating circumstances, sir. A public trial would not have been in the best interests of this country. So we had to take matters in our hands. Duly authorized of course by your predecessor."

The president sat back and fingered his teacup. "Different times back then, I suppose. Dirty business."

"Yes sir. That sort of thing is no longer done, of

course," Gray said quickly. "However, the termination attempt failed. And now I think it's come back to haunt us."

"How so?"

"It seems clear that the man behind the deaths of the three former CIA agents is Carr."

"Why do you think that?"

"They were the ones who turned him in. And now he's exacting his revenge."

"Why would he wait three decades for that?"

"I can only speculate there, and that would hardly be a good use of your time, sir. However, there's only one man who had grievances against all three, and that's John Carr."

"And he tried to kill you? Why?"

"I managed his unit. I was the one who brought him up on *internal* charges, in fact."

"You ordered him terminated?"

"My superiors did with, as I said, all appropriate authorization." Gray told this lie as though it was perfectly true. Perhaps he had convinced himself it was.

"Are these superiors still around?"

"No, all dead. As is, as you know, the president in office at the time."

"How does this tie into Solomon and this Lesya person?"

"That was the reason Carr was terminated. We believed he'd been turned by Solomon and Lesya."

"But Solomon died. Suicide, I think the report said."

"Yes, but presumably Lesya is still out there. And I recall that Carr and Lesya had grown especially close. They could be working together now."

"Why would this Lesya help Carr kill the CIA's former Triple Sixes?"

Inwardly Gray sighed. This president was not as stupid as others he'd served under. "Let's put it this way, sir. Rayfield Solomon officially committed suicide. But that's only the official version. It could be that he had help."

"Help? From us?"

"He was a traitor, sir. He cost many Americans their lives. He would've been executed in any event. He's on the 'Wall of Shame' at Langley next to Aldrich Ames and other spies. The lives he cost this country, incalculable. A venomous traitor if ever there was one." It pained even Gray's hardened conscience to say these things about his deceased friend, but Solomon was dead. Gray wanted to remain alive.

"So we terminated *him*, too!"

"It was, as you said, a different world then. I for one applaud the more open and public face of the CIA and the government in general that we have today. But back then we were fighting against the possible annihilation of the world."

"So Carr and Lesya may be out there. Anyone else on their target list?"

"Only one—Roger Simpson."

"That's right, he was with the CIA way back. So Roger was involved with this?"

"Only tangentially. We've taken appropriate precautions to ensure his safety."

"I certainly hope so. We don't have much of a majority in the senate. Every vote counts."

Gray's features remained inscrutable, but his mind did reflect for a moment on the president's concern for maintaining a majority in the Senate over the life of an individual senator. "Certainly," he said. "I can see why that's important to you."

The president said quickly, "Of course a man's life has to take priority."

"I never doubted that," Gray said. He suddenly wondered if there were recorders in the room and the commander in chief was making that statement for posterity.

"So what do you propose? John Carr's name has been all over the news. The man must've heard about it by now. I don't think I would have done it that way, Carter. I would've kept it on the QT while I hunted for him."

The president didn't know that Gray knew exactly where John Carr lived and that he was now known as Oliver Stone. Stone certainly would have found out by now that his grave had been dug up and his secret exposed. He was no doubt now on the run. As quick-witted as the man was, he'd also probably deduced that Gray was alive and actually plotting against him. Gray *could* have kept it on the QT, and then simply gone to Stone's cottage and arrested him. Or killed him. But he couldn't do that, because Stone had a piece of incriminating evidence against him. And Gray wanted it back. Now he had something to bargain with: the evidence in exchange for letting John Carr live. He had wanted Carr to know. He had wanted Carr to go on the run, with Gray's men keeping him on a long leash. It would make him more amenable to negotiating.

Gray said, "In hindsight that would probably be the best strategy. But we have to keep in mind that we need to avoid dredging up a lot of Cold War history with Solomon, Lesya and the others. Russia is in a fragile state right now, and the last thing we want is for accounts of our old skirmishes to surface. Frankly, sir, both sides played dirty back then, and public sentiment needs to be kept in check here and in Russia. Contact has been made with the Russians and they understand what is at stake. They've pledged their support to eliminating the problem."

"Of course. Well, you can count on my full support too, Carter. Good to have you back in the saddle. Never understood why you resigned in the first place."

"Perhaps neither did I." *And I never would have if it hadn't been for John Carr.*

Gray was taken by chopper back to his bunker. He

looked out the window of the helicopter as it soared along over the Maryland countryside. Down there Carr was running hard, with Gray's men right behind. And Lesya's son was probably planning his next attack: on that same John Carr. Which was why Gray had wanted this to become public; he *wanted* Carr to become a target.

Now all he had to do was get to Carr first, pretend to give him back his life in exchange for the evidence, and then Lesya's son could have him. And then they would kill the son and Lesya and finally put an end to this once and for all. As for Roger Simpson, he didn't care whether the man survived or not.

Admittedly, it was a complicated plan. Yet in Gray's world, nothing seemed to be simple.

60

When Annabelle returned to the hotel, Paddy was waiting for her in her room.

She sniffed the air. "You haven't been smoking."

"I tossed them in the trash can."

"Why?"

"I need to be in fighting shape when we go up against Bagger."

He looked so determined and yet so frail, like a stubborn little boy hell-bent on standing up to a bully, that for an instant Annabelle's heart went out to him. She felt her hand reach out and touch him on the shoulder. And then the moment passed and she withdrew her fingers.

Yes, he was dying. Yes, he hadn't technically let her mother die. But he was not suddenly the greatest father on earth. And he would be dead in six months. She was not going to let herself go down that road. She had grieved long and painfully for her mother's passing. She would not do the same for him.

"Any luck with getting us some help?" he asked.

"Maybe."

"Tell me about it."

"Secret Service agent, Alex Ford. Oliver asked him to step in."

"This bloke Oliver has some damn fine connections. Who the hell is he? I mean, living at a graveyard and all."

"I'm not really sure who he is," Annabelle said truthfully.

"But you said you could trust him."

"I do trust him."

Paddy looked hopeful. "Secret Service, that's good stuff. Maybe they can pull in the FBI."

She slipped off her sandals and sat down in a chair across from him. "I never thought I'd hear you sound so enthusiastic about having feds around."

"Circumstances change. Right now, I'd take every bloody cop in the country marching in lockstep with us."

"With Bagger, it might take that. So if I can get the cavalry how do we do it? I need details now, not generalities. How do we get him to confess?"

"You ran a long con on Jerry."

"Right, so?"

"So you must have his telephone number."

"I do. And again, so?"

"I'm going to call him and make him a deal he can't refuse. I'm going to sell you down the river, Annabelle. He'll offer cash, a ton of it. But I'll tell him that's not what I want."

"So what *is* your motivation?"

"You bad-mouthed me to the con world after your mum died. Haven't had a decent gig in years."

"You'd have to sell that line one hundred percent."

He stared across at her. "Not a problem, since it happens to be the truth."

"So you ship me down the river, then what?"

"That's where the cavalry comes in." He added, "Obviously that's a critical part of the plan."

She stared at him suspiciously. "Obviously."

"I've got the delivery all worked out."

Annabelle hunched forward. "Tell me every detail of it so I can tell you it'll never work."

"Don't forget, I've run a con or two in my day."

When he'd finished, she sat back, impressed. It had holes, like all initial plans did, but nothing that couldn't be sufficiently tweaked. It was actually pretty good.

"I've got some ideas we can add to it," she said. "But the underlying concept is sound."

"I'm flattered."

"Jerry will do everything in his power to make sure once they leave the pickup spot they won't be followed."

"I realize that."

"Well, since I'm the bait I have a heightened reason for making sure that we *will* be able to follow him."

"He'll send his boys to do the pickup. He won't be there, just in case it's a setup," Paddy pointed out.

"I know that. And that's our way in, actually."

"How do you figure?"

The answer that had shot into Annabelle's head made her smile. "We get to Jerry first."

"How are we supposed to do that?"

"You're going to do it."

"I am?" Paddy snapped his fingers. "On the phone call?"

"On the phone call."

"But we still need the cavalry or none of it does us a damn bit of good," he added.

She put her sandals back on and grabbed her car keys. "Then I'll go get it."

61

They sat at a table in a coffee shop near M Street and Wisconsin Avenue, barely a mile from Stone's empty cottage. Annabelle gazed out the window while Alex kept his eyes on her. He was trained to read people's expressions and body cues. This lady was tough to decipher, but it was clear she was under considerable stress.

"So why the sudden call?" he asked. "I didn't figure I'd be seeing you again."

"What can I say, I'm a sucker for tall cops."

"Does that translate as a cry for help?"

"How much do you know?"

"Oliver asked me to dig up stuff on this Bagger guy and I did. It seems Milton and Reuben went to Atlantic City, presumably to the Pompeii Casino. Oliver said they were laying low now. They're friends of mine too, so if they're in trouble I'd like to know about it so I can help them while I'm helping you."

"Is that what you do, run around helping people?"

"That's what it says in my job description. So tell

me about you and Bagger. And why did Oliver go to Maine?"

"You already seem to know everything."

"Everything and nothing. But if you really want my help you're going to have to trust me." He cocked his head as she stared moodily off. "I take it trusting people is not something you do well."

"That's a philosophy that's served me incredibly well over the years."

"I don't doubt it. But just so you know, I've covered Oliver's back, more than once. And I'd trust him with my life."

"I know, he told me. He said he'd go to war with you any day."

Alex sat back. "There you go. So maybe I *can* help you, if you can bring yourself to trust me."

Annabelle took a deep breath. Enlisting Alex's aid was critical to her father's plan to get Bagger. Yet even with that goal in mind this was so damn hard for her. She was sitting across from a cop—no, not just a cop, a federal cop! Someone who could bust her in a second if she misspoke. On the drive over it had seemed so simple. Now it appeared impossible.

Come on, Annabelle, you can do this.

With one more deep breath, she decided to do something she almost never did. She swallowed her principles and decided to tell the truth. At least part of it.

She quickly went through the main points. Bagger killing her mother. The fact that he was now in town.

That she had teamed with her father to bring him down. Alex already knew that they'd been kidnapped and almost killed by Bagger's men. She added, "I don't have evidence of any of this. Nothing that would stand up in court. But it's the truth."

"I believe you. But my cop friends were a little pissed when they showed up to arrest the guys and found no one home."

"No less pissed than I was."

"Why is Bagger after you now?"

Annabelle went automatically to lie mode. "He knows I'm trying to nail him for my mom's murder. He found out I went up to Maine where it happened. He doesn't want me to find something that could put him away for good."

Alex sipped his coffee and studied her some more. Either she was the best bullshitter he'd ever run across or what she said was legit. "And so you're teaming with your old man? How exactly do you propose sticking it to Bagger?"

"My dad's going to pretend to double-cross me with Bagger. Bagger gets me, I get him to confess, and the cops are there to nail him."

"That's your plan?"

"Yeah, why?"

"Because it has about a million holes in it, that's why. And all of them end up with you dead."

"That's just the broad concept. It's all in the details. It's always in the details."

"You really think you can make this work?"

"I sort of have a knack for it. My old man's not that bad either."

"Uh-huh. I'm going to need a little bit more than that if I'm going to be able to get you the backup you need."

"I tell you what. We'll get everything in place, you can take it to your people with a big nice bow, and then you can decide? Then if you say no, I die. That do it for you, big fella?"

"Hey, I'm just trying to be realistic here."

"No, you're being a classic bureaucrat. You look at how you *can't* do something instead of how you can."

Alex managed a tight smile. "Actually, the Secret Service is pretty can-do."

"Good. Show me."

"Give me a break here. I'm doing you the favor. I'm going out on a really big limb and it's a long way down."

Annabelle nervously balled her napkin up. "I know, I'm sorry. It's just . . ."

"The good news is the Justice Department really wants something to stick on Bagger. If I can dangle a big enough carrot in front of them, we should be able to get some FBI support. Bagger's been involved in a lot of questionable stuff. Several murders in fact, but the evidence just wasn't there."

"I know of a few more, but without his tripping himself up, nothing you can use."

"Just so you understand, I've only believed about half of what you've told me."

She started to say something but Alex said, "But I'm not going to press it."

Annabelle eyed him curiously. "Why not?"

"Because Oliver told me not to ask too many questions. He said you were a good person with an imperfect past."

Annabelle studied him closely. "So who was John Carr?"

"He worked for the U.S. government doing some highly specialized work."

"He killed people, didn't he?"

Alex looked around but the place was empty and the girl at the counter was too busy reading about Britney Spears' latest comeback in *People* to waste time eavesdropping on them.

"He doesn't do it anymore. Not unless he has to. Not unless someone's trying to kill him, or his friends."

"I saw him kill a man," Annabelle said. "He did it with a knife. Just a flick of his wrist and the man was dead. But the guy was trying to kill us." She fiddled with her coffee cup. "Do you have any idea what's really going on with him?"

"Did you hear about Carter Gray's house blowing up the other night?"

"Yeah, I read about it."

"Well, Oliver and Gray go way back, and not in a

good way. Oliver was at his house, at Gray's request, shortly before it blew up. And it was no accident. Oliver had nothing to do with it, but somebody else did. Somebody else who might just have Oliver on his target list."

"So he's got someone looking to kill him too?"

"Looks that way. And that's why he didn't want to hang around any of us."

"And I was really upset that he abandoned me."

"Hey, he called me in. I might only be the JV, but I've been known to get a few good punches in from time to time."

"That stuff I said before about you being a bureaucrat."

"I believe the exact phrase was *classic* bureaucrat."

"Yeah, well, I take it back. I appreciate your help."

"I need to make a few calls. And then I can help you fill in some of the details now that we have the *concept* nailed down."

She returned his grin. "I've never met a fed like you before, Alex Ford."

"That's okay, you're a new one in my book too."

62

As the night settled in Oliver Stone knew he was still being followed. Well, now was the time to say goodbye to the shadows. He ran for a cab and gave the driver an address in Alexandria. With deadly men in pursuit of him he was heading to a rare book store.

The taxi dropped him off in front of the shop on Union Street a block from the Potomac River. With the hunters behind him Stone hurried inside, nodding at the owner of the place, Douglas. The man had used to be called simply Doug, and had once sold pornographic comic books out of the trunk of his Cadillac. Yet he harbored a secret passion for rare books and a desire to be rich. That dream had gone unfulfilled until Stone had hooked him up with Caleb. Now *Douglas* ran a successful high-end rare book store. As part of the bargain Stone was given access to the place at all times, and had a room in the cellar area that he used to store some of his most important possessions. And it also provided something else that Stone was going to use right now.

Stone reached the cellar, unlocked a door and

entered the room where an old fireplace sat, long unused. He reached inside the fireplace opening, where next to the damper switch was a small pull cord. He tugged and a door on an old priest's hole-like chamber swung open. The room was filled with boxes stacked neatly on shelves, well above the flood line.

Stone opened a box and pulled out a journal that he stuffed in his bag. From another box he drew out a set of clothes, including a floppy hat, and changed into them. From a small metal box he took out an object that was more precious to him than all the gold in the world. It was a cell phone. A cell phone with a very special message carefully preserved on the built-in recording device.

When he left he did not reverse his path and go upstairs. He walked down a different passageway, toward the river. He unlocked one more door, passed through, knelt down, pulled on an iron ring that was seated into the floor, yanking hard, and a square of floor came up on hinges. He dropped through, traversed a dark tunnel that smelled of river, dead fish and mold, clambered up a set of rickety stairs, unlocked another door and came out behind a clump of trees. He passed along a footwalk by the river and plopped into a small boat owned by Douglas that was docked at one of the slips.

He engaged the Merc outboard and headed south, his white stern light the only sign of him in the darkness. He ran the boat up on the shore about two miles north of Mount Vernon, George Washington's home, tying its bow line to a tree. He hoofed it to a gas station and called a cab from a pay phone.

On the ride back to town, Stone read through the journal. These records represented a significant part of his distant past. He had started keeping them almost immediately after he was recruited into the CIA's Triple Six Division. He had no idea if the CIA still had the division operational and didn't know if the men who'd attempted to follow him tonight were part of that element. However, he assumed that if they were ordered to kill him they would carry out the task with suitable skill.

Page after page of the journal was turned as Stone took a painful walk through his past work for the U.S. government. Then he focused on several photographs he'd pasted on one page along with his handwritten notes and some bits of the "unofficial" record he'd managed to snag.

He was staring at the photos of his three Triple Six comrades, all now dead: Judd Bingham, Bob Cole and Lou Cincetti. And then he looked at the older bespectacled man in the picture at the bottom of the page.

"Rayfield Solomon," he said to himself. The hit had been quick and efficient but still one of the most unusual of Stone's career. It had been in São Paulo. The orders had been clear. Solomon was a spy, turned by the legendary Russian operative Lesya, last name unknown. There was to be no arrest and no trial; it would be too embarrassing for the American public to endure; not that lengthy explanations were ever given to the Triple Six teams.

Stone remembered the man's expression as they burst in the door. It was not fear, he recalled. At best it was mild surprise, and then his features hardened. He politely asked who had ordered him to be terminated. Bingham laughed, but as the leader Stone stepped forward and told Solomon. There was no official requirement to do this. Stone simply felt every doomed man had a right to know.

Rayfield Solomon was a man of average height and build, more professor than secret operative in appearance. But to this day Stone remembered those wondrous eyes that burned into him as he raised his pistol. It was a gaze that bespoke a brilliant mind behind it, and a man who was unafraid of the death knocking on his door. He was no traitor, Solomon said. "You will kill me, of course, but understand that you kill an innocent man." Stone was impressed at how calmly the man spoke while four armed men encircled him.

"You will have been told to make it look like a suicide of course," Solomon said. This too stunned Stone because those had been his exact orders. "I am right-handed. As you can see, the hand is larger, stronger, so I'm not lying to you. Thus, place the shot in the right temple. If you wish I will also hold the gun and place my finger on the trigger so that my prints are on the weapon." Then he turned to Stone with a gaze that froze even the veteran killer. "But I will not pull the trigger. You will have to do the killing. Innocent men do *not* commit suicide."

After it was over, the men left as quietly as they had come. An overnight ride on an American cargo plane operated by a shell company of the CIA carried them back to Miami the next day. Bingham, Cincetti and Cole went out partying that night because the team had been given a few days off, as a reward for a job well done. Stone did not join them. He never did. He had a wife now and a young child. He stayed alone in his hotel room that night. He stayed up all night, in fact. The image of Rayfield Solomon would not leave his mind. Every time he tried to close his eyes, all he saw was the man's gaze ripping into him, the words eating away his soul.

I am an innocent man.

Stone hadn't wanted to admit it then, but all these years later, he could. Solomon had been telling the truth. Stone *had* killed an innocent man. Somehow he had known that this death would come back to haunt him. In fact, the Solomon case was one of the reasons Stone decided to leave Triple Six. It was a decision that ultimately destroyed his family.

They had called him a traitor, just like they had Solomon. And just like Solomon he'd been innocent. How many more Rayfield Solomons might have wrongly died by his hand?

He closed the journal and the cab dropped him off a few minutes later. He called Reuben, because if Gray couldn't find Stone he would use any means possible to flush him out, including kidnapping his friends.

Stone said calmly, "The big man we thought was gone isn't. Is your phone listed in your name?" Stone thought he knew the answer because he knew Reuben very well.

"Nope, I'm actually piggybacking on a friend of mine's service," Reuben said evasively.

"Luckily you just recently moved and don't have an official address. Otherwise I would've already had you relocate."

"I got *evicted* from the other place, Oliver. Left in the middle of the night because I wanted to avoid a certain rental dispute."

"Now everyone needs to lay low because friends of mine are valuable to him. I'll check in later."

He needed information from the inside and he needed it now. There was only one man who was in a position to give it to him. Stone hadn't seen the fellow in thirty years, but figured now was a good time to get reacquainted. Indeed, he wondered now why he hadn't made the visit decades ago. Perhaps he'd been afraid of the answer. Now he was no longer scared.

He had focused on the Rayfield Solomon case because, in his long career, it had been the one Stone felt the most regret for. After he'd been assigned to kill the man, Stone researched his background. He hardly seemed like a traitor, though that was not Stone's case to make. He'd heard of Solomon's personal link to the legendary spy Lesya. And if she'd survived and was still out there, the woman might be exacting her revenge on the people who'd killed Solomon. An innocent man.

63

Max Himmerling closed his book, yawned and stretched. Ever since his wife, Kitty, had died of cancer two years ago, his routine rarely varied. He worked, he came home, he ate a simple meal, he read a chapter in a book and he went to bed. It was an unexciting life, but his life at work was exciting enough. He had grown bald and fat in the service of his country. A nearly forty-year veteran of the CIA—he'd started there right out of college—his job was totally unique. Blessed with the most orderly of minds, he was like a central clearinghouse for the most diverse sort of matters. How would a coup in Bolivia or Venezuela orchestrated by the U.S. impact on the West's interests in the Middle East or China? Or if oil dropped another buck a barrel, would it behoove the Pentagon to open a forward military base in such-and-such country? In a time of supercomputers and servers filled with trillions of bytes of data and spy satellites that stole your secrets from outer space, it made Max feel good that there was still a strong human element in the work of his agency.

He was unknown outside the corridors of Langley, was considered only a low-level bureaucratic grunt within it, and would receive neither wealth nor honors. Yet to the people who mattered, Max Himmerling was an indispensable asset to the world's most elite intelligence-gathering agency. And that was enough for him. Indeed, after his wife's passing, it was all he had left. His importance to his agency was represented by the two armed men who guarded the exterior of his house when he was home. Himmerling would retire in two years and dreamed of traveling to some of the places he'd analyzed all these decades. He was worried, though, that his money would run out before his life did. The government provided a good package and first-rate health care, but he hadn't saved much on his own, and to continue living in this area, which he very much wanted to do, was expensive. He supposed he would cross that bridge when he came to it.

He lifted his tired, fleshy body from his easy chair and started up the stairs to his bedroom. He never made it.

The figure came from nowhere. The shock of the man standing in his living room nearly gave Max a heart attack. That was nothing compared to the shock he received when the intruder spoke.

"It's been a long time, Max."

Max put a hand against the wall to steady himself. He said in a shaky voice, "Who are you? How'd you get past the guards?"

Stone stepped into the small wash of light from a table lamp. "You remember the Triple Sixes, don't you, Max? How about John Carr? That name ring any bells for you? If it does, even after all these years, you can pretty much figure out how I got past the two idiots lying unconscious outside that you call *guards*."

Max stared up fearfully into the face of the tall, lean man standing across the room from him. "John Carr? It can't be. You're dead."

Stone stepped closer to him. "You know everything that goes on at CIA. So you knew John Carr wasn't in that grave they dug up."

Max slumped back down in his chair and looked pitifully at Stone. "What the hell are you doing here?"

"You're the great brain. You always figured out the best logistics for our missions. They almost always went off without a hitch. And when they didn't you were always thousands of miles away. So what the hell did you care? It was our asses on the line, not yours. So tell me, great brain, why am I here? And don't disappoint me. You know how I hate to be disappointed."

Max drew in a sharp breath. "You want information."

Stone glided forward and put a vise grip on Max's arm. "I want the truth."

Max grimaced from the pressure on his arm, but there was absolutely nothing he could do about it. His strength was mental, not physical. "About what?"

"Rayfield Solomon. Carter Gray. And anyone else you know who had his finger in that debacle."

Max had shuddered at the mention of Rayfield Solomon. "Gray's dead," he said quickly.

Stone's long fingers tightened on the man's arm until a bead of sweat broke over Max's forehead. "That's not what I meant by being truthful."

"His home was blown up, damn it!"

"But he wasn't in it. Now he's out there, plotting and planning, just like he always did. Only I'm the target. Again. And I don't like it, Max. Once was enough." Stone squeezed harder.

"Look, you can crush my arm if you want, but I can't tell you things I don't know about."

"I'm not going to crush your *arm*." Stone let go and slid a knife out from his coat sleeve.

Max wailed, "John, you're not a killer anymore. You got out. You were always different. We all knew that."

"That didn't seem to help me back then. My wanting to get out almost cost me my life."

"Things were different back then."

"So people keep telling me. But once a killer, always a killer. I did it very recently, in fact. In self-defense. But I still killed a man. Slit his throat from ten feet away. And he was a former Triple Six. I guess they're not making 'em like they used to."

"But I'm defenseless," Max pleaded.

"I *will* kill you, Max. And it *will* be in self-defense.

Because if you don't help me, I'm a dead man. But I'm not going alone." He placed the edge of the blade against Max's quivering carotid artery.

"For God's sake, John, think what you're doing. And I lost my wife recently. I lost Kitty."

"I lost my wife too. I didn't have her nearly as long as you had your Kitty. But then you probably were the one who worked the logistics of the hit on me out on your nice, neat paper."

"I had nothing to do with that. I only learned about it after the fact."

"But you didn't go running to the authorities about it, did you?"

"What the hell did you expect me to do? They would have killed me too."

Stone pressed the blade harder against the man's flesh. "For a genius you sometimes say stupid things. Tell me about Rayfield Solomon before I lose my patience. Because this is all about Solomon, isn't it?"

"He was a traitor and you killed him, on orders."

"We did kill him, as ordered. Roger Simpson said it came right from the top. But there's obviously more to it. A lot more. Was Solomon innocent? And if he was, why were we ordered to kill him?"

"Damn it, John, just let it go! The past is dead."

Stone's knife cut into Max's skin a millimeter beside the artery, and a drop of blood appeared. "Was Solomon innocent?" Himmerling said nothing. He just sat there with his eyes closed, his chest heaving.

"Max, if I sever this artery, you will bleed to death in less than five minutes. And I will stand here and watch while you do."

Himmerling finally opened his eyes. "I've kept secrets for nearly forty years, and I'm not going to start talking now."

Stone swung his gaze around the room and stopped at the pictures on the mantel. A young boy and girl.

"Grandkids?" he asked with an edge to his voice. "Must be nice."

A trembling Max followed the man's gaze. "You . . . you wouldn't dare!"

"You people killed everyone I loved. Why should you get any better treatment? I'll kill you first." He pointed at the pictures. "And them next. And it won't be painless."

"You bastard!"

"That's right. I am a bastard. CIA-built, owned and operated. You know that as well as anyone, don't you?" Stone looked once more at the photos. "Your last chance, Max. I won't ask again."

And so for the first time in four decades, Max Himmerling let a secret slip out. "Solomon wasn't a traitor. He knew some things, but he didn't know all of it. People were afraid if he found out the truth, he'd talk."

"People like who? Gray? Simpson?"

"I don't know."

Stone made another nick on Himmerling's skin. "Max, I'm losing my patience."

"It was Gray *or* Simpson. I never knew which."

"And the secret?"

"Not even I knew that. It involved a mission Solomon and the Russian Lesya handled against the Soviet Union. The whole thing's on the front burner now. I don't know why."

"One more question. Should be an easy one. Who ordered the hit on me?"

"John, please—"

Stone violently seized the man around the throat. "Who?"

"All I can say is you have the same choice as with the last answer," Himmerling gasped.

So Gray or Simpson. Not that he was surprised.

Stone put the knife away and said, "If you try and tell anyone I've been here, you know what will happen. Gray will find out and he'll suspect you told me things. And you can't lie to him. He knows ways to get the truth out of the toughest people, much less someone like you. And when he finds out what you told me, guess what, Max?" Stone placed an imaginary pistol against the man's head and pantomimed pulling the trigger. "Enjoy the rest of your evening."

"Would you have really killed my grandkids?" Himmerling asked in a quavering voice.

"Just be glad they don't have to find out."

64

After Stone left, Max Himmerling breathed a sigh of relief; it caught in his throat. *The guards. They'll know someone came. They'll contact . . .* He ran to pack a bag. He had long ago worked out a doomsday scenario of having to flee. Ten minutes later he was on his way out the door, boarding pass printed out, fake ID in his pocket. The ringing phone made him stop. Should he answer it? Something told him to. He picked it up. The voice on the other end was very familiar to him.

"Hello, Max. What did you tell him?"

"I don't know what you're talking about."

"Max, you're a brilliant man, but a very bad liar. I don't blame you. I'm sure he threatened you, and we both know what a dangerous man he is. So what did you tell him?"

Once more Himmerling spilled his guts.

"Thank you, Max, you did the right thing." The line went dead.

Himmerling dropped the phone as the back door opened.

"Please," he said. "Please."

The silenced gun fired and the bullet hit him in the forehead. The body was placed into a black bag. In a minute the truck had carried it away. Officially Himmerling would be reassigned to a foreign post on short notice. When the next American chopper went down anywhere in the world, it would be recorded that Max Himmerling had been on it, his body burned beyond recognition. Thus would end the man's near forty years of service to his country.

At least he would no longer have to worry about outliving his pension.

In his bunker Carter Gray smacked his fist into his palm. The loss of Himmerling was a heavy if unavoidable one. Gray knew he should have anticipated it, but he hadn't.

He looked back at the computer screen in front of him. He had received the birth records from hospitals in major Canadian cities for the year in question. Even electronically they were voluminous. He had to separate the wheat from the chaff. Fortunately, he had known Rayfield Solomon well. They had been good friends, and friendly rivals. Indeed, it could be said that Solomon was the only man of his generation who could match Carter Gray in ability. Gray had to concede that in the field, Solomon might well have been his superior. So uncovering the man's tracks wouldn't be easy, but he did have the advantage of knowing him intimately.

He had focused his efforts on the name of the father listed in the birth records. Lesya would not have used her own name, of course. The name of the son would not help either, since Gray was sure that it would be different today. So it came down to the father. Rayfield Solomon was very proud of his Jewish heritage. Though the demands of his work did not allow him to practice his religion in a traditional fashion—critical missions could not be interrupted even for the exercise of his faith—Solomon had been an ardent scholar of his religion. He and Gray had had numerous discussions about theology. Gray's wife had been a devout Catholic. Gray had not been particularly religious until his wife and daughter had been killed on 9/11. Solomon had often told him, "Find something to believe in, Carter, other than your work. Because when you leave this life, you leave work behind. If that's all you have, then you have nothing. And eternity is a long time for nothing."

Wise words the man had uttered, though Gray had not necessarily believed them back then.

His fingers skimmed over the computer keys, trying this and that search combination. The list of names was further and further reduced. He continued to scan the names until he came to rest on one proud father.

David P. Jedidiah, II.

He smiled. *You blundered there, Ray. You let personal trump professional.* Over the years since his family's death Gray had also become a keen reader of the Bible, so the name of *this* father had particular relevance for him.

Solomon was the *second* son of David, his first legitimate child with Bathsheba. Jedidiah was the name that Nathan, the future King Solomon's teacher, called him. And in Hebrew Solomon means "Peace," hence the middle initial, *P.* Rayfield Solomon had used the name David P. Jedidiah, II, in the birth records. Carter Gray looked at the mother's name, and then at the son's. He picked up the phone and relayed this information. "Trace the son," he ordered.

He put the phone down and said aloud, "So where are you now, son of Solomon?"

65

It was morning, with a chill in the air. Harry Finn stood by himself, hands in pockets, and stared at it: the empty hole in the ground at Arlington National Cemetery, where John Carr was supposed to be resting, for all eternity. That had been a lie. And why was Finn surprised? The government always lied about the most important things.

Even though he previously believed the man was dead, Finn had researched John Carr's background. As a Navy SEAL he had done joint intelligence work with the CIA. Using the same skills that he made his living with today, he had slowly unearthed much of the history of his father's last days, and also the pasts of the men who'd been involved in killing him.

Judd Bingham's, Bob Cole's and Lou Cincetti's histories were pretty much the same. They had worked for the CIA, seemed to relish their duties in fact, until they'd retired to a life of comfort and leisure. Retirements that Finn had abruptly ended.

Only Carr was different. Officially, he had been killed while a member of an army unit, in the type of skirmish that popped up from time to time around the world and to which the United States was morally if not technically required to respond. Before becoming a member of the CIA's Triple Six Division, John Carr had been one of the most decorated veterans of the Vietnam War, including four Purple Hearts, and none of them for hangnails. There was even talk of his receiving the Congressional Medal of Honor, the highest military award of all. Every soldier who earned it had instantly attained a place of immortality in the eyes of professional warriors, though many had been awarded the honor posthumously. This had led some to dub it "The medal you'll never get to see."

Carr had certainly seemed an ideal man for the military equivalent of an Olympic gold medal. Finn had read the official report with both thrill and horror. Carr had single-handedly saved his ambushed platoon of soldiers in a murderous firefight with a far larger mass of North Vietnamese backed by artillery support. Sergeant John Carr had personally carried four wounded men to safety on his back, repeatedly going back into harm's way to do so. He had been hit twice by enemy fire and still somehow managed to kill a dozen Viet Cong, three of them in hand-to-hand fighting, while shooting several more out of trees with a marksman's skill that the report described as nothing short of supernatural.

Finally, manning a machine-gun post, Carr had repelled repeated attacks, survived multiple mortar rounds exploding all around his position and still managed to call in an airstrike that had driven the enemy back, allowing his men to safely retreat. He had walked off the field of battle under his own power despite his uniform being soaked in his blood. Finn could not help feeling a certain level of respect for the man. He had always considered himself to be a soldier of the highest level, but he was thinking that John Carr had perhaps surpassed him on the ability scorecard that all professional military people kept in their heads.

Yet Carr had not been given the medal. Finn didn't know that it had to do with politics rather than heroics on the battlefield. He didn't know that John Carr's growing ambivalence about the war had turned his superiors against him. His CO had not even recommended him for the medal until others had stepped in. Yet somewhere along the line, folks even higher up the command chain prevented a deserving soldier from receiving the military's highest honor.

Instead Carr had disappeared from the ranks of the army until resurfacing years later, only to die in that minor skirmish and supposedly be buried at Arlington. Finn knew what Carr had been doing in the interim. He'd been killing, on orders from his government. Yet he was a man who had been on the receiving end of death too.

It had taken two years of foraging on databases he was not supposed to have access to, but Finn had learned that Carr's wife had died one night when their house was supposedly burgled. The couple had had a daughter, but she had simply disappeared too. Finn was smart enough to read between the lines. The "burglary" had CIA hit written all over it. Carr must've angered his superiors somehow. Finn had been glad initially to learn that John Carr was dead. He had no interest in killing war heroes who had never gotten their just rewards, nor a man with the courage to buck the most powerful spy agency in the world.

But now perhaps Carr wasn't dead. And if he wasn't Finn knew what he had to do. What his mother expected him to do. Whether he liked it or not. And regardless of what sort of man John Carr was, he'd killed Finn's father. For nothing.

Finn left the graveyard. He had work to do.

For now, John Carr would have to wait.

66

It was a nontraditional penetration so Finn had grabbed a couple of guys from his office who normally sat behind a desk analyzing the data that he and his team of specialists routinely gathered. However, the client on this case had wanted low-level people headed up by someone who knew what he was doing—namely Finn. This was because the facility that manufactured vaccines for several man-made biological germ agents was not considered a high-priority target for terrorists. Still, they wanted to see how it measured up. Enter Finn and company.

They had no trouble scaling the unguarded fence at the rear of the facility, though one of the office boys, a hefty fellow named Sam, had a bit of trouble hoisting his bulk over. Finally, with Finn's help, he managed.

They were able to enter the facility from the rear through an unlocked door. A door being unlocked in a building housing valuable vaccine was something that sounded impossible but that nevertheless happened every day in countries all over the world. Why, indeed, would someone take home a laptop with the personal data of millions of military veterans only to see it stolen during a burglary? It's what kept bad guys in business and the good guys on antidepressant drips.

Inside, they spread out, their cover stories having been worked out in advance. Finn had donned a white lab coat he'd carried in a duffel bag. An ID was on a lanyard he put around his neck. He also carried an electronic pad for inputting notes. Thus outfitted, he worked his way to the front entrance area. To the guard stationed there he mentioned the name of a scientist who worked in the building. Finn had gotten the name off the Internet, knowing full well that the chap was on vacation. He'd obtained this bit of intelligence by going through the man's garbage one night and seeing a copy of the detailed travel itinerary for him and his family that the "genius" had cavalierly thrown away. When he was informed that the scientist was away, he said, "That's right. Bill told me he was taking the family to Florida." He then mentioned another name he'd pulled off the building directory. He had pulled this maneuver with the guard to both gain credibility and put the security person at ease. Both of these things were usually accomplished by concocting a personal connection with someone who worked at the place he was targeting.

"I can just pop up and see him for a few minutes," he told the private security guard. "I know the way. I have some test results to go over for the A/B run they did last week on the two new microbe trial vaccines. You in the loop on that?"

The guard, a kid barely out of his teens who proudly wore the standard-issue sidearm, said, "No, I'm not in the loop on that," and went back to his coffee and computer screen on which Finn caught sight of an online dating service's latest offerings.

Finn waited patiently inside the elevator car until someone came along. He held up a plastic card he had just taken out of the slot. "Damn RFID's malfunctioning again," he said, referring to the encrypted smart card that was needed to access the elevator. "Third time this month. And every time they said they fixed it. Yeah, right."

"I know the feeling," the other man said as he swiped his card through the slot and the doors closed. "What floor you want?" he asked.

"Fifth," Finn replied, as he put his son's plastic library card back into his pocket.

He got off on the fifth floor and found the door he wanted right next to the elevator bank. It also required a smart card for entry. He slipped inside a nearby bathroom and dabbed some water on his pants leg. When he heard the elevator ding, he opened the door to the bathroom, pretending to be rubbing his wet hands dry as the doors to the elevator slid open. The woman stepped off and swiped her card in the secure door as Finn stood behind her, his library card in hand.

The woman glanced at him and smiled. "Looks like I beat you to it."

Finn put his card away. "Hasn't been a great morning. I spilled coffee on my pants leg on the drive over." He pointed to the wet stain.

The woman smiled again. "Bet that woke you up."

"Oh, yeah," said Finn as he followed her in.

"You here to see anyone in particular?" she asked.

Finn shook his head and held up his phony but genuine-looking ID tag that had the imprint of Homeland Security. "Just a random drop-in. Feds need to see how the tax dollars are being spent."

"Don't I know it. Have a good one," she added as she walked off.

Finn strolled around the lab, surreptitiously taking pictures with his buttonhole camera and nodding to people as he walked along jotting down notes on his electronic tablet with his stylus. It really did amaze him. If you looked like you belonged, people never challenged you. He even had several people give him helpful details on certain vaccines' potencies. He left and made his way back down to the main entrance, courtesy of the help of another clueless Good Samaritan. When he exited onto the main lobby, however, he froze.

Sam, the fat kid from his office, was up against the wall and the security guard was doing a very unprofessional pat-down. Any person who knew what he was doing could have taken the guard's gun in a second with no trouble.

"What's going on here," Finn called out as he headed over.

"Spy!" the guard said. "Caught him red-handed. I'm calling the cops."

Finn had no choice now but to pull his credentialing letter and alert their contact inside the building that they'd been uncovered. He didn't like to have to make that call, but when you brought rookies with you, it sometimes happened. At least Finn had penetrated to where he needed to go. That's how it would have finished if Sam hadn't done something incredibly stupid. Panicked at the sight of the gun, he pushed the guard away and started to run.

The guard pointed his pistol at Sam's broad back and shouted, "Stop!"

"Don't," Finn screamed as he hurtled forward. The guard fired his weapon just as Finn collided with him. In an instant Finn had the gun away from the man and pushed his credentialing letter in his face. "Call John Rivers in security, he knows all about—" He broke off what he was saying and stared down the hall. Sam was lying on the floor, blood pouring out of a wound on his back.

"Son of a bitch!" Finn jumped up and raced to Sam.

67

The ambulance pulled away thirty minutes later. After reaching Sam, Finn had stanched the bleeding and then performed CPR on his colleague when Sam had ceased breathing and his heart had stopped, perhaps from shock. The EMTs had arrived and taken over from there. Sam would live, but his rehab would take a while because it looked like the bullet had done some nasty damage to a few of his organs.

Finn watched the red rack lights until they disappeared. Standing next to him was John Rivers, the head of security, who had apologized profusely for the guard's shooting Sam in the back when he was not being threatened.

"Thank God you were there, Harry," Rivers said. "Otherwise he'd be dead."

"Yeah, well, he wouldn't have gotten shot if I hadn't dragged him here."

"They give us no money or time to train our guards," Rivers complained. "They spend billions on the facility and security *technology*, but then they put a gun in the hands of a punk who's earning ten bucks an hour. It makes no sense."

Finn wasn't really listening. He had never had anything like this happen before. Sam was a good man but strictly a desk jockey. Finn had never liked taking inexperienced folks with him on these outings, and had voiced that opinion several times. Maybe now they would listen to him.

He drove home and later took Patrick to baseball practice, silently watching his athletic middle child field all balls hit his way and later mercilessly pound the automated pitches in the batting cage. Finn didn't say much on the way home, letting an animated Patrick talk about his day at school. Over dinner that night, Susie recited her lines from the upcoming play—although it didn't appear that trees were given much to say, a fact her two older brothers ribbed her about. She took the kidding well before finally telling them both, "Stuff it, dorks." That comment drew a warning from Mandy, who'd had her hands full lately with the three because Finn had been so buried at work.

David said, "Hey, Pop, you coming to the soccer match on Friday afternoon? Coach is gonna let me play goalie."

Finn said absently, "I'll try, son. I might be tied up." He had to go visit his mother. His wife would not be happy about that.

Mandy gave David some pocket money for when

his class went downtown on their field trip the next morning. She took a small bite of food and looked over at her husband, who was obviously not mentally with them.

"Harry, you okay?"

He stirred. "Just some stuff at work." There had been no news coverage of the incident, even though the police had been called, because Homeland Security had stepped in to put the kibosh on it. Having Finn exposed in the press would put a severe crimp in the red cell contract work that his company did for Homeland Security, work that was critically important to national security. With DHS in Finn's corner, the local cops had quickly rolled over. The young security guard had not been charged with anything other than being stupid and undertrained, and his gun had been taken away. He had been reassigned to a desk job and told that if he said anything to anyone about what had happened he would regret it for the rest of his life.

After dinner he drove to the hospital to see Sam. He was in the ICU after surgery, but his condition had stabilized. He was on heavy meds and didn't even know Finn was there. His parents had been flown in from New York that afternoon and were in the ICU waiting area. Finn sat with them for an hour, explaining the situation and downplaying Sam's complicity in getting shot by stupidly running away from a nervous kid with a big gun.

He left the hospital and drove around for a while with the all-news radio station on. He finally turned it off after bad news became awful news and then moved on directly to terrible. What a world they were leaving for the next generation.

He headed downtown, because he didn't want to go home to the Virginia suburbs just yet. He could tell from the expression on Mandy's face at dinner that she wanted to talk about things, but he really didn't want to. He didn't know how he was going to break the news of having to visit his mother again. With the kids' busy schedule, his being gone really left his wife scrambling. And yet he had to do it, particularly after the John Carr revelation.

He crossed over the Theodore Roosevelt Bridge, passing the island named after the very same president. He kept straight and headed down Constitution Avenue, arguably the capital's second most famous street behind the one named Pennsylvania. Hooking left, he headed up toward the White House before turning right onto F Street and working his way through a congested shopping and business district that was crawling with renewed nightlife. To his right stood the concrete-and-steel skeleton of an uncompleted building whose developer had gone bankrupt. As Finn waited at a red light he stared up at the new residential condo building on his left. His gaze went up seven stories, drifted to the corner unit of the luxury high-rise, and that's when he stiffened slightly. He had not come here by accident. The drive-by was completely intentional; he did it often.

The lights were on and as he watched a tall figure passed by one of the windows.

Senator Roger Simpson from the great state of Alabama was home.

68

Annabelle stood next to Paddy who was slumped in a chair in her hotel room. Daughter nodded at father and on cue he picked up the phone.

Before he punched in the number, she put a hand on Paddy's shoulder.

"You sure you're ready for this?" she asked.

"I've been ready for this for years," he gamely replied, his voice cracking a bit.

He didn't look ready, she thought. The man seemed tired and scared.

"Good luck," Annabelle said.

As soon as the number was placed, Annabelle picked up another phone and listened in.

"Hello, Jerry," Paddy said. "It's Paddy Conroy. Long time no kill. But then again, maybe that's not entirely accurate. Hear you've been busy on that score."

Annabelle stared at her father. Paddy's entire manner had changed. His smile was wide, and his voice was confident. He was sitting up big and fearless in the chair.

Bagger was not a man easily shocked. But when he heard that name, he felt his knees slightly buckle. The next emotion he had was far more familiar. He nearly crushed the phone in his hand and screamed, "How the hell did you know how to reach me, you bastard?"

"I just looked in the phone book under A for assholes."

On that remark, Annabelle had to stifle a laugh.

"Seen that bitch of a daughter of yours lately?"

"Heard she ripped you for plenty. Enough to get the wind up at the Jersey Control Commission. I must've taught her good."

"Yeah, maybe you're behind the whole thing. And if you are, all I can promise you is a skin peel that takes about two days."

"Stop talking dirty, Jerry, you're getting me horny."

"What do you want!"

"I want to help you out."

"I don't need help from a two-bit, washed-up con."

"Don't be so quick on the draw, Jer. The definition of help is when I have something you want. And I do."

"Like what?"

"Care to guess?"

"Care to have me rip your balls off?"

"I have Annabelle. You still want her or you gotten

over her making you look like the world's biggest idiot?"

"You'd turn over your own daughter to me, knowing what I'm going to do to her?"

"Not going deaf on me, are you? That's what I said."

"And you're doing this out of what, the goodness of your heart?"

"You know me better than that, Jerry."

"So how much do you want for your little girl?"

"Not a dime."

"Excuse me?" Bagger said in disbelief.

"I don't need any more money."

"So what then?"

"You have to promise me that if I give Annabelle to you, you'll never come after me again. I got a little time left on this planet and I don't want to spend it looking over my shoulder for the likes of you."

"Let me get this straight. You'll give me Annabelle so long as I leave you alone?"

"That's right. I know you've been on the lookout for me ever since I ripped you off for that lousy ten grand. And I'm getting tired of it."

Bagger screamed into the phone, "*You're* getting tired of it?"

"Is it a deal? And I want your word. Because I know you're a lot of things, but you've never gone back on your word. You get Annabelle and you leave me alone, forever."

Bagger stared down at the floor, the veins throbbing in his neck.

"I want to hear you say it, Jerry. I *have* to hear you say it."

"I'll pay you millions for her."

"Yeah, sure. Say it, Jerry. Say it or no deal."

Paddy stared over at Annabelle, who was holding her breath as she clutched the phone.

"Why do you hate her so much?" Bagger finally said.

"Because she's blamed me all these years for what happened to her mum. You killed the woman but I've paid the price. Ain't been one bloke in the whole con world who'd give me the time of day since. She ruined my life. It's payback time. *My* payback time." Paddy glanced over at Annabelle and smiled weakly.

"How are you going to set her up? She's not stupid. So I know she doesn't trust you."

"Leave that to me."

"I haven't agreed to nothing."

"But you will. You're too smart not to."

"I can just catch her myself. I came close the other night. And maybe you too if I get real lucky."

"Then go for it. And two weeks from now when you realize she's long gone, you can't say old Paddy didn't tell you the truth. Because the longer you wait, the more time she has to hide, and we both know the girl is good at what she does. Take your time, think about it. I'll call you back."

"When?"

"When I want to."

In one motion, Paddy and Annabelle put down their phones.

She gripped his shoulder. "You did great. You baited him just right."

He put his hand on top of hers. "We'll give him a little time to stew on that. That'll give your friend some time to get his end in gear. I have to say, I was surprised he agreed to help us, no questions asked."

"Like I told you, he's not your typical fed. One thing." She paused, worried. *Was her father really not up to this?* "You didn't poke around about where Jerry might be staying."

He looked at her, a smile playing across his lips. "I'm not losing my touch, Annie, if that's what you're thinking. You don't push too hard on the first go-round. Old pro like Jerry will sniff that out every time. Next call, I'll let him make the slip. Then I'll hit it."

"Sorry, I didn't mean you didn't know what you were doing."

"Ninety percent of the con is preparation. The other ten percent is seat of the pants, being able to adapt on the fly."

"But without the ten the ninety is worth shit."

"Exactly."

"That stuff you said to Bagger. About my ruining your life?"

"I ruined my own life, Annie. All I'm doing now is trying to get a little piece of it back."

He gripped his daughter's hand tightly. He now looked old, sick and scared; his body collapsed into the chair again. "You really think we can pull this off?"

"Yes," she lied.

69

Dressed in the outfit of a Capitol Grounds maintenance crewman, Harry Finn stood outside the Hart Senate Office Building with the remote detonator in his hand. He stared up the façade of the building until his gaze came to Simpson's office. In his other hand was a small device that looked like an iPod. Actually, it was the receiving unit for the wireless pin video camera he'd hidden in Simpson's office. The images on the small screen were razor-sharp. Simpson was meeting with several of his staff, no doubt reporting back on his vital "fact-finding" mission to the Caribbean.

Finn was waiting until Simpson was alone in his office, for only Simpson was going to die today. He tensed as the staff people rose and left. He then watched as Simpson checked his hair and face in the mirror on one wall, adjusted his tie, walked to his desk and sat down.

The end had finally come. Finn's finger was poised over his BlackBerry. He would send the e-mail first. He would be able to tell from Simpson's reaction on the screen that he had seen the photo of Rayfield Solomon, right before he died.

Finn's thumb descended on the BlackBerry key. *Good-bye, Roger.*

"Hey, Dad!"

Finn glanced up, recognizing the voice. "Damn it," he breathed.

David Finn came running up to him, smiling. "What are you doing here?"

Finn quickly slipped the devices into the duffel slung over his shoulder.

"Hey, Dave, what are *you* doing here?"

His son rolled his eyes. "You going senile on me, Pop? The school visit to the Capitol? You signed the permission slip? Mom gave me the money last night at dinner?"

Finn's face paled. *Oh shit.* "Sorry, just a lot going on, son."

David noticed his dad's clothes. "What's with the uniform?"

"I'm working," he said quietly.

David's face brightened. "Cool, you mean you're undercover?"

"I really can't talk about it, son. In fact, you better get going. It's not really great that you're here actually." Finn's heart was beating so hard it was a miracle his son didn't seem to hear it.

David looked disappointed. "Hey, sure. I get it. Secret stuff."

"Sorry, Dave. Sometimes I wish I had a normal job."

"Yeah, me too." He jogged back to his friends.

When Finn looked back at the screen, Simpson had left his office.

He stared over at David and his friends. His son glanced over at his father once and then looked away. The group of students marched down the sidewalk toward the Capitol.

Finn walked off in the opposite direction. He would have to try another day. Now he had to see his mother. He'd been hoping to report to her the news of Simpson's death. So intent was he on what he was doing that he never saw the man emerge from behind a nearby tree and start following him.

After what Max Himmerling had told him the night before, Oliver Stone had come here to check out the office of Roger Simpson too, at least from a distance. Either Gray or Simpson had ordered Solomon's death and the hit on Stone. Since he couldn't get to Gray, Simpson was the next best thing. Now, however, there had come a detour. Stone had heard and seen enough of Finn to make him more than a little curious. Finn was good, to Stone's experienced eye. Others around the area, even the police officers, would have noticed nothing suspicious about the man. But Stone was not like other people. He had run down many leads that led to nothing. His instinct told him this would not be one of them.

When Finn hopped on the subway at Capitol

South, Stone did the same. The men rode it to National Airport. Stone followed Finn in. The latter went into a bathroom and came out dressed in street clothes, the duffel still over his shoulder. Now Stone believed that his hunch had just struck gold.

Finn bought a round-trip ticket for a short flight to upstate New York. Standing within earshot, Stone later did the same, using the fake ID and money Annabelle had given him. He went through security, his heartbeat ratcheting up a bit as TSA agents scrutinized his picture on the ID. They let him through and he allowed Finn to pass from his line of sight. He knew which gate the man was going to, after all.

Stone bought some coffee and a magazine. The flight was called. Finn was in the front of the full plane, Stone the rear. Forty minutes later they were wheels up. Less than an hour later, they touched down. Now it got dicey. The airport was small and the patrons few. Finn seemed preoccupied, but Stone couldn't be certain. If he was the man running around murdering highly skilled killers in their own right, Stone could not underestimate him.

Stone was debating what to do when Finn surprised him. He bypassed the small rental car counter, ignored the taxi stand out front and walked down the road away from the airport.

Keeping an eye on him, Stone stepped over to a taxi and leaned in the window. "Got a layover. Anything within walking distance of here?"

"Some residences, some shops, a nursing home," the driver said as he idly read his newspaper.

"Nursing home?"

"Yeah, you want to go there for a little R and R during your layover?" He chuckled.

Stone slid in the backseat. "Just drive for now, *slow.*"

The driver shrugged, put down his paper and the taxi pulled off.

70

Herb Daschle was a veteran employee of the CIA. He'd done years of fieldwork, seen the world, ridden a desk for the last decade and then accepted his current position. It was not all that exciting, and the public was totally unaware of it, but it was vital to the security of the CIA and thus the nation. Or so said the Agency's internal manual.

For two months Daschle had been coming to this nursing home three times a week and sitting in a chair in the private room of a man who was lying unconscious in the bed. The man was very high up in the CIA and his head was filled with secrets that could never be revealed to the public. Unfortunately, he'd had an aneurysm and was not quite himself. He could say things without knowing, disclosing vital national secrets unintentionally.

That could not be allowed, so men like Daschle came out and stayed with incapacitated Agency employees possessing such sensitive knowledge. There had been a man in the operating room when the surgery was done to relieve the pressure on the brain. There had been an agent stationed in the post-op, and there was 24/7 surveillance here at the nursing home, where it was hoped the man would eventually recover. Even the man's own family was never allowed to be left alone with him. This had come as quite a shock, because the family was not aware that this husband, father and grandfather even worked for the CIA.

Twelve o'clock came and Daschle rose from his seat as a fellow agent, his replacement for the next shift, sat down. The two men exchanged pleasantries and Daschle mentioned a few items from his watch, nothing of importance. He left the room, dying for a cigarette, and wandered down the hall toward the snack room to buy a can of soda and some crackers before he left. The voices coming out of one room that he passed stopped him. It seemed to be Russian. Daschle knew that language well, having been stationed in Moscow for nearly nine years. Although if what he was hearing was Russian, it was a particularly mangled version. It actually sounded like an amalgam of several Slavic languages. He'd also been stationed in Poland and Bulgaria for a time. He edged closer to the door of the room, which was open just a crack, and listened a bit more. Then he heard enough to make him hustle out of the building. And it wasn't for a cigarette.

As soon as he was gone, Oliver Stone stepped from

around the corner where he too had been listening. He watched the fleeing man.

Damn.

Inside the room Lesya was speaking while Finn sat quietly in his chair.

"So now John Carr rises from the dead like the Phoenix," she said in her tortured Cyrillic mishmash.

"It seems so," Finn said. "But I can't be sure."

"And the senator still lives."

"Not for long."

"What about Carr?"

"I'm working on it. I told you that. But I have no idea where he is or even if he's really alive. They just dug up his grave. That's all anyone knows."

She coughed hard. "Time grows short."

For you or me? Finn wondered. He was still thinking about the encounter with his son. *So close. Too close.*

"But you will find out. I will help you find out."

"Let me handle it."

"I can tell you what I know about the man."

"I know a lot about him already." He paused. "I don't think he's like the others."

She looked at him sharply. "What do you mean by that?"

"I think the Agency tried to kill him. I think they killed his wife. And perhaps his daughter. I believe he's suffered a lot. And he was a war hero too."

"He is *just* like the others. An evil man. A murderer!"

"Why, because he followed orders and killed my father and your husband?"

"You have no idea what you're saying, Harry. No idea."

"You know, I was just about to kill Simpson this morning, when David showed up. He almost caught me."

"David your son?" Finn nodded and his mother clamped a hand to her mouth. "Good, God. Did he suspect?"

"No, but I promised myself that I would never let this part of my life impact on that part of my life. And now it has!"

Lesya sat down next to him, grasped his hand with her bony one. It felt slightly repulsive to him now.

"Harry, my son, my loving son, it will soon be over."

"You can't possibly know that. And it might end with me dead."

She slowly withdrew her hand from his. "So what now?"

"Simpson and then Carr."

"You will do this. You swear?"

Finn nodded.

His mother scrutinized him a bit longer and then shuffled over, opened her drawer and removed a photo. She handed it to him. "For Carr," she said bitterly as she spat on the floor. Then she lay back on her bed. "Let me tell you a story, Harry."

He sat back, but for the first time ever he wasn't listening.

When the door to the room opened, they both turned to look.

"What do you want?" Lesya said angrily in English. "I have a visitor."

When the man started speaking in Russian, the breath caught in her throat.

"Who are you?" Finn asked in English.

"They used to call me John Carr," said Oliver Stone. He looked at Finn. "You're right. I'm not like the others. And you both need to get out of here, just as fast as you can."

71

When Paddy called back, Bagger answered after the second ring.

"Yeah?" Bagger said.

"Have you had time to decide that I'm right?" Paddy began politely.

"Do you know how many times I've killed you in my mind since we talked?"

"It's nice to be popular. But I need to hear your answer."

"How do you want to do this?" Bagger said bluntly.

"We don't do nothing until I hear from you what I need to hear."

"Come over to my hotel and I'll tell you in person. I know she's in D.C., so you must be too."

Paddy smiled and said, "What, after you've put a bullet in my brain? Don't think so. Besides, I don't go into the shitty parts of town, Jerry. You casino dicks always trend to the scum side."

"Yeah? I make more money in one second than you've made in your whole life."

"Money ain't everything, Jerry. It can't buy class. I

don't care if you're staying at the bloody White House, though I doubt they'd let the likes of you in the door."

"Well money is everything if you want a *view* of the White House like I got. That costs a grand a night."

Paddy smiled and pointed at Annabelle, who gave him a thumbs-up sign.

"You going to give me your word or do I hang up? 'Cause once this line goes dead, I won't be calling back."

Bagger swore under his breath and then said very slowly, "If you get me Annabelle, I give you my word that I will never come after you again."

"And that you and your people will never cause me any harm. And you give me your word."

"Okay."

"I need you to say it, Jerry."

"Why?"

"Because I know once those words come off your tongue I'm really safe."

"And that me and my people will never cause you any harm. I give you my word." This last part was so painful for Bagger that he slammed his fist down on the table next to him.

"Thank you."

"You still haven't explained how I get her."

"She's going to walk right into your arms, Jerry. I'll see to it."

Paddy hung up and stared at Annabelle, a smile creeping across his face.

"Grand a night with nice views of the White House. Can't be many of those."

"Can't be," Annabelle agreed.

72

"Can you get me a list of the hotels in D.C. that have views of the White House and cost a grand a night?" Annabelle asked Alex as they sat in the same coffee shop as their previous meeting.

"Why?"

"It's all part of those details I talked to you about."

"I'll get the list. You need any help?"

Annabelle started to say no and then stopped. "How good are you on your feet?"

"Excuse me?"

"Are you quick on your feet?"

"I'm a Secret Service agent. That's what we do."

"Then you can help me."

Later that day Annabelle walked into the second hotel from the list provided by Alex. She approached the front desk and discreetly flashed her phony FBI credentials to the clerk there.

"What is this about?" he said nervously.

"Potentially a big problem for your hotel, but we

might be able to work around that if you cooperate. I've got a strike team standing by outside."

The astonished clerk immediately looked over Annabelle's shoulder.

"You can't see them," she said. "That would sort of give it away, wouldn't it?"

"I think I should get my supervisor," the clerk said nervously.

"No, I think you should stand right here and answer my questions, William," she said quietly, eyeing his nametag.

"What sort of questions?"

"Do you have a guest staying here named Jerry Bagger?"

"I can't possibly give out that sort of information. It's confidential."

"All right, I guess we'll have to do this the hard way." Annabelle took a small walkie-talkie from her pocket that she'd purchased from a sporting goods store. "Bravo One to X-Ray strike team. Are you in position to crash all entry points? Affirmative. Squad leader, rules of engagement, no gunfire unless absolutely necessary. Repeat, unless absolutely necessary. There's potential collateral damage throughout the lobby."

"What is this, some sort of joke?" the clerk snapped.

On a cue from Annabelle, Alex, who'd been standing behind a pillar in the lobby, walked over. The tall agent looked down at the clerk.

He held out his Secret Service creds and showed the badge and gun on his belt. "Is there a problem?"

The clerk pointed at Annabelle. "She said she's with the FBI and she's looking for some guy and they're going to send a strike something-or-other."

Alex leaned down close in to the shorter man. "It's not a strike something-or-other. It's called a strike *team*. And I'm heading it up. We're part of a joint antiterrorist unit. I've got twenty-five agents in heavy Kevlar body armor with MP-5 submachine guns ready to bust into this place because this 'some guy' is number two on our most wanted list right behind Osama. I've been after this 'some guy' for two years of my life, and I'm not about to let a little prick like you screw it up. So you either get on your computer and tell us if he's here, or your ass will be the first one I arrest for obstruction."

"Holy shit!" the clerk exclaimed. "You can do that?"

"With a smile on my face."

Alex turned to Annabelle and he nodded. "Proceed, Agent Hunter."

Annabelle took a sheaf of papers from her pocket. "We have a search and arrest warrant for Mr. Bagger and his associates." She eyed the clerk sternly. "We don't like putting innocent people in harm's way, William, but this Bagger is a killer, into drugs, arms dealing, every bad thing you can think of. But if you cooperate we can put a tail on him and take the bastard *outside* the hotel. I think your supervisor would probably approve of that."

William stared at her for a few moments and then started clicking on his computer. "We don't have a Bagger listed," he said in a shaky voice.

"I would be astonished if he used his real name." Annabelle described Bagger to him in detail. "He'd always come and go with a bunch of muscle."

Alex added, "I would think a guy like that would tend to stick out here, am I right?"

William nodded. "He *is* staying here, under the name Frank Walters. He has the best suite in the hotel. Wonderful views of the White House."

"I'm sure. Okay, thanks for the assist, William. But don't say a word to anyone. You understand me?"

"Absolutely, best of luck, Officer," he said weakly.

Alex nodded, gave him a hard slap on the arm and left with Annabelle.

Outside Alex called in a team to cover the hotel. Now where Bagger went, so would they.

As they were leaving in Alex's car Annabelle said, "You *are* quick on your feet. That was great in there."

"Coming from you that's a real compliment. So now what?"

"So now we pull the trigger."

73

Finn, Lesya and Stone just stared at each other for a long time. Then Lesya uttered a curse and slowly rose from her chair. She gripped a small wooden box on her nightstand and looked ready to hurl it at Stone's head. "John Carr," she spat out. "You? Here? You murderer."

Stone turned to Finn. "A man was eavesdropping on you both. From his expression he understood some or all of what he heard. He ran out of here. I saw the room he originally came out of. I 'accidentally' looked in that room. There was another man in there keeping watch over a patient."

Finn hadn't moved a muscle. "Who is the man?"

"At the CIA we used to call them crypt keepers. An agent with a serious brain injury who might reveal secrets is watched over by other agents until the person either dies or recovers. I believe that's what's going on here."

"The CIA here?" Lesya hissed, an incredulous expression on her face.

"And the other man was also a crypt keeper presumably going off duty. He overheard us and he understood what we were saying?" Finn said slowly.

"The language you were speaking provides a good cover. Almost no one would understand any of it."

"But you did?" Finn said.

Stone nodded. "Language skills came with the territory. And that's why we have to leave. Now."

Finn glanced at his mother, who was still staring at Stone with loathing. "And why should we trust you? You could be leading us right into a trap."

"That's right," Lesya said. "A trap. Just like they did to your father."

"If that were my intent I would simply have waited until *you* left here," Stone said, indicating Finn. "And shot you on your way back to the airport. There's a stretch of woods in between that's particularly convenient. As for your mother here, this place is not well guarded. An unlocked door, a pillow, a brief struggle." He shrugged. "And if I worked with the CIA I wouldn't have come here and warned you. I would've just let them take you."

"How did you know to even come here?" Finn said.

"I followed you from Washington. I saw you outside Senator Simpson's office building this morning. You seemed a bit suspicious-looking."

"I didn't think I was that obvious."

"You weren't. I've just been trained how to look."

"And why were you at Simpson's office?"

"Because a man told me, against his will, that the matter of Rayfield Solomon had become a priority for the CIA again."

"And why is that?" Finn said warily.

Stone sized him up. And came away with a clear impression. *He reminds me of me, all those years ago.* "If you kill for revenge, you want the victim to know why. So you either send them something ahead of time or give it to them right before you pull the trigger. I think that was done with Cincetti, Bingham and Cole. And it was also done with Carter Gray. And he knew that it was tied to Rayfield Solomon. But of course Gray didn't die."

"What!" Lesya screamed and then looked accusingly at her son.

Finn didn't even blink. "Carter Gray is alive?" he said.

Stone nodded. "And no doubt the man who ran out of here is—"

"Going to get the message to Gray," Finn finished for him. He grabbed his mother's bag from under the bed and stuffed her few belongings in it.

"What are you doing?" his mother said.

Finn grabbed her arm. "Let's go."

"Where?"

"Out of here," Stone said.

Finn glanced at him. "Plane?"

Stone shook his head. "No doubt covered by now. They don't know about me, at least not yet. I'll rent a car from the airport. That stretch of woods I mentioned? I'll pick you up there in twenty minutes."

"You can't trust him, Harry! He is a killer. He killed your father." Lesya said this in pure Russian.

Stone answered her in Russian. "Everything you say is true. I led the team that killed your husband. Now I know that he was innocent. I lost *my* wife and daughter violently because of what I used to do for my country. I have spent the last thirty years of my life trying to make amends. I doubt I have enough years left to settle my debt. I know you have no reason to trust me. But I swear to you that I will sacrifice my life to save both of you."

"Why? Why would you do this?" Lesya said, though her voice was calmer and now she spoke in English.

"Because I simply followed orders without question. Because I took the life of another human being and I had no right to do it. And because you've suffered enough."

Five minutes later, they left the nursing home by a back entrance. Even with her walker, Lesya managed to keep up a brisk pace. She was not as immobile as she had led people to believe.

Stone left them hidden in the woods, hustled to the airport and rented a car using the credit card Annabelle had given him. He could already see subtle activity all around him that did not bode well for their escape. He drove off with the car, picked the pair up, and with Finn reading a map and guiding, they made their way through a series of back roads to the interstate.

"Where to now?" Finn asked.

"Washington," Stone answered.

74

Jerry had nearly paced a trench through the rug in his hotel room.

When the phone rang he jumped for it and then immediately calmed. He was Jerry Bagger and the Conroys were shit. Yet he would have to settle for the daughter, because Paddy was off-limits now. The thought made Bagger want to tear his own heart out. He would just take it out on Annabelle, giving her enough pain for two.

"Hello, Jerry," Paddy said. "You ready to dance with the princess?"

Bagger said, "You got her? Prove it."

"You'll see for yourself soon enough."

"Put her on the phone."

"Well, she's a wee bit tied up right now. And duct-taped."

"Then un-duct-tape her," Bagger said firmly. "I wanta hear her voice."

A minute later she said into the phone, in a beaten voice, "I guess you win, Jerry. First Tony, now me."

Jerry smiled and sat down. "Annabelle, don't even

mention yourself in the same sentence with that screw-up. But I wanted to let you know that I'm really looking forward to seeing you."

"Go to hell, you prick!"

"Still kicking to the end. It's a shame, it really is. We could've been a great team."

"No we couldn't, Jerry. You killed my mother."

"And you ripped me off for forty million, bitch!" he shouted. "You cost me respect. You cost me everything I've worked my whole life for."

"And it still wasn't enough for me. All I want is your fat, ugly head on a stick."

With an immense effort Jerry calmed. "I tell you what. I'll let that remark slide. People close to death, they say stuff. And I'll tell you something else. I was going to make you feel pain like you never felt before. But instead I'll do you fast, not slow. *After* you tell me where my money is. You know why I'm doing that? Out of respect. For your talent. Your *wasted* talent. If you'd learned that little concept of respect you might've lived longer."

"Tell me something. How much did you pay my old man to set me up?"

"That's the best of all. Didn't cost me a dime. You're one cheap date."

"Good-bye, Jerry."

"No, not good-bye, baby. This is just hello."

Paddy came back on the phone. "Okay, Jerry,

you've exchanged your pleasantries. Now it's time for business."

"Where and when? And don't say in front of the White House or the Washington Monument or some Hollywood bullshit like that or the deal's off. For me agreeing to leave your ass alone I want privacy."

Paddy said, "They're building a new ballpark in town near the Anacostia River."

"So I heard. What's that got to do with anything?"

"They're tearing down a bunch of buildings and neighborhoods around there. Lot of abandoned places. At eleven o'clock tonight I'll call with the address of an old parking garage. There'll be a white van parked on level two. Inside that van will be Annabelle tucked neatly in a roll of carpet. The keys will be in the van."

Bagger hung up and looked at his men.

Mike Manson said, "This could be a setup of some kind, boss."

"Gee, Mike, you think so? Not that I believe for one minute that Paddy Conroy is working for anybody other than Paddy Conroy, but I'm not stupid. He may have a big beef with his daughter about Mom getting killed. And that may be why he's willing to hand her over to me so I'll leave him alone. But nothing's for sure with that son of a bitch."

"So how do we do it?"

"We wait for the address. Then you guys are going to do the pickup at midnight. Bring her to a place where I'll be waiting. A place that's a lot more private than an abandoned parking garage."

"And we just drive off with her? What if they tail us?"

Bagger smiled and picked up his newspaper. "Says in here there's a World Bank conference today downtown and then fancy dinners and speeches all over the city. Big muckety-mucks flying in from all over the globe."

"So?" Mike said.

"So I say that's some great timing if you got the right exit strategy."

75

Carter Gray had risen from his bunker once more and wondered if his beloved Agency had grown so weak and incompetent that he was going to have to pull the damn trigger himself on Lesya and her son. After a fruitless nationwide search they'd had a wonderful, absolutely golden opportunity at the nursing home in upstate New York of all places, and it had come to naught. The room was empty, mother and son gone. And a third person had been seen with them. Something told Carter Gray that John Carr had gotten in his way once again after losing Gray's men and getting to Himmerling. And Gray now had to change his original plan to bag all three.

The description of the old woman left no doubt in Gray's mind that it was Lesya Solomon. Age had not been kind to her; she was no longer the beautiful, enticing Soviet spy. But it was Lesya, Gray just knew it.

Yet what would John Carr have been doing with the very people who wanted to kill him? Had he lied about his identity? Had he taken them by force? Had they teamed up? *That might actually make my job easier.*

Gray looked out the window of the chopper as it soared over the Virginia countryside on its way to Langley. With the overpowering force of the president's authorization burning a hole in his pocket, he would take command of the search. No questions would be asked. Still, the mission required delicacy, stealth and, when the target was sighted and then fixed, an unstoppable show of force. He would one-up the military on what shock and awe really meant.

He studied the topography below. Carr, Lesya and her child were down there somewhere. Only three people marshaled against him, one of them a woman in her seventies. Gray had unlimited people, assets and money. It would only be a matter of time. David P. Jedidiah's son was now being sought with the combined might of America's intelligence empire. And there was another way to speed up the process. As soon as the chopper landed at CIA, Gray started implementing his attack.

With Finn driving they crossed into Maryland that evening. Lesya sat in the backseat looking tired and frightened. Stone heard her keep muttering in Russian, "They will kill us all."

He glanced over at Finn, who was staring ahead,

but Stone noted that his eyes kept checking the rearview mirror.

"You have a family?" Stone asked.

Finn hesitated and then said, "Let's stay focused on the task at hand."

Lesya leaned over the front seat. "And what is that? What are we focusing on now? You tell me."

"Staying alive," Stone answered. "And with Carter Gray after us, that's not going to be easy."

"They dug up your grave," Finn said as they traveled around the Capital Beltway.

"Gray's doing, to flush me out."

"He knew you were alive?"

"Yes. We reached an understanding of late. He left me alone and I left him alone."

Lesya pointed an accusatory finger at Stone. "You see, you see? They are allies, son. They are working together. We are in the hands of the enemy."

Stone turned around in his seat to stare at the woman. "Lesya, you were one of the greatest spies the Soviet Union ever had. It was said that you turned more foreign agents than anyone ever had."

"I am Russian. I worked for my country. As you did yours, John Carr. And you're right, I was the best."

He was silent as he saw the pride creep into her hollow features. He allowed her to feel it for only a few seconds before he snapped. "Then start *acting* like it. Stop with the hysterical and stupid comments, because we're going to need all the help you can give us if we're going to survive this. Or are you just going to sit there and let your son die?" he finished bluntly.

She stared coldly at him, the sudden anger narrowing her eyes. And then her expression cleared. She looked at Finn and then back at Stone. "You are right," she said matter-of-factly. "I am being stupid." She sat back. "We need to formulate a plan, keeping in mind that Carter Gray has enormous resources at his disposal. Only sometimes, enormous resources cannot move with agility, while we can. They may find that we have a trick or two they didn't anticipate."

Finn stared at his mother in the mirror. He had never heard this tone of voice, seen this calm confidence before. Her Russian accent was completely gone. It was as though she had taken thirty years off her life. She was even sitting up straighter!

Lesya continued, "They may not know of my son's involvement, at least not yet, but they will before very long."

"How?" Finn asked.

"They will check the flights into the airport today. Match descriptions. It is a small place, it won't take long."

"I didn't use my real name. I had a fake ID."

"Video surveillance at the airport," Stone said. "They'll match your face to some database. I assume it's in at least one." Finn nodded. "Then your family may be compromised."

"Call them, now!" Lesya urged.

Stone could see the enormous pressure the younger man was under as he gripped the phone.

In a shaky voice Finn spoke into the phone. "Please, honey, no questions now. Just get the kids and take them to a motel. There's a cell phone in my desk drawer. Use that to call me. No one can trace it. Get cash out of the ATM. Don't use your credit card or your real name at the motel. Stay there. No school, no baseball games, soccer or swimming, nothing. And don't tell anyone. Please. I'll explain later."

Stone and Lesya could hear the woman's frantic responses.

A bead of sweat slid down Finn's forehead. His voice dropped still lower and finally his wife calmed. "I love you, sweetie. I will make this all right. I swear it."

He clicked off and slumped back. Lesya slid a hand on his shoulder and squeezed.

"I'm sorry, Harry. I'm sorry for doing this to you. I . . . I . . ." Her voice trailed off. She removed her hand and eyed Stone.

"You say Gray knows you're alive, Carr? He flushed you out of the grave, as it were. Do you have anyone he can use to get to *you?* To flush you out again? Because as I said, undoubtedly someone at the nursing home saw us leave and will already have given a description. He will know you are with us. He will know the easiest way to get to us is to get to you. So tell me, is there?"

"I do have people he can exploit, but I already warned them, *before* I went to the hospital."

She shook her head. "A warning is meaningless unless it's acted on with skill. They are capable people who can take care of themselves, follow orders, these friends?" she asked as she scrutinized him. "Don't color the truth. We need to know exactly how it stands."

"One of them is and he's with another friend of mine. But there's a third friend . . ." *Caleb, please don't do anything stupid.*

"So that is the flank Gray will exploit. Tell me, how close do you value this friend?"

"Very!"

"Then I am sorry for you and your friend."

Stone leaned back against the seat and felt the smacks of his heart. He hated what the woman was saying and yet he knew she was absolutely right.

She added, "And if it comes down to it, will you trade us for your friend?" Stone turned around to find her looking at him. He had never seen a more piercing stare than the one Lesya was giving him now. No, he was wrong about that. He had seen a gaze like that once before: on Rayfield Solomon, right before Stone killed him.

"No," he said. "I won't."

"Then let's work to ensure it doesn't come down to that, John Carr. And maybe you *can* redeem yourself for killing my husband."

She glanced out the window and said, "And I *was* the best agent the Soviet Union ever had. But Rayfield was even better."

"Why?" Stone asked.

"Because I fell in love with him. And he turned *me*."

"What?" Stone blurted out.

"Didn't you know? I was working for the Americans when you murdered him."

76

Jerry Bagger had been working the phones ever since he'd talked to Paddy Conroy. The casino chief had been thinking a lot in the last few hours and he'd arrived at a decision. Normally, in any confrontation, Bagger's instinct was to trade blow for blow until he or the other guy fell down. He wasn't going to do that this time, for a lot of reasons. Chief among them was the fact that he'd seen Annabelle in action. He knew how good, how convincing she could be. And there was a little tickle in the back of his brain that reminded him that a jab-jab-jab was a great setup for a left hook, a haymaker that had put many an opponent down permanently. He didn't intend to be on the receiving end of one of those.

Yet he couldn't bring himself to *not* go through with the whole thing, because the opportunity of getting his hands on Annabelle—in the event Paddy was playing straight with him—was too good to let pass. If he had a shot at getting the lady, he had to go for it. But you always had to have a backup plan, because the first plan almost never went perfectly.

And sometimes it went so badly you weren't sure if you were going to wake up the next day. Annabelle had taught him a valuable lesson by ripping him off. Unpredictability was a powerful thing.

He first called his money guy, instructing him to park a ton of cash in a safe place offshore with instant access for Bagger, and untraceable by anyone else. With money you could do anything. He had his jet fly back to Atlantic City to pick up some things for him, including his passport, and land back at a private airstrip in Maryland.

Next, he phoned another associate of his, a very trusted colleague who had one unique talent. He could make anything go boom. Bagger told him what he wanted and the man said he could have it ready in two hours, delivered. Bagger offered to pay his asking price and added a five grand bonus on top of it.

"You must need it bad," the colleague said.

It was true, Bagger really did need the boom bad. Ironically, such devices almost always killed people, lots of people. Yet in this case, it might just let one person live.

Me.

"Okay," Annabelle said to Alex and her father. "We need to get me to that van."

Paddy stood and shook his head. "Afraid not, Annie."

"What?" she said quickly with a sharp glance at Alex. He seemed as puzzled as she was.

"You're not going to be in that van. *I* am," Paddy said.

"That's not part of the plan. Jerry wants me, not you."

"I'll tell him you got the better of me. He'll buy that. He damn well knows how smart you are."

"Paddy, I'm not letting Jerry near you."

"You've got your whole life ahead of you, Annie. If something goes wrong and I'm the one who buys it, so what?"

"Why didn't you tell me this part before?"

"Because I knew you wouldn't go along with it, that's why. Now we've gone too far to turn back."

"Alex, talk to him."

"Well, what he's saying makes sense, Annabelle."

"You'll put me in the van," Paddy continued. "I'll buy some time with Jerry telling him how you outsmarted me, but I can still get to you if he lets me have another chance."

"Paddy, he'll kill you as soon as he sees you."

"I've known Jerry a lot longer than you have. I know how to play the fella, you just have to trust me on that one."

"I'm not going to let you do—"

"I have to do this. For a lot of reasons."

She looked from her father to Alex and back to Paddy. "What if something goes wrong?"

"Then it goes wrong," replied Paddy. "Now let's get this show on the road. I'm not getting any younger." He pointed a finger at Alex. "But one thing. No cavalry until the bastard admits to killing Tammy."

The call came at eleven o'clock with the address. At midnight Bagger's men went into the parking garage and found the white van on the second level. In the back, neatly hidden in a roll of carpet, was a person.

"Shit!" Mike Manson said as he shone his light on the person's head. "It's some geezer."

They unrolled the carpet and there was Paddy Conroy. He was apparently so weak from being bound up that they had to help him stand.

Manson shoved a gun in his sweating face. "What the hell is going on? Who the hell are you?"

"What's going on is that my damn daughter screwed me."

A smile eased across Manson's face. "You're Paddy Conroy?"

"No, I'm the king of Ireland, you dumb-shit."

Manson shoved him across the van and Paddy hit the sidewall and slumped down. Manson got on the phone and relayed the news to Bagger.

The casino boss was delighted at getting ahold of his old nemesis, but he also didn't like this abrupt change in the plan. No, he didn't like it at all, because that meant Annabelle was out there somewhere.

"Bring him," he instructed Mike.

Manson clicked off. "Now we go for a little ride. But first."

The two men expertly searched Paddy for any surveillance devices.

A minute later the white van roared out of the garage, hit a hard left, sailed down an alleyway, turned right and slid to a stop behind three black SUVs parked there in a column.

Paddy was hustled by Mike Manson into the middle one. All three trucks fired up and sped out of the alley. One turned left, one right and the third went straight.

The vehicles reached main roads and Bagger's plan quickly became evident. Everywhere there were motorcades of black SUVs carrying World Bank conference attendees to or from important events. Bagger's three SUVs were readily absorbed into this crush of dignitaries and bureaucrats.

At ten-thirty that evening Bagger left his hotel with his men. They drove to a disused warehouse that Bagger's men had located in a run-down industrial area in Virginia. There they waited until the black SUV with Paddy Conroy and Mike Manson pulled into the warehouse.

As soon as Bagger saw Paddy he walked over to him and belted him right in the mouth. Paddy fell back against the vehicle and then tried to get to Bagger, but Bagger's men held him back.

"That was for the ten grand you stole from me. Been waiting a long time to pay you back on that one."

Paddy spat blood out of his mouth. "Best ten grand I ever took."

"Yeah, we'll see how you feel about that in a few minutes. You got no idea how good I feel. You see, no Annabelle means my agreement not to go after your ass is *null and void*, as the prick lawyers say."

He studied Paddy's gray, gaunt features and his threadbare clothes.

"Looks like life's been treating you real well. You sick, poor or both?"

"What's it to you?"

"I'm insulted. I mean even you at the top of your game might not be good enough. You think it was smart coming after me wearing rags and looking like you're knocking on the grave?"

Paddy looked around at the armed men surrounding him. "Right this minute, not particularly smart, no."

Bagger sat down on a packing crate, his gaze never leaving Paddy's face. "So Annabelle outsmarted you? How'd she manage that, Paddy?"

"Like I said before, I guess I taught her too good."

"You sure about that?"

"What's that supposed to mean?"

"Maybe father and daughter got together to screw me. How about that theory?"

"My daughter hates my guts."

"So you say."

"So I *know.* But if you believed otherwise, why do the deal at all?"

"You know why. But now here you are and no Annabelle. So where is she?"

"No clue, Jerry."

Bagger stood slowly. "I think you can do better than that. So you and me are gonna have a little chat."

"I'm not in the chatting mood."

Bagger took a serrated knife out of his jacket pocket and slipped on a plastic glove. "Oh, I can be pretty damn persuasive." He looked at his men and nodded. A minute later, Paddy's pants and underwear were off and Bagger was sizing up the man's privates for cutting.

"I used this technique on a little asshole named Tony Wallace in Portugal after I *chatted* with the people he'd hired to run his mansion with my *money.* And let me tell you something, he talked and talked right before we beat his brains out. In fact, that was the way I was able to track down Annabelle. And now you're gonna do the same thing for me, old man. You know where Annabelle is and now you're gonna tell me. And when you do I kill you fast, no pain. If you don't talk? Well, you just don't wanta go there, trust me. "

Paddy struggled against his captors, but they were too strong. As the knife came closer and closer to a spot no man would want a sharp instrument to be, Paddy cried out, "For Chrissakes, don't! Just put a bullet in my brain."

"Tell me where Annabelle is, and I promise I'll kill you fast. That's the only deal you're getting now. And if you really hate your daughter, you should have no problem telling me where she is, right?"

"If I did know do you think I'd be here, you idiot?"

Bagger slapped him across the face. "You show some respect."

"Here's my respect." Paddy spat in his face. "That's for Tammy."

"Right, your old lady you left behind for me."

"I was in jail on the night you murdered her, you bastard. Otherwise you'd have had to go through me to get to her. She was the only thing I ever loved in my whole life. And I swear to God above, before this was all over, I was planning on putting a bullet right into *your* brain just like you did her."

"Was that before or after I killed your daughter?"

"Any price I had to pay to get you, I was willing to do it," Paddy screamed at him.

"But Annabelle screwed that all up, didn't she? Didn't she, old man?"

"Can't blame her for turning the tables on me."

"Since you were planning to whack me for killing your wife, why don't I fill you in on her last minutes of life? Would you like that?"

"I'll find some way to kill you, Jerry. I swear it."

"I'll take that as a yes. We crashed her house, and she recognized me right away. And you know what she said? She said, 'Why are you doing this, Jerry? Why are you going to kill me? I didn't do nothing to you.' And you know what I told her? I said, because your chickenshit husband ripped me off and left you holding the bag. That's how much he loved you, you dumb broad. And then I pumped a round right into her brain. Now, anything else you want to know about it before I start carving you up?"

"No, that's about it," a woman's voice said.

They all turned as Annabelle and Alex walked out from behind a stack of crates. Alex had his gun pointed right at Bagger, while eight guns held by Bagger's men pointed back at him and Annabelle.

Bagger said, "How the hell did you get here?"

"I came with the FBI," Annabelle said.

"Nobody could've followed my boys."

"We didn't tail them. We followed *you*. The place is surrounded, Jerry. You've got no way out."

"Yeah? Working for the FBI now? Look, baby, you con me once, shame on you, con me twice, shit on me." The man's voice was confident, but his look was something less than that.

"She's telling the truth, jerk-off," Alex yelled. "So just lay your weapons down before you don't have a choice in the matter."

"Kill 'em," Bagger said.

A split second later doors on all sides of the warehouse burst open and two dozen men in body armor came barreling in, sub-machine guns in hand.

"FBI, put down your weapons. Now!"

Bagger dropped the knife and his men quickly put down their guns in the face of the overpowering show of federal force.

Bagger's gaze went from Annabelle to Paddy. "Two con artists working with the feds?"

"You do what you got to do, Jerry," Paddy said as he hastily pulled his clothes back on.

Bagger looked at one of the FBI agents and immediately regained his swagger. "That bitch ripped me off for forty million. She bother mentioning that to you while she was playing snitch?"

"That's not my concern."

"Oh yeah, so what exactly am I being charged with?"

"Aside from kidnapping and assault, you're being charged with the murders of Tammy Conroy, three people in Portugal and Tony Wallace, who died yesterday."

Bagger snorted. "I got a dozen eyewitnesses who'll testify I wasn't around when any of those people got killed."

Annabelle held up a video recording device. "We've got your whole confession right here, Jerry. I have to hand it to you, you speak very clearly." She gave the device to the lead agent.

Bagger looked at the FBI men, Paddy, Alex, and then his gaze came to rest on Annabelle.

"Well, I guess this is it, then," he said. His hand slipped to his pocket.

"Hold it," an FBI agent said. "Take that hand out very slowly."

Bagger did so. His hand was cupped around something. He said, "This is a detonator, folks. My thumb comes off this thing, I got a chunk of C4 in the SUV right behind me that'll blow everything and everyone within a hundred yards sky-high." He nodded at the lead agent. "See for yourself if you don't believe me."

The lead agent nodded to one of his men. The man looked in the back of the vehicle. His glance back at his commander said it all.

Bagger said, "Now here's what we're going to do." With his free hand he pointed at Paddy and Annabelle. "They're coming with me."

"We're not letting you leave this building," the commander said.

"Then I'm going to blow us all to kingdom come."

"I don't believe that," the FBI agent said.

"Best I can hope for is lethal injection, right? Well, I ain't going alone. So if you don't think I'll do it, you don't know Jerry Bagger." He glanced at twin snipers who had placed red dots on his forehead. "And your boys shoot me, hot-shit FBI man, this thumb is coming off whether you like it or not."

The commander gazed uneasily at Alex and then Annabelle.

She stepped forward. "Okay, Jerry, you win. Let's go."

Alex stepped forward too. "I'm going too."

"No you're not, Alex," she snapped.

Bagger smiled maliciously. "Alex? Alex, is it? You sound like you finally found a friend, Annabelle. And I don't want to take your friends from you." He looked at Alex. "Congratulations, *jerk-off*, you get to go too."

Bagger eyed the commander. "Just so you know, I'm a fair guy, so you can keep a few of my boys to make you look good." He pointed to Mike. "Including Mike there."

"Mr. Bagger!" Mike started to protest.

"Shut up," Bagger snapped before turning to Annabelle and the others. "Get in the SUV." Several of his men retrieved their weapons and everyone climbed in.

Alex, Annabelle and Paddy slid into the middle seat. Bagger and one of his men got in the front seat, three others in the rear.

Bagger rolled down the window. "I see one car or hear one chopper following us, I start popping people, understand?" He waved to the FBI agents as the vehicle sailed out of the warehouse.

"Where to, Mr. Bagger?" the driver asked.

"Private airport in western Maryland where I had them park the jet. I thought I might need to get away on short notice. I'm calling ahead right now to tell them to warm it up." He glanced at Annabelle. "I'm sorry to say you three *won't* be joining us."

77

Carter Gray was a remarkable fisherman. Only he had not caught the fish he most prized, and that was because he could not find the right bait. He had burned thousands of man-hours and looked at a mountain of digital files until his eyeballs were ready to fall out. And yet for all that trouble he only had one name to show for it: Harry Jedidiah, son of Lesya and Rayfield Solomon, a.k.a. David P. Jedidiah the second.

He had tried to find Oliver Stone's ragtag band of freaks: the big man and ex-military Reuben Rhodes that Gray remembered from Murder Mountain; the mousy librarian Caleb Shaw who had not been to his home or job at the Library of Congress in recent days; and Milton Farb, the cherubic genius with OCD. Gray had a dossier on each man, and yet they had simply vanished. Farb and Shaw hadn't used their cell phones and Rhodes didn't have one registered in his name. And Rhodes had recently moved and left no forwarding address. Nor was wherever he was living listed on any real estate records, because Gray's men had checked. Still, with Carter Gray's resources no one should be able to simply vanish. No wonder these terrorist sleeper cells were proving nearly impossible to uncover. America was too damn big and too damn *free*. In some ways the Soviets had had it right: *Spy on everybody because you never know when a friend might turn into an enemy*.

He now turned his attention to locating Lesya's son. And he had focused on one aspect in particular as the point of least resistance. He rose from his chair in his bunker and flipped on the TV. Then the intelligence chief hit a button on the remote he was holding.

The scene he was looking at was from the Hart Senate Office Building. Roger Simpson clearly would be a target of Lesya's son. If so he could hit the senator either at his home or at his office. Gray had already checked the surveillance cameras at Simpson's condo building and found nothing helpful. Now he had turned to the office.

He watched hour after hour of people coming and going into the building. There were many and their numbers tended to dilute everyone down to useless silhouettes. Then Gray thought of a second angle. He put in another DVD, sat back and started watching the hallway outside Simpson's office. He spent three hours doing this, methodically checking out each person coming into frame.

Finally. He sat up and viewed it again. The man working on the door to Simpson's office. He zoomed in on the man's face. Penetrating disguises was something Gray had been long trained in. In the cheekbone was that a touch of Solomon? The chin, the eyes, that of Lesya? Contrary to what he'd told the president, he knew the woman well.

He made numerous calls, and the story came into focus quickly. No one from Simpson's office had called for a government repairman for the door. Simpson's receptionist, though, reported that that's what the man had said—that he'd been told to come. Yet he hadn't gone in the office in the footage Gray had, and a review of the other surveillance discs turned up no such penetration. A bomb-sniffing dog was brought in but found nothing at which to bark. No one bothered to check for bugs, because a bug couldn't kill a man.

The next step was to take the picture of the door repairman, pare it down to its essentials and run it through every database the government had. They were doing the same with the video feed from the airport and the descriptions that had been received from the nursing home. Even though the computer age had infinitely speeded this process up, it would still take a little time, something Gray did not have an abundance of. Allowing Lesya to be taken by the authorities was not an option. She had far too much she could tell. It was certain that she had passed this knowledge on to her son. And if Carr was with them, none of them could be allowed to live. It would be cataclysmic for the country, for the world. And for Carter Gray.

78

Bagger ordered his man to take a route through the city instead of getting on the Beltway to Maryland. They stopped once and switched out the license plate on the SUV in case the FBI had it. Then they drove on, blending in with dozens of other similar vehicles on the road.

Bagger sat back with a contented look as he clicked a button on the detonator, disarming it.

Paddy sat very still in his seat, his gaze on Bagger. Annabelle kept her eyes forward. Like Paddy, Alex was watching Bagger, or more precisely, the man's thumb.

Annabelle said, "A bomb, Jerry? And it doesn't seem your style to run like this."

He smiled. "You taught me that lesson. Unpredictable. Sometimes you learn more from getting your ass kicked than you do from winning. You came right at me with the long con instead of targeting the casino. So I gave you some of your con stuff right back at you. Jerry Bagger never backs down, always stays and fights. Well, not this time, baby. And how sweet it feels."

"Glad I could be such an example for you," she said dryly.

"So what's the plan?" Alex said. "Dump us in the woods on the way to the plane?"

"What the hell does it matter to you? You'll be dead."

"But once you get rid of us, you've got no more hostages. You think they're going to let you just fly away?"

"They got no idea I have my jet here or where it is. I'll be outta the feds' jurisdiction in a couple of hours."

"We have extradition with just about everybody."

"I know the gaps there, trust me."

"And the Pompeii goes down the tubes."

Bagger turned around to grin at him. "You think a guy like me doesn't have plenty stashed away somewhere?"

"I'm sure you do. But you're still not going to get away."

"Yeah, right. Who says?"

"I do."

"You're in a real good position for that." Bagger glanced at Annabelle and tapped his temple. "You really should've gotten some class-A talent, Annabelle. I mean, first Tony Wallace and now this whack job."

"Would you like to know why you're not going to get away, Jerry?" Alex said.

"Yeah, tell me, I'm just dying to know."

Alex looked out the window. They were crossing over the Potomac. "Because the FBI knows exactly where you're going."

"Really? How? They telepathic now?"

Alex and Paddy exchanged a glance and the Irishman's body tensed.

Alex undid a few buttons on his shirt and opened it. Underneath was revealed a wire. "You ever think about searching your hostages for bugs, *moron*?"

"Shit!" Bagger screamed, right as Alex shot forward and slammed the casino boss into the driver, in turn whipping the man's head into the door glass. Paddy lunged forward and wrenched the detonator from Bagger's hand. The driver fell limp across the wheel, his foot pushing forward on the gas. The SUV careened out of control and flew across a lane of oncoming traffic.

In the same motion, Alex kicked the passenger door open, grabbed Annabelle and jumped. Annabelle reached out for her father's hand and clutched it. A second later she was falling out of the truck as her father, with a strength that had stunned his daughter, pulled his hand free.

The last thing Annabelle saw before hitting the street was her father with the detonator in hand looking at her.

The next instant she and Alex hit the pavement, with her landing on top of him. A second later the

SUV slammed into the side of the concrete bridge, broke through and went airborne.

Alex and Annabelle jerked up as the explosion rocked the air. The SUV was blown apart as it sailed toward the river below.

Alex covered Annabelle with his body as parts of the truck rained down around them. Thirty seconds later they rose, bruised and bleeding, on shaky legs, staggered to the side of the damaged bridge and gazed over. What was left of the SUV and the men inside was already disappearing into the Potomac.

As the last part of the vehicle slid beneath the water, Annabelle turned and walked slowly down the road. She seemed shell-shocked.

People stopped their cars on the bridge and raced to the side to gawk. Others rushed at Alex and Annabelle.

One man said, "Are you hurt, mister?"

Another, an old gent, exclaimed, "What the hell happened, lady?"

Alex flashed his badge at these folks. "Secret Service. Get back in your cars and drive on. Now!" Then he hustled forward, put a protective arm around Annabelle, flashed his badge at another group of onlookers to back them off and the pair walked quickly off into the night.

79

The three were in a cellar of a building that hadn't been occupied in over a decade. It was a rat-infested, malodorous place, but right now it was the only location where they felt safe. The light was from a battery-powered lantern, the only chairs mounds of junk. It was the place of last resort for Oliver Stone. He only came here when he had nowhere left to go.

Stone leaned against a dank brick wall and stared at Lesya, who sat on a pile of old carpet, obviously lost in thought. Finn hovered by the door, every sense on alert. Stone turned his gaze to the younger man. "You killed Cincetti, Bingham and Cole, and you tried to kill Carter Gray by blowing up his house with an incendiary bullet after filling the place with gas. You climbed up the cliffs to get to his house and then jumped off the cliffs to make your getaway."

"Don't answer him," Lesya said sharply, shooting Stone a suspicious glance. "I agreed to work with this man to keep us alive, but that doesn't mean we have to trust him."

"I wasn't expecting an answer," Stone said. "I was

just expressing my admiration. It's not easy to take out killers like that."

"So do you think you deserve to die then?" Lesya said sharply. "You were a killer too."

"Frankly, I've been dead for a long time."

"They murdered your wife, didn't they?" Finn said.

"Because I wanted to get out. And they almost killed me. To make matters even worse, Roger Simpson adopted my baby daughter. She never knew I was her father."

"Simpson!" Lesya spat on the floor. "That is what I think of Roger Simpson."

"You said you were working for us all those years ago," Stone said. "But we were told that you had turned Solomon and that you both were working for the Soviets. That's why he was targeted for termination, because he was a traitor."

"They lied to you," Lesya said simply.

"I know that now. But if you both were working for us, why would they want to kill you? Or him?"

"Because of a highly dangerous and confidential mission which Rayfield and I were given. We carried it out successfully with a group of Russians loyal to me."

"What was this mission?"

"I haven't told anyone all these years, not even my son."

"Why?"

"I was a spy. We do not give up our secrets easily."

"If I'm going to help you, I need to know the truth."

"You, the killer of my husband, you make demands of me?"

"We can't outresource Carter Gray. Yet together we might be able to outthink him. But before I help you I need to know the *whole* truth."

Lesya did not look convinced.

Finn stepped in front of his mother. "I've already scared my family to death. I have no idea if they're really safe. If I try to go to them, I could be leading Gray right to their door."

"I told you there would be risks, many of them."

"Like there was ever a question that I would turn my back on you," Finn said angrily. "My whole life you've prepared me to do this. That it was my duty to make it right. That I was the only one who could do it."

"Every man has a choice," Lesya said. She pointed at Stone. "Like this man. He chose to follow rather than question orders and he killed an innocent man."

"He was a soldier. He was *trained* to follow orders."

"So were Bingham, Cole and Cincetti," his mother pointed out. "Why is he different?"

"Because he came to warn us. But for him you and I would be dead now. That's the difference. I think he's earned our trust. *Your* trust."

"I've never trusted anyone in my life, other than your father."

"And me," Finn said.

"And you," she conceded.

"Well, if you really trust me, listen to me! You can't go through your whole life thinking everyone is against you."

"That philosophy served me well for many long years."

"And if you hadn't trusted Rayfield Solomon?"

Lesya fell silent, studying her son closely. Then she slowly turned her attention to Stone. "How well do you know your Soviet history?"

"I was there a lot if that means anything."

"Do you know the two heads of the Communist Party before Gorbachev came to power?"

Stone nodded. "Yuri Andropov and Konstantin Chernenko. Why?"

"Soviet leaders were generally known for their longevity. Yet Andropov lasted barely thirteen months, Chernenko roughly the same."

"They were old men in ill health," Stone replied. "They were filler after Brezhnev died. No one expected either of them to last long."

Lesya clapped her hands together. "Precisely. No one expected them to last long, so when they died, no one was surprised."

"You mean they were killed?" Stone said.

"It is not that difficult to kill old, sick men. Even when they're Soviet premiers."

"On whose orders were they killed?"

"Your government's."

Finn stared at her in amazement. "That's impossible. Under U.S. law it's illegal to assassinate a head of state."

She scoffed. "What does that mean when you're trying to prevent a nuclear war that will wipe out the planet? Andropov and Chernenko were old men, yes, but they were hard-line Communists. They were in the way. No real change would occur under them. And the Soviet Union was crumbling. Its back was against the wall. There was growing talk of very desperate measures that the Communist Party leadership was considering taking to restore its place as a superpower. That could not be allowed to happen. Gorbachev had to be given a clear field. Because even though early on Gorbachev seemed to be the same as the other party leaders, *we* knew he was very different. We knew things would change under him. He was still a Communist and we knew he would not dissolve the Soviet Union, but we also knew that the threat of war would go down considerably with him in power. Then Yeltsin came along after Gorbachev. No one could have predicted that, but it was under Yeltsin that the Soviet Union was dismantled.

"But we had to get rid of the old Communist Party leaders. We had to! And we told the Americans our beliefs about this. They agreed with us. And Rayfield thought the same. He knew as much about the inner workings of the Soviet Union as any American alive. But we did not come up with the assassination plot. That was the Americans." She eyed Stone. "You believe it's true, don't you?"

"Heads of state have been assassinated before," Stone admitted. "But are you saying Gorbachev knew of the plot?"

"Of course not. Only a very few of us did."

"How did your orders come on this?" Stone asked.

"From our contact on the American side."

"Who was that?"

"Does it not seem obvious? Roger Simpson."

"And you and your team killed Andropov and Chernenko?"

"Let us say we helped them to their graves prematurely, yes."

"And Rayfield Solomon was involved?"

"Deeply. The Soviets thought he was working for them."

"How do you know this was approved by the U.S. government?"

"I just told you. We received the instructions from Simpson. He was our case manager. And he reported directly to Carter Gray. And Gray to the head of CIA."

"So you just followed orders, without question."

"Yes."

"And killed Andropov and Chernenko, two innocent men?"

Lesya and Stone exchanged a long look. "Yes," she said slowly.

Finn said, "Why would the Americans kill my father and try to kill you if you completed your assignment successfully? Why would they try to paint you as traitors?"

Stone answered. "Because the American government *didn't* order the assassinations. Possibly it was the CIA, or Simpson and Gray could have done it on their own. And once the deed was done they had to discredit and then get rid of anyone who knew about the murders." He looked at Lesya. "Isn't that right?"

"Yes," said Lesya. "And what do you think they would do to prevent *that* truth from coming out now? It could cause war between Russia and the United States. What do you think they would do?" she asked again.

Finn answered. "They'd kill anyone they had to."

"And unfortunately we are David and they are Goliath," Lesya added bitterly. "The Americans are always Goliath."

"But David beat Goliath. And so can we if we get to them first," Stone replied.

"Just the three of us?" Lesya said skeptically.

"We're not alone," Stone said. "I have friends."

If they're still alive.

80

Alex had hailed a cab and he and Annabelle had driven off. He had decided not to wait for the other feds to show up. The charred truck and the floating corpses that awaited them would be self-explanatory in any event. He did call the FBI lead commander and let him know what had happened and that he and Annabelle were the only survivors. "If you need us, we'll be at my house," he told the man. "I'm in the book."

The commander protested but Alex cut him off. "We've had enough for one day. Go and clean up the pieces and talk to us later. It's not like you have to take Bagger to trial. He gets to go before a higher judge now."

The cab dropped them off at Alex's house in Manassas, a one-story rancher with a single-car garage, set off by itself down a gravel drive. Inside the garage was Alex's fully restored '69 fire red Corvette, the only extravagance the Secret Service agent had ever allowed himself. His fed cruiser was parked out front.

"You hungry?" he asked Annabelle, but she merely shook her head.

"I guess asking if you're okay would be pretty stupid right now."

"I'll get through this."

"I'm sorry, Annabelle."

She sat down in a chair. "All these years I've hated my father because I thought he just let my mother die. Then I find out he didn't . . ." Her voice trailed off.

"And now you lose him too," Alex finished for her. "But at least you found out before he died, Annabelle. And he knew that you knew."

"He could've gotten out of that truck. He could be alive right now."

"For six months of the cancer eating him away?"

She stared up at him. "For six months of being with me. I would've taken care of him. I guess he thought blowing himself up was a better alternative."

"No, maybe he wanted to get Bagger even worse than you did. Maybe he was willing to die to avenge his wife and your mother. At the very least you have to admire the guy's courage."

"I do," she finally said. "But I still wish he hadn't done it."

"And he gave you that scar. He wasn't the world's greatest father."

"But he was my father," she said quietly.

"And a criminal."

"Alex, *I'm* a criminal."

"Not to me, you're not." There was an awkward pause before Alex added, "You said you weren't hungry, but I'm going to make some coffee. And when you're ready to talk, we'll talk. How does that sound?"

"Can I take a shower first? I feel really, really dirty."

He showed her to the bathroom that was off his bedroom, and then he went into the kitchen, washed up, put on a pot of coffee and cleaned himself up. By the time he was done, she was out of the shower. She walked into the kitchen wrapped in one of his bathrobes.

"Hope you don't mind," she said.

Her hair was wet and hung down straight.

"Shower make you feel better?"

"Not even close."

They drank the coffee mostly in silence. Then Alex built a fire in the living room fireplace, and Annabelle sat on the floor in front of it, holding her hands out to the flames.

She said in a low voice, "I guess the FBI will have a bunch of questions for me."

"Some. But I can help you field them, if you want."

"Thanks for helping me."

"You put your life on the line too."

She gazed up at him. "Can you sit with me? Just for a little while?"

Alex got down on the floor and they sat quietly in front of the fire as the flames slowly died.

Carter Gray was brooding. None of Carr's people had been located. Then another possibility occurred to him: the Secret Service agent, Alex Ford. He and Stone were tight. They had been at Murder Mountain together. He knew as much of the truth about what Gray had done as did Stone. If he got Ford, used him as bait? It would be a little tricky. The man was a federal agent. He couldn't just kidnap him. Or maybe he could if he somehow discredited him first. This was a favorite tactic of Gray's. Destroy the reputation of the victim first—indeed, make him appear to be a criminal—and then seize him at his most vulnerable. It was far easier to do than most people would have thought. And by the time it was all figured out, it wouldn't matter. Gray made a couple of calls and put the operation into motion.

He quickly received a call back from a mole of his at the FBI. The man there had some interesting news. He told Gray the details of what had happened that night with Ford and Jerry Bagger. And also that Ford had a woman with him, a woman apparently of questionable past. They had walked away from a fiery explosion in Washington. Ford had told the FBI that he would talk to them tomorrow. He had presumably gone home with the woman.

Gray thanked his spy and hung up.

This new intelligence changed things remarkably.

Alex Ford's career was just about to take a nasty turn for the worse.

81

After Annabelle went to bed, Alex sat up in the kitchen drinking another cup of coffee. He glanced every now and then in the direction of the bedroom as he thought things over. But what really was there to think over? The case was done, the bad guys vanquished. This was where the movie ended, the credits rolled and maybe some outtakes played. In the real world, of course, it wasn't quite that simple. There would be enough paperwork to fill out to clear-cut a small forest. And then an internal investigation to ensure that nothing Alex had done had improperly led to a bunch of men getting blown up over the Potomac. Explanations would be made and corroborated and Alex was confident that relatively soon, many months from now, it would all be over.

Yet he didn't want it to end. Not really. Because that scenario would mean that Annabelle would be on her way. He sighed. She would probably be on her way regardless. And maybe that was a good thing, at least officially. After all, she was a con, and he was a cop, and if that wasn't human oil and water, he didn't know what was.

He glanced in the direction of the bedroom once more. *No, it just isn't that simple, is it?*

When she woke up what could he do? Ask her to please stay? He could invent some lie. *You have to stay until the official inquiry is complete.* That sounded totally bogus even to him. Annabelle would see right through it.

The next second he stopped thinking about that issue. They were just about to receive visitors, unwelcome ones from the looks of things.

Alex bent low, slipped to the window and looked out. Down the gravel drive, nearly out of sight, was a vehicle that he didn't recognize. It was a nondescript black van. Alex hated nondescript black vans. They often carried nondescript men with large guns and bad attitudes. This fear was confirmed when he grabbed a pair of night binoculars from a shelf and used them to take a closer look. There was a small satellite receiver pod on the roof of the van. And if he'd still had lingering doubts, the movement in the bushes next to his house erased them. People in the bushes, satellite vans, maybe the glint of rifle optics in the moonlight—none of it was making Alex feel too good right now. And he'd thought nearly losing his life once already tonight was enough.

Yet this was a tad different from the encounter with Jerry Bagger. This had government strike team written all over it. And why would the government be bothering with one of its own? Alex nearly instantly answered his own question.

Carter Gray couldn't find Oliver Stone so he'd decided to cast his net wider. Whether this was actually true or not, Alex wasn't going to wait to find out. He had already had one near-death face-off with Carter Gray at Murder Mountain; he had no desire to go for a second round.

He grabbed a set of keys off the hook over the kitchen phone and raced to the bedroom. Clamping a hand over Annabelle's mouth in case she screamed at being awoken from a dead sleep, he whispered, "Someone's outside. Get dressed. Fast. We have to roll."

Annabelle had barely thrown on her clothes and grabbed her bag when two men came through the front door and another pair through the rear. They had body armor and MP-5s and Alex's pistol would be no match for them. So he opted for going out the door off the kitchen leading to the garage.

"Stop!" one of the armored men called out to them from the hall.

Alex had no intention of doing anything other than running like hell. He only bothered to open the garage door enough to let his Corvette scoot underneath, clearing it by about an inch. He grabbed another gear and they shot down the gravel road past the van right as the front door of his house burst open.

As the Corvette spat rocks in all directions, bursts of machine-gun fire zipped over their heads. Annabelle ducked down in her seat.

"Damn it!" Alex cried out.

"Are you hit?" Annabelle said anxiously, as she sat back up.

"No, but I think one of the shots hit the car."

He screeched onto the main road, keeping his foot mashed to the floor. He looked in the mirror and breathed a sigh of relief. There was no one back there.

"Alex, what's happening?"

"I wish I knew, Annabelle."

"Where are we going?"

"I wish I knew that too. Hold on."

He speed-dialed one of his buddies at the Service's WFO, or Washington Field Office, where he was stationed.

"Bobby, it's Alex. Something really weird is going on, man."

"Like what?"

Alex filled him in. "I don't know who those guys were, but they were carrying some serious hardware. Find out anything on your end and then call me back."

He hung up and looked at Annabelle. "Bobby's good, he'll be able to dig up something to help us."

"Why don't you just go to your headquarters or whatever you call it? We should be safe there."

"I would except for one little tiny problem."

"What's that?"

"I've seen the jumpsuits those guys were in before."

"Where?"

"At a joint exercise the Service did down at Camp Peary."

"Is it that bad?" she said, looking at him uneasily.

"It's one of the CIA's main training facilities, known as the Farm."

"The CIA!"

"Their paramilitary units wear that sort of gear."

"The CIA has paramilitary units?"

"Yeah, is that a secret outside the Beltway?"

"So you're saying our own government might be after us?"

"That's right."

"We got rid of a psychopath casino owner, my father just blew himself up and now the CIA's on our ass?"

"That sums it up pretty accurately."

"I have to say you're taking it very calmly."

"If nothing else, the Service teaches its agents to remain cool. But I have to admit, it's getting more difficult by the minute."

"It's nice to know you're human. What now?"

"As much as I hate to do it, we have to ditch my Corvette and find a place to hole up. Then we wait to hear back from Bobby and hope it's good news. But I sort of doubt it will be."

82

They jettisoned Alex's Corvette, grabbed a cab to Old Town Alexandria and then walked to a nearby motel. Annabelle checked in paying cash and using her fake ID while Alex hid outside. They went to their room and bolted the door.

An hour later Bobby called back. That he was whispering told Alex all he needed to know.

"The official story we just got in is you opened fire on federal agents who were attempting to make an arrest at your house. And that you're harboring an unnamed fugitive, a woman. None of us believe it, Alex, but the director's going nuts. Word is he and the CIA director just had a dustup on the phone."

"Those *federal agents* were either trying to kill or kidnap *me*, Bobby! And the only thing I'm harboring is a strong desire to kick somebody's ass to get some answers."

"Hey, I'm on your side. You didn't walk out of the office today and become a felon. But you still better come in and give your side of things." He paused. "Alex, *do* you have someone with you?"

Alex stared over at Annabelle, who looked anxiously back at him. "Thanks, Bobby. I'll be in touch."

He clicked off and threw the phone down on the bed in disgust. "Okay, we've obviously been teleported to an alternate universe where all the good guys are screwed."

Annabelle sat down on the bed next to him. "Thank you."

"Look, sarcasm I can do without right now."

"I'm not being sarcastic. I'm thanking you for saving my life tonight. *Twice!*"

"I'm sorry, Annabelle. I just didn't see this twist coming until it was too late."

"But why would the CIA target us?"

"The only thing I can think of is that I have a connection to Oliver."

"But why come after Oliver now?"

"A while back when the president was kidnapped and the U.S. was on the verge of a nuclear strike—"

"Oliver was involved in that!"

"We both were. And not by choice. But when that happened, Carter Gray was also involved. And not in a good way. Oliver's the reason the guy ended up resigning."

"So Oliver had something on Carter Gray and used that to make him quit his job?"

"You got it."

"But Gray's dead."

"They never found his body."

"So maybe the man's plotting from beyond the grave."

"That's what it looks like. And we're trapped right in the middle of it all."

"We have to find Oliver."

"Won't be that easy. If the CIA is involved you can bet they've put the hammer down on the other agencies either to cooperate or stand down."

"But we just helped the FBI," Annabelle countered.

"Doesn't matter. National security trumps everything else. So that means our movements will really be restricted. And unlike in TV shows and the movies, it's almost impossible to run from the cops. You have millions of eyes watching and somebody will see something and then that's it. And they sure know what I look like."

Annabelle held up her bag. "I can do something about that. Step into the changing room." She had Alex sit on the commode in the bathroom while she pulled out a small box from the bag and readied some items. It took an hour, but at the end of sixty minutes Alex Ford no longer looked like Alex Ford.

He gazed at himself in the mirror. "You're good at this stuff."

"Comes in handy. Tomorrow morning we can find a wig shop and get a few other clothes and things to improve the disguise. Give me a little more time with you and I doubt Mrs. Ford would recognize her husband."

"That wouldn't be hard since there isn't a Mrs. Ford."

She packed the kit back up. "I suddenly realized I'm starving."

"I saw a McDonald's down the street."

"Super-size me," Annabelle said.

As Alex was walking to McDonald's he got a call from Stone. "Bagger's history but Gray almost nailed us," he told Stone. "Paddy's dead. Annabelle's taking it kind of hard."

"I'm truly sorry to hear that, but I'm afraid I need your help, again."

Alex listened for a few minutes and then told Stone that he and Annabelle would meet him two nights from now, allowing things to settle down a bit.

He clicked off and hoofed it to the McDonald's, where he super-sized them both. On his way back, his arms full of artery-busting food, he wondered if this might be one of his last meals.

83

For one of the few times in his career, Carter Gray screamed in uncontrolled fury after being told that Alex Ford had escaped.

With a disgusted look he dismissed the stone-faced men standing in front of him. They'd missed Carr, Lesya and her son, and now this! Such incompetence never would have happened in the old days, he told himself. When he had men like John Carr . . .

Three deep breaths later and Gray was all business again. It was a setback, but only a setback. He had gotten another intelligence breakthrough barely thirty minutes ago. He'd discovered over the years that they tended to come in bushels.

They had matched the man's face to a database. The gentleman with Carr and Lesya was named Harry Finn, a former Navy SEAL who now performed consulting work with the Department of Homeland Security as a member of a red cell team. Or he *did* such work. Gray couldn't envision the man's career continuing, because he was undoubtedly Lesya Solomon's son. And that meant he was a murderer. And he had to die before he ever came to court.

Gray had already dispatched a team to Finn's home. He lived in a cozy place in the suburbs; had a lovely wife and three darling children. He coached soccer in his spare time and from all accounts was a model citizen. And Gray was sure that when his men got to the house it would be empty. A phone call he received ten minutes later confirmed this.

However, his team didn't come away entirely empty-handed. In a safe in the garage they discovered some interesting details. They also found some paperwork about a storage unit. When they got there, they hit the treasure trove. It was filled with the histories of Bingham, Cole and Cincetti. And Carter Gray and Roger Simpson. And finally John Carr. Though nary a scrap of information could be found about Rayfield and Lesya, Harry Finn was undoubtedly their man. Only where was he now? And where were his wife and children? In hiding, of course. And it was up to Carter Gray to flush them out. He only hoped he would have better luck.

Yet he sensed that he would. It was completely counterintuitive for them to do it, but for some reason Gray felt as though Stone, Lesya and Harry Finn were very close by. And if they were, they would succumb to a mistake at some point. It would not necessarily be *their* mistake. There was another factor to be put into the equation: Finn's very ordinary family.

He lifted his phone. "Put a trace on every credit and debit card and every cell and hard-line phone registered to the Finn family. You know where he works, so put surveillance on all his co-workers and his office. Watch the kids' schools and Mom's book club group. If they show themselves, take them. Move heaven and earth, but get them."

84

They had passed another day sitting in the cellar and now the darkness was settling in. Stone, Finn and Lesya had spent the time developing a plan of action. The next night Stone's team would assemble and they could execute that plan.

Finn, who'd been pacing in increasing agitation suddenly said, "I have to see my family. Now."

Lesya started to protest but Stone asked, "Where are they?" Finn told him.

Stone turned to Lesya. "You stay here. I'll go with him."

"You're going to leave me here, alone?" the old woman said.

"Just for a little while," Stone added. "You'll be safe."

The two men left the cellar.

"How bad is your wife?" Stone asked once they were outside.

"Bad! And who the hell can blame her?"

"We can get to them on the Metro and then it's a bit of a walk."

"You were Army Special Forces in Nam," Finn said. "I looked it up."

"And you?"

"How do you know I was anything?"

"I can just tell."

"SEAL. Look, we need weapons. They'll have searched my house by now. I have a storage unit with some stuff in it, but they'll have found that too."

"I have a place with guns," Stone replied.

Thirty minutes later, Stone waited outside while Finn entered the motel room in a run-down area of south Alexandria.

His children immediately flew to him, nearly crushing him against the wall. Even George the Labradoodle got in the act, barking and jumping on his master. As Finn hugged his kids tightly, all their tears mixing together, he saw his wife through a tiny crevice between David and Susie. Mandy was sobbing too but made no move toward him.

After a few minutes of hugs and cries, Finn managed to get his kids to sit down on a bed. Susie clutched the bear her grandmother had given her, tears trickling down her plump cheeks. Patrick nervously chewed on his bloody, bitten-down nails. He did that before every test and every ball game, Finn knew. And it pained him that his son was now doing it because of something his father had done.

David eyed his dad nervously. "Pop? What's going on?"

Finn took a deep breath. He could no more tell them the truth than he could jump to the moon. On the way over he had thought of the lie he would use, but it didn't seem so plausible now. He could never say, "I'm a killer, kids, and the cops are after me." No he could never say that, because these were his children. They and Mandy were all he had. Mere justice didn't constitute an adequate defense of what he'd done.

"Something happened at work, Dave," he began as Mandy looked on. In her eyes was stark fear, but also something else that devastated Finn: distrust. He put his hand out to her, but she drew back a little.

He decided to abandon his cover story. He rose and leaned against the wall. When he was finally ready to speak he looked directly at them.

"Everything you know about your grandparents, my mother and father, is a lie. Your grandfather didn't come from Ireland and die in a car accident a long time ago. Your grandmother wasn't from Canada. And she's not in a nursing home because she belongs there." He took another deep breath, trying not to focus on his family's collective astonishment.

And he told them. Their grandfather's real name was Rayfield Solomon. He'd been a spy for the Americans. Their grandmother's name was Lesya, a Russian, who'd been a spy for her country until coming over to the American side with Solomon and also marrying him.

"They were framed by some people at the CIA," he said. "Rayfield Solomon's picture hangs on the wall at Langley, the 'Wall of Shame' they call it. But he doesn't deserve to be there. He was killed by these same people so the truth would never come out. Your grandmother survived but has been in hiding ever since."

To their credit and Finn's relief, his children seemed to readily accept his explanation, even be excited by the revelations. "But what is the truth?" David asked. "What were they framed for doing?"

Finn shook his head. "I can't tell you, son. I wish I could, but I can't. I only found out a short time ago."

"Where's Grandma?" Patrick asked.

"I'm going back to her after I leave you."

Susie flung herself around Finn's leg. "Daddy, you can't leave. You can't leave us," she wailed. The sounds were cracking Finn's heart in half. He could barely breathe as the tears streamed down his daughter's face. He lifted her up and held her. "I'm sorry, baby, but I promise you one thing. Are you listening? Can you listen to Daddy for just a minute? Please, baby, please?"

Susie finally stopped crying. She and her brothers stared at their father. They were so still, it didn't seem like any of them were actually breathing.

"I promise you this: that Daddy will fix everything. And then I'm going to come and get all of you and we're going to go back home and everything will be like it was. I promise you. I swear to you that it will."

"How?"

Everyone looked at Mandy, who now moved toward her husband.

"How?" she said again, her voice rising. "How will you fix it all? How will you make everything like it was? How can you possibly fix this . . . nightmare?"

"Mandy, please?" Finn glanced at the kids.

"No, Harry. No! You've been deceiving me, the kids, for how long? How long, Harry?"

"Too long," he said quietly. He added, "I'm sorry. If you just knew—"

"No, we don't want to know." She took a struggling Susie from his arms. "I called Doris, our next-door neighbor. She said men came to our house today and searched it. When she tried to ask them what was going on, they said they were looking for you, Harry. They said that you were a criminal."

"No! NO!" Susie screamed. "Daddy is not a criminal. He's not, he's not!" She started hitting her mother. Finn grabbed Susie away and clutched her tightly. "Susie, you never do that, you never hit your mother. She loves you more than anyone in the whole world. You never do that. Promise me."

A tearful Susie said, "But you're not a bad man, are you?"

Finn looked desperately at Mandy and then at his

sons, who stared at him, their faces pale, their eyes wide in fear.

"No, he's not, Susie. Your father is not a bad man."

They all turned to look at Oliver Stone, who had just come quietly in the door. George the dog hadn't made a peep. He just sat next to Stone looking up at him.

"Who are you?" Mandy demanded fearfully.

"I'm working with your husband to try to right some wrongs. He's a good man."

"I told you, Mommy," Susie said.

"What's your name?" Mandy asked.

"That's not important. What is important is that Harry has told you the truth, or as much of it as he can and still keep you safe. It was incredibly dangerous for him to come here tonight, but he insisted. He even left his mother, who is old and frail, to come and see you, because he was so worried. He had to see you." He looked at Mandy. "He had to." Mandy's gaze went from Stone to her husband. Finn slowly put out his hand. She slowly took it. Their fingers instantly gripped like steel.

"Can you right these wrongs?" Mandy asked, looking at Stone anxiously.

"We're going to try our best," he said. "That's all we can do."

"And you can't go to the police," she said.

"I wish we could, but we can't. Not yet."

Finn put Susie down and picked up the bear she'd dropped. "I told Grandma how much you love your bear." Susie clutched it with one hand and her father's leg with the other.

After twenty minutes, Stone told Finn they had to leave. At the door Mandy slid her arms around her husband and they hugged while Stone and the children kept a respectful silence.

"I love you, Mandy, more than anything in the world," Finn said into her ear.

"Just make things right, Harry. Make things right and come back to us. Please."

After they left, Finn turned to Stone. "Thanks for what you did in there."

"Families are the most important things there are."

"You sound like you speak from experience."

"I wish I did, Harry, I wish I did. But I don't."

85

David Finn was very upset about the events of the night before and he welcomed the opportunity to get out of the motel room and go to the grocery store. The room they were staying in had a kitchenette and their mother had been fixing their meals there.

When he was in the checkout line he realized that he didn't have enough cash, so he pulled out the debit card his mother had given him for safekeeping but then told him not to use. But what could it really hurt, he thought.

A lot, as it turned out.

As soon as the card was swiped through the receiver, an alert signal was received electronically in a room two thousand miles away. It was then relayed to CIA headquarters and nearly instantly thereafter to Carter Gray. Within two minutes' time four men had been dispatched to the location where the card had been swiped.

David was barely halfway back to the motel when the car pulled over and two men got out. The tall boy was swallowed up between their bulk, thrown in the car and it was rolling, all in less than five seconds. Thirty minutes later he was twenty miles away in a dark room secured to a chair. His heart was pounding so fast he could barely breathe. He said in a low voice, "Dad, please come and help me. Please."

The voice came out of the darkness. "Dad's not coming, David. Dad's not coming ever again."

Stone, Finn, Lesya, the rest of the Camel Club and Alex and Annabelle were congregated in the cellar. Standing in the center of the room, Stone made introductions, and then told them the entire story. They sat back, an enraptured audience. Several of them occasionally glanced over at Lesya or Finn.

"My team and I killed Rayfield Solomon," Stone concluded. "We killed an innocent man."

"You didn't know that, Oliver," Milton protested, a response that Reuben and Caleb echoed.

Stone had noted gratefully that his fellow Camel Club members had taken his frank admission of being a former government assassin attached to the Triple Six Division of the CIA without much surprise.

As Caleb had pointed out, "We knew you weren't a retired librarian, Oliver. I can sniff those folks out pretty easily."

Lesya said, "Why do they call you Oliver? Your name is John Carr."

Milton, Reuben and Caleb all exchanged curious

glances. Stone looked at Lesya and said, "Have you kept your real name all these years?" Lesya shook her head. "Well, neither have I. For obvious reasons."

Stone next looked over at Alex Ford. "Alex, you're the only lawman here. And since what I'm proposing isn't exactly lawful, you can bail out now."

Alex shrugged. "I care about the truth as much as the next person." He shot Lesya a glance. "But to play devil's advocate for a minute, how do we know her story is true? We only have her word for it that all this happened. What if Solomon really was a spy? What if she didn't come over to the American side? I mean, I've heard of Rayfield Solomon. And it seems like the gent was guilty as charged."

All eyes turned to Lesya.

Stone said, "I have my own reasons for believing her, including someone at the CIA who would know."

"Granted," Alex said. "But we're all going to be risking pretty much everything here. So I'd like to know it's for the right cause. I mean, if she was this terrific spy she must be a pretty damn good liar."

Stone started to say something else, but Lesya put up a hand and rose. "I will defend myself if you don't mind. I'm actually surprised the question is only coming up now." She gripped her walker, flipped it upside down, took off the foam booty and unscrewed the covering on the metal tube. Out came two rolled-up pieces of paper.

"These are the written orders we received from the

CIA. We insisted on it because of the magnitude of what we were being asked to do."

They all read through them. They were each on CIA letterhead, addressed to Lesya and Rayfield Solomon. The first instructed them to carry out the assassination of Yuri Andropov; the second, that of Andropov's successor, Konstantin Chernenko. Each had Roger Simpson's signature at the bottom. Everyone looked stunned.

"I take it you didn't trust Simpson," Stone said.

"We only trusted each other," she replied.

"That's Simpson's original signature," Stone said. "I know it well."

"There's no countersignature from the president?" Alex said incredulously. "Are you telling me you killed *two* heads of the Soviet Union on the orders of, what, a low-level case manager?"

"Do you think the president of the United States would actually put his signature down on such an order?" Lesya said with equal incredulity. "Our chain of command was what we worked with. If it came down that chain we had to rely on it being approved from the top. If we couldn't rely on that, we couldn't do our jobs."

"She's right about that," Stone said. "Triple Six operated the same way."

He was examining the letter against the lightbulb. He glanced at Lesya. "There's a code line next to the watermark."

She nodded. "That special encoded paper was only available from at least one level above Simpson."

"Carter Gray?"

"Yes. We knew the orders had really come through Gray. And it was our experience that if they came through Gray, they had come from the top. We didn't trust Simpson that much. He was a loose cannon."

"But Gray might have played you for the fall guy too," Stone pointed out. "The president might not have authorized the killings."

She shrugged. "There is always that possibility. I am sorry but I did not have the opportunity to go to your White House and ask the president personally if he wanted me to kill two Soviet leaders," she added in a bristling tone.

"Why didn't you take this letter to the authorities back then?" Alex said.

"I had no reason to even think of doing so until Rayfield was killed. Even then I didn't know he'd been murdered by the Americans until much later. Then an attempt was made on my life when Harry was still a child. At that point I knew we had been betrayed. We had to go into hiding. I spent decades finding out the truth, the people responsible. But even so, how could I use this evidence? I was a Russian spy. It was only Rayfield, Simpson and Carter Gray who knew I was a double agent. If I had come in from the cold even with this evidence no one would have believed me. They would have just killed me."

She paused and looked at each of them as they stared back at her in some disbelief. "You think your people would hold back from doing something like that?" She glanced at Stone. "Ask him."

"I believe you, Lesya," Stone said. "I know it could have happened exactly *that* way."

"Rayfield and I were married in the Soviet Union. I was already carrying Harry. We couldn't tell anyone we were married, either Soviet or American. We assumed double lives, new names, eventually settled in America. Rayfield spent as much time with us as he could. When Harry was still small Rayfield severed almost all ties with us. Someone was after him. He knew this. His fear was confirmed in São Paulo. He was still working for the Americans, his own country. And they killed him."

"Wasn't there an investigation?" Alex added.

"What did I care for investigations that went nowhere? I didn't want the truth covered up. I just wanted revenge." She took Finn's hand. "We both did."

Alex said, "Oliver, can't we just take this evidence to the authorities now?"

"That's what I was thinking," Annabelle added.

Stone shook his head. "We don't know that the CIA and the president at the time didn't order those assassinations. If they did, others, who are still in the government, may know too."

"And we go waltzing in with it," Alex said slowly.

"And are never seen again," Lesya said. "Look what happened to my poor husband."

"And making this public now may start World War Three," Stone said. "With the state of Russia right now and the tarnished global image of the U.S., I doubt the Russians would take kindly to us having killed two of their leaders even if it did lead to the fall of the Soviet Union."

"So what's your plan?" Alex asked.

"We have to get to Carter Gray," he said. "And I think I know how to do it."

Stone had just started to lay out his plan when Finn's phone buzzed. He listened, clicked off and looked at the others. His face had gone very pale. "That was Mandy. David didn't come back from the store."

Lesya said quietly, "Carter Gray has taken him. As bait."

Finn stood. "Then it's over. I'll trade myself for my son."

"The only result of that will be *both* of you will die," Stone said. "Gray never allows for leaving witnesses if he can help it."

"I have to get my son back," Finn snapped.

"We will get him back, Harry. I promise," Stone said.

"How?" Lesya exclaimed. "How will you do this if Gray has him? You just said the man does not allow for survivors."

"We need someone else to trade David for other than you and Harry."

"Who would that be?" Reuben asked.

"Someone Gray can't afford to lose."

Lesya said instantly, "Roger Simpson."

Finn whirled around to stare at Stone. "And I know just how to get the son of a bitch."

86

Roger Simpson was sitting at his desk in his office at the Hart Building working when his computer screen went blank. A second later a picture appeared on it.

Simpson gasped. It was the image of Rayfield Solomon materializing across his screen. *How can that be?*

Typed letters next appeared on the bottom of the screen. "I hope you recognize your old friend."

"What the?" Simpson said, looking around. "What the hell is this?"

"What the hell is this?" a voice said, sending Simpson nearly out of his chair. It was coming from the wireless unit Finn had hidden there when he'd broken into the senator's office.

"Who are you? *Where* are you?" Simpson said fearfully.

"What's important is that there's a bomb hidden inside your computer."

"What!" Simpson exclaimed, half rising from his chair.

"And if you try to leave the room it will detonate."

Simpson immediately sank back down. "But they swept my office for bombs."

"Unscrew the back of your computer. There's a screwdriver in your desk drawer, I checked when I was in here."

"But I—"

"Do it!"

Hands shaking, Simpson retrieved the screwdriver, undid the back cover and stared at the device Finn had put there.

"It's designed to use the chemical and electronic components in the CPU to cause a chain reaction and then a big boom. By the way, I can also see everything you're doing, so if you try to disarm the bomb I'll blow you up. Understood?"

Simpson slowly nodded.

"Don't just nod, I want to hear you say it. Do you understand?"

"I understand. For God sakes, I understand."

"A man will come to your office shortly. You will go with him without resistance. If you try to warn anyone I will detonate the bomb and your whole office disappears. Once out of your office, if you try anything, say anything to anyone to try and get away, your wife is dead. Do you understand that?"

"You have Donna?"

"The former Miss Alabama is doing very well right now. That status could change, depending on your level of cooperation. Do you understand?"

"Yes," Simpson said in a defeated tone.

"Good. Now compose yourself and wait for him to come. I'll be listening and watching until he does. He'll explain that he's taking you to an emergency meeting at Langley to cover a crisis that just came up, one that the chairman of the Intelligence Committee needs to be in on. You will confirm to your staff that this is true. Understood?"

"Yes."

A few minutes later there was a knock at Simpson's office door. Shortly after that the pale but composed senator was escorted down the elevator by Stone dressed in a black suit; he was also wearing sunglasses. They got into a car driven by Reuben. As the car pulled away Stone took off his sunglasses and stared at Simpson.

"Hello, Roger, it's been a long time."

"Do I know y—?" Simpson's breath caught in his throat as Stone's gaze bore into him.

"I guess I haven't changed as much as I thought," Stone said. "Actually, I think I did all my aging while working for you and Gray."

Simpson stammered, "John, please, you have to believe me, I had nothing to do with what happened to you or your wife." He added quickly, "And we took care of Jackie. We loved her very much."

Stone elbowed the man hard in the ribs. "*My* daughter's name was *Elizabeth*, not Jackie."

"Gray gave her to us. He didn't tell us she was your daughter. He only told me the truth recently."

"So who did order the hit on me?"

"I have my suspicions," Simpson said.

"Gray?"

Simpson said slowly, "Could have been. He said you wanted to leave Triple Six. He didn't like that one bit. That's the truth."

"Apparently neither did a lot of people. You ordered the hits on Andropov and Chernenko, didn't you?"

Simpson almost choked on his own breath. "Who told you that?"

"Did you?"

"That's in the past. But if I did anything of that magnitude, which I'm not admitting that I did, it would have been duly authorized from the highest possible level."

"I'm sure you covered your ass. I talked to Max Himmerling before he died."

A tic started at Simpson's left temple. "Himmerling?"

"Yeah. I'm assuming Gray had him killed because he knew he'd tell me everything. And Max knew where all the skeletons were buried."

"What all did he tell you?" Simpson asked nervously.

"Everything I needed to know," Stone said quietly.

"Like it was either you or Gray who ordered the hit on me."

Simpson could barely speak now. "Are you going to kill me?"

"That depends on you, doesn't it?" Stone put on his sunglasses and sat back. "*And* how much Carter Gray values your *friendship*? If he doesn't take the bait, you're of no value to me."

"I could well be the next president of this country!" Simpson snapped.

"Like I said, no value to me at all."

87

Simpson spoke slowly into the phone. His words had been scripted. If the man had any desire to deviate from that script, Stone was holding a gun against his head to dissuade him.

"They want to meet, Carter," he said in a strained voice.

"I have no idea what you're talking about," Gray said. "*Who* are you talking about?"

"You know who!"

"Well, tell them, whoever they are, that if they're recording this conversation, I wish them luck in trying to use it against anyone."

"Carter, dammit, they've kidnapped me!"

"I can call 911 if you'd like. Any idea where they might be holding you?"

"They have something you want."

"Really?"

"They know about David."

"Again, I don't know what you're talking about."

"They have the orders I signed, you know the ones."

"No, I really don't."

Simpson said angrily, "You authorized that order, Carter."

"Again, without possibly knowing what you're really talking about I can try to make a trade."

"Me for the boy."

"No, for the orders."

"What about me!"

"What about you, Roger?"

"They'll kill me."

"I'm very sorry to hear that. But you've lived a fairly long and full life. Where do they want to do the exchange?"

"You son of a bitch!"

Stone took the phone. "We'll call you back with the place and time. And we'll throw in Simpson for no extra charge. I have no desire to keep him."

"John, nice to hear your voice. Do you know how difficult you've made things for me?"

"It seems to be the only thing I live for anymore."

"And of course you won't be lying in wait to ambush me."

"You'll have to take your chances, just like I will."

"And what if I don't show up?"

"Then the orders for Andropov and Chernenko's assassinations get sent to five people in D.C., none of whom you'd call a friend. And then we can let the distinguished senator sell you out to save himself. I think he'd make a great witness."

"After all these years you think anyone will really care?"

"Fine, if you don't think it matters, why bother coming? We'll just messenger them out and let the chips fall. Take care, Carter."

"Wait!"

A few moments of silence passed.

Stone said, "I don't hear anything."

"Where did you get these orders? Lesya?"

"You don't need to know. Roger has seen them. And judging by the paleness of his skin I'd say he thinks it matters a lot."

"He was always a bit excitable. Not like you and me. All right, John, but if you really want to do a deal, you'll have to sweeten the pot. I want the original recording you took at Murder Mountain."

"That's not negotiable."

"Oh, but it is. You cost me my career. I want it back. And don't try to run and make copies. We have technology now that shows that."

"And if I don't?"

"I don't have to tell you the consequences, do I?"

Stone looked at Finn. "All right. I'll call you back with the time and place. And you have to be there in person or it's no deal."

"Then I'd prefer to pick the location."

"I know, that's why *I'm* doing it. One more thing. Anything happens to David Finn, you won't walk away alive."

"You're not what you once were, John. I have fifty men as good as you ever were."

"Make that forty-nine. I ran into one of your *best* about a month ago, an ex–Triple Six turned spy."

Gray put down the phone and wiped a trickle of sweat from his face.

88

Mandy and the rest of the Finn family were moved to other quarters by Reuben, Caleb and Alex that night, after taking great precautions to make sure they weren't followed. They also brought Lesya to stay with them. Caleb was left on guard with strict instructions to phone immediately if anything seemed suspicious. Then Reuben and Alex left to help the others with the preparations for the exchange of Simpson and David Finn.

Back at the cellar Stone quickly made it clear that only he and Finn would be directly involved in the exchange.

"Oliver," Alex said. "You have no idea how many people Gray's going to be bringing. If you remember Murder Mountain, it was a lot of guys with submachine guns."

Stone said, "This time we'll have the advantage." He looked at Annabelle. "However, we need someone to lead David out. For a number of reasons, you fit the bill. Are you game?"

Alex stepped between them. "Wait a minute. If

anyone's going in there with you, it's going to be me, not Annabelle."

"She will only be involved in getting David out of the building. We have a way to do that that doesn't involve confrontation with Gray and his men." He looked at Annabelle again. "I know you have a great deal of nerve. But I wouldn't ask you to do this if I could think of any other way." He added quietly, "And you have no reason to help me. I certainly abandoned you in your time of need."

She looked at Stone and then over at Alex. "Well, your handpicked replacement did a pretty good job. So I am game. Where is this all going to go down?"

Finn answered, "The Capitol Visitor Center."

"It's not finished yet," Milton said.

"Which is exactly why we're using it," Stone answered.

Finn explained. "The company I work for has been targeting the visitor center for a penetration. We do that under contract to Homeland Security as a way to evaluate the security of a particular facility. We do penetrations on airports, shipping ports, nuclear reactor facilities; highly sensitive and strategic operations like that."

"But the visitor center isn't even open, like Milton said," Reuben added. "Why would Homeland Security want you to test its defenses now?"

"Because that's exactly what a terrorist might think. Hit it now before it's fully up and running. But the more important reason is that the visitor center is connected by tunnel to both the Capitol building and to the Library of Congress. Terrorists might use that to attack either of those buildings from below ground. I've already done extensive reconnoiters of the visitor center. I have a way to gain access and also a way to get my son out."

"When is all this going to happen?" Annabelle asked.

"Tomorrow night," Stone answered.

Alex said, "But that's the night of the mock terrorist attack on Capitol Hill. We got that notice a while back. The place will be total chaos, Oliver. Ambulances, police, fire trucks, casualties, total bedlam."

"Chaos always makes it easier to escape," Stone noted.

"*If* you escape," Annabelle said. "The two of you are basically going into an unfinished building with limited exits to meet a heavily armed force of government killers led by a guy who sounds about as brilliant and ruthless as they come."

"You've summed it up nicely," Stone said.

"How do you know Gray won't just kill Simpson? He might be pretending to agree to do an exchange and then his men will just kill all of you." They all turned to stare at Milton as he finished speaking. "When you've been around Oliver long enough you do tend to get a bit paranoid."

Stone smiled before answering. "Milton, you're

absolutely right. In fact, I don't think Gray would have any trouble killing Simpson and then blaming it on us. But I do have something he really wants. And I knew he'd ask for it."

"The evidence you used to make him resign," Alex said.

"That's really the only reason he's coming. The orders we have only tie Simpson to the assassinations of Andropov and Chernenko."

"So Gray comes with a lot of firepower and the exchange is made. Once he has what he wants, how are you going to get David and yourselves out of there safely?" Annabelle wanted to know.

"There is a way," Stone said. "And we're going to need help from all of you to do it."

89

Finn's red cell team had prepped a tractor-trailer rig for use on its planned penetration of the visitor center. Those plans had been put on the back burner due to the incident involving Sam. Yet the truck was ready to go and when Finn told Stone about the rig's capabilities, the ex–Triple Six had bluntly replied, "Go get it."

And Finn had, with very little trouble actually since he had the keys to the tractor and access to the secure storage facility where it was housed.

He was now driving the rig through the middle of the capital. As he pulled into the entrance to the visitor center he could see preparations for the mock terrorist attack unfolding all around him.

He brought his truck to a stop in the loading dock alley and hopped out. He wore the requisite uniform and had the proper ID and shipping orders, all phony but good enough to fool a very bored government gunslinger. He showed the manifest to the guard and then popped the back door of the truck. The guard inspected the cargo, even pulling the tops off some of the boxes and peering in before closing them back up.

Finn had arrived here at half past six because he knew the construction workers were scheduled to go off duty promptly at six because of the mock terrorist attack. The next shift came on the following morning. The exchange with Gray would be set for midnight as soon as the call was made two hours from now by Stone. This would give them an opportunity to put their exit plan in place and give Gray very little time to make his own preparations.

Down the street Milton was sitting in a parked car with a cell phone in hand. He was the failsafe. If everything seemed to be going to hell, he was to call the police, the FBI, the fire department and anyone else they could think of. Since they would all be in close proximity, their response time should be very fast, although it still might not be fast enough. Caleb was back at the hiding place keeping watch over Lesya and the rest of the Finn family. Reuben and Alex were nearby, waiting for word from Stone.

"This is going to take some time," Finn told the guard. "I not only have to offload the equipment, but I have to unpack it too. And my helper called in sick."

"How long is long?" the guard asked.

"Probably after midnight before it's all done."

"You better get to it, then," the guard said, walking away without bothering to offer to help.

Finn used a power-driven hand truck to offload the

boxes of HVAC equipment and take it inside the visitor center. Four of the cargo boxes had compartments cleverly concealed in the bottom. Out from one box popped Stone, and from another, Annabelle. From another box they pulled a gagged and bound Simpson. From the fourth box Stone and Finn retrieved their weapons, including sniper rifles that Stone had used when he worked as a Triple Six. Finn looked at them doubtfully.

"They still work just fine," Stone assured him. "Despite their, uh, vintage."

"No night-vision equipment?"

"No."

"Gray's men will have them, state of the art," Finn said slowly.

"I'm actually counting on that."

"And body armor, latest generation."

"I always aim for the head."

They put the bound Simpson behind a crate of ceiling tiles and Finn showed Stone and Annabelle the interior rooms, most of which were unfinished.

Stone stopped at one room and looked up. "Balcony?"

Finn nodded. "This is the Great Hall. It looks down on the main visitors' area. There's also the atrium, the congressional auditorium, exhibition gallery, theaters and dining area."

"I like this room," Stone said firmly as he stared at

the waist-high concrete wall along the balcony. "High ground is always good ground. Now show me where the closest power supply is."

After that was done, Finn led them through a series of doors that ended in a long hall that was closed off. "That's the underground corridor leading to the Capitol. It's totally blocked off for now."

"So how do I get David out of here?" Annabelle asked.

Finn nodded and pointed overhead. "The ventilation ducts. That was going to be the focal point of our penetration. That duct there will carry you directly into the Capitol. I've drawn up a map." He handed it to her and went over various points, including how the duct ended in a small storage room.

"You only have to walk down a short hall and there's an exit door there. It's not guarded and you can open it from the inside. I had an associate go through it when we made an initial penetration. It was a tight fit for him, but he was bigger than you and David. You two should have no problem; you're both very lean."

Stone looked at Annabelle. "That's why you fit the bill. There's no way Reuben or Alex could have fit in there. Caleb and Milton are small enough, but—"

"I know," Annabelle said. "If we run into any problems I can try and talk my way out."

"Alex and Reuben will be stationed near the exit you'll be using. If need be, Alex can use his Secret

Service credentials to get you past any security checkpoints."

"So where do you want me to be, Oliver?" Annabelle said.

"Right here next to the entrance to the ductwork. We'll bring David to you."

She looked at the tall and broad-shouldered Finn and Stone. "But I don't understand. Harry and you obviously can't fit in the ductwork, so how are you two going to get out?"

"Let us worry about that, Annabelle," Stone said.

90

For the next two hours, Stone and Finn choreographed what would happen later that night. Finn was highly experienced when it came to work like this, but he finally had to admit to himself that when it came to killing other people while putting oneself in the best possible position to survive, Oliver Stone was his clear superior.

And then they were as ready as they were going to be. Stone made the call to Gray and then they both took up their positions and waited. Stone knew that Gray would send in an advance guard to recon the place. Sure enough, two hours later, men came sniffing and poking around, with the security guards out front no doubt either tied up or suitably intimidated by the men's badges.

Then the man himself appeared. Carter Gray was looking chunkier than usual. From his sniper's post Stone instantly discerned why: body armor. That didn't bother Stone in the slightest since, as he'd told Finn, he always aimed for the head. People couldn't survive without a brain. Although it did seem that more than a few people in Washington managed to do so quite nicely.

Next to Gray was a man pushing a hand truck with a bag on it. He unzipped the bag and helped the boy out. David Finn was blindfolded and had sound mufflers over his ears. Wobbling, he stood next to Gray, who looked around the vast interior of the uncompleted Great Hall.

"Well," Gray said to the emptiness. "We're here."

Harry Finn walked out into the room, a gagged Simpson in hand. "Give me the boy."

Gray looked mildly annoyed at being talked to in such a manner. "Harry Finn, Lesya and Rayfield's son. You take after your mother more than your father."

"Let me have my son!"

"Where are the orders? And where is my recording?"

Finn pulled a set of papers and a cell phone from his jacket pocket. He held them up. "I want David next to me."

Finn pushed Simpson toward Gray. The senator jogged the last few steps. When he reached Gray the intelligence chief immediately had the gag and hand bindings removed.

The guard pushed David toward his father. Finn hugged his son. "It's okay, Davey, I've got you." He took off the blindfold and sound mufflers.

"Dad!" David said in a trembling voice as he squeezed his father tightly.

Gray held out his hand. "Give them to me. Now!"

Finn tossed the items to him. Gray looked at the orders. "It's hard to believe these have survived all these years."

"Lots of things have survived all these years, including my mother," Finn said as he edged David behind him. He could sense everyone's fingers edging toward triggers.

Gray listened to the recording on the cell phone, then handed it to a man next to him, who placed it in a small electronic device and played it again. He read off the result displayed on an LED screen on the side of the device. "It's the original, copied once."

Stone had given one copy to Gray previously.

Gray smiled, pocketed the cell phone and looked at Finn. "And how is your mother?"

"A widow, thanks to you."

Gray looked around. "John, I know you're out there. Perhaps you have your little ragtag regiment with you. But just so you understand the playing field, I have this place surrounded and sealed shut. And it has been placed off-limits to the police, FBI, Secret Service and anyone else you might be counting on. I'm sure you know there is a mock terrorist attack going on outside right now. That's probably why you selected this place tonight. You no doubt hoped it would help you to escape. But what it does, instead, is ensure that if there is any shooting in here, no one outside will hear it, or if they do, they won't bother to investigate."

As they listened, the sounds of staged sirens, gunfire and bombs exploding, all part of the drill, reached them.

Gray glanced back at Finn. "And you might want to thank this young man, John. He killed Bingham, Cincetti and Cole. You have no way of knowing this, but it was your three former colleagues who were part of the team sent to kill you. They missed, of course, but they did get your wife. Cole claimed he was the one who killed her, but Bingham disputed that. They actually volunteered for the job. I guess you weren't too popular with them."

Only silence greeted this verbal right cross from Gray.

Gray waited a moment and then added, "You also might want to see who else I stumbled on while I was on my way here."

91

Finn's heart sank as he saw Milton being marched in between two of Gray's men.

From behind the concrete parapet on the balcony Stone's finger eased near the trigger of his rifle. He could take both men out before they could harm Milton. The only problem was he didn't know where the rest of Gray's strike team was. He needed to flush them out.

Finn said quietly, "I think that concludes the exchange."

Gray shook his head. "Actually, Harry, it's just starting."

He nodded to his men as he backed out with Simpson. When they reached safety, Simpson called out, "By the way, John, I was the one who ordered the hit on you. No one leaves Triple Six voluntarily. My only regret was we didn't get you then. But good things come to those who wait."

From the balcony Stone stared down at the spot where Simpson was speaking from. The senator was smart enough to have put a thick wall between them.

For an instant Stone's mind went blank, then everything clicked back on. He had a job to do and nothing Simpson could say would interfere with that. He raced over to a large powered winch they'd set up earlier.

On cue, Finn grabbed his son and flung him down, pulling a gun from his waistband and shielding David with his body. The next instant a large object dropped from the rafters. It was a heavy Jersey wall they'd hoisted up earlier. Stone had just let it go and hustled back to his shooting position.

The barrier hit its mark perfectly, landing a foot in front of Finn and his son. The impact nearly broke it in half but they immediately took cover behind it.

Gray's two men took aim at Milton, the easiest target. Before their fingers could squeeze the triggers, two rounds from Stone's weapon fired a second apart killed them.

Next to Stone was a long electrical cord attached to a power strip. He hit a button and the entire room went black.

Stone raced down from the balcony. He had memorized the number of steps and turns, so the darkness didn't slow him much. He dropped on top of a flat roller that they'd found in a storage room, the kind that mechanics use to glide under cars. He slid across the floor of the Great Hall, heading toward Milton. The original plan had been to get Finn and his son out this way. But Milton was in the most immediate danger.

He called out, "Finn! Cover!"

Finn immediately started laying down fire.

As he rolled along, Stone blinked rapidly, making his eyes adjust to the absence of light. He hit one dead body, his fingers snagging the NV goggles off the dead man's belt. As he put them on he said, "Milton!"

"Over here," Milton answered weakly.

Stone powered on the goggles and looked to his right. Milton was lying there, his hands over his head. The other dead man had fallen on top of him.

Stone asked, "Are you hurt?"

"No."

Stone pulled the body off his friend and, "double-decking" on the roller, they slid across the room toward the stairs to the balcony while Finn emptied two clips from his pistol to cover their escape.

Stone said to Milton, "I'm taking you to Annabelle. She, you and David will get out via a duct that leads to the Capitol. It'll be a tight fit, but you can make it."

"Oliver, I can't go out that way."

"Why not?"

"I've got claustrophobia."

Stone sighed. "All right, then you can leave with me."

"No tight places," Milton said nervously.

"It's all tight places in here, Milton," Stone snapped. "Did you see how many men Gray brought with him?"

"A dozen."

"Then he has ten left."

Stone knew that the next part of their escape involved running through quite a bit of open space. Gray's men were certainly watching for any sign of them through their NV goggles. Stone was actually counting on that. The goggles were wonderful tools, but they had one Achilles' heel.

Stone pulled off his goggles, tensed and then hit the button on the power strip again. Lights blazed on all over. He heard voices calling out in pain. Gray's men. When bright lights came on and you were caught wearing your NV goggles, the result was you wouldn't be seeing anything except hot stars for at least a minute.

He and Milton ran for it.

No sooner had they gotten behind cover than Gray's men recovered and opened up with overwhelming firepower. Stone left Milton and raced off again. Finn and his son were still behind the barrier, pinned down by fire. Stone grabbed the motorized hand truck full of commercial HVAC equipment and made his way to Finn and David. The bullets fired by Gray's men bounced off the heavy metal.

With this shield they made their way back to relative safety and collected Milton. They sprinted down the hall and through a series of doors, handing a terrified David off to Annabelle.

Annabelle saw Milton and said, "My God, what are you doing here?"

"Long story and no time to tell it," Stone said.

"You and David can get out through the ducts. Milton will come with us."

Finn hugged his crying son, who kept his arms tightly around his father.

Finally Finn eased the boy off and told David he had to go with Annabelle. "You have to help your mom," he said. "I'll be there as soon as I can."

"Dad, they're going to kill you. They're going to."

"I've been in tougher spots than this, believe me," Finn said, managing a smile.

Annabelle looked at Stone, took his hand and squeezed it. "Don't die, Oliver. Please don't die."

They helped her and David into the duct. Finn led Stone and Milton to another tunnel paralleling the one they had been in. It had been put in in case construction workers had to evacuate the place and they couldn't get out for some reason through the visitor center's exit.

They came to a stop at a secured door. Stone shot the lock off, and Finn opened the door, revealing a long passageway.

"That'll take us to the Jefferson Building," Finn said.

Stone nodded. "Caleb told me how to get out of the Jefferson without anyone seeing us. Harry, you go first, Milton in the middle and I'll bring up the rear."

Milton peered down the long, dark corridor. "Are you sure it's safe?"

"As safe as—"

Stone never knew where the shot came from. He

barely heard it. He never saw Finn raise his gun and fire. He never saw the sniper fall.

All he saw was the look on Milton's face. The eyes widened slightly, as though he was only mildly surprised. Then he dropped to his knees, still looking up at Stone. The blood started dripping from his mouth. He only said one word: "Oliver?"

Then Milton Farb dropped face-first to the hard floor, his body twitched once and he lay still, the large hole dead center of his back oozing red.

Stone had seen many wounds just like that one, all of them fatal.

Milton was dead.

Finn stared down at the body. "My God."

Stone knelt down, lifted his friend's body up, carried it over to a corner and placed him gently down. He closed the blank eyes and put the small, slender hands over the still chest. Then he rose, clenched his weapon and walked past Finn without a word. He wasn't heading toward safety. He was heading back to the visitor center.

Harry Finn eyed the door to the Jefferson Building and freedom. His son was safe. He could join him in a short time if he left now. This wasn't his fight anymore. John Carr had killed his father. What did he owe the man?

Everything. He saved me, my mother and my son. I owe him everything.

He gripped his gun and raced after Oliver Stone.

92

It wasn't mild-mannered, middle-aged cemetery caretaker Oliver Stone who strode out into battle that night. It was a killing machine called John Carr, thirty years younger, with all the skills and ferocity of a lifetime spent ending other people's lives in ways unimaginable to most people. He used every one of those skills that night. And yet there seemed a greater power at work. Bullets that should have ended his life numerous times missed by less than an inch. Disaster that should have struck never did. Maybe it was finally his time for justice. He only thought about that later. Tonight, he just killed. And the unfinished visitor center ran red with blood. Finn had killed only one more man. Stone had finished off the other six, two with shots that Finn had never seen anyone make before. He still couldn't fathom how Stone had done it. It seemed the man had simply willed the bullets to find their marks.

To Stone, there was another explanation as to how he had survived. Undoubtedly, Gray's men were younger, stronger, faster, superbly trained. These days they always had overpowering force before they attacked. They had killed thousands of times—in practice.

It was altogether different when one did it for real. And counting Vietnam, Stone had probably killed more people than all of Gray's men combined. And he had never had overpowering force. He had often only had himself. That just made you better than the other guy.

When the last man had dropped, Finn and Stone left via the emergency exit, reaching the Jefferson Building and leaving from there as Caleb had told them. An anguished Stone carried Milton's body over his shoulder. While he waited behind some bushes with the body, Finn managed to sneak out and snare a spare EMT uniform from a body recovery truck stationed near the epicenter of the mock terrorist attack. Next he spotted an ambulance that was parked near the library with the keys still in the ignition. A few minutes later Milton's body was loaded into the ambulance by Stone and Finn on a gurney, a sheet placed over his face. With all the chaos going on everywhere around them, no one could tell a fake corpse from a real one. With Stone riding in the back, Finn drove away, the ambulance lights flashing.

Finn glanced in the rearview mirror. Stone was sitting next to his friend, his head hanging down. He had not escaped the battle unscathed. A bullet had sliced through his right arm, leaving a bloody gash.

Another had left a crease on the left side of his head. The man took no notice of them. Finn had had to bandage them up using gauze and tape from the ambulance's supplies while Stone had just stared down at his dead friend.

Stone lifted the sheet, took Milton's still warm hand in his and squeezed it. He started mouthing words that Finn could not hear clearly, but he instinctively knew what the man was saying.

"I'm sorry, Milton. I am so sorry."

A tear trickled down from Stone's weathered face and dropped onto the sheet.

Finn didn't want to break into this very private moment but he had no choice. "Where do you want to take Milton?"

"Home. We're taking him home, Harry."

Leaving the ambulance about three blocks from the house, they carried Milton's body through the woods at the rear of his neighborhood. Stone placed him gently in his bed and turned to Finn.

"Give me a minute."

Finn nodded and respectfully withdrew from the room.

Stone was a man who had suffered more heartbreak in life than any human being should have to. He had done so stoically, trying to look ahead rather than focusing on the past. Yet as he gazed down at his friend's body, every memory of every personal tragedy in his life came charging at him from the darkness.

And for one of the very few times in his life, Oliver Stone sobbed without restraint. He cried so hard his knees buckled and he ended up on the floor, his body curled tight like a child in distress, suffering the anguish of a million nightmares that had collected inside him all these decades, nightmares that had suddenly been released, like the crush of water over a collapsed dam.

Thirty minutes later he had no more tears left to shed. Stone rose and touched his friend's face with his hand. "Good-bye, Milton."

93

After the exchange, Gray and Simpson had left the Capitol area quickly.

Simpson said, "How soon will you know when Carr and Lesya's son are dead?"

"Anytime now. You know, it was quite ballsy of you to confess to Carr that you were the one who ordered his execution."

"I didn't want him to die without knowing. It would have left me unfulfilled."

"Still, I wouldn't have done it," Gray said.

Simpson took the old orders from Gray and studied them. "The world is better off because of what we did."

"I agree. Two dead Soviet leaders. We cleared the way for peace."

"We never got the credit we deserved, though."

Gray said, "That's because it wasn't authorized. We took matters into our own hands."

"Patriots have to do what they have to do. So what now?"

"The orders and this cell phone will be destroyed." He took the papers back from Simpson.

"What's on the cell phone? I couldn't hear."

"Be glad you couldn't, Roger. Otherwise, I would've had to kill you too."

Simpson stared at him with an incredulous expression. "You're joking."

"Of course I am," Gray lied.

At four o'clock in the morning, Carter Gray received the news. His men had been wiped out. Carr and Finn had escaped. Carr, the killing machine, obviously hadn't lost his touch. He immediately called Simpson.

"Well?" Simpson asked.

"Just like we planned, Roger. Carr and Finn are dead. There'll be nothing in the news. We'll cover it all up."

"Excellent. Now we can finally put this behind us."

Gray hung up. *Right.*

He met with the president later that day after he had taken care of sanitizing the visitor center.

The commander in chief was not particularly happy about these events. "What the hell happened there last night? I was told they found blood in there and evidence of a gun battle."

"Sir, we were able to track down John Carr and Lesya's son at the visitor center."

"My God, in the middle of the Capitol!"

"I have no idea how they got in there, but they

did. We received a tip, went down there with a detachment of paramilitary and had a very intense shoot-out."

"And what the hell happened?"

"The appropriate people were terminated," Gray said vaguely.

"Did we take any casualties?"

"Yes, unfortunately. Families are being notified."

"Where are the bodies?"

"We're having them flown overseas for discreet disposal. We have to keep this hush-hush, sir. The press would have a field day with all this."

"Look, Carter, I am the president. I want to know what all *this* is. And I want to know right now."

Gray sat back. He had of course been expecting this. He pulled the orders from his pocket. He'd destroyed the cell phone, but these orders were too valuable. Valuable principally because they didn't have his name on them.

The president read through the documents. "Roger Simpson?"

Gray nodded. "Let me tell you the entire story, sir." It was mostly fabrication, but Gray delivered it with such authority and assurance that when the president sat back, it was clear he accepted all of it as truth.

"And Lesya and Rayfield Solomon's involvement?" the president asked. "Solomon has been labeled a traitor to this country. Was he? If not, we have to make this right, somehow."

Gray hesitated. "I cannot say with assurance that he was a traitor, sir."

"But you said he was terminated. You said he was a traitor."

"Back then it seemed clear that he was. Now, perhaps less so. I have to investigate further."

"You do that, Carter. You do that. And if the truth is that this man was innocent, we will make it right, do you understand?"

"I'd have it no other way. Ray Solomon was my friend."

"My God, two Soviet leaders assassinated by this country. I can't believe it."

"Not many of us could, sir."

"You're saying you didn't know?" the president asked sharply.

Gray chose his words carefully. "Things operated differently back then. We had evidence of Soviet plots to kill U.S. presidents from time to time, but we took measures to counter them. The truth couldn't come out because it might have led to nuclear war. They were never official plots of the Soviet leadership, you have to understand, but the Cold War was played for all it was worth."

"So who the hell ordered the assassinations of Andropov and Chernenko?"

"The orders didn't come through me."

"Are you telling me that Roger Simpson, who if I recall was merely a case agent, did this on his own?"

"No, not at all. He never would have done something like that by himself. He must have received authorization from higher channels."

"Channels that circumvented you? Why? You were his superior, were you not?"

"Not for all matters, sir. And my feelings on assassinations of foreign leaders was clear. There was an executive order making it illegal, and that was where I drew the line."

"Well, perhaps I should talk to Roger about this directly."

"I'm not sure that's wise, sir. He's going to make his own run for the White House. He's a fellow party member of yours. You start making inquiries, then there're leaks to the press and eventually everything comes out. As you know it's much harder these days to keep secrets."

"Damn whistleblowers; yes, I know."

"And what would Senator Simpson say? His signatures are on these orders. He will claim that higher-ups ordered the killings. He might even say I knew about it. You can hardly blame him for trying to cover his tracks. But the matter is over. Two men were killed. Illegally? Probably. Did the result justify the means? I think humanity would judge that it did.

I say we let sleeping dogs lie, Mr. President. Just let sleeping dogs lie."

"I'll think about it, Carter. But keep me informed of further developments."

"One more thing, sir."

"Yes."

"I'd like to come back to work. As the intelligence chief. I want to serve my country again."

"Well, as you know, that slot is presently unfilled. So it's yours if you really want it. I doubt the Senate will have any problem confirming a Medal of Freedom winner."

"I really want it, Mr. President."

He shook Gray's hand. "I appreciate your frankness today, Carter. You're a true patriot. Wish we had more like you."

"I'm only doing my job, sir." Actually, Gray was thinking that with Carr still out there, he wanted to be surrounded by as many heavily armed men as possible.

"You know, I believe you'd make a good president."

Gray laughed. "Thank you, sir, but I don't think I have the right qualifications." What Gray left unsaid was he believed he was *overqualified* for the job. Plus, he wanted a position with *real* power. All a president could really do was start wars, and those came along all too infrequently. Other than that, the office was fairly impotent, Gray felt.

He left the White House and climbed into his chopper. As it rose into the air, he knew he should feel good, victorious. Yet he didn't. In fact, he had rarely felt this depressed in his life.

94

Oliver Stone didn't attend Milton's funeral, though most of the others were present and grief-stricken. Caleb was so distraught at his friend's death that Alex and Annabelle had to hold him upright. Harry Finn had wanted to come but he was still in hiding with his family.

Alex had checked in with his supervisor and had found that all of his problems had gone away. "I don't know what the hell it was all about," the supervisor said, "and I don't think I want to know."

They all gathered a week later at Caleb's condo to honor Milton's memory. This time Finn came with Lesya.

"I can't believe Oliver missed Milton's funeral," Reuben said, staring down into his beer. "Can't believe it," he said again, his eyes red.

Annabelle looked at Alex. "No word from him at all?"

Alex shook his head. "Harry, you were the last one to see him. Did he say anything about where he was going? What he was going to do?"

Finn shook his head. "I know he blames himself for Milton's death."

Caleb said angrily, "And I read in the paper where Carter Gray is going to be the head of the intelligence community again. Isn't that just wonderful? We all know what he's done. We know, but we have no proof." He slumped down in a chair and stared at a photo of Milton that he'd placed on a shelf for all to see. Tears slid down his fat cheeks.

Finn said, "My family and I will have to leave the country, somehow. Gray won't stop until he gets us."

"I think not. It is time to end this foolishness."

All eyes swung around to Lesya, who sat in one corner.

From her bag she pulled an item, a very unusual object for an elderly woman to be carrying around. It was a bear.

"My granddaughter's beloved bear. My beautiful Susie's bear that I gave her when she was very little."

Everyone simply stared at her, no doubt wondering if she had at that very instant lost her mind.

"It is with Susie's permission that I do this." She took a small penknife from her purse and cut the stitching holding the bear together. She parted the seam, reached in and pulled out a small box.

"I had a craftsman in Russia make it for me." She took out a key, unlocked the box and took out a thumb-size electronic device with a USB port. "Does anyone here have a computer?"

The scene on the computer screen was a small sparsely furnished room. Four people were seated around a wooden table. A younger Lesya and Rayfield Solomon were on one side. Across from them was Roger Simpson as a young man. And next to Simpson was another man who hadn't really changed all that much.

"Carter Gray," Alex said.

Lesya nodded. "It was Rayfield's idea to secretly film this. The mission was so monumental, you see."

As they watched the four discussed the assassination. It seemed that Andropov had already been killed, and they were now focusing on Konstantin Chernenko as the only man standing in the way of Gorbachev's rise to power.

"You did wonderfully the first time, Ray and Lesya," Gray was saying. "There wasn't the slightest doubt that Andropov died from natural causes."

"There are certain poisons that leave no trace," Lesya commented. "And there are those high up in the Soviet Union who were not sad to see poor Yuri go."

"Perhaps it will be the same with Chernenko," Simpson said, "now that he's been named the general secretary."

Gray cut in. "But wait a bit. At least a year. It will allow us time to arrange things on our end and cut down on suspicion. All roads now point to Gorbachev taking power after Chernenko dies."

"If we wait, Konstantin may accommodate us without poison. He is not a well man," Solomon pointed out.

"So we give it a year," Gray said again. "Then if he's still alive, you and Lesya can make sure he isn't living much longer."

"And the director and the president are on board with this too?" Solomon asked.

Simpson answered, "Absolutely. They see it as critical to world peace and the destruction of the Soviet Union. As you know, there are many on the Soviet side who want this too."

Gray was beaming. "You'll both be heroes," he said. He turned to Lesya. "Your coming over to our side has made all the difference. If there is peace between the U.S. and what's left of the Soviet Union, it will be in large measure because of you. And though it can never be made public, you will have earned the eternal gratitude of your adopted nation. You and Ray have risked your lives countless times on behalf of this country and I bring a message directly from the president that he expresses his heartfelt gratitude for all that you've done for America."

The film ran for a few more minutes and then stopped. Lesya said, "I have never seen any human beings who could lie as well as your Carter Gray and Roger Simpson. Next to them, I was but a rank amateur."

"Why the hell didn't you show us this before?" Alex demanded.

"When you gave us the written orders?" Finn added.

"Only fools give up all they have on the first go-round. You keep something back always. I had the film saved and put on this device before I placed it inside the bear and gave it to Susie."

"My God, people died, Milton died," Caleb said in a hushed tone.

"I could do nothing about that," she said simply. "If we had given them this too, where would we be? People would still be dead. Your friend would still be dead. And we would have nothing."

"But what do we do with this?" Alex said.

"I want to meet with Carter Gray."

"What!" Finn exclaimed.

"Gray and I must sit down face-to-face."

"What if he won't?" Alex said.

Lesya smiled. "Let me talk to him on the phone. Then he will see me."

95

"It's been a long time, Lesya," Gray said as the two sat across from each other. They were in a motel room in Fredericksburg, Virginia. "You've changed quite a bit," he added politely.

"Given recent events it is clear that you haven't changed at all."

"You said on the phone that you had something I needed to see?"

"I know you have men outside. You always have men outside, Carter."

"Yes, in my line of work one has to take precautions. The thing you wanted to show me? I don't have a lot of time."

Lesya opened the laptop computer she'd brought with her. Gray sat watching it until the screen went dark. He looked over at her.

"Was the film Rayfield's idea?"

"Yes."

"If he suspected the truth, why did he carry out the plan?"

"He was loyal. You were not. But he really did it

to protect me. He knew how vulnerable I would be. He at least had the cover of the Americans. I had nothing."

"What happened to you and Rayfield was something that I've always deeply regretted, Lesya. In many ways he was the best friend I ever had."

"He trusted you, Carter. I did not, but he did. It was Simpson he was always wary of."

"He was a good judge of character." Gray sat forward, seeming eager to finally tell the truth. "Lesya, I did not order his death. That was Roger's doing. I never would have done that to Ray. Never. I was furious when I found out, but there was nothing I could do. And I tried with all my might to have Ray's name removed from the Wall of Shame at CIA. But Roger had fixed that up too neatly. He had built a very convincing story of Ray's treason. And with Ray dead, and unable to defend himself, there was nothing I could do."

"I don't want your explanations, Carter. What's done is done. Nothing can bring my husband back."

"But the right result was achieved. You of all people understand what that meant for the world. Ray would have understood that."

"Oh yes, he would. But my husband died. And his name is now synonymous with traitor in the country of his birth. He died for his country and they call him a traitor. This I cannot live with."

"If there had been anything I could do about that,

I would have. But my hands were tied. If I exposed Roger, I would have exposed myself. He knew that. He may be dishonorable, but he's not stupid."

"So you would not expose yourself to save the reputation of *your* 'best' friend? You would not give up your career to do that? Rayfield might have been your best friend, but you were clearly not *his* friend."

"I admit that I was weak and selfish not to give myself up for Ray."

"Yes, you were," she said bluntly. "So the assassinations were not authorized by your government? It was you and Simpson and a few others. None in political leadership positions. I know you won't answer my question, but it is the truth. I've had many decades to think about it." She sat back and studied him. Gray's normally confident demeanor had faded markedly.

He said, "Roger was afraid that if Ray found out the plan wasn't authorized he would have exposed him. And the truth is Ray would have. Regardless of the damage it would have done to him personally."

"That is exactly right. My husband was an honorable man. And yet he was murdered and Roger Simpson has a fine career as a senator of this country."

"Lesya, you know how things were back then."

With a wave of her hand, she cut him off. "Things back then were exactly the same as they are today. Nothing has changed except the people. And the people who play these games are all the same. They talk of doing good, of making the world a better place. That is all bullshit. It is about power and about protecting their interests. That is all it is ever about. Always!"

Gray sat back. "So what do you want? I'm sure you've thought about that too over all these decades."

"Oh yes, I have thought about it. And I know exactly what I want. And I have been waiting to tell you for thirty years, you son of a bitch. And you're going to sit there and listen. And then you're going to do *exactly* as I say."

When she had finished, Gray rose to go. "Can I expect to have the original of that film and all copies in return for doing what you've asked?"

"No, you cannot. You only have my word that I will take it to my grave. And you and Simpson should consider yourselves fortunate. I could destroy you both. Nothing would make me happier. But I am a person who actually thinks of things besides my own happiness. And that is the only thing that has saved you and the miserable Simpson. Now leave me. I do not want to see you again. Oh, but you can tell the good senator something for me."

"What's that?"

"I've heard he wants to be president."

"Yes, he intends on running."

"Well, you can tell him to rethink his plans. Unless

he wants to explain the contents of that film to the American people. You will tell him that."

"I will. Good-bye, Lesya. And for what it's worth, I'm sorry."

With another wave of her hand she dismissed a man who would shortly be running America's intelligence empire once more.

Rayfield Solomon's picture was taken down from the Wall of Shame at CIA. A bogus reason was given for his revised history. It was hidden under the rubric, "New evidence coming to light." And then the CIA classified the evidence. Scholars might get a shot at it in a hundred years or so. Solomon was then posthumously given the CIA's highest award for fieldwork. Never again would his name be spoken in the same sentence as traitor.

Lesya Solomon was awarded the Medal of Freedom, the first time it had been given to a former Russian spy. Again the reasons for this were classified, but it still made the national news. She even gave an interview praising the progress in American-Russian relations. She finished by saying that she wished her heroic husband, who did so much to end the Cold War, could have lived to see it. She refused all other interviews and once more disappeared.

Not surprisingly, Gray's nomination to be the intelligence chief sailed through the Senate. A chopper flew him from his highly secure Maryland retreat to his office in Virginia every day. His life was once again filled with clandestine activities, hard decisions that influenced the entire world. One word from Carter Gray and nations trembled, it was said. The man was in his element once more.

But for those who knew him well, he had changed. The overpowering personality, the absolute intolerance for the smallest mistake, the stunning confidence front and center all these years had diminished. He was seen sitting in his office from time to time staring at the wall, an old photo in his hands. No one had ever seen what that picture was, because he kept it locked in a safe.

In the photo Lesya, Rayfield Solomon and Carter Gray were decades younger and looked happy and full of life. They were doing exciting work, risking their lives so that billions could live in peace. In those countenances one could see the friendship, even the love that had formed among them. Sitting there staring at that photo, Carter Gray would occasionally cry.

96

Six months passed and no one had heard a word from Oliver Stone. Caleb returned to work at the library, but the old books that had given him so much pleasure now seemed just like, well, old books. Reuben went back to work at the loading dock and then came home and sat on his couch, beer in hand, and yet he never drank any of it. He would pour it down the sink and go to bed.

With one member dead and its leader having disappeared, the Camel Club seemed officially disbanded.

Harry Finn rejoined his red cell team and started doing work for Homeland Security again. Because of Lesya's demand and the evidence she held, it was certain that Carter Gray would make no move against him or his family ever again. And it was also certain that Finn would never stand trial for killing three men and attempting to kill Carter Gray.

Yet Finn did not have the soul of a killer, and what he had done haunted him. He finally took a six-month leave of absence. He spent all his time with his family, shuttling his kids to school and sports, and holding his wife as she slept. He kept in contact with his mother, but she refused his pleas for her to come and live with them. He wanted to come to know her in a way that didn't involve secrets and plotting violent deaths, but his mother apparently didn't want this. If this wounded Finn, he did not show it.

Annabelle could have left D.C. and spent the rest of her life living on the millions she'd conned from Bagger, but she didn't. After she and Alex finished explaining things to the FBI about Bagger and Paddy Conroy, an explanation that left out any details of Annabelle's multimillion-dollar rip-off of Bagger, the lady worked another con. The target this time was the church that owned Stone's cottage. She convinced them that she was Stone's daughter and she volunteered to move in and keep the cemetery in decent shape until her father returned from what she described as a much-needed vacation.

She had the place fixed up, brought new furniture in, all while carefully preserving Stone's things. Then she started taking care of the grounds. Alex came by to help her often. They would sit on the porch in the evening.

"Amazing stuff you've done to this place," Alex said.

"It had good bones to start with," Annabelle said.

"Most cemeteries do." Alex gave her a sideways grin. "So you think you might hang around here for a while?"

"I've never really been able to call a place home before. I used to kid Oliver about living in a cemetery but I sort of like it here."

"I can show you around town. If you want."

"Save me, now date me? You're quite the full-service cop."

"All in the line of duty."

"Right. I'm the con, remember? That's my line."

"Let's make that 'retired' con, okay?"

"Absolutely." For once she didn't sound that convincing.

They sat back in their chairs and looked out over the tombstones. "Do you think he's still alive?" she asked.

"I don't know. I hope so, but I just don't know."

"Will he come back, Alex?"

He said nothing, because only Oliver Stone could make that decision. He had to want to come back. And with each passing day Alex was growing more certain that he would never see his old friend again.

97

When Carter Gray had informed Roger Simpson of Lesya's demand, the senator's initial response had been predictable.

"There must be something we can do," Simpson had wailed. "I've worked my whole life to make this run for the White House." He eyed Gray hopefully.

"I don't see what can be done," Gray replied.

"You know where she is? If we can—"

"No, Roger. Lesya has suffered enough. This is about more than you or me. She gets to live out what's left of her life in peace."

It was clear from Simpson's expression that he was not in agreement with this. Gray gave him one more warning to leave it alone and then left.

Months passed and still Simpson brooded. Solomon's name cleared. Lesya given a medal! Gray was back in power. It was all so unjust. This all gnawed at the man, making him even more morose and insufferable than usual. Indeed, his wife started spending more time in Alabama; friends and colleagues avoided him.

In the predawn hours one morning Simpson sat moodily in his bathrobe, which he typically did, after retrieving the newspaper from outside the front door of his condo. His wife was visiting friends in Birmingham. That had been another thing that had infuriated him. No one had kidnapped his wife. That simply had been a bluff that Finn and Carr had used to get him to go quietly. Once out of his office and away from the bomb he could have had Carr arrested immediately. Only he had been too afraid. This just made him angrier.

Well, he'd really had the last laugh. Both Finn and John Carr were dead. Simpson had not bothered to check up on Finn, and Carr *had* vanished. Yet it was also true that he would now only be a senator, his shot at the Oval Office gone. The destruction of his lifelong dream made Simpson throw his cup of coffee against the wall.

He slumped down at the kitchen table and stared out the window into the darkness; the sun was still hours away from making its creep up the wall of the eastern seaboard.

"There must be a way, there must be," he told himself. He could not let a former Russian spy, who by all rights should be dead, deny him the highest office in the land, an office he felt he was predestined to hold.

He sighed, opened his paper and froze.

Staring back at him was a photo that had been

taped inside the front page of the newspaper he was holding.

As he stared at the picture of the woman, it suddenly occurred to him who she was.

Then her head disappeared. Left in its place was a large hole. Simpson gasped and then looked down at his chest. Blood was pouring out of it from where the bullet had entered after passing through the newspaper and neatly obliterating the identity of the woman. By any standard, it was a hell of a shot.

His eyes started to flutter as he stared out the window where the glass had been cracked by the bullet. He looked at the shell of the building across the street, the one that had never been finished. As he pitched forward, dead, onto his kitchen table, the thought did occur to Simpson of who had just killed him.

98

In quickly rebuilding Carter Gray's cliffside house overlooking the Chesapeake Bay, great pains had been taken in ensuring that the intelligence chief would be safe and secure. This goal, obviously, included preventing someone from blowing up the place a second time. With that in mind, and taking into account some of Oliver Stone's observations, the windows were all now made from bulletproof glass and the gas regulator was no longer accessible from the outside. The guards still slept in the cottage near the main house and the underground chamber and escape tunnel had been rebuilt as well.

Gray rose early and went to bed late every day. He put many miles on his personal chopper that landed in the rear grounds at all hours. He had a private jet at his disposal that carried him to hot spots all over the world. He knew that he would retire in a few years with his reputation intact as one of his country's greatest public servants, and that meant a lot to the man.

The storm was fast approaching from the bay; the rumbles of thunder reached Gray's ears as he dressed in his bedroom. He checked his watch; it was six o'clock in the morning. He would have to hurry a bit. There would be no chopper ride today; the winds were too strong and unpredictable and lightning was already starting to flash across the sky.

He climbed into a three-SUV motorcade; his vehicle was in the middle. A driver and guard were in his Escalade; the other two SUVs carried six armed men in total.

As the cars pulled out of the estate and onto the road, the rain began to sprinkle lightly. Gray studied a briefing book open on his lap in preparation for his first meeting this morning, but his thoughts truly were elsewhere.

John Carr was still out there.

The motorcade slowed to round a curve and that's when Gray saw it. He rolled down the window to get a better look.

Set into the grass next to the road was a tombstone with a small American flag stuck into the ground in front of the white grave marker. They were exactly like the ones used at Arlington National Cemetery.

An instant later, Gray realized what he had just done. Before he could even scream, the round from the long-range rifle slammed into the side of his head, ending his life.

The armed men exploded out of the truck, guns drawn and swinging in all directions. Yet there was nothing to see, no shooter to kill.

As several guards sprinted in the direction of where the shot probably had come from, another one opened the passenger-side door and a bloodied Carter Gray slumped out, still encased in his seat belt.

"Son of a bitch," muttered the guard, before punching in a number on his cell phone.

99

Oliver Stone had shot Gray from such a long distance away that he did not need to sprint away from the man's bodyguards. In truth, he had made even more difficult shots in his career, but none that meant more to him. He made his way slowly back through the woods to the dead man's home. As he walked along the rain started coming down harder, and the flashes of lightning and accompanying cracks of thunder picked up their pace.

He'd killed Simpson from the unfinished building across the street, his sniper rifle perched on an oil drum. The photo Stone had taped inside the newspaper was of his wife, Claire. He wanted Simpson to know. He'd placed the photo at a precise spot on the page, gauged his shot accordingly, leaving behind no evidence of who was in the picture.

Stone had driven here right after the shooting because he had to kill Gray before Simpson's murder was discovered and Gray went deep into hiding. He'd checked the forecast the night before. The approaching storm front from offshore was critical. Choppers didn't take off in such weather. That limited Gray to his motorcade. Stone had set the tombstone and flag by the side of the road, certain that even a cautious man like Gray would roll down the window to get a good look at it. That few seconds was all Stone had needed. With his scope and trusty rifle, and killing skills that one never really lost no matter how many years passed, it was a near certainty that he would get his man. And he had.

He skirted the edge of Gray's property, his gait steady but unhurried. He knew Gray's men would be coming soon, but in many ways he'd waited his entire adult life for this moment. He did not intend to rush it.

He reached the edge of the cliff and looked down at the dark water far below. Racing through his mind was the image of a young man very much in love, holding his wife in one arm, his baby girl in the other. The world seemed to be theirs. Their potential seemed unlimited. And yet how very limited it had all become. Because the next mental image was one of John Carr killing as he ran from one brutal murder to the next over a span of a decade.

He had built his life on lies, deception and swift, violent death with "government authorization" as his sole justification. In the end it had cost him everything.

He had lied to Harry Finn that day in the nursing home. He'd told Finn that he, John Carr, was different from the likes of Bingham, Cincetti and Cole. Yet he really wasn't. In many ways, he was *just* like them.

He turned and walked away from the edge. Then John Carr whipped around and ran straight toward the edge and over it. He sailed out into space with his arms spread wide, his legs splayed. It was thirty years ago and he had just killed another man. It was a successful hit, only there were dozens of men intent on killing him. He had run like the wind; no one could catch him. Faster than a deer he was. He had run straight to the edge of a cliff three times as high as this one and without a second thought had jumped into nothing but air. He had plummeted down, bullets raining all around him. He'd hit the water cleanly, come up and lived to kill another day.

As the water rushed toward him, Carr's arms and legs came together in perfect form. Some things you just never forgot. Your brain didn't need to send a message; your body just knew what to do. And for most of his life, John Carr had known just what needed to be done.

An instant before he hit the water, Oliver Stone smiled, and then John Carr disappeared beneath the waves.

AUTHOR'S NOTE

DON'T READ THIS UNTIL YOU'VE FINISHED THE BOOK

Hope you enjoyed *Stone Cold.* One note so people won't e-mail telling me I made a glaring mistake: I've played with the time-line, putting Yuri Andropov and Konstantin Chernenko in office as heads of the Soviet Union so it would match Oliver Stone's career as a government assassin. As a fiction writer, I have full latitude to do so. It's an entitlement actually granted to me by the Novelist's Bill of Rights, under the subsection "Why Bother with the Truth When You Can Just Make It Up?" It was duly enacted by Congress, an august body that has enviable experience in same.

ACKNOWLEDGMENTS

To Michelle, the ride continues, and there's no one else I could ever do it with.

To Mitch Hoffman, here's to the first of many.

To Aaron Priest, Lucy Childs, Lisa Erbach Vance and Nicole Kenealy, who let me focus on writing. And for always giving it to me straight.

To David Young, Jamie Raab, Emi Battaglia, Jennifer Romanello, Martha Otis and all the wonderful folks at Grand Central Publishing, for being with me every step of the way. New name, same great people.

To David North, Maria Rejt and Katie James at Pan Macmillan, for leading me to the top across "the Pond."

To Grace McQuade and Lynn Goldberg, on a great new partnership. Thanks for all your hard work. It really paid off.

To Shane Drennan, for all your expert advice. I hope I did it justice.

I owe the craps table scene to Alli and Anshu Guleria and Bob and Marilyn Schule. Thanks, guys. See you in Vegas.

To Deborah and Lynette, the stellar Starship *Enterprise* crew.

And to the millions of Camel Club fans for seeing light when others only saw the darkness.

divine justice

To the memory of my father

ACKNOWLEDGMENTS

To Michelle, the ride continues. And your incredible enthusiasm always keeps me going.

To Mitch Hoffman, for another superb editing job. Your thoughtful comments guided me to where I needed to go.

To David Young, Jamie Raab, Emi Battaglia, Jennifer Romanello, Martha Otis and all the rest at Grand Central Publishing who take such good care of me.

To Aaron and Arleen Priest, Lucy Childs, Lisa Erbach Vance and Nicole Kenealy for good counsel and warm friendship.

To Tom and Patti Maciag and their wonderful children, Stephen, Colleen and Emily. The Tall Family truly rocks.

To Maria Rejt and Katie James at Pan Macmillan for always being there.

To Grace McQuade and Lynn Goldberg for letting the world know.

To Dr. Catherine Broome, Sohan Makker, Dr. Alli Guleria, Mark Poplawski and Harvey Watkins for technical support and making a cool scene even cooler.

To Bob Schule, for his boundless knowledge of all

things political and his incredible generosity in sharing it.

To Tom DePont, for being a great friend, wonderful advisor and the guru of NASCAR for yours truly.

To Lynette, Deborah and Natasha for always steering the good ship Columbus Rose straight and true.

1

The Chesapeake Bay is America's largest estuary. Nearly two hundred miles long, its watershed covers an area of sixty-five thousand utopian square miles with more than a hundred and fifty rivers and streams barreling into it. It's also the home of myriad bird and aquatic life, and a haven for legions of recreational boaters. The bay is indeed a creation of remarkable beauty, except when you happen to be swimming in the middle of the damn thing during a thunderstorm in the veiled darkness of early morning.

Oliver Stone cracked the surface of the water and gulped in the thick salty air, a thirsty man in the center of a trillion-ton ocean. The long dive had caused him to go farther down than was particularly healthy. Yet when you throw yourself off a thirty-foot cliff into an angry ocean, you should be thankful just to have a heartbeat. As he trod water he looked around to gauge his bearings. Nothing he saw was too appealing right now. With each streak of lightning sparking to earth, he eyed the three-storey-high cliff he'd been standing on. He'd been in the bay less than a minute yet the chill was already drizzling into his bones despite the full-body wet suit he wore underneath his clothes. He stripped off his water-logged pants, shirt and shoes and then kicked off swimming east. He didn't have much time to get this done.

Twenty minutes later he cut toward shore, all four limbs cement. He used to be able to swim all day, but he wasn't twenty anymore. Hell, he wasn't even fifty anymore. Now he just wanted land; he was tired of impersonating a fish.

He pointed himself at a cleft in the rock and shot toward it. He slogged free of the breakers and jogged toward a large boulder where he snagged the cloth bag he'd previously hidden. Tugging off his wet suit, he toweled dry and changed into fresh clothes and a pair of tennis shoes. The sodden articles were pushed into the bag, tied to a rock and hurled into the storm-swept bay where they'd join his decades-old sniper rifle and long-range scope. He was officially retired from the killing profession. He hoped he would live to enjoy the experience. Right now it was barely even money on that score.

Stone carefully picked his way up the rocky path to a dirt trail. Ten minutes later he reached a fringe of woods where shallow-rooted pines leaned away from the punishing sea wind. A twenty-minute jog after that carried him to the batch of ramshackle buildings, most closer to falling down than not. The cloud-encrusted light was just beginning to topple the darkness as he slid through the window of the smallest hut. It was no more than a lean-to, really, though it did have such luxuries as a door and a floor. He checked his watch. He had ten minutes at most. Already dog-tired, he once more pulled off his clothes then slipped into the tiny shower with rusted piping that only delivered a thin stream of lukewarm water, like a fountain on its last dying spurt. Still, he scrubbed hard, wiping away the stink and briny clutch of the angry bay—wiping away evidence, actually. He was on auto now, his mind too numb to lead the way. That would change. The head games were about to start. He could already envision the boots coming for him.

Stone was listening for the knock on the door; it came as he was dressing.

"Hey man, you ready?" called the voice. It shot through the thin plywood door like a cat's paw into a mouse hole.

In answer Stone smacked one hand hard against the ragged plank floor as he slipped on his shoes, shrugged into a frayed coat, tugged a John Deere cap low over his head and put on his thick glasses. He ran a hand over the bristly gray beard he'd grown over the past six months, then opened the door and nodded at the short, squat man facing him. The fellow had a beer keg frame and a lazy right eye along with teeth yellowed by too many Winstons and double-pop Maxwell House coffees. This was clearly not café latte land. The top of his head was covered by a Green Bay Packers knit cap. He wore faded farmer's bibs, dirty work boots and a threadbare, grease-stained coat along with an easy smile.

"Cold one this morning," the man said, rubbing his chunky nose and slipping a lit cigarette from between his lips.

Tell me about it, Stone thought.

"But it's supposed to warm up." He drank from an official NASCAR tankard of java, letting some dribble down his chin when he pulled it back.

Stone nodded as his bearded face drooped and his normally attentive eyes grew vacant behind the smudged lenses. As he walked behind the other man Stone's left leg bent outward with a chicken-wing limp that stooped him into being several inches shorter.

They were loading an old banged-up, bald-tired Ford F-150 with firewood when the police car and black sedans slid into the driveway, propelling pebbly gravel in all directions like fired BBs. The trim, muscled men who climbed out of the rides wore blue slickers with "FBI" stenciled on the back in gold lettering and pistols with fourteen-round clips in their belt holsters. Three of them walked up to Stone and his buddy, while a chubby uniformed sheriff with polished black boots and a Stetson hustled to catch up.

"What's the deal, Virgil?" Green Bay asked the uniform. "Some sonofabitch break outta prison again? I'm telling you, you boys oughta start shooting to kill again and screw the pissant liberals."

Virgil shook his head, worry lines rising on his forehead. "No prison. Man's dead, Leroy."

"What man?"

One of the FBI slickers snapped, "Let me see some ID."

Another said, "Where were you and your friend an hour ago?"

Leroy looked from one Fibbie to the next. Then he stared over at the uniform. "Virgil, what the hell's going on?"

"Like I said, a man's dead. Important man. His name's—"

With a slash of his hand, a slicker cut him off. "ID. Now!"

Leroy quickly slid a thin wallet out of his bib's pocket and handed over his license. While one of the agents punched the number into a handheld computer he'd slipped from his windbreaker, another agent held out his hand to Stone.

Stone didn't move. He just stared back with a vacuous expression, his lips gumming and his bum leg doing an exaggerated deep knee bend. He looked confused, which was all part of the act.

"He ain't got no license," Leroy said. "He ain't got nothing of nothing. Hell, can't even talk, just grunts."

The FBI agents closed around Stone. "He work for you?"

"Yessir. Four months now. Good worker, strong back. Don't ask for much money—room and board is all, really. But he got a bad leg and not too much upstairs. He's mostly what you call unemployable."

The agents looked down at the protruding angle of Stone's leg then back up at his bespectacled face and bushy beard.

One of them asked, "What's your name?"

Stone grunted and made several jerky motions with his hand, like he was showing off a bastardized martial art for the federal men.

"Sign language, least I think it is, or some such," Leroy volunteered wearily. "Don't know sign language myself so's I don't know his real name. Just call him 'Hey man.' Then I show him what needs doing. That seems to work. It ain't like we're doing heart surgery up here, just throwing shit in a truck mostly."

A slicker said, "Tell him to lift up his pants leg on his *bum* wheel."

"What for?"

"Just tell him!"

Leroy motioned to Stone to do so by drawing up his own pants leg.

Stone bent down and, with improvised difficulty, mimicked Leroy's action.

The men all stared down at the ugly scar marching across the kneecap.

"Damn!" said Leroy. "No wonder he can't walk good."

The same FBI slicker motioned with his hand for Stone to roll his pants leg back down. "Okay, fine."

Stone never thought he'd be thankful for the old bayonet wound a North Vietnamese soldier had given him. It looked a lot worse than it actually was because the surgeon had had to fix Stone up on the floor of the jungle in the middle of an artillery barrage. Understandably the doctor's hands had not been at their steadiest.

Sheriff Virgil said, "Leroy and me grew up here together. He was the center and I was the quarterback on the high school football team that won the county championship forty years ago. He's not riding around killing anybody. And that feller there, easy to see he's not the sharpshooting type."

The FBI agent tossed back Leroy's license and looked at his fellow feds. "Clean," he muttered in a disappointed tone.

"Where you headed?" another slicker said as he glanced at the half-loaded truck.

"Same place I'm always headed this time of the morning this time of the year. We take us some wood down to folks who ain't got time to chop their own, and sell it before the cold weather sets in. Then we get down to the marina and work on the boat. Maybe take it out if the seas clear up."

"You got a boat?" one agent said sharply.

Leroy looked over at Virgil with a comical expression. "Yeah, got me a big-ass yacht." He pointed behind him. "We like to take us a ride in that there Chesapeake Bay and maybe catch us a few crabs. I hear tell they like that shit round these parts."

"Cut the crap, Leroy, before you get yourself in trouble," Virgil said quickly. "This is serious."

"I believe it is," Leroy shot back. "But if a man's dead, you best not waste any more time jawing with us. 'Cause we ain't know nuthin' 'bout nuthin'."

"You see anybody pass this way this morning?"

"Not one car till you folks come tearing up. And we both been up before full light."

Stone limped over to the truck and started throwing wood in the cargo bed.

The agents looked at each other. One of them mumbled, "Let's roll."

A few seconds later they were gone.

Leroy walked over to the truck and started tossing wood in. "Wonder what man be dead?" he said, really to himself. "Important man, they say. Lot of important men in this world. But they die just like the rest of us. God's way of making life fair."

Stone let out a long, loud grunt.

Leroy looked over at him and grinned. "Hey man,

now that's the smartest thing I heard all damn morning."

When the day's work was over, Stone pantomimed to Leroy that he was heading on. Leroy seemed to take it well. "Surprised you lasted long as you did. Good luck." He peeled off a few faded twenties and handed them over. Stone took the money, patted the man's back and limped off.

After packing his duffel, Stone set out on foot and hitchhiked to D.C. in the back of a truck, the driver unwilling to let the scruffy Stone ride with him in the warmth of the truck's cab. Stone didn't mind. It would give him time to think. And he had a lot to think about. He had just killed two of the most prominent men in the country on the same day, literally hours apart, using the rifle he'd earlier chucked into the ocean before taking the dive off the cliffs.

The truck dropped him off near the Foggy Bottom area of the capital and Stone set out for his old home at Mt. Zion Cemetery.

He had a letter to deliver.

And something to pick up.

And then it would be time to hit the road.

His alter ego John Carr was finally dead.

And the odds were awfully good that Oliver Stone might be right behind him.

2

The cottage was dark, the cemetery darker still. The only thing visible was the mist of Stone's exhaled breath as it mingled with cool air. His gaze penetrated to every square inch of the cemetery because he could not afford any screwups now. It was stupid coming here, but loyalty was not a choice he felt, it was a duty. And it was who he was. At least they couldn't take that away from him. He'd waited nearby for about a half hour to see if anything looked strange. His place had been watched for a couple months after he'd abandoned it. He knew this because he'd been watching the watchers. However, after four months of him not being around, they'd given up their sentinel and moved on. That didn't mean they wouldn't come back. And after the events of this morning, they probably would. All cops would tell you that every violently ended life was worth the same level of investigation. Yet the reality was, the more important the victim the more diligent the hunt. And based on that maxim they would be bringing an army on this one.

Finally satisfied, he crawled underneath the fence at the back of the cemetery and crept to a large headstone. He yanked it over, revealing underneath the small compartment scooped out of the dirt. He took the box hidden there and put it in his duffel bag, then set the stone back in place. He patted the grave marker affectionately. The name of the deceased who lay here had long since been worn away by time. But Stone had researched the people who'd been buried at Mt. Zion and knew that this was the final resting place of one Samuel Washington, a freed slave who'd given his life to help others like him to freedom. He felt a certain kinship with the fellow because in a way Stone knew just what it was like to not be free.

He eyed the cottage in a dusk rushing headfirst to nightfall. He knew Annabelle Conroy had been staying there. Her rental was parked at the front gate. And he'd been inside the cottage when she'd been absent from it a couple months ago. The place looked far better than when he'd lived there. Yet he knew he could never reside at Mt. Zion again unless it was in a supine position approximately six feet underground. With the two early morning pulls of the trigger he'd become the most wanted man in America.

He wondered where she was tonight. Hopefully, out enjoying life, although since the news of the two murders was everywhere, he knew that his friends would easily deduce what had happened. He hoped they didn't think less of him. That actually was the real reason he was here tonight.

He didn't want to leave his friends hanging out there for him. The feds weren't incompetent. They would be coming this way eventually. Stone wished with all his heart he could do more for the Camel Club, after all they had done for him. He had thought of simply turning himself in. But there was such a core of survivor mentality built into his psyche that his essentially walking to his own execution was not an option. He could not let them win that way. They would have to work a little harder.

The letter he held was carefully worded. It was not a confession because that would put his friends in an even greater dilemma. Granted, Stone was caught in a classic catch-22, but he owed them something. He should have known that with the life he'd led there was only one possible conclusion.

This.

He slipped the letter from his pocket and rolled it around the hilt of a knife he pulled from another pocket, securing it with string. He took aim from the darkness of the side yard and let fly. The knife stuck into the porch column.

"Good-bye."

He had one more place to visit.

A few moments later he was crawling back under the fence. He walked to the Foggy Bottom Metro station and climbed on the train. Later, a thirty-minute walk brought him to yet another cemetery.

Why was it he was more comfortable with the dead than the living? The answer was relatively simple. The dead conveniently never asked questions.

Even in the darkness he quickly found the grave he was looking for. He knelt down, brushed some leaves away and gazed at the tombstone.

Here lay Milton Farb, the other member of the Camel Club, and the only deceased one. Yet even dead, Milton would forever be part of that informal band of conspiracy theorists who'd insisted on only one thing: the truth.

Too bad their leader hadn't honored that principle.

The only reason his beloved friend was dead was because of Stone.

My fault.

Because of him, the brilliant if quirky Milton was resting here for all time now, a large-caliber round having ended his life underneath the United States Capitol. It nearly equaled the grief Stone felt for the death of his poor wife decades ago.

Stone's eyes moistened as he remembered that final, awful night at the Capitol Visitor Center. How Milton had looked at him after the bullet struck; those wide, pleading, innocent eyes. The memory of his friend's last seconds of life would remain with Stone until *his* dying day. And there had been nothing Stone could do, except avenge his friend. And he had. He'd killed many heavily armed, expertly trained men in close confines that night, and he hardly remembered doing any of it, so overshadowed was it all by that one stunningly improbable death. Yet it hadn't come close to making up for the loss. That was what the killings this morning had been about, at least partly. And neither of them had made up for losing Milton either. Or his wife. Or his daughter.

He very carefully cut out a chunk of grass and dirt on top of his friend's grave, laid the box in it, and put the grass back on top, pushing it down firmly with a shove from his foot. He removed all evidence that the ground had been disturbed and then stood very erect and saluted his dead friend.

A few moments later Stone slowly walked back to the Metro and rode it to Union Station, where he bought a train ticket south with most of his remaining cash. There were a few police and plainclothes officers around and Stone duly noted the location of each one. No doubt the heavy artillery was at the three local airports doing their best to nab the killer of a well-known U.S. senator and the nation's intelligence chief. The lowly American train system obviously didn't warrant such a level of scrutiny, as though assassins wouldn't deign to ride the decrepit rails.

Thirty minutes later he climbed on the Amtrak Crescent, destination New Orleans; it was a spur-of-the-moment decision as he had looked up at the marquee. The train was a few hours late leaving, otherwise he would've not been able to take it. Not a naturally superstitious man, he had considered that an omen. He jammed himself into a small bathroom, trimmed off the beard and removed his glasses before going to his seat.

He'd heard construction jobs were still plentiful in New Orleans after Katrina. And people, desperate for workers, didn't ask for tricky things like Social Security numbers and permanent addresses. At this point in his life Stone did not like questions or numbers that would lead anyone to know who he really was. His plan was to lose himself in a mass of humanity trying to rebuild from a nightmare not of its own making. He could relate to that very well, because he was basically trying to do the very same thing. Except for those two final shots. Those he'd intended with every pulsating nerve of anger and sense of justice denied he possessed.

As the train bumped along in the darkness Stone sat in his chair and stared out the window. In the reflection he studied the young woman who sat next to him holding a baby, her feet perched on a battered duffel bag and a pillowcase crammed with what looked to be bottles, diapers and changes of clothes for the infant. They were both asleep; the child's chest nestled against its mother's swollen bosom. Stone turned to look at the child with its triple chins and doughy fists. The baby suddenly opened its eyes and stared at him. Surprisingly it didn't cry; it didn't make one sound, in fact.

Across the aisle a rail-thin man was eating a cheeseburger he'd bought in the station, a bottle of Heineken cradled between bony knees covered by patched denim. Next to him was a young, tall, good-looking man with brown, tousled hair and a few days' worth of stubble on his unmarked face. He had the lean, lanky build and confident moves of a former high school quarterback not yet run to fat. This was not exactly a guess on Stone's part, because the kid was wearing his high school varsity jacket dripping with medals, letters and ribbons. The year stitched on the jacket told Stone that the kid had been out of high school for a few years. Long time to be holding on to the glory days, Stone thought, but maybe that was all the kid had.

To Stone's eye the young man also had the look of someone who was certain that the world owed him everything and had never bothered paying its bill. As Stone watched, he rose, climbed over the cheeseburger man and headed to the rear of the car and through the door into the next train car.

Stone reached over and gently touched the baby's fist, receiving a barely audible coo in return. While the infant's life was all in front of him, Stone's was drawing closer to the end.

Well, they would have to find him first. He owed that to an authority that was often callous to the people who served it with the greatest loyalty, with the most quietly suffered sacrifice.

He leaned back in his seat and watched Washington disappear as the train rattled on.

3

Joe Knox had been reading in the small library of his town house in northern Virginia when the phone rang. The speaker was economical with his words and Knox, from long experience, did not interrupt. He hung up the phone, laid aside his novel, pulled on his raincoat and boots, grabbed the keys to his scuffed up ten-year-old Range Rover and headed out into the foul weather for an equally foul task.

An inch over six feet with the thick, muscular build of the undersized linebacker he had once been in college, Knox was in his fifties with thinning hair that he still had barber-shop cut and then slicked back. He also possessed a pair of pale green eyes that were the human equivalent of an MRI: they missed nothing. He gripped the wheel of the Rover with long fingers that had pulled just about every trigger there was while in service to his country. From his secluded, forested neighborhood he turned on to Chain Bridge Road in McLean, Virginia. The traffic would still be heavy on the Beltway this time of morning. Actually, there was really no longer a time when the asphalt noose around the capital city's neck *wasn't* strangled with cars. He pointed his SUV toward the District and backtracked his way to eastern Maryland from there. Eventually he smelled the sea, and with it he envisioned the murder scene. All in a day's work.

Three hours later he was walking around the truck as fat raindrops pelted down. Carter Gray still sat in his seat-belt harness, his head destroyed and his life ended by what appeared to be a long-range rifle round, although the postmortem would confirm that. While police, FBI and forensic teams buzzed everywhere like bluebottle flies, looking for some place to land and do their business, Joe Knox squatted in front of the white grave marker and small American flag planted in front of it by the side of the road. It was on a curve. The motorcade would have slowed here. A curious Gray had obviously seen these two items and rolled down his window—a fatal mistake.

Grave marker and American flag. Just like at Arlington National. An interesting and perhaps telling choice.

The fact that the windows rolled down showed Knox that the vehicle wasn't armored. Such vehicles' windows were phone-book thick and did not move. Gray had made his second mistake there.

Should've asked for the armor, Carter. You were important enough.

This wasn't baseball, Knox knew. In his business, it never took more than *two* strikes to finish you.

Knox looked off into the distance, tracing in his mind the trajectory of the lethal round. None of the protection detail had seen any sign of a shooter, so he had to cast the potential flight path out farther where the optic and muzzle signatures would be nearly invisible to the naked eye.

Thousand yards? Fifteen hundred? To a target inside a vehicle revealed only through a barely two-by-two-foot opening in the dark and drizzle. And planted the bullet right in the brain.

Remarkable shot any way you look at it. No luck there. A pro.

Revealing again.

He rose and nodded at one of the uniforms. Knox wore his ID badge on a lanyard around his neck. When everyone had seen what his official ties were they had been deferential and also given him a wide berth, like he had an incurable and contagious disease.

And maybe I do.

The cop opened the door of the Escalade and Knox peered inside. The shot had hit dead center of the right temple. There was no exit wound. The round was still in the brain. The postmortem would dig it out. Not that he needed the autopsy report to tell him what had killed the man. Blood and bits of flesh and skull had embedded in parts of the SUV's interior. Knox doubted the government would be reusing this ride. It would probably go the way of JFK's limo. It was bad luck, bad karma, call it what you would, but no other VIP would want to rest his butt in the dead man's seat, sterilized or not.

Gray didn't appear as though he were sleeping. He simply looked dead. No one had bothered to close the man's eyes. His glasses had been blown off on impact from the kinetically energized round. The result had Gray perpetually staring at whoever looked back at him.

Knox lifted one of his gloved hands and shut the eyelids. It was out of respect. He'd known Gray well. He hadn't always agreed with the man or his methods, but he'd respected him. If their positions were reversed, he hoped Gray would've done the same for him.

The briefing papers Gray had been reading had been collected already by the CIA. National security trumped even homicide. Knox highly doubted that whatever the CIA chief had been reading at the moment of his death would be connected to his murder, but one never knew.

Yet if they could have read the man's mind in his last moments of life? When he stared out at that grave marker and that flag?

Knox's gut was telling him that Gray knew exactly who had killed him. And maybe others at the Agency did too. If so, they were letting him go through the motions on his own. He wondered why for a second and then stopped. It was tricky business trying to figure out what the hell went on behind closed doors at Langley. The only thing you could count on as the real truth was as convoluted as anything you'd find in popular fiction.

He left the corpse and mentally processed the facts as he stared off toward the Atlantic.

Gray's home had been blown up over six months ago, the man barely escaping with his life. Knox had been briefed via secure phone on the drive over. Any suspects involved in that matter were not to be considered to be involved in Gray's murder, he'd been told. This directive had come from the highest levels and he had no choice but to defer to it. Yet, still, he filed that away in the back of his head. For him the truth should not come with qualifiers or conditions, if for no other reason than that he might need it as ammo to cover his own ass at some point.

He drove to Gray's home, made a brief inspection of the interior, found nothing of interest there, and then walked toward the cliff at the rear of the property. He stared down at the thrashing water of the bay below before glancing out at the fully formed storm front that was not making the nearby murder investigation any easier. Knox eyed the fringe of woods that ran by the right side of the house. He walked through the trees and quickly calculated that a path through here would take one up to the gravel road that Gray's motorcade had used.

He looked back at the cliffs.

And wondered if it was possible.

With the right man there was only one answer to that question.

Yes.

He climbed back in his Rover and headed to the second murder scene.

Roger Simpson.

The great state of Alabama was suddenly one senator short.

And without even seeing the circumstances of Simpson's death, Knox instinctively knew he was looking for only one killer.

Just one.

4

As soon as Annabelle stepped on the front porch she saw it. Alex Ford did too. They'd just gotten back from dinner at Nathan's in Georgetown. It had become a favorite haunt of theirs.

She pulled the knife free, unfolded the letter and then glanced around, as though she expected the person who'd delivered it to still be nearby.

She and Alex sat in front of the empty fireplace while she read it. She finished and passed it across to him, waiting in silence while he read it through.

"He says for you to pack up and move. That people would be coming to ask questions. You can stay at my place, if you want."

"I guess we knew it was him, didn't we?" she added.

Alex looked at the letter. "'I've had many regrets in my life,'" he said, reading from it. "'And I've lived with them all. But Milton's death was my fault alone. I did what I had to do. To punish those who needed to be. But I will never be able to punish myself enough. At least John Carr is finally dead. And good riddance.'" He looked up. "Sounds like a man who did what he believed needed to be done."

"He asked us to tell Reuben and Caleb."

"I'll do it."

"They deserved it, you know. From all that Finn told us that happened that night."

"Nothing gives someone the right to murder someone, Annabelle," he said firmly. "That's vigilantism. That's wrong."

"Under any circumstances?"

"One exception destroys that rule for good."

"So you say."

"Burn the letter, Annabelle," Alex said suddenly.

"What?"

"Burn it now, before I change my mind."

"Why?"

"It's not a confession but it's still evidence. And I can't believe I'm saying this. Burn it. Now!"

She grabbed a match, lit the paper and tossed it into the fireplace. They watched the letter curl and blacken.

"Oliver saved my life, more than once," he said. "He was the most decent, reliable person I've ever met."

"I wish he'd stayed to talk to us."

"I'm glad he didn't."

"Why?" Annabelle said brusquely.

"Because I might have had to arrest him."

"You're kidding. You just said he was the most decent person you'd ever met."

"I'm a lawman, Annabelle. I swore an oath, friend or not."

"But you knew he killed people before. And you didn't seem to have a problem with it then."

"Right, but he did that on orders from the U.S. government."

"So that makes it okay in your eyes? Because some politician said it was?"

"Oliver was a soldier. He was trained to follow orders."

"But even he felt guilt for that. Because some of the people he was 'ordered' to kill were innocent. You saw how that crushed him."

"I respect his morals. But that wasn't his call."

Annabelle rose and looked down at him.

"So he kills two people who *did* deserve it, but because he didn't have 'government authorization' you're suddenly prepared to arrest him?"

"It's not that simple, Annabelle."

She flicked her long hair out of her face. "Sure it is," she snapped.

"Look—"

She walked over to the door and opened it. "Let's call it a night before we say something we'll regret. Or at least I do. Besides, I have to pack."

"Where are you going to go?"

"I'll let you know," she said in a tone that left much doubt whether she meant it.

Alex started to say something but instead rose and walked out, his features clouded and his lips set in an uncompromising line.

Annabelle slammed the door behind him. She sat down cross-legged in front of the fireplace and studied the blackened bits of Stone's final message to them. Tears trickled down her cheeks as in her mind she went through the letter's contents again.

She glanced toward the door. Alex and she had become very close over the last several months. When they had heard of Gray's and Simpson's murders they both had instantly suspected the truth. Yet they hadn't said anything about their feelings, afraid perhaps that if they did acknowledge that they believed Stone had killed the two men it would make that suspicion an intractable truth. Now their two very different interpretations of the man's perceived actions had just driven a wall right between them.

Annabelle packed her few belongings, locked up the cottage for what she was sure would be the last time, climbed in her car and drove to a nearby hotel. She got undressed and climbed into bed. She would be moving on now. There was nothing to keep her here any longer. With Oliver gone, her father dead and Alex revealed to be something other than what she thought, she was alone once more.

It seemed to be her natural state.

Good luck, Oliver Stone.

Annabelle was very sure of one thing. He would need all the luck he could get.

Maybe they all would.

5

Joe Knox would have preferred to have been back at his town house drinking a beer or maybe even a couple digits' width of Glenlivet while sitting in front of a toasty fire and finishing reading his novel. Yet here he was. The chair was uncomfortable, the room cold and ill-lighted, the waiting unpleasant. He eyed the opposite wall but his thoughts were far from this place.

His tour through Roger Simpson's murder scene hadn't taken all that long. Like his former boss at CIA, Simpson had still been sitting in death, only with him instead of a car seat it was a ladder-back chair in the kitchen that was now all mottled with the dead man's blood. The shot had come from the unfinished chunk of construction across the street. The hour of execution—for Knox was certain that's what this was all about—had been an early one. And eyewitnesses had been in damn short supply.

The only item of interest, really, had been the newspaper. Simpson had been shot right through that morning's edition of the venerable *Washington Post*, taking the round smack in the chest. As had been the case with Gray, most snipers aimed for the brain as the gold standard of all possible killing shots. Sure, you pack the right ordnance and a torso hit would also likely be fatal, but the head shot was like a faithful dog in a professional killer's world because it just never let you down.

So Gray in the head; Simpson in the chest. Why?

And why through *the newspaper?*

That had really bothered Knox. Not that having to penetrate the few pages would've screwed the shot, but the shooter would've had to more or less guess where his round would impact. And what if Simpson had had a thick book on his chest, or a cigarette lighter in his breast pocket that the paper had concealed? That *could've* fouled the shot. Most snipers Knox had known didn't like to guess about anything other than who they'd kill next.

Yet when he'd examined the paper he understood quite clearly why the chest shot had been used. A snapshot of someone had been taped to the inside of the newspaper. The shot had taken the person's head in the photo right off. As Knox looked more closely, the remaining part of the picture showed the torso to be that of a woman. There were no marks or writing on what was left of the photo to help him figure out who it was. He'd talked to the paper carrier to see if he'd seen anything suspicious, but he hadn't. And Simpson's building didn't have a doorman. Yet the killer *had* put that photo in the paper, Knox was certain of it.

And that meant only one thing. This hit had been personal. And the killer had wanted Simpson to know exactly why he was going to die and also who was doing the deed. Just like the flag and grave marker with Gray. His grudging admiration for the assassin increased even more. Gauging the shot accurately enough to take out that picture required remarkable skill, planning and simply a level of confidence that not even most professional sharpshooters possessed.

He'd instructed the medical examiner to let him know if anything showed up in the wound that was out of the ordinary. They almost certainly wouldn't be able to reconstruct the burned bits of photo now plastered into the senator's chest cavity by a high-velocity rifle round. But one never knew. Knox understood from experience that it was the little shit that brought most criminals down.

He straightened up and stopped thinking about gunshots and dead men as the sounds of the footfalls trickled down the narrow hall toward him. There were two men, both in suits, and both carried equally grim expressions. One of them held what looked like a large safety deposit box. He set it down on the table with a loud clunk. It gave added gravitas to a situation that didn't really need any more, at least to Knox's thinking.

The older man was very tall and broad with a

crown of thick white hair. Yet he was also weathered and beaten down by innumerable crises spread over decades. There were no safe harbors here; the hitch in his step, every wrinkle on his face and the bow in his shoulders bespoke that essential truth. His name was Macklin Hayes, a former army three-star who'd matriculated to the intelligence side a long time ago, though his ties to military intelligence, Knox understood, were still strong. He had never heard anyone refer to the gentleman as Mack. It was just not something you'd ever consider doing.

Hayes nodded at him. "Knox. Thanks for coming in."

"Didn't really have a choice, did I, General?"

"Do any of us?"

Knox waited, choosing to say nothing in reply to this.

"You understand the situation?" Hayes said.

"As much as possible considering the short time I've been on this sucker."

Hayes tapped the lid of the box. "The rest is in here. Read it, absorb it, memorize it. When it's all over, you are to forget every last bit of it. Understood?"

Knox slowly nodded. *That part I always understand.*

"Any preliminary thoughts?" the younger man asked.

Knox didn't know this gent and wondered why he was even here. Perhaps just to carry Hayes' goody box. Yet he'd asked a question and probably expected an answer.

"Two executions performed by one sniper who knew his business, probably ex-military with some kind of grudge and he wanted Gray and Simpson to know it. He left the grave marker and flag for Gray and a photo of a woman taped to a newspaper for Simpson. He shot the senator first and then came to Maryland to nail Gray, probably before word of Simpson's murder got out and Gray was forewarned."

"You're sure not two shooters?" queried the younger man. "And you're certain of the sequence?"

"I can't be *sure* of anything right now. You asked for my prelim, there it is."

"Escape? He couldn't have left by any road. He would've been seen."

Knox hesitated. "Off the cliff."

Hayes spoke up. "Apparently you're not the only person to suggest that."

"Who was the first?"

"Read the file."

A burn developed in Knox's gut but he held his tongue on that command. "Did Gray say anything in the days leading up to his death?"

"He was involved in something about six months before he was killed. What exactly is so classified even I haven't been allowed a full briefing. Gray, as you well know, was a man who kept things very close to the vest. And he was in the private sector at the time, so that also limits what we know. It's a bit muddled to say the least."

Knox nodded. Gray and secrecy just naturally went together. "Is that connected to the usual suspects who have now been taken off the table? I have to say that revelation was a little out there."

The younger man answered. "But not all of us agree with that decision."

Knox looked from young man to old. "So what exactly does that mean? Are they off-limits or not?"

Hayes cast off a smile that was impossible to read. The man could have made a fortune with chips and cards in Vegas, thought Knox.

"Hard to say. As my colleague here mentioned, there's a split decision about that in the corridors that matter."

"So where does that leave me?"

"Treading cautiously, Knox, treading very damn cautiously." He tapped the box. "I was able to collect some things that I've placed in here. Including a few off-the-record items."

"You mean things that technically I'm not supposed to be privy to?" Knox was now missing his book and cozy town house even more.

"We'll just assume that's the case."

"I'm not looking to take a slug in the back of my head over this."

"I would add that neither am I."

"That doesn't give me a lot of comfort, sir, because

if *you're* watching your back, I'm probably already dead."

"I want you to read everything, leave here, go home and think. Then call me."

"With questions or answers?"

"I would hope both."

"The guy's probably long gone by now." *Real pros exit as well as they kill.*

Hayes lightly tapped the tabletop with his long, bony fingers. To Knox they looked like miniature Medusas in the dim light. "Perhaps."

"Look, I can spin my wheels and report back zip. You tell me the parameters, General. I've played this game too long to get the rookie runaround."

Hayes rose, as did his companion; the master and his puppet. "Read, think, call. Good night, Knox. And best of luck."

Knox glared after the pair until they disappeared down the hall, the aircraft carrier and its faithful destroyer chugging through the storm-tossed seas of American intelligence. He lifted the lid of the box, pulled out a fistful of documents and started to read.

Best of luck said the cobra before it struck.

These were precisely the sorts of days where Knox wished he'd followed his old man into the plumbing business.

6

Stone's brief sleep was suddenly disturbed by what sounded very much like a fight. He blinked awake and looked around. The woman next to him was comforting her crying baby. Stone stared over several rows of seats at the cause of the ruckus.

It looked to be three against one, all in their twenties, where the testosterone surge frequently overrode all safety valves. Two held one while the third pounded away. Some of the passengers were making halfhearted calls for the men to stop, but no one had climbed from their seats to really do anything. Stone looked around for the conductor but didn't see anyone in uniform.

The kid being held was the one Stone had seen before, the former high school quarterback who held an angry chit against the world. His handsome face was taking another right cross to his already swollen left cheek. Blood ran down his nose as he struggled to free himself. He kicked and spit and lunged, but couldn't break loose as the third fellow laughed and landed a kick to the gut that doubled over Mr. Quarterback.

Okay, that's enough.

Stone sprang up from his seat, and when the hitter swung back to let fly with another blow, he grabbed the fist and pulled hard, almost knocking the fellow off his feet. He jerked around and stared at Stone, his anger dissolving to amusement.

The kid was at least five inches shorter than the six-two Stone, but nearly forty years younger and fifty pounds heavier.

"You want some of it, old man?" the kid mocked, raising his fists. "You want some of this?" He danced and juked around, his belly jiggling, his meaty arms flapping and the bling on them jingling. It was all Stone could do to keep from laughing.

"Just let him go and we call it square."

"He's a card cheater!" yelled one of the other punks as he gripped the quarterback's hair and ripped his head upward. "He cheated at poker."

"And I think you taught him a real tough lesson. So why don't you let him go."

"Who the hell are you giving orders?" the beefy kid with the cocked fists said.

"Let's just call it a day, fellows. You made your point. He's banged up pretty bad."

"Yeah, but you're not."

"Just trying to make the peace." Stone looked at the other passengers, many of whom were elderly. "You've scared everybody pretty bad."

"You think we give a shit?" He pointed at Stone.

"Now, what *you're* gonna do, old man, is say you're sorry for bothering us and you're gonna turn yourself around and go sit down if you know what's good for you. Otherwise I'm gonna have to kick your ass too. Hell, I just might do it anyway 'cause I feel like it. How 'bout that?"

It had been a long day and Stone was already pissed that he couldn't even get ten minutes of sleep, so he said, "Just you? Or with your two buddies there helping?"

The kid smiled. "Oh, just me, granddad. But I tell you what, just so's my kicking your ass won't be over too fast, I'll only use one hand." He gave a little jab and Stone darted his head out of the way.

"Oh, looky here, pops can dance. You a good dancer, pops?" The kid suddenly kicked at Stone, who seized the leg and held on to it with an iron grip.

Beefy's face now turned scarlet as he hopped around on one leg. "Let me go, or I'm gonna hurt you bad. Let me go!"

"You get one more chance," Stone said.

The kid swung a fist out. And missed.

Stone's elbow to the side of his head didn't. Neither did the blow to the nose, with the kid's bone breaking on impact. The punk crumpled to the floor moaning and twitching.

The other two dropped the quarterback and started forward. One fell like he'd been axe-cleaved when

Stone's foot smashed his crotch and then collided with his head. The other never saw the fist slam into his gut and then shoot up and crush his chin. He ended up on the floor of the train car next to his friends, holding his stomach and his face.

"What the hell's going on here?"

Stone turned to see the rotund conductor racing down the aisle, walkie-talkie and ticket puncher in hand and his Amtrak cap bouncing on his head.

Before Stone could say anything one of the punks he'd laid out yelled, "He attacked us."

The other passengers immediately started talking, telling their version of what had happened, but it all came out pretty garbled.

The harried train conductor looked over the mess of bodies on the floor, then turned to Stone and said, "You're the only one left standing. So did you hit these men?"

"After they attacked me. They said they caught that one cheating at cards," Stone said, pointing to the "glory days" kid who sat on the floor holding his bloody nose. "They wouldn't stop pounding the crap out of him and then they came after me." He pointed to the crowded floor. "You can see it didn't turn out the way they probably intended."

"Okay, let me see some ID," the conductor said.

"What about their IDs? I'm just the Good Samaritan. Ask any of these folks."

"That may well be. But I'm starting with you and

I'll work my way through all of them. How's that for a plan?"

Stone didn't want to give the man his ID, because he knew if he did it would end up in an official record somewhere that the folks coming for him might be able to find and use. Besides it was a fake ID and wouldn't pass muster under a database check.

"Why don't you start and *end* with them while I just take my seat? I wasn't really part of any of this."

"Either give me some ID or I radio ahead for the cops who'll be waiting at the next stop." He pointed to the young men. "You too."

The quarterback gave a groan and spit up some blood.

"He needs some medical attention," Stone said quickly. He knelt next to the young man and put a hand on his shoulder, only to have it thrown off.

"I don't need any damn help from the likes of you!"

Stone rose and said to the conductor, "I think we need to call in a doctor."

"If he wants medical attention, we'll get it, but I'm still waiting for your ID, sir," the Amtrak man said stubbornly.

He just isn't going to give up, is he?

"I'm getting off this damn train at the next stop," said the quarterback. He rose on shaky legs.

"That's fine. You can all get off as far as I'm concerned," the conductor said.

"What is the next stop?" said Stone.

The man told him. "And you either show me some ID or I radio for the police."

Stone thought for a moment. "How about I get off the train at the next stop too?"

"Works for me," said the conductor, staring at him intently. Stone did not like the look on the man's face; it was full of suspicion.

The conductor pointed at the young men lying on the floor. "Now all you get back in your damn seats and stay there or else you're going to jail, and I mean what I say."

The beefy kid Stone had pounded first wailed, "What if I want to press charges against this son of a bitch?" He pointed at Stone.

The conductor said, "Fine, and then that feller"—he pointed at the quarterback—"can press charges against you. And this man," he added, indicating Stone, "can press charges against you too and your buddies, because what I'm hearing from all the other passengers is that you came after him first. So what's it gonna be, mister bloody nose?"

Beefy's cheeks quivered. "Screw it, just forget it."

"Smartest thing to come out of your mouth yet. And next time you want to brawl just make sure it's not on my train. You don't want to mess with Amtrak, sonny boy." The conductor turned and stalked off.

Stone retook his seat, inwardly fuming. Why the hell had he gotten involved? Now he'd lost his ride.

The woman next to him leaned over and said, "You sure were brave to do what you did. Where'd you learn to fight like that?"

"Boy Scouts," Stone said absently.

Her eyes widened. "Boy Scouts? You're kidding?"

"The Scouts were a lot tougher in my day, ma'am."

But then he grinned weakly and she laughed. "That was a good one," she said.

Stone stopped smiling.

Not really. Because now I'm screwed.

7

Caleb Shaw and Reuben Rhodes had been depressed before Alex Ford came to Caleb's high-rise condo and dropped the latest news on them. Now their attitudes sank right through the floor.

Caleb poured himself a sherry and started popping greasy potato chips in his mouth as fast as possible, a longtime nervous habit of his, and he was the possessor of many. "How much more tragedy are we expected to endure?" he exclaimed.

Reuben said, "So he killed Simpson and Gray?"

"He didn't come right out and say it in the letter, but that looks to be the case," Alex said.

"Pricks deserved it," Reuben said staunchly.

"It was still murder, Reuben," Alex pointed out.

"And look what they did to him. Anybody get one day in jail for that? Hell no."

Alex looked ready to debate the point as he had with Annabelle but then seemed to think better of it.

"Where do you believe he is?" asked Caleb.

"Running," answered Alex. "And don't be surprised if the FBI shows up on your doorstep asking questions."

"If they do, I don't know nothing," Reuben stated firmly.

"Be careful on that score," Alex warned. "A perjury charge can get you a few years in a federal lockup."

"I'm not saying anything that'll get these bastards caught up with Oliver, Alex. And I'd expect you to do the same."

"My situation is a little different," Alex said defensively.

"Are you Oliver's friend? Didn't he save your life?"

"Yes. And I returned the favor, unless you've forgotten."

"And isn't he the reason you got that special commendation for busting that spy ring?"

"I get the point, Reuben."

"No, obviously you don't," the big man said, rising up to stand next to the tall Secret Service agent. "Because if you say anything to help them find Oliver, you're a traitor, plain and simple."

"There's nothing simple about it, Reuben. I'm still a federal agent. I took an oath to uphold the law."

"What does Annabelle think about that?" Reuben demanded.

"What the hell business is that of yours?"

"She thought it sucked too, didn't she?"

"Please," Caleb pleaded. "I'm sure Oliver would not have wanted this to drive a wedge between us."

"There's no wedge, Caleb. There's just the right way to be a friend and a wrong way," Reuben pointed out. "And I just want supercop here to be real clear on which side he needs to come down."

Alex did an eyeball-to-eyeball with Reuben. "Is that some sort of threat?"

"Oliver has been through hell and back because of Simpson and Gray. I'm glad they're dead. I would've put a round in their heads myself."

"Then you would've gone to prison."

"Right, under your way of thinking I guess Hitler deserved a trial."

"What the hell is your problem? You're making it seem like I'm against Oliver."

"It sounds to me like you are!"

"Alex, maybe you should leave, before things get out of hand," Caleb said. "Please."

Alex looked from the red-eyed Reuben to the distressed Caleb and walked out the door.

So much for the Camel Club, he thought. That was over. Done. Dead. And he was reasonably certain he would never see Annabelle again.

So preoccupied was he that Alex never saw the two men watching him from their car. When he drove off they followed. Meanwhile, another pair waited outside Caleb's apartment. The hunt apparently had already started.

8

As the train pulled out of the station that was basically a few planks thrown together and poorly lighted at that, Stone looked at the quarterback. Then he eyed the three punks, who were staring at them both with looks of unfinished business they wanted to jump right on.

Stone heaved up his duffel bag and grabbed the young man's arm. "Let's go."

He jerked back. "I ain't going nowhere with you."

"Then you can stay here and let them finish what they started," Stone said, nodding at Beefy and his boys.

"They'll wanta jump you mor'n me. You kicked their ass."

"*Your* ass, on the other hand, they were kicking pretty easy. So which road do you think they're going to pick?"

For the first time Stone saw some element of reason slide across the young man's features.

"Okay, now that I seem to have your attention, why don't you start by telling me where you're coming from?"

"Home. Just getting away. Make my own life."

"I know the feeling. But as things stand right now it might make more sense to go back home, get patched up and then start your trip over. You got parents?"

"Got a mom."

"Where's home?"

The kid looked angrily over at the gang of three, who hadn't moved a muscle.

"I don't want to go back there. I just got away from that damn place."

Stone ran his gaze over the kid's jacket. "Looks like you were some athlete."

"Best ever to come out of that little shithole, and look what good it did me."

"Not many people make it in professional sports. That doesn't mean it wasn't worth it, or that you're some kind of failure."

"Thanks for the pep talk, changed my whole life," the kid said scornfully.

Stone let out a heavy sigh. "Look, son, I've got my own problems, so I'm about five seconds from leaving your ass to the hyenas over there unless we get an attitude adjustment real fast."

"What do you want me to do?" he snapped.

"Tell me your name and where you're from."

"Danny. Danny Riker," he said grudgingly. "Satisfied? And what's *your* name?"

Stone didn't hesitate. "Ben." That had been his father's name. "From where, Danny Riker?"

"*Divine*, Virginia. Little coal-mining town just this side of hell."

"How far from here?"

"About here to the moon."

Stone sighed again. "Is your mother still there?"

"That's right."

"So you just left her in the little hellhole all by herself?"

"She's not alone, trust me."

"You got money to get back home?"

"Maybe."

"You sure, or did you lose it all in the poker game? They say you were cheating."

"They just said that because they can't play cards worth shit." He glanced over at Beefy and cracked a smile. "Ain't that right, fat boy?"

"Where were you headed to on the train?" Stone asked.

"Where there ain't no coal to mine."

"You worked in the mines?"

Danny looked around. "I'm hungry."

He walked off toward a greasy spoon visible about a block away. It had a neon sign spelling out "restaurant" in cursive, with only the final "T" still lighted. In his head Stone instantly dubbed it the "One T."

Stone glanced back at Beefy and his battered goons. Beefy had a knife in his hand. If Stone left Danny alone now he was certain the men would finish him off. He'd killed many men over the years. Perhaps it was worth a bit of a detour from his plans to save one.

They ate at the counter with Stone occasionally looking over his shoulder to stare at Beefy and his boys sitting at a booth gobbling up their burgers and fries and shooting nasty glances at them from over their beer mugs.

When Stone went to pay the check Danny dropped the cash on the bill and rose.

"Thanks for helping me out back there," he said, without a trace of an attitude.

"You're welcome."

"You fight pretty good for a geezer." Somehow this statement did not come out as an insult.

"I might not be as old as you think. I've just had a tough life."

"Ain't we all."

"So where to now?"

"Gotta keep rolling or else you die. Think somebody important said that once."

Not bad advice to live by, Stone thought. *I'm a rolling stone right now.*

As they left the One T Beefy confronted them outside the door, his two mates right behind him.

"Where the hell you two think you're going?"

"You know, I can set your nose back in place if you want," Stone said amiably.

"You lay another hand on me, you son of a bitch,

I'll cut you bad." He brandished a knife. Well, it was technically a knife, but it was so small and the guy was handling it so awkwardly that Stone had trouble thinking of it as actually being a weapon.

"Okay. Good luck then."

He and Danny started to walk past when Beefy slashed at them with the blade.

A second later he dropped to his knees holding his belly. Danny rubbed his fist and looked down at his attacker.

"Not nearly as much fun when it's just one-on-one, is it, chunko?"

Beefy weakly threw a punch at Danny, catching him lightly on the knee. Danny wound up to nail him again, but then just pushed him away. He grinned at Stone. "Can't hit a man when he's down. Ain't sporting."

Stone glanced sharply at Beefy's two friends, who seemed to be deciding whether to attack or run. He said, "I'm done with you guys. So if you don't take your friend here and get the hell out of my life right now I'm going to beat both of you into a coma."

He knelt down, picked up the knife, and with a flick of his wrist tossed it ten feet where it embedded neatly in the wooden façade of the One T. Seconds later his two sidekicks were helping Beefy down the street as fast as they could go.

Danny was staring at the knife stuck in the wood,

his mouth agape. He pulled it out and tossed it in a trash can. "Where'd you learn to throw like that?"

"Summer camp. So what's it going to be, Danny? Home to get patched up, or running around on that gimpy leg watching your back for those a-holes?"

"Home. Couple days. No more."

"Sounds like a plan."

"What about you?"

"Flop here for one night. Wait for the next train south. Tired of the cold." *Just tired.*

The men started walking down the street.

"I wasn't cheating at cards."

"I believe you."

"How come?"

"You don't seem dumb enough to cheat when it's three against one. How you getting to Divine? The train go there?"

Danny laughed. "Hell, nothing *goes* to Divine. Bus goes near it. Walk or thumb it from there. Won't be the first time for me."

Stone's gaze caught on a black sedan that pulled slowly down the street. It stopped next to a police car and the driver of the sedan rolled down his window and started talking to the cop. Stone's eyes dropped to the white government plate on the sedan.

Bureau car? Here? Did the train conductor suspect something and make a call?

Stone turned to face Danny. "Divine a pretty isolated place?"

Danny's gaze drifted to the twin cars and then back to Stone. He'd clearly noted Stone's reaction to the police car. "Isolated? Let me put it like this. Divine's the sort of place you got to really want to get to if you want to find it. Although why anyone would beats me. And once you do find it then the only thing you want to do is get the hell out of there."

"Sounds good."

"What?"

"Let's go."

"You're kidding, right? I'm telling you, man, it's hell."

"I don't think so, Danny."

"What makes you a damn expert?"

Because I've actually seen hell. And it wasn't in Virginia.

9

Joe Knox climbed in his Range Rover and drove slowly home, deep in thought. He'd gone over every scrap of paper in that box and each held a startling revelation. Yet while the sum total of information was considerable, the investigative leads flowing from this intelligence were negligible. The CIA was exemplary in covering its tracks, and the Agency had outdone itself here. However, Knox had been able to piece a few things together.

The reason that Gray's home had been blown up six months ago seemed tied to an unauthorized CIA operation targeting the Soviets back in the 1980s. Exact details were not available and probably never would be. The connection in between was anything but clear. No names were available. One page in the box had stunned even the veteran Knox. There apparently had been a gun battle at the unfinished Capitol Visitor Center around the same time that Carter Gray's home had been destroyed. An unknown number of CIA paramilitary personnel had been killed, the real circumstances of their deaths hidden from public view by the Agency's very efficient disinformation machine. It seemed that Gray, then technically out of government, had been behind this mission. Who had killed the agents and why they were there in the first place remained a mystery.

A shoot-out in the middle of the Capitol? Gray must've been insane.

There was an indication in the file that Gray had met with the current CIA director, a man Knox considered a useless political appointee who had started at the Agency but had been brain-drained by his later years in the Congress. Whether Knox could get in to see the man was not a given. As Macklin Hayes had made clear, there was a difference of opinion at the Agency as to how this matter should proceed. Or *not* proceed.

Gray had also been given a secret audience with the president at Camp David. Knox suspected this piece of information was one of the ones Macklin Hayes had gotten hold of that he wasn't supposed to know about. Knox realized that the odds of his interrogating the president of the United States about this meeting were about the same as his spontaneously combusting while in the shower.

One of the most interesting pieces of information he'd gleaned from the file had to do with the now defunct Triple Six Division of the CIA, or its "political destabilization" arm as it unofficially had been known to the CIA rank and file. The less polite term of course was "government assassin." Triple Six was one of the CIA's most closely guarded secrets. Officially the CIA did not kill, torture or falsely imprison. Or, for that matter lie, cheat or steal. Unfortunately, the media had made some inroads into the Agency's past, resulting in some embarrassing revelations. Officially, Knox had followed the company line and been upset that the press had ferreted out some of this skullduggery. Personally, he'd never had much use for that side of the Agency. While it was true that the United States was better off with certain people dead, Knox had felt the CIA's best use of resources was in intelligence gathering, not authorized murder or stringing people up by their toes or making them believe they were drowning to induce them to talk. His experience had been that tortured people would tell you anything to make the pain stop. There were far more effective ways to get to the truth.

Gray had apparently concluded that several retired Triple Six assassins had been murdered. Whether these deaths were tied to the unauthorized mission in the former Soviet Union he had no way of knowing. According to one of Gray's bodyguards, the former intelligence head had met with a man at Gray's home on the very night it had been blown up. That man worked in a cemetery in Washington, D.C., and had been questioned by the FBI in connection with Gray's believed murder. And it was this man—the one Macklin Hayes had alluded to—who had suggested the bomber of Gray's home might've jumped off the cliff into the Chesapeake Bay.

Knox smiled grimly as he thought of the name the man had given the FBI agents.

Oliver Stone.

Was he a lunatic or something else? Since Carter Gray was not known to summon mentally unstable people to his home, Knox opted for the latter. Oliver Stone had been accompanied by a Secret Service agent when he'd visited Gray's demolished house. That too was interesting. He would have to get acquainted with Agent Alex Ford.

The last bit of interesting information had to do with a recent disinterment at Arlington National Cemetery. The grave of a man named John Carr had been dug up on orders from Gray. The coffin had been taken to CIA headquarters. Knox did not know the results of that action or actually who had ended up being in the coffin. He had seen some of Carr's confidential military record, and it was an exemplary one. Yet then the man had simply disappeared.

Knox's instincts told him that a man like Carr, with proven killing skills, would've made a productive member of Triple Six. Many of their members had come from the military. And right around the time Carr had vanished from public record was when Triple Six had been at the height of its activity. That had raised more questions than answers.

He reached his house and pulled into the garage.

A moment later his daughter, Melanie, opened the door to the kitchen. She'd earlier phoned him to say she was coming over to take him to dinner. After he'd gotten the summons from Macklin Hayes he'd called her back saying he couldn't make it, so he was surprised to see her.

The aroma of a cooked meal reached him from the kitchen. She gave him a hug and ushered him in, taking off his coat and hanging it up.

He said, "I didn't think busy lawyers in private practice had time to cook for themselves, much less anybody else."

"Reserve your judgment until after you've eaten it. I don't watch the Food Network and I don't hold myself out as any sort of cook. But the intent was honorable."

Melanie had taken more after Knox's deceased wife, Patty, than she had her father. She was tall and lithe with reddish hair that she usually wore pulled back. She was a graduate of UVA Law School and a rapidly rising young star at a D.C. powerhouse legal firm. The older of his two children—his son, Kenny, was currently in Iraq with his fellow Marines—Melanie had taken it on herself to make sure her father did not starve or wallow in pity over the recent death of her mother and his wife of thirty years.

The meal was eaten in the sunroom where they shared a bottle of Amarone and Melanie filled him in on the latest case she was handling. Over the years his children had quickly learned that their father never discussed his work with them, or anyone else. They knew he traveled the world, often on very little notice, and was gone for long periods of time. This was explained as him serving his country in a minor capacity with the State Department.

He had once told Melanie, "I'm unimportant enough to where they can call on me whenever they like, and I just go."

That line had worked all the way through middle school. But once his precocious daughter had reached high school Knox could tell she no longer believed it, though she never tried to uncover the truth. His son had just accepted his father disappearing from time to time as the way life was. Now, as a Marine lance corporal serving overseas and trying to stay alive day by day, Kenny Knox had more on his mind, his father hoped, than worrying about what his old man did for a living.

"When you called to cancel," Melanie began, "I was sure you'd be on a plane somewhere. I got the idea of cooking dinner when you said you'd be back home tonight."

Knox simply nodded at this, while he sipped his wine and stared out at the trees in his backyard as they were whipsawed by yet another approaching storm.

"So everything going okay at work?" she asked tentatively.

"Just looking over some old papers. Not that enlightening actually."

It was hard, he knew, for her. Most kids knew exactly what their parents did for a living and consequently could have cared less. While his children were growing up Knox had declined all invitations to parents' career day at school. After all, what would he have said?

"Given any more thought to retiring?"

"I pretty much already am. One foot in the professional grave."

"I'm surprised the *State Department* can function without you."

Father and daughter exchanged a brief glance and then each looked away, focused on their wine and last bites of roast beef and potatoes.

As she was leaving Melanie let her hug linger around her father's broad shoulders. She whispered in his ear, "Take care of yourself, Dad. Don't push the envelope too hard. Dangerous times out there."

He watched her walk to the cab she'd called to take her home to her condo in D.C. As it drove way, she waved to him.

He waved back, fleeting images of the last thirty years racing through his mind and ending with the image of Macklin Hayes telling him to tread carefully.

His brilliant daughter was right. It *was* dangerous times out there.

He would call Hayes in the morning. Early. The

general was on rooster time. And like the rooster, he believed the sun rose because he did too. He had no answers and many questions. How the general would react to that he didn't know. In the military Macklin had the rep of always getting the job done, by any means possible, which often included excessive losses. After becoming a battalion commander in Vietnam, Hayes still held the record, Knox believed, of having the highest casualty count of any field officer in the war. Yet because those losses often came with victories, at least victories measured in the taking of small hills or even yards of turf, sometimes only for hours, Hayes had swiftly moved up the command chain. Still, Knox did not intend on becoming one of the man's statistics on his way to yet another triumph. The best he could hope for was to thread his way through the minefield, keeping his eye firmly on the target and watching his back at the same time. Macklin was a superb infighter, connected in all the right ways, and a man who excelled at putting other people's necks at risk while protecting his own flanks with skillful dexterity. Competitive past all reason, he reportedly thrashed men half his age in racquetball at the Pentagon's courts. What he lacked in speed, quickness and stamina he more than made up for with sheer guile and peerless vision.

His exact title in America's intelligence empire was unknown to Knox. The man performed a curious—and as far as Knox was aware an unprecedented—

straddle between military- and civilian-sector intelligence factions. It was a powerful position and anyone under his control had to play by his rules or risk the consequences. He had been a close friend and protégé of Carter Gray, and no one could have had a better mentor. Knox would do his best to gauge the general's true intentions and then hope to fulfill them. Any way one looked at the task it was a formidable challenge.

He closed the door, stoked up the fireplace and picked up his novel with the intent of finishing it tonight. He might not get another chance for a very long time. When the wheels started to spin in his profession, they tended to spin very fast.

And from what Knox had seen in that box of secrets tonight, this time things could easily spin right out of control.

10

Knox watched the earth disappear from underneath him as the tri-engine Falcon Dassault jet shot skyward with enormous thrust. The luxurious, wood-paneled interior of the plane only held three occupants, other than the two pilots up front—Knox, Macklin Hayes and a uniformed steward who'd discreetly disappeared as soon as the plane leveled off and the coffee and continental breakfast was served. When Knox had called Macklin at seven a.m. he'd been told to report to a private airstrip near Front Royal, Virginia, that he had no idea even existed. Five minutes after he'd pulled up in his Rover, the plane had lifted from the tarmac.

Hayes had an office in some building in some undisclosed part of Washington, Knox knew, but the man obviously preferred conducting his meetings at thirty-five thousand feet, as though the altitude made for better decision-making, or at least fewer opportunities to be spied on. Knox knew that just the fuel burn for this flight would have paid for some really nice digs in the heart of D.C. Yet it should have come as no surprise that some high-up government folks treated the U.S. Treasury as though it would never run out of dollars. At least it kept gainfully employed the feds who sold T-bills to the Chinese and the Saudis to keep America running.

The former general was dressed in civilian government standard issue, namely a boring suit and an equally boring tie and black wing-tips on the feet. His socks were too short, Knox noted, and revealed pale ankles and the bottom of a hairless calf. The man had definitely not scaled the walls of power based on his fashion sense. He'd done it, Knox was well aware, on nerve and brains. The only sign of his former illustrious military career were the three stars on his tie clip.

They made casual conversation while munching an overabundance of carbs, and then the white-haired Hayes took a final sip of coffee and sat back in his leather seat looking expectant.

"Impressions from your reading session?"

"Many. None of them crystallized. I have to say the record is about as garbled as any I've seen. There're enough holes to fly a jet five times the size of this one right through it without even nicking a wingtip."

Hayes nodded approvingly. "I had the same *initial* reaction."

Knox didn't bother asking about the significance of the emphasized word because he knew from past dealings with Macklin that he would get zip for his troubles. "And I have to say I'm still not clear on the agenda. Where do you want this to go?"

Hayes spread his long, bony arms. "Where? To the truth. I suppose."

"You don't sound convinced of that," Knox said warily.

"But that could change, depending on what you find out. You know how this drill works, Knox."

"Gray and Simpson are dead. Do we let sleeping dogs lie?"

"We need to know. What we do after we know? Now that's another question entirely and one that does *not* involve *you*."

The man has always been subtle about putting subordinates in their place.

"So I go full-bore on this? Is that what you're telling me, sir?"

Hayes simply nodded. It struck Knox that the former general might have suspected Knox was somehow taping this conversation.

If only I had the balls to.

Knox decided not to press the man on actually verbalizing his answer. For all he knew there was government muscle hidden on the jet somewhere who might be summoned to relieve him of his ride at nearly eight miles up if he pushed Macklin too far. Farfetched? Perhaps. But Knox didn't want to find out.

"Tell me how you'll proceed."

"I've got some leads I can follow up. I take it DCI is off-limits," he said, referring to the director of Central Intelligence.

"I doubt he'd be much good to you anyway. Intelligence begins at home and his house is unfortunately empty."

Okay, he definitely knows I'm not taping this.

"Then the FBI agents who investigated the bombing at Gray's house. The Secret Service agent Ford. What about Triple Six?"

"What about it? Officially it never existed."

Knox had tired of the word games. Even his natural deference to the man had its limits. "There were subtle references in the papers intimating that somebody was popping retirees from the division and that Gray was aware of it."

"You can run that down if you want, but a dead end is what you'll find."

"How about the unauthorized Soviet op from decades ago?"

"History not worth repeating or dredging up. None of us would look good."

"You're not making this easy, General."

A smile eased across Hayes' face. "If it were easy why would we call you in, Knox?"

"I'm not a magician. I can't make things just appear or disappear."

"We have the disappearing end quite well covered.

All we need to find is what we need to make vanish. How about the man Gray met with on the night his home blew up?"

"The famous film director, Oliver Stone?" Knox could not hold back his smile.

"He used to have a little tent in Lafayette Park. Was there longer than anyone else. I believe his sign read, 'I want the truth.'"

"Looking for the truth right across from the White House? Sort of like hunting for Nazis in a synagogue. You consider him important?"

"The fact that he is no longer where he used to be, yes, I consider him important."

"What else do you know about him?"

"Not nearly enough. That's also why I consider him somewhat important."

"The grave being dug up at Arlington?"

"I was actually in the office on the day Carter Gray ordered that."

"Did he say why he wanted it done?"

"He was always better at giving orders than explaining them."

"So who was in the coffin? John Carr? Another body?"

"Neither. In fact there was nothing in the coffin."

"So Carr might still be alive?"

"He might."

"Was he a Triple Six? I read part of his military record. He would've fit the bill."

"Take that as your working hypothesis."

"So that would be the connection to Gray. Do you have reason to believe that Carr and Stone are one and the same?"

"I have no reason to believe that they're not."

"So why would Carr kill Gray and possibly Simpson?"

"Not all Triple Six personnel ended their deployment there on good terms. Carr may have been one such."

"If so, he waited a long time to pull the trigger. And he had just been to Gray's house. Did he have anything to do with blowing it up?"

"We don't think so."

"He could've killed Gray when he met with him."

"Maybe he didn't have the motivation then."

"So what changed?"

"That's for you to find out, Knox. There was the flag and grave marker. A clear sign, I think, that it's connected to this John Carr and his grave being dug up."

Knox marveled at how Hayes had gone from knowing very little and letting him find his own way in the investigation to, in a few short moments, shepherding him down the path he wanted. "I don't disagree. The man just seemed to have done it ass-backwards."

"Maybe he had his reasons. Regular reports, usual channels. But check back in with me tonight. If you need support, don't hesitate. We'll do what we can. Within limits, of course. As I said, not everyone is on the same page over this. Nothing I can do about that. Consensus in intelligence circles these days is as elusive as sectarian peace in Iraq."

That's reassuring. The right hand tells me to charge ahead while the left hand uses a knife to slit my throat.

Macklin pressed a button on the armrest of his seat and Knox felt the plane begin a tight bank to the right. Apparently, the flight and discussion were over.

To bolster that deduction Macklin rose without a word and made his way down the aisle to a door at the back of the plane. It clicked shut behind him.

Knox watched the clouds pass by as the plane began its descent through the Virginia sky. A half hour later he was tearing east on Interstate 66 in his Rover.

He would begin with Alex Ford and work his way through the usual suspects. But from what Hayes was both saying and leaving unarticulated, it seemed that all roads might lead right to a man named Oliver Stone.

If Stone had been a Triple Six and was good enough to take out both Simpson and Gray all these years later, Knox wasn't sure he wanted to run into the gent. Yet those sorts of encounters just came with the territory. And Knox was still standing.

But so, apparently, was Oliver Stone.

Dangerous times indeed.

Retirement was looking better and better. If only he could survive that long.

11

Greyhound didn't travel to the vicinity of Divine, Virginia. Yet a rusting bus on wobbly wheels with the name "Larry's Tours" crudely hand-stenciled on the side did. Stone and Danny sat in the back, next to a man who had a chicken in a crate on which he was resting his bare, swollen feet, and a woman who gave Stone far more attention than he would have liked, which included telling him her life story, all seventy-odd years of it. Fortunately, she got off before they did and was picked up by a man driving an ancient station wagon that was missing two of its doors.

They were finally let out at what Stone could only describe as the side of the road in the middle of nowhere. It made the one-horse stop Amtrak had dropped them at resemble a glittery metropolis on full throttle.

"Now what?" said Stone, shouldering his duffel while Danny clutched his small suitcase.

"Now we walk and thumb. Maybe we get lucky, maybe we don't."

Though it was not yet two in the morning they did get lucky and rode into Divine in the back of a pickup truck, with what the driver told them was a prizewinning hog named Luther who kept pushing his pink snout in Stone's crotch.

In the distance Stone saw the silhouette of some massive facility. Narrow towers and three-story buildings rose into the dark sky. In the weak moonlight something glinted along the perimeter of the place.

"What's that?" he said, pointing.

"Some place you never want to end up. Dead Rock. Supermax prison."

"Why do they call it Dead Rock?"

"It's built on the site of an old coal mine where about thirty years ago twenty-eight miners lost their lives in a cave-in. Their bodies are still in there somewhere 'cause they could never get to them. So they just sealed it up. They send the scum of the scum to Dead Rock. Least that's the official story. Hell on earth."

"You know somebody in that place?"

Danny looked away without answering.

Stone continued to stare at the complex until they rounded a curve and it disappeared from his view. He realized that the glint he'd seen must've come from the moonlight bouncing off the slash-your-ass wire that surrounded the place.

After the truck dropped them off their transportation became their own feet. Divine was still mostly dark at this hour, but Stone could see lights here and there as they trudged down the street. A truck passed them going east. And then another followed. And then another. Stone saw eight in all. Through the dirty truck windows Stone spied lean silhouettes of the drivers as they hunched over their steering wheels, cigarettes dangling between fingers, the windows cracked to let the white cancer-causing vapor escape into the frosty air. All around him he could sense the shadows of the nearby mountains, darker even than the night.

He checked his watch. It was barely two a.m. "Folks get an early start here?" Stone asked, nodding at the mini-caravan of dirty Fords and Chevys.

"They're miners."

"Going to work?"

"Nope. Next shift starts at seven. Those boys are heading to the clinic to get their methadone pop for thirteen bucks. Then they go to work."

"Methadone?"

"Some folks have cereal for breakfast, miners have methadone mixed with OJ in a cup. Just the way it is around here. Lot cheaper than snorting oxy up your nose or banging it into your feet. And that way you don't get dinged for dirty urine and lose your miner's license." Danny pointed up ahead to a small storefront set next to a clothing shop on one side and a hardware store on the other. Apparently Home Depot and Wal-Mart had not yet seen an opportunity in the isolated hamlet of Divine.

"That's my mom's place."

Stone eyed the sign. "Rita's Restaurant and Bar. So your mom's name is Rita?"

Danny wagged his head and grinned. "Nope. Rita ran the place before her. My mom never had enough money to switch the sign out. Then when she got some cash she figured why bother changing it. Everybody already knew it was her place. Her name's Abigail, but everybody calls her Abby."

Danny put a key in the front door of the restaurant and motioned Stone to follow him in.

"Does your mother live here?"

"Nope, but there's an apartment above the restaurant. You can crash there for what's left of tonight."

"What about you?"

"I got things to do, people to see. Get myself patched up." He touched his face and his leg.

"A doctor at this hour?"

"Don't need no doctor. Hell, just feels like Friday night after a football game. Can't let it screw up your life. I got the quick fix all right."

"You sure it's okay that I stay here for the night?"

"Oh, yeah. I'll be back about the time Mom opens up for breakfast. Get it all straight with her."

Stone looked around the interior of the place. A

long, polished mahogany bar with stools in front that was set at one end, with a deuce of pool tables and a 1950s-era jukebox anchoring the other end. In between were tables with checkered tablecloths and wheel-back chairs. The place didn't smell like a bar; it smelled like lemons and fresh air. From the looks of things Abigail Riker kept her place of business orderly and clean.

"Danny, is there any place around town I can do some work? I'm a little short on cash."

"I'll see what I can do."

Danny led him upstairs and a few minutes later an exhausted Stone was asleep on the small bed there.

A few hours later he woke up when he felt something hard touch his cheek.

It got his full attention.

Twelve-gauge shotgun muzzles usually did.

12

"Who in the hell are you?"

Stone didn't move. Swift motion in the face of a big-bore weapon was never advisable.

"Are you Abigail Riker?"

"I'm asking the questions."

Stone saw her finger slide to the trigger.

"My name's Ben. Danny Riker said I could sleep here."

Stone saw her finger slide to the trigger as her scowl deepened. "You're lying. Danny's gone."

"Well, he's back now. I met him on the train. He got in a fight with some guys. I helped him out. He's a little beat up so he decided to come back here for a bit. I just came along."

The woman was in her early forties, petite, five-three, with narrow hips and the lean body of someone to whom food was not of much interest. Her braided hair was long and dark with hints of silver. Her cheekbones were high and tight. Her face was lovely but her wide green eyes flashed at Stone as she snapped, "How beat up is he?"

"Not that bad, mostly bruises. Can you get the shotgun out of my face? An accidental discharge would do a little more damage to me than that."

She stepped back but kept the muzzle pointed halfway between the floor and Stone's head.

"You said you helped him? Why?"

"It was three on one. Didn't seem all that fair. You mind if I stand up? My back is really starting to ache."

She took another step back as Stone stood and stretched. They heard feet on the stairs and a moment later Danny Riker appeared, his handsome face with the swollen cheek grinning as he sized up the situation.

"See you two already got acquainted."

"Yeah," Stone said tersely, eyeing the gun. "It was a nice way to wake up."

His mother had seemed dumbstruck to see her son. She found her voice and said, "What the hell's going on, Danny? You talked and talked about getting out, broke my heart, I did my crying and now you're back?" She swung the shotgun in Stone's direction. "And this man says only for a little bit."

"Took a detour, Ma. Shit happens."

"Yeah, well, shit seems to happen a lot to you." She lowered the shotgun and looked at Stone. "This man says he helped you in a fight. And from the looks of your face he's telling the truth."

"He did. Took three guys out all by himself. And he throws a knife like I've never seen."

She now seemed to appraise Stone in a different light. "You look a little old to be running around like Rambo."

"Trust me, I feel it this morning," said Stone. "I take it you are Abigail Riker?"

Instead of answering she said, "Guess you two are hungry. Come on, coffee's hot and so are the eggs."

They followed her downstairs where Stone could see the restaurant was already mostly full. Many of the customers were middle-aged men with coal dust rings under their eyes dressed in coveralls with reflective stripes on them.

"Miners off the night shift," Danny explained.

If Stone hadn't known better he would've thought he'd just walked into a hospital ward. Most of the men sat bent over, in obvious pain. Their hands, arms, legs, backs were all wrapped with something. Butchered fingers were curled tight around mugs of coffee. Cracked plastic safety helmets were on the floor next to feet that were encased in steel-toed boots. The men's eyes were red and unfocused. Lung-shattering coughs filled the room.

"Hell of a way to make a living," said Abby in a low voice as she led them to an empty table near the counter. She'd obviously observed Stone's amazed look.

She made plates for them and a famished Stone took the next ten minutes to devour two helpings and drink down three cups of piping hot coffee.

Abby drew a chair up next to them. She eyed her son and waited until he bit into a fourth piece of toast before cuffing him on the ear.

"What was that for?"

"You left and now you're back."

"Don't worry, I'll be heading out before you know it. Nobody needs to get pissed off."

"I didn't say I was pissed off."

"Well, are you?"

"Yes!"

Stone observed this exchange and then, simply to break the tension, said, "Where are you headed to?"

"Don't know. See where it takes me."

"Where what takes you?" Stone asked.

He shrugged. "Dreams. Everybody's got dreams. Might end up in California. Maybe in the movies. I'm tall and good-looking enough. Maybe I'll be a stuntman."

Abby shook her head. "How about college? That dream ever flit inside that big head of yours?"

"Ma, we've had that talk."

"No, *I've* had that talk and you decided not to enter the discussion."

"If my knee had held up, I'd be playing ball for Virginia Tech right now. But it didn't. So what good is college gonna do me? It's not like I was such a great student in high school."

"You're not stupid!"

"Never said I was. Just not book smart."

She looked over at Stone. "Did you go to college?"

He shook his head. "Wanted to but I ended up going to war instead."

She said, "Vietnam?" He nodded.

"So that's why you fight so good. You ain't one of them crazy vets with a metal plate in your head, are you?" said Danny, grinning. "A walking time bomb?"

"The man fought for his country, Danny, don't make that into a joke," scolded his mother.

"I made it home without any metal plates," Stone said.

"Ever get shot?" Danny asked eagerly.

Stone said, "I agree with your mother. College should be on your radar."

"Well, I'll just go sign up right now. Just give me a check for a hundred grand for Harvard, Ma, and I'm out of here."

Abby started to say something when the door opened. Stone could sense the quiet chatter in the restaurant fading away. When he looked up he saw the big man standing in the doorway, his uniform sparkling and his Stetson perched at an angle on his head. His skin was leathery and lined from wind and sun. But it was a handsome face, its jaw tight and jutting like the lower half of a medieval helmet. The curly fringes of his dark hair stuck out from under the rim of the Stetson. His right hand rested over the top of his holstered pistol like a road scavenger's claw over its kill.

His gaze swung around Rita's until it came to rest on Abby Riker. He smiled. Then he saw Stone sitting next to her. And the big man stopped smiling.

13

Alex Ford was heading out to grab some lunch when the man approached him on the street outside of the Secret Service's Washington Field Office.

"Got a minute?" the fellow asked, flashing his creds.

Alex flinched when he saw the Agency insignia.

Great, here we go.

"What's this about, Agent Knox?" But he really already knew of course.

"We need to talk."

"Now?"

"Now."

The two men started off and soon they reached a small park where Knox sat on a bench and motioned for Alex to join him.

Knox spoke for some minutes, mostly telling Alex things he already knew.

"Your friend's not at home," Knox said.

"Really? I haven't been by to see him lately."

"But according to my sources you have been by to see the lady that was staying there. Funny, she's gone too. What can you tell me about her?"

"Not much."

"Let's start with a name."

Alex drew a shallow breath. *This could get real complicated real fast.* "What's her involvement? Or my friend's?"

"That's what we're trying to figure out. Her name?"

"Susan. Susan Hunter."

"Do you know where she is?"

"No." *At least that's the truth.*

"What's your relationship with her?"

"Just friends."

"And why is your friend gone now?"

"Who knows? Here today, gone tomorrow. She's just that sort of person."

"Your other *friend* Oliver Stone received a commendation from none other than the FBI director for helping to break up a spy ring here in D.C."

"That's right. I was involved in that at the end. But he deserves the credit."

"And he used to have a tent in Lafayette Park. A White House protestor. And he was caretaker at a cemetery. And he helps break up spy rings. Interesting career choices."

"He's an interesting guy."

"What else can you tell me about this interesting guy? Like his connection to Carter Gray?"

"Carter Gray?" Alex did his best to appear baffled even as the sweat gathered under his armpits. By lying to a federal officer he'd already committed several felonies. He was digging his professional grave deeper with each word.

"Yeah. Carter Gray. Stone went to see him on the night his house was blown up. You came out the next day with him to the crime scene. I've talked to the FBI agents who were out there with both of you."

"Right, right. Well, I knew that Oliver had gone to see Gray because he told me he had. I don't know why. He asked me to come with him to meet the FBI agents. So I did. As far as I know that's where it was left."

"How'd you two meet?"

"Anybody who's pulled White House Protection Detail knows about Oliver Stone. He was a fixture in Lafayette Park for a long time."

"You happen to know his real name, or is the famous film director moonlighting?"

"I don't know his real name."

"I thought Secret Service agents were more inquisitive than that. Guy was right across from the White House and you don't even know his real name?"

"It's a free country. He never did anything threatening. Just exercising his right to protest. We just thought he was an eccentric."

"So the name John Carr ring any bells?"

Alex had been expecting that follow-up question. "No, but it sounds familiar for some reason."

"It was the name of a soldier whose grave was dug up at Arlington Cemetery. On Gray's orders."

"That's right. I read about it in the papers. I wonder what the hell that was about?"

Knox just stared at him.

Finally Alex broke the silence. "I don't know what to tell you, Agent Knox."

"The truth would be helpful."

The migraine started in the center of Alex's forehead. "I'm *telling* you the truth."

Knox looked down and shook his head slowly. When he glanced back up his features were sad. "You aiming to scuttle your career over this guy, Ford?"

"I know him as Oliver Stone. That's it."

"You know his buddies. Reuben Rhodes and Caleb Shaw?"

"Yes. They're my friends too."

"And one recently died." Knox looked at a little notebook he held. "Milton Farb. Killed in his house over six months ago."

"That's right. We were all really upset about that."

"I'm sure. Police never solved the crime?"

"That's right, they didn't."

"And you were also working with the feds on nailing the casino king Jerry Bagger. Only he ended up blown to pieces in the Potomac River."

"I almost ended up there myself."

"You're a busy man. And your friend too, what did you call her, Susan Hunter?"

"I called her that because it's her name. And that's right, she was there too."

"And how did you get involved with a guy like Bagger? Through the lady?"

"It's pretty complicated and I'm not at liberty to divulge what happened. But the FBI can probably fill you in. And really I was just helping out a friend again."

"Man, you got lots of friends."

"Better than lots of enemies," Alex shot back.

"Oh, I think you got a few of those too." Knox rose and handed Alex a card. "You think about any more bullshit you want to tell me, give me a buzz. Meantime, I'll check everything you just told me out seven ways from Sunday. And just to show my good faith, I'll give you a two-minute heads-up before they serve you with the arrest warrant for obstruction of justice. How's that sound, Ford? You have a good one now." Knox walked off.

Alex just sat there on the bench because his legs, at that moment, didn't have the strength to support his body.

Thanks, Oliver, Thanks a lot.

14

Knox's next stop was the Library of Congress' Rare Book Reading Room where he found Caleb Shaw placing some priceless tomes on a rolling cart. Five minutes later they were sitting in the same small room where Caleb had been interrogated by casino owner Jerry Bagger. On seeing Knox's credentials Caleb said coolly, "And you want to see me about what?"

"Your friend, Oliver Stone?"

"You call him a friend. I call him an acquaintance."

"That's just semantics."

"I'm a librarian. Semantics are my life. Besides, I haven't seen him in a long time. I'm afraid I don't know anything that could help you."

"Well, sometimes people know more than they think."

"If I knew more than I thought, then I'd know it."

His patience clearly exhausted, Knox said, "Okay, let's cut to the chase, Shaw. I don't have all day to pull this story together so just answer my questions. Who is Oliver Stone really? And where is he now?"

"Oliver is Oliver. He used to have a tent in Lafayette Park. He's the caretaker at Mt. Zion Cemetery. But I don't know where he is. I haven't seen him for over six months. You can water-dunk me and I'd tell you the same thing."

"You mean *waterboarding*, and we don't do that to people," Knox said firmly. "Because that constitutes torture."

"Oh, really?" Caleb replied with both eyebrows tilted to the ceiling. "Then you might want to let your friends in the government know. There seems to be some confusion on that particular topic."

Ignoring this, Knox said, "Does the name John Carr mean anything to you?"

"Yes, it absolutely does."

Knox perked up. "Tell me about him."

"John Dickson Carr is a very famous mystery writer. Well, he's dead now, but I can recommend several of his works to you. Good stuff."

"I'm talking about John Carr the soldier, not the writer," Knox snapped.

"I don't know anyone by that name. There is of course John le Carré, but he's also a writer, though he did work in British intelligence at one point. And le Carré is only a nom de plume. His real name is David Cornwell. I could recommend some of his works as well."

Knox ground his teeth together and reminded himself that beating to death a public servant was not in the best interests of either his investigation or a future peaceful retirement. "This soldier was an *American*. Very distinguished record in Nam. He died. He was buried. This was over thirty years ago. Then they dug up his grave at Arlington and there was no body in it."

"Good Lord! I don't like to disparage my employer, but the federal government really has become so sloppy recently. But to lose an entire *body*? That really is outrageous."

Knox stared at him for a moment, then said, "Maybe the body was never in the grave, Shaw. How does that theory grab you?"

"Interesting, but what does that have to do with me?"

"Maybe John Carr and Oliver Stone are one and the same?"

"Well, I don't really see how that could be. But then again, Oliver never talked about his past and I respected his privacy. He's a good man, though, one of the most loyal friends anyone could ask for."

"You sound pretty sure for him just being an *acquaintance*."

"I'm a quick and accurate judge of people."

"How about your buddy, Milton Farb? Was Stone loyal to him?"

"Milton's dead," Caleb said firmly.

"I know. I'd like to know how he died."

"He was murdered."

"I know that too. Any idea who might've killed him?"

"If I did, the police would know, I can assure you."

"He dies and your buddy Oliver disappears?"

"If you're thinking that Oliver had anything to do with it, you're sadly mistaken. He loved Milton like a brother."

"Right. Anything else you can tell me?"

"Not unless it has to do with rare books."

He handed Caleb a card. "Call me if you *don't* think of anything else."

He left the room.

At another time in his life Caleb probably would've have fainted dead away after such an encounter. However, he was a different person now, especially after Milton's death.

He simply rose and went back to work, tucking the card into his pocket.

Knox drove to the warehouse where Reuben Rhodes worked, but the big man was not there, nor had anyone seen him for some days. They also did not have an address for him.

"How do you pay the man without a home address?" he asked the foreman.

"He picks up his check in person. I never mail it. That's the way he likes it."

"How about his year-end tax documents?"

"I give him that too. In person."

"I take it the man doesn't want people to know where he lives?"

"I'm not putting words in Reuben's mouth but I'd say that was a fair assessment."

"What can you tell me about him?"

"Good worker, nice sense of humor. Doesn't like rules too much. Likes the government even less."

"Did you know he worked in military intelligence for years?"

"He never mentioned that. I knew he was in the army. Helluva soldier, I bet. Man's strong enough to strangle a bear. Wouldn't want to get on the bad side of him."

"I'll try to keep that in mind."

"Mister, if I were you, I sure would. Four fellows jumped him leaving work one night. Three of them ended up in the hospital and the fourth fellow would've too, but he ran too fast for Reuben to catch him."

Knox climbed back in his truck and headed off. A moment later he received a text message from Macklin Hayes. They had just tracked down the woman who'd been staying at Stone's cottage. She was at a hotel in downtown D.C.

Knox floored it. Right now he had one lying Secret Service agent and one federal librarian who acted clueless but wasn't and an AWOL loading dock worker with a grudge against the U.S. government who could probably break Knox's neck with ease.

Knox could only hope the lady would tell him what he needed to know. Yet he doubted it would be that easy. If he'd learned nothing else about this Oliver Stone character it was that he commanded a great deal of loyalty from his friends.

Knox would just have to see how long that loyalty would endure. He was very good at pushing such things to their limits. And beyond.

15

The big man swept off his hat and ambled forward to the table where Stone, Danny and Abby were sitting. He had the smooth gait and perfect build of the natural athlete. Along the way he shook the gnarled hands of some of the customers and patted many a back like a politician scavenging for votes.

"Hello, Abby," he said as he stopped at their table. He eyed Danny. "Thought you were heading out to make your way in the world, young man."

"Got sidetracked, Sheriff. You know me, short attention span."

The policeman gave him an easy grin. "That include getting your face busted up? Girl or guy?"

"If it'd been a girl I'd have a little bit of lipstick on me," Danny said slyly. "Before she got pissed and slugged me."

"He'll be heading back out soon," Abby said. "So he says."

The sheriff turned his attention to Stone. "Who we got here?"

"New friend of mine," said Danny quickly. "Ben, this here is Sheriff Lincoln Tyree."

Tyree put out a big hand. "Just call me Tyree, everybody does, Ben. Got a bunch of Lincolns in my family. Like most folks round here the Tyrees fought for the Union. Pleased to meet you."

Stone shook his hand. There was great strength in the man's fingers, he noted. But he didn't attempt to crush Stone's hand. The grip was measured, confident but not aggressive.

Tyree pulled up an empty chair and sat down, laid his hat on the table and motioned to the waitress to bring him a cup of coffee.

"When'd you get back, Danny?"

"Late last night or early this morning, depending on how you want to call it. Got in a little tussle on the train. Some fellers jumped me. And Ben helped me out. In fact, he laid all three of them out without any help from me."

Tyree nodded at Stone, a new level of respect on his features. "Thank you for that. We were all worried when Danny told us he was leaving. We're pretty insulated here. Outside world's different from our little town."

"Places are different and also the same," Stone said. "Some bad and some good everywhere you go."

Tyree chuckled. "Well, I hope we've got more good in Divine than bad, right, Abby?"

She fingered her coffee and nodded absently. "Nice town, good place to raise a family," she said.

"Hell, yeah," exclaimed Danny. "I mean, look how I turned out."

Abby's face flushed and Tyree silently drank his coffee that the waitress put down in front of him.

"You gonna be staying around, Ben?" Tyree finally asked. "We don't get many visitors up here. Most people here have been here all their lives. Unlike Danny here, they tend to stay in Divine till they die."

Danny snorted at this comment.

Stone shook his head. "Just wanted to see that Danny got home okay. I'll be heading on soon."

"You're welcome to stay," Danny said. This comment made both Abby and Tyree stare uneasily at him, something Stone was quick to note.

"I doubt he'd find much to keep him here," Abby said.

"You never know, Ma. Ben here might be looking for a little peace and quiet."

Stone stared at Danny for a moment. Was the kid a mind reader? "Thanks, but I'll be moving on soon." Stone wasn't going to stay and he didn't like sitting next to a lawman, small-town or otherwise.

"I do appreciate what you did for Danny. And you can stay in the room upstairs tonight, if you want," Abby said.

"You've done enough for me," Stone said. "Bed and a good breakfast."

"Ben needs some work to do," Danny said. "Needs some cash because he got thrown off that train along with my sorry ass."

"I'm sure I can find something for you to do, Ben," Abby said.

"I appreciate it."

The sheriff said, "You know, you're welcome to stay over at the jail."

"Behind bars?" Danny said, laughing.

"On the cot in the back," said Tyree with slight annoyance. "Probably keep you okay for *one* night. Real quiet. No prisoners in lockup now."

"Yeah, they're all up at old Dead Rock," said Danny. "We passed it coming up. Looks real pretty at night," he added sarcastically.

Tyree nodded. "Put it on a mountaintop in the middle of nowhere, and for good reason. City folks don't want supermaxes in their backyard. But they'll dump them here. Not complaining, it brings jobs to folks, and Lord knows we need them." He motioned to the door where two burly young men in blue uniforms walked in and sat down at a table. "There're two of them right there. Probably be heading up to the prison after they fill their bellies."

"If you ain't working in the mines or the prisons, you ain't making a living 'round here," said Danny. "Because everything else is for shit."

Tyree scowled at him. "Now, Danny, you know that's not true. We got us a whole line of shops up and down that street outside that are doing real good. Folks can earn a decent living in Divine, hold their heads up and take care of each other. It's not like that in most places."

"I can vouch for that," Stone said.

As there was a pause in the conversation the picture on the TV hanging on a wall behind the counter caught their attention; Stone's more than anyone else's. It was about the murders in Washington. The FBI had leads they were running down. Several persons of interest were being questioned. And though no one at the Bureau would be specific, apparently there was a theory tying together the killings of Simpson and Gray.

Tyree said, "Hope that they catch the bastard. I think it's some terrorist plot."

"Towelheads on the run," said Danny, chuckling. "Well, if they come here they'll be pretty easy to spot."

"No laughing matter, Danny. These crazies are trying to take over the world." He touched his gun. "But I tell you what, if they do show up in Divine, they can expect some good old American justice."

Stone turned to Abby. "What sort of work do you need done?"

Tyree stood, the rubbed leather of his gun belt squeaking slightly. "Danny, come see me later, boy, okay?"

It really wasn't a question.

Danny grinned, nodded and went back to his over-easy eggs and grease-fried bacon.

"Supplies need to be brought in from the back," Abby told Stone. "Storage room picked up. Windows washed, floor mopped. One of my dishwashers called in sick so you can pitch in there too."

Stone nodded, wiped his mouth with his napkin and rose. "Just give me a quick walkthrough and I'll get to it."

"Don't you want to know your pay scale?"

"I'll leave it up to you."

"You're a trusting man," chuckled Tyree before he left.

No, I'm not.

As Stone followed Abby to the back room Danny's grin eased off his face as he looked at the dirty, tired men staring back at him. He finished eating, slurped down his coffee, jumped up from the table and made his way to the door. Before he got there, a lanky man rose from his table and blocked his way. He had greasy hair, three days of beard, a coal-dusted face, and eyes that were just begging for trouble.

"Hey, Lonnie," said Danny. "You're looking like shit just like always."

"What you doing back here? Heard you bought yourself a ticket on the train. Had enough of Divine. Ain't that right, Danny boy? Had enough of us?"

"Didn't you know? Got the FBI on my ass for

robbing that damn train. Came here to hide out. You'll cover for me, right?"

"You think any of that's funny?" said Lonnie as he slipped a wedge of chew into his mouth, pushing his fingers so far in it was a wonder he didn't gag.

"I try to find the humor in everything, Lonnie. Makes life a lot more bearable."

"You staying this time or not?"

"Why, you gonna miss me if I leave again? Best watch out. People might think you got a weird-ass thing for me, dude."

Some of the men at the other tables laughed at this. Lonnie's hands balled to fists, but Danny gripped his bony shoulder. "Just joking around, man. Ain't made up my mind whether I'm going or not. Soon as I do you'll be one of the first I tell. Now, I got to go. While I'm standing here flapping my jaw with you, I could be making millions of bucks out there in the big city of Divine."

He skirted around Lonnie, who suddenly became aware that all eyes were now on him. As the door slammed shut behind Danny, Lonnie quickly sat back down and with a defiant look shot a wad of chew into an old coffee can sitting on the floor.

Behind the bar, Stone set down a load of boxes. He had heard most of this exchange. Divine was turning out to be quite a peculiar town.

Get the cash and hit the road. Before twitchy trigger finger Tyree finds out I'm *the towelhead.*

16

Six hours later Stone had finished his work and Abby pronounced herself satisfied with what he'd done.

"You've got a lot of energy," she said. "And you don't waste time. I like that in a person." She smiled and for the first time Stone registered on how lovely she actually was.

"What now?"

"There're some more chores to be done at my house. All outside work. You interested? It's a dirty job."

"Just tell me how to get there. And what you want done."

He grabbed his duffel bag and a few minutes later left the restaurant. For the first time Stone got a good look at Divine in daylight. It surprised him.

Right out of Andy Griffith's Mayberry but with a Hollywood veneer, something the Disney people might have put together, he concluded. The storefronts were all freshly painted and the wood new-looking; the windows were clean, the brick sidewalks smooth and swept, the roads recently laid with black asphalt. Folks walked past waving at each other, friendly "hellos" floated all around him, though none were directed at Stone, apparently the only stranger here.

He passed what looked to be a new brick building that was the town's library. He peered through the glass doors and saw shelves of books and rows of shiny computers. It occurred to Stone that he couldn't even get a library card. He walked on.

The cars and trucks that passed by him as he made his way through the downtown area were all relatively new. He gazed up at the two-story jail, constructed of red brick with white columns out front and tubs of pansies guarding the entrance, and Coke and snack machines set against the wall. It was the most inviting entrance to the shackled life Stone had ever seen, though. Next door was a larger building, built of red brick too, with a clock tower and "Court House" stenciled on the outside.

A jail and a courthouse in such a little hamlet? With a supermax prison not that far away? But the supermax was for the deadliest of the deadly, not small-town criminals who probably stole car batteries and hit their bar mate while shit-faced.

As he was thinking this a small man with snowy white hair came out of the courthouse, perched a soft felt driving cap on his head and ambled down the street away from Stone.

"Want me to introduce you to the judge?"

Stone turned around and saw Tyree standing behind him. He must have come out of the jail. The big man moved quietly. Stone didn't like that stealth.

"The judge?" *A lawman and a judge*. Just what he needed. They could both arrest and try him for murder right now.

Tyree nodded and called out, "Dwight, got somebody here you might want to meet."

The small man glanced around, saw Tyree and smiled. He headed back toward them.

"This here is Ben," Tyree said. "You got a last name, Ben?"

"Thomas," Stone said quickly.

"Okay, this is the Honorable Dwight Mosley."

Up close Stone had the impression that he was talking to a smaller version of Santa Claus with a trim beard in place of the bushy one.

Mosley chuckled. "I'm not sure how honorable I am or ever was, but it does indeed come with the title of a judge."

"Ben was the one who saved Danny Riker's butt when he got into some trouble on a train."

"I heard Danny was back. Well, thank you, Ben. Danny can be, well . . ."

"Hotheaded?" suggested Stone.

"Impetuous."

"A nicer word, but means the same thing," Tyree pointed out with a laugh.

"Fine-looking courthouse you have there," said

Stone, glancing away from the judge. "I guess you have a lot going on?"

"You wouldn't think a small town like this would have need of a courthouse or a judge," Mosley said, apparently reading Stone's mind. "But the fact is it does because my jurisdiction covers a large geographic area in addition to Divine. It's not just litigation, though we have a fair amount of that, mostly over mineral rights and such and mining accidents resulting in personal injury. And federal law just changed a few months ago that required coal-mining companies to file what are termed recertifications for all their property and operational aspects. Unfortunately for me, I'm the judge who has to review all of it." He pointed at a delivery truck pulling into the small alleyway that led to a parking area behind the courthouse.

"Unless I'm much mistaken that's another load of boxes filled with said recertifications. It's been a boondoggle for mining lawyers, but I get paid the same regardless."

"Monotonous work, I imagine," said Stone.

"You imagine correctly. We're also the repository for land deeds, surveys, rights-of-way, easements and the like, which also come to the court boxes at a time. But on a more personal level folks come to me with legal questions or counseling from time to time and I try to do the best I can."

"Being neighborly," said Tyree.

"That's right. It is a small town after all. For

example I helped Abby Riker get the restaurant and other property put into her name after Sam died."

"Sounds like you keep pretty busy."

"Yes, but I find time to do some hunting and fishing. And I like my walks. My walks take me all over. Beautiful countryside here."

They paused for a moment as a mother and two kids walked by. Tyree tipped his hat to her and rubbed the heads of the kids while the judge gave them all a gracious smile.

After the family had passed Stone said, "Well, I better be going."

But Mosley said, "Where are you from, Ben?"

Stone's gut clenched. It wasn't what Mosley had said, it was the way he'd said it. Or had he just become overly paranoid? "Here and there. Never had much inclination to put down roots."

"I was the opposite of that, at least for a while. I called Brooklyn home for the first thirty years of my life. After that I spent time in South America and then Texas, near the border. But I've never seen any place as pretty as this."

"How'd you end up here?" Stone asked, resigned at least for the moment to play the casual conversation game so as not to make the judge suspicious.

"Complete coincidence. Drove through on my way back to New York after my wife died, and my car broke down. By the time it was fixed a few days later, I'd fallen in love with the place."

"And lucky for us he did," said Tyree.

"The town has reciprocated," said Mosley. "It certainly helped me get over my poor wife's passing." He added, "Are you going for a walk too?"

"To Abby's actually. She has some work out at her house she wants me to do."

"A beautiful place that is, A Midsummer's Farm."

"Is that what she calls it?" Stone asked.

Mosley nodded. "A variation on the Shakespeare play. A dream, you see. I guess in a way all of us up here are living a dream, isolated as we are from the rest of society."

"Not such a bad thing," Tyree noted. "The rest of society isn't all that great. Divine is just what it sounds like, at least it is for me."

Mosley passed by them and continued on down the street.

Tyree took off his hat and swiped his hair. "Well, you have a good one, Ben. Don't work too hard."

Tyree went inside the jailhouse and Stone continued on his way to Abby's.

Or A Midsummer's Farm.

Or a dream.

Or a nightmare.

17

As Stone passed down the main street of Divine, he quickly observed that the shops seemed prosperous and the customers happy-looking. It was hard for him to reconcile this image with that of broken-backed, gnarled-handed, dirty-faced miners with the coal-caked lungs having breakfast in Rita's Restaurant. And then his thoughts refocused on what he'd seen on the TV.

Leads. People of interest. Ties between the two murders.

As he glanced through one storefront window he saw it. Ubiquitous for so many decades, it was now rare to find one anywhere, at least one that worked. Yet Divine apparently was a bit slow in following the rest of the country's lead.

He slipped inside and looked at the payphone on the wall and then at the sign behind the front counter: "Appalachian Crafts." The store's shelves bulged with sculptures made from wood, stone and clay. On the walls were paintings and photos of mountains, valleys and little tin-roofed shacks clinging to the sides of hills. Behind the counter a large, red-faced woman was pecking keys on her computer.

She looked up and smiled. "Can I help you?"

"I just wanted to use the phone. Do you have change for a five?"

She gave him the money and he retreated to the rear of the store and loaded the quarters in the phone's slots. He dialed the one person he knew had a truly untraceable phone number: Reuben. This was because he didn't have a phone in his own account but rather used minutes of piggybacked phone time from hundreds of different people. Stone had always assumed it had been something Milton had shown him how to do.

The big man answered on the second ring. He nearly shouted when he heard it was Stone. After telling Reuben that he was fine and that he would not under any circumstances tell him where he was, Stone asked him about the investigation.

"Guy named Joe Knox from CIA has talked to everybody but me. Real bulldog apparently. He knows you and Carr are one and the same. He knows you're on the run. If they find you you're not going to trial, Oliver."

"That had already occurred to me, Reuben. How is everyone holding up?"

"Okay. Alex is being a shit about all this, though."

"He's a federal agent, Reuben. He's caught right in the middle."

"Well, he did tell Annabelle to burn the letter you left behind. I guess I should give him some points for that."

"Tell him I appreciate that. I really do."

There was a brief pause and then Reuben said, "Oliver . . ."

"I'm not going to tell you that I did it, Reuben. That would do no good at all. I just want you to know that you were a better friend than I deserved. All of you were. And I'll be watching the news. If it even looks like any of you will be harmed because of this, I'll turn myself in."

"Listen to me, we can take care of ourselves. They can't touch us. But if you turn yourself in to the cops, CIA will swoop in, scream national security, and your ass will disappear."

"Let me worry about that. And I know it doesn't do you justice, but thanks for everything."

Reuben started to speak but Stone had already hung up, replacing the receiver with a smack of finality. *It's like I just cut off my right arm. Good-bye, Reuben.*

He glanced up to see the shopkeeper staring curiously at him. He had been speaking so low that there was no risk of being overheard.

"Call go through okay?" she said pleasantly.

"Just fine. Thanks." She kept staring at him so he finally said, "You have some nice pieces." Pointing to a painting on one wall, he added, "Who did that one?"

The woman's face fell. "Oh, that would be Debby Randolph."

"She's talented."

"Yes." She added quickly, "I'm Wanda. Haven't seen you around here before."

"I just got here. Came in late last night with Danny Riker."

"Danny?" she said, startled. "Heard he'd left town."

"Well, he's back, but I think it's just temporary. So how's business?"

"Really good, especially on our Web site. Lot of folks like the Appalachian stuff. Takes 'em back to a simpler time, I suppose."

"I think we could all use a bit of that. Well, thank you."

"Hope you come back. Got a sale on black bear cubs sculpted from chunks of coal. Makes a right fine paperweight."

"I'm sure."

Stone walked out of the "feel-good" shop feeling like he was navigating the last few yards to his own death. He really was all alone again.

18

The asphalt road gave way about a half mile out to macadam. Stone passed by a stone church that had a small steeple with a dry-stack stone wall encircling the property. Next to this house of worship was a graveyard. The former graveyard caretaker Stone took a moment to walk through the burial plots. The same family names kept popping up on the headstones. Stone saw the grave of Samuel Riker. He'd died five years ago at the age of forty-one.

There were many Tyrees also sprinkled around. One tombstone, darkened by age, was the resting place of Lincoln Q. Tyree. He'd died in 1901. Stone thought it must be a bit disconcerting to pass by a graveyard with a marker already bearing your name, but perhaps the good sheriff didn't come this way often.

Two graves still had fresh flowers on them and the mounds of dirt looked new. Rory Peterson had died a week ago. The name on the other grave made Stone do a double take. Debby Randolph had gone to her Lord a day after Peterson had died. That's apparently why the woman at the shop had acted a little strangely. Peterson was forty-eight while Debby had only been twenty-three.

Stone walked on, turning left at a fat oak with thick sprawling branches that resembled more Atlas holding up the world than a mere tree. Hanging from one of the branches was a sign that read "A Midsummer's Farm" with an arrow pointing to the left. He went on for another hundred yards down a crushed gravel path until he came to the house, although that term clearly didn't do it justice. He wasn't sure exactly what he had been expecting, but it wasn't this.

"Antebellum" was the first word that jumped to mind. It was large, constructed of white clapboard and sections of stone with black doors and shutters and no fewer than four stone chimney-stacks. A broad front overhang supported by rows of elaborately milled columns offered up a fine porch with rocking chairs, sturdy tables, hanging plants and an upholstered swing anchoring one end. The landscaped yard stretched on and on with the perimeter bordered by stacked stone walls. In a cobblestone-paved motor court was parked a muddy pickup truck along with a Mini Cooper in racing green with a white top.

All this from the revenue produced by a restaurant with ten tables, eight barstools, two pool tables and a jukebox?

The work to be done was in the stables that were

almost out of sight from the house. He spent the next several hours mucking out stalls and sorting bridles and reins and other equipment as several horses whinnied and stamped their hooves in other stalls.

Stone was rubbing his aching back when he heard the horse's hooves pounding his way. The fifteen-hand-high chestnut drew up next to him and Danny jumped down. He pulled two beers from his jacket pocket and handed one to Stone. "Heard from Ma you were out here."

He popped the can lid and a bit of the liquid spewed out. "Horse riding and beer delivery ain't a good fit," he said.

"Knee looks to be okay," Stone noted.

"I'm a fast healer. What are you doing?"

"Mucking stalls among other things."

"I'll help you."

"You sure?"

"Got nothing else to do right now."

They went into the stables and Danny grabbed a shovel after tethering his horse to an iron ring stuck in cement in the ground.

Stone eyed a bruise on the side of the man's face. "It was the other side that fellow nailed on the train, wasn't it?"

"Duke was too fast for me in the stall this morning. Clocked me in the face when I was trying to bridle him. Damn horse."

"But a beautiful one."

"You ride?"

"Not if I can help it. You call this place a hellhole? Which part— the pool, the mansion or the cool car parked in front?"

"I'm the exaggerating type."

"Seriously, why would you want to leave something like this?"

"It's hers, not mine." Danny slung horse manure into a wheelbarrow.

"You're her son. You'll inherit someday."

Danny stripped off his shirt, revealing a lean, muscled physique. "Who says I want it?"

"Okay, fair enough. You an only child?"

"That's right."

"I saw your father's grave coming up here."

"That's why we got all this stuff."

"How so?"

"Lawsuit against the damn coal company that killed my old man. See, coal companies almost always win those things, or else settle for pennies on the dollar 'cause they got all the good lawyers wrapped around their little finger. But Mom held on, proved her case. Coal company appealed but in the end she kicked their ass, they caved and she got her blood money. And the only thing it cost us was her husband and my dad." Danny tipped another shovelful of horse manure into a large wheelbarrow and banged his tool against the metal side as if in exclamation.

"And your mom still runs the restaurant?"

"She likes to keep busy, and people need to eat."

"The whole town looks pretty prosperous."

"Coal prices highest in decades and there ain't enough miners to do the job. When demand's higher than supply, wages go up. About doubled in fact over the last five years. High wages, low cost of living equals prosperity for the common man. Simple."

"You sound like an economics major."

"Nah, just a dumb ex-jock, but I got eyes, ears and a little bit of common sense. Where you bunking tonight?"

"Must be a motel or something around here?"

"Back in town, couple blocks from my ma's place and around the corner from the courthouse, there's a place that has rooms to let. Cheap but clean. Bernie Sandusky runs it." He laughed. "Tell old Bernie that Danny sent you."

"Why, that'll get me a reduced rate?"

"Nope, more likely get your butt kicked out the door."

"Why's that?"

"Bernie has a real cute granddaughter named Dottie. Few years ago he caught me and Dottie in one of his rooms working on our *biology* homework." He laughed and pitched a big load of manure into the wheelbarrow. "Okay, I'm done shoveling shit. You're on your own, dude."

Stone watched until Danny and his ride disappeared from sight. He finished his work and later idly followed a path that wound around a small hill covered with scrub pines. Abby's property seemed to have no end. He reached another gravel road that headed back out another way. As his eye followed its path he reckoned it would go back out to the main road at some point, on the other side from where he'd come to the farm.

A few minutes later Stone followed a dirt path that was worn black and finally led to an old barn that looked close to falling down. Inside was an old gray pickup truck, bales of rotted hay, and rusted tractors and other farm equipment.

He perched on the bumper of the pickup and counted his meager cash. An act of kindness on his part to help Danny had really cost him. The train ticket hadn't been cheap and the bus ride just to the vicinity of Divine had cost him still more precious dollars. Danny had offered to pay but Stone had refused. And he still had to rent a room in town. He prayed that rich Abby would be generous with her payment for the day's work so he could move on.

Yet should he even still be thinking of escape? Maybe when he'd jumped off the damn cliff, he should have just sucked in a chest of water and ended it. What did he have to live for anyway?

What do I have to live for?

He heard a vehicle skid to a stop outside. He hopped off the bumper and walked outside in time to see Abby step from the truck cab.

"Taking a stroll around the place?" she said, not smiling.

"I finished up at the stables. Beautiful property you have here."

"Okay," she said, her features unreadable.

"Doesn't look like this place gets much use anymore," he said, looking toward the barn.

"This was my momma and daddy's place for fifty years. They ran it as a farm, but we haven't done any farming here for thirty years. Their house was just down there," she said, pointing to the left. "Burned down a long time ago. Only thing left is the chimneystack. I oughta just knock it down, but I can't do it. I mean, it's really the only thing I have left of them."

"I can understand that."

"You can, huh?"

"The past is hard to let go of, particularly when the future is a little uncertain."

"You're wasting your talents mucking stalls, Ben. You ought to be a philosophy teacher."

"I was just heading back to town."

"I need to pay you. Why don't you ride with me back to the house? You can get some supper and your money."

"You don't have to do that."

"I know I don't." Her tone did not seem to invite dissent.

A few minutes later they pulled into the driveway.

"Beautiful house."

"Came at a damn steep price."

"Danny told me a little about that."

"Expect you want to take a shower and change your clothes. Mucking stalls isn't the cleanest job in the world."

"Thanks. I'm sorry about your husband."

"Uh-huh," she said.

She slammed the truck door behind her and headed up the steps.

Stone slowly got out and trudged after her.

He could have landed in any town in the country. And it had to be Divine, Virginia.

Damn, I can really pick 'em.

19

Knox collared Annabelle Conroy as she was leaving her hotel.

He flashed his creds and asked her to go with him.

"I don't think so," she said.

"Excuse me?"

"Those creds could be faked and you could be a rapist. Go call a cop and I'll go with both of you if he's satisfied you are who you say you are. But until then, get the hell away from me."

"How about a cup of coffee in the restaurant over there? If I put my hand up your skirt, you can start screaming and kick me in the balls."

"Just so you know, I kick really hard."

"I have no doubt."

"Will this take long? I'm sort of busy."

"As long or as short as you want to make it."

Over two cups of strong coffee Knox explained what he wanted.

"I don't know where Oliver is," she said truthfully. "We became friends, and I stayed at his cottage, but now he's gone and he didn't tell anybody where he was going."

"How did you become friends and why were you staying at his cottage?"

"Simple enough. He helped me with a problem I had and after he left I wanted to keep his home going for him in case he came back."

"So your problem was with Jerry Bagger, now deceased?"

"I see you do your homework."

"Wasn't that hard actually. What exactly was your beef with Bagger, Ms. Hunter?" Knox didn't believe for a moment that that was her name but he was willing to play along, for now.

"What's it to you?"

"Humor me."

"Why the hell should I?"

He pointed to the cup she was holding. "How about I take the prints off that and run them through a database. Would I pull up the name Susan Hunter?"

"There's no law against changing your name."

"Right, but the *reason* for changing your name, now that might be illegal."

"Bagger hurt someone I cared about and I wanted to nail him for it and I did."

"With Alex Ford and Oliver Stone's help?"

"Yeah. Bagger was a crook and a sociopath. The FBI and Justice Department had been after him for a long time. He got what he deserved. So what's wrong with that?"

"I don't really give a crap about Jerry Bagger. I want Oliver Stone. Or John Carr. I don't know which name you refer to him as."

"I only know him as Oliver Stone. I have no idea who John Carr is."

"When was the last time you saw him?"

"About six months ago."

"You heard about Carter Gray's and Senator Simpson's murders?"

"I watch the news."

"Stone had a relationship with Gray."

"Didn't know that."

"Alex Ford never bothered to tell you? Because he knew all about it."

"We're just friends, and friends don't share everything."

"Why'd you leave the cottage?"

"Got tired of living with dead people."

"You wouldn't have happened to have heard from Stone? Maybe he told you to take it underground?"

"Why would he do that?"

"You tell me."

"How can I tell you about something that didn't happen?"

"I think your buddy's on the run."

"From what?"

Knox stood. “Okay, my BS alarm is clanging so hard it’s hurting my ears. So like I told your friend, Ford, I’ll be in touch. And don’t try to leave the city. That would not make me happy.” He walked off.

20

Macklin Hayes did not seem particularly pleased. He and Knox were sitting in front of a fire in the library of a luxurious late-nineteenth-century brownstone in the heart of D.C. that Hayes had access to 24/7. Spy kings, it seemed, had gold-plated perks.

"So you've run around interviewing all the usual suspects today and have *no* progress to show for it."

"I'm not just going through the motions, General. I did my little dog-and-pony show with all of them except for the Reuben Rhodes character, and I'll catch up to him at some point. They're all lying. They all know more than they'll admit. That's progress right there as far as I'm concerned. At some point they'll make a slip and then we move in."

"I seriously doubt the man left them a copy of his travel itinerary."

"I doubt that too, but Carr is a loyal guy. If we can nail his friends on something, put them at risk for prison time, then that may flush him out."

"Meaning he'll come running back here to save his friends? You really believe that will happen, Knox?"

"I've studied the man, gone over his career, talked to his friends. Yeah, I think that might happen. And what's the downside if it doesn't work?"

Hayes finished off his glass of wine and stared into the fire. "Let me speak frankly, Knox. Hopefully it will be instructive and won't bore you too much."

"I doubt anything you have to say would bore me, sir. And you know I'm a sucker for *truthful* information."

Hayes ignored the barb. "Carr is a killer, clearly. He was at the Capitol Visitor Center that night. We know he murdered Gray and Simpson. That part is simple, the rest is not."

"And do I finally get to hear the rest?"

Hayes rose and poured himself another glass, this time of scotch, and sipped it while standing in front of the fire. Gazing at this tall patrician figure dressed in a three-piece suit with his beautiful snowy hair, square jaw and twinkling eyes and holding his cut-crystal snifter made Knox fantasize he was in a Hollywood spy film.

Let's see, how does that story go again? Oh, yeah, bright, refined, patriotic people recruited from Ivy League schools doing their noble best to keep their country safe while nattily attired in their Brooks Brothers suits, bedding all the beautiful women, sucking thoughtfully on their sweet-smelling pipes and remaining high above the riff and the raff. Like me. And John Carr. The riff and the raff.

Knox had quickly found that that notion was

indeed a fantasy. Intelligence was a nasty, dirty business and necessitated each side to get as filthy as the other. The only rule was there never had been any rules at all. No, actually he was wrong. There was one rule. People like Macklin Hayes did remain above it all. Untouchable. And yet that rule was not absolute. Look at Carter Gray. John Carr had pulled him right down into the trench shit with him.

You go, John.

Hayes said, "Unfortunately, Carr is also probably in possession of certain information, perhaps even proofs of actions taken by this country at sensitive times, that might, in unforgiving hindsight, mind you, place us in an awkward situation. I'm sure Gray was aware of that as well. I believe he attempted to get to Carr, but as we know, Carr got him first."

"So in other words he has the goods on us so this is not a case for the law courts?"

Hayes smiled. "I've always loved your perspicacity, Knox. Saves so much time."

"I'm not a hired killer, sir. You ordered me to find him. I will do my best to do so. But that's it."

"And that's all you need do. Others will take over from there."

"If Carr is as smart as I think he is, he knows all this. He might have devised a way that his violent death will trigger the very disclosure you don't want. A packet of information to the *New York Times* perhaps in the event a bullet slams into his brain?"

"Find him, Knox, and I believe we can persuade him that such action would not be advisable."

"What leverage would you have over him at that point?"

"As you said, he's a very loyal man."

Knox considered this for a moment. "So his friends are his Achilles' heel? Only in your version instead of coming back and going to jail he takes the bullet, he falls on the sword *silently* so his friends can what, live?"

"That's certainly one scenario."

"One or the *only* one?"

"Just find him, Knox, that's all you have to do. Any leads of interest?"

"The *friends* have given me squat, and if we have to do this outside the law now it comes back to following the physical evidence as far as it takes me."

"Back out to the crime scenes then?"

"Yes."

"Time is not on our side."

"It never is. This information would have been helpful earlier, sir, in all candor."

"I'm sure it would have. But there you are."

"So I'm competing with the cops on this one too? What if they get there first?"

"We've taken certain actions that will preclude that from happening."

"And if some detective gets lucky?"

"That's highly doubtful because they know

nothing of John Carr or his ties to Gray and Simpson. So you have a tremendous advantage there. But if the police get to him first, we will make sure that he will disappear from their custody. National security trumps all, Knox."

"Of course. Can I inquire as to what the chain of command is on this, sir?"

"You report to me, no one else," he said sharply.

"No, I mean who do *you* report to, General?"

Hayes finished off his drink and carefully put the glass down on an antique side table. "I'll pretend I didn't hear that. Good luck. Regular reports."

"Absolutely," Knox said, with more edge to his voice than he would have liked. One could push Macklin Hayes only so far, but Knox was getting sorely tempted to push as hard as possible. Like off a cliff.

"One more thing. John Carr is probably the best assassin this country has ever produced. The fact that he was able to singlehandedly kill a dozen of our best paramilitary field agents thirty years after he left Triple Six speaks volumes. God, he must have been something else indeed in his prime. What an honor to have commanded such a killing machine. Gray was lucky in that regard. The meteoric rise of his career was tied, in no small way, to Carr's ability to hit the bull's-eye time after time."

"And you're telling me this why?"

"Just want you to understand the playing field. We

need him alive, Knox. We need to know what he has before the sword falls. Never forget that. There may need to be sacrifices, of course."

As Hayes left the room Knox did indeed understand the playing field. They clearly needed Carr alive.

Sacrifices? But they didn't necessarily need Joe Knox still breathing when the dust settled, did they?

Knox left the brownstone, climbed back in his Rover, and drove off in pursuit of apparently the greatest assassin his country had ever produced, while a cagey former general who had no problem allowing his foot soldiers to die to achieve his goals was crowding his rear flank.

Whoopie.

21

Very early the next morning, Knox started with the caretaker's cottage at Mt. Zion Cemetery. He went over every square inch of it, pulling up loose floorboards, emptying every drawer, checking inside the fireplace, and poring over the books Stone kept there, many in different languages.

"If the guy can speak all these languages, he might have already left the country," Knox told himself. Other than that, the cottage was a bust. The guy had obviously cleaned it out before fleeing. He next set about searching the cemetery. Here he was a bit more fortunate, though it ultimately turned out to be nothing. His sharp eye discerned that one tombstone had been recently moved. He yanked it over and found the small compartment carved in the earth. Whatever had been there, though, was now gone.

The "dirt" Macklin Hayes had hinted at?

Two hours later found him standing in the rear grounds of Carter Gray's former home. Knox had decided not to go by Simpson's murder scene. The vacant construction site had not given up any clues on the first go-round and he'd wisely decided that it was probably not going to give up any simply because he went back.

He stared out at the bay. Stone had told the FBI agents that the person who'd blown up Gray's house might have escaped by jumping off the cliff. He walked to the edge and peered down. Hell of a long dive, but probably easy for someone like Oliver Stone/John Carr.

Okay, he tosses his rifle into the water and jumps. Then where did he go?

He did not for a second believe that Stone had committed suicide. One did not plan hits so meticulously to merely end it all with a plunge off a cliff. He had lived. Knox was sure of that.

Carrying a knapsack over his shoulder, Knox walked along the cliff's edge, following on land what might have been Stone's journey in the water. He passed through woods, open fields, and then more woods, all the while keeping his eye on the shore below. Finally, he stopped. There was a bit of a beach down there. Stone had shot Gray before seven a.m. Knox had checked the tide charts. That time of morning would largely mirror the tide he was looking at right now. He eyed the boulders, then spotted the cleft in the rock, the trail coming up. He followed it to where it reached the top of the cliff. There was a path there. He took it. A half hour later he came to the series of shacks.

"Can I help you?"

Knox looked over at the short, squat man in the Green Bay Packers knit cap and greasy coat who was staring at him from beside an ancient tractor with one wheel off.

Knox approached. "I was over at Carter Gray's house." He held up his creds. "I'm Agent Knox."

"Good for you. They call me Leroy because that's my name. Gray, huh? The important fellow what got himself shot?"

"That's right. I take it someone's been by to see you."

"Hell, yeah. But like I told them, I don't know nuthin' 'bout nuthin'."

"You live here by yourself?"

"That's right, ever since my Lottie went to meet her Lord four years ago."

"Sorry to hear that. Nobody to help you around here? What is it that you do, by the way?"

"Anything I can to make a little money. Had me a helper but he went on."

"When was that?"

"Same day that man got shot."

Knox looked anxious but Leroy held up his hand. "Don't get yourself excited. He was here when them FBI folks come by. You can ask them. He's old, bum leg, bad eyes and feller couldn't even talk, just grunted."

"Tall, short? Fat, thin?"

"Skinny, though with the bad leg it was hard to tell how tall he was. Lot taller'n me, that's for sure. Big beard and thick glasses."

"Why'd he leave?"

"Who the hell knows? Been with me about four months. Then he just went moving on. It's not like I had him locked into no million-dollar long-term contract." Leroy laughed and shot a glob of spit at the ground.

Knox looked around. "Did he stay in one of those buildings?"

Leroy nodded and pointed at the one closest to the path.

"Mind if I take a look through it?"

"What agency you with again?"

"Federal."

"I know that. But which one?"

Knox held up his "public" creds close to the man's face. "*That* one."

Leroy took a step back. "Go on ahead then."

Knox inwardly smiled. That was at least one perk you got doing what he did. There weren't many others.

The search of the shack turned up only one significant fact. There wasn't a single fingerprint in the place and Knox had brought equipment with him that would show if there were. That alone told Knox that he was probably on the right track. Most people, including gimp-legged, nearly blind mutes, were not known to be so meticulous about wiping away such identifiers.

He left the shack and found Leroy puttering around.

Knox said, "I'm going to have an artist come up here and he's going to do a composite drawing based on your description of the guy."

"I'll do my best."

"I know you will."

22

The dinner was delicious, mostly fried and filling. Abby had cooked it herself and Stone had helped her serve it. It was only the two of them. He'd taken a shower in an upstairs bathroom decorated like something out of a design magazine. The coal company must've really paid through the nose.

"So you're a fan of Shakespeare?" Stone said.

"I read his plays in high school. I could never relate to them before."

"And now you can?"

"Maybe. He's got all of what life has to offer, especially the negatives, but I've lived the real thing too much to be impressed anymore by a fiction of it."

Danny came in halfway through the meal, took one look at Stone and his mother in the dining room with their linen napkins and fancy plates, and turned back around without a word. Then a door slammed. Loudly.

Stone glanced after him and then turned back to Abby. "I'm sure he keeps you busy."

"That's one way of putting it. You have children?"

"I did. She's not alive anymore."

"Sorry to hear that. Danny's used up about seven of his nine lives and I feel like he took mine right along with his."

"Were you against him going away? You said you cried a lot."

"What mother wouldn't with her only child saying good-bye?"

"Then you're glad he's back?"

"I wouldn't go that far. Besides, it's more likely than not that he'll be gone again before too many more suns come up. Won't break my heart again, at least I keep telling myself that."

"Has he left before?"

"Talked about it a lot, but never pulled the trigger. I guess I'd made up my mind it always would be talk. Then he threw me a curve." Her voice shook a little as she said this last part.

"Any particular reason he decided to do it this time?"

"It's hard to tell why Danny does anything. Bull-headed, just like his father."

"Danny said he died in the mines."

Abby took her time putting the last forkful of pie into her mouth. "He did. You said you lost a child. How about your wife?"

"Died too. Long time ago."

"What've you been doing with yourself since?"

"This and that. Never stayed in one place too long."

"Did you get out of the army right after Nam?"

"I hung around for a while. Nothing too exciting."

"No pension from Uncle Sam?"

"Didn't stay long enough."

Their conversation trailed off and a while later Stone took his leave, resisting her invitation to drive him back to town. There was sorrow in that house, despite the luxury and designer touches, for one simple reason: the source of the wealth was death.

"I guess you'll be heading on soon," she said as she stood by the front door.

"I'm a lot older than Danny and I still haven't made up my mind what to do with the rest of my life. So I think I better get to it."

"Thanks for helping my son."

"He seems like a good young man, Abby. Just needs a little direction."

"It would've been real good if the direction had taken him out of here and kept him there."

She closed the door, leaving Stone standing there puzzled. Telling himself again that this was not his business, he walked out to the road and made his way back to town. The sky was lit with stars, which was the only light there was. As he drew closer to town, he heard something. At first it seemed to be the moan of an animal and it occurred to him that in this part of the country it would not be unheard of to run into a black bear or maybe even a mountain lion. As he continued to walk along the moan became more recognizable.

Stone picked up his pace. The church and the graveyard were just ahead.

He cut across the road, entered the churchyard, made a beeline for the graveyard, and then stopped when he saw it. Or rather him.

The sobs racking him, Danny was lying sprawled on top of the fresh grave of Debby Randolph.

23

The tall man slipped inside the building, hung a left, grabbed an elevator, rode it down, entered the tunnel, skimmed along underneath the streets of Washington, D.C., arrived at another building and turned down a long hall. When he passed one door, it opened and a big hand grabbed him and yanked him inside, slamming the door behind him.

Reuben Rhodes let Alex Ford go. The agent smoothed down his jacket collar and turned to scowl at the others there arranged on busted-up government-issued furniture and packing crates.

"You said the second door on the *left*," Alex snapped.

"Brother Caleb got it wrong," Reuben said. "He meant the first door on the right and we didn't want to call you on your cell in case they put a trace on it."

"They need a court order for that," Annabelle said.

"Like hell they do," Reuben shot back.

Alex looked at Annabelle. "He's actually right about that. As a federal agent my life and cell phone are not my own."

"Sorry about the mix-up, Alex," Caleb said shamefacedly. "I was a little nervous. I'm not really sure why, though." He glared furiously at Reuben. "Oh, now I remember. It was when Reuben called and screamed that I had to find a place for us to meet ASAP or we were all going to die and it would be my fault!"

Reuben shrugged. "I didn't say die. I said we were all going to go to prison for the rest of our lives. And I just said it would be *mostly* your fault."

"How do you figure that?" asked Annabelle.

"This Joe Knox character already met with Caleb."

"So? How do you know I told him anything?"

"Caleb, you'd spill your guts if a Girl Scout got the drop on you."

Annabelle stood. "Okay, we don't have much time. It seems Knox has grilled me, Alex and Caleb."

"And I know he went to the loading dock, but luckily I took a few days off," Reuben added.

"Reuben, I understand that Oliver called you," said Alex. "Did he tell you where he was?"

"He wouldn't tell me where he was calling from." Reuben went on to tell them about his conversation with Stone. "And he did want me to tell you that he appreciated your burning the letter."

Alex nodded slowly but said nothing.

Caleb said, "Is there any way to trace the call he made to Reuben?"

Reuben shook his head. "I sort of have an unusual cell phone arrangement. A little convoluted."

"You mean you steal other people's minutes," declared Caleb.

"Anyway, I had a buddy I trust try and do it for me. He's a real pro with that stuff and it went nowhere."

"Well, let's compare notes on what Knox said and see where we stand," Annabelle suggested.

Alex went first, followed by Annabelle and then Caleb. When they'd finished, Reuben said, "Caleb, I apologize. It looks like you stood your ground pretty well."

"Apology accepted," snapped the federal librarian.

Alex said, "Okay, Knox knows Oliver is John Carr. He knows what he did at CIA. He knows that he killed Simpson and Gray. And he wants him badly."

"And he thinks we can lead him right to Oliver," Caleb replied. "But we can't. Thank God."

"Don't be thanking God yet, Caleb. He knows where we are and our connection to Oliver. They'll use that."

"How?"

Annabelle answered. "Leverage. To reel Oliver in."

Caleb exclaimed, "What do you mean? Use us as bait? That's preposterous. We are United States citizens. Knox is a public servant."

"That line didn't even work in the fifties," said Alex. "He's a public servant with a job to do. Nail Oliver. And while he's on the run, we're left as targets."

"So should we all go into hiding?" Annabelle asked.

Alex said, "That's pretty much impossible for me to do. But Annabelle, you definitely should dig a deep hole and get in it. Reuben too. Caleb, how about you?"

"Why would Oliver have left us in this impossible situation?" Caleb groused.

"He didn't have much choice," Reuben answered. "If we're right, he popped two giant VIPs on the same day. You don't go have coffee after that and wait for the SWAT team to tap on your door with a battering ram."

Caleb shook his head. "Even if Oliver did kill them—and despite the letter he left behind, I bet he didn't leave any evidence for them to find."

"Damn it, what point aren't you getting, Caleb?" Reuben exclaimed. "These guys don't care about prosecuting his ass. They just want him. They'll squeeze whatever useful information he has out of him and then put a round in his brain. He was a former government hit man who had to go on the run because Gray and Simpson screwed him over and tried to kill him." Reuben said this last part while staring at Alex. "Oliver's been on the run for thirty years. And then they killed Milton. And don't forget, Harry Finn told us that Simpson admitted that he was the one who ordered the hit on Oliver and his family way back when. If ever a man had a reason to kill somebody it's Oliver, to hell with what the law says."

"So they might be afraid of what Oliver might know about past government missions," Caleb said. "And they'd want to silence him?"

"Now you're thinking like a librarian," noted Reuben wryly.

Annabelle said, "But there might be another way, I mean instead of us going underground."

Alex leaned against the wall. "What do you have in mind?"

"We find Oliver and help him really get away."

"Forget it, Annabelle. We'd be leading these guys right to him," protested Alex.

"And besides," added Reuben, "I'm sure Oliver had a nifty escape plan."

"Really? No ID. No money. I gave him a credit card. I checked on it. It hasn't been used in months. He can't get on a plane. He can only run so far."

"Before they catch him," said Reuben quietly.

"Maybe that's what he wants," stated Alex. The other three stared at him. "He got Simpson and Gray. He felt terrible guilt for Milton. He may feel he has nothing else to live for. He runs, but not that hard. He knows they'll catch up to him and he's prepared for what that means."

Annabelle said, "I'm not going to let his life end that way."

"Annabelle, stonewalling the CIA is one thing, but you get mixed up in actively helping Oliver elude the authorities then you're looking at prison time too. A big chunk of it."

"I don't care, Alex. Look what he did for me. He risked everything to help me."

"He's done that for all of us," added Reuben.

"You wouldn't be here either, Alex," Annabelle said, eyeing the man. "Except for Oliver."

Alex sat down on an old desk. "Guys, I hear you, but I'm a federal agent. I can only go so far."

"We don't want to get you in trouble, so you don't have to do anything," said Annabelle, though her tone was less gracious than her words.

"Except look the other way," added Reuben.

"How would you even go about finding him?" said Alex.

"That's for *us* to figure out," said Reuben coldly. He glanced over at Caleb. "You're a *federal* employee too, but are you in?"

Caleb nodded. "I'm in."

Alex, his features grim, rose. "Well, I guess this is where we part company. Good luck."

"Alex—" Annabelle began, but the door had already closed behind him.

The three remaining members of the Camel Club simply looked at each other.

"Screw him," exclaimed Reuben. "So how do we find Oliver?"

She gazed at him. "The fox is on the hunt, right?"

"Right. So?"

"So we follow the fox."

"You have a plan?"

"I always have a plan."

"Annabelle, girl, I love you."

24

Stone was about to approach Danny Riker when someone else appeared from the other side of the graveyard. Stone shrank down behind the stone wall as the man stepped clear of the shadows and into the moonlight. At first, Stone thought the big fellow was going to attack Danny, so stealthy was his approach. Indeed, Stone was preparing to spring out when the other man gently touched Danny on the shoulder.

"Come on, boy, no good you being here."

Danny looked up into the face of Sheriff Tyree, who bent down to help him up.

"Not right. Ain't right," Danny sputtered, as he leaned against the large frame of the lawman.

"A lot in life isn't fair, Danny. But you can't let it eat you up, boy."

"I want to die."

Tyree slapped Danny across the face. "Don't let me never hear you say that again, Danny. The girl's dead. Nothing you can do will bring her back."

He pointed at the dirt. "You call that fair?"

"You get your head on straight. She had a choice. She killed herself. This ain't doing nobody any good. Now you want me to give you a ride home?"

Danny wiped his face and shook his head. "You're a stupid man if you think that," he snapped.

Tyree studied him. "You know something I don't?"

"I know lots you don't. So what? Ain't worth shit what I know."

"I mean about Debby?"

Danny dropped his head and his defiant tone. "No. I don't know nothing. Just talking is all. Talking and saying nothing, really."

"You said I was stupid if I believed that. What, that she killed herself?"

"You putting words in my mouth now, Sheriff," Danny said, his face whitening a bit.

"I just want to hear what you have to say."

In response, Danny turned and walked off.

"Danny, you come back here."

"Stop yelling, Sheriff, you'll wake the dead."

"Right now, boy."

"I'm not a boy, Tyree, in case you hadn't noticed." Danny turned to look at him. "And unless you want to put a bullet in my back, I'm going home."

Tyree laid a hand on top of his pistol as Stone stooped as low as he could. He didn't want to give either man a chance to spot him.

He waited for Danny to disappear down the road

and then watched as Tyree stalked back to his patrol car parked nearby and drove back toward town.

Should I just leave now? Why wait until morning?

Yet Stone walked to town and got a room at the tiny house Danny had recommended. He climbed the stairs, put his bag away and sat on the soft bed and stared out the window toward the main street of Divine.

What he'd seen at the graveyard had puzzled him. Had Danny been in love with Debby Randolph? Had she killed herself? Why had Danny left and then come back?

"It's not my problem," Stone finally said aloud, surprising himself with the force of the words. He checked his watch. It was nearly ten o'clock. He had a small transistor radio in his bag. He pulled it out and turned it on. It took some twisting of the tuner knob, but he finally found a station that had a national news roundup program at the top of the hour. He sat back on his bed. The murders weren't the lead story, but they were a close second to another salmonella outbreak in some vegetables.

The announcer's voice seemed breathless as he recounted the latest on the high-level D.C. killings.

"The FBI and Homeland Security have combined their efforts in this investigation. The murders of Senator Roger Simpson and intelligence head Carter Gray are definitely connected and are apparently tied to events from decades ago when both men worked at the CIA. The killer is reportedly a former colleague of the two men and was believed to have died years ago. Authorities are watching all airports, train and bus stations and border crossings. We will bring you more developments as they break in what is shaping up to be the manhunt of the decade."

Stone turned off the radio, rose and stared out the window once more. They hadn't announced the name of the killer, but they might as well have.

They know it was John Carr and they know what I look like and they have every escape route bottled up.

He had never really dwelled on his eventual capture. He even imagined that he might make it to New Orleans, start a new life and live out the rest of his years in peaceful obscurity. But that was apparently not to be. The one thing that bothered him was that everyone would believe him to be a criminal. Was revenge always wrong? Was righting an injustice outside the law never condonable? He knew the answer to those questions. He would never have the luxury of facing a judge and jury. They would never let him because then he could tell his side of the story. No, that could never be allowed.

Stone put on his jacket. He needed air. He needed to think. Could he even leave Divine now? He should call Reuben, but he would have to wait until tomorrow. Now he just wanted to walk in the darkness and peace of Divine. And think.

He reached the main street, turned right and

walked at a brisk pace. He soon left the little downtown area behind. The trees grew thicker and the lights of the small houses that dotted the perimeter of Divine finally disappeared.

Five minutes later Stone had decided to turn back when the scream reached him. It was from up ahead. It was a man. And he sounded beyond terrified.

Stone started to run.

25

After leaving Leroy's place in Maryland Knox did not drive home. One question had been bothering him so badly that he had to have an answer. He headed not for Langley, but for a nondescript building in the heart of Washington. He'd called ahead and was admitted without issue, what with his military background and government credentials.

He entered a vast room filled with long, scarred tables where gray-haired men, probably grizzled vets of past wars, along with some bow-tied historians, sat reading through piles of yellowed documents. It was windowless and seemed nearly airless as well. As Knox looked around, the one emotion he sensed was misery. This place contained the recorded and too brief lives and violent deaths of far more people than one would ever want to think about.

The main collection center for U.S. Army records was in St. Louis. Unless you were next of kin, to get access to an enlisted person's complete service record there required either that person's permission or a court order. However, Knox had learned something unknown to most people: The St. Louis facility didn't have *all* the records. There were some in D.C.—and, indeed, copies of some of the ones housed in St. Louis. And they weren't simply records of enlisted personnel. Here were housed documents chronicling America's wars. That was why many historians came here to do research, many with FOIA requests in hand, since the military only reluctantly revealed anything about itself.

Many of the records he wanted to look at had not been computerized yet, but some had. Still, after Knox showed his creds, the attendant was able to pull the boxes he wanted very quickly and showed him how to access the computerized files. His butt parked in front of a PC, Knox started with the digital ones first, flicking from screen to screen. He had a hunch and he wanted to see if it was true. What had been bugging him was why Macklin Hayes would want to get to John Carr so badly. If Carr had killed Simpson and Gray, he was now on the run. He was not going to hold a press conference and start blabbing about secrets from the past. Knox could understand Hayes wanting him to nail Carr before the police did. If the cops caught up to Carr he might start talking in exchange for a deal. But Hayes had also said that the cops had been put on a short leash on this investigation, giving Knox, in essence, a clear field in which to operate. And even if the police somehow got to Carr first, the CIA could, like Hayes had said, just swoop in and take him away under cover of national security interests. Carr would never even reach a press conference or make a phone call to his lawyer.

So why the all-out necessity to get this guy? Aside from the moral issue of letting a killer escape justice, in some ways letting him go away and die peacefully made the most sense strategically. The bottom line was, Hayes was acting somewhat irrationally and he was not an irrational man. There had to be another reason.

Knox stared at the screen, reading the military records of the men and women who had served in Vietnam. He exhausted the digital trail and had to resort to the boxes after consulting with another attendant who helped him narrow his area of search. He went through thirty of the boxes without success. He was about to call it a day when his hand gripped a sheaf of papers, the top page getting his immediate attention.

As Knox leaned forward, the rest of the room seemed to slowly disappear around him. He was reading the official history of a soldier named John Carr, an enlisted man who'd quickly risen to the rank of sergeant. The account Knox was enthralled with was Carr's heroic actions during one five-hour period nearly forty years ago.

Outnumbered dozens to one, Carr had almost single-handedly turned back an attack by the enemy, saving his company and carrying several of his wounded comrades to safety on his back. He'd killed at least ten enemy soldiers, several in hand-to-hand fighting. Then he'd manned a machine-gun nest to hold back the North Vietnamese while mortar and rifle rounds hit all around him. He'd left that post to radio in air support to allow his men to retreat safely. Only then had he walked off the battlefield drenched in his own blood and permanently scarred by bullet and machete wounds. Knox had experienced combat in those jungles and knew the confusion and horror that such confrontations almost always held. He'd been wounded. He'd been scarred. He'd been routed in action thinking this was surely his last day on earth. And he'd been part of successful attacks in the last days of America's participation in that war in South-east Asia, although by that time little victories in the field meant nothing. If they ever did.

Yet Knox had never read or heard of any soldier doing what Carr had done that day. It was beyond miraculous. It was beyond human, in fact. His respect, along with his fear of the man, notched upward even more.

With such heroism there must've been reward. The military was often slow in many ways, but it was quick at awarding bravery and selflessness in the field if for no other reason than to inspire other soldiers. And such accounts also made for great PR. The extraordinary heroism and extreme gallantry Carr had demonstrated that day not only *easily* qualified him for the Distinguished Service Cross, the second highest award the army could bestow, but, in Knox's judgment, it should have earned him the country's highest award for military heroism, the Medal of Honor. John Carr a Medal of Honor winner? Hayes had not mentioned any of that in his briefing. Nor had that piece of background made its way into press accounts when the man's grave had been dug up at Arlington.

Knox flipped through page after page and explored several more boxes before he was able to piece the story together.

Carr's Purple Hearts could not be denied him because the wounds alone were proof enough. All told, he received four of them, counting injuries received in other battles. Then there had been talk of awarding him a Bronze Star, but the date of this document was long after the fact of Carr's miraculous actions in the field. And the Bronze Star—while certainly prestigious—didn't come close to recognizing what the man had done, Knox felt. The Bronze was a bit of a hybrid in Knox's mind. It could be given out for bravery in battle with a Valor device attached, but also for acts of merit or meritorious service. The Silver Star, Distinguished Service Cross, and Medal of Honor, the acknowledged triumvirate of recognition for the fighting soldier, were for bravery and heroism *in combat*, pure and simple.

He finally found a sheaf of documents showing

that Carr's immediate superior *had* recommended Stone for the Medal of Honor. The man had filled out all the requisite documents and assembled all the required proofs and eyewitness accounts. He'd then sent it up the chain of command. The date on the documents showed it to be shortly after Carr's actions in the field, long before the documents talking about awarding him the Bronze Star. What the hell was going on?

And nothing had happened. It apparently had stalled out at that point. Knox could find no other documents that touched on it. But why? It was a perfect story. The man was a hero. Instead Carr had disappeared from the ranks shortly thereafter. Knox thought he knew why. That's when he'd been enlisted by the CIA for its Triple Six Division. The spooks, Knox was aware, often trolled for their assassins in the ranks of the military's best.

He put the documents back in the box. And that's when he noticed it. Two pieces of paper stapled together that had slid down in between the interior flap of the box and the exterior cardboard wall. Knox almost didn't read it, so disgusted was he at the military's injustice to a man who should have been one of the most legendary recipients of its highest award.

But Knox did reach for the papers.

It was an order, a simple one. It shut off any further consideration of John Carr receiving the Meals of Honor or any other commendation. As Knox read through the document it was filled with official mumbo jumbo about unreliable evidence and inconsistent eyewitness accounts and conflicting background documentation. It made no sense at all until Knox's gaze reached the signature line where the name of the officer appeared.

Major Macklin D. Hayes.

26

Knox slowly drove his Range Rover into the garage of his town house. Before he hit the button on his remote to close the door, he scanned the street in his rearview mirror. They were out there, he was pretty sure, watching him. Hayes typically covered all the bases.

The former general trusts me about as much as I trust him.

There might come a time when Knox would have to give those boys the slip, and when and if the time came, he hoped he was up for the challenge.

It might seem bizarre to ordinary citizens that a government agent like Knox would be nearly as fearful of his employer as he was his quarry. Yet Knox was only called in when things had gone to hell and people were already pointing fingers at each other and essentially building their "blame" strategies. He sometimes compared his job to that of an internal affairs officer in a police department. No matter what you did, someone was going to be pissed at you. And being pissed off and taking somebody's life as payback did not require a great leap of thought. Sometimes, it simply needed a walk across the street, a decisive trigger pull and a good cover strategy.

And from what Knox had learned about John Carr's military past, Hayes was definitely playing his own agenda on this one. He had clearly lied to Knox already. He'd commented on what an honor it would have been to command a killing machine like Carr. Well, the man *had* commanded him. In his murderous prime. And denied him the honor that was surely his. What had Carr done to tick the man off? Hayes was known to hold grudges for decades, and it seemed like that reputation was proving true here.

Knox had spent several more hours in the records room trying to find an answer to that question, but had come away with nothing more than speculation.

The dark thoughts going through his mind right now were nearly as numbing as what he'd experienced in his last nights in a Vietnam jungle before his country had called it a war and gone home. Knox's battalion had been one of the last to be sent to Southeast Asia. He'd been there all of eleven months and it had felt like eleven years. When he'd gotten back with a piece of shrapnel in his left thigh and a truck load of recurring nightmares as reminders of his time there, he'd decided that war was not a particularly smart way to decide global issues, especially when politicians rather than the grunts on the ground were calling the shots. That's when he'd worked his way to the Defense Intelligence Agency and from there to the civilian side and CIA.

Now his official home was a specialized piece of that agency that John Q. Public had never heard of and never would. He had two sets of creds: one for the public that showed him to be with Homeland Security and was suitably intimidating; and another set that he showed only to certain fellow federal agents. That evidenced his association with OSM, the Office of Special Matters. It was made up of personnel from five of the major intelligence agencies, though it was controlled by a handful of folks at Langley. "Office of Special Matters" sounded a little hokey, Knox thought, but what they did was far from it. Knox had been up to his ass in "special matters" for years, often handling six crises of international melt-down range at once.

In fact he'd been involved in every major op OSM had been handed over the last decade, including some paramilitary action that had gotten him back into the field with a gun and lives to take care of, and others simply to take. He'd narrowly avoided the "WMDs that never were" fiasco and then had spent six years in the Middle East doing things he would never write down and had done his best to forget about since.

He'd been thousands of miles away when his wife had died from a brain hemorrhage. He got back just in time for the funeral to say a hurried, mumbled good-bye to his life partner, the only woman he'd ever loved. To this day he felt like he had cheated her.

Twenty-four hours after burying her, he was back in Iraq trying to figure out where the next suicide blast was coming from and paying yesterday's enemies with good American cash so they'd kill extremists instead of U.S. troops. When the money eventually ran out Knox knew he didn't want to be within five time zones of the place. Then he'd gone back to his safe room in the Green Zone and wept for the love of his life in the privacy of his own nightmares.

It had been more than a challenge and in the last year Knox had seriously contemplated retirement after talking his way out of the Middle East where no Muslim trusted anyone with light skin who held a firm belief in the supreme holiness of the Lord Jesus Christ. He'd pulled enough time. He could go out on his terms. He was actually on a short sabbatical when Hayes had called. And now look at him. And the same old question had raised its ugly head once more:

Will the sun come up for me tomorrow?

He walked into his kitchen, tossed his keys on the counter, opened the fridge and popped a beer. He sat down in his small study and considered what he did and didn't know, the latter unfortunately being far more voluminous than the former. He slipped the pages from his pocket. He'd taken the two-page order with Macklin Hayes' signature on it. It was probably a felony stealing government property but Knox really didn't care at this point. He looked at the precise signature of the man.

What were you thinking when you signed that order, General?

He now had a connection between Hayes and Carr. That changed the dynamic of his mission, Knox just wasn't sure how. Yet it did explain one thing.

He was told he'd been ordered to track down Carr because the former Triple Six held secrets that would embarrass the U.S. government, or at the very least the CIA. Sometimes, for Knox, it was hard to tell the two apart. Hayes had said that Carter Gray had been concerned about that too. And that he'd been after Carr, but Carr had evidently gotten to him first.

That's what hadn't made sense. Carr had *been* at Gray's house the night it was blown up. So he'd evidently already known where Carr was. And on top of that Carr hadn't opened his mouth these last thirty years. So why would Gray or Hayes and the CIA be worried that the man was going to open it now?

Perhaps Gray had been after Carr for some reason, but not to kill the man. Ordering his grave to be dug up? Was he trying to flush him out, make him run? But why? Knox had a hunch the answer lay in the area he was prohibited from looking into. But he'd been "ordered" from doing things before. And he'd still gone ahead and done them.

And Hayes too had some strong reason for getting Carr out of the way. He must've thought Carr was dead all these years. Reading the man's face, Knox could tell he'd been out of the loop when the grave was dug up. And then to have no body in the coffin? All these years Hayes had probably felt safe. Now he didn't, and he was using Knox to take care of the problem for him.

And what exactly had happened at the Capitol Visitor Center? Had Carr really killed all those men? If so, why? Were they trying to kill him? Knox thought back to the notes he'd read about someone dispatching retired Triple Sixes. Had Stone been on that list? Had they gone after him for some reason? That was part of the puzzle that he apparently was not going to be allowed access to. Well, he would see about that.

If Carr had something on Hayes? Something personal? Now, that might be an interesting line to hunt down, if only to cover his backside when the time came. But he'd have to straddle the fence. If Hayes found out—

He'd turned the radio on in his study while he'd been thinking, and the news story caught his attention. Authorities knew who the killer was. They were closing in. All escape routes blocked.

What the hell?

He made the call. Hayes picked up on the second ring.

"I just heard the news," Knox said. "I thought the feds were being left off this one. If I've got an FBI posse breathing down my neck I'd like to know it."

"Not to worry, Knox, I had that story planted. It would be inconceivable for a man like Carr not to be listening to the news carefully. I want him to think he's trapped. Trapped men do stupid things. Then we move in. Just making your job easier."

Hayes clicked off.

"My ass you are," Knox said to the dead line.

The buzzing phone cut off his thoughts on what Hayes had just told him. He didn't recognize the number.

"Hello?"

"Mr. Knox, this is Susan Hunter. I'd like to meet with you, about Oliver."

Knox sat up. "Can we do it over the phone?"

"No. You never know who might be listening."

He couldn't argue with her about that. Someone probably was listening.

"Fair enough. When do you want to do it?"

"Right now."

27

Annabelle was standing on the street corner in Georgetown when Knox pulled up thirty minutes later. He popped open the passenger door and she climbed in. He drove off, heading east toward the downtown area.

Knox glanced at her. The woman's face was flushed, her eyes red. He couldn't know it was from a little rouge and a little eye irritant deliberately applied.

"You okay?" he finally said.

She wiped her eyes. "Not really."

"So let's talk about it."

"I don't want to get in trouble."

"I don't want that either."

"Yeah, but can you guarantee it?"

"If you've done nothing wrong, I can. And even if you have screwed up, depending on what you tell me, you might very well get a walk."

Annabelle started twisting her fingers. "It's complicated."

"Trust me, my job never involves anything remotely simple."

"What exactly is your job?" she said bluntly.

He pulled over and parked on the street and turned off the truck. "Let's get one thing straight. This is not an information exchange. You talk, I listen. If it's good, I help you. If you're screwing me over, well, just don't."

She drew a long breath and plunged in. "Oliver was very secretive. Nobody really knew anything concrete about his past. But we could all tell he was special, different. You probably saw the books in his cottage. He spoke different languages. He just carried himself in a different way.."

"His past I'm reasonably well-informed on. It's his current location that I'm most interested in."

"I don't know that."

"So why'd you call me?"

"Oliver had some information on Carter Gray. That was why Gray resigned when he did."

"What kind of information?"

Annabelle shook her head. "He never said, but he visited Gray and the next day Gray resigned, so it must've been pretty incriminating."

"But then Gray got his old position back."

"That's because he got the evidence that Oliver had back."

"The Capitol Visitor Center?" Knox said sharply.

"I think so. It wasn't like I was there. It's just something Oliver said right before he vanished."

"What else did he say?"

"That it's better no one ever finds out the real truth. That it could hurt this country and he would never want that."

Knox smiled. "You'd make a great witness for the defense."

"Do you know about his military service?"

"Guy was a helluva soldier. So what about Senator Simpson? What's the connection there?"

"Oliver said he worked for the CIA before he got into politics."

"That's right, he did. So Oliver knew him back then?"

"I guess. If he did work for the CIA, I mean. I have no proof that Oliver ever did."

"Let me worry about the proof. Does the term Triple Six mean anything to you?"

"I heard Oliver mention it once, but he never explained what it was."

"I bet he didn't."

"He was a good man. He helped break up a spy ring. He got a commendation letter from the FBI director."

"Good for him. So why do you think he killed Gray and Simpson?"

"I have no reason to believe that he did."

"Come on, Susan, or whatever your real name is, you're obviously not stupid. You know Carr and Stone are the same person. He's been hiding out for thirty years."

"If that's so, why do you think he's been hiding out?"

"You tell me."

"Maybe people were after him."

"What people?"

"People looking to kill him, I think."

"Is that what he said?"

"He told me once that with some agencies, even if you want to leave, they won't let you. They'd rather you'd be dead than not working for them."

This remark hit Knox like a hard slap but he didn't show it. *That one I can believe.*

"So let's assume for the moment he was a Triple Six who wanted out. They didn't want him to leave?"

"I know he was married and had a daughter. But he said they were both dead now."

Knox sat back against the seat, his fingers still gripping the steering wheel. "Suggesting that whoever was after him killed them?"

"I don't know. Maybe."

Knox let go of the steering wheel and stared out at the traffic whipping by down Pennsylvania Avenue. His thoughts turned momentarily to his own son and daughter. Maybe his son was safer in Iraq than his daughter was in Washington. *That* was a brutally numbing thought.

"Do you have a family?" she asked.

Knox snapped back. "What else can you tell me?

His last few days with you? Anything that might show where he went?"

"If he did kill Gray and Simpson they probably deserved it."

"That's not what I asked, and, by the way, talk like that could wind you up in jail."

"I owe Oliver my life."

"That's you, not me."

"So when you find him are you going to kill him?"

"I work for the federal government. I'm not a hired killer."

"So you're telling me that if you do catch him he'll end up being tried, in a court of law?"

Knox hesitated. "That's not my call. A lot of it depends on him."

"Yeah, I thought that might be what you'd say."

"We're talking about a killer, Ms. Hunter."

"No, we're talking about my friend who was pushed past all human limits."

"You know that to be a fact?"

"I know him. That's how he's built. Was he capable of violence, of killing? Sure. Was he a cold-blooded killer? No."

"I have information that says otherwise."

"Then your information is wrong."

"What makes you so sure?"

"My gut."

"Your gut? That's it?"

"Yeah, the same gut that's telling me you really

don't want any part of this job. I'm betting you have a family and a dream of being retired. But you got called into this shit and now you don't know which side is playing you for a fool."

It was a testament to Knox's iron-hard nerves that he didn't even blink in the face of this spot-on observation.

"Unless you have anything to add, I'll drop you back off."

"So am I in trouble?"

"You'll be the first to know."

Back in Georgetown she climbed out of the Rover. Before she closed the door he said, "With something like this, Ms. Hunter, everybody needs to watch his back."

He drove off.

Annabelle pulled her coat tighter around her and watched, stone-faced, as Reuben's truck edged past her and took up the tail on Joe Knox.

The fox had now become the hunted.

A minute later an ancient Chevy with a stuttering tailpipe stopped at the curb, Caleb at the wheel. Annabelle climbed in and they drove off in the opposite direction.

Annabelle glanced at Caleb and he looked at her.

"We're being followed too, you know," Annabelle said.

"Story of my life," Caleb replied without a trace of a whine.

28

Stone hustled down a clay-packed path, really no more than two truck tire tracks wide, as he followed the cries. From out of the darkness loomed a long shape. The double-wide trailer was no longer "mobile" since it had a cinderblock undercarriage. The hulks of old cars and trucks, like the skeletons from faded battlefields, flew past as Stone hurried to the trailer. It had long strips of vinyl siding dangling off and the front steps were blackened railroad ties nailed together. Stone went from the bottom to the top step in one leap as the screams picked up.

The door was locked. He pounded on it.

"Hello, what's going on? Do you need help?" He suddenly wondered if the frantic calls were coming from a TV set turned up far too loud.

A moment later the door was thrown open and an old man stood there, his body trembling as though he was in the throes of a Parkinson's meltdown.

"What's going on?" Stone exclaimed.

The next moment Stone was knocked aside as a young man burst past his trailer mate and sprang into the air, landing hard on the ground. Stone recovered his balance and stared after him.

Aside from the fellow's obvious agitation, he was remarkable for having no clothes on. He stopped next to one old wreck in the yard, moaned and fell to the ground, writhing in the dirt like he was being Tasered.

The old man grabbed Stone's arm.

"Help him, please!"

"What's wrong with him?"

"He's got the DTs. Coming off the pills or something. Went crazy. Ripped off his clothes. Tearing up the place."

Stone raced to the fallen man's side. His breathing was shallow, his eyes unfocused. His skin was cold and clammy.

Stone yelled over his shoulder, "Call the ambulance."

"Ain't none up here."

"Where's the hospital?"

"Hour drive."

"Is there a doctor around?" Stone was holding on to the stricken man, trying to calm him.

"Doc Warner's place is on the other side of town."

"You have a car?"

"Truck right there." The old man pointed to a battered old Dodge. "Is he going to be okay?"

"I don't know. Who are you?"

"His grandpa. Come to check on him. Then this happened."

"Can you help me get him in the truck?"

Together they lifted the young man into the cab and Stone covered him with a blanket. The old man was still shaking so badly he couldn't drive. Stone took the wheel and followed his directions to the doctor's place.

"What's your grandson's name?"

"Willie Coombs. I'm Bob Coombs."

"Where are his parents?"

"My son—his daddy—is dead. His momma ain't much good."

Stone glanced at Willie. He'd stopped thrashing and screaming and was now lying quite still. Stone again checked his pulse, slammed on the brakes and grabbed a flashlight off the dash to look at his pupils. They were pinpoints.

"Shit!"

"What is it?"

"He's not in withdrawal. He overdosed. And his heart's stopped."

Stone pulled Willie out of the cab, set him on the ground and started doing CPR. He checked his pulse and then looked desperately around while he continued to push down on the man's chest. There was nothing but woods here, not even the wink of a house light in the distance.

"Come on, Willie. Come on! Don't die on me. Breathe."

Stone checked his pulse.

Bob Coombs looked at him. "Is he okay?"

"No, he's not. He's technically dead. And we've got maybe sixty seconds before there's brain damage."

Stone ran to the truck and threw open the hood. The battery didn't throw off the juice he would need, but something else in the engine did. He ran to the cargo bed and started tossing items around there. His hands seized around a set of battery cables, masking tape and a nail.

He turned to see Bob staring at him anxiously. "Whatcha gonna do with that stuff?"

"I'm trying to get his heart restarted."

Stone ripped out a spark plug wire leading from the distributor cap and jammed the nail in the end of it, securing it there with the tape. He attached the positive end of the battery cables to the nail while he grounded the negative clamp onto a metal part of the engine. He knelt next to Willie and placed the other ends of the battery cables onto his right and left fingers respectively.

He called out, "Bob, fire the truck up!"

Bob looked at the cables leading from the truck to his grandson. "You gonna fry him!"

"We're out of time, Bob. This is our only shot. Just do it! Now! Or he's dead."

Bob jumped in the truck.

Stone looked down at Willie, reached over and made sure the connections were solid. The young man was already turning blue. They only had seconds left.

Stone had done this once in Nam with a fellow soldier who'd gone into cardiac arrest when a massive round had sheared a chunk of his torso off. Stone had gotten his heart going again, but the man had bled to death on the way to the field hospital.

The truck started.

"Rev the engine," Stone screamed out.

Bob smashed the gas to the floor and the engine roared.

Even though he wasn't touching Willie, Stone could feel the surge of current. The effect on the young man was far more intense.

His legs and arms came off the ground and Willie sucked in an enormous breath. He sat up and then fell back, choking and coughing.

"Cut the engine," Stone yelled and Bob instantly did so. The only sound now was a miraculous one. A dead man was breathing.

Stone ripped the cables off and checked the pulse. Pretty strong and steady.

Bob and he lifted Willie into the truck. Stone put the spark plug wire minus the nail back in place, threw the battery cables in the back, and drove off. They made it to the doctor's home office five minutes later and carried him inside. Warner worked on

Willie after Stone told him what he'd done. Warner was not Stone's image of a rustic country doctor. He was barely forty, trim, with a clean-shaven face and wide, intelligent-looking eyes behind a pair of wire-rimmed glasses. He gave Willie an injection and made a phone call.

He said, "That injection should stabilize him for now. But can you get him to the hospital quick as you can? I called ahead and I'll follow in my car."

Stone nodded. "But if his heart stops again on the way? I don't want to rely on the truck's juice again."

Warner opened a cabinet and pulled out a portable defibrillator. "If it happens again, pull off the road and we'll use this."

As they were loading Willie back in the truck the doctor said, "You saved his life, you know."

Bob placed a hand on Stone's shoulder. "I can't thank you enough, Mr. . . . ?"

"Just call me Ben. And he's not out of the woods yet. Let's go."

They arrived at the hospital less than an hour later. Stone went in with them, but after Willie was checked in, he came back outside and leaned against the truck, sucking in the crisp, cool mountain air.

The hospital was big. It probably had to be since it was probably the only one for a few hundred square miles.

He walked around the parking lot trying to push back the adrenaline rush. He spotted the squat one-story cinderblock building next to the hospital and walked in that direction.

When he saw the sign on the building Stone realized this was the methadone clinic, where the truck parade came every morning. As he watched he noted the armed security guard patrolling in front of the building. When the man saw Stone standing there, Stone smiled and waved. The man neither smiled nor waved back. Instead he put a hand on his holstered gun. Stone turned and walked back to the hospital. He assumed the presence of the guard meant that the clinic was a target for either drug dealers or druggies. Stone knew that liquid methadone on its own couldn't deliver a high, that's why it was used to wean addicts off drugs. But when combined with other drugs, like anti-anxiety pills, it could produce an often deadly cocktail.

About an hour later Bob came back out and explained that Willie was out of danger and was being admitted.

"So what did they find out?" Stone asked.

"They said he overdosed on something."

"That I knew. You have any idea what?"

"The emergency room doctor asked that too. I saw a crack pipe in Willie's hand when I came in the trailer. He tried to hide it from me, but I still saw it."

Stone shook his head. "Crack's a stimulant. His eyes would've been dilated, not pinpoints. He overdosed, but on a depressant, not a stimulant."

"Well, I guess I could be wrong about what he took," Bob said hesitantly.

Stone looked at him curiously but the old man didn't seem inclined to add anything to what he'd already said. Stone drove Bob back to Willie's trailer where he'd left his truck. He tried to pay Stone for his help but Stone refused.

Bob dropped an exhausted Stone off at the rooming house. As Stone slowly walked up the stairs he figured that despite the massive manhunt after him he would have to get out of Divine pretty soon, just to get some rest.

29

By the next morning nearly everyone in Divine had heard of Stone's heroics. Apparently Bob Coombs had told everyone he encountered of the stunning rescue, and the story had quickly spread.

"Cool a hand as I ever seen," he repeated over and over, referring to Stone.

"Heard he was in Nam," another man said. "Good under pressure."

"A true American hero," said one lady. She added in a lower tone while talking with a girlfriend of hers, "Too bad it was wasted on Willie Coombs."

Sheriff Tyree came to Stone's room that morning to congratulate and thank him. "Willie's a good young man except for the pills."

"He's a coal miner, right?" said Stone.

"How'd you know?"

"Scars and banged-up hands. And he had coal dust embedded in his skin. Does his mother know?"

"Shirley? Doubt she'd care."

Stone chose not to ask about that. "Bob Coombs said his son, Willie's father, was dead."

"Yep. Hunting accident. Didn't have his orange slicker on and somebody thought he was a deer. Abby told me to tell you she's got some more work you can do. Same pay scale."

"I'll head over there right now." After the news on the radio last night he was even more uncomfortable being around the lawman.

When Stone arrived at Rita's Restaurant Abby had breakfast waiting for him. When he walked in customers smiled and waved at him. A few miners came over and clapped him on the back, thanking him for helping their fellow miner.

"How's it feel to be a hero?" Abby asked, pouring him a cup of coffee.

"I'm just glad he's okay. But he's got a long road ahead of him. Apparently he has a drug problem."

"Most miners do. Willie Coombs is actually a good young man. He and Danny played ball in high school together. Best of friends but then they had a falling-out."

"Over what?"

"When we were all poor, that was one thing. Then when we got the settlement money Willie seemed to think Danny owed him. We gave him some money, sure, but most of it went up his nose so we stopped."

A tall, thin man came over to them. He was the only man in the place dressed in a suit and tie. His gray hair was neatly parted and fashionably cut. His eyes were gray and alert and his face was deeply lined, carrying the gravitas one usually found in scholars.

Abby said, "Ben, this is Charlie Trimble. He runs the *Divine Eagle*, the local newspaper."

It was all Stone could do not to leap up and run out of the place.

A smiling Trimble said, "I would love to interview you about your experience with Willie, Ben. Not only because it's an amazing story but it shows why we need to reinstate the volunteer rescue squad program here."

Abby looked at Stone. "Is that okay?"

Stone said slowly, "What I did wasn't all that special. And I'm not looking to get any publicity just because I helped someone."

Trimble smiled more broadly. "And modest too. That will work well in the story angle. It's just a few questions, Ben. We can even do it here or back at my office."

Stone stood. "Abby, if you have some more work for me to do that would be great." He looked at Trimble. "I'm sorry, Mr. Trimble. I'm sure Bob would love to talk to you. He helped as much as I did. Maybe more."

Trimble looked put off. "Just a couple of questions?"

"No, I'm sorry."

Abby gave him a list of jobs to do while Trimble sat at his table, drinking a cup of coffee and staring at

Stone. And Stone could feel the burn of the man's gaze.

Stone worked half the day at the restaurant and the other half at Abby's home. And every minute he was desperately trying to think of some way out. If he left Divine he would probably be caught. If he stayed in Divine someone might put two and two together and one morning the feds would rumble into town. For one of the few times in his life, Stone did not know what to do.

On his way back to his rooming house that evening he saw Bob Coombs standing in front of it. The old man looked nervous, rocking back and forth on his heels, hands shoved in his pockets as he studied the pavement. Stone crossed the street.

"Hey, Bob, is Willie okay?"

Bob looked nervously around. "Can we talk somewhere private?"

Stone led him up to his room. "What's up?"

"Talked to Willie this morning and the docs over at the hospital and some things don't make sense."

"Like what?"

"It was sort of like you said. Drugs Willie said he took don't add up to what happened to him."

"Was it crack?"

"That's what Willie said he was on."

"He might have made a mistake."

Bob was shaking his head. "I know some folks

think Willie's nothing but a pillhead, but he's not. He's a smart boy but killing himself in the mines. Started there right out of high school and looks like he's been there thirty years, just the way it is. But if he said it was crack, it was crack, you can count on it."

Stone studied him, not really sure why the man was telling him this. "Well, if you think something's wrong, Bob, you should let Sheriff Tyree know."

"I was wondering, sort of, if you could maybe step in."

"Me? Step in what exactly?" Stone said cautiously.

"You saved Willie's life. Easy to see you been around, know stuff. I was just hoping maybe you could talk to Willie, get his side of things and see what you can find out."

"I'm not a PI."

"Lost my son, see. Willie's the only thing I got left. Can't lose him too. Well, that's all I got to say. If you go see Willie, I thank you. And if you don't I still thank you for all you done."

"Has that fellow Trimble from the paper been by to see you?"

"Yep. Had some questions. Told him what you did. He said he's writing up the story. Said you wouldn't talk to him."

"I'm not much into tooting my horn. Is he from Divine?"

"Oh, no, he retired here. Got a little place up near the river and then took over running the newspaper here."

"Was he into journalism before?"

"Oh, yeah."

"Where?"

"Somebody told me once. The *Washington Post.*"

Oh, shit.

"Look, Ben, I can pay you if you'd look into it."

"Bob, go see the sheriff. That's his job. Not mine."

"But—"

"I'm sorry, Bob. I can't."

30

Later, Stone walked to the craft shop and did something he really didn't want to, but he was out of options. He called Reuben.

"Oliver, tell me where you are," he said immediately.

"Just listen, Reuben. I need some information."

Another voice came on the line. It was Annabelle.

"Oliver, we want to help you. But you've got to tell us where you are."

"I'm not getting you involved in this, Annabelle. So stop trying to help me. I don't deserve it anyway."

"I don't care if you killed those men. What I care about is you."

Stone took a deep breath. "I appreciate that, Annabelle, I really do." Stone glanced up to see Wanda, the shopkeeper, eyeing him from across the room. He smiled and turned away from her.

"Oliver, are you there!"

"Look, it means a lot to me that you want to help,

it really does. But if I'm going to go down, it's going to be just me, not all of you."

"But—"

He cut her off. "If you really want to help me, put Reuben back on."

He could hear her accelerated breathing for a few seconds and then Reuben said, "What do you need?"

"Has Knox or anyone else been back?"

"No." Technically Reuben wasn't lying since Annabelle had gone to see Knox, not the other way around. In fact, they were parked out on Knox's street right now watching and waiting for the man's next move.

"The news said that they have all the airports, train and bus stations under watch."

"I heard that too."

"That's a lot of ground to cover, even for the FBI."

"They're working with Homeland Security on this, which has opened up all local resources as well. Lot of street cops out there looking."

"You said Knox knew it was John Carr, and that he and I were one and the same."

"That's right. Though nothing in the press has said anything about John Carr now being Oliver Stone."

"Have any photos of me been circulated?"

"Not to my knowledge. At least publicly. But who knows what's going on behind the scenes."

Stone leaned against the wall and studied a miniature black bear formed from a lump of coal. *Coal is king. Stone is dead.* "Any idea if they think I'm still in the area?"

"Are you?"

"Reuben!"

"Okay, slit my throat for caring. Nothing specific, but you can count on the fact that any place within a few hundred miles of D.C. will be under close watch."

Stone sighed. "Thanks for the info, Reuben. I hope I won't have to call you again."

"Oliver, wait—"

Stone hung up the phone and walked toward the front of the shop, managing a smile at Wanda as he passed her.

She said, "Heard about Willie. That sure was real smart of you."

"I'm just glad I could help."

"I told my husband about it. He was in the army. I told him I heard you were too. He wanted to know which part."

"The part that fought in Vietnam," Stone said as he closed the door behind him.

He went back to the rooming house and packed his few belongings. The bus ride to the vicinity of Divine had taken three hours from where they had gotten off the train. He remembered the general direction they'd come, but the corkscrew roads and hairpin curves were impossible to recall with any specificity. He thought back to the night he and Danny had come here via hog truck. He remembered the towers of Dead Rock prison. The main street of Divine. The warm bed above Rita's. The shotgun in his face the next morning. Abby Riker's scowl that had somehow turned to a smile.

He waited until it was well dark and then headed out of town. His route carried him past the road leading to Willie's place. A few minutes later he saw the burn of car headlights coming his way and he quickly stepped off the main road and onto the dirt one leading to Willie's trailer. He quickly retreated into some bushes lining the dirt drive as he waited for the car to pass. He only got a glimpse at the driver as it sped by and continued to watch as the car kept on going before it rounded a curve and its rear lights vanished.

Stone looked back at the main road and then glanced the other way. He was on his way again when yet another car came along the main drag, forcing him to scurry once more back down the road to Willie's place. He obviously hadn't waited until it was late enough. Right now, for him, every car could be a state trooper with his digital picture painted on the laptop computer in the cruiser.

He hustled down the dirt road and stopped. The car was parked in front of Willie's trailer and there was a light on inside. He glanced at the car; it was a small red two-door Infiniti. He looked inside. There was a purse on the front seat and the smell of cigarette smoke was heavy. He peered around at the trailer. The front screen door was partially open. He heard a small crash from inside.

He quickly moved up the steps and said, "You okay?"

"Who is it? Who's there?" It was a woman and her voice trembled.

She appeared at the door a moment later; a tall bleached blonde with a spare tire wedged into slim jeans and spiky heels. A cigarette dangled from her left hand. She looked to be in her late forties, although the amount of makeup she had on made it difficult to tell.

"I'm Ben, the man who helped Willie last night." Her features looked familiar. "Are you Willie's mom, Shirley Coombs?"

She took a drag on her cigarette and nodded absently, but the suspicious look only deepened. "How'd you know that?"

"You look like each other." Stone glanced over her shoulder into the trailer.

She followed his gaze and said hurriedly, "I came over to check on things when I heard 'bout Willie. Got folks round here that might take advantage of him being laid up in the hospital. Messing with his stuff and all."

It occurred to Stone that Mom might've been messing with her son's stuff too.

"Have you seen Willie yet?"

"Planning to get over there soon. Long drive. And my car's not too dependable."

Stone glanced back at her car. "Looks to be pretty new."

"Yeah, well, it's a piece of crap. Keeps stalling out on me."

"Everything look okay in there?" he asked.

"Willie's not the neatest person in town, so it's hard to tell, really. Looks okay, I guess."

"You need any help?"

"No," she said quickly, a beat too quickly actually. "I mean, you've helped enough. Willie would be dead except for you. I thank you for that."

"I'm glad I was around. But Bob helped with Willie too."

Her features turned dark. "Yeah, old Bob is real good about helping folks. At least ones he likes."

"He doesn't include you in that group?"

"You could say the whole town doesn't include me in that group."

Okay. "I was sorry to hear about your husband."

She stiffened. "Who told you about him? Bob?"

"No, Sheriff Tyree. He mentioned the hunting accident. Pretty tragic."

"Yeah, real tragic."

Stone looked at her quizzically. "I hope Willie will be okay," he said, after an awkward silence.

"Hell, he'll be fine. He's got four shotguns, a deer

rifle, two hunting bows, a pickup truck, his own double-wide, cable TV and propane to keep warm, a camp stove to cook on and folding money from the mine. What's not to come home to? My boy aimed high in life, didn't he?" She smiled. But then it quickly faded. "Look, I got to go," she said. "Thanks again for saving my baby."

She closed the door behind her and moved past Stone.

He watched as she got in her car and drove off.

He hoisted his bag and walked back to the main road.

Five minutes later the truck almost hit him as it flew by. He dodged out of the way, rolled and came up in time to see a man throw himself out of the truck cab and land hard in the road. Stone raced toward him and turned him over.

It was Danny. He was badly beaten but still breathing. And then Stone looked up. The truck had stopped. As he watched it turned and headed toward him, stopping a few feet from where he knelt next to Danny. Three men climbed out and each one carried a baseball bat.

31

Joe Knox sat in his town house having a cup of coffee and pondering his next move. The idiot Agency artist he'd requested to do a composite had gotten lost on the way to Leroy's place. And when he'd gotten there Leroy had gone off on his damn boat. Leroy didn't have a phone so the best Knox could do was send another agent up there to try and pin the man down. Until he had a picture to show around, Knox was at a standstill in his investigation. And if Leroy had been involved and was now on the run after Knox had conveniently warned him?

There will be no way to explain such a junior mistake to Hayes.

He decided to run through again what he'd learned at the military records center, in case it might suggest something. A half hour later he was no further along. Maybe he should go back to the records center and go through some more documents. The attendant had been able to easily find the other boxes for him. It probably wouldn't take—

Knox slowly set down his coffee cup. The next

moment he was racing to the phone. He got the number for the records center and punched it in. A minute later, after being forwarded along to several extensions, he heard the voice of the man who'd helped him before. Knox identified himself and then asked the question.

"How did you find what I wanted so easily? It was like the boxes were already out."

"Well, actually they were," the man replied a bit sheepishly. "I mean, they'd been checked out some months back. Maybe six months or so, and I'm a little embarrassed to say that no one had filed them away yet. And we've been a bit shorthanded as of late," he added quickly, as though suspecting that Knox might actually be some sort of military archives inspector trying to pull a slick one.

"So someone else was looking at those records?" Knox said slowly. "Can you tell me who?"

The man excused himself for a minute. When he came back on the line he said, "Guy named Harry Finn. Says here on the sign-in log he used to be with the Navy SEALs. He had the credentials and top secret clearances to get access to the boxes you looked at. That help you any?"

"That helps me a lot, thanks." Knox clicked off and spent the next hour tracking down Harry Finn, former SEAL.

An hour later he pulled his truck to a stop, got out, walked up to the steps and rang the doorbell. A few moments later it opened and he was staring across at a tall young man whose gaze burned back into his.

"Harry Finn?"

Finn didn't answer. His gaze instinctively checked behind Knox.

"I'm alone. Well, as alone as is probably possible on something like this."

"Something like what?"

"Can I come in?"

"Who in the hell are you?"

Knox flipped open his creds. "I'm here to talk about Oliver Stone. Or you might know him as John Carr."

"I've got nothing to say."

"I'm not sure why you were looking up the guy's military record, or whether you're his friend or not. But he's on the run and somebody's going to get to him at some point. And when they do." Knox simply shrugged.

Finn was about to say something when Knox's cell phone rang. He'd been half expecting it actually, even as he glanced over his shoulder and saw the black sedan parked down the road. His expert gaze, however, did not pick up the nondescript white van parked farther down. It was Macklin Hayes on the phone, and as usual he got right to the point.

"What the hell are you doing there, Knox?"

"Where?"

"Harry Finn is off-limits."

Knox backed down the steps and turned away from Finn. "Nobody told me that."

"I'm telling you now. How did you get on to him? Anything to do with your visit to the military records center?"

"And why do you find need to follow me, sir?" Knox turned and waved to the men in the black sedan.

"What did you find?"

"Not much. He fought in Vietnam. He was a good soldier. Then he just disappeared. Probably when he was recruited for"—Knox glanced at Finn and smiled—"for that thing that doesn't exist."

"You are to leave that house now and never go back."

The phone went dead. Knox put it back in his pocket and turned to Finn.

"You'll be happy to know that you're officially off-limits, or so my boss just told me. But just keep in mind that something really screwy is going on with Carr. I've already gabbed with his friends, including the lady who calls herself Susan Hunter. She told me Carr had the goods on Carter Gray but that Gray got it back probably at the Capitol Visitor Center. You probably already know that from your suitably blank expression. Maybe you were even there. All I can tell you is I've been assigned to track Carr down. That's all. But when I do track him down, and rest assured I will, other people will show up and take over. And I doubt they'll have his best interests at heart. Whether you give a shit or not, I don't know and really don't care."

He put out a hand for Finn to shake. When he did, Finn came away with a business card with Knox's contact information on it.

"You have a good day, Mr. Finn."

Knox walked back to his truck while Finn stared after him.

Knox didn't know exactly why he'd done that. Well, maybe he did. John Carr had gotten his ass shot up for his country and they'd screwed him. Whatever else the man had done, that just wasn't right.

In the white van, Annabelle punched in the number. A moment later Harry Finn answered. He relayed to her what Knox had told him and she in turn filled him in.

"Do we trust this guy, Annabelle?" Finn asked.

"I didn't at first, but now I'm not so sure. He seems to be caught right in the middle."

"So what do we do?"

"Sit tight. I may need your help later. Or more to the point, Oliver will."

"I owe Oliver everything. So I'll be there if you need me."

32

Stone rose, his right hand undoing his belt as he did so. He slipped it off and held it by the buckle. The silver pointed end dangled a few inches from the road.

The men circled him, holding their bats ready.

"Odds don't look too good for you, pops," said one of them.

An instant later he was on the ground, his face covered in blood from where the belt point had bitten into his eye.

As he writhed and screamed with his hands over his face, one of his buddies took a step toward Stone and swung his bat with all his strength. Stone ducked under the blow and snapped his belt against the side of the man's face, gouging it. The fellow yelled in fury and came at Stone again, his bat whipping back and forth. Stone dodged out of the way, but one of the wild blows caught him squarely on the arm. He dropped his belt, rolled and snatched up the fallen man's Louisville Slugger with his good arm. One smack to the man's knees brought him down; the second to the base of his neck kept him there.

The remaining attacker dropped his bat and ran. Stone turned and threw the bat he was holding. It whipsawed through the air and nailed the guy in the back. He screamed, dropped to the road, picked himself up and kept going. Stone started to go after him but stopped when Danny moaned. He raced back to his side even as the truck sped off.

"Danny, Danny, can you hear me? Can you get up?"

Stone looked around. One man unconscious. The other still rolling around on the ground. He was worried the third attacker would go get reinforcements. And his arm was killing him.

"Danny, can you walk?"

Danny finally focused on Stone and nodded. Stone heaved him to his feet, the pain shooting across his injured limb. He was still able to support Danny as they made their way down the road. They reached Willie's trailer. Stone loaded Danny into the truck and raced into the trailer. He found Willie's truck keys, ran back out, fired up the truck and pulled off.

He drove first to Doc Warner's office but no one was there. He changed direction and headed to the hospital.

Danny lay against him in the front seat. His face was bloody and one arm hung limp. "Hold on, Danny, we're going to the hospital."

Danny mumbled something.

"What?"

"Call my mom."

Stone watched as Danny slowly dug his hand in one pocket and drew out his phone. Steering with his knees, Stone flipped it open, found the number on the speed dial and hit the key.

It took a few rings but she finally answered. "Hello?"

"Abby, it's Ben. I've got Danny. He's been attacked by some guys with baseball bats. I'm taking him to the hospital. Meet us there."

To her credit the woman didn't scream or start crying. All she said was, "I'm on my way."

Less than an hour later Stone once more pulled into the hospital parking lot. He half carried Danny into the emergency room entrance. While they were working on him Abby screeched to a stop in the parking lot, jumped out of the Mini Cooper and rushed in. Stone met her at the door and took her to Danny, who was lying on a gurney in the triage room.

Tears gathered in the corners of her eyes as she held her son's hand. "Danny, what the hell happened? Who did this to you?"

He murmured, "Just an accident, Ma. Don't worry. I'll be good to go. Took better hits on Friday game nights."

Abby looked at Stone. "An accident?"

He shook his head.

The doctor said, "We need to get him admitted and have some tests run. He seems stable now, but he may have internal bleeding."

"Will he be okay?" Abby said anxiously.

"Ma'am, we need to run some tests. We'll take good care of him. And we'll let you know how he is."

A moment later they whisked him away.

Abby stood there, teetering a bit. Stone put an arm around her shoulders and led her to a chair in the waiting area.

"He said it was an accident."

"It was no accident. Three men. Big and mean with baseball bats."

"How do you know that?"

Stone didn't answer her immediately. Something had just occurred to him. One of the men he'd beaten up had looked familiar. He tried to think where he'd seen him, but couldn't place him.

"Ben?"

"What? Oh, because they came after me when they were done with Danny."

"How'd you get away?"

Stone touched his waistline. "It cost me my belt, but I hurt two of them pretty bad. One of them got away. I need to call Tyree and report it. Do you have his number?"

She handed him her phone and he made the call.

After he explained things to the sheriff and described the men and their truck, he nodded at something Tyree said. "Right, we'll be here," he replied.

Stone handed the phone back to Abby. "He's going to come here to get a statement after he checks out the crime scene."

"I can't believe this is happening." But there was a hollow ring to her words that puzzled Stone.

"When I called you didn't sound all that surprised that someone had attacked Danny."

She didn't look at him.

"Abby, I know I'm a stranger here, but I saw those guys up close and personal. If Danny hadn't managed to throw himself out of the truck, he'd be dead. And they might come back to finish the job."

She touched her eyes with one of her hands, brushing away the tears. "There's some things been going on in Divine. Strange things."

"Like what? Was that why Danny left? And now someone's upset he's back?"

"I don't know why he left. He wouldn't tell me."

"Abby, I saw Danny crying his heart out over the top of Debby Randolph's grave."

She looked at him strangely. "Debby Randolph?"

"Yes. Did he know her? Did he love her?"

"They dated a couple times in high school. But she was Willie's girl now."

"How did she die?"

"Committed suicide. With a shotgun in a little shed behind her parents' house."

"Why would she have killed herself?"

"I don't know. I guess she was depressed. Tyree's looking into it."

"But right after she died, Danny left Divine?" Abby balled a tissue between her fingers and nodded slowly. "Did he ever mention Debby to you recently?"

"No." She dabbed at her eyes again.

"So what strange things are you talking about?"

"Just things."

"Abby, can't you be more specific?"

"There was a murder right before Danny left."

"Murder? Who?"

"Fellow named Rory Peterson."

"I saw his grave too. Who murdered him?"

"Don't know. Tyree's still looking at that one too."

"Who was Peterson?"

"An accountant. He also helped run the town fund."

"Town fund?"

"Divine has been through enough booms and busts so we decided to try a different approach. Everybody kicked in some money, businesses, regular folks. I put in more than most because I had more money. We put it all in an investment account and it's done real well. Rory did the books. The fund pays out quarterly dividends. It's been a godsend to folks around town. Kept businesses going that otherwise wouldn't be able to make a go of it. Allowed folks to keep their houses, pay off their debt, survive the lean times."

"You said Peterson did the books. Was he maybe skimming and somebody didn't like that?"

"I don't know. I know Rory had some contacts in New York. That was where he was from originally. That was another reason the fund was doing so well. He got us piggybacked on some of those private equity people's investments up there. At least that's what he said. Hitting stuff out of the park, at least according to the dividends I get."

"Would Danny be mixed up in that somehow? Or Debby?"

"Don't see how. Danny's never been what you'd call financially savvy. His interests are a lot more basic. Debby was an artist. She had nothing to do with the fund."

"Well, those guys tonight didn't seem like the Wall Street types either."

Abby's phone buzzed. She answered it and then passed it across to Stone. "It's Tyree," she said.

The sheriff said, "Ben, I went to the place you said. Nobody was there. Didn't find nothing. No bats, no blood, no belt."

"They must've come back and cleaned it all up."

"How's Danny?"

"Getting some tests run."

"Did you ask him who did it?"

"He said it was an accident."

"And you're sure it wasn't?"

"Not unless you categorize three guys with baseball bats doing you bodily harm an accident."

"I'm heading over to talk to Danny. How's Abby?"

Stone glanced at her. "She's holding up."

Stone passed back the phone. "I'm going to get a cup of coffee, you want one?"

She shook her head and tried to smile. "No thanks. I'm just going to stay planted here until they tell me Danny's going to be okay."

Stone walked off looking for a vending machine, stretching out his sore arm as he did so. Then the rather obvious occurred to him. Willie Coombs was still here.

Crack and pinpoint pupils. And now Danny beaten nearly to death. And a dead woman in the middle of it all.

The coffee could wait. He needed to talk to Willie.

33

Knox's cell phone buzzed. The caller ID came up as blocked.

He hesitated and then answered it.

"Hello?"

It took a second for Knox to place the caller's voice. "Finn?"

"I thought about what you said and I thought you might want to know something."

Knox snatched a small notebook off the kitchen island and uncapped a pen. "I'm listening."

"I *was* at the Visitor Center with Stone. That won't come as a surprise to the folks at CIA. Carter Gray was there too, as was Senator Simpson."

"What were you all doing there? Having a pre-opening party?"

"We were doing an exchange. My son for Senator Simpson."

Knox caught a breath. "CIA snatched your kid?"

"And we grabbed a U.S. senator in return."

"Why Simpson?"

"He, Gray and Stone have a history. Not a good one."

"I didn't think they were all best buds."

"Anyway, we did the exchange, gave Gray all he wanted, including a cell phone with a recording on it that Stone had."

"What was the recording of?"

"Don't know. But whatever it was, it's the reason Gray resigned his post as intelligence czar."

"Some dirt?"

"Seems to be."

"I take it after the exchange was made they weren't going to let you walk away?"

"You could say that Gray had a different idea as to how we were going to leave the place."

Knox was writing fast and scribbling questions in the margins. "Let me ask something. Was Milton Farb a casualty in this little skirmish?"

"He's dead, isn't he? Stone was getting us all out on a prearranged route. He knew Gray would try and screw him so he had a backup plan. But while we were getting out of there, Milton was killed by one of Gray's men. Stone didn't leave after that. He went back in." Finn paused. "I went with him."

"Why?"

"He saved my son. He saved me along with everyone I cared about. I owed him."

"Okay. I can see that." Knox clenched the top of the pen between his teeth.

"One more thing. Before Simpson left the building he called out something to Stone."

"What was that?"

"He told him that he'd been the one to order the hit on Stone and his family when Stone was with Triple Six and Simpson was with CIA. His wife was killed and his daughter just disappeared during the hit. Stone got away and he's been on the run ever since. They took everything he had, Knox. Everything."

"Why would they want to torpedo one of their own?"

"He wanted out. He'd had enough. Only they didn't want him to leave," Finn said simply.

Knox settled down in a chair and peered out the window into his small front yard as he digested this. "Why are you telling me all this?"

"Two reasons. Owing to something that happened a long time ago involving Gray and Simpson, my family and I are bulletproof so far as the U.S. government is concerned. They're not coming after us no matter what I say or don't say."

"Yeah, I got that impression. And the second reason?"

"I've still got contacts on the inside and I checked you out. I peg you as a good guy in a tough spot. You may need a lifeline more than anybody before this is all over."

"I hope you're wrong but I appreciate the assist."

"Here's another one. If you are trying to find Oliver Stone, I'm not going to wish you luck."

"I can understand that."

"It's not just for the reason you think."

"Come again?"

"That night at the Capitol Visitor Center he had a thirty-year-old sniper rifle and a shitty scope. There was a seasoned CIA paramilitary force on the other side loaded for bear with a six-to-one advantage over us. We walked out, they didn't. I've never seen anything like it, Knox, and I was a SEAL who pulled time in just about every flame point there is in the world. Oliver Stone is the most stand-up guy you'll ever meet. He'll never let you down. He's a man of his word and he'll lay down his life for his friends without hesitation. But with a gun or knife in his hand the guy's no longer human. He knows ways to kill people I've never even heard of. So if you do run into him the chances are pretty high that you won't be the one walking away. Just thought you ought to know."

Finn clicked off and Knox sat there looking out his window, his pen now making nonsensical doodles on the paper.

This intelligence from Finn, while compelling and interesting, should not have made a difference to Knox insofar as his mission was concerned.

But it did.

It had come as no shock to Knox that his agency

had less than clean hands. That was just the nature of the business. But though Knox was a veteran of the intelligence world, there was something in his gut—perhaps as deep as his soul—that had recoiled in anger with every fact that Finn had revealed about John Carr and how his country had repeatedly ripped the man's life apart.

There was right and wrong, although those lines got blurred all the time. Justice and injustice too were often all over the place, he knew. There were no easy answers and whatever road you took, be it the high, low or more likely somewhere in between, half the people would hate the result and half would applaud. And the hell of the thing was in a way they'd both be right.

However, as Knox dwelled on all this, it seemed to him that John Carr, no matter what he might have done on that rainy, gray morning a few days ago, deserved to live out his life as a free man, but that was not Knox's decision to make. His investigator mind told him to verify what he'd been told. Then he would just have to see.

34

Visiting hours at the hospital were long over, but Stone found a sympathetic nurse who let him into the ward after he explained his connection.

"That's right," the nurse said. "Doc Warner mentioned that. Who would've thought to use a car engine to start somebody's heart?"

Somebody who's been in a war.

Willie was propped up in the bed and hooked up to an IV drip. Other cables connected to his body ran to a monitor where lines and numbers darted across.

When Stone walked in Willie opened his eyes and said, "Who the hell are you?"

"Ben. I helped your grandfather get you here."

Willie put out a hand. "Gramps told me about that. I guess I owe you my life."

"You look like you're doing better."

"Don't feel all that much better."

"Did they tell you how long you'll be in here?"

"No. I still don't know what the hell happened."

"You overdosed."

"I know I did. I just don't know *how* I did it."

"So what'd they find in your bloodstream?"

"Docs said oxycodone along with some other stuff."

"That would do it."

"But I didn't have any. That shit is expensive unless you got a prescription. You're talking a couple hundred bucks a pill on the street."

Stone pulled up a chair and sat next to the bed. Willie Coombs had longish brown hair and a good-looking face though tiny lines were already massing around his eyes and lips. He looked like Danny Riker, only more worn. "All right, what did you have and what did you take?"

"Hey, you some kind of undercover cop?"

"Well, if I were it'd be a pretty clear case of entrapment."

Willie let out a long sigh. "I'm too tired to give a shit. What I usually do is get me some fentanyl patches, shuck 'em in two, squeeze out the juice, cook it up and inject it in my feet. Gives you a nice pop, like heroin."

"Fentanyl? China white, right?" Stone said.

"You sound like you know your drugs."

"You said that's what you *usually* do?"

"Prescription ran out. So I just got me some run-of-the-mill street crack. Never had no trouble like this."

"Bob told me it was crack."

Willie looked surprised. "Well, if he told you, why the hell ask me?"

"I always like to confirm things with a corroborating source."

"You sure you ain't a cop?"

"Not even close. But crack is a stimulant. Your pupils would have been seven or eight millimeters, not pinpoints."

"I don't know what to tell you."

"How can you take crack and then go to work in the mines?"

"Had a couple days off. Sick leave," Willie added hastily.

"You sure you didn't take any oxycodone that night?"

"I wouldn't have taken any even if I had it."

"Why not?"

"Doc Warner put me on it when I busted up my arm in the mines couple years ago. Got some kind of reaction to it so I don't use the damn stuff."

"Did you take anything else? Anything you can remember? Eating or drinking?"

"Had a couple beers. Picked up some takeout at Rita's."

Stone perked up. "What sort of takeout?"

"Burger and fries and a platter of grilled nachos."

"So you ate, drank and then did the crack?"

"Yep. Started acting jumpy and shit and rambling on, but I was by myself, so that was okay. Before I was going to bed I took some Tylenol. I always take Tylenol anyway, every night. Just turned twenty-three, but I feel like I'm sixty some days."

"Tylenol?"

"Then I remember Gramps showing up. Then things really started getting weird."

"Who knew you took Tylenol every night?"

"Ain't like I kept it a secret. Lot of folks take pills up here."

"Yeah, I'm starting to see that," Stone said dryly. "So anybody really could've known?"

"What the hell are you getting at, mister?"

"If somebody replaced your Tylenol with oxycodone pills, that could explain how it got in your system. How many did you take?"

"A couple, least I think."

"Were there any left in the bottle?"

"A few."

"Do you remember if they looked like Tylenol pills?"

Willie sat up, pulling the IV lines and cables taut. "You saying somebody's trying to kill me? Who the hell would wanta do that?"

"You'd know that better than me, Willie."

"I doubt somebody's coming after me for my double-wide, guns and hunting bows. Other than that, I ain't got much."

"Forget the money factor. Anybody have a grudge against you?"

"'Bout what?"

"Did you tick somebody off? Steal somebody's girl?"

"I had a girl," Willie snapped. "But she's dead."

"Debby Randolph?"

"How did you know that?"

"Small town. I heard she committed suicide."

"Yeah, that's what they say."

"You think different?"

"What the hell reason did she have to commit suicide? Tell me that."

"I saw some of her work at the craft shop. She was talented."

Willie's face assumed a proud look. "She could draw and paint. And make stuff out of clay. She had a studio set up in a storage shed behind her parents' house. That's where her momma found her," he added quietly. "That's why I took some sick leave. I went back to work after the funeral, but, man, my head was all messed up."

"I can understand that, Willie. I really can."

"You wanta see a picture of her?"

Stone nodded and Willie reached into the drawer of his night-stand and pulled out his wallet. He slid a photo out and passed it over to Stone.

Willie and Debby were standing next to each other. The tall Willie towered over the petite Debby. She had dirty blonde hair and an infectious smile with eyes full of warmth.

"You can tell from her face she's just a really nice person."

Willie slowly nodded as he stared down at the dead woman's face.

As Stone gazed at the picture, an obvious point clicked in his head. "She doesn't look like someone who would kill herself."

"I'd asked her to marry me and she said yes. Happy as can be. Then the next thing I know she's dead." His face trembled and the tears started to slide down his thin, pale cheeks. "That's why I got back on the drugs after she died. I had nothing left."

"Did you tell people she and you were getting married?"

"No, I asked her not to till I had time to get a ring. I wanted to show her momma and daddy that I was serious. I'd saved up 'bout all I needed. Then I'd just come off the shift at the mine when I heard. Couldn't believe it."

"What time was she found?"

"Early in the morning. She'd been dead awhile they say."

"And no one heard the shot."

"They live in a little holler, nobody close."

"But you said it was in a building behind the house."

"Her momma didn't hear nothing 'cause she's about deaf without her hearing aids in. Her daddy Toby's a trucker and he was on the road in Kansas when Debby died. So unless he's got himself elephant ears, he didn't hear a damn thing either."

"Whose gun was used?"

"Toby's ten-gauge."

"Did you tell Sheriff Tyree about your doubts?"

"Till I was blue in the damn face. He just kept saying, 'Where's the evidence, son?' Her prints and her daddy's prints were the only ones on the gun. She was all alone. Nobody had no reason to kill her so they decided she must've done it herself. Real damn smart."

"Can you think of any reason why someone would want to kill Debby?"

"She never hurt nobody. Sweetest thing under the sun. And she's all I had."

"Before she died, was she upset or nervous about anything?"

He shrugged. "No, not that I could tell."

"When's the last time you talked to her?"

"Around eleven that night. She sounded fine."

"Would it surprise you if I told you that Danny Riker was really upset that she was dead?"

Willie wiped his eyes with some tissues, balled them up, and threw them in the wastebasket. "I guess not."

"You guess not?"

"Danny and her even dated before we got together. But Danny dated every girl in the high school so there wasn't nothing there really."

"Danny's here in the hospital too."

"What! What happened?"

"Some guys busted him up, bad. Any ideas there?"

"No. Danny and me weren't that close anymore."

"But you two *were* friends."

"Best friends." He paused. "He came to see me here."

"When was that?"

"Yesterday afternoon. We had a good talk. High school football and all."

"You two were teammates."

Willie grinned and Stone could suddenly see the young man under the coal dust. "Man, we *were* the team. He threw thirty-seven touchdown passes his senior year and twenty-eight of them were to me. We both could've played for Virginia Tech. But I got a damn DUI and they rescinded my scholarship and Danny hurt his knee. Glory days all right." His grin disappeared and the young man was gone as quickly as he'd appeared.

"So Danny didn't say anything that might explain why he got attacked?"

"No, nothing like that. He said he was real sorry about Debby. And he told me to keep off the pills. Said he was thinking about heading out again and he wanted me to come with him. We'd go west and start over."

"Were you interested?"

"Maybe. Ain't nothing keeping me here now."

"I understand things changed between you two when the Rikers came into all that money?"

"I got my head turned around over that. I mean, they had a lot and I ain't got nothing. But I should've just sucked it up. They didn't owe me nothing. And he lost his daddy over that and all. I know how that feels."

"I heard your father was killed in a hunting accident. Did he work in the mines too?"

"No, he was a guard up at Blue Spruce Prison. It was one of his best friends that accidentally shot him."

"Who was that?"

"Rory Peterson."

"Peterson? And then he ended up being murdered."

"Yeah, but that was just recent. My daddy got killed over two years ago."

Stone checked his watch and rose. "I need to get going."

"Is Danny going to be okay?"

"I don't know. They got him pretty bad. But you need to worry about yourself."

"What are you talking about?"

"If somebody tried to kill you by switching those pills, they're likely to try again."

35

Knox made a late-night trip to Langley to talk to some folks he'd known for a long time. He trusted these people as much as he trusted anyone these days. And, more important, they had no love lost for Macklin Hayes. He asked the questions he needed to ask and got the answers. Some surprised him, some didn't. It was only a start, but it was more than he'd had a few hours before.

The CIA had lost a human asset about the time that John Carr was disappearing. Nicknamed "Einstein" by his colleagues, Max Himmerling had been nearing retirement when he'd died in an overseas chopper accident, his body burned so badly it had been identified through dental records. The reason this interested Knox was because that sounded like a typical Carter Gray maneuver in disposing of an agent who had committed an unforgivable act. Himmerling was nearing seventy, with the physical ability of a cow and who'd been assigned stateside at Langley for the last thirty years. So his turning up in a flamed-out chopper somewhere in the Middle East did not make sense. Yet no one at CIA or the U.S. government dared question the circumstances of the man's death. What Himmerling had done must have been particularly egregious because he'd been a valuable asset for the CIA and Carter Gray. And though no one would say it out loud, from what Knox was able to find out, that *something* might have to do with John Carr. And he'd found something else out. The records of the Triple Six Division hadn't been destroyed, like he'd thought. The CIA, apparently loath to part with any documented part of its past, no matter how politically incorrect it might seem in hindsight, had moved those records somewhere.

And that led Knox to the next phase of his "parallel" investigation.

It took him to several different locations and he was aware that Hayes' men were following him every step of the way. Yet he had pretty decent cover, he *was* conducting an investigation on the man's behalf. After many twists and turns along the investigative trail, he reached his final destination. The fairly new and ultra-secret CIA underground records complex was in the middle of three hundred bucolic acres twenty miles west of Thomas Jefferson's Monticello near Charlottesville, Virginia. The CIA had purchased the property over two decades ago for an exceptionally good price that set the American taxpayer back a mere eleven million dollars. That had been, by far, the cheapest part of the project.

The property had barns, stables, paddocks and even a stately brick colonial manor house that was *ostensibly* owned by a multinational corporation headquartered in Belgium that *ostensibly* used it for corporate retreats. Indeed, several times a year, long convoys of limos and SUVs with camera-toting, Flemish-speaking executives could be seen heading to the estate along the winding gravel path. The CIA spent about one million bucks a year to perpetuate this myth and considered every dollar well spent.

High-speed elevators inside the manor house and two of the barns allowed access to an elaborate underground labyrinth of concrete tunnels, bunkers and rooms that were protected against any type of eavesdropping. It sounded very James Bond–like, and yet the reality was there were several facilities like this across the country. On two occasions curious souls had managed to open the doors of these structures—one in the Pacific Northwest and one in Nevada—and seen what was actually going on inside. Knox had never known what had happened to those unfortunate folks. Abducted by aliens was probably the myth spread by Agency disinformation teams. It was just the cost of doing business and keeping Americans safe. Well, except for folks who unfortunately opened doors they shouldn't have.

When complete the underground labyrinth had only set the American people back over one billion dollars, not a cent of it acknowledged in any budget of the U.S. government. The construction workers were relocated, without really ever knowing exactly where they'd been. Yet keeping secrets was an expensive proposition and the CIA had more secrets than most. And governments had hundreds of billions of dollars to spend on projects like this. For that level of coin one did not rent space at Storage Town USA; one built cement cities underneath crappy barns.

As Knox rode the elevator down he carefully went over for the hundredth time his next step. He had pretty much every security clearance one could have, but he did not have the necessary authorizations to get to where he believed he needed to go right now. One person who could give him that authority was Macklin Hayes. To get the man to cooperate entailed Knox both tricking the spy chief and outthinking him. The sweat under his armpits continued to spread even as the elevator hurtled him downward to where the temperature was a constant sixty-one degrees.

A few seconds later, Knox was walking steadily toward his destination. Along the way he endured increasing scrutiny as stern-faced men checked him out from every angle before reluctantly passing him along. Apparently, spies didn't even like fellow spies coming to visit them and going through their stuff. Knox had one advantage. He had a friend who worked here, Marshall Saunders. Knox sat in this man's office a half hour after going through the identification gauntlet.

"Been awhile, Joe," Saunders said, rising from his desk and shaking his visitor's hand. Everyone down here wore sweaters, and indeed Knox felt himself shivering despite his jacket.

"You've gussied up the place from the last time I was here, Marsh," Knox said.

"Budget cuts have yet to come our way. Just lucky. I guess."

It was far more than a matter of mere luck, both men knew. You couldn't cut what you never saw.

"I won't waste your time. I'm doing some under-the-radar work for Macklin Hayes."

"So I've been informed. How is the general by the way?"

"The same." Knox left his friend to interpret that remark however he wanted. Marshall, whom everyone called Marsh, had served three years directly under Hayes' command. That meant if he ended up going to hell when he died, he would have a pretty good idea of how it would be.

Knox told him what he wanted to look at and his friend's features turned uncomfortable. "That'll take a phone call to the man."

"I'm aware of that," said Knox. "I actually just thought of it on the way over, or else I would've gotten the okay already. I don't think it'll be a problem." He added with as big a smile as he could manage, "On the other hand, if I end up disappearing you'll know I was wrong about that."

Marsh didn't even grin at this crude joke and Knox felt his ass suddenly clinch.

The call was made and the man passed the phone over to Knox.

As though a distant rumble of thunder heralding the approaching storm, he heard Hayes bark, "What's going on, Knox?"

"Just thought of this new angle, sir, but I need to check out a couple more pieces."

"Explain this new angle. But tell Marsh to leave first."

Knox glanced at his friend who got the sign immediately, rose and left. If he felt any anger for being kicked out of his own office, the savvy agent was too smart to show it.

Knox hunkered down, gripping the phone tightly. "I turned a lead that got me thinking about something in Carr's past."

"Where *exactly* in his past?"

Knox didn't hesitate. "Triple Six days."

"Knox—"

"I know what you said before, but here's my theory. If Carr was with Triple Six and colleagues from his past were being killed—"

"That's out of bounds."

Knox said, "I know Finn and his back story are off-limits, but if I'm going to track Carr down, I need to understand where this guy came from."

"I don't think that's relevant—"

Knox had anticipated this question and broke in. "With all due respect, if you're deciding what's relevant or not on this case, get somebody else to tackle it for you."

"I'm not trying—"

"If you want results, General, then I need some control over *my* investigation. You called me in to do a job. Then let me do it!"

Knox waited for the man's response, trying to breathe normally. He was betting the farm that Hayes would react one way, but the truth was, Knox could just as easily go down hard for this insubordination. *Real hard.* As in his butt being catapulted to Afghanistan, where he could spend a little quality time in the mountains with Osama's boys on the Pakistani border.

"I'm listening."

Knox went on autopilot. "Carr knows we're going to be on him. He's been on the run for a long time now. He's loyal to his friends like you said. He'd want to keep as far away from them as possible. But he still needs cover. He still needs help." Knox paused here to allow the bait to sink in. He wanted Hayes to say it. The man had to say it.

"You think he might turn to some old Triple Sixer for help?"

Thank you, God. "Well, General, look at it from his point of view. He pops Gray and Simpson and makes his initial escape. He can't go near his civilian friends. He knows the machine is on his ass, so he has to look somewhere for cover. These Triple Six guys would be retired by now and deep underground. If I can get a lead on any that Carr was close to and either shadow them or beat it out of them, we might turn this guy. It's a shortcut, but it might just work. I know you don't care how we get there, so long as we get there. You know as well as I do the longer Carr is out there, the greater the odds that he does something that will hurt *us*."

When Knox said *us* he of course meant *you*.

He waited again. He could almost hear the former military man's synapses firing off, weighing from virtually every conceivable angle what Knox had just proposed.

Virtually every conceivable angle. Just hopefully not the real one.

"It might be worth checking," Hayes said finally.

"And just so we're clear, this will only be a tangential line of inquiry." Knox wanted to feed the man a comfort bone, however disingenuous. "I'll be following up other leads at the same time. We can only hope that one of them will pop for us."

"Put Marsh on the phone so I can give him the necessary authorizations."

"Thank you, General." *You bastard.*

Hayes did his thing with Marshall and twenty minutes later Knox was being led into one of the most secure areas of one of the most clandestine facilities the United States of America had.

36

Stone had rejoined Abby when Tyree burst into the emergency room.

"How's Danny?" he said when he spotted them.

"Doctor just came out and said the x-rays look okay," Abby said shakily. "And they don't think there's internal bleeding."

Tyree knelt down and held her hand. "Well, thank God for that. Have you talked to him any more?"

"No."

Tyree looked over at Stone. "You seem to always be in the right place at the right time. First Willie and now Danny."

"Any leads on the guys who attacked him?"

"I'm hoping to cut to the chase and get Danny to tell me. Any chance of me talking to him?"

Stone pointed at a man in a white coat. "There's the doctor over there."

Tyree hurried over to the man while Stone turned to Abby. "Do you want me to drive you home?"

"No. I'm going to stay here. I'd just worry myself sick if I left."

"Then I'll stay with you."

"You've done enough. You saved Danny's life. Again. I really don't know how to thank you."

"Abby, I talked to Willie a few minutes ago. He said Danny came to visit him yesterday. He talked about him and Willie heading out of town together. Going west."

"Did Willie know why anybody would want to hurt Danny?"

"No, but I asked him about Debby Randolph. He said she and Danny dated some in high school, but it wasn't serious."

"I'm not sure Danny can get serious with a girl. It's all fun and games for him."

"But Willie doesn't think that Debby committed suicide. You see, he'd asked her to marry him. And she'd said yes. He talked to her around eleven the night before she was found dead. She was in good spirits."

"I didn't know he'd proposed."

"I guess they were keeping it secret. So we have Willie in the hospital with an overdose of a drug he didn't take. Debby killing herself for no reason, and now Danny nearly died. There has to be a connection."

"I can't see one."

"Willie also said that his father was accidentally shot by Rory Peterson."

"But that was over two years ago."

"It could still be important."

"Can we go outside for a few minutes? I need some air."

They walked out in time to hear the *thump-thump* of the aircraft going over. Stone looked up.

"Chopper?"

She nodded, staring up too. "Going to Dead Rock. Prisoner transport."

"Why not just drive them?"

"Most of the prisoners spending the rest of their lives up there come from pretty far away, lot of urban areas. Roads are pretty crappy around here and lots of places for ambush. Hard to bust your buddy out of jail thousands of feet up there."

"I can see that."

She turned to face him. "So what were you doing when you ran into Danny?"

Stone stared over at Willie's pickup truck where his bag was in the back. "I was heading out of town," he said a bit guiltily.

"Okay. Does this have something to do with Trimble wanting to write a story about you?"

Stone tried hard to look surprised. "What are you talking about?"

"Danny told me that you came along with him because a government car pulled into the town where you two got off the train."

"I think he made a mistake."

"If you're in some kind of trouble—"

"I'm in no trouble, Abby."

"I was going to say if you are in trouble, I want to help you."

"Why? You barely know me."

"You saved my son. And I can't explain exactly why, but I feel like I've known you all my life."

Stone looked down, stubbed the sidewalk with the toe of his shoe. "I appreciate the offer, Abby, I really do."

"But you're leaving anyway?"

He shot her a glance. "I didn't say that."

"But you didn't *not* say it either. Everybody's got problems. You have no obligation to stay here and help us. Hell, it's not your battle."

"Why don't you just leave here? You've got plenty of money."

"Run out of my hometown? No thank you. I'm not built that way."

"But Danny left."

"He didn't want to go. I made him."

Stone looked stunned. "What, why?"

"This is no place for him. What's he got here? Work in the mines or the prison?"

"Is that all? Or how about the strange things happening here you mentioned?"

"It's not your fight, Ben. If you need to move on, you move on." She hesitated. Stone thought she was going to say something else. "I better go back and check on Danny. And I'll look in on Willie too."

She left him there. Stone sat down on a low brick wall. An hour later he was still there, trying desperately to make sense of what he should do.

As he watched, the miner brigade began pulling in for their methadone pop. He checked his watch. Not even five in the morning yet. He continued to watch as the bone-thin men climbed out of their rides and straggled into the clinic before leaving to pull twelve hours in the pits of hell, contorting their bodies way past all sane levels. That only led to more pain, and more painkillers, and the cycle just kept on spinning.

All so the lights remain on in this country.

He looked on a few minutes later as the zombie-eyed men headed out in their dusty Chevys and Fords.

I'm going to start using candles and cook my food over a fire.

He was still sitting there when Tyree came out and reported that Danny had refused to say anything about who had attacked him.

"Sheriff, I think I've seen one of the men before. But I just can't remember where."

"Soon as you do remember, call me."

An hour after Tyree left, Abby finally came out, bleary-eyed and hunched over.

"Danny's going to be fine. They're moving him to a room pretty soon. I think the one next to Willie's."

"That's great, Abby."

"He said you beat those men up pretty good."

"I got lucky."

"Lucky once, maybe. Lucky twice, I don't think so."

"I guess the army did teach me a thing or two. Do you want me to drive you home?"

"No, but you can follow me there. I'll make us both some breakfast."

"Abby, you've been up all night. You don't have to do that."

"Just follow me home, Ben, unless you want to head on out of town right now."

They eyed one another.

Stone finally said, "I'll be staying, at least for now."

37

After he finished up in Charlottesville Knox made a quick trip to downtown D.C., his mind spinning from all that he'd learned. John Carr *had* been a member of Triple Six. Three members of his team had been killed about six months ago. The case had not only remained unsolved but apparently abandoned too. Knox wondered if Harry Finn's immunity was connected to that outcome somehow. However, he didn't wonder about that for long. It was not his problem. He had enough of his own.

There was nothing in the official record about Carr wanting out of Triple Six. Knox didn't expect that there would be. Personal feelings, and certainly hostile personal feelings, would never be officially acknowledged. Carr had had a family, though. That sort of information had been duly noted in the records, if only for security and threat assessment purposes. Carr had been technically listed as MIA on a certain date over thirty years ago. Cross-referencing these records with other info he'd collected previously, Knox was able to piece together that only a few days later Sergeant John Carr somehow miraculously reenlisted in the army. He then quickly died under mysterious circumstances and had been laid to rest at Arlington Cemetery. It was amazing, really, how history could be effectively rewritten on both large and personal scales.

Stone and Carr were one and the same. Long suspected, it was nice to have confirmation. Stone had fled Triple Six. A short time later an empty coffin had been put into the ground at Arlington with Carr's name on the white marker.

Later that morning Knox poured himself a cup of coffee and drank it at his kitchen counter as his gaze ran over the personal items in the room that had been his wife's. He hadn't changed it much after her death. The home had been both of theirs, but it had really been Patty's. Knox had spent more time in other countries than he had his own. It just came with the job. This was her space. In a sense, after her passing, Knox felt he was merely renting it.

The place he'd gone to in downtown D.C. was a news archive center maintained by the federal government. The feds burned a lot of money, without doubt, but some of what they purchased was actually useful. In his last days at Triple Six Carr had been assigned to a post in the Brunswick, Georgia, area with his official cover being that of an instructor at the then relatively new FLETC, or the Federal

Law Enforcement Training Center. From the daily logs that Knox had found, Carr was gone a lot from his post. On several occasions Knox had discovered that when Carr had been missing from FLETC, somewhere else in the world, a person of interest to the United States had died or disappeared.

Knox had canvassed the archives looking for one item in particular. After an hours-long search, but aided by his knowing the week span he was looking for, he found it. An obscure item in the local Brunswick paper detailed the disappearance of a local couple and their two-year-old daughter. A grainy photo of a woman was identified as Claire Michaels. Her husband, John, and their daughter, Elizabeth, had also vanished. John Michaels had been employed as an instructor at FLETC, the article said. There were rumors that some local federal cop-haters might have been involved and had targeted the Michaelses because of John's occupation. Knox searched for additional stories or any possible break in the case, but found none. The CIA had effectively buried it all, deflecting suspicion onto a logical if bogus source.

Knox stared at the old black-and-white image of Claire Michaels that he had taken a copy of from the archives. He wondered if the fragments of another picture of the woman currently resided inside the ballistics entry in the chest of a senator from Alabama. If he were a betting man, he would've laid down a stack of hundred-dollar chips that the photo taped to Senator Simpson's newspaper the morning he died was of Claire, John Carr's wife.

Okay, Finn had been telling the truth. They'd killed the man's family because he wanted out. Knox didn't want to believe that his government would treat a man who'd served them faithfully for many years in such a way, but the reality was it certainly could've gone down like that.

Knox walked to his book-lined study. He was chasing a man who'd been betrayed by his own government. True, the evidence was compelling that Carr had killed Gray and Simpson. Knox stared over at a photo of his wife on one wall. Yet what would he have done if he'd found out the two men had killed Patty? He sat down in a chair and stared at the floor. He couldn't say he wouldn't have done the very same thing.

And if that wasn't enough, Carr had been screwed in Vietnam by the very man Knox was working for. The war hero had never gotten his just due. The military man in Knox took great umbrage at that. It was hard enough to fight. It was hard enough to survive without some prick denying you something you'd earned fair and square. And Knox still didn't know why Hayes had cheated Carr out of his medal. Yet if he had to guess, he would have concluded that the fault rested with Hayes and not the heroic enlisted man.

The real question became: what did Knox do now? He had to keep looking for the man. But maybe what he did when he got there might change. And that meant he was now basically a traitor to his own agency. Helping the enemy. It could tank his career, ruin his retirement, perhaps cost him his freedom or maybe even his life.

For a man he'd never even met, but one whom he felt he probably knew better than many he'd called a friend.

Was John Carr worth it?

He didn't have the answer to that. At least not yet.

38

Abby and Stone had just finished breakfast. Stone had been famished while Abby barely touched her food.

He looked at her nearly full plate and said, "Remember that Danny is going to be okay."

"For now, yeah. He never should have come back here."

"And you're saying you only wanted him to go because there were no decent jobs here? You've got plenty of money."

"It's not the money! He hated how I got it anyway."

"They killed your husband, Abby. What other way was there for you to get justice? You can't exactly imprison a company."

"For what they did to my husband somebody should've gone to jail."

She rose, poured another cup of coffee and sat down next to him.

"You know much about digging coal out of the mountains?"

"Only that I probably wouldn't want to do it for a living."

"My husband worked at a dog hole mine. I guess you don't know what that is?"

"No."

"Small-scale shops, usually only a single shift crew and a foreman. Doesn't pay as well as the big shops and you get no health insurance. But if you've failed enough drug tests the dog holes tend to be more forgiving than the big outfits. Nice fallback."

"So your husband had a drug problem too?"

"The men are beat to hell from digging in the earth on their hands and knees. Sam had three back surgeries before he was forty. Got a hand caught in a grinder machine that they use to chew up coal seams. Even after a bunch of surgeries his hand was still a mess. Out of his mind with pain and the meds the clinic gave him didn't do anything after a while. He was snorting six hundred dollars' worth of crushed-up oxycodone up his nose every day."

"Can't they get help for their addiction? Other than the methadone juice?"

"I kept begging until Sam tried. Tore my heart to see him all wormed over after a few days in withdrawal. But he could never hold it."

"I'm sorry, Abby."

"The mining companies don't care so long as you pass your pee test and show up for work. They make their money and America stays warm."

"Abby, how did your husband die?"

She put down her cup and gazed past Stone, perhaps all the way to the past when her husband's life had abruptly ended. "Lot of things to worry about when you're sitting a thousand feet under rock, but there are two big things to keep in mind besides the earth falling on top of you. One is carbon dioxide and the other is methane gas. The first one will suffocate you and the second one will blow you up. The methane got Sam because the meter the company gave him to use to check out a new seam line was faulty. And they knew it. Explosion caused a cave-in. That was it."

Stone didn't know what to say, so he just stared down at his hands.

"Yeah, we're going through a real boom right now, coal and natural gas just pouring out of the mountains. Funny thing, though."

"What's that?"

"Most folks around here use propane or wood to warm themselves and cook with, *not* coal or natural gas. Maybe nobody else knows the real cost of digging that stuff out of the rock, but we sure as hell do, you hear what I'm saying?"

"Yes."

"A young man right out of high school with clean urine can start in the coal mines at twenty dollars an hour. Never get that kind of money anywhere else. But by the time they're thirty-five they'll be broke-backed and worn out, looking closer to seventy with lungs full of shit."

She finally looked over at him and her eyes seemed to refocus. One large tear was perched at the corner of her right eye.

"So you staying or going?"

"I'm not going to leave you like this, Abby." If Stone was startled by his words he didn't show it.

She reached over and squeezed his arm. He involuntarily grunted in pain.

"What's the matter?" she said in an alarmed tone.

"Nothing, just . . . it's nothing."

"Ben, what is it?"

"One of the guys with the bat got me a little bit on the arm."

"Oh good Lord, why didn't you say anything?"

"Abby, it's nothing."

"Take off your shirt."

"What?"

"Take it off."

He slowly peeled it off and she exclaimed, "Oh my God."

There was a lumpy black bruise the size of a walnut on his left upper arm and the discoloration had spread down to his forearm.

She ran to the freezer and grabbed an ice pack and placed it over the bruise. "You're a hero, okay, you don't have to be stupid," she scolded. "And if—"

She was staring at his chest and other arm. Stone

followed her gaze to the old knife slashes and bullet pocks.

She looked up inquiringly.

"Coal miners aren't the only ones with scars," he said quietly.

A half hour later, she came back into the room. He noticed that she'd changed her clothes and the scent in the air spoke of a shower and shampoo. She gave him an unfathomable look as she checked his arm. "Does it feel better?"

"Yeah, it's fine."

"Good." She leaned down and kissed him. In the same motion her arms slid around his middle and he felt her nails dig lightly into his back. Before he realized it, Stone felt himself kiss her in return. Abby's lips tasted sweet.

Stone felt his hand slide to her back and squeeze but then he pulled back.

"Abby, I don't think—"

She put a hand against his mouth. "That's right. You don't have to think at all. Come on."

Abby took his hand and led him up the stairs to her bedroom. She closed the door and motioned for him to sit on the bed. She stood in front of him and undressed.

She was fit and fleshy in all the right places and Stone felt a small gasp jump from his throat as he took all of her in. He noted that she had a small tattoo of a cross near her left hip bone. She pressed against him, her warm breasts pushed flat against his own hard chest; her hands began massaging his shoulders and back even as she made soft moaning sounds in his ear. She nimbly worked his pants off. A minute later he lay down beside her on the bed.

Later, they lay back, side to side, her hand clasping his arm, lightly rubbing the hairs.

"I haven't been with anyone since Sam died." She rolled over on her stomach, her arms supporting her chin. "Not once."

"There must've been opportunities, Abby. You're . . . beautiful."

She kissed him on the cheek and smiled. "Opportunities, yes, desire on my part, no."

"Not even Tyree?"

"It's not like that with us. We've known each other since we were little kids. Went on exactly one date in high school and we didn't really click. I think he might want more now. He never married, but I don't feel the same way."

"It's been a long time for me too. A long time." He wondered if Claire would have disapproved of what he had just done. After decades of loneliness for him, perhaps she would have understood.

"Opportunities or desire lacking?"

"Both."

He rolled over on his side and rubbed her back.

She stretched and smiled and Stone smiled back as he watched her do this. The braids in her hair had come out and several tresses dangled in her eyes. He carefully moved one away, revealing a green pupil looking at him.

"You ever think about leaving Divine?" he said.

"All the time."

"Why'd you never do it?"

"Scared, I guess. Divine's a little pond but I know it well. Hard to prove yourself all over in a new place."

"I suppose."

He rolled onto his back.

She curled next to him and slid her leg up and down his. "You ever think about settling down somewhere?"

"Lots of times. In fact I thought I had the place to do it, but it turned out it wasn't."

"What happened?"

"It just wasn't."

The phone rang. Abby looked at the clock. "Who could that be at this hour?"

"The hospital?"

"I just talked to them before we had breakfast. And to Danny. He was okay."

"Maybe it's the restaurant. People want their breakfast at Rita's." Stone was glad of the change in the conversation's direction.

"I already called there too. I got my helpers opening the place."

She climbed over Stone and snatched up the phone. Stone put a hand on her butt and gave her a gentle squeeze. She smiled, grabbed his hand and gave her backside a hard slap with it. Then she let go.

"What? Um." She glanced at Stone. "No, he's not here. Right. If I see him I could ask him, sure. Okay, right."

She put the phone back in the cradle, pulled a pillow into her lap and sat cross-legged facing him.

"Who was that?"

"Charlie Trimble. He heard about Danny and what you did. He wants to ask you some questions. And he seemed very determined."

"Great, well, my position hasn't changed. I'm not answering any questions."

"Ben, listen to me. If you don't want to do it, fine. But if you keep saying no to Charlie he's going to start digging. And unless you've got nothing you care about him finding, it might be smart to just talk to him. That way he can focus on what happened here instead of on you."

Stone opened his mouth and then closed it. "How come you're beautiful *and* smart? That's hardly fair."

"Just the luck of the draw, I guess."

"You have his number?"

"Yes, or you can just go to the newspaper. It's around the block from the restaurant. Can't miss it."

"Call him and tell him I'll be there sometime this afternoon."

He rose to get dressed.

"This afternoon? We can do a lot in that amount of time," she said playfully.

"As great as that sounds, I've got something I really need to do."

"What's that?" she said, sounding a little hurt.

"I'll let you know if I find it."

He finished dressing and drove Willie's truck back to the trailer. A few minutes later, after a thorough search, he found the bottle of Tylenol. It was empty. Had Willie taken the last few pills but forgotten? *Were* they oxycodone tablets? But why leave an empty medicine bottle in the drawer? As he looked around at the mess Willie Coombs called home, he concluded an empty bottle left in a drawer in this pigsty was hardly compelling evidence of anything. But still, it might be important. Maybe this was what Shirley Coombs had been looking for.

He pocketed the bottle, left the trailer and started to climb in the truck.

The next instant Stone lay unconscious on the ground, blood seeping from the wound in his head.

39

Stone rose slowly to a sitting position, his limbs shaky, his head throbbing and his belly queasy. He touched the knot on his head. The blood was dried solid over the wound. He'd been out for a while, apparently. He sat on his haunches for a bit, breathing slowly, trying to keep from puking.

He finally staggered to his feet and looked around. Or tried to. He could move his hand a foot in front of him and be unable to see it. He put a hand up and it nicked the hard, low ceiling.

He was in a cave. He breathed in and nearly gagged. No, he was in a mine. A coal mine. He took a few tentative steps forward and then stopped.

Rattle-rattle.

Stone took a slow step back from the sound. It seemed like more than one snake actually. Standing in the pitch black with rattlesnakes within striking distance probably constituted a pretty decent nightmare. Most people would have been frozen to the spot, waiting to be bitten and die. Stone was not stupid, so he was scared. But he wasn't paralyzed.

He moved both arms out from his sides. One hand brushed wall, his left nothing but air. He leaned toward the left and his fingers now grazed the rough side of the mine. That the mineshaft was not very wide was not much help since he couldn't exactly walk on walls. He reached up again and his hand hit the low ceiling. Rattlers could not see very well in the dark, he knew. But they could register his body heat and also sense any movement he made from the vibrations on the ground.

He was in grave danger of being fanged repeatedly with no way to get out. How long before they found his body? Or his bones? And then it dawned on him. That's why they hadn't just killed him and left his carcass to be found. Here he would die and never be discovered. People would just assume he had left town. No explanation or cover-up required. And yet there was more to it, he sensed. Whoever had done this could have just left him in the mine-shaft with no way out; they didn't have to use snakes too. Or they could have just shot him and left him here. There was a desire here to cause not only death, but terror as well. They wanted him to die horribly, and alone, and in the dark. Then the panic did hit him. But not for the obvious reason.

Abby.

He'd been with her. They might know that. They might think he had told her things. What things he wasn't sure. But they might go after her just in case.

Stone felt around the ceiling until his fingers touched what he deduced was a support beam. The beams helped hold up the ceiling, preventing tons of rock from raining down and crushing him, for which Stone was understandably grateful. Yet more important, there was a light cage attached to the beam by a sturdy metal plate. The light obviously wasn't working. Yet he didn't need light, just the cage.

He moved backward, away from the rattles, holding his arm up to the ceiling. Roughly four feet later his hand grazed another beam and another caged light. Four feet later, another.

Figuring that the snakes would've been placed between him and the exit to the mine, Stone slowly moved back toward the sounds. A rattler was deaf so it couldn't even hear its own rattles, but it was an instinctive signal to prey or predator that the snake was there, coiled and ready to strike. With each hesitant step he took Stone braced for the venom shooting into his legs. When he reached the first ceiling beam he'd touched, he reached up and gripped the metal light cage. Praying that it would be strong enough to hold his weight he lifted himself into the air, his legs bent and raised to chest-high. His injured arm ached badly, but he simply focused on what he was doing and willed the pain away. The Triple Six Division had been great at beating that technique into him at the Murder Mountain training facility, because they'd been expert at inflicting all types of agony, both physical and mental.

He swung back and forth and then lunged forward in the air, his hand outstretched like he was working the monkey bars, as he had in basic training. His hand closed around the next metal cage. Keeping his knees high, he let go of the first cage and kept moving. He had no idea if a rattler would strike upward and nail him in the ass, but he also didn't want to find out.

Four beams later, and after he missed one cage and almost fell, he stopped and listened, dangling there, his knees still bent to his chest. The rattles had stopped. But he didn't want to drop to the ground just yet. He kept swinging until his lead hand went out and touched nothing but rock wall.

Shit!

Had he actually gone the wrong way? Or had the snakes perhaps moved past him while he'd lain unconscious? Or had whoever put him here out-thought Stone and placed the snakes on the side opposite the exit? Or was this actually a nightmare and he would wake up any moment now?

His arms growing heavy, Stone cautiously lowered his legs and stood on firm ground. He put out his arms again, trying to gauge the width of the shaft here. He touched what he believed was the dead-end wall, but nothing was on the other side. He kept moving to that side, but nothing was there. Puzzled for a moment, the truth finally struck him.

Idiot.

This was a turn or bend in the mineshaft. He got his bearings, walked his fingers along the wall and moved forward, listening carefully for more rattles. Ten minutes later he ran smack into wood.

The mine entrance must've been boarded up, because he could see a thin line of light at the bottom edge of the wood. He considered his options. That was relatively easy, because he had none. He took a few steps back and ran full tilt at the wall. All that did was land him on his butt with a bruised shoulder. He started to rise and then froze. His fingers had grazed against something metallic half-buried in the dirt. It was long and slender. As his hand closed around it, Stone could tell it was a pole with a flat end, like the shaft of a screwdriver.

He worked the bottom edge of the pole into one side of the wooden wall and started to lever. He felt the nails in the frame start to give a bit. He probed at another spot and pushed his weight against the pole, his feet slipping and sliding with the effort. Twenty minutes and much sweat later, the top right edge of the wooden wall gave way and a big shaft of light lit the mine. Encouraged by this breakthrough, Stone really put his shoulder to the effort and only another twenty minutes passed before he was able to force the board enough away from the frame to squeeze out and fall on his back in the dirt.

Free.

He let out a deep, relieved breath. Then, blinking rapidly, he looked around to see if he recognized where he might be. He didn't. There was a dirt road here that was actually colored black. It took him a moment to realize why. Years of coal trucks carrying the stuff away. Their tires had ground the black dust and bits of rock into the red clay and the black had won out. He looked down at his clothes. The black had won out on him too. He brushed himself off and walked down the road, keeping alert in case whoever had sucker-punched him was still watching to see if he escaped the snake party.

A mile later he cleared the trees and turned onto a gravel street. As soon as the stuff crunched under his feet something occurred to him and he put his hand in his jacket pocket. The empty bottle of Tylenol was gone. Great. His skull felt like it was cracked, and now he'd lost the only real clue he'd found in pounding the increasingly dangerous streets of Divine.

He hitched a ride on a truck to Rita's and went in through the back but found out that Abby wasn't there. Then he called her house from the restaurant but there was no answer. He ran to Willie's trailer, grabbed his truck, drove pell-mell to Midsummer's Farm and caught her as she was walking out to her car.

When she saw him she said, "What the hell happened to you?"

When he told her, she simply stared at him. "Oh my God, Ben," she finally managed to stammer. "What is going on?"

"Have you talked to Danny?"

"Just a bit ago. I was just now going to see him."

"I tried calling you from Rita's."

"I thought I heard the phone ringing, but I was drying my hair. What are you going to do?"

Stone thought about that. What *was* he going to do? "I'm going to see Trimble. And then I'm going to hook up with Tyree to see what he found out." He took her by the arm. "Abby, I want you to be careful. I know you have the shotgun. How about a pistol?"

"Sam had a couple. They're upstairs in the closet."

"You know how to fire one?"

"You're asking a girl from the mountains if she knows how to fire a gun?"

"Okay, I'll take that as a yes. You said you had a couple of guns. Mind if I borrow one?"

"I can't think of anybody right now who needs it more."

They went in the house and Stone got the pistols. He loaded them both and handed one to Abby.

"I'd like to keep in close contact with you, but I don't have a cell phone."

"You can use Danny's. I brought it home from the hospital." She looked at his filthy clothes. "You can't go see Charlie like that. You can shower here and change your clothes."

Stone looked toward the truck. He hadn't thought to check. He looked in the cargo bed. His duffel was gone.

"I, uh, I don't have any clothes to change into."

"Come on. You're about the same size as Danny."

She led him to Danny's room and picked out some clothes for him. When he came out of the shower they were all neatly packed in a bag except for a pair of pants, shirt, socks and skivvies.

Dressed with phone and gun in hand, Stone gave Abby a hug. "Thanks, I'll meet you at the hospital later," he said.

He watched her drive off. Then he sped off in the opposite direction to keep his appointment with Trimble. Then he would go see Tyree. He had to play this just right. Or the only future he'd have would be either six feet under or else making calendar scratches on the walls of a federal prison.

40

A truck drove up and a man got out and sprinted to Knox's front door. He answered and the man handed him a package and left.

Knox sat in his office, put the DVD into his computer, and the images spread over the screen. The artist and Leroy had finally hooked up. The digital sketches of presumably a bushy-bearded John Carr looked back at him. The artist had also, on Knox's instructions, done images where the beard and glasses were removed. Knox compared these to old photos of John Carr from his military days along with more recent pictures that he had obtained from CIA files. They looked like the same guy to him. He printed out multiple color copies and hustled out the door.

The wheels squealing on his Rover, Knox sped out of his driveway.

From down the street, Caleb started the van and followed.

"Looks like our hound might have a lead," Annabelle said as she lowered her binoculars.

Knox went to National Airport first and Annabelle followed him in. An hour or so later he got back in his truck and drove off.

Annabelle jumped back in the Chrysler.

"Looks like he got zilch at the airport, though. Let's see where he goes next."

Knox's next stop was Union Station. Normally he would've flooded the area with the images of the altered John Carr, putting them on the metro database, with all the airlines and law enforcement agencies, but he couldn't do that here. If the FBI recognized the bushy-bearded man as one they'd allowed to slip through their fingers, they would wonder about CIA's interest in him. And despite Hayes' assurances that he could keep the FBI at bay, you never knew.

Inside the station Knox hit what might have been the jackpot. A ticket clerk believed she recognized the composite drawing of Stone with the bushy beard and glasses. He'd paid in cash for a coach fare but the clerk couldn't remember what name was on his ID.

"Do you remember which train he took?"

"Yep. Don't have many people who pay in cash. He booked the Crescent. To New Orleans."

"How can I get in touch with somebody who was on that train? A conductor, maybe?"

The woman picked up a phone. Minutes later Knox relayed his request to a supervisor in his office. The man made some calls and told Knox he was in luck. One of the conductors who'd been on that train had just gotten back to town. He came in an hour later to the station after the supervisor phoned him. He was shown the picture but didn't recognize the man. Knox handed him another composite with the beard and glasses removed.

"Yeah, this could be the guy who got in the fight."

"Fight?"

"Laid out three guys a lot younger than him on the train."

"Is that right?"

The conductor went on to explain what had happened, ending with Stone and the other men getting off at the next station. He told Knox the name of the town.

"He wouldn't give me any ID. Offered to get off the train instead. Little suspicious, I thought."

"Did you get the names of the other guys?"

"Nope. They said they'd get off the train too and they did. No skin off my nose. Saved me from filing a police report. Damn punks."

"Give me descriptions of all of them."

After Knox finished writing this information down he glanced at the supervisor. "Can you pull the ticket records for that train trip?"

"Yeah, but we can't match them to faces on that train."

"I'll take a list of the names anyway. Something might turn up."

The manager printed out this information and gave it to Knox.

"So is this something big?" the conductor asked eagerly.

"So big you'll probably never hear anything about it ever again. And I'd strongly suggest that you two gents forget I was ever here."

Knox hustled out of the station with Annabelle following. His truck rumbled off from the parking lot and the van eased after it.

The Rover picked up its pace and threatened to leave Caleb and Annabelle behind. When Caleb started cutting in and out of traffic in an effort to keep up, Annabelle told him there was no need.

"But we'll lose him."

"No we won't." She pulled a small device from her bag. "When I was in his truck in Georgetown, I placed a transmitter under the seat. It has a range of about twenty miles."

"Why didn't you tell me that before?"

"I'm sorry. I've had a lot on my mind."

Caleb grumbled for a bit but then said, "That was a pretty good idea. Putting that in his truck."

"And that way we can hang back a little just in case he's checking."

"He strikes me as a man who checks and often."

"Me too."

"So Oliver took a train?"

"Appears to be."

Knox's Rover turned on to Interstate 66 heading west. After traveling out past Gainesville, the Rover exited off the highway.

"I don't believe the train goes this way," Caleb said.

"Let's just see where he's headed."

Twenty minutes later Annabelle said, "Shit! There goes my perfect record."

They watched as Knox climbed into a chopper and it rose from the ground in a whirl of power.

"Now what?" Caleb asked.

"Back to Union Station, just as fast as you can." She glanced at Caleb with a quizzical look. "Wait a minute." She grabbed her camera. "Take off your ball cap and that sweater."

"Why?"

"I need to take your photo."

She snapped his picture. "We'll stop on the way into town at a photo place. And then I'll need to grab a laminator and some other supplies."

"What are you going to do?" Caleb said as he put the van in drive.

"You're about to change careers."

41

The chopper dropped Knox off about thirty miles from the town where Stone had detrained. A truck was waiting for him there. The aircraft had come courtesy of Macklin Hayes, who had sounded heartened over the phone that Knox finally had grabbed hold of a solid lead.

His instructions to Knox had been clear. Locate Carr but do not move in.

"Phone me and I'll take it from there."

I'm sure you will, General.

When Knox pulled into the town he decided he'd better hit the first place that looked promising. His prayers were almost immediately answered. The sign of the One T restaurant loomed ahead. He parked, went in, settled himself at the counter and ordered some food. There weren't many people in the place, but still, Knox figured if Carr had come by to eat after ditching the train someone could remember seeing him. He showed his composite and asked his questions and thirty minutes later he walked out, not knowing much more than when he'd gone in.

Neither the people behind the counter nor the customers were the observant type apparently, or else didn't like to volunteer any information about anybody. All he got in response to the artist's comp were dull shakes of the head. Even the flash of Knox's creds had not helped matters. In fact, it might have hurt. Knox had to keep in mind that around here the federal government was probably only a bit more popular than Osama bin Laden.

There was a bus station, he found, though it was now closed and wouldn't reopen for a while. Apparently folks up here didn't need to travel every day.

Knox sat in his truck and studied his map. The terrain around here was rugged and the towns few and far between with the roads connecting them two-lane and serpentine. He decided to find a place to sleep and start anew in the morning. He would have to come back to the bus station when it reopened. He'd asked around about the people that worked there, but they operated on some sort of circuit basis and wouldn't be back in town for a couple days. Yet Knox was counting on the bus station to pop for him if nothing else turned up in the meantime. There were probably limited ways out of this dump, and a bus was at least one of the more promising ones. Carr might have taken one after losing his ride on the train.

The motel was yellow-painted concrete and crummy, the rates so low they were easily covered by his government per diem. Crackers and a soda constituted room service that he grabbed out of the vending machine outside the tiny office. He showed the artist's comp to the manager but the man shook his head and went back to his TV and can of Bud. Knox spent another hour roaming the streets, showing the picture to passersby and shop owners. Either no one had seen the man or else they wouldn't confess to it.

Knox sat fully clothed on the bed in his room, crunching his miniature cheese and peanut butter sandwiches and sipping his diet Coke. He channel-hopped from wars to natural disasters to corruption scandals to ESPN, NASCAR, and finally settled on the TV Land channel watching, of all things, a decades-old episode of *Happy Days*.

Carr was the hunted and Knox the hunter. Those were the official roles anyway. In reality those identities could be switched at any time, and with Carr's skill level, the odds that they would reverse at some point were pretty good. And after what he had learned, Knox had quite the misgivings about his exposed rear flank, because there lurked the master of the ambush and blame game, Macklin Hayes.

He pulled out his phone and punched in the number.

"Hello?"

"Melanie, it's Dad."

"Hey, I was just thinking of you. Do you want to get together tomorrow night? I've got center orchestra seats. *Wicked* is playing."

"I'm sorry, sweetie, I can't. I'm out of town."

"Where are you? Paris? Amsterdam? Kabul? Tikrit?" Her tone sounded light and upbeat, but Knox knew his daughter well enough to sense the anxiety behind the casual words.

"I'm a little west of you. And a little rural."

"Terrorists hiding out in the hollers, Dad?"

"You never know, honey. Have you heard from your brother lately?"

"I got an e-mail from him this morning. He sounds good. He sent some pictures. There was some bad news, though. His deployment was supposed to be up in four weeks but they just got notice of extension for another six months. Apparently the Taliban is really coming back with a vengeance. Mark said they're pulling twenty thousand troops from Iraq to send to Afghanistan and he might end up there."

Knox swore under his breath. "I know he can't say exactly where he is, but is he in the line of fire at his current position?"

"He only said he was keeping his head down and trying to do his job."

Knox slumped back on the bed. "Look, what do you say we all plan to do something together when he gets back? Go away somewhere. Maybe the Mediterranean. Just the three of us. Wind down and take a breather. My dime."

"That sounds great. But the Med is expensive and I probably make more money than you. How about

I chip in too? Mark's the poor one. Serving his country doesn't even get him minimum wage."

"Nope, *my* dime. And you need to save your dollars."

"Why?"

"To take care of me in my old age. I won't be doing this crap forever."

There was a change in his tone when he said this and his daughter was quick to pick up on it.

"Dad, is everything okay?"

"Fine, sweetie. And a piece of advice, you don't waste premium theater tickets on old farts like me. You get a nice young man to join you in seeing *Wicked*. I want grandchildren, okay? I'm not getting any younger here."

"Okay, sure."

"I'll talk to you soon, honey."

"Good-bye, Dad. And . . . take care of yourself."

"Always."

"Dad?"

"Yeah?"

"Are you sure you're okay?"

Knox didn't want to hesitate, but for some reason he did. "Everything will be fine, Mel."

Knox clicked off and dropped the phone on the bed. Now he felt worse than he did before he'd called. He knew he'd frightened his daughter and there was nothing he could do about it now. Maybe he wanted to scare her. Or at least prepare her for when he didn't come back home, or even for when she might have to come and ID his body.

He looked around the dismal interior of his room. How many crappy hole-in-the-walls, how many effed-up towns, how many shitty countries had he spent the majority of his life in? The answer was clear: way too many.

He lay back on the bed feeling lonelier than he ever had.

Wicked? Yeah, I can tell you all about wicked, honey. But then I'm afraid you'd hate your old man, and I'd rather eat a machine-gun round.

His cell phone buzzed.

It was Hayes. He knew without even looking. He didn't want to answer it but he had to. Official protocol, meaning he didn't want to be transferred to undercover duty in, say, Tehran or Pyongyang.

"Joe Knox."

Hayes snapped, "Where are you?"

"On the hunt."

"On the hunt precisely where?"

"Southwest Virginia."

"That's not precise enough."

"To tell you the truth, I'm not even sure where I am and the reception up here is lousy, sir, I can barely hear you."

Hayes raised his voice a few notches. "Have you sighted him yet?"

"If I had I would've already called you. I'm just

trying to run some leads down and get a more pinpoint location."

"Why didn't you have the chopper take you all the way in?"

Because then you'd know exactly where I was. "A bird dropping a fed in the middle of this place would've aroused a little bit of suspicion. If Carr was around he wouldn't have been much longer. I'm going to poke around and then get back to you."

"I'm not exactly on board with how you're handling this, Knox."

"Flying by the seat of my pants, sir. Doing the best I can, what with all the *prohibitions* on what I can look at or the roads I can go down."

"The minute you know anything, Knox. The very minute!" He clicked off.

Knox looked up in time to see the Fonz deliver his trademark line on TV.

"Sit on it, asshole," Knox said in his best Arthur Fonzarelli voice.

42

Annabelle and Caleb marched into Union Station and went straight up to the clerk that Knox had talked to. Annabelle flashed her fake FBI badge.

"Agents Hunter and Kelso. Was there a man in here earlier asking questions and showing you a photo? He would've identified himself as Joe Knox? Said he was with Homeland Security?"

"Yes, that's right," the woman said nervously.

Annabelle let out an audible sigh. "Then we have a big problem."

The woman looked anxiously at her. "What was the problem? We helped Agent Knox as best we could."

Caleb spoke up. "The problem is his name isn't Knox and he isn't with Homeland Security."

The woman blanched. "Omigod."

Annabelle said, "Omigod is right. I need to speak to everybody he talked to, right now!"

A few minutes later Annabelle and Caleb were seated in the supervisor's office. The train attendant was there too, having stayed behind at the station to catch up on some paperwork and been summoned when Annabelle had made her demand of the manager.

"We thought he was a fed."

"I'm sure. He probably told you not to say anything to anyone about what he'd told you, right?" said Annabelle.

"That's right, he did."

"Standard operating bullshit, I'm afraid."

"But his credentials looked authentic," the Amtrak supervisor said.

Caleb held out his creds so they could look at them closely. They were still a bit warm from Annabelle having just created them in the van on the way over. "*I'm* with Homeland Security. Did you note that in the upper-right-hand corner of the picture there's a small 'e' done in reverse like there is in mine?"

The train men looked at each other and shook their heads. The supervisor said, "I didn't know to look for that."

"That's because it's a secret," Annabelle chimed in. "To prevent people from successfully duplicating our creds. It's a double-edged sword, I know. It's a secret so the public isn't supposed to know. But I thought a notice had gone out to certain levels of the federal government about it. You're a federal agency, right?"

"Quasi-governmental," the supervisor replied. He

added, “And let me tell you, nobody from the federal government tells us shit about anything. Hell, a lot of them question why the country needs trains at all. What with the highways suffocated and the skies filled to overflowing and every civilized country in the world building trains and rails at record paces, you’d think they could figure it out for themselves.”

“We’ll put in a good word for Amtrak at the next budget meeting,” Caleb said sarcastically. “But right now we need to find this jerk-off, fast.”

“Wait a minute, aren’t you guys supposed to wear jackets with your acronym on the back?” the train conductor said.

“Yeah,” Annabelle said impatiently. “When we’re knocking down somebody’s freaking door to make an arrest! Not when we’re undercover trying to nail a spy.”

Caleb gave her a sharp and totally choreographed glance along with a quick shake of the head.

“He’s a spy?” exclaimed the supervisor.

“Yeah, he is,” she admitted. “Now, I need to know exactly what you told him.”

The two men filled her in while Caleb took notes. When they were done, she said, “I don’t blame you for what happened. And hopefully we’ll be able to run him down with the intel you just gave us.”

“Wish us luck,” Caleb said sourly. “We’re going to need it because he’s got quite a head start.”

The pair quickly left and returned to the van.

"Nice job in there, Caleb," Annabelle said admiringly.

"I was in the thespian club in college. I had dreams, you know. Not Hollywood, God forbid. The stage."

"So you wanted to be on Broadway but ended up a librarian? How come?"

"I loved acting but there was a downside I could never get over."

"What was that?"

"Stage fright. I was sick for hours before every performance. I lost so much weight and went through so many costumes I finally had to give it up."

"Well, today you were a star."

43

The interview with Charlie Trimble was going better than Stone had expected. His questions were polite but prepared. And then it began to change. The reporter sat in his old swivel chair, a piercing expression in his gaze, one that was making Stone extremely uncomfortable.

"You seem familiar to me, Ben. Have we met before?"

"I don't see how."

"You ever been in Washington?"

"Never."

Trimble sat back and drummed his fingers on his desk. "Why'd you come here?"

"Just making sure Danny was okay."

"That's all?"

"Why not?"

Before Trimble could launch another question, Stone pounced. "What do you know about Debby Randolph's and Rory Peterson's deaths?"

At first, Trimble seemed taken aback by this, but

his expression became bemused. "Why do you want to know?"

"Some people tried to kill Danny. I think somebody tried to OD Willie."

"I talked to Bob Coombs about that. Do you have any proof?"

"Just what Willie told me and what the doctors found in his system."

"Willie's a drug user, not the most reliable people in the world."

"Have you talked to him about that?" Stone asked sharply. Trimble shook his head. "Then you're not really in a position to gauge his credibility, are you?"

Trimble's face flushed but then he smiled. "You make a good point. I do need to talk to him."

"So getting back to my question. Danny and Willie both are targets. They both knew Debby. Willie was engaged to marry her."

"I didn't know that."

"No one apparently did. Debby supposedly commits suicide. Willie thinks that's impossible. He talked to her the night before she was found dead. She sounded great."

"Sheriff Tyree looked into all that. It did seem crazy that Debby would do that, but all the evidence pointed to suicide."

"It's pretty easy to make murder seem like suicide if you know what you're doing."

Trimble shot him a penetrating look. "You know about such things?"

"I'm just trying to get to the truth, Mr. Trimble."

"Call me Charlie. And why are you so set on doing that? You've only been here a short while."

Stone rubbed his shoulder and then his head. "Let's put it this way, I don't like being pushed around." *And then there's Abby.* "How was Peterson killed?" he asked.

"Gunshot. Probably during a robbery. There was a safe in his office that had been forced. Cash, some files, and his computer were stolen. Tyree's been working that one too, but he's not come up with much, at least that he's confided in me. He's the entire police force, you know."

"He could call in the state police."

"He might do that." Trimble smiled. "Or maybe his brother."

"His brother?"

"Howard Tyree. He's the warden up at Blue Spruce Prison."

"He never mentioned that."

"Well, I'm not sure the two get along all that well. So my suggestion of him calling in his brother to help was a poor attempt at a joke. Tyree's on his own."

A few minutes later Stone left the *Divine Eagle* office and headed to see the sheriff.

He found him in the jail building going over some papers.

When he told Tyree what had happened to him in the mineshaft, the lawman nearly came out of his chair. As Stone continued explaining, Tyree started to nod.

When Stone finished he said, "The hospital confirmed that Willie had oxycodone in his system. Willie *was* allergic to it. He never would've voluntarily taken it. Plus it's pretty expensive without a prescription."

"So somebody did try to kill him," Stone said.

"Looks that way. And a smart way to do it, actually. Prescription drug abuse is rampant around here. I spend a lot of my time with that crap. Black stain on what is otherwise a nice place to live. But you can't lock everybody up who's addicted. Hell, there wouldn't be any miners left to work. You try to rehab them, get their methadone pop every day, but it's not enough. Every cop up and down the Appalachian mining country knows we're fighting a losing battle. But we don't have enough resources. We're overwhelmed."

"This area is pretty remote. Where do they get all the drugs? It's not like there's a pharmacy on every corner."

"They can get it from any number of sources. Sham pharmacies on the Internet, pipeline from the Mex border. Many a miner has sucked away his life savings and his marriage over that crap. Old saying up here is, 'Methamphetamines keep you awake and oxy keeps you high.'"

"Sheriff, I believe there's a connection between Danny, Willie and Debby Randolph's death." Stone went on to tell him about Willie proposing and then him talking to Debby the night before she was found.

"I didn't know about the engagement, but I knew Willie was convinced she hadn't killed herself. He was all over me about that.

But all the evidence pointed to suicide."

"Who performed the autopsy?"

"Doc Warner. He's not a full-time pathologist, but he's a qualified medical examiner. And it seemed straightforward. She put a shotgun in her mouth and pulled the trigger."

Tyree didn't look at Stone when he said this last part. Stone noticed this and said, "I'm not telling you how to do your job, but it's rare for a woman to kill herself with a gun. And with so many drugs around here, you'd think she would've just popped some pills and gone quietly."

"I know. That's been bugging me too."

Stone began cautiously, "I saw Danny lying on top of Debby's grave that night."

Tyree looked surprised. "Where were you?"

"Behind the stone wall. I heard something and came to see what. I was going to go to Danny when I saw you walk up."

Tyree looked uncomfortable. "Craziest thing I ever saw. I didn't understand what he was even doing there. I just put it down to Danny being Danny."

"Meaning what exactly?"

"Meaning unpredictable."

"Abby made him leave town."

Tyree sat back in his chair and scowled at Stone. "She never bothered telling me that," he said in a hurt tone. "And she told you?"

"She was afraid for him, I guess. And from what happened to him once he got back, it seems she was right. And maybe she was afraid to tell you."

"Why?"

"You're the law. Maybe Danny was mixed up in something not quite legal."

Tyree's anger faded away. "I guess I can understand that. By the way, that description you gave me of the men, I'm sending it around to the state police and to sheriff's offices in other towns. But they didn't ring a bell with me and I know just about everybody around here."

"Well, it was dark and things were happening pretty fast. I didn't get that good of a look at them so my description wasn't all that great. But I caught Shirley Coombs snooping around Willie's trailer right before Danny was attacked. I think she was looking for something."

"Like what?"

Stone told him about the Tylenol bottle. "And

Josh Coombs was shot by his friend, Rory Peterson. Quite a coincidence."

Tyree nodded dumbly.

"Those are a lot of pieces dangling out there," noted Stone.

"But how do you tie it all together? That's the thing."

Stone stood up. "I'm heading over to the hospital to see Danny and Willie."

"Well, you tell Danny he needs to start telling me the truth. He's the way we get to the bottom of all this. I'm convinced of that. And once his story comes out, those boys won't go after him again."

"I'll tell him."

As he was walking out, Stone noticed a long-barreled shotgun resting on a table with a tag on it.

"What's that?"

"The shotgun Debby was killed with."

"Do you mind?"

"Go ahead."

Stone picked up the gun, first holding it by the stock and then by the muzzle. When he laid it back down his face was puzzled.

"What?" asked Tyree curiously.

"Not sure. I'll let you know."

Actually Stone was sure. He was six-two with exceptionally long arms. He had gauged that with the muzzle perched in his mouth he could have managed to pull the trigger. Barely. He thought back to the photo of Debby that Willie had shown him. There was no way the petite Debby could have done it.

Someone *had* killed her.

Stone walked outside. That's when he noticed the sign on the one-story building across the street.

Peterson's Accounting Service.

He crossed the street and peered in one of the windows. He saw a desk, file cabinets and shelves and a dead corn plant. Other than that the place looked to have been cleared out. There wasn't a computer, printer or fax machine in sight. He noticed some people passing by on the street who were staring at him. He smiled at them and ambled off. Crossing back to the other side of the street, he pretended to be window-shopping. He passed by the bakery and decided to go inside when he saw Bob Coombs standing at the counter.

"Hey, Bob, how's Willie doing?"

Bob smiled and said, "Docs say he'll be coming home real soon."

"I'm going over to see him today. I've been using his truck. Hope it's okay."

"After what you did, you can use anything of his you want."

Bob bought a cup of coffee and some donuts while Stone admired the half-finished mural of a country meadow scene on the wall behind the cash register. Bob offered to buy Stone a coffee but he declined.

The two men walked outside where Stone said, "I

ran into your daughter-in-law the other night. She told me that the whole town blames her for something. Any idea what?"

Bob's features turned dark as he bit into his donut. "It was because of Josh's death. He wasn't even supposed to be hunting that damn day. Shirley had been nagging him about not killing any deer that season. Now, Josh was a good hunter, but the truth was Shirley didn't give a crap about eating venison. Couldn't cook it worth nothing, all gamey. It was just her way of cutting Josh down. Well, she wouldn't stop nagging and Josh finally headed out that morning by himself. He was real upset."

"How'd you learn all that?"

"Josh called me when he was driving over to the woods and told me what had happened. Hour later my boy was dead."

As the two men parted company, Stone glanced over at the courthouse. There was a white Cadillac parked in front with the license plate HCDJ. Then Stone froze when he saw her.

Why was Shirley Coombs going into the courthouse?

44

After a long drive Annabelle and Caleb had arrived in the town where Stone had gotten off with Danny. Annabelle had done a quick recon of the small downtown area and then settled herself at the counter of the venerable One T. A few other butts were parked next to hers, all of them male. She got more than one look from some of the younger men at the counter. She shot back a smile here, a nod there to keep the interest stoked in case it came in handy later.

"Where you coming from?" the waitress asked her as she poured coffee into Annabelle's mug.

"Winchester, Virginia." To Annabelle, mentioning that area was good enough to give her a bit of rural cred.

"Got a cousin lives up that way. Horse farm."

"It's pretty country," Annabelle agreed, sipping her coffee and ordering off the menu. "Kind of reminds me of around here, only a little flatter."

The man next to her chuckled. He was big and broad and wore a checkered shirt, jean jacket with Dale Earnhardt Sr.'s image on it and boots with all the shine worn off. "Just about anything's flatter than 'round here."

"You been out to see the Rockies?" Annabelle said.

"No, ma'am, can't say I have."

"They're a lot bigger than these mountains, but not nearly as pretty. Just chunky and brown with a top hat of snow. Not many trees. These mountains are green."

"You just passing through or looking to mark yourself out a piece of green?" said the waitress, coming back to them after placing Annabelle's order.

"Neither, really. I'm looking for somebody. Maybe you've seen him?"

The waitress and Annabelle's stool mate glanced at each other.

"Who might that be?" said the man warily.

"Son of a bitch ex-husband who skipped town owing a year's worth of child support for our two kids."

"Prick," said the man. "What's he look like?"

Annabelle gave them a description of Knox.

"Sounds like the feller who was in here asking questions right before I finished my shift," said the waitress as she made doodles on her order form. "He was a fed. Least he said he was. Asking questions. Didn't like that."

Annabelle said, "He *is* a fed. And I know Uncle Sam's paying him enough to keep his kids clothed, with food on the table. Got a tip he was working on something up this way. That's why I'm here. Tired of the man coming and going when he pleases. You think he gives a crap I can't even afford proper meds for our son? He's got really bad asthma. Almost died once."

"Prick," the jean jacket man said again as he pushed a forkful of biscuits and gravy in his mouth, and chewed with a force to match his choice of words.

"If you see him, don't say anything," Annabelle warned. "He's armed and prepared to use it. Don't get him pissed. Believe me, I've been on the receiving end of that."

"Are you telling me the asshole struck you?" the jean man asked as he swallowed his mouthful and partially lifted his wide butt from his narrow seat.

Annabelle said, "Just be real careful around him, you hear me?" Every time she spoke her voice picked up more of a drawl, as though she was absorbing their twang whenever they opened their mouths. She edged him back on his stool with her hand.

"So what's your plan?" said the waitress, obviously taking an avid interest in this little drama.

"I'm going to find his ass." Annabelle handed her a slip of paper. "You see him, call me on this number please."

The waitress nodded. "My old man did that crap

to me too. Took me eight years but I got my money."

"Hope I'm as lucky. Any place to stay around here?"

"Don't go to Skip's Motel down the street," said the waitress, a smile playing across her lips.

"Why not?"

"'Cause that's where he's staying, honey. Or at least he asked for a place to crash and I told him about that one. Try Lucy's at the other end of town. She's got a couple nice rooms for let."

"Thank you. Skip's, huh?"

"You got it, sweetie."

The waitress grabbed Annabelle's plate off the pass-through counter and put it down in front of her. "So what's your plan to nail the scumball, honey?"

"I brought someone with me," Annabelle said. "He works for the government too and he specializes in bagging other feds who pull crap like this."

"Shit," said jean jacket man. "They got a department for that too? No wonder our taxes are so damn high."

"Hush up, Herky," said the waitress. "Can't you tell this young lady's distressed?"

"Sorry, ma'am," said Herky, his gaze downcast as he stuffed a whole sausage patty in his mouth.

"So you gonna nail the little weasel good?" said the waitress eagerly.

"Something like that. Just give me a call if you see him and meantime I'll check out Skip's too. Thanks for the tip."

Annabelle finished eating and ordered some take-out for Caleb.

She walked out of the diner, looking cautiously around for Knox. She made it back to the van and told Caleb what had happened.

"Apparently he's staying at this Skip's Motel. We can ease down there and see if we pick up his trail. If not, I've got friends in high places here now."

Caleb looked at the platter of food. "It's all fried," he said in dismay.

"I'm sorry, Caleb, that's all they had."

"Not even any yogurt? Or fruit? Do you have any idea what my LDL cholesterol count is? And my triglycerides are off the charts. I could literally drop dead at any moment, Annabelle."

"It's a *diner*, Caleb. There're enormous men in there eating entire sides of beef without a fruit cup in sight, okay? Besides, what happened to the new, old Caleb? The dangerous come-at-me-with-both-guns-blazing Caleb?"

Caleb stared darkly at her. "Oh, what the hell. We're probably going to end up dead anyway." He made a face and then crunched down on a thick slice of sugar-cured bacon.

45

There was no one in the front office of the courthouse when Stone walked in. He waited a moment and then eyed the stacks of boxes against one wall. He slipped over to them, pulled one off the top, and looked inside it. It was filled with legal documents. This must be one of the shipments of mining recertification documents Judge Mosley had told him about. He picked up what looked to be a shipping manifest. Eighty large boxes. Stone looked at the cardboard towers and wondered how Mosley had any sanity left after going through that mind-numbing mountain of legalese.

He heard someone coming, dropped the manifest on top of one of the boxes and hurried back to the front of the large desk in the middle of the room. A moment later Shirley Coombs walked through an interior door, her gaze on a mess of papers in her hand. She looked up and gave a little cry when she saw Stone standing there.

"You work here?" he said.

She nodded, one hand on her chest. "You startled me."

Stone glanced around the space. "Are you the court secretary?"

"The court *clerk*. Have been for years. Why? Don't I look like a court clerk?" she said icily. "Or do I just look like a secretary?"

"I went to see Willie. He's doing okay."

Shirley busied herself with some papers on her desk. "I'm going over to see him soon."

Sure you are. "There's a Caddy parked out front with a vanity plate."

"HCDJ?"

"Yep."

"That's Judge Mosley's car."

"What does HCDJ stand for?"

"Here comes da judge." She said this as though Stone were an idiot for not having figured it out on his own.

"By the way, did you get everything you needed at Willie's trailer?"

"Excuse me?"

Stone said, "I think you left a bottle of Tylenol at Willie's trailer. I had it with me, but then I lost it." He stared at her pointedly and then rubbed the back of his head. *Why be subtle at this point?*

Shirley looked like Stone was pointing a gun at her. "I didn't leave anything behind."

"You sure?"

"Sure I'm sure. And I use Advil. Have ever since they had that pill scare with Tylenol."

"Willie thought there were pills left in the bottle, but when I found it, it was empty. And now it's gone. Maybe someone wanted it."

"Wanted an empty bottle? What for?"

"Well, there might have been some residue in there."

"Residue of what?"

Stone could tell she was lying. It was in every twitch of her face and shake of her voice. It had been her. She'd tried to kill her own son.

Now, who threw me into the snake pit, because it wasn't Miss Court Clerk with her stilettos and Pall Malls.

"You can't believe anything Willie says. Boy's always high."

"He was high on a stimulant, not a depressant. But the hospital said he had oxycodone in his system. That's a depressant."

"Willie doesn't know half the crap he's on. Probably forgot he took it."

"Or somebody wanted it to look that way."

She looked at him sharply. "What's that supposed to mean?"

"Just that somebody might have wanted to make it look like he'd OD'd accidentally."

She scoffed, "Why would anybody waste time trying to kill Willie? I mean, what'd be the point. It's not like he's got any money."

"That's not the only reason to kill somebody."

"What then?" She said this almost fearfully.

"Willie told me he'd asked Debby Randolph to marry him. Did you know about that?"

Shirley flushed at this information. She fumbled in her purse and pulled out a cigarette and a lighter. "No, I guess Willie didn't see fit to tell me that, his own mother."

"I take it you knew Debby?"

"Everybody in Divine knows everybody else," she said resignedly as she lit up.

"Would anybody in town have a problem with that happening?"

She blew smoke out and stared up at him. "What the hell does it matter to you? You're not from here. You don't know us. And just because you helped Willie doesn't mean I have to answer your damn questions."

"I thought you might want to help me, in case someone *is* trying to kill your son."

"Mister, no one is trying to kill Willie."

"But seeing as how he almost died and he says the drug that almost did him in he didn't take. Well, it does make you wonder."

She glanced at the wall of large boxes stacked a half dozen high and ten across. "I got a lot of work to do."

"Right. You want some help? I hire out cheap."

"I think you need to leave. Right now."

Stone turned and walked out.

As soon as he'd left another door opened and

Judge Dwight Mosley walked slowly into the room. His tie was undone and his shirtsleeves were rolled up.

"Shirley, was someone here? I thought I heard you talking."

"Just to myself, Judge. Just to myself. You know how I get sometimes."

"Yes, I know." He smiled and went back through the door.

Shirley puffed on her cigarette, staring thoughtfully at the wall.

46

Joe Knox lay in his underwear on a thin piece of puffed-up nylon masquerading as a mattress while he tried to connect the dots. Carr had killed a deuce, a mighty prominent deuce, and hit the road after slipping past the feds disguised as a bushy-bearded, gimp-legged village idiot. He'd gotten sidetracked on the train and ended up in this cluster of shacks. Where he was now, Knox had no clue. By asking around he'd discovered that the bus had headed out the very night the man had gotten to town, lucky, lucky him. By now, he could be pretty damn far away.

He sat up, jerked on his pants, socks and his Timberlands. He washed his face, finger-brushed his teeth and smoothed down his hair with the palm of his hand. If he was going to be on the chase much longer, he'd grab some clothes and toiletries other than the small travel bag he always carried with him. He slipped on his shirt and checked his cell. No messages, though the bars were looking a little jumpy at this altitude in the middle of nowhere.

Hayes was the show-runner on this dramatic piece;

Knox his faithful attack dog. Well, the "faithful" part was in serious doubt right now. Knox chewed some gum and stared out the window of Skip's Motel. Checking in last night he'd actually run into said Skip, an ancient man who said little, but his hand had shot out for the cash that was required to stay here with the jab speed of a welterweight in his prime. Old Skip apparently did not believe in the merits of consumer plastic.

Hayes had a hard-on for Carr for reasons he had not bothered to share with Knox, but which were growing a little clearer each time Knox thought about the possibilities. If Hayes had his way when Knox caught up to Carr, the man would not be read his rights, have his call to a lawyer or his day in court. But why kill the Medal of Honor man? It would have been a feather in the cap of then Major Macklin Hayes' career to have had such a soldier in his ranks. Carr had certainly pissed off his leader somehow. The paper trail had demonstrated that the lower chain of command had had no issue with Carr getting the mother of all American medals pinned to his chest. It had stopped at Hayes. What had Carr done to merit that sort of stonewall; a grudge that had apparently lasted over thirty years?

Now Knox's dilemma was obvious. If he did his job successfully and found Carr, he would, in essence, be delivering him to his executioner. A part of Knox said that was neither his business nor his battle to fight. Turn him over, be done with it and start collecting your pension. Rome in summer, his kids, sailing in the Med, the wine, the food. His kids.

If only that damn aneurysm in Patty's head hadn't popped—

The other part of Knox fell down on this theory like a four-hundred-pound WWE monster coming off a wrestling-ring rope. If Carr had killed the men, he would have to be proven guilty of those charges and then punishment could be meted out. Once you let way too smug and smart men like Hayes call those kinds of shots, play God for all seasons and all reasons, it was over. You might as well pull the democratic tent poles and phone in for Joe Stalin to make a comeback. The old US of A was finished. And Knox would not be a party to that. Twenty years ago the answer might have been different. But not today, not now. It was funny and a little ass-backwards, but he believed in the principles that made America what it was more strongly now than when he'd first started out in this line of work. Back then he was a raw, snot-nosed kid fresh from the military grunt side itching to carve out a credible rep as an intelligence op. He did anything and all to accomplish that goal, many things just over the line and a few that obliterated it. Looking back, he was not particularly proud of those moments, but he also took some solace in the fact that his work had saved lives and also that he'd eventually come around to the good side again. He knew many others who had never accomplished that last step. Hayes was clearly one of them.

It wasn't that he wasn't cynical. You couldn't do this job as long as he had and not cross that line a long time back. Experience without cynicism was a sure sign your brain had dry-rotted and you hadn't bothered to notice. He went into every high-level meeting these days knowing there were at least three agendas and also knowing he'd only be told one of them.

He put on his jacket and fingered his wallet with one hand, his rental truck keys with the other. He could also run, head for the hills, let Hayes find another lackey to do this job. There were plenty waiting in line. And truth be known, Knox was finding his enthusiasm for locating Carr waning the more he learned about the man and the more he found out about Hayes' probable reasons for taking down a war hero who'd never gotten his due.

He went down to his truck and debated whether to go to the One T and give it another whirl. He decided that might be worth it but he would do it later. First, he wanted to take a drive around and see what the night had hidden from him. He highly doubted one of those things would be John Carr. He had started out wanting no more than to find the man. Now a part of him was hoping it would never happen. And not just because a run-in with Carr, the grizzly bear of government assassins, would probably not end well for Knox.

It had something to do with justice, a concept Knox had not entirely forgotten, even if his boss apparently had.

47

"There he goes," said Annabelle. They watched from inside their van parked at the corner as Knox drove off.

"What do we do?" Caleb asked.

"Follow him." She held up a device. "I've got another tracker I can put in that truck."

Caleb put the van in gear. "You come prepared, I'll give you that."

"Just wait till you see what Reuben's bringing."

They followed from a discreet distance as Knox did a sweep of the area before parking at the One T and going inside.

"This should be interesting," said Annabelle with a grin.

Knox sat down at the counter. Herky, who was two seats down and working on his third plate of food, looked up, scowled and moved over next to Knox as the same waitress hurried over to take his order.

"Back again?" said the waitress.

"Thought the night might have refreshed your memory," Knox said.

"Only thing it refreshed was me knowing I was right to tell you to blow it out your butt."

Knox dialed back his natural anger and tried his best to keep it light. "Hey, give Uncle Sam's guy a little more respect than that, will ya?"

Herky moved slightly and bumped Knox in the arm. He glanced over at the big man. "Is there a problem?"

"No problem," said Herky, whose menacing features clearly said otherwise.

The waitress moved away to make a phone call.

"So you got any kids?" said Herky.

Knox looked surprised, but said, "Yeah, two, why?"

"So why don't you take care of 'em?" Herky snapped, stuffing a biscuit in his mouth.

"What the hell are you talking about? My kids are grown and gone. They should be taking care of me."

"Asshole," said Herky between bites.

"What?"

"You leave your wife and kids with nothing. Asshole," he said again.

"Herky!" the waitress said as she rejoined them. "Shut up!"

"Doris, this man is letting his wife and kids starve."

"Starve! My wife's dead. Who the hell have you been—"

Herky bumped him again. "I got a mind to take you out back and teach you some manners, mister."

"I wouldn't advise that."

"Advise this!" Herky swung a big fist. Knox caught it, twisted it around Herky's back and then slammed the man's face into his grits and eggs.

"Hey!" the waitress screamed as other men in the One T started rising from their chairs to help their friend.

Knox pulled his badge and his gun. "Everybody sit their butts back down in their chairs unless they want to spend some quality time in a federal prison a long way from here."

The men froze, all except Herky, who was snorting out grits and egg yolks. Knox looked at the waitress. "Who the hell told you that I—"

The waitress committed the mistake of glancing toward the door.

Knox burst outside, his gaze sweeping up and down the street.

Annabelle peered back from inside the van, the front of which was just barely in Knox's line of sight. She was still holding her phone from when the waitress had called her. "Damn it, they must have tipped him off somehow. Caleb, put the van in reverse and very slowly back up."

Caleb did so, and then once out of Knox's sight

he backed into a parking lot, shifted to drive and sped off.

"That was close, but at least I got the tracker on his truck while he was in the One T." She looked at a small device in her lap. "He's on the move. Let's go, but take it slow."

Knox knew that someone was on his trail, but he wasn't sure who. Hayes would have most likely taken a direct route. Was it one of Carr's friends? The chick with the fast tongue? The Secret Service agent? But how could they have possibly followed him here? He kept gazing in the rearview mirror as he drove to the bus station. It wasn't due to be open for another day, but Knox was done waiting. He didn't like the sensation of people creeping up behind him. He would tear up this whole town and find somebody who could tell him something.

He banged on the door of the bus station long and loud enough till a middle-aged man looking very put off came into view. Knox plastered his creds against the glass. When the man saw them he paled and quickly unlocked the door.

"Can I help you?" he said in a trembling voice.

"You better hope to hell you can."

Twenty minutes later he had his answer and was rushing back out to his truck.

The man had recognized Carr. He'd been traveling

with another man, younger. They'd taken a bus heading even farther southwest. The man had gotten hold of the driver at home. He'd remembered where he'd dropped the pair. Basically in the middle of nowhere, but it was a start.

Knox floored it.

He was coming to realize that maybe the only way he was going to survive this was to find John Carr.

48

Knox was motoring down the road trying to fathom how somebody had been able to follow him up here. Not even Macklin Hayes with all his support had been able to accomplish it. It was like they knew exactly where—

He nearly swerved off the road. He cut the wheel hard and turned off into a dark path. He put the truck in park, threw off his seat belt and went over the interior of the cab meticulously. He found nothing. But his examination of the truck's exterior was far more productive. He held up the small tracking device with the magnetized side. It had been placed inside one of the rear wheel wells. As he held the tracker, a smile crept across his face.

Annabelle was driving and Caleb was staring at the tiny screen.

"How we doing?" she asked.

"He's up there about a mile ahead, going straight." They had a vertical slab of mountain on one side of them and on the other a drop of nearly a half mile with not a guardrail in sight. "Seems like Oliver took a bus."

"Judging from the way Knox ran out of the bus station, I'd say that was a pretty safe bet."

He glanced over at her. "What about Reuben?"

"I talked to him. He's back there somewhere," she said. "He'll eventually catch up to us the next time Knox stops."

Caleb stared out the windshield. "Pretty isolated place."

"What, did you expect Oliver to take up residence in the suburbs?"

"Sometimes the best place to hide is with a lot of people."

"Yeah, and sometimes it's not. For all we know he could be up in those mountains somewhere. It worked for that abortion clinic bomber in North Carolina."

"But they finally caught him," Caleb pointed out.

"Okay, but—"

"Oh, damn!"

"What?"

Caleb was staring at the tiny screen that registered the movements of Knox's truck.

"He's turned around. He's coming right at us."

Annabelle glanced at the screen and, sure enough, the red blob of light representing Knox was flying right at them.

"Quick, pull off," Caleb cried out.

"Where? Into the side of the mountain or over the edge and two thousand feet down?"

"There!" Caleb stabbed his finger in the direction of a tiny sliver of dirt that ran between a stand of trees on the left where the mountain slab receded a bit.

Annabelle zipped into that crevice. They both turned around and watched the road. A minute later an Exxon tanker truck flashed by.

Caleb stared down at the screen. "We're in trouble."

Annabelle followed his gaze. "He found the tracker and put it on the fuel truck. Shit!"

Caleb nodded absently before tossing the useless contraption down on the seat. "Now what do we do?"

Annabelle put the van in gear and backed out onto the road and floored it. "We drive and we watch. And with any luck we'll pick up his trail again."

"I don't think I'm that lucky."

"Well, I am."

"Why?"

"I'm Irish. We always keep some reserve in the tank."

49

Joe Knox was feeling good for the first time in a long time. He'd ditched the tail and could now move on. He looked at the map on the seat next to him. The guy at the bus company had given him fairly precise directions to where the bus had dropped Carr and his friend off. Knox did a rough estimate in his head. He was probably an hour or so away.

When he got there he slowed the truck and looked around. It really was the middle of nowhere. Yet maybe not. He punched in some buttons on his navigation system and on the screen sprang up a number of different locations in the relative vicinity. "Tazburg, Mise, Divine, South Ridge." He read the names off the screen. All these places were scattered in different directions. So which should he take? And what should he do when he got there? His experience in the last tiny town had not been good. He swore he would not flash his federal badge, for one thing. And he was a stranger, so they would be suspicious anyway. If Carr were still in one of these places he might have already ingratiated himself with the townsfolk. Knox could be walking into something he would end up not liking. And the bus driver had said that Carr had a young guy with him. Was he from one of these towns? If so, he hadn't told the driver which one.

Knox pulled off the road and left the engine running as he stared at the navigation screen. He sighed. Hell, even for intelligence experts it sometimes came down to something as simple as this.

He closed his eyes and stabbed the screen with his finger. When he opened his eyes and pulled his finger back the town's name was revealed. He had a twenty-five percent chance that it was right.

Tazburg, Virginia, here I come.

He put the truck in gear and pulled back on the road.

While Joe Knox was enjoying a rare moment of exuberance Annabelle was slamming her hands down on the steering wheel. They'd been driving round and round trying to pick up the scent, but when they pulled past the same gas station for the third time, she'd driven into the parking lot, ripped the van into park and was now scowling at a dog that was sunning itself next to the air pump, only rising every few seconds to investigate its private parts.

"This isn't working, is it?" said Caleb.

"You think!" snapped Annabelle.

"Do you have another idea?"

She glared over at him. "Why do *I* always have to come up with the ideas, Mr. Librarian of Congress?"

Caleb said imperturbably, "I only asked because I happen to have one, an idea I mean."

She drummed her fingers on the steering wheel and looked at him expectantly.

"Do you want to hear it?" Caleb said tersely.

"Yes!" she shouted at him.

"I don't appreciate being yelled at."

She leaned into him. "Will you appreciate it more if I pull you out of this hunk of junk and kick the shit out of you instead?"

Caleb put one hand on the door lever and looked ready to sprint for it. "How about I just tell you my idea?"

Annabelle gripped the wheel so hard her forearms quivered. "That would please me very much," she said between clenched teeth.

"You see, civility is really not that difficult." She gave him such a ferocious look that he hurried on. "Okay, we go back to that town where they serve heart attacks instead of meals. You go to the bus station, do your usual bushelful of lies routine, maybe show some leg, buy a ticket and get the driver to drop you off at the exact same spot he did Oliver. He might have even overheard where they were headed. I'll follow in the van, and when you get there I'll pick you up and we go from there. At the very least it'll put us in the general vicinity of where Oliver was. How does that sound?"

Actually it sounded pretty good, Annabelle had to admit. She put the van in gear and pulled onto the road, setting a course back to the town.

Caleb's cell phone buzzed. It was Reuben. He spoke for a few minutes and then clicked off.

"Well?" said Annabelle.

"He's about two hours away, he said. I filled him in on the plan and he'll meet us there."

"Good."

"So you like my idea?"

"I'm doing it, so I must think it has *some* merit," she snapped.

"Annabelle, can I make a personal comment?"

She took a deep breath. "Go ahead."

"You really need to do something about your anger issues."

She stared over at him with an incredulous look. "I've been in this van so long I can't even remember when I haven't been in this van. I'm tired, I'm filthy, I'm worried and I'm frustrated. Okay? I don't have anger *issues*."

Caleb smiled knowingly. "That was a good first step to getting your feelings out. Only then can you achieve real progress."

"Can I share another feeling with you?" she said pleasantly.

"Of course."

"Either go back to being the mildly amusing testosterone Caleb, or else your ass can walk back to D.C."

Predictably, they drove on in silence.

50

Knox cruised into Tazburg and passed the local police station. He parked the truck and watched uniformed officers come and go, some on foot, others climbing into old mud-splattered Ford LTDs and speeding off to somewhere. The downtown area consisted of brick and clapboard buildings, a few leaning into each other, with old telephone lines running to them, while cars were parked slantwise in front of them. He'd passed through a long tunnel cut straight through a section of mountain on his way here. It felt like a border crossing.

What country am *I in?*

He pulled out the photos of Carr and mentally absorbed them one more time. He put the truck in gear and slowly pulled off. He would grid the downtown area street by street. From the look of the place that would take all of five minutes. Then he would get something to eat at the local place. He wouldn't pull his badge or show his photos. He would just watch. He had one big advantage. He knew relatively well what Carr looked like, while Carr had no idea who he was. He would press that to his full advantage. If that didn't pay off, he would eventually go to the police and work through them. It was a plan at least.

Three hours later and after having sat his butt down in four hole-in-the-walls and downed more cups of coffee than his stomach or bladder cared for, he concluded that he had struck out.

He parked in front of the police station, went in, flashed his creds, explained his mission to the extent he could, meaning it was mostly refined by-the-spook-book gobbledygook, and got zip for his troubles from the lawmen who were understandably excited that a dangerous desperado might be in their midst, but not very helpful. No one had seen anyone remotely resembling the man in the photo. Although one young deputy did mention that a fellow that looked just like that had lived in Tazburg for sixty-three years and happened to be his daddy. Knox thanked them politely and nearly sprinted back to his truck.

Before he'd gotten the door of his truck closed, his cell phone rang.

It was Hayes. The spy chief was not happy. But then again, Knox had never known the man to be really happy about anything. Knox had been with him when the Berlin Wall had come down. While everyone else had been raising their champagne flutes and making victory toasts, Hayes had only sipped on club soda and grumbled, "About damn time."

"Yes, sir?"

"Have you ever known me to give an idle command?"

"Can't say that I have."

Hayes bellowed, "When I ordered you to give me regular updates, I didn't mean at such wide intervals that obviously seem to appeal to you."

Knox punched the gas and rapidly left the good hamlet of Tazburg behind. He didn't want the megaton blast that he sensed was coming from Hayes to flatten the place.

"Well, General, you're a busy man and if I'd had something of substance to report you'd be the first to know." Before Hayes could send off another broadside he added, "But in fact I was just going to call you. I've narrowed the search area to four places. I just cleared one and I'm heading on to the second one now."

"Give me the locations."

Knox knew that one was coming. "With all due respect, sir, can I ask why?"

"Why *I* want to know where your investigative search is going on? Are you on drugs, Knox?"

"Stone cold sober, I can assure you. But if your plan is to flood the area with agents, that would definitely be a bad move in my opinion. We're looked on with suspicion here, and for all I know Carr has already gotten cozy with some folks around here and they may provide him with cover."

"Why would they do that?"

"Big bad government coming after a persecuted Vietnam vet. He could've made up any lie about his background. Believe me, sir, I've passed enough pickup trucks with shotguns and deer rifles in the window rack and bumper stickers that read, 'Thanks for visiting, now get the hell out,' to know an unfriendly atmosphere when I see it. There was even a ten-foot-tall graffiti sign on a train overpass that said, 'The Feds Suck!' I couldn't fail but note by the faded paint that it had been there apparently a long time without a single attempt to wash it off."

"Where are you, Knox? Now!"

Okay, here comes Plan B. Knox sped up, rolled down the window and stuck the phone out so it was blasted by the wind. He leaned out the window and spoke into the phone. "General . . . mile . . . border . . . hour . . . berg."

"Knox!" Hayes roared. "You're breaking up."

Knox pretended not to hear. In for a dime, in for a dollar. Maybe his lawyer daughter could represent him in his criminal insubordination trial. Although Hayes probably wouldn't bother with a trial. Knox would simply just disappear.

"Next . . . then . . . report. . . . investigation . . . west . . . lead." This was so absurd he had to work hard to keep from laughing his guts out, he really did.

"Damn it, Knox!"

Knox turned the phone off, wound the window back up, patting his hair back into place. With any luck Hayes was so apoplectic they would find him facedown on his desk, the unfortunate victim of a Joe Knox–induced fatal cardiac blast.

He pointed his ride to the next town on the list.

51

As Stone walked down the hospital corridor he heard laughter. When he reached Willie's room he understood why. Danny was in the bed next to his friend and Abby was sitting between them.

They all looked up when Stone walked in.

Danny's head was bandaged and one eye was swollen and there were cuts on his face. When he sat up he moved slowly and stiffly. Still, when he saw Stone he grinned in his usual cocksure manner.

"Looky what the cat dragged in. Dudley Do-Right. Savior of mankind, or at least two sorry-ass mountain boys."

Abby smiled. "The 'boys' seem to be doing a lot better ever since they were put in the same room."

"I can see that." Stone pulled up a chair and sat down next to her. "Danny, how you doing?"

"Thinking better than ever. See, couple knocks on the head straightened my brain out."

Willie piped up, "Too bad it didn't happen when we were playing football. Remember that godawful play you called in the state semis our junior year? I was wide open but you threw it right to the safety. Almost cost us the game."

"Play was fine. Only problem was I was checking out the other team's cheerleaders when I let go of the ball. One of 'em kept bending over. Trying to distract me, I expect."

"Some things never change," said Abby wearily. "Boys never grow up, they just get bigger with more hair and people start calling them men."

Stone said to Danny, "Tyree told me he came by to see you."

Danny's look changed. He glanced toward the window but uncharacteristically kept his mouth shut.

"Those men almost killed you, Danny. They almost killed me."

"I'm sorry about that, Ben. Sure wasn't your fight."

"Who were they?"

"Can't really remember. Docs say I got a concussion." He looked back and his face brightened. "Had a few in high school. Didn't I, Willie?"

"Hell, yeah. He always held on to the ball too long."

"Had to so your sorry butt could get open. If you'd run a little faster my brain would be doing better."

Willie grinned.

"Once we get out of here me and Willie are heading to California. Ain't that right, Willie?"

Willie nodded. "We talked it over last night. Got it all worked out."

"You sure it wasn't the painkillers talking?" said Abby.

"I'm sure. Divine ain't big enough for the two of us, is it, Willie?"

"No way."

"He's getting out of the mines and I'm gonna be a movie star. Willie's going to be my agent."

"What do you two know about any of that?" asked Abby with an incredulous look.

"Actors are just paid liars, far as I can see. They memorize a bunch of lines and then just say 'em. And, Ma, you've always said I could spout the biggest load of crap you've ever heard."

"He's got a point there, Mrs. Riker," said Willie.

"California is a long way away," she said slowly.

Danny looked over at her. "You want me to stay here?"

"No, I mean, I want you to be happy, honey. And safe. So if that means California, then so be it. Maybe I'll come and visit."

"Hell, when I hit it big I'll buy you a place next to Brad Pitt. But you got to let me use it too so I can sneak peeks at Mrs. Pitt."

"Okay, Danny, okay," she said quietly, but looking anxious.

Danny seemed to notice this. He slid a hand out from under the covers and took one of hers.

"Ma, it'll be okay. All right? I promise."

"Sure. I know."

"You can't remember anything about last night?" said Stone persistently.

"No," Danny said firmly. "But you'll be the first to know when and if I do."

Stone was about to say something else when a nurse walked in. "Willie, the doctor's releasing you. We're getting the paperwork done up. You have a way to get home?"

Stone said, "I drove here in your truck. I can take you back."

"Okay, but I'll call Gramps. He'll want to be there when I get home."

"Hey, Willie, don't you forget now. California here we come."

"I'm there, man."

The two did a little knuckle smack to seal the deal.

Stone said to Abby, "How long are you staying here?"

"A few hours. Why don't you come by for dinner tonight?"

Danny said, "Hey, you two got something going on?"

"Look, Mr. Movie Star, you're not the only one with dreams," said Abby, who blushed slightly as she said this.

*

On the drive back to town, Stone asked Willie something that had been puzzling him.

"You said Debby called you the night before she was found dead. Where from?"

"The bakery. She was doing some work there. They liked her to come after hours. Folks coming in to get muffins and cookies don't want to smell paint. Ain't good for business."

Stone thought of the half-finished mural he'd seen on the wall there. "And the bakery is right across the street from Rory Peterson's office."

"That's right. So?"

"So he was killed too."

"But in town. And the night before. Debby was out at her folks' house."

"No. Debby's body was *found* the next morning. But you said she'd been dead awhile. Maybe she was killed the night before. The same night Peterson was. His body was probably found that same morning too."

"Okay, but her parents' place is a good fifteen miles from town."

"But at eleven o'clock she called you from the bakery in good spirits. Let's say Peterson was killed around then or a bit later. The mural she was painting was in front of the store, with a good view of the street and the buildings opposite."

Willie sat up straighter. "Are you saying she maybe saw who killed Peterson?"

"At the very least she might have seen someone go in his office. Then she might have gone to investigate or the killers saw her and grabbed her because she was a potential witness. They take her back to her parents' house, kill her, make it look like suicide and no one thinks to connect the two together."

"Damn," Willie said slowly. "That makes a lot of sense. We gotta tell Tyree about this."

"I plan to."

When they pulled into the front yard of Willie's home they saw Bob Coombs' truck parked there. Willie got out as the front door opened and Bob was standing there smiling and waving. Willie hurried up the steps to embrace his grandfather while Stone, who'd been following Willie, turned and walked back to the truck to grab Willie's bag.

He had just closed the truck door when the force of the explosion knocked him off his feet and slammed him facedown into the mud. As debris rained down around him, a dazed Stone lifted up his head. Where the trailer had been there was now nothing. He could see straight through the gap to the trees behind. Something large landed next to his head, smoke rising off its sizzled surface. He didn't recognize it. And one could hardly blame him.

They were the earthly remains of Willie Coombs, what little there was of him left.

Stone's head dropped back into the mud and he lay still.

52

Annabelle and Caleb had returned to the bus station and discovered that, somewhat ahead of the regular schedule, the same driver was just about to head out with a load of people on the route Stone had taken. Annabelle snagged a seat right behind the driver and peppered him with questions while Caleb followed in the van. A half hour into the ride Annabelle saw the 1924 Indian motorcycle with the rare left-hand sidecar pass the bus, drop back and then fall in behind the van.

She sighed with relief. Big Reuben Rhodes had arrived. They might very well need the man's muscle. She'd told Reuben to bring quite a few things with him that she'd thought they might need. She noted with satisfaction that the sidecar was filled with items.

A few hours later Annabelle climbed off the bus in the middle of a curvy road bracketed by a mountain on one side and a typical sheer drop on the other. This was where Stone and his friend had gotten off, the driver told her.

Before she left the man had added, "Lot of interest in those two. What's going on?"

"Can't talk about it. National security."

"National security, huh? They looked like a couple of bums."

"If you were on the run from the feds, what would you dress like?"

"I guess I see your point."

"And you're sure you don't remember anything they said about where they were actually going?"

"Kid just got up and told me to drop him off here. The older guy got off with him." He paused. "The kid was wearing a varsity jacket. You know, for sports."

"Did you get the name of the school? College? High school?"

"Didn't pay that close of attention."

Annabelle held up a sheet of paper where'd she taken notes during her conversation with the driver. "And these are the towns nearby? All of them? You're sure?"

"Lady, there ain't that many of them. That's it. Happy searching."

He closed the door and the bus pulled away.

Annabelle met up with Caleb and Reuben and filled them in on what she'd learned. "Knox is doing exactly what we are, only he has a head start," she said.

"Yeah, but there are three of us," Reuben said. "We can split up. I'll take two of the four places and you guys hit the others."

"Good idea," said Caleb.

"And you brought everything I told you to?" asked Annabelle.

"Yeah, but I feel like I'm running a damn Hollywood prop department."

"You just never know when something might come in handy. We can load it in the van." After they were done she looked at the sheet. "Caleb and I will do Mize and Tazburg. Reuben, you can hit South Ridge and Divine." She pulled maps from her bag and handed them to Reuben. "I got these from the bus station. The towns look to be anywhere from two to three hours apart. They're not far as the crows fly, but all the roads are back roads and switch backs with chunks of mountain in between."

"Winding roads. Perfect cruising turf for the Indian," Reuben said, affectionately patting the motorcycle's gas tank.

"They just make me queasy," said Caleb. "Not that I'm complaining," he quickly added as Annabelle shot him a look.

"We'll keep in touch via cell phone. Whoever finds something positive, we can hook up within a few hours." She handed a photo to Reuben. "This is a picture of Knox, just in case you run into him."

"Thanks," said Reuben as he climbed on his bike and put his helmet and old-fashioned goggles back on.

"What if we find Oliver at the same time that Knox does?" asked Caleb.

"Then we persuade him to let Oliver go with us," Reuben said.

"He's not going to do that, Reuben."

"He will if we're *really* persuasive."

"We can't take out a fed," Caleb said. "Even new testosterone Caleb draws the line at that."

"Caleb," Annabelle said, "let's worry about that only if we have to. Right now, all I want is to find Oliver. And the longer we stand around here the better the chances are that Knox will find him first."

Reuben kick-started the Indian and the engine roared to life. He gave them a little salute, glanced at one of the maps and took off heading east.

Annabelle started to climb in the driver's seat of the van but Caleb stopped her. "I'll drive," he said, hopping in and putting the keys in the ignition.

"Why?"

"You don't know how to handle curves. Too herky-jerky. That's why I was feeling sick."

"Really? What if the time comes where we need to drive really fast, Caleb?"

"Get in!"

"What?"

Caleb fired up the van and Annabelle had to hustle

around and jump in before he roared off. He accelerated so fast she tumbled into the backseat.

"What the hell are you doing?" she cried out as she struggled back up.

"When the time comes, I'm your wheelman."

She managed to clamber into the front seat and quickly buckled up as he took one curve and then the next at almost sixty miles an hour. When she glanced over she noted how professionally he was maneuvering the steering wheel and then realized how smoothly the bulky van, which was clearly not designed for this sort of terrain, was handling the road.

"Caleb, how are you doing that?"

"I can drive, okay? You should have seen me at a guy named Tyler Reinke's house. I took the Nova airborne."

"I can see that you can drive. But how?"

He sighed. "Why do you think I kept that crappy Nova all these years?"

"I don't know. I just thought you were either cheap or had no taste. Or both."

"Well, I am cheap, but I actually do have taste. No, it was about my father."

"What are you talking about?"

"My dad was a stock car driver."

"No way!"

"After he retired from racing he worked on a NASCAR pit crew for Richard Petty."

"King Richard?"

Caleb nodded. "I was his protégé."

"What?"

"You heard me."

"You were Richard Petty's protégé? Get out of here."

"Annabelle, I started racing Go-Karts when I was six. Then I moved up to dirt track racing, and then on to ARCA where I was the top rookie. After that I finished number one in the Late Model Sportsman Series, which is like the junior circuit for NASCAR. I was just about ready to launch my career in the big leagues with Petty's help. I was going to be the number two driver on Billy Nelson's Chevy team out of Charlotte. They'd won the Winston Cup three years in a row and Bobby Mallard, their number one driver and a four-time Daytona 500 winner, was going to be my mentor. It was all set up, and then it all went to hell."

"What happened?"

"I was doing a qualifying lap at Darlington. Some call it the 'paper clip' because it's shaped like one. Others refer to it as the 'Lady in Black.' That's what it was for me."

"Why, what happened?"

Caleb's features turned somber. "The Lady in Black is very unforgiving. I came out of turn number four at 185 miles an hour, let my wheel drift and the car bumped the wall. I left half my paint on the wall, the 'Darlington Stripe' they call it. Then my right front tire blew and I was completely out of control. This was before the roof flaps era so my car flipped over and then went airborne. There are two interior walls at Darlington, the inside and pit walls. I cleared them both and slid right into a pit crew."

"Oh my God."

"*My* pit crew," Caleb said solemnly. "My *personal* pit crew."

Annabelle gasped. "It wasn't your father, was it?"

Caleb turned to look at her, his eyes watery. "I walked away from the crash with a few bumps and bruises, but he was in the hospital for months before finally pulling through. But after that, I couldn't do it anymore. Couldn't shift a gear, couldn't mash an accelerator, couldn't even slide in the car. So I just walked away from it all. Turned my life around. Went from speed to being a librarian. As far away as I could get from that world. But I kept the Nova. It was one of the first cars I ever raced in. I painted it that shitty gray to cover up the numbers and stripes. The number twenty-two car, Double Deuces, they called me. It didn't look like much but under the hood it had muscle, that car. Dual carbs, overhead cam, four hundred–plus horses and a gas pedal that never let me down. Whenever I needed to bring it, it was there. Years ago, late at night, I used to run it on straightaways when Centreville was still cow country. Got it up to 150 more than once. Those were the days."

"Caleb, I'm so sorry." She gently squeezed his shoulder.

A few moments of silence passed.

"Hey, I really got you, didn't I?"

She glanced back over at him. He was smiling broadly.

"Come on, Richard Petty's protégé? Me?"

"You made that all up? You shit!" She smacked him on the shoulder hard. But there was admiration in her features.

"What? You think you're the only one who can lie really well? I've spent my adult life surrounded by stories at the library, Annabelle. I can 'fiction' with the best of them."

"That still doesn't explain how you can drive like this."

"I grew up on the side of a mountain in Pennsylvania. First thing I ever drove was a Bobcat down a dirt road that would make this stretch of gravel look like the Autobahn." He paused. "And I did do some stock car racing when I turned eighteen. Mostly junk on dirt tracks. But after my third near-fatal accident, I decided to go into library science. But I'm still a big NASCAR fan."

"Caleb, I'm seeing a totally new side to you."

"Yes, well, everyone has their secrets."

"The Camel Club more than most, I'm finding."

53

Stone opened his eyes and felt rather than saw the people around

him.

"Ben?"

He turned to the right and focused on Abby standing there, holding his hand. He gazed over her shoulder and realized he was in a hospital room.

"What the hell happened?" he said, trying to rise up.

Abby and someone else gently pushed him back down.

"Just take it easy, Ben."

This was Tyree, who was standing on the other side of the bed.

Stone leaned back against the pillow. "What happened?" he said again.

"What do you remember?" Abby asked.

"Driving Willie home and then waking up here."

"It blew up," Tyree said quietly. "His trailer, I mean. It blew up."

"Willie? Bob? He was there too."

Abby gripped his hand. "They're both dead." Her voice broke as she said this.

"How did it happen?"

"They think it was his propane tank. Only thing that could've blown like that," Tyree said. "Another few feet and you would've been gone too. You're lucky you were standing on the other side of that truck. It took most of the blast instead of you."

Stone thought for a moment. "I remember something falling right next to me."

Abby and Tyree exchanged glances. "Just some debris," she said quickly.

"How did the gas thing happen?"

"I'm checking that out right now," said Tyree firmly. "He apparently had a cookstove and some propane tanks in his trailer along with a lot of ammo."

"I don't care about that. It can't be an accident," said Stone. "It can't be."

"I'm inclined to agree with you," said the sheriff. "I just need some proof."

Stone managed to sit up a bit. "Wait a minute. On the drive home, Willie and I talked about Debby." He went on to tell Tyree and Abby what he had figured out about Debby seeing who had killed Peterson.

Tyree rubbed his jaw. "I never saw the connection there, but Willie never told me she was at the bakery that night either. But I knew Debby hadn't killed herself."

"How?" asked Stone and Abby together.

"Her arms weren't long enough to put the muzzle in her mouth and still pull the trigger."

Stone looked at him with new respect. "I actually thought of that when I saw the shotgun. Willie had shown me a picture of Debby. I saw how petite she was."

"Tyree, you never mentioned you believed Debby was murdered," said Abby.

"That's because I didn't know who killed her. Or why. Figured it had to be somebody local. Might as well let the murderer think I'm a clueless country bumpkin. He might make a mistake, and it lets me snoop around under the radar too."

"You're clearly no country bumpkin," said Stone, and Tyree gave him an appreciative look.

"Does Danny know about Willie?" asked Stone.

Abby nodded. "He was so upset they had to give him something to calm him down. He was bawling like a baby."

"No more California dreams," said Stone.

"What?" asked Tyree.

"Long story," replied Abby.

"We need to get to work, Tyree, before somebody else gets killed." Stone started to get up again.

Tyree pushed him back down. "Whoa, now. You just got yourself nearly blown up and the doc says you need to stay quiet for a day or two."

"We don't have a day or two."

"I'm going to poke around some. With what you told me I got some new angles I can work."

"Danny and Abby need protection," said Stone.

"Me?" said Abby.

"Look at what happened to Bob. They don't care who they kill."

"I agree," said Tyree. "I got a couple of men I've deputized in the past. I'll have one here with Danny and another with Abby."

"Tyree, you don't have to do that."

"But we're gonna do it, Abby. Anything happens to you, I couldn't live with myself. I mean, well, it's just not going to happen. Understand?"

The strength of his words seemed to surprise even the sheriff. He reddened slightly.

"Okay," she said meekly.

Stone said, "What are you going to do?"

Tyree sat down and drew up a chair. "You said three men beat up Danny. Now, he won't talk to me about it but I think at least one of them was a miner."

"Why?" asked Stone.

"When I came to see Danny at the hospital like I said he zipped his mouth. But that didn't stop me from looking at his clothes. They had coal dust on them. I figure it came off at least one of the boys who jumped him 'cause Danny's never been in a mine that I know of."

"That's true," said Abby. "But why would a miner go after Danny?"

"Damn, I knew I'd seen him before," exclaimed Stone. They both looked at him. "The first day I was at your restaurant. Tyree had left, and Abby, you'd gone in the back. Danny had finished eating and was leaving when this big guy blocked his way. Asked Danny if he was going to stay this time or run out on them again. He's one of the guys with the baseball bats."

"This guy have a name?"

Stone thought for a moment. "Lonnie."

"Lonnie Bruback?"

"Describe him." Tyree did. "That's him," said Stone. "He'll have a wound on his face from my belt."

"Lonnie works a floating shift at the Cinch Valley Number Two Mine. I didn't even know he and Danny hung around with each other."

"They didn't as far as I knew," added Abby. "He's never come to the house. He's not, well . . ."

Tyree said, "Abby's too polite to say that Lonnie is definitely white trash. He's come my way a few times, petty crap, stealing gas, poaching, and then there's the addiction thing of course. Thanks for the tip, Ben. I better go check it out."

"Has anybody told Shirley about Willie and Bob?" Abby said.

"I haven't, but I expect she knows by now. But I'll check in with her too."

"I'd check her real well too, Sheriff," Stone said.

"You think Shirley's involved in this somehow?"

"Let me put it this way, you don't nag your husband about deer hunting only to see him go out and get shot. What are the odds?"

"You think it was premeditated?"

"I wouldn't necessarily except the shooter was Rory Peterson, who ended up murdered."

"Right." Tyree tapped his gun holster with his thumb. "Who'd ever thought the town of Divine would end up like the damn Wild, Wild West?"

He left and Abby pulled her chair closer to Stone and laid a hand on his. "I brought your bag with the clothes I packed for you. It's in the closet."

"Thanks, Abby."

"And I took Danny's cell phone from your pocket and put it in your nightstand."

"Won't Danny need it back?"

"I don't think he wants to talk to anybody right now."

"I'm sorry about everything that's happened to you."

"I think you've suffered a lot more than me."

"It seems so complicated, I wonder if we'll ever get to the bottom of it all."

She looked down as she said this and Stone thought he knew why. "If Danny is involved in something not quite legal, Abby, I'm pretty sure it didn't involve murder."

She looked up. "You're a mind reader too? Sort

of unsettling." She sighed. "I know my son, or at least I think I do. But there's also the chance he might be involved in something really crazy."

"Let me tell you something. When those guys on the train came after us again, Danny dropped one of them with a gut shot. The kid was beaten but he punched Danny again. Your son could have landed a haymaker but he didn't. Said it wasn't sporting to hit a man when he was down. That doesn't sound like a cold-blooded killer to me."

"I lost Sam. I can't lose Danny too."

He gripped the woman's arm and pulled her to him. "You won't, Abby. I promise."

54

Reuben was in trouble. He'd driven into South Ridge and had nearly run into Joe Knox as the man walked down the streets of the small, plain town. After about an hour, he'd climbed back in his truck and driven off. An excited Reuben had phoned Annabelle and filled her in. Then, on the way out of town while barely keeping Knox in his sights, Reuben had blown a tire on the Indian. He'd pulled off the road and phoned Annabelle again.

"Sit tight, Reuben," she'd said. "We're going to finish up the two towns and then we'll pick you up."

"Why not come now and we can tail Knox?"

"He'll be long gone by the time we get there. And if he didn't find Oliver in South Ridge, we might find him first. What town do you think he's headed to next?"

Reuben checked the map and looked around to gauge things. "If I had to guess, I'd say this Divine place."

"Okay, call back if anything else comes up."

Reuben clicked off, looked sourly at the flat tire and then kicked it. After all these years the Indian had finally let him down. And the thing was he usually carried a spare in the sidecar, but he'd taken it out so he could fit all the crap Annabelle had asked him to bring.

He sat on the side of the road and figured the odds. If this was the first town Knox had cleared, he still had three more to go. So the odds that Oliver was in Divine were one in three. Not great, but not terrible either. He would just have to keep his fingers crossed that Divine didn't turn out to be the jackpot for the federal agent and a probable death sentence for Oliver.

Melanie Knox had tried calling her father several times. The fact that Joe Knox had not answered or called her back wasn't surprising. Yet her last conversation with him had left her feeling disturbed. There had been something, well, fatalistic about his comments. A seize-the-moment sort of thing as though he was doubtful there would be many more tomorrows.

On impulse she took a cab to his town house and asked the driver to wait. When she unlocked the door, she was surprised that she didn't hear the alarm warning sound. Her father was scrupulous about setting the security system when he was away. When she turned on the lights, Melanie had to fight the impulse to scream.

The place had been trashed. Initially she thought it had been broken into and her first inclination was to run out in case the burglars were still here. To be safe she raced back to the cab and explained to the driver what she'd found. She told him that if she wasn't out in five minutes to call the cops. She hurried back in, picked up a heavy vase in the foyer and moved cautiously forward, leaving the front door open just in case.

It took less than five minutes for her to discover that the place was empty. She leaned out the front window of the upstairs bedroom and waved to the cabbie that all was okay. Melanie ducked back inside and started doing a more thorough search. She knew that her father kept two safes in the house. One was in the bedroom and the other was behind a panel in the garage; both had been undisturbed. Nor did it appear that anything of value had been taken.

That left only one possibility. Whoever had broken in had been searching for something other than valuables. And whoever it was had her dad's alarm code.

She went into her dad's study and looked around. She knew this was where he kept items from work, although she was also aware that her father did not routinely leave any important items lying around. She turned on the light, bent down and started going through the piles of papers on the floor. Thirty minutes later she had found only one thing of interest. It was a list with names on it. She didn't recognize any of them, but one did capture her attention.

Alex Ford was a Secret Service agent working out of the WFO. Why he was on a list in her father's house she didn't know. But she did know one thing: she was going to call him and find out if he knew anything about what her father was involved in.

She ran back out to the cab after locking the door and resetting the alarm. As she sat back breathless in the taxi she had the sickening feeling that her father's "job" had finally come back to bite him. Hard.

55

Alex Ford was sitting in his kitchen working his way slowly through a bowl of soup and a beer. He had been largely going through the motions at work since his last meeting with the Camel Club, or what was left of it. He'd driven past the cottage at Mt. Zion Cemetery in the hopes that Annabelle might have returned. He'd tried to call Reuben several times without success. And Caleb had been absent from the library. Unexpected personal issues, he'd been told when he called for him there.

He knew what they were up to. Working together to try and save Oliver. And a big part of him hoped they were successful.

When the phone rang he groaned. It was probably his boss trying to scrounge up some overtime drones to pull some low-level protection duty. Well, tonight he was busy. He had TiVo reruns to catch and tomato soup to finish and beers to pour down his throat.

"Hello?"

It *was* his boss, but he wasn't looking for overtime. He told Alex that he would be receiving visitors any moment now. And that he was to cooperate fully with them.

"Who are they?"

But the man had already hung up.

The knock on the door came barely thirty seconds later, which told Alex that his boss was in communication with his "visitors" and had just given them the all-clear. He poured the rest of his beer down the kitchen sink, tucked in his shirt, quickly adjusted his tie and opened the door.

Alex was six-three but the white-haired, bony-faced fellow facing him had him by at least two inches.

"Agent Ford, my name is Macklin Hayes. I'd like to have a word with you."

Alex stepped back and motioned the man in, peering behind him to see if he was alone. There wasn't anybody else, but Alex knew enough about Hayes to understand that the man went nowhere by himself. He closed the door and indicated a chair for Hayes to sit in.

"Thank you."

Alex plopped down across from him and tried to appear nonchalant.

"What can I do for you, sir?"

"I believe that one of my subordinates, Joe Knox, came to see you about a certain matter?"

Alex nodded. "He did. Had some questions about someone I knew."

"John Carr?"

"He asked about Carr, but I don't know anyone by that name."

"Oliver Stone then? You do know the man calling himself Oliver Stone?"

"Most Secret Service agents who've pulled White House protection duty do."

"But you were closer than most?"

Alex shrugged. "I'd call him an acquaintance."

"You were far more than an acquaintance. And you're going to tell me everything that you knew about his plans to assassinate Carter Gray and Senator Simpson. And whether you helped him to escape. At worst that makes you a coconspirator. At best, an accessory before and after. In a matter as grave as this one, either one gets you put away for life."

Well, the man doesn't waste any time, does he? "I don't know what the hell you're talking about."

Hayes drew a slip of paper from his coat and glanced at it. "Nearly twenty years in the Service, good record. You were the one guarding the president in Pennsylvania when he got kidnapped."

"I was the only one left standing."

"So you were there when he disappeared. Did you have anything to do with his reappearance? And more to the point, did your friend Stone?"

"Again, I—"

Hayes didn't let him finish. "Ever heard of Murder Mountain? A vanished CIA agent named Tom Hemingway? A piece of evidence that your friend Stone held over Carter Gray? Or a former Russian spy named Lesya?"

Alex, of course, knew about all of these things, but stayed silent because what could he possibly say that would do him any good?

"I'll take that as a yes."

"Oliver helped break up a spy ring operating in D.C. It involved one of your employees. Maybe you heard of it? He received a commendation from the FBI director."

"Wonderful for him, but I doubt that will carry much weight when he's caught and prosecuted for two murders."

"What exactly do you want from me?"

"I want to know what Knox asked you, and I want to know what you told him."

"Can't you just ask him yourself? I'm sure he has it down in some nice, neat report and—" Alex stopped. "Do you not know where Agent Knox is?"

"I'm not here to answer questions, merely to ask them. I believe you received a phone call from a superior at the Secret Service telling you to cooperate fully."

Alex spent the next two minutes telling Hayes what he and Knox had discussed.

"That's all?" Hayes said in a clearly disappointed tone. "I must have Knox go through an interrogation refresher course."

"He said he'd be coming back around to ask more questions. I'll be sure to tell him you're looking for him," Alex said, getting in a subtle jab.

Hayes rose. "One piece of advice. If I find that any of what you've told me tonight is untrue, or if I discover that you withheld anything of importance from me, you can catch up on your solitary confinement skills at the Castle."

"The Castle? That's the military prison at Leavenworth. I'm not military."

"Actually, it's also for prisoners convicted of national security crimes. But to more directly answer your question, you're anything I want you to be."

As soon as the door closed behind him, Alex realized he'd been holding his breath. He let it out with a gush and stood up on wobbly legs. He might as well have banded with the Camel Club to help find Oliver since it looked like he was headed to prison anyway.

The phone rang again. It was probably his boss telling him he hadn't been particularly cooperative and how did suspension without pay sound?

But he was wrong. The caller ID readout surprised him.

"Agent Ford? My name is Melanie Knox. My father is Joe Knox. Someone broke into his house and I can't get hold of him. The only thing I found was a list with your name on it."

"When's the last time you heard from him?" She told him. "I spoke to him before that. I haven't heard from him since. It could be a burglary. You should call the cops."

"Nothing of value was stolen. The two safes he had weren't even touched."

"I'm not sure what I can do about it."

"What did he talk to you about?"

"I'm afraid I can't disclose that."

"Agent Ford, I am really worried about my dad. The last time I talked to him he sounded, well, he sounded like maybe he was talking to me for the last time. I really think he might be in trouble."

Maybe that was why he'd gotten the visit from Hayes. His faithful dog had gone off the scent and the old man was operating blind. "When you talked to him did he give you any indication of where he might be?"

"He said something about being west of here, only a little more rural. I joked about terrorists in the hollers. And he said you just never knew."

"This isn't really my bailiwick, Ms. Knox."

"I'm a lawyer in private practice with lots of connections, and while my dad has never mentioned what he actually does for the government, I know it's not some State Department crap, that's just a cover. Can you at least confirm that? Please?"

Alex hesitated, but the pleading sound in her voice

finally got to him. "As best I can figure he was doing investigative work for the CIA, or at least in connection with them somehow."

"Over something critical?"

"Critical enough. He's trying to find somebody who doesn't want to be found."

"Can this person be dangerous?"

"Most people who don't want to be found are dangerous."

He thought he could hear a groan from her. "What should I do?" she said. "My mom's dead. My brother's in the Marines in Iraq. What should I do, Agent Ford? I don't know anybody else to call."

Alex sat there staring off. It was as though his nearly twenty years in the Service had simply disappeared from his memory. If Hayes had had his way, that would be more true than not. So why sit here waiting for the nuke to hit him in the head?

"Give me a number where I can reach you anytime. I'll poke around and see what I can find."

"Oh, God, thank you so much."

"I can't promise that if I find out anything it'll be what you want to hear."

"Agent Ford, I know you don't know my father, but if you were in trouble there wouldn't be anybody else you'd want covering your back more than Joe Knox. He's as straight as they come. I hope that means something to you."

"It does," Alex said quietly.

56

Later that night Stone sat up in his hospital bed staring at the wall opposite. He checked his watch and then slipped open the nightstand next to his bed and pulled out Danny's phone. He called Abby first and Tyree next. Abby was working at the restaurant and Tyree was out in the field trying to track down Lonnie Bruback, who, he said, seemed to have disappeared. They had found nothing in Willie's trailer other than a couple of torn-apart propane tanks and the remnants of the cookstove, he told Stone.

"I've got a bomb squad guy from the Virginia State Police coming to examine the scene. I know you don't want to hear this, but it might have been an accident. Willie was gone, maybe the propane was leaking and Bob lit a cigarette when Willie came through the door, and boom."

"If the propane was leaking, it would have exploded before then. I saw Shirley there like I told you and she *was* smoking a cigarette. And you would think Bob would've smelled the propane. The odor they put into the gas is pretty pungent for that very reason."

"I know. But why would they want to kill Willie so badly?" Tyree asked. "First an overdose and now a bomb?"

"He knew Debby didn't kill herself. He was going to keep making noise until the truth came out. Somebody obviously didn't like that."

"But now that they killed him we know there's something going on," Tyree pointed out.

"But these people are good and we have no proof that a crime's even been committed. So in their eyes it's better."

"Well, I'm not giving up until I get to the bottom of this."

"Tyree, everybody needs to watch their back here, and that includes you."

"I hear you."

Stone clicked off and stared down at the phone. Danny had a late-model Verizon cell phone with all the bells and whistles, including e-mail. Stone had never been into mail that didn't involve pen and paper. He scrolled down Danny's contact list. The names there were mostly female. He'd even made annotations by each entry indicating the lady's strong suits, and each contact also came with a digital photo of the woman. Several of the pictures would have qualified as pornography, at least in Stone's estimation.

He shook his head. Danny needed to seriously upgrade the quality of his female companions.

He looked outside. It was dark. He slowly eased himself from the bed. He was pretty stiff and sore but the more he moved around, the better he felt. His butt was already numb from lying in the damn bed all those hours.

He walked out of the room and over to the nurses' station. After being chastised for being out of bed, he asked and was told where Danny's room was.

He walked down that hall and saw a man sitting outside of Danny's room. When Stone approached the man stood. "Can I help you?"

"You the deputy Tyree put on Danny?"

"That's right. Wait a minute, you're that Ben fellow, aren't you?"

"Yes. I wanted to see Danny?"

"Seeing as how you saved his life, sure, go on in."

When Stone popped his head in, Danny was sitting up in bed, his face red and his eyes puffy slits.

"Danny? Can I come in?"

He looked over at Stone. He didn't say anything but waved him in with a feeble sweep of his hand.

Stone pulled up a chair and sat down. "I'm really sorry about Willie."

Danny didn't look at him but kept his gaze on the pillow he held over his midsection. When he did speak his voice was heavy and slow. The meds, Stone thought.

"He didn't deserve to die that way."

"Nobody does."

Danny glared at him. "Some people do."

"I guess you're right. Maybe some people do."

"He never hurt anybody, you know that?"

"I know."

"And Bob. I mean he's a damn old man. And they blew him up too?"

"Who blew him up, Danny? Who are we talking about?"

Danny glanced at Stone. "Why ask me?"

"Why'd you leave Divine?"

"Fresh start, like I told you."

"And why'd you come back?"

"My business."

"You want to tell me about Debby Randolph?"

"What's to tell? She was Willie's girl. He loved her, man. They were going to get married."

"So you knew about that?"

Danny nodded absently. "I was all over his case to get off the drugs. Mine work was killing him. He was in pain, okay, I get it. But I saw what the shit did to my old man. I didn't want that happening to Willie. And then Debby came along and she got him back on the right track, you know what I mean? He was doing all right. Called me up out of the blue, told me he was thinking about proposing. Asked me what I thought. Part of me wanted to say, 'No man, run the other way, you're too young. We got stuff to do.

Girls to bed.' But deep down, I was jealous, man. I got pieces of meat on my plate. He had a woman who loved him."

"So what'd you end up telling him?"

"I told him to go for it. I knew Debby. She was a great gal. And great for him. He asked me to be his best man."

"Sounds like you two had patched up your differences."

"We never had any real differences. It was just crap really."

Danny fell silent and Stone sat back in his chair and watched him for a while as the darkness fell more heavily outside.

"I saw you crying over Debby's grave. You want to tell me about that?"

Danny's head snapped up. "Nothing to tell. I was sorry she was dead. And I knew Willie was all busted up about it."

"You know who killed her, don't you?"

"If I did I would've told Tyree, wouldn't I?"

"Would you?"

"I'm tired, man. Going to sleep."

"You sure you don't want to tell me?"

"Sure as I'm lying here doing nothing."

Stone returned to his room but did not get back in the bed. Something was gnawing at him. Something he'd seen, heard or maybe both. Something that just did not add up.

He absently pulled out Danny's phone. He went through the contact list again, to see if anyone on there would provide him with a clue and explain why Danny refused to tell him what had happened. Yet nothing stuck out.

He continued pressing buttons, pushing the phone's memory into advanced fields of content. Then he stopped as the screen came up with only one name and phone number on it. *Tyree.* Yet the phone number next to the name was not the one Stone knew for the lawman. He punched it in. A few rings later a voice answered.

"Danny?" the man said.

Stone immediately clicked off. It was Tyree. He'd recognized the voice. Why would Danny have the man's name and a different phone number hidden in his phone's memory? And if this number was to be a secret, why not just memorize it? Why input it where someone like Stone could find it? He looked back at the regular contact list. Even on here he saw the numbers for Abby's house, the restaurant, numbers Danny should have easily remembered. On impulse he called Abby and told her about his conversation with Danny, though he didn't tell her about finding Tyree's number on her son's phone.

"Abby, does Danny have trouble remembering numbers?"

"Ever since high school. Doctors said it was from

the concussions he got playing ball. I told him to stop playing but he loved it too much. Killed him when his knee wouldn't let him play for Tech. Why do you want to know?"

"Just sitting here with too much time on my hands. Thanks."

He clicked off and then heard a rumbling sound coming from down the hall and glanced over in time to see an orderly passing by with a load of boxes. That ordinary sight produced an extraordinary reaction in Stone.

It came together in a neat little box all its own.

Sixty, not eighty boxes. Black dirt instead of the normal red clay. And miners who left town to get their methadone pop long before the crack of dawn.

It seemed like a spontaneous revelation, but it really wasn't, Stone knew. This stuff had been swirling around in his subconscious for a long time now. And it had finally percolated to the surface.

He grabbed his bag from the closet and quickly changed into clean clothes.

"Come on, let it be there," he said to himself as he searched the bag some more. He remembered putting it in there.

His hands finally closed around the gun Abby had loaned him. He stuffed it in his waistband and covered the bulge with his shirt. A moment later he peered out the door. When the nurses' station was empty he bolted down the hall. When the nurses came that night to give him his meds they would find his room vacant.

He had no way of knowing that they would find the very same thing in Danny's room. An hour earlier, the young man had juked his guard and made his escape.

57

Knox rolled into Divine not really knowing what to expect. It was late and it was dark and hardly a light burned on the town's main street. He drove down the road looking to the left and right, although he doubted he'd see John Carr loitering on the corner awaiting his arrival. He passed a restaurant named Rita's. There was a courthouse and jail, both seemingly deserted at this hour. Knox contemplated whether to wake up the local constabulary to help him in his quest, but he'd found the other town cops to be useless at best. He would try a different approach this time.

He turned off the main drag and headed east, at least according to his vehicle's compass. Knox's own internal direction monitor had long since given up trying to keep track of his heading after meandering through the boxy Appalachians all this time.

He slowed the truck when he saw what looked to be the remains of a trailer home. At first he thought it must have been a tornado passing through that had destroyed the place, but the trees and earth around it had not been disturbed by a twister's route. He stopped the truck, got out and inspected the site.

The blackened and jagged remains and the diameter of the debris field told him that an explosion of some kind was the cause. That was a little unusual. Of course it didn't mean that John Carr was in the vicinity, but it was at least something out of the ordinary.

He did a circle of the downtown area and drove back through. That's when he spotted the little rooming house. He parked down the street from the entrance and did a slow walk up, keeping his gaze alert for any sign of Carr.

He knocked on the door and kept tapping for another five minutes until he heard the steady if unhurried footfalls heading his way.

The door opened and the little old man with tufts of white hair standing on the other side of the threshold looked up crossly at him. "Do you know what time it is, young man?"

Knox hadn't been called a young man in at least twenty years. He hid his smile and said, "I apologize. But I got in a lot later than I thought I would."

"You mean you were *heading* to Divine?" the old man said incredulously.

"Is there a law against that?" Knox said, now smiling broadly and, he hoped, disarmingly.

"What do you want?" the man said gruffly.

So much for disarming. "Right now, a place to sleep, Mr. . . . ?"

"Just call me Bernie. Sorry, but I'm all booked up."

Knox looked over his shoulder. "This the high season in Divine?"

"I've only got two rooms to let."

"I see. Thing is, I was supposed to meet a buddy of mine up here. Maybe you've seen him, tall, lean guy around sixty with close-cropped white hair."

"Oh, you mean Ben? He's got one of the rooms, but he's not there right now."

"Any idea where he is?"

"Over at the hospital?"

"What's he doing there? Did he get hurt?"

"Almost got his butt blown up. Killed Bob and Willie Coombs, and your buddy came real close to meeting his maker."

Knox kept his voice calm and level. "So where is this hospital? I want to go see if he's okay."

"Oh, he's okay. We're all glad of that. Ben's a real hero."

"How's that?"

"Helped a couple of our own. Danny Riker when he got in trouble on the train. And Willie Coombs when he almost died on drugs. Ben saved 'em both. Right good fellow. And then Danny got attacked here in town. And Ben saved him again. Beat up three guys, or so I heard."

"Wow, that sounds like Ben all right. He was always in the middle of all the action. I'll give him your best when I see him at the hospital. And where was that again?"

Bernie told him. "But visiting hours are long over."

"I'll try to talk my way in. But if I can't, anybody else around here that can help me?"

"You can try Abby Riker out at her place, Midsummer's Farm." Bernie gave him directions. "From what I heard she and Ben got real tight."

Knox slipped a twenty into the old gent's hand when they shook.

"You're welcome to sleep in the front room," Bernie said, indicating the space behind him.

"Thanks, I might take you up on that."

He walked back to his truck trying to keep his nerves steady. He climbed in the rig, fired it up and pulled away. As he steered one-handed along the winding country road, he used his free hand to flip open the glove box. He pulled out his nine-millimeter pistol and laid it on the seat next to him.

John Carr here I come.

58

Annabelle looked down at her vibrating phone. "Who would be calling me in the middle of the night?"

"Maybe it's Reuben?" said Caleb as he drove along.

"No. I don't recognize the number." She flipped open the phone. "Hello?"

"Annabelle? How's it going?"

She snapped, "What the hell do you want?"

Alex Ford said pleasantly, "It's nice to hear your voice too."

"I'm a little busy, Alex."

"I'm sure you are."

"Wait a minute. Where are you calling from? I didn't recognize the number."

"A payphone."

"Why a payphone?"

"Because I'm pretty sure my home, cell and office phones are being tapped."

"And why is that?" she said slowly. "Is Knox on your case still?"

"That's why I'm calling. I got a frantic phone call

from Knox's daughter, Melanie. She's a lawyer in D.C. Her dad's disappeared."

"No he hasn't. He's after Oliver and we're after Knox."

"And where is all this taking place?"

"In the boondocks of southwest Virginia. So you can tell little Melanie that her daddy is just fine. For now at least."

"That's not all. His house was turned over by someone looking for something, and I'm not talking your random burglary. And on top of that I had a visitor, a man named Macklin Hayes."

"Doesn't ring a bell."

"No reason it should. He's a former army three-star who's now on the intelligence side. His rep is like a Carter Gray only more sinister and evil. He's also Knox's boss and he doesn't know where his guy is, which means Knox is roaming free."

"Why would he be doing that?"

"He might if he found out something that made him uncomfortable about what was really going on with all this. I don't think Knox is a killer. He's a tracker, and if Hayes put him on Oliver, he must be the best they have on that score. It seems clear that when Knox finds Oliver, he was to call in Hayes' heavy artillery to finish the job."

"What would Knox have found that would make him start freelancing?"

"No clue. How close are you to finding Oliver?"

"Hard to say. We narrowed it down to four towns up here—at least we think that's the case. We've cleared two of them and we're heading to a third now."

"Caleb and Reuben with you?"

"Of course. We're the Camel Club, remember?"

"Or what's left of it."

"Yeah, we seem to be dropping members like flies in a jar. Of course some chose to leave, others had no choice."

"Annabelle, I'm trying to help here, okay? I'm taking a big risk just talking to you about this."

"Nobody's asking you to take any risk, Alex. Just go back to your nice, safe federal job."

"What is it about you that pisses me off so much?"

"My girlish personality?"

"Well, keep this in mind, *girly*. If Knox is on his own then in Hayes' eyes he's become a target just like Oliver. Hayes will take them both out and anybody else who's standing around."

"The three of us are willing to take that risk."

"I know *you* are, but have you bothered to ask the other two?"

"I don't have to ask. The fact that they're with me right now is all the answer I need. Unlike some people."

Caleb glanced nervously over at Annabelle.

"Okay, just don't say I didn't warn you."

"Yeah, thanks for all your help." She clicked off and threw the phone down.

"I take it the conversation didn't go all that well," Caleb said.

"You can take it that way, yeah."

"So what did he say?"

"Hang on a minute. There's Reuben."

The big fellow was waving to them from the side of the dark road. They pulled over and in a few minutes had loaded the motorcycle into the back of the van. As they resumed driving Annabelle filled them both in on what Alex had told her. At the mention of Hayes' name Reuben's face turned a shade paler.

"Macklin Hayes?"

"Yeah," she said. "Do you know him?"

Reuben nodded. "I served under him at DIA. Also did some fieldwork for him in certain parts of the world, where the good general had a well-deserved reputation of leaving his men out to drown when things went to hell. I happened to be one of his little sacrifices. But no dirt ever splashed on him. Which is why the asshole sits where he does today."

"Well, he's apparently after Oliver *and* Knox now."

"So Hayes' plan *is* to take out Oliver then?" Reuben said slowly.

"But we're ahead of the dude on that score," said Annabelle, noting the nervous look on Reuben's face.

"And since he screwed you this would be a perfect way to settle things, Reuben," she added.

"You don't settle things with a guy like Macklin Hayes, Annabelle," he said. "He's got an army behind him and, while the man's heart is as black as they come, he's also smart and cagey as hell. I've never known him to lose at anything."

"Reuben, we can beat this guy."

Caleb said, "But we really don't know if Knox is on the run from Hayes. That's just Alex's opinion. They could still be working this thing together. Maybe Hayes' visit to Alex was a ruse."

"That makes no sense, Caleb," Annabelle snapped.

"It makes as much sense as us running around the country trying to find Oliver while the CIA is too. I mean, do we actually think we can beat them at this? And what if we do find Oliver first? Then what? We just make him disappear without a trace with all those people looking for him? We're not experts at that."

"I am," Annabelle retorted.

"Fine, *you* are. I'm not. So we make Oliver disappear. Then what? I go back to my job at the library after being inexplicably absent? You don't think they won't be all over me?" He looked over at Reuben. "And if they waterboard me, I'll spill my guts. I'm not naïve enough to believe that I can withstand that crap. And then I go to prison for the rest of my life. Great!"

"If that's what you thought, why the hell did you even come with me?" Annabelle said hotly.

Reuben answered, "We came because we care about Oliver and we wanted to help him."

"And you've changed your mind?" she said.

"It's not that simple, Annabelle."

She said fiercely, "Sure it is, Reuben. The question hasn't changed. So your answer must have." She looked between him and Caleb. "So what now? You two want to give up? Go back to town? Fine, go! Get the hell out of here. It's not like I need you."

Reuben and Caleb glanced guiltily at each other.

"Pull over the van, Caleb," she said. "I want out of here."

"Annabelle, just calm down," Reuben said in a slightly raised voice.

"No, I won't. I can't believe that you two and Alex are such wimps that—"

Reuben roared, "Shut the hell up!"

Annabelle looked as though he'd popped her in the mouth.

Reuben stared at her, his eyes those of a man barely in control of his anger. "I fought in wars for my country. I got my ass shot up for my country. I've almost died about twelve times following Oliver on his little adventures. I love him like a brother and he was there for me when I didn't have anybody else. I walked into a death chamber called Murder Mountain with him and we almost didn't walk back out alive.

And you know who was right there beside us? Alex Ford. He put his career right on the line when he could've just walked. And he also got his ass shot up, stood up to a team of freaking Korean ninjas looking to slit our throats, took a round for the president of the United States and pretty much single-handedly got us out of that hellhole." He glanced over at Caleb. "And this guy's been kidnapped, knocked out, almost asphyxiated, nearly blown up and saved me and Oliver's ass on several different occasions. And we both had to deal with one of our closest friends in the world getting blown away. And all we did was hold up our heads and try to keep going. And now we're out here in the middle of frigging nowhere trying to keep Oliver alive while an asshole that would make Charlie Manson look like a soccer mom is breathing down our backs. So if that's your definition of a wimp, then we're wimps with a capital W, lady."

For the next minute all that could be heard in the confines of the van was the heavy breathing of Reuben Rhodes.

Annabelle stared at him, a series of emotions competing on her features until one finally won out.

"I'm an idiot, Reuben. I'm sorry. I'm really sorry."

"Yeah, well. Hell." Red-faced, he looked down at the floorboard and punched the seat with one of his massive fists.

Before Annabelle could say anything, Caleb spoke up.

"Maybe we should keep going."

A red-eyed Reuben looked over at him and smiled grimly. "Won't be the first time. Or hopefully the last."

Annabelle reached out and took each man's hand in one of hers. "I just realized something," she said.

"What's that?" Caleb asked.

"That I should probably keep my big fat mouth shut. I've been acting like I'm the leader here, but I'm not even a full member of the Camel Club yet. I haven't earned it."

"You're getting there," said Reuben, giving her a quick smile. She squeezed their hands and gave him a smile back. Reuben said, "So what's the next town on the list?" Caleb looked at the sheet. "Divine."

59

Stone crouched low with his pistol out. He didn't like doing this alone, but with Tyree now implicated in whatever was going on here, he didn't have many options for assistance. The trucks were already lining up. The methadone pop brigade. Rusty trucks and rustier miners looking for their joy juice. Only they wouldn't find it here. The men came out of the old barn at the rear of Abby Riker's property carrying large boxes. They were loaded in the back of each truck with a tarp over them. After that, the drivers pulled off.

Stone mentally kicked himself for not realizing the truth sooner. The very first night he'd arrived in town and seen this caravan of miners heading to the methadone clinic, Danny had told him that they got up this early because they had to get back in time to start the seven a.m. shift at the mines. Yet it was only a two-hour round trip from the clinic back here. Stone had made the trip himself to the hospital several times. He'd actually seen the men roll into the methadone clinic at nearly five in the morning.

At the courthouse he'd seen the manifest for the delivery of legal documents. It had listed eighty boxes, but there had only been sixty there. Six high, ten across. That had meant nothing to him until he'd thought of the discrepancy in time with the miners going to and from the clinic. At least three extra hours, missing boxes and one more thing.

He glanced at the grass in front of the barn. He'd seen it while he was here working, yet had really thought nothing of it. The carpet of grass was worn down and blackened, blackened by the filthy tires of the coal miners' trucks as they came here to pick up their cargo. Just like the road in front of the snake-filled mine from which he'd barely escaped. Black dirt, black grass; he should have seen it sooner.

So the big question was, what was in the boxes?

After connecting all the dots Stone thought he knew the answer to this too. But would he get the chance to find out for sure?

There was one truck left. The boxes were put in the cargo bed. Right before he tied the tarp over them, the driver opened one of the boxes and pulled out what looked to be a small black bag. Stone had seen each of the other drivers do the same thing. He closed the box and was about to secure the tarp when one of the other men who'd been helping load the boxes called to him. They went into the barn together.

Stone slid his pistol in his waistband and crept out

of the woods, keeping as low to the ground as he could. There was a bright full moon that had made the night far less dark than usual. He reached the truck, glancing at the barn as he did so. He moved the tarp away and slowly slid a box toward him. Fortunately it wasn't taped shut, just closed up. He opened it and peered in.

He'd been right. Clear baggies filled with what looked to be prescription drugs. Probably in the oxycodone family. Two hundred bucks a pill on the street, Willie had said. Based on that he was looking at millions of dollars in this box alone.

And the *black* baggies the druggie miners had taken were probably their payment for driving the boxes to what was probably the next step in the pipeline, with the final destination being some major urban area on the East Coast. It was pretty powerful leverage when all your employees were addicts. They'd do whatever you told them to get the pain meds they couldn't otherwise afford. It was also pretty damn heartless—not surprising with drug dealers.

With the sixth sense that he possessed, Stone reacted to the presence he suddenly felt behind him. Yet it was still a fraction of a second too late.

The gun muzzle was next to his head and Stone heard the man say, "You move, you die."

Stone could feel the man's other hand expertly pat him. His gun was yanked out of his pants, dropped to the dirt and kicked under the truck.

Stone didn't move. He just stood there with a baggie of pills clutched in one hand.

The man said, "What the hell is that?"

"Illegal prescription drugs," Stone said, confused. "Why, who the hell are you?"

"Joe Knox. Central Intelligence. And you're John Carr."

Stone didn't know whether to feel a bit of relief that it was the CIA who'd caught up to him and not the drug runners. However, the end result might not be all that different. "Well, Mr. Knox, you just walked into a drug transport going down."

"What?"

"I suggest we carry on this conversation somewhere else." Stone pointed to the men coming out of the barn.

"Hey!" one of them screamed when they saw the pair next to the truck. Shotguns and pistols appeared in the men's hands even as other men rushed out of the barn to join them.

"Run, Knox!"

Using the truck as a shield, Knox and Stone sprinted off, hurtling into the woods. The men raced after them, taking aim with their weapons.

Running next to Stone, Knox snapped, "What the hell is going on?"

"Your timing was as bad as my selection of towns to hide out in." Stone glanced behind them. "Look out." He grabbed Knox by the sleeve and pulled him off the path they were on. A moment later a shotgun blast ripped the limb off a tree that Knox had been next to.

Knox pointed his pistol over his head and fired four shots in a wide swath to buy them some time. The only thing it bought was a barrage of bullets, one of which burned a crease in Knox's right arm but didn't go in.

"Damn it!" He clutched his wounded limb but kept running.

In a flash Stone grabbed the pistol from his hand, whirled around and emptied the clip at the men coming for them. He hit one of them and placed his shots so well that the other pursuers were forced to take cover.

Stone said, "This way, quick!"

They cut across a gulley, hit the asphalt road, crossed it in three leaps and plunged into the woods on the other side.

"How's the arm?"

"I've had worse."

"Got another clip?" Stone asked.

Knox dug in his pocket and flipped it to him. "Damn sorry I took your gun now."

"Me too." Stone slapped the ammo clip in and held the gun ready.

"We can't outrun them," Knox said, panting, even as he nervously eyed the gun in Stone's hand.

"No, we can't. They look a lot younger than we are."

"You're a damn good shot."

"I don't think it'll matter this time."

"You are John Carr, aren't you?"

"He's dead."

"I'll take that as a yes."

Another bullet blast came at them, forcing them to turn east. They raced up a slope, both men's breaths coming in gasps now even as they slowed. Stone slipped on some mud and fell down. Knox stooped and helped him up.

They were nearly at the top of the hill.

Stone said, "Get behind that tree, Knox. We've got some high ground here and I don't want to waste it."

Knox took cover and watched as Stone nimbly scaled an oak, shimmied out onto a thick branch, took aim and when the first man appeared out of the brush he opened fire. The man yelled out and went down. Two other men appeared behind him. When they raised their weapons, Stone shot one of them in the leg. A moment later a barrage of gunfire erupted from the woods. Stone returned it, spraying shots all across the front of the tree line. He jumped to the ground, rejoined Knox and handed him back the gun.

Knox looked surprised. "You do understand that I'm here to arrest you for the murders of Carter Gray and Senator Simpson?"

"Yeah, I do."

"So why are you giving me back my gun?"

"Because it's empty."

They ran hard, or as hard as two middle-aged men could manage over hilly terrain.

Knox said, "Shit!"

Up ahead they heard the men coming.

"They outflanked us," Stone gasped.

They stopped running as four men with shotguns broke through the brush and took aim. Behind them four more men stood, panting, guns fixed on them.

Knox held his pistol up in a surrender position. "Would it make a difference if I told you I'm a federal agent with a shitload of backup heading your way?"

One of the men placed a shot that came within an inch of taking off Knox's right ear.

"That answer your question?" the shooter said. "Now put your gun down real slow."

For a number of reasons Stone had half expected to see Tyree standing there, but he didn't recognize this guy.

"I'm just here to take this man into custody," Knox said, indicating Stone. "I don't give a damn what else is going on."

"Right, and then we just go about our business and trust you and your friend to keep quiet. Drop the gun, I ain't asking again."

Knox bent down and placed his pistol on the

ground. One of the men stepped forward and pocketed it along with his wallet and cell phone. They did the same with Stone.

The man who'd fired the shot flipped open the wallet and checked the ID. He looked up at Knox and slowly shook his head in disbelief. He spoke into a walkie-talkie.

"We got a big problem down here."

After a minute or so of conversation the man put the walkie-talkie away on a holder on his belt.

"Do we kill 'em here?" one man asked.

"No, we don't kill 'em here," he snapped. "We got to get this figured out." He motioned to his men. "Tie 'em up."

They shot forward and expertly bound Knox and Stone together. They carried the pair back to the road, where they were laid facedown in the cargo bed of a pickup truck. It drove off while the other men piled into other vehicles that had pulled up behind the truck.

Five minutes later the truck raced off the road and into a clearing, where it spun to a stop in a swirl of dirt and ripped-up grass.

Stone heard it before Knox did.

"Chopper."

It landed next to the truck, its prop wash so strong that, roped together as they were, Stone and Knox had a hard time keeping their balance as they were pulled out of the truck and loaded into the aircraft.

Two armed men climbed in with them and the chopper lifted off.

"Where are we going?" Knox said.

When the men didn't answer he looked over at Stone. "Any ideas?"

Stone glanced around the interior of the chopper. He'd only seen one other chopper up here before. "I think we're going to Dead Rock."

"What the hell is Dead Rock?"

Stone looked out the window. "That."

Knox crowded next to him and gazed down at the lights of the prison.

"Supermax prison," Stone volunteered.

"Why the hell are drug runners taking us to a super—" Knox broke off, his face ashen. "We're screwed."

"Yes, we are."

60

As the van drifted down the street early the next morning, Annabelle, Caleb and Reuben eyed the people walking by on the sidewalks; several of them stared back with suspicion.

"Not a very welcoming lot, are they?" said Caleb.

"Why should they be?" growled Reuben. "They don't know who we are or what we want. All they know is that we're not from here."

Annabelle nodded thoughtfully. "We'll have to tread carefully."

"We may not have time to tread carefully," Reuben pointed out. "Knox had a big head start. He might have already gotten to Oliver for all we know."

"There's an obvious starting place," Caleb pointed out.

The three of them stared at the sheriff's office and jail next to the courthouse.

"Stop the van, Caleb," said Annabelle. "I'll go in."

"You want some backup?" Reuben wanted to know.

"Not now. We need to keep something in reserve in case things go to hell."

"How are you going to play it?" Caleb asked. "FBI or wronged woman?"

"Neither. New angle."

She checked her face and hair in the rearview mirror, slid open the door and climbed out.

"If I'm not back in ten minutes, pull off and I'll meet you at that end of the street."

"What if you don't come out at all?" asked Reuben.

"Then assume I blew it, just start driving and don't stop."

She slid the door closed and walked into the building.

"Hello?" she called out. "Hello?"

A door opened and Lincoln Tyree stepped into the small waiting area.

"Can I help you, ma'am?"

Annabelle stared up at the tall lawman resplendent in his crisply starched uniform and highly polished boots with a leading man's jaw and brooding eyes.

"I sure hope so. I'm looking for someone." She drew a photo out of her pocket and showed it to him. "Have you seen him?"

Tyree studied the photo of Oliver Stone but made no immediate reaction. "Why don't you step on in here?" He held open his office door.

Annabelle hesitated. "I just need to know if you've seen him."

"And I need to know why you're looking for him."

"So you have seen him?"

He indicated the open door.

Annabelle shrugged and walked past him and into the office. There was another man seated there. He was in a seersucker suit with a red bow tie.

"This here is Charlie Trimble, runs the local paper."

Trimble shook Annabelle's hand.

Tyree closed the door and motioned for her to sit. He plopped behind his meticulous desk, still clutching the picture.

"Now why don't you tell me what this is all about," said Tyree.

"This is sort of confidential," she said, looking at Trimble. "No offense, but I'd like to speak to the sheriff in private."

Trimble got up. "We can talk more later, Sheriff." He glanced over at the photo. From this angle he could see it was the man he knew as Ben. "Maybe you and I can talk later too, ma'am."

Once he'd left Annabelle said, "My name is Susan Hunter. Here's my ID." She handed him across a professionally done and totally fake driver's license. "The man in the photo is my father. He might go by Oliver or John, or maybe another name."

"Why so many names?" asked Tyree as he studied the license before handing it back.

"My father worked for the government many years ago. He left under somewhat unusual circumstances. Ever since then he's sort of been on the run."

"Unusual circumstances? Is he a criminal?"

"No, these unusual circumstances are that enemies of this country are looking to kill him because of what he did to them."

"Enemies? Like who?"

"Like governments, the names of which you would recognize. I don't claim to know the whole story, only that between the ages of six and when I started college, we moved fourteen times. Different names, histories, jobs were lined up for my parents, we had handlers."

"Then y'all were sorta like in witness protection?"

"Sort of, yes. My dad was a real American hero who did incredibly dangerous work for his country. That work came with a price, though. We've been paying that price for a long time."

Tyree rubbed his chin. "That might explain a lot."

Annabelle leaned forward eagerly. "So he has been here?"

He leaned back in his chair. "He was, yes. Called himself Ben, Ben Thomas. How'd you track him up here?"

"Something he managed to send me, a coded message. But it hasn't been easy. I've been to just about every small town in the general vicinity. I was running out of hope."

"Well, like I said, he was here, but he's not here now."

"Where did he go?"

"He was in the hospital the last time I saw him."

"Hospital? Was he hurt?"

"Got himself nearly blown up. He was okay, though. I went by the hospital early this morning to see him but he was gone."

"Gone voluntarily?"

"I don't know the answer to that."

"You said he was nearly blown up?"

"We've had some strange things happening here. Haven't gotten my arms around it. Your dad was helping me. And he's not the only one missing. Fellow named Danny Riker was at that hospital too. Had a guard posted to watch him because some folks tried to kill him. But Danny slipped by my guy and he's gone too."

"And you have no idea where my father might be?"

"No ma'am, I don't. Wish I did. I'm a one-man police force in over my head. But if he was in protection why is he on the run now?"

"A few weeks ago an attempt was made on my father's life. He made sure I was okay and then he left. The way the attempt came I believe he thought it was an inside job."

"Well, if he was looking to hide out here and get a little peace and quiet, he was sorely mistaken."

"What are you talking about?"

Tyree took a few minutes to sketch out what had happened in Divine since Stone arrived there.

Annabelle sat back, thinking fast. She didn't want to get bogged down in whatever was happening in Divine. Yet if these events were connected to Oliver's disappearance it also might be the only way to find him.

She rubbed her hands nervously over the arms of her chair. "Has anybody else been in town, another stranger, asking questions about my father?"

"Not that I know of. He was staying over at Bernie's, that's a little rooming house right around the corner from here. You could check there."

"I will, Sheriff, and thanks." She rose and so did Tyree. "Anybody else in town you think I should talk to?"

"Well, there's Abby Riker. She owns Rita's just down the street. She and Ben seemed to get on right good."

Was it Annabelle's imagination or did she detect a note of jealously there?

"Thanks." She handed him a card. "Here's my phone number in case you think of anything else."

She left Tyree standing in his office looking troubled.

Outside the jail the man had obviously been waiting for her.

Charlie Trimble said, "I couldn't help but see the

photo of the man you were looking for. I interviewed him in connection with some of the things occurring in town. Perhaps the sheriff explained that to you?"

"Murders and suicides and people getting blown up, yeah, he filled me in. You say you talked to him? What did he tell you?"

"Well, perhaps we could have a bit of negotiation there."

"Excuse me?"

"I own a newspaper, ma'am. I thought when I moved here and started running the little town paper that the most exciting thing I'd have to report was when someone drove his truck off a mountain road or a mine cave-in. Now with all that's going on I feel like I'm back in Washington."

Annabelle looked impatient and felt more than a little disgusted at his gleeful tone. "What exactly do you want?"

"You tell me things and I tell you things."

"Like what?"

"Like who Ben really is."

"And if I do, what can you tell me?"

"We have to have a bit of good faith there. But I can tell you that he struck me immediately as not being your typical drifter. He was too well-spoken, too cunning. And his physical abilities spoke for themselves. According to what I've learned, he beat up three men on a train, saved a man's life using battery cables and fought off three other men wielding baseball bats. Not your typical wandering soul."

"He had some special skills, yes."

"And your relation to him?"

"My father."

"Excellent. I'd heard he was in the military."

"Vietnam."

"Special Forces."

"Very special."

"And does he make a habit of wandering the countryside?"

"He had a job in the government for a while but got tired of sitting behind a desk."

Trimble gave her a patronizing smile. "I doubt your father ever sat behind a desk. If you don't tell me the truth, I have no reason to accord you any."

"Well, it seems like I've told you a lot already. How about some action on your end?"

"All right, that seems fair actually. Your father has been spending a lot of time with Abby Riker and her son Danny. He's a troubled youth. Sort of the epitome of the high school poster boy who reached his prime when he was eighteen and everything's been downhill since."

"Is he a druggie? A boozer?"

"Not drugs, but he does like his alcohol. His mother won a big lawsuit against a coal company involving an accident that cost her husband his life.

So they have a lot of money, live in a big house, but Danny's life has been off track for a while."

"The sheriff says he's missing too."

"Your father struck me as a good man trying to do the right thing. My advice would be to not assume that anyone else here has those same intentions, including Danny, even though your father saved his life."

"Would that caveat include you too?" she said.

"I'm a fairly recent arrival here. I called Washington home for forty years. I still have a lot of friends there, get regular updates. And—" Trimble broke off, his eyes seeming to look right through Annabelle and on to something of far greater interest.

"Mr. Trimble?" Annabelle did not like that look at all.

He seemed to refocus on her, but his eyes showed his mind was still elsewhere. "Excuse me, I have something I need to check right now." He hurried off.

Annabelle raced down the street to the van and climbed in. She quickly filled them both in on what Tyree had told her and her run-in with the reporter.

"You think he suspects who Oliver really is?" asked Caleb.

"I wouldn't bet against it. And right now our margin of error is zero."

"Damn, Oliver can't buy a break, can he?" exclaimed Reuben. "The one town he picks turns out to be teeming with killers."

"Let's hit the rooming house fast. The clock is running."

A few minutes later Annabelle had charmed the entire story out of Bernie Sandusky.

She got back in the van. "Knox was here. He found out about Oliver. Bernie told him that Oliver was in the hospital or else he could try Abby Riker's place, A Midsummer's Farm. If Knox went to the hospital and found Oliver gone he might have tried Midsummer. Let's roll."

61

Stone and Knox sat, manacled to metal chairs that were bolted to the slab floor, in a windowless cement block room painted gray. They'd been here for many hours now and the room was so cold that they were both shivering. They jumped when the door banged open and the group moved in. There were five of them, all in blue uniforms and all armed with pistols and billy clubs dangling from thick belts. They formed a semicircle of flesh behind the pair of prisoners, arms folded across their muscular chests.

So fixated were Stone and Knox on this little army that they didn't hear the other man come in until he closed the door.

When Stone turned to look at this new arrival, he flinched.

It was Tyree. Only it wasn't Tyree. Not Lincoln Tyree anyway. It was a shorter, stouter version of the man.

In an instant Stone made the connection—Howard Tyree, the older brother who was also warden of this place. He wore a navy blue polo shirt, pressed khaki pants and tasseled loafers; wire-rimmed glasses covered his clean-shaven face. He didn't look like a rottweiler warden at a supermax. He looked like an insurance salesman on a golf holiday.

"Good morning, gentlemen," said Tyree.

Stone's heart sank with the words. It was the voice he'd heard when he'd made the call on Danny's phone. He and the sheriff sounded nearly identical.

Son of a bitch!

The other men had instantly come to attention when Tyree walked in. He sat down behind a small table opposite Stone and Knox. The warden held a file in his hand, opened it and read through the contents.

A minute later he slipped off his glasses and gazed across at Stone. "Anthony Butcher, triple murderer, fortunate enough to have done it in a state that does not believe in capital punishment. So you received a life sentence without possibility of parole instead of the execution you so well deserved. Transferred out of four different correctional facilities over the last twelve years, including the supermax in Arkansas, because you have an anger issue." He glanced down at the file. "And a problem respecting authority."

Stone glanced at Knox and then back at Tyree, his *anger* at what was being done to them building beyond all hope of containment. Stone knew he shouldn't but he also couldn't stop himself. "How much does one of those scripts cost, Howie? They must come in real handy in your line of work."

The warden tapped his thumb on the table and one of the guards handed him his billy club and a towel along with a bungee cord. Tyree stood, took his time wrapping the towel around the head of the club and secured it there with the cord.

The next instant Stone was slumped sideways in his chair, blood running down his battered face.

Tyree sat back down after dropping the bloody club on the table. He resumed looking at the file after methodically wiping a speck of Stone's blood off his glasses with a handkerchief he pulled from his pants pocket.

"With the towel it doesn't really leave much of a mark," he murmured in a casual tone. "We find that helpful in keeping order here. Prisoners have far too much time to complain about trivial things."

He thumbed through more pages of the file and then pointed at Knox. "You're Richard Prescott, a.k.a. Richie Patterson from the great state of Mississippi. Killed two people in an armed robbery in Newark twenty-one years ago and one more since you came into the correctional system. The Garden State didn't want you anymore so you're now our guest for the rest of your natural life." He said all this as though he were reciting tedious lecture notes to an auditorium full of bored college freshman.

"My name is Joseph P. Knox of the Central Intelligence Agency. And in about twenty-four hours there'll be an army of feds at this place, and the next thing you know, you assholes are the ones who'll be rotting in a supermax."

Tyree hit Knox so hard with the billy club that the chair tore loose from its underpinning and he fell over unconscious onto the slab floor.

Tyree closed the file. "Get 'em up."

The guards unhooked them from the chair shackles and pulled the men to their feet.

Tyree looked at the unconscious Knox. He said in a weary tone, "Wake him up, George. He has to hear this."

A bucket of water was thrown in Knox's face. Gagging, he came to, spitting up water and his own blood.

Tyree waited for Knox to catch his breath and then paced in front of the two with his hands clasped behind him.

"This is the Blue Spruce Supermax Prison. It is unlike any prison you gentlemen may be familiar with. My name is Howard W. Tyree. I am privileged to be the warden of this outstanding facility. Here, we receive from all over prisoners who have problems adjusting to the life of incarceration, or simply who have problems in general. Our sister prisons sent you here because at Blue Spruce we specialize in being problem solvers. We have never had any disruptions here or, needless to say, any escapes. We are a professional organization. So long as you follow the rules, you will have no reasonable cause for concern for your personal safety either from your fellow prisoners or the fine men who guard this place."

Blood from both Stone and Knox dripped onto the floor as Tyree was talking. He impatiently flicked a finger at one of his men, who quickly cleaned it up with the billy club towel.

"Excessive force is only used here when absolutely necessary. Just so we're clear on the boundaries, I will demonstrate."

He stopped pacing and faced the two men.

"If a prisoner does not instantly obey a command from a guard, this level of force can and will be utilized."

Tyree took the billy club from the guard and slammed it point first into Stone's gut. Stone bent over, throwing up what little there was in his belly, and then dropped to the floor.

Tyree calmly kept going. "Please keep in mind that at Blue Spruce, unlike other correctional institutions, warnings to inmates of any kind are not required and typically will not be given. Unauthorized action on the part of any inmate will be met with immediate consequences." Tyree paused to let Stone be wrenched back to his feet, still heaving and gasping for air.

Continuing, Tyree said, "If a prisoner in any way verbally abuses a guard, this level of force can and will be utilized."

Tyree slammed into the still dazed Knox, knocking

him to the floor. He pushed the billy club against his throat until the man turned blue and his body started to spasm from lack of oxygen.

Tyree got up, tossed the club to one of the guards and a gagging Knox was heaved back to his feet.

Dusting off his pants, Tyree went on. "If a prisoner in any way threatens bodily harm to and/or physically attacks a guard, deadly force can and will be utilized without prior warning."

Tyree nodded at one of his guards, who pulled out his pistol and handed it to the warden. He checked to make sure there was a round in the chamber, popped off the safety, lifted the gun up and aimed at Stone's head.

"For Chrissakes! Don't!" screamed Knox through his busted mouth.

The door opened and a tall black man was hauled in, his face bloody and swollen, and his hands and legs chained together, forcing him into a prisoner shuffle. The guards slammed him up against a section of wall that was paneled in a rubbery material covered in pockmarks and then moved away.

Tyree explained, "This man attacked a guard barely five minutes ago. He felt it violated his civil rights to be beaten for extending his middle finger to one of my men because he'd made a silly little joke about this fellow's mama."

Tyree swung the pistol around and fired a round into the black man's head. He slumped to the floor, an exit crater blown into the back of his head. A part of his brain along with the slug was embedded into the rubber wall behind, leaving another large pockmark.

"And he was shot while trying to escape after taking a hostage, all of which we have duly documented for regulatory review."

Tyree handed the gun back and resumed his pacing. "Those are basically the rules here. We keep them short and simple so that you will have no trouble remembering and thus following them. Please also keep in mind that here you have no privacy, no rights, no dignity and no reasonable expectation of anything except what we say you can have. At the moment you walked into this facility you ceased to be human beings. Indeed, because of the crimes that you have committed against humanity you have forfeited all rights to be considered human beings. No guard at this prison will have any compunction about ending your life at any moment and for any reason. You now will be officially processed into this prison's inmate population. If you give us no trouble, I can reasonably assure that you will live out your lives here in relative peace and security, though I cannot say how long that life will be. Supermax facilities are by their very nature dangerous places. We of course will make all reasonable attempts to ensure your safety, but there are no guarantees." He paused and faced them. "Welcome to Dead Rock, gentlemen. I *can* guarantee that you will not enjoy your stay with us."

62

Annabelle walked into Rita's, pausing at the door to survey the landscape. Half the tables were filled, as were all the stools at the counter.

"Can I help you?" A man came around the bar and was looking at her.

"I was looking for Abby Riker?"

"She's not here. She's at home."

"Midsummer's Farm?"

"Who are you?"

"Sheriff Tyree told me to come and see her."

"Oh, well I guess that's okay then. You might want to call out to the house and talk to her."

"Do you have her number?"

Annabelle made the call. When Abby answered it was clear that she had been crying. She didn't want to talk to Annabelle until she mentioned the man Abby knew as Ben.

"He's my father." Annabelle quickly told her the same story she'd told Tyree.

"He told me his daughter *and* his wife were dead," Abby said coldly.

"My mother *is* dead. Has been for decades. He told you I was dead because that's how he protects me."

"Government spy type? I knew there was something about him. Just different, you know?"

"Yep, that's my dad. Different. Do you have any idea where he might be?"

"He was at the hospital yesterday. Along with my son, Danny. Now they've both disappeared. I'm worried sick for a lot of reasons."

"Sheriff Tyree told me about what's been happening around here. I guess you have good reason to worry. Can I come out to see you?"

"Why?"

"Right now you're the closest lead I have to my dad."

"I told you I don't know where he is. Or my son either."

"But you might remember something if we keep talking about it. Please, it's my only shot."

"All right." Abby told her how to get to the place and a little while later Annabelle was seated across from Abby in her living room. Caleb had parked the van well back and had stayed there with Reuben. Annabelle tried various lines of questioning and Abby answered each of them, but nothing she learned helped her.

"Had you two become friends?"

Choosing her words carefully, Abby said, "He's a good listener. Not judgmental. I find that a rare combination. I hope he's all right." A tear slid down her cheek. “He had a way about him too. Just made you feel good about yourself.”

“Do you think he and your son might have left the hospital together?”

“I don’t know. Danny was pretty beat up. If it wasn’t for Ben.” She stopped and looked at Annabelle. “What’s his real name?”

Annabelle hesitated, but Abby appeared to be genuinely concerned about Stone. “Oliver.”

“If it hadn’t been for Oliver I wouldn’t have my son at all, so whatever I can do to help you I will.”

“If you think of anything that might be helpful you can reach me at this number.” She handed Abby a card, gave her hand a reassuring squeeze and left.

Back in the van, she sat lost in thought in the passenger seat.

“What do we do now, Annabelle?” asked Caleb, while Reuben stared at her curiously.

“You okay?” he asked.

She started and looked at him. “What? Yeah, I’m good.”

“Boy, Abby Riker has some big bucks,” said Reuben as he glanced back at the enormous house.

“Yeah, only thing it cost her was her husband.”

“What do we do now, Annabelle?” Caleb asked again.

Annabelle didn’t say anything, because she didn’t have an answer.

Where the hell are you, Oliver?

63

Being processed into Dead Rock included standing bent over naked with your butt cheeks spread as painfully as possible while a group of men and one woman looked on. The woman was also videotaping the proceedings, which added considerably to the dignity of the event. The body cavity search completed, their heads were then shaved.

Suspicion of lice, Stone heard one guard say, while another chuckled about a weapon perhaps being concealed in their hair roots.

They sat crouched in a corner naked while men scrubbed them raw with stiff brushes that felt steel-tipped. After this a fire hose blasted them with such force that they were pinned against the wall like ants at the mercy of a berserk garden hose.

Dressed in orange jumpsuits, cuffed and shackled, they were led down a stone hall to a cell. Guards held stun guns an inch from their prisoners' sides, seemingly just praying for a reason to hit them with a 50,000-volt tickle. The cell door was solid two-inch steel with a food and cuffing slot cut into the bottom half and a small viewing window in the upper half. They were pushed in, the shackles removed, the jagged links stripping at their skin, and then the door slammed shut and was loudly bolted behind them.

Knox and Stone slumped down next to each other as their gazes drifted dully over the eight-by-twelve-foot space. There was a steel toilet and sink unit bolted to the wall with no knobs that could be fashioned into weapons. There was also a steel slab for a desk and two steel slabs on the wall with a thin plastic mattress and pillow on each. A six–inch vertical slit in the thick concrete block and rebar wall constituted the sole window.

For the next half hour each man groaned and moaned and rubbed at innumerable bruises, cuts and bumps on their bodies.

Knox finally sat back against the wall, wiggled a loose tooth in the back of his mouth with his finger and looked over at Stone. "Whatever the hell happened to due process?"

"It seems to be growing less popular these days," Stone replied as he rubbed at a knot the size of a quarter on the side of his head.

"I'm surprised they put us in here together. I'd assumed we'd be segregated."

"They did it because they don't care what we tell each other."

"You mean because we're never getting out?"

"We don't really exist. They can do anything they

want. And he murdered a man right in front of us. That shows he doesn't expect us to be a witness anytime soon. You think the cell is bugged?"

"I doubt they care that much, but you never know."

Stone drew closer and lowered his voice to a whisper and tapped his shoes against the walls to disrupt any audio surveillance. "Any chance your agency will find you?"

Knox joined in the wall-tapping. "There's always a chance. Looks like the only one we've got right now. But even if they do, you realize how many places there are to hide us here. Like you said, we don't exist."

"And they can always kill us. Invisible in life, nothing in death. Who sent you after me?"

"I guess it would sound pretty stupid to say that's classified under the present circumstances. Macklin Hayes."

A tiny smile crept across Stone's face. "I guess that makes sense."

"You served under him."

"If you want to call it that."

"What would you call it?"

"I didn't serve under him, I *survived* him."

"You're not the first to tell me that."

"I'd be surprised if I were."

"You earned that medal. Why didn't you get it?"

Stone looked surprised. "How'd you find out about that?"

"Did some digging. You were a slam dunk for the big one."

"Every soldier in my company would've done the same for me."

"That's bullshit and you know it. I was over there too. All soldiers are not created equal. So why didn't you get it? I looked at the paperwork. It stopped at Hayes."

Stone shrugged. "I haven't given it that much thought over the years."

"You did something to really piss off the man, didn't you?"

"If I did, it doesn't matter now, does it?"

"Tell me."

"No, I'm not going to tell you!"

"Okay, next subject. I know you killed Gray and Simpson."

"Good for you."

"Is that a confession?"

Stone picked up the intensity of the tapping. "Right now we need to come up with a way to get out of here. Because if we don't it won't matter to either of us what I did or didn't do."

"Okay, I'm listening," said Knox.

"And I'm still thinking. But if we do escape, what are you going to do?"

"What do you mean?"

Stone's eyes flashed. "You know what the hell I mean. About me?"

"If I had to answer you now I'd say I was going to complete my assignment and turn your ass in."

Stone took this in and finally nodded. "Okay. Fair enough. Just so we know where we stand."

"So fill me in on the events leading up to us ending up here."

Stone started talking. A half hour later he was finished as both pairs of shoes continued to drum against the wall.

"Damn!" Knox said. "You weren't kidding about picking the wrong town to hide out in." He rubbed at a cut on his face. "I talked to your buddies, by the way."

"Which buddies?"

"You know which."

"Are they okay? Tell me the truth. No bullshit." Stone looked Knox directly in the eye.

"I didn't do anything to them. And as far as I know, they're fine."

"They don't know anything and did nothing. If we manage to get out of here you put that down in your report. This is about me, not them."

"Okay." He leaned close to Stone and whispered in his ear. "But they still managed to follow me up here."

"You're sure? You saw them?"

"Not exactly, but it couldn't have been anyone else. At least the chick is up here. Susan, not that that's her real name. Pretty sure she spun a story at a local diner that almost got my ass handed to me."

"If she did, it was only out of friendship to me, Knox. She's not worth going after. You've got me. That's all Hayes wants anyway."

"But still, you think they might figure out we ended up in here?"

"I'm not sure because even I can't believe we're here."

Knox slapped his hand against the hard wall. "So how do you think they're running a drug op from a supermax prison?"

"Haven't gotten that all figured out yet. But it's not like they have to worry about witnesses. They sort of have a *captive* audience."

"And the prisoners might not even know. But I guess all the guards are in on it."

"That's not necessarily true," said Stone thoughtfully.

"Why?"

"There was one guard who used to work here. He was killed in a deer hunting accident that I don't think was so accidental. His name was Josh Coombs and I believe he stumbled onto what was going on here and paid the price for it."

"Coombs? Also the name of the folks who got blown up."

"Yeah. Willie knew Debby Randolph hadn't killed herself. His mom's in on it, I'm pretty sure. They used her to try and kill him with an overdose. When that didn't work, they went for essentially a homegrown IED."

"Mother killing her own son?"

"In a town called Divine. Yeah."

The door to the cell was hit with a massive blow. Both men staggered to their feet and backed away.

"Shut up in there!" a man screamed through the door.

"Okay, we're shutting up," Knox said.

"I said shut up, assholes."

Knox and Stone said nothing, just stared at the door.

"One more word and we're extracting your asses."

Silence.

"Okay, you asked for it. Walk over to the cuffing slot, turn around and extend your hands through the opening. Now!"

Stone and Knox looked at each other. Stone went first, extending his hands through the slot with his back facing the door. He was cuffed hard, his bony wrists slammed together and cut by the edge of the slot. Then Knox did the same.

"Now move away from the door," the same voice barked.

Knox and Stone retreated to the back of the cell.

The door was opened and what happened next was only a blur.

Five body-armored men with face masks poured in carrying two huge inch-thick Plexiglas shields. They hit Knox and Stone hard, slamming them against the stone wall. Pepper spray hit them both in the eyes, even as Taser shots paralyzed them. They went down, wanting to claw at their eyes, but with limbs electrified stiff as a corpse *and* cuffed hands that wasn't an option. They were stripped of their clothing, lifted into the air and hustled down the corridor. Thrown in a shower, they were hit with blasts of water, which at least helped ease the agony of the eye spray.

Picked up again, they were carried to a room that had two steel slabs covered in what looked to be urine and feces. They were smashed down on these hard cots and put in five-point restraints. Before the guards left they were Tasered once more.

"What the hell was that for?" Knox managed to scream as the current pounded him.

A guard with one stripe on his sleeve hit him in the mouth with his fist. "Not obeying orders. This ain't like other prisons, old man. This is Dead Rock. Don't know what prison you come from but you get no warnings up here, boy. No damn warnings. And just so's you know, I can Taser your ass just for the hell of it. 'Cause my old lady didn't blow me, or 'cause my dog shit on the rug."

"I work for the CIA."

"Sure you do. Hey, fellows, we got us a spy right here. Bet your friend is KGB."

He walked to the next slab and smacked Stone in the face. "You KGB, Grandpa?" The guard reached a gloved hand down to Stone's crotch and squeezed. "I asked you a question, old man."

Stone didn't say anything; he just looked at the guard, remembering every detail of his face through the clear mask. And he suddenly recognized him too. He was one of the men with the baseball bats who'd beaten up Danny and then come after him. This was the third one, the coward who'd run for it, but Stone had still managed to nail him in the back with one of the bats.

"You ever tell your buddies you ran out on them?" he said quietly as the Taser sting wore off.

The guard gave a nervous, hollow laugh under the burn of Stone's gaze, glanced at the other guards and took his hand away. As he was leaving the room with the other guards, Stone managed, despite the restraints, to turn his head just enough to keep his eyes on the fellow. Then the door closed.

"I guess they're trying to break us quick," groaned Knox.

"They'll have to work harder."

"You think so, do you?"

"Yeah, I do."

Something in his voice made Knox glance over at him. "Were you ever a POW?"

"Six months. This place is actually pretty nice compared to what the Viet Cong thought was humane. All I had there was a pit with a sheet over it, beatings whenever they felt like it, along with an interrogation technique that would make waterboarding seem like dunking for apples. And the food they threw down once a day would not be considered edible by any stretch of the imagination."

"But we're not twenty years old anymore, Carr."

"Call me Oliver, Carr is dead."

"Okay, but we're still not twenty."

"It's all in the mind, Knox. It's all in the mind. If we don't believe they can break us they never will."

"Yeah, sure," Knox said, clearly unconvinced of this.

"You got any family?"

"Son and daughter. My boy's in the Marines stationed in the Middle East. My daughter's a lawyer in D.C."

"I had a daughter. But she died. How about your wife?"

"Dead."

"So's mine."

"Brunswick, Georgia? Claire?"

Stone didn't say anything.

"Guy named Harry Finn said that Simpson admitted

to having her killed. That he ordered a CIA hit on you and your family."

Stone stared at the ceiling, slowly flexing his limbs against the thick leather bindings. "Harry's a good guy. Knows how to cover your back."

"I'm sorry about your family . . . Oliver," he murmured.

"Get some sleep, Knox. Just get some sleep. You're going to need it."

Stone closed his eyes.

A few minutes later an exhausted Joe Knox did the same.

64

"We're running out of time," Caleb said.

The three of them were sitting around an old picnic table in a small clearing off the main road to Divine. A meal Annabelle had purchased at Rita's was on the table. Reuben gnawed on a piece of fried chicken while Annabelle glared at Caleb.

"I'm open to suggestions," she said.

"Maybe Alex can help," suggested Caleb as he carefully picked the skin off his piece of chicken.

"Help what, screw things up?"

"We talked about Alex, Annabelle," retorted Reuben. "He's as professional and brave as they make 'em. And I think Caleb's got something."

"What do you expect him to do, come running to help us? It'll mess up his career. You heard him."

"You can always ask."

"Why me?"

"Okay, I'll do it," said Reuben. "*Anything* to help Oliver."

Annabelle stared at each man, sighed and pulled out her phone. "No, I'll do it."

A minute later she said, "Alex?"

"Annabelle? You okay?"

"I—" She stopped. "*We* need a favor."

Five minutes later she clicked off.

"Well?" Reuben and Caleb asked together.

"He's going to help us. He's coming up here, in fact."

Reuben slapped Caleb on the back, almost sending him headfirst into a tub of potato salad.

"I knew it. Friendship *is* thicker than official duty."

"Yeah, well, we'll see, won't we?" she murmured. "But in the meantime we can't just sit on our butts. We need to keep digging away."

Reuben tossed the bones of his chicken breast into the woods, wiped his mouth and balled up his napkin. "I'm ready to roll. I'll do a recon of the area, see if anything hits me."

"And me and Caleb?"

"Talk to some more people in town. And Caleb stays with you. Remember there's a killer on the loose. We'll meet back here later."

"I'm worried about that reporter," said Annabelle. "Even if we find Oliver, that guy could screw it all up. I didn't like his look. It was like he'd just suddenly figured something out."

Caleb said, "Well, maybe we have to convince him it would not be in his best interests to follow any of that up."

Annabelle considered this suggestion. "I think you might be right."

Reuben drove off on his Indian while Caleb and Annabelle headed back into Divine. When they reached the main street Annabelle had Caleb park near the courthouse.

"The sheriff told me that Willie Coombs' mom works at the courthouse as the clerk. I want to see if I can get a word with her."

Caleb looked around and his eyes brightened as his gaze fell on the library.

"I think I see something *I* can do," he said. "But if you need a bodyguard, I can hang with you. Like Reuben said, there is a murderer on the loose."

She gave him a gracious smile. "I appreciate the offer, killer, but I think I'll be fine. The sheriff's office is just right next door."

Caleb headed off and Annabelle went inside the courthouse.

Shirley Coombs looked up from her desk when the door opened. Annabelle introduced herself and said why she was there. Though Annabelle couldn't know it, Shirley Coombs looked as though she'd aged several decades.

"I'm really sorry about your son."

Shirley eyed her suspiciously. "Did you know Willie?"

"No, but Sheriff Tyree told me what happened."

"Parents aren't supposed to outlive their children," she said in a hushed tone and then lit up a cigarette; her fingers shook so badly she was barely able to work the Zippo.

"No, ma'am, they're not."

"Lost my husband too. In an accident," she said quickly. "And my daddy in a mine cave-in."

"God, that's awful."

"Yeah, life is just awful, ain't it?" she said sarcastically. "What can I do for you?"

"I was hoping you could tell me something about my dad."

"I never met him," she said immediately.

Annabelle studied the woman closely without appearing to do so.

Okay, that was a lie.

She looked over at the stack of boxes.

Shirley said, "Got a lot of work to do."

"I'm sure. I'm really worried about my father."

"Somebody told me he was heading out of town."

"Who was that?"

"Don't recall. Probably heard it over at Rita's."

"You're friends with Abby Riker?"

At that moment an interior door opened and Judge Mosley ambled out. He wore a suit and held his driving cap in one hand.

"Shirley, I'm—" He broke off when he saw Annabelle. His smile was instant.

"Well, who is this?"

Annabelle shook his hand and felt his fingers linger just a beat too long on hers. She explained who she was and why she was here.

"Ben seemed to be a very interesting man," said Mosley. "I wish I'd gotten to know him better. I hope you find him. Well, I have to be off."

"Up to the prison, Judge?" said Shirley.

"That's right." He turned to Annabelle. "I go up there once a week and resolve disputes between the prisoners and the guards. And there are many, I'm afraid."

"I'm sure."

"Rehabilitation is the key," he said. "Although not many of the folks at Blue Spruce will ever see the light of day as free men, they still deserve some respect and dignity."

"That's what Josh thought," blurted out Shirley.

They turned to look at her.

She reddened. "My husband. He was a guard up there." She glanced at Annabelle. "He's the one who died in the . . . accident. He thought you should treat folks with respect regardless of what they've done, prisoner or not."

"Exactly," said Mosley. "I would be the first to admit that Howard Tyree is not exactly sold on that concept, but that's why it bears repeating. And my weekly presence I hope lets everyone see that common ground in fact can be reached."

"Howard Tyree?" said Annabelle sharply.

"He's the sheriff's brother," answered Shirley. "The warden up at Dead Rock."

Mosley smiled at Annabelle. "Its official name is Blue Spruce, but folks 'round here call it Dead Rock."

Shirley snapped, "They call it Dead Rock because a bunch of miners got trapped in a cave-in. Never could get to them. Sealed up in there and they built a damn prison on top of them. And one of 'em was my daddy."

Tears smeared Shirley's mascara while Annabelle and Mosley looked politely away. The judge finally said, "Mining is a very dangerous business."

"I can see that," replied Annabelle.

"Well, good day, ladies."

After he'd gone, Annabelle rose. "I guess I'll let you get back to work."

"Sorry I couldn't help you," Shirley said gruffly.

Oh, you already have, lady.

65

Stone and Knox were kept in the restraints for nearly six hours and slept the whole time. The guards who came to take the pair back to their cells seemed chagrined that they'd navigated the ordeal so easily.

They were dressed back in orange jumpsuits and hauled back to their cells. Each man had to exercise considerable self-control in the face of the guards' taunts. Knox had to bite the inside of his lip while Stone just stared straight ahead unblinking and telling himself that an opportunity would present itself if he were patient.

An hour later, they were strip-searched again, cuffed and shackled and led to the cafeteria, where the cuffs were taken off so they could eat.

Knox's belly was rumbling as they sat down at an unoccupied table. They stared around at the sea of other prisoners. Quickly counting, Stone arrived at nearly five hundred inmates, with well over three-quarters of them black, while all the guards he could see were white.

Some of the prisoners stared back at them with an array of expressions that ranged from curious to indifferent to hostile. Only a few people were talking. Most focused on their meals. Knox looked down as his food was slid in front of him.

After the attendant walked off he said to Stone, "I wonder if they have a nice cabernet to go with this slop?"

"Humor, Knox, I like that. Helps the time go by. What do you see out there?" He indicated the inmate population.

"Sorry asses just like us, only we haven't committed any crime. Correction, *I* haven't committed any crime."

Stone took a bite of his food with a limp Styrofoam spoon that was the only utensil provided. "You've seen the insides of prisons before, haven't you?"

"Yeah, but not as an inmate."

"So what's different? Think about it."

Knox looked around. "Well, they seem a pretty quiet bunch to be the baddest asses in the land."

"That's right. Subdued, beaten down, scared. Anything else?"

Knox stared at one group closest to them. Four men, all black, who sat there idly prodding their food and not bothering to even look at each other.

Knox squinted at them, following their lethargic movements and glassy eyes. "And drugged?"

"And drugged. We know they have enough pills to do the job."

"Do you think that's where the pill shipments are coming? Here?"

"No. That stuff was all for street sale probably in New York, Philly, Boston, D.C. and other big cities up and down the East Coast. They probably just use a little overflow to knock these guys down."

"Drugging prisoners involuntarily? That's got to violate about a million rights."

Stone suddenly bent down and started shoveling food in his mouth. Sensing why, Knox immediately did the same. The footsteps came up behind them and stopped.

"Manson, are the new prisoners adapting to our routines?" Howard Tyree said to the burly guard standing next to him.

Manson had an eye patch over his right eye. And as he glanced up Stone knew why. Manson was the one he'd hit in the eye with his belt.

This is just getting better and better.

"It's taking some work, but we'll get them where they need to be, sir."

Stone watched as Manson curled and uncurled his fingers as he stared at Stone with his one remaining eye. The man's look was one of unconcealed homicidal intent. He lifted his billy club out of its holster and stuck its end against Stone's jaw and pushed.

"This one here will take a little *extra* work, but we'll get him to understand our ways."

"Good man," said Tyree.

When Manson pulled the club back he did it in such a way that a jagged edge of the wood tore at Stone's face. It started to bleed, but Stone didn't make a move to wipe it away.

Tyree said, "You know, at most supermax prisons the prisoners eat in their cells and recreation time is only done one inmate at a time. But here at Blue Spruce we're a little more liberal than that." He surveyed the deadly quiet room. "Here, we allow our inmates to experience some human touches. A nice meal together, some camaraderie."

Tyree placed a hand on Stone's shoulder and squeezed lightly. Stone would've taken the bite of the rattlers in the mine over this man's repulsive touch. Yet he didn't flinch and Tyree finally released his grip.

"And because of our compassion and understanding on points like that," Tyree continued, "sooner or later they all learn our ways. But I'd be the first to admit that the route can get bumpy at times."

As he walked along with a wall of guards every inmate stared down at his plate, as though it was the most wonderful cooking they'd ever seen.

These guys are not only drugged, they're terrified, thought Stone, *because they know this guy will kill them, and there's nothing they can do about it.*

He can kill me too. And probably will. Unless Manson gets to me first.

Only when Manson and Tyree had left the room did he wipe the blood off his face with his napkin.

66

After the meal they were allowed thirty minutes outside. Outside being a floor of concrete in the middle of the prison courtyard with a sheet of razor wire as a roof and a lone and netless basketball hoop and patched ball as apparently the sole recreation.

So much for the liberal human touch, thought Stone.

Some of the prisoners slowly jogged in tight circles, one bounced the ball, yet most just stood there staring down at their shoes. Up on the tower walks were the guards, their AK-47s, shotguns, and sniper rifles at the ready and clearly visible to every man down in the pit. Stone noticed that there was a blue line that ran around the concrete field.

"You cross that line, put one toe over it, the man up there shoot you." This came from a small, twitchy inmate with a bristly gray mustache, wild hair and eyes that didn't promise much of anything behind them.

"Thanks for the scoop," Knox said. "They forgot to mention that in the orientation class."

Twitchy looked at Knox and laughed. "Hey, that's a good one. That's a damn good one." He looked at Stone. "You boys ever getting out?"

"Doesn't look that way," Stone answered. "You?"

"Life, life, life," Twitchy said in a singsong voice. "Three life sentences to run consecutively instead of concurrently. That's a big-ass difference. Oh yeah, I found that out. Both begin with the letter 'c' but that's where the similar shit stops, man."

"I can see that." Stone methodically eyed the position of each tower walk, and the shooting angles available to the guards up there. He came away impressed with the design of the place. It wouldn't take great skill to kill any man down here before he even had a chance to piss on the concrete, much less make a break for freedom.

"Is that what most people are here? Lifers?" Knox asked.

"Everybody I know is, and I been here eleven years. Least I think it's been eleven. Used to keep a calendar but I ran out of wall space. It ain't matter. No parole for old Donny boy."

"What'd you do, old Donny boy?" Knox asked, the distaste clear in his tone though Donny boy seemed oblivious to it.

"Killed me three little kids," he said as matter-of-factly as though he were merely giving his date of birth. He blew his nose in his cupped hands and then wiped them on his thighs.

"And why the hell would you do that, Donny boy?" Knox asked as his fingers curled into a fist.

"'Cause the bitch told me to, that's why. They was her kids from her second marriage, man. Insurance money. Least that's what she said. Seduced me. That's right. Gave me some ass. High on shit when I killed 'em too. You'd think that'd be a defense, wouldn't you? But hell no it ain't. I was robbed, man, robbed. I mean, where the hell is the accountability?"

"Accountability?" Knox said incredulously.

"Yeah, man. Lawyers, judges, bitches giving ass to make you do shit. Nobody wants to take responsibility for nuthin' no more. It's a damn disgrace. God bless America but we need to get our shit together in this country."

Knox clenched his teeth. "Did *she* get three life sentences?"

"The bitch? Hell no! Blamed it all on me. And she's married again and sitting pretty with all that insurance money, while my ass rots in here. Called me a *maniac* at my trial. And we had cocktails together, man. I swear to God."

"Sounds like you needed a better lawyer. But then again I think you're right where you need to be, *Donny*. Now why don't you go find another corner to hang out on?" Knox said, taking a menacing step toward the man.

Before Donny could move, Stone hooked him by the arm even as one of the tower guards stared down at them, his hands perched on the trigger guard of the AK.

"Hey, Donny, you been in many prisons?" Stone asked.

"Me? Hell yeah. This here's my fourth one. And my second supermax," he added with pride.

"Why'd you get sent to Dead Rock?"

"Hit a guard. They ain't like it when you hit *them*, but they sure as hell don't mind busting our asses, do they?"

"Yep, life's real unfair," Knox exclaimed.

"I bet you're a guy notices stuff. Notice anything weird around here?" Stone said.

"Notice stuff? Man, we only get one hour out a day. Half for chow, half for this recreation shit. Twenty-three hours and two meals in the old eight-by-twelve after that. Ain't much time to notice *stuff*."

While they were talking the man bouncing the ball let it get away from him. It rolled past the blue line. He went to get it.

"Oh, hell," said Knox, who had just noticed this. "Hey, buddy!"

The man either didn't hear him or didn't care. He crossed the line and the bullet hit him right in the back. He went down, face first. Stone and Knox started to run toward him, but other shots were fired and they pulled up.

As they watched, two guards sauntered over and picked the man up. There was no blood, Stone noted.

Donny said, "They use those damn dummy bullets if it's your first time. Hurt like hell. Knock your ass out, but it ain't kill you. Now, if it's your second time, well, you ain't gonna be around for a third time, get my drift?"

They returned to their corner as the unconscious man was carried away.

Stone continued their previous conversation. "What about the prison library? Classes? Workshop? You notice anything there?"

Donny snorted. "What, you been watching reruns of *Escape from Alcatraz*? Look around, man, ain't no Clint Eastwood 'round here. They been promising a library the whole time my ass has been here and I ain't seen one damn book yet. Supposed to have GED classes on TV too, but they say it keeps breaking down. Ain't no workshops. Ain't no nuthin'. Get a shower three times a week for five minutes and they stick a damn poker up your butt every time they do that, like you gonna pull a bazooka out your ass somehow and blow 'em away. I'd rather stay dirty. Ain't like I got nowhere to go."

He popped a piece of gum in his mouth and chewed it hard with the few teeth he had.

"Visitors, phone calls home? Lawyers?"

Donny chuckled. "At Dead Rock you got to earn your visits. Get a max of two a month. You screw up the least little thing, guess what, you ain't getting no visitors. And guess what else? From what I hear ain't been nobody earn a visit at this place in the last five years. I sure as hell ain't. Not like there's many folks lining up to come see me, but still. And you got to call collect if you even get near the damn phone. And not even my damn momma is gonna pay for a collect call from me. And ain't no lawyers coming up here. Ain't no more appeals for these boys. Everybody's forgotten us. We ain't anybody no more. We Dead Rock. Gonna die here, just the way it is. Better get used to it." He swallowed his gum and hacked up some phlegm.

Stone looked around at the other prisoners. "People seem a little mellow here." He eyed Donny. "Little too mellow."

Donny cracked a smile and drew closer. "You noticed that too? Most of these boys ain't never caught on to that crap."

"So what drug do they use?"

"Ain't know, but it's pretty strong."

"Do they put it in the chow?"

Donny nodded.

"Which meal?"

"Lunch or dinner, but that's the thing. You never know which one."

"So why do you seem so chipper?"

Donny's eyes twinkled. "I could let you in on my little secret, but what you gonna gimme me for it? Now that's the sixty-four-zillion-dollar question."

Stone started to say something but Knox broke in.

"Tell us and if I ever get out of here, I'll take you away from old Dead Rock."

"Right, shit you will. And besides, you ain't never getting out of here."

"I'm a fed, Donny. Assigned to look into corrupt prisons. You think this place is corrupt?"

"Sure as hell is. But if you a fed why would you be getting *me* out of here?"

"Feds can do anything, Donny. You help me, Uncle Sam helps you."

Stone added, "And it's not like you have a lot to lose by doing it."

Donny considered this. "Okay. Not that I believe you're a fed, but what the hell." His voice sank lower. "Any meal you get, don't eat the damn carrots, just flush 'em down the toilet and then practice your dumbshit look for the boys with the billy clubs."

A guard started to move their way and Donny skittered off.

Knox said, "Well, that was informative but not particularly helpful except for the carrots. You believe him?"

"Maybe." He gazed once more up at the walls. "They designed this place well, Knox. I don't see many weaknesses."

"Day gets better and better."

A horn sounded and the prisoners started shuffling in.

Stone said, "The only way I see—"

The shot hit the cement right next to him, shards of concrete splattering up and slicing Stone and Knox in the lower legs. Both men grabbed at their calves even as another shot hit close to them. These were clearly no dummy bullets.

"Get your hands up!" screamed a tower guard through a bullhorn as the shooter stood next to him, his scope crosshairs dead on Stone's brain.

They both whipped their hands in the air as the blood trickled down their pants and into their shoes.

"What the hell—?" said Knox.

"Ain't walking fast enough, boys," Donny cackled over his shoulder.

"What the hell happened to the dummy bullet for first offense rule?" Knox snapped as they hustled after the group.

"Apparently, that doesn't apply to us."

"Yeah," Knox snarled.

A female nurse came to their cell later. They were stripped, searched and then shackled while she stood and watched surrounded by guards.

Through the open door and into the hallway outside, Stone could see a video camera bolted to the wall. He gauged that whenever a cell extraction was done the camera was perfectly positioned to, at best, capture a nice shot of the guards' backs while they pounded the crap out of the unseen inmate.

Invisible for sure.

The nurse cleaned their injuries and bandaged

them up while the guards made snide comments about sissy wounds.

Neither Stone nor Knox said a word.

However, when the nurse was finished Stone did say, "Thank you, ma'am."

He was instantly hit in the mouth with a toweled billy club, the blow felling him. "You don't talk to the lady, asshole," screamed Manson the one-eyed guard as he leaned down into Stone's bleeding face.

The nurse smiled graciously at her defender as they headed out.

Knox helped him to his feet. "We've got to get out of here, Oliver, or we're dead."

"I know. I know," said Stone as he wiped fresh blood off his face, and then he froze.

The guard was looking in at him, his hand curled around the cell door as he was closing it. He wasn't a young punk one-striper. He was older, and gray hair peeked out from under his cap as he stared at Stone. Right before the door clanged shut the guard gave one brief nod at Stone.

67

When Reuben hooked back up with Annabelle and Caleb later that day at the campground, the big man didn't have much to report. Yet he did have one observation.

"We been to all these little towns up here, but Divine is different."

"Different how?" asked Caleb.

"There's money here," answered Reuben. "Thriving shops, new cars, renovated buildings, a courthouse and a jail. Went to the church, even did a little praying. I talked to the padre, he said it was all done in the last few years."

"What cover are you using?" Annabelle asked.

"Said I was a writer looking to set a novel in a small mountain town. Everybody seemed to accept it okay. I guess I look like a writer," he added smugly.

Caleb stared up at his giant friend with the long, curly black hair and beard shot with gray. "I'd say you're more bohemian-looking, but that's probably just splitting hairs. But I think I see what you're saying. The library was really beautiful. The librarian said it had been recently redone too. Brand-new media center, computers, the works."

"And who'd you tell 'em you were?" asked Reuben gruffly.

"A wandering bibliophile. I think I fit that role rather well."

"You really told them that?" asked Annabelle.

"No, I actually said I was looking for work as a short order cook and was checking the classifieds. For some reason she accepted that without question, though I hardly look like a Fry Daddy connoisseur," he added stiffly.

"Sure you don't. What'd you find out, Annabelle?" asked Reuben.

She told them of her conversation with Shirley and Judge Mosley.

"The woman knows something, that's for sure. I think we should follow her and see what else we can find out."

"Sounds like a plan."

"When will Alex get here?" Caleb wanted to know.

"Soon, at least I hope."

"Missing the lawman, are we?" Reuben asked.

"No, I'm just tired of doing all the thinking."

"Well, here's another one for you to think about. Where are we going to be crashing?"

"Not in town," she said. "How about we just sleep in the van out here?"

"In the van?" said Caleb with a stricken look. "What about bathroom facilities?"

Annabelle pointed to the woods. "Nature's own."

"Oh, for Chrissakes," began Caleb.

Reuben held up a hand. "Caleb, if a bear can shit in the woods so can a librarian."

"And what about that reporter?" Caleb pointed out.

"I've sort of got a plan, but I need Alex's help." She turned to Reuben. "So why do you think Divine is so prosperous?"

He said, "Maybe if we answer that, we can explain why people keep getting murdered and/or blown up."

"Do you think something's happened to Oliver?" Caleb asked.

"I've never met anyone better able to take care of himself than Oliver," Reuben answered quite truthfully.

At least we can hope, thought Annabelle.

68

When Shirley Coombs left the courthouse it was already seven in the evening and the darkness had fallen solidly on mountain-bound Divine. She stopped at one store, and when she came back out she toted a plastic bag full of wine bottles. She put this in her car and then walked into Rita's. When she came back out a couple hours later she climbed in her late-model red two-door Infiniti where it was parked behind the courthouse. Apparently so absorbed was the woman in her thoughts that she never saw the white van behind her as she pulled on to the road and sped off.

She arrived home and went inside, staggering slightly.

Caleb pulled the van to a stop a little ways down from the house. Shirley Coombs lived in a one-story vinyl-sided house with a small front porch decorated with tubs of pansies. A gravel drive led to a detached garage. Twenty yards behind the house was thick forest. In a side yard a vegetable garden had been laid out, though the only things planted in it now were a couple of bare and leaning tomato stakes. A pile of rusted lawn chairs and a stack of firewood dominated the small backyard. The lady had no neighbors; hers was the only house down here.

Reuben hunched forward between the two front seats and stared at the house as lights came on inside.

"Do we wait till she passes out and search the place?"

"Why don't you go and see if you can get a look inside one of the windows," said Annabelle.

"I'll go with him," said Caleb.

"Why?"

"Four eyes are better than two."

They slipped out of the van and headed to the house, keeping to the tree line until they neared the house. Then the two made a beeline for the back porch.

Five minutes later they were back in the van.

"Talk about your diamonds wrapped up in a tin can," said Reuben.

"What do you mean?" asked Annabelle.

"What he means is the inside of Shirley Coombs' humble abode hardly matches the outside. The furniture is all high-end, the paintings on the walls are real oils, a couple by artists I recognized, the rugs are authentic oriental, and she's got at least one sculpture that is museum quality."

"Shirley the small-town court clerk is living high on the hog," added Reuben.

"But not so anyone can see it," said Annabelle. "Crappy on the outside and I bet she doesn't encourage visitors."

"She must just like to be surrounded by nice things," ventured Caleb.

"I'd like to get a look at her bank statement," said Annabelle. "What do you want to bet it shows she's loaded?"

"And still staying in this place," said Reuben. "Why?"

"Greed," said Caleb, and they both stared at him. "She's doing something up here, something at that courthouse, and she's getting paid for it. But she wants more and she won't get it if she leaves."

"I bet you're right, Caleb. Nice deduction. She did strike me as the greedy type."

"The thing is, do we know it's connected to whatever happened to Oliver?" asked Reuben. "We could be wasting time with her and meanwhile Oliver might be in serious trouble."

"I think they are connected, Reuben," said Annabelle. "From what the sheriff told me, Oliver was right in the middle of all this stuff. I can't believe a small town like this would have two completely unconnected major secrets. Whatever Shirley's got going on has to be tied to all the other stuff. It has to. It's the only thread we've got."

An hour went by and then another. Finally, the front door to the house opened and Shirley came out.

She was dressed in jeans, a long-sleeved blouse and flats and carried a bag. The way she meandered to her car indicated that at least some of the wine she'd purchased had made its way down her throat.

"She's going to drive like that, up here?" Caleb said worriedly.

When Shirley shot out of her drive, Caleb followed. They headed back to town and through it. Shirley finally turned off and drove up a dirt road, pulling the car to a stop in front of the demolished trailer.

She popped open the car door, grabbed her bag, and staggered up to what was left of the front steps and sat down. She opened the bag, pulled out the bottle of wine and chugged it. It went down badly and she ended up throwing most of it back up. She tossed the bottle down and lit up a cigarette. Then she started to weep, her head resting on her knees.

"Willie! WILLIE!" she sobbed.

"Can I help?"

Shirley jerked up and saw Annabelle standing there. She wiped her face with her sleeve, stared at her suspiciously for a moment and then shook her head wearily. "Nobody can help me, not now." She indicated the destroyed mess behind her.

"Was this where your son . . .?"

Shirley nodded and dragged on her cigarette. "What the hell are you doing here?" she slurred.

"Just driving around looking for my dad and heard

someone crying. I'm sorry, Shirley, I really am. I know how you feel. The loss and everything." Annabelle sat down on the steps next to her.

"Why come here?"

"The sheriff told me my dad had helped Willie. I don't know, I thought there might be some clue here. At this point I'm basically grasping at straws."

With this earnest explanation Shirley's suspicious look faded. She flicked her cigarette away and rubbed at her eyes. "He *was* curious about what happened to Willie," she said slowly. "Came to see me about it."

"He did?" Annabelle said quickly. "I thought you two hadn't spoken."

"I lied to you," Shirley said bluntly. "I didn't know who you were and all," she added vaguely.

"Sure, I understand that."

Shirley's hands nervously slid back and forth over her thighs. She pointed straight ahead. "Lot of things out there in the dark, can't see 'em till it's too late."

"Right. What did he talk to you about?"

"Said somebody had tried to kill Willie. Said they'd put stuff in his Tylenol. I think he thought I did it. But I never would've done that to Willie. I even went to Willie's trailer one night to check on what pills he had there. I was thinking somebody was trying to get some crap in Willie's system that shouldn't be there. That's when I ran into your daddy, and he got all suspicious. But I loved my boy. Never would've done anything to hurt him."

She started sobbing again and Annabelle put a comforting hand on her shoulder. "I'm sure my dad was just trying to help."

Shirley wiped her eyes dry and sucked in some fresh air, calming down. "I know that now. And he was right. Somebody killed Willie, sure as I'm sitting here talking to you."

"Do you have any idea who would've done that?"

"I got ideas, sure." Shirley's cheeks quivered.

"Can you tell me?"

"Why?"

"Shirley, whoever killed your son might have gone after my father because he was trying to help Willie."

"Sure, that makes sense, I guess. Oh, I don't know. Just don't know anymore."

"I'll try to help too. If you can just trust me."

Shirley gripped Annabelle's hand. "Lord, girl, do you have any idea how long it's been since I trusted anybody around this damn place?"

"Trust me and I'll help you. I promise."

Shirley glanced back at what was left of Willie's trailer. "When my daddy got buried up in that mine cave-in, we were all sick in our hearts. People die, sure, but you get to say good-bye, bury 'em proper, at least you're supposed to. But not with cave-ins. You know what you get? A condolence letter from the mining company that some damn lawyer wrote so a company executive wouldn't say anything actionable or that could be used against them. You know, admitting liability? I work for a judge, I know about that crap."

"Absolutely, it's terrible," Annabelle said encouragingly, continuing to hold the older woman's hand tightly.

"Mining company wouldn't do nothing, so the rest of the miners got together and dug a parallel shaft up there with the idea that maybe they could cut over to where the trapped miners were. They worked day and night, borrowing and begging equipment from everybody they could. This was long before the Internet and most folks up here didn't even have TVs or nothing, and there weren't any news trucks with satellite crap or nothing like you see everywhere when some movie star gets drunk and goes to court. So nobody knew what was really going on. My momma and I and all the rest of the women set up a kitchen and laundry and had cots and such for the men while they dug. And God did they dig. Ran a shaft all the way up there and were about to cut over when there was an explosion in the other shaft. Probably methane. Half the mountain dropped on top of my daddy and the others. After that, you couldn't risk it. And we all knew they were dead anyway. Nobody could've survived that blast. So they just sealed it up and built a damn prison on top of it. Some damn grave marker for my daddy that was.

"And when my husband Josh got a job there, I didn't like it one bit. But like he said, it was either the prison or the mines. And I sure as hell didn't want him digging for the same black rock that killed my daddy. So the prison it was. He wanted to get Willie a job up there too, but the boy went into the mines instead. Josh was working hard on him to get him out when he got killed."

"You said it was an accident?"

Shirley snorted. "Accident? Yeah, it was 'bout as much an accident as this was." She pointed to the trailer's remnants.

"You're saying your husband was murdered? Who? Why?"

Shirley stared at her, bleary-eyed. "I shouldn't be telling you this. I shouldn't be telling anybody this. It's been a hole in my heart for two years now."

"I just want to help. I just want to find my father. You've lost your son and your husband. Shirley, it's time the truth came out."

Come on, lady, tell me.

"I know you're right. In my heart I know you are."

"Then you know you should tell me."

Shirley took a deep breath. "I'm just so tired. And this has gotten way out of hand."

"Please, Shirley."

Shirley's red eyes seemed to finally focus as she stared out into the black night. "We get big shipments at the courthouse all the time. Lots of boxes. But the manifest and the boxes never match up."

"How do you mean?"

"I mean if the manifest says fifty boxes, there's only thirty that show up."

"Do you know why?"

"I'm not looking to get into trouble."

"I'm not the police, Shirley. I just want to find my dad."

"I've been poor all my life. You see this town now, it's doing good. Everybody is happy. Why shouldn't I get my piece? You know."

"I know. It's only fair."

"Damn right it is. I wanted to go to college. My brother got to but not old Shirley. We didn't have the money."

"I'm sure," Annabelle said patiently.

Shirley took another swallow of wine. Now she didn't even appear to remember that Annabelle was there. She seemed to be talking to herself. "And was I supposed to know that Josh would get killed when he went hunting deer? Rory just said to make Josh go and then call him. And so that's what I did. How was I to know? You tell me that."

"You certainly couldn't have known. But about those boxes?" prompted Annabelle.

"There's a big drug addiction problem up here. People'll do anything to get their pop."

"Is that what's in the missing boxes. Drugs?"

If Oliver ran into the middle of a major drug ring he's

probably already dead. But if he isn't, he might not have much time.

"Prescription pills. Throws off a lot of damn cash."

"How are they transferred? I mean from the missing boxes with the pills to wherever they're going?"

Shirley lit up another cigarette and eyed Annabelle shrewdly. "Missy, we got us a bunch of drug addict miners go to get their methadone pop over at the clinic every morning so they can get back and hit seven a.m. shifts at the mines."

"Okay," Annabelle said. "But how does that tie in with anything?"

"They start out about *two* a.m. I know that because I've seen 'em. It's less than an hour drive each way, and it takes about a minute to get the pop. Anybody sees them and asks why so early, they tell 'em they can't sleep, just go to the clinic and shoot the breeze. But I know for a fact that doesn't happen. What happens is those boxes get driven a good ways from here and are dropped off at designated spots."

"Okay, but where do they pick them up?"

Oliver might have found that out and gone there.

Shirley stood and stumbled down the blackened timbers to her car.

"Shirley, where are you going?"

"Where I'm going is getting the hell out of here. I'm done with Divine. Should've left a long time ago."

Annabelle raced after her, grabbed her shoulder. "Please, Shirley, it's my dad. Please. He's all I've got left."

"I already said way too much. Booze talking."

"Can't you tell me something? Anything? To at least point me the right way?"

Shirley hesitated and then looked at the ruined trailer and then back at Annabelle.

"Okay. But you'll have to think about it real good."

"All right."

"When is a bottom changed into an ass?"

Annabelle immediately looked puzzled. "What?"

Shirley let out a drunken giggle. "Like I said, you think about it. When is a bottom changed into an ass? You want to find your daddy bad enough, you'll come up with it."

She staggered to her car and got in.

"Are you okay to drive?"

Shirley poked her head out the window. "Hell, honey, I been driving drunk since I was thirteen."

Shirley peeled off and Annabelle raced to the van, which was hidden down the road and behind some trees. When she got there she found four men waiting for her instead of just two. And the new pair had guns.

69

Dinner came right at six-thirty; two trays pushed through the slots. Knox and Stone took them, sat down on their cots and started to eat.

Knox pointed at the carrots on the plate. A few moments later the toilet flushed and the vegetables spun down the metal bowl and out of sight.

Stone was cutting his meat, which was a little difficult considering he only had a flimsy spoon to work with, when his eye caught on the edge of white poking out from under his plate. He nudged Knox with his elbow as he slid the piece of paper out. He unfolded it and began to read, while Knox looked anxiously over his shoulder.

I was the guard at the door when the nurse finished with you. I was a friend of Josh Coombs. Tomorrow in the rec yard. Just follow my lead. Flush this note.

Knox and Stone glanced at each other. Knox took the note, read it once more and then sent it sailing down into the prison's sewer to join the drug-laced carrots.

"What do you think?" Knox said in a low voice as

they resumed eating. They both tapped their feet against the floor to cover their conversation.

"I saw him glance at me when he was at the door. And he nodded. Didn't know exactly what was going on, but I was hoping."

"Follow his lead?"

"He'll have to cover himself. And we'll do exactly as he says when the time comes."

Twenty minutes later something hit their door. "Trays," bellowed a voice.

They pushed them through and sat back on their cots.

"Why do you think they're even keeping us alive?" Knox said. "They don't know that folks won't show up for me."

"Anybody comes near this place, they'll know long in advance. Then they either kill us or hide us. Plenty of places to do that here."

"So why not kill us now? Not that I'm glad they're not," he added hastily.

Stone thought about being left in the mine with the snakes. He was certain now that had been Tyree's handiwork. "Killing is fast, a second of pain and then it's over. We're free of this place. That's apparently not good enough for Howard Tyree. He wants to control us, every second of our lives. I'm sure he'll kill us at some point. But in the meantime he's looking forward to making our lives as miserable as they can possibly be."

"Guy sounds like a serial killer."

"He is, only on the wrong side of the bars."

Knox stretched out on his steel cot. "So now we wait?"

"I don't see another option right now, do you?"

Their door was hit with a hard object. "Hands through the cuff door," yelled a voice.

"Aw shit, what now!" moaned Knox.

Stone whispered, "Just remember that we've been drugged, so act punchy."

"I'm so tired I won't have to act."

They were cuffed, stripped, searched and probed. This had quickly become almost as natural as taking a piss. Both men hung their heads and acted as listless as possible without overdoing it.

They were herded down the hall, guards and Tasers on either side while they shackle-shuffled along. They climbed stairs until there were no more stairs to climb. Stone figured they were in the west tower of the prison but he couldn't be sure. His usually reliable internal compass wasn't working all that well in here.

The room they were brought to was circular-shaped with a table and two chairs in the very center. Three-inch-wide slits in the wall revealed the dark outside. A fluorescent light bubbled overhead. They were placed in the chairs and the guards stood back, waiting.

So were Knox and Stone. With apprehension.

They didn't know what was coming, only that it would be painful.

The door opened and Tyree walked in followed by four more guards, including the one who'd grabbed Stone by the balls and Manson, the one-eye.

"Gentlemen," said Tyree. "We need to talk."

Stone stared up at him with a dull expression. Knox kept his gaze on the table as though he hadn't understood the man.

One guard whispered into Tyree's ear. He nodded. "Right. Of course. Give them a pop then, because I need their undivided attention."

A guard pulled a syringe from a black bag he carried. Stone was swabbed and then injected in the upper arm. The needle was cleaned with alcohol and Knox was hit next.

Whatever they'd been given, the effect was immediate. Stone could feel his heart racing and every nerve he possessed was on overdrive. He glanced over at Knox and saw he was having the very same reaction.

"Good," said Tyree. "Now get 'em hooked up."

A duffel bag was opened and out of it came two thick leather belts with black wires attached. They were placed around each man's middle and padlocked down. Tyree was handed a black box with buttons on it.

He depressed one of the buttons and a green light

came on. He stood in front of the men and then turned his attention to Knox.

"All right, Mr. CIA. Does anyone know that you came to the town of Divine?"

"Yes."

Tyree depressed the button and Knox stood straight up, screaming as the voltage entered him. Tyree released the button, and like a marionette that had lost its handler, Knox slumped back down in the chair, panting and swaying.

Tyree looked at Stone. "What is your real name?"

"Oliver Stone."

A second later, Stone was involuntarily on his tiptoes, feeling like both his brain and his heart were going to explode.

Tyree removed his finger and Stone dropped back down, missed the chair and hit the floor. The guards grabbed him and slammed him back in his seat.

Tyree turned back to Knox. "Does anyone know that you came to the town of Divine?"

"NO!"

The blast hit him again. After he was slumped back in his chair, he barked, "What the hell answer do you want?"

"The truth."

"Well, one of those answers *had* to be the truth, you dickhead!"

Tyree held the button down so long that Stone

feared Knox would not come back. But he did, sweating and swearing.

Tyree turned to Stone. "Oliver Stone?"

Okay, buddy, let's see if you can take it as well as you can dish it out.

Speaking as steadily as was possible after having his organs fried, he said, "My real name is John Carr. I used to be a government assassin, decades ago, tasked to a special division of the CIA so classified not even the president knew about it. I had a falling-out with my superiors. I've been on the run ever since. Agent Knox is one of the best men the intelligence community has. He was assigned by the president of the United States himself to hunt me down because they believed that I murdered Senator Roger Simpson and Carter Gray. I'm sure you heard about that. Well, Knox is as good as his rep, because he found me. Now we're here at Dead Rock being beaten and tortured by a bunch of drug dealers masquerading as prison officials." He glanced around at the guards. "But I'm sure you have nothing to worry about. The president will probably just forget the matter and do no follow-up. I doubt they care what happens to me. Or one of their best agents."

Stone could now see just the reaction he was hoping for. Sweat. Sweat and nervous glances, particularly from the one-striper and Manson, who looked ready to piss all over their Gestapo boots.

The next instant Stone was on his feet, the current

thundering through him. When Tyree released the button, Stone took a little while to recover, panting and gasping for air, his muscles twitching uncontrollably.

He gasped, "You can do a polygraph. I'm sure you're set up to do that what with all the electronic gizmos you guys seem to enjoy so much. I can tell you enjoy the pain thing, but it's not getting you what you want. So be smart about it, Warden. Ask me the question again. *Who am I*, while I'm strapped to the meter. Then you'll see what the truth really is. But again I wouldn't worry. I don't see how sixteen intelligence agencies plus the Department of Homeland Security, with thousands of highly trained agents and collective budgets of about a hundred billion dollars, will ever find us here."

Now, finally, Stone could see the twitch in the warden's eyes too. Tyree fingered the box but did not push the button again. He also did not meet Stone's gaze.

Later that night after their hearts and other organs had settled down from the pounding, they were both hooked to polygraphs. Questions were asked and answered. And results were read. The squiggly lines from the polygraph did not appear to please the warden. Stone could see that clearly from the man not looking at him as he ordered them back to their cell.

Let *him* sweat tonight.

They lay there on their cots staring up at the ceiling, recovering from their ordeal by electric shock and each no doubt daydreaming about their strong hands closing around the throat of one Howard Tyree and crushing the life out of him.

"Smart thinking, Oliver," Knox said, finally breaking the silence. "I loved it when he followed your *order* about the polygraph. And you saw the guards' expressions when you hit 'em with the facts?"

"I saw."

"What do you think they'll do now?"

"Snoop around and see if anything might be coming their way. That gives us the one thing we really need."

"Time," answered Knox.

"Time," agreed Stone.

They heard a sound at the door and both men braced for another painful extraction. Yet the only thing coming in was a slip of paper through the cuff slot. It drifted down to the floor. Knox snagged it and passed the note to Stone.

Stone read it. "Next chow, watch out for Manson."

Stone glanced up at Knox. "You thinking what I'm thinking?" he said.

"Absolutely, but they could kill us or at least mess up our chance with this guard."

"Not if we do it the right way."

70

"Harry, what are you doing here?" Annabelle looked from Harry Finn to Alex Ford as they sat crammed in the back of the van.

"Alex filled me in on what was going on. Sounded like you could use some help."

Harry Finn, while perhaps not as lethal and skilled as Oliver Stone, was worth at least five ordinary men in his ability to fight and think at the same time.

"What did you get from old Shirley?" asked Reuben.

"A lot." She quickly filled Alex and Harry in on all that they'd found out, including her conversation with Shirley.

"How does a bottom turn into an ass?" said Alex. "What the hell kind of clue is that?"

"It's a very clear one," answered Caleb, who was in the driver's seat. Everyone turned to stare at him. "Nick Bottom is a character, a weaver actually, whose head is transformed into an ass's head by Puck the Hobgoblin."

They all stared at Caleb in befuddlement before

Reuben said, "Are you on some kind of librarian crack?"

"No, it means that drunk Shirley is actually fairly well-read because that's a scene from Shakespeare's *A Midsummer Night's Dream*."

"Abby Riker's place," exclaimed Annabelle. "A Midsummer's Farm."

"Sounds like a plan," began Alex, but he stopped talking when Harry held up a hand. They all listened.

"There's someone out there," hissed Caleb.

Harry and Alex pulled their weapons. Alex tossed a spare gun to Reuben, who took up position near one of the wide windows.

"Caleb, are you okay driving—"

They were nearly knocked over when Caleb rammed the accelerator and the van crashed through some bushes and hit the road even as bullets pinged against the sides of the vehicle.

Alex shoved Annabelle to the floorboard and then he ducked down.

Reuben slid open the window, took aim and fired behind them. Alex and Harry did the same from the other side.

Caleb hit a straightaway and pushed the van to its max.

"Eighty is all the juice this shit-can has," he barked. "Next time give me a decent ride if you want me to outrun the suckers. I can't make tomato sauce without tomatoes, for godsakes!"

Confused, Alex eyed Harry and then looked down at Annabelle.

She said wearily, "You don't want to know."

Over the next five minutes Caleb took hairpin turns barely on four wheels, cut down this road and that, and ran around one curve where the van's left-side tires were nearly kissing air over a vertical drop. He finally slowed.

"No lights back there for the last two minutes," he said. "Where to now?"

"The farm," answered Alex. "Fast, but without killing us, please."

Keeping alert, they made their way slowly back and drove through downtown Divine. When they reached the other side they saw the red rooftop lights of the cop car that was parked on the side of the road near a long drop-off. Other vehicles, including a fire truck, were parked next to it. Men were milling about, and a fire hose extended down the slope.

Annabelle said, "Stop, Caleb. That's Sheriff Tyree."

Caleb pulled off the road and Annabelle climbed out of the van and hurried over to Tyree, who was standing there, hands in his pockets and seemingly studying his boots with little interest.

"Sheriff, what happened?"

He glanced at her and scowled. "What are you doing around here this time of night?"

"Still looking for my dad." She stared down the

steep slope where she could see smoke rising and some men tethered to ropes looking over the remains of a car. Then she noticed where the dirt shoulder had been torn up. "An accident?"

He nodded. "Shirley Coombs, or what's left of her."

Annabelle gave a sharp intake of breath.

He eyed her sternly. "What?"

"I was talking to her not more than an hour ago."

"Where?"

"At her son's trailer, or what's left of it."

"What were you doing there?"

"I was driving by and heard somebody sobbing. It was Shirley. I was trying to comfort her."

"Had she been drinking?"

Annabelle hesitated but then said, "Yes."

"Damn fool woman ran off the road."

Annabelle looked around and saw the tire marks and then a bit of gray metal lying on the road under the glare of lights. She bent down to pick it up.

"Don't touch that!" snapped Tyree.

She stood quickly. "But Shirley's car was red."

Tyree grabbed her by the arm and hustled her away from the accident scene and across the road while several of the men looked on curiously.

She exclaimed, "Sheriff, what is going on? That wasn't an accident. Someone hit her car."

"I know that. I just don't want other folks to."

"But why?"

"Because I said so, that's why! Now, what did Shirley tell you that would get her killed?"

Annabelle nervously licked her lips. Shirley had made it clear that she trusted no one in this place. So how could Annabelle?

"Ma'am, I want to get to the bottom of this whole thing. It's my town and I need to make things right."

Annabelle had a great BS meter and it was making no noise. "Come over here."

She led him to the van and opened the back door, revealing the others inside. She introduced them one by one and said, "Sheriff, you got some time to hear what we know? It's going to take a while."

"Let's get on over to my office then. Too many ears 'round here."

An hour later, sitting in Tyree's office, the lawman rubbed his face, stood and glumly stared out the window. "So he's not your father but he did work for the government and has been underground for years. And you and your friends are FBI agents tasked with bringing him safely back?"

"That's right," said Annabelle. She'd of course made no mention of Joe Knox being after Stone for the murders of Simpson and Gray. Yet she had told the lawman as much of the truth as she could, which for Annabelle was a new way to operate.

"You lied to me once and now I'm just supposed to believe you? How about I call the FBI in D.C. Will they know who you are?"

Alex stood and held out his ID. "I'm not FBI. This is a joint task force. So how about you call my headquarters in D.C. and verify I am who I say I am. We'll wait here while you do. But if you're going to do it, do it now. We need to find him, fast."

Tyree eyed Alex's creds and then shook his head. "I believe you." He stepped back to his desk and perched on the edge while Annabelle shot Alex a grateful look. "And you think it has something to do with Abby Riker's farm?"

"The clue clearly referred to her place," said Caleb.

"But you're not saying Abby has anything to do with it. That's crazy."

Annabelle said, "I'm not accusing anyone of anything. But her son *is* missing."

"A drug ring operating out of Divine," said Tyree. "And if Shirley said the boxes were coming to the courthouse with some missing, the judge must be in on it too. Pretty slick, because who's going to check legal documents going to a courthouse? And using the miners going to get their methadone? Who the hell thought of that?"

There was a knock on the door and a man came in. Charlie Trimble was dressed in khaki pants and a striped button-down shirt.

"I know it's late but I saw your light on, Sheriff—" He broke off when he saw the other people with him.

"I'm sort of busy, Charlie."

Trimble looked keenly at Annabelle. "Ah, the daughter. Still looking for your *father*?"

Annabelle did not like the emphasis the man put on the last word.

"No, he's actually not my father." She turned to Alex. "He's the man I was telling you about. The reporter looking to make a fast scoop."

"I see. At the expense of national security, I don't think so."

"National security?" said Trimble, taken aback. He glanced at Tyree. "What are they talking about?"

"Apparently Ben isn't who we thought he was."

"I know that," said Trimble excitedly. "But I think I do know who he is. I've got the story all ready to go. But I—"

He shut up as Annabelle shoved her ID in his face. Alex did the same. "Trimble," she began, "you're not going to print one syllable of anything having to do with this matter."

Trimble said in a defiant tone, "Don't think you can intimidate me."

"We're not trying to intimidate you, just give you a fair warning," said Alex.

"Warning, about what?"

"If you print your story and something happens to our guy, your butt will end up at the Castle."

"The Castle? What castle?"

"Leavenworth."

"Leavenworth? That's for military crimes. I'm not in the military."

"Actually," said Alex, barely able to conceal a smile, "it's also for national security crimes. And just for the record, you're anything I want you to be."

"What about the first amendment?"

Reuben towered over him. "What about the *second* amendment?" he said menacingly, the pistol in his belt clip clearly visible.

"I . . . I mean, uh, nothing, nothing."

Annabelle hooked him by the arm. "Trimble?"

"Yes?" he said shakily.

"Go home. Now! Before you get hurt."

The journalist nearly shot out of the room.

She turned to Tyree. "I think it's time we go to see where a bottom turns into an ass."

71

Tyree led the way in his patrol car with the van behind. About a quarter mile from the farm he pulled off and the van slid in behind him.

Getting out of the car, he said, "We'll make the rest of the way on foot. Don't want to spook anybody. We got time before the miners come."

They threaded their way through the woods until they came to the outskirts of the farm and set up an observation post near the house, which was dark. Abby's pickup truck and the Mini Cooper were parked out front.

Tyree said in a near whisper, "There's another back road into the farm that leads to an old barn. We should probably post some folks there too just in case."

Reuben, Harry and Caleb headed that way following directions Tyree gave them.

Both groups hunkered down and waited. And waited some more.

Finally, Alex checked his watch. "Four in the

morning. I don't think it's happening. Maybe they don't transport every night."

Tyree stretched his limbs. "They killed Shirley so maybe they postponed the shipment."

At that moment Harry came hurrying up to them.

"Did you see anything?" Alex asked excitedly.

"Not a person, but we did see something. Come on."

They hurried after him. When they reached the spot where Caleb and Reuben were waiting, Harry pointed to the woods at a spot right across from the entrance to the barn. "You can see somebody's gone crashing through there. Brush and low tree limbs all busted up."

"Let's follow it," said Tyree, taking the lead. He pulled out a flashlight and slipped another off his belt and handed it to Alex.

"Never worked with a fed before."

"It's sort of a first time for me too, Sheriff," Alex said wryly.

They came to a dirt road in the woods.

"Look," said Annabelle.

It was Joe Knox's truck.

They ran to it and looked inside.

"No rental docs," said Tyree. "Any idea who it belongs to?"

Annabelle glanced at the others, her thoughts moving rapidly. *Does this have nothing to do with the drug dealers? Has Knox gotten to Oliver, killed him already? But why would Knox's truck be here then? Has Oliver killed Knox?*

"No," she said.

Tyree saw the bloodstains in the woods a bit later. "There, and there, and over there," he said, making stabbing motions with his light.

"That's not good," Caleb said quite unnecessarily.

Annabelle's spirits sank further. It seemed like one of the men had been hurt or killed. But which one?

They followed the trail across the road and up the slope. There were more bloodstains here. They moved across some more ground and then stopped. There were lots of footprints in the soft mud and more dark stains. Annabelle's gloomy expression changed now and she became more alert. As they followed the marks they came to a spot where it appeared as though the people had marched in lockstep.

"Or carrying something. Or somebody," Alex deduced.

They followed the trail back down to the road but at another spot. There were more dark stains here, and also what looked to be a slick of oil.

"It looks like someone was put in a car or truck," said Harry.

"A truck," noted Tyree. He flashed his light on the asphalt. "Tire ran over some of that oil and left a mark. That's a tire tread from a truck. Maybe we can track it that way."

As the edges of the night began to lift around them they hustled down the road, desperately looking for more clues.

Reuben was the first to see it. "The truck cut across here." He pointed to the smear of oil on the road. "And went into that field."

They rushed into the open space. It was quite easy to see the ruts the truck had made in the soft earth here. As they got to the middle of the field, Alex swept his light in a wide swath.

Harry said, "Stop. Hold it right there." Alex did so and Harry knelt down and grazed his hand along the top of a long depression in the dirt.

He looked up. "That's a mark from a chopper's skids." He eyed Tyree. "Who has a chopper around here?"

Tyree's light was square on this mark, his features were very grim.

"Tyree, does anybody you know up here have a chopper?" Alex said, tugging at the lawman's arm.

"Yeah," he said slowly. "My damn brother."

There was a buzzing sound. Tyree reached in his pocket and pulled out his phone.

"Tyree?"

The tall lawman's legs buckled. "What? When?"

Annabelle said, "What is it?"

"I'll be right there."

He clicked off and looked at the others.

"What is it?" Annabelle demanded again.

"That was a fellow I deputized to look after Abby Riker. He just came to."

"Just came to?" Alex said uneasily.

Tyree was already rushing back to the road. "They've got Abby," he yelled.

72

Knox and Stone ate their breakfast in silence, doing their best to act as lethargic as the rest of the prison population actually was from their drug dose the day before. Both men's gazes were in fact sweeping the cafeteria.

Near the end of the meal, Knox, who was sitting across from Stone so they could watch both sides of the room and not be surprised from the rear, gave a little rehearsed cough and his gaze darted to nine o'clock. An instant before the blow struck, Stone lifted his tray up and used it as a shield. The shiv glanced off the hard plastic. In the next motion, Stone had hooked Manson's leg with his own, and the big guard's momentum caused him to slide across the table. He crashed through plates and plastic cups until he toppled to the floor on the other side, taking two prisoners next to Knox down with him. In the commotion that followed, Knox edged his plate off the table with his elbow and his uneaten grits plopped directly on Manson's head.

When the other guards came running they found

Stone and Knox sitting there calmly, but with bewildered expressions, and staring at the pile of bodies on the floor.

When the guards pulled Manson to his feet, he was still holding the shiv.

"Frank, what the hell are you—" began one of the guards before Manson roughly pushed him away. With an enraged scream he tried to jump over the table at Stone. Only Knox had stood on his foot at that precise moment and his leap turned into an abrupt fall. His chin slammed down on the table in front of where Stone was sitting. As if on cue, Knox stood, blocking the view of the other guards.

"Let me get out of your way so you can deal with the psycho guard," he said politely.

In that instant, Oliver Stone delivered a crushing blow to the back of Manson's neck with his elbow. When the guards finally got around Knox, Stone had slipped to the other end of the table and seemed to be innocently watching the events.

Manson was carried off on a gurney unconscious and barely breathing. Even the most comatose con in the room had a smile on his face at the sight.

Later that morning Stone and Knox were standing in the rec yard. No one had come after them about what had happened to Manson, though Stone had been popped once in the head for apparently chewing too loudly.

"How hard did you hit him?" Knox asked.

"Hard enough."

"I like your style."

Donny boy smiled at them as he passed by. He gave a stupid thumbs-up to Stone. The guards on the pod towers were making their rounds, eyeballing the gaggle of cons with binoculars and scopes on stationary tripods. And the guns. The guns were always front and center. The power. The deterrent. Stone thought this as he leaned against the cement block wall and wondered how the older guard was going to accomplish it, whatever it was.

Knox kept checking the periphery without seeming to do so as he stood next to Stone.

One inmate was bouncing the ball. He made a layup, caught the rebound and went back for a jumper. Like most of the inmates Stone and Knox had seen, he was black, young, tall and muscular. He seemed to have all his wits about him, so maybe Donny had let out his secret to others about the carrots. He missed the jumper and Stone stiffened as the black guy jogged to get the ball that had rolled past the blue line.

Before he could get there though, another inmate crashed into him, knocking the man across the line where he landed on the ball. The two men got up and faced off. A horn sounded. And the rifle-men on the towers took aim. A shot was fired, but it didn't come from the tower. The guards looked everywhere for the source of the round.

As if on cue one inmate hit another inmate, sending him down with a bloodied nose. Another shot was fired. Whistles erupted, horns blared and a cluster of cons in the middle of the concrete playground bolted, screaming. Two guards who ran up to stop this human stampede were run over, their caps and billy clubs disappearing beneath the tidal wave of fleeing prisoners.

Hands closed around Stone's and Knox's wrists and they were pulled forward.

"Back to your cells, now!" barked a voice.

Stone's gaze fell on the older guard, the one who'd nodded at him. He was pushing Knox and Stone toward one of the entrances into the prison.

As they passed a throng of prisoners standing there watching the melee, Knox spotted Donny, who was smiling and cheering on the fighters.

Knox sucker-punched him and old Donny boy, the killer of three kids, slid unconscious to the cold concrete lawn of Dead Rock.

"Now, that's what I call accountability," Knox muttered as he followed behind Stone.

Inside the building the guard herded them up a set of stairs and into a small room, where he closed the door.

"Turn around."

They did so, a little hesitantly.

He quickly cuffed and shackled them, then spun them back around to face him.

"We don't have much time. I was Josh Coombs' best friend. I heard you helped Willie."

"I did. He's dead now, I guess you heard. Bob too. Blown up."

The guard nodded. "Any idea what's going on?"

"Drugs." Stone gave him the thirty-second version and ended with, "And Josh was murdered because he'd found out."

"I kind of figured something like that. I've heard things, seen some weird stuff, but nothing I could prove. But I sure as hell know you two weren't prison transfers."

"How many guards think like you?"

"No more than two or three. The rest are in Tyree's pocket."

Knox said, "I'm with the CIA. My name is Joe Knox. I need you to contact a guy named Marshall Saunders and tell him where I am. His phone number is—" He broke off and stared at Stone. "You can tell him I'm alone," Knox finished.

"I'm not going to let you do that," said Stone.

"You don't have a choice. That's why I'm calling my buddy Marsh and not Hayes."

"We both know Hayes. If he finds out you screwed him, your next stop will be a torture center in Afghanistan, and you won't be the one doing the interrogating. So go back to your family. And finish your life on your terms, not his."

"Oliver, do you know what he's—"

Stone broke in, "I've always known. Some things never change."

"Guys," the guard said nervously. "Hurry the hell up."

Knox gazed for another moment at Stone and then gave the phone number to the guard and the fact that he had a man named John Carr with him. "Call Saunders just as soon as you can and tell him where we are."

They were hustled back to their cells as the entire prison was put in lockdown.

As the pair sat shackled in their cell, Knox said, "I'll do all I can do to ensure you get a fair shake. I'm not going to let Hayes make you disappear."

"I've already disappeared. I've been invisible for the last thirty years, in fact."

A few moments of silence passed.

"Why didn't Hayes let you have that damn medal?"

Stone scooted up to a standing position and leaned back against the wall. "It was so many years ago, I don't think I remember anymore."

"Sure you do. That place you never forget. Ever."

Stone glanced at him. "When were you in Nam?"

"Last eighteen months of the war."

"I was more on the front end." Stone gazed down at the floor as he spoke. He had never really told anyone about this before, but he also knew it really didn't matter anymore. They would either die in this place or Stone would die in another prison, if he wasn't executed.

He looked up at Knox. "Macklin Hayes had one way of fighting. Throw as many grunts into the meat grinder as he could find, and see where the chips fell. But regardless of the outcome he saw to it that the reports that went up the line all detailed his brilliance on the battlefield. Although I believe the closest he ever got to actual combat was the occasional dustup in the officers' mess."

"I had some brass just like that. Talked a great game but never wanted to come up to bat."

"Hayes believed that I cost him a fast promotion to lieutenant colonel. And maybe I did."

"How?"

"There were three villages on a patch of dirt that the higher-ups suddenly decided we had to own. I guess so they could make it seem like we were winning the war back home. They gave the assignment to Hayes. A nice little carrot for his next bump up the line to the one-star. He ordered three companies forward, one company to hit each village. The night before we were going in Hayes called a meeting of all the sergeants."

"What about the captains?"

"They were all dead. We ran through captains and second lieutenants like you wouldn't believe. Anyway, he ordered us to flatten the places. Nobody left."

"No soldiers, you mean."

"I mean nobody, Knox, men, women and children. Nobody. Then we were to put a torch to the place and say that the Viet Cong had done it. It was some disinformation bullshit campaign that Hayes had come up with. He was constantly pulling that crap. Guy was like Machiavelli reincarnated. I think he saw it as a career enhancer."

"What happened?"

"Two of the three companies followed orders. One didn't."

"And Hayes came after you?"

"He tried. But I told him if he did I'd tell everybody the truth. It wasn't like he could say I'd disobeyed orders, because the orders he gave should have landed him right in front of a court-martial. See, I knew how he played the game. The brass upstairs might look the other way if the mission went off, but any hiccup that the journalists could get hold of and they'd eat him alive. Anyway, with one village left, the command chain wasn't pleased. So it took old Hayes a little longer to get his cluster of oak leaves."

"But he found another way to hurt you. The medal."

"I really didn't give a shit at that point. I'd been fighting a war that had no end. Every friend I'd ever had over there was dead. I was tired. I was sick of Southeast Asia, the rain, the heat, every minute of every day of my life spent taking and giving up a hundred yards' worth of dirt and jungle, and for what? For what, Knox?"

"Is that when you joined Triple Six?"

Stone hesitated. "I guess you've earned the right to know."

"I promise you it won't go any further. If they convict you it won't come with any help from me."

"Yeah, that's when Triple Six came, although I wouldn't say I joined. They made it clear that was my only option. I just ended up trading one hell for another. I was always lucky that way."

"I'm assuming you were great at your job. So why did the CIA turn on you?"

"The years went by and I married Claire and we had our little girl. Best thing that ever happened to me. Without getting too sappy about it, it was like a whole new world of possibilities opened up for me.

And I decided I didn't want to play the game anymore. I just couldn't pull the trigger, Knox. I couldn't stand my own stench. I couldn't fly halfway around the world, pop someone in the brain and come home and hold my little girl and kiss my wife. I couldn't do it anymore."

"And they didn't appreciate that?"

"Men like that think they own you forever. And maybe they do."

Stone slid back down to the floor, tipped his head back and closed his eyes.

"I'll help you, Oliver. I swear it."

"You just help yourself, Knox. It's too late for me. And all I'll be getting is exactly what I deserve."

73

They'd all caught a few hours' sleep at Tyree's home about two miles from downtown Divine. It was a modest-size plank house on a nice piece of land set on a hill with a long meadow behind.

Tyree made a big pot of coffee and put together some breakfast. The big sheriff's eyes were red and puffy.

"I apologize for the sorry state of the vittles. I'm not used to having this much company."

"This is all the *vittles* I need," said Reuben, gulping from a large mug of straight java.

They'd gotten to Abby Riker's place and the scene there had easily told them what had occurred. Front door busted in. Furniture overturned and the deputy sitting in the middle of the floor with blood running down his face. Besides that there was no clue who had taken Abby or where they'd gone. Tyree had put out an APB but they'd heard nothing yet. And every hour that slipped by did not bode well for the woman's safe return.

"I can't believe I didn't think of that," said Tyree guiltily.

"You had a man posted to guard her, Sheriff," Annabelle pointed out.

"Earl isn't much good in situations like that. But he's all I had. I should've been the one to protect her. If anything happens to her—" He broke off and stared down, and a tear fell from his eye onto the kitchen table.

"Why do you think they took her?" Alex asked quietly after an awkward silence.

Tyree wiped his face and looked up, clearing his throat loudly. "Been thinking about that. Danny's out there somewhere. Maybe they were afraid of what he'd do. So they took his mother as insurance. That boy loves his mother."

"Do you think Danny was involved in the drug-running?" asked Annabelle.

"Don't know. Fact that they were using that old barn makes me think the answer to that might be yes."

"But you said he left town."

"After Debby died. Maybe he drew the line at folks murdering his friends."

"Any word on the judge?" asked Alex.

"Surprise, surprise, he's gone too."

"So he must've been in on it and got tipped off," said Harry.

Tyree nodded. "He'd been a judge down in Texas.

And he spent time in South America, least that's what he told me."

"They know drug dealing real well there."

Tyree added, "See, I been reading about how easy it is to ship stuff up from Texas that comes over the Mexican border. Seems there's two ways to deal prescription drugs. Steal it or make it."

"*Make* prescription drugs?" said Caleb, looking astonished.

"Drug labs in Colombia in particular have been producing oxycodone knockoffs by the ton and smuggling them in here," Alex explained. "The stuff isn't pure, of course. It's not like a filthy drug lab has the same quality control as a legit pharmaceutical manufacturer. And that's why it's so dangerous."

Tyree nodded. "So maybe our friend the judge had connections down there. Maybe the place was too hot to hold him. And when he stumbled across old Divine he thought he'd found a good place to lie low for a while."

"So the judge has the pipeline connections. Would your brother have big-city connections for distribution purposes?"

"Eighty percent of the prisoners up there are from big cities and most of 'em were in the drug business and killed somebody. That's what got them to Dead Rock. So, yeah, he might have distribution contacts."

"But if your brother is involved in this, how did they get together? Were they friends?"

"Mosley went up to the prison once a month to mediate. I thought that was right funny when I first heard about it."

"Why?"

"My brother's not much into compromise. It was always his way or the highway."

Annabelle said, "You don't seem all that surprised to learn your brother might be a criminal."

Tyree gave a weak smile. "I was the son who won all the sports awards and Howard was the one who got all the academic scholarships. The dumb jock and the smart older brother. But he had another side to him. Cruel, I guess you'd call it. Before I got bigger than him, he would put the hurt on me if I did something he didn't like. That's why him and me have never been that close. And he always liked to live well. And while he's the top dog up there, it's not like wardens make a ton of money, even at a supermax."

"Peterson was an accountant. Maybe he was doing the books for the ring. Maybe he was skimming and they found out," Alex suggested.

Tyree rubbed his hand along his chin. "There might actually be more to it than that."

"What do you mean?"

"We have a town fund here. An investment fund that Peterson was doing the books on too."

"A town fund?" said Annabelle.

"Yeah, people and businesses pooled some money. Abby kicked in quite a bit; she had more than anybody else. It's done real well over the last few years. Paid quite a dividend."

"Which is why Divine is a lot more prosperous than other towns like it," added Reuben.

"But it might not be because of great investments," ventured Harry.

"No," said Alex. "It might be for another reason: they're using the town fund to launder the drug proceeds."

Annabelle said, "And it's a perfect way to do it. Lots of little checks cut. A town in the boonies. Who'd suspect? The cash comes out pure white."

Tyree said, "What if your guy is up at that prison, how do we get to him? It's not like we have enough to get a search warrant."

Annabelle snapped, "Screw a search warrant. What we need to do is just get up to that prison and get him out fast if he's there."

They all stared at her, Tyree looking the most nervous.

"I'm not sure that's such a good idea, ma'am. My brother is a pretty smart guy. And if he is involved in all this, you can bet he won't let us waltz into the place and look around."

"That's okay, Sheriff, I rarely go in the front door. Shirley told me about those miners getting killed and that's why they call the prison Dead Rock. She mentioned a parallel shaft. I wonder where it is and how far it went in?"

Tyree said, "I don't know the particulars."

"I can check at the local library," Caleb offered.

"And find out everything you can on Dead Rock prison," she added. She looked at Tyree. "And I'd appreciate everything you can tell me about the place too."

"I'll be glad to, but there're lots of places to hide folks up there," Tyree pointed out.

"I'm sort of counting on that," said Annabelle.

74

There *was* another chopper in the vicinity of Divine and it soared along the treetops before landing in the parking lot of Blue Spruce Prison.

Only one man got out of the bird; he walked unhurriedly toward the prison.

It took a few minutes of processing at the front entrance and a phone call. And for such a special visitor, the warden himself came down.

Macklin Hayes shook hands with Howard Tyree.

"What does the CIA want here?" Tyree said in a surly tone.

"I think you have one of my men here," the CIA chief answered pleasantly.

"I have no idea what you're talking about."

"All right, we'll play the game. For now, anyway. His name is Joe Knox. He's about six-one, two-twenty, with slicked back salt-and-pepper hair. He should have another man with him. A little taller, leaner, white hair, cut short. Answers to the name Oliver Stone or John Carr depending on the day and the situation."

"There's no one here who fits that description. Now, I'm going to have to ask you to leave. This is a supermax prison and unauthorized visitors are never welcome even from the CIA." Tyree's men clustered behind him.

Hayes looked slightly alarmed. "You seem to have me outnumbered. My goodness, what was I thinking?" He put the slim briefcase he was carrying down on a table, popped it open and drew out a slim file. From it he took several slips of paper. "Drug-running, was it? Yes, that's right." He gave a mock shiver. "I'm sure you all are suitably tough and dangerous, so I must watch my step." He pressed his long, bony fingers against the pages. "These documents are awaiting signature by the attorney general to authorize a lock-down of this prison and all personnel here."

"On what grounds?"

"On the grounds that your drug-dealing operation is funneling monies to terrorist organizations that have infiltrated the United States."

"That's ridiculous."

"Actually, we already have the proof ready to go. This document," Hayes continued imperturbably, "is an arrest warrant for Joseph Knox, John Carr *and* Howard Tyree. You can see that it's duly signed."

The warden didn't even bother glancing at the papers. He said, "You might be a big deal in Washington, but in case you haven't noticed this isn't Washington. So I'm not going anywhere."

"That's the whole point," said Hayes. "Let me see Knox and Carr and you'll have no more problems."

"Right. If they were here, and I'm not saying they are, how do I know they wouldn't tell you some bullshit story that you'll use to come after me? Tell me that?"

Hayes looked at his watch. When he glanced back up, his smile was gone. "I don't give a shit about your little drug operation. In the grand scheme of things you don't even rise to the level of a hemorrhoid on my *ass*. You have one minute to take me to these men."

"Or what?" snapped Tyree.

"You really are tiresome." Hayes reached slowly in his pocket, lifted out his phone and pushed one button.

A second later there was an explosion in the prison's front parking lot.

Tyree and his men raced to the window and looked out at the smoldering remains of the car. Smoke was still rising off the chop per's side cannon muzzle.

"That was my damn Cadillac," screamed Tyree.

"I know. We checked the registration. I wouldn't have wasted a cannon round that expensive on a mere guard's ride. Let me make this as clear as I possibly can. *This* is a national security issue. Not even the president himself could stand in the way. And *you*, my little friend, are no president. Take me to see them. Now!" He added in a softer tone, "And Uncle Sam will even buy you a new car."

Stone and Knox sat shackled at the table. Everyone in the prison had heard the explosion outside, but no one knew what was going on. When the door opened and he saw the man, Knox cried out, "Oh shit!"

"It's nice to see you too, Knox." Hayes smiled at them both and sat down.

"What the hell are you doing here?"

"I had anyone you might contact on a surveillance list. When Marsh got the call I was ready. And don't waste time wondering if he'll come to your aid. He's already been transferred out of the country. You shouldn't have played me for an idiot, Knox. You really shouldn't have."

He gazed at a stunned Knox for a moment longer and then turned to Stone.

"It's been a long time, John. I can't say the years have been kind to you."

"They've been better to me than they have been to you, *Mack*."

"Tell me, how did it feel to kill our old friends? Did your chest puff with pride when you finished them off?"

"That's right, you wouldn't know how it felt to kill somebody. You always got other people to do it for you."

Hayes opened his briefcase and took out a single piece of paper. He held it up for Knox to see. It was the order signed by Hayes cutting off further discussion of John Carr receiving the Medal of Honor.

"When you called and told me that the 'country' folks around this filthy hole in the ground might rally around the *persecuted* Vietnam vet, I wondered what you might have meant by that. *And* how you found out about it. I went to the military archives. They were very helpful in showing me what you'd looked at. Unfortunately, the boxes weren't inventoried, but this page had left a bit of the print on the inside of the box wall. It was enough to have my people search your house. And they found this. I thought it had been destroyed a long time ago. Just goes to show that no one is truly omniscient."

He glanced over at Stone. "And I'm sure John here has told you all about our little disagreement in the jungle."

"I've told him nothing. He was working for you. You think I'd trust his ass?" Stone snapped.

Hayes sat back and rested his hands on his lap. "John, you're a much better killer than you are a liar. Prevarication is my bailiwick. And I could always sense it in others."

"You could never let it go, could you?"

"Why should I? You hurt me a long time ago. Where's the justice in that?"

"Justice?" bellowed Knox. "You kept him from getting the Medal of Honor!"

"And he kept me from the promotion that was rightfully mine."

"You're comparing what this guy did on the battlefield to making you wait a couple extra months to get your crappy pair of oak clusters?"

"He was a grunt. We had millions of them. But there weren't that many officers of my caliber. I'm certain he hurt the war effort by doing it."

"You really think we would've won the Vietnam War if you'd been made lieutenant colonel sooner?" Knox said in disbelief.

"I admit I have an ego."

"That's not an ego. That's freaking psychotic."

Hayes pulled out a lighter, clicked it against an edge of the old paper and in a few seconds it crumpled to ash.

"Now let me get this right." He pointed at Knox. "You're an armed robber and murderer. Nasty business. If I'd only known." He turned to Stone. "And you're Anthony *Butcher*. At least that idiot warden has a sense of humor if not style. Triple murderer. How perfect, though that tally hardly does you justice."

He rose and clicked his briefcase shut. "I believe that's all. I'll leave you two to serve out your debt to society. I've told the warden to be especially attentive to you both. I'm sure you appreciate the significance of that."

"Hayes!" Knox screamed as he strained against the shackles. "There is no way in hell you can pull this off. Not even you."

Hayes stopped at the door. "Well, the fact is, I just did. Oh, and one more detail. The guard who contacted Marsh on your behalf? I wouldn't wait around for his help again. You see, we traced the call to his home phone. I've shared that information with the good warden. I'm certain he'll follow up in an appropriate manner."

He closed the door softly behind him.

75

"The Human Rights Watch people and Amnesty International, among others, have been trying to get into Blue Spruce for years," Caleb said after he'd informed them of many particulars of how the prison was run. They were all back at Tyree's house, which they were now using as a base.

"The list of alleged human rights violations there is very lengthy," Caleb continued. "But the prison has refused all requests for visits by Amnesty and other organizations. God, even Russia has allowed those folks to visit its prisons. And when several inmates had stun guns used on them at Blue Spruce, lapsed into comas and died, additional requests were made to enter the prison, but they were denied."

Alex looked at Tyree. "I know he's your brother, but all that going on right next door and you never did anything about it?"

"That's another reason Howard and me aren't close. Who do you think turned Amnesty International on to the place?"

"You?" said Caleb.

"I went up there once on a prisoner transport. Poked around a bit when nobody was watching me. I guess my big brother thought I could be trusted. Stuff I saw, heard. Yeah, I called it in. Howard found out later. That was the official end of our brotherly love and I haven't been invited back to Blue Spruce since."

"Let's just call the place by its *real* name, okay?" said Annabelle sternly. "Dead Rock!"

"With all that stuff how come the Justice Department or the Civil Rights Division hasn't opened an investigation then?" said Harry Finn. "Or at least the Virginia Department of Corrections?"

Caleb looked at his notes. "Apparently, the current state and federal administrations don't have the rights of prisoners as a priority. There was talk of a state inquiry but it went nowhere, and the Justice Department has nothing pending. And for the last two years the prison has been more or less shut down to all visitors."

"So Howard Tyree has his own personal little fiefdom and can do what he wants. Including selling drugs," growled Reuben. "And holding innocent men."

"Looks that way," said Caleb.

"What about the mineshaft?" asked Annabelle.

"I did find some info on that," Caleb answered as he pulled out some pages he'd printed off at the library. "It was cut on a parallel course to the shaft the miners were trapped in. I read a couple newspaper articles about it and then compared it to records I was able to access about the prison construction. I can't be certain, mind you, because it's not like they publish the blueprints for supermax prisons online. But it seemed to me that that rescue shaft ran all the way up that ridge because that's where the miners were trapped. When the explosion happened it collapsed the tunnel the trapped miners were in, but the rescue tunnel survived. I know that because the other miners were able to get out okay. It says that the mine was sealed up at the entrance, but it doesn't say anything about the rescue shaft entrance."

Reuben said, "But if you build a supermax on top of a mine and you know there's a shaft running underneath, you sure as hell are going to plug it up."

"Plug it up, sure, but maybe in a way that allows you to unplug it," replied Annabelle as she paced the room in front of them.

"Howard was involved in the construction planning, that I know," said Tyree. "It would be just like him to allow himself some flexibility."

"But why would anybody do that?" asked Alex. "Prisoners could escape that way."

Annabelle turned around to face him. "From what Caleb has been telling us about Blue Spruce, there's no way that escape is that serious of an issue. Every prisoner is kept segregated, and then shackled and searched when they need to take a leak. There are almost as many guards as cons, and they only get one hour out of their cells a day. The setup is perfect for a drug-dealing operation that requires some of his men to routinely leave the prison in the middle of the night to take care of business."

"But if some of the guards are involved why wouldn't they just leave from their houses?" asked Caleb.

"Howard Tyree sounds like a real control freak to me. He'd want every man right under his thumb."

"You're right about that," agreed Tyree.

"If these shipments come in routinely to the courthouse with some of the boxes diverted, where do you think those boxes are going?" asked Alex.

"To the prison," answered Tyree simply. "It's easy enough. Prisons get deliveries every day of food, supplies."

Alex added, "And the courthouse records filings are a great way to ship the drugs. DEA or ICE agents would just let it right on by."

"So they make the switch somewhere en route," reasoned Annabelle, "and the diverted boxes go to the prison until they're ready to be shipped out using addicted miners as couriers. Which brings me back to my point. You're not going to have a bunch of guards walk out the front door every night with boxes of illegal pills. And you can't fly the chopper out every night, because people will start wondering."

Harry said, "So you go out the back door."

"You go out the back door," echoed Annabelle. "Which I believe is that mineshaft."

Alex looked at her incredulously. "So we're going to find this mineshaft entrance, get in somehow, even though it's been sealed, and then somehow make it through there alive? And then break into a supermax prison where there are guards armed to the teeth and who also happen to be drug dealers?"

"Sounds like a plan," said Reuben eagerly.

"It sounds like suicide," shot back Alex.

"Actually," said Annabelle, "you're both wrong."

76

"I swear if it's the last thing I ever do, I'm going to kill Macklin Hayes," Knox muttered to Stone. The two men were back in their cell and many hours had passed since Hayes had come to put the proverbial nail in their coffins.

"But that would be against the law. And people will come and hunt you down and put you away," said Stone, as he peered out the slit the prison called a window. It overlooked the front parking lot but it was very difficult to see through because of the opaqueness of the window covering attached to the bars.

"Yeah, I realize the irony, trust me, but I'm still going to do it."

"*If* we get out of here."

"Yeah, I also realize the impossibility of that at the moment."

"I think you might be wrong about that."

Knox sat up. "Really?"

"Don't get your hopes up. It's for a bad reason, not a good one."

"What are you saying?"

"Have you noticed that ever since Hayes left they haven't bothered to feed us or let us out of the cell?"

"Yeah, my stomach is reminding me of that pretty much every second. So?"

"So that tells me that our stay here is coming to an end."

"Don't waste food on corpses? How unlike our esteemed warden."

"There's no reason to keep us here any longer. There's always a chance that someone might show up and search the place. Why risk it?"

"Where do you think they'll take us?"

"I know from firsthand experience that there are abandoned mines around here. A drop down an old shaft, seal it back up. Apparently people up here are used to dead men being inside these mountains. That's how this place got its name, in fact."

Stone pressed his face against the wall, trying to wedge it between the edges of the slit so he could see out better. He squinted and could see the outline of the mountains in the distance. They might as well have been on Mars. Three feet of concrete, a hundred yards of open space, killer wire and a battalion of snipers with aggressive trigger fingers was all that stood between them and freedom.

No way out.

Knox said, "You get into this business you know any day your number could come up. And you deal with that. But you keep going because it's your job, a job you swore to do to the best of your ability. Serve your country to the end."

"Or until your country screws you," amended Stone.

"When I was assigned to come after you, I really didn't know what to expect. I knew you were a dangerous guy but figured you'd just gone bad like some do. But the more I found out . . . Well, if anyone ever deserved an apology from his country, you sure as hell do."

"Funny, I was thinking the same thing about you, Knox."

"My friends call me *Joe*, Oliver."

Stone turned back to look at him. Knox was standing and holding out his hand.

Stone took it and the two condemned men shared a brief but heartfelt handshake.

"When do you think they'll come for us?"

"Tonight." Stone looked out the slit again. "And best as I can tell that's about six hours away—" He stopped talking and then desperately tried to squeeze his head into the slit. He was barely making out a group of people climbing out of a car and heading to the prison entrance. Yet one tall, bushy-haired gent stood out from the others.

It has to be.

"What is it?" Knox said, "what do you see?"

Stone turned to look at him, a smile spreading across his face. "I see hope, Joe. Damn if I don't see hope."

77

"Mr. Tyree, I think you better come down here, sir," the guard said into the phone.

"What is it?" barked Tyree as he sat behind his large desk with a bird's-eye view of his little kingdom. "I'm busy."

The guard turned to the group facing him.

"He said he's busy."

Alex Ford yanked the phone out of the man's hand.

"This is Alex Ford, United States Secret Service. I'm here with a joint federal agency task force and we have some questions for you, Warden. And if you don't get your butt down here, the next person you'll be talking to is a U.S. attorney as he reads the charges against your ass."

In his office Tyree nearly dropped the phone. "I have no idea—"

"Get down here, now!"

Sixty seconds passed and then Tyree walked stiffly into the front entrance area.

Alex flashed his creds before motioning to the

others. Reuben, Caleb and Harry Finn wore blue FBI windbreakers. Annabelle had on a DEA jacket. "Agents Hunter, Kelso, Wright and Tasker."

"What the hell is this about?" said Tyree angrily.

Alex looked askance at him. "You really want to do this out in the open? Wouldn't you prefer some privacy, or is every son of a bitch here in on it?"

"In on what?" Tyree said indignantly.

"Tyree, you can't be that stupid. In fact, I've got a file on you an inch thick that says you're a pretty smart boy."

Tyree glanced at the nervous-looking guards and hurriedly motioned Alex and the others into a small room off the main entrance.

Alex shut the door behind them. "Okay, your little drug ring is falling apart."

"What drug ring?"

Alex looked at Annabelle. "Agent Hunter?"

Annabelle walked up to the diminutive Tyree, towering over him. "I thought you'd be a bigger guy. I rarely see shrimp like you in charge of an op this large."

"I am the warden of this prison. You will address me—"

"Screw you! You're lucky I'm not cuffing your scrawny ass right now. We have the shipments coming up from down south. Either the real oxy or manufactured pills. They're addressed to the courthouse, which gives them cover. That's where the old judge came in. The old judge on the run. When we find his ass he'll turn government witness faster than I can say lethal injection. And you can kiss your butt so long, unless you killed him too. Like you did Shirley and Bob and Willie Coombs. And let's not forget Debby Randolph and your bean counter in crime Rory Peterson. How much did he skim off the top before you stopped him?"

"You're a lunatic!"

"I'm just getting warmed up. Then you'll see how crazy I can really be when I have your ass with a grand jury indictment painted all over it. So where was I? Oh, then part of the shipment is peeled off en route and comes here. Maybe in the chopper rides where you *transport* prisoners. Then the stuff gets moved out to the back edge of the Riker farm. And the miner train comes by and picks it up in the dark of night, and slings it on up the pipeline under the guise of the poor addicts going to get their methadone. And the money comes pouring in." She glanced at Caleb. "Agent Kelso?"

Caleb stepped forward. "And then the town *investment* fund is used to launder the drug proceeds. That's where Rory Peterson came in. He kept the cooked books and parceled out checks to the good folks of Divine, with you and your partners keeping the lion's share of the profits. What the citizens of Divine thought were payoffs from brilliant bets in the stock market were really drug monies. I believe that an investigation will show that you all have an ownership interest in all those businesses. Then you dump the laundered funds into offshore accounts. Peterson was killed because he was skimming. Josh Coombs was killed because he got wind of what was going on up here. You killed Shirley because after you killed her son you figured she might just turn on you."

"Why the hell would I kill her son?"

Annabelle looked confident, because Tyree had told them what Stone had figured out. "Because he was close to Debby. She saw whoever killed Peterson because she was working at the bakery across the street from his office. Your goons killed Peterson and Debby and made her death look like a suicide. But Willie never believed she killed herself. He was making a lot of noise. You were probably afraid Debby might have called him back and told him something about what she saw before she was killed. You tried once to get him and failed. The second time it worked."

Tyree slumped down in a chair.

She counted off on her fingers. "So let's see, that's at least half a dozen murders in addition to the federal drug charges. And on top of that we have reason to believe that you're holding two federal agents here against their will."

"What?" Tyree snapped.

"Right, I forgot to tell you that part. Where are they? One answers to the name Joe Knox, the other John Carr."

Annabelle studied him closely. The man was a good poker player, but she saw the truth simply in how his blinking kicked up a notch and his fingers quivered just a hair.

"These accusations are ridiculous. And where's your proof?"

"Our proof will be when we search this place and find our two agents. And the rest of the puzzle is coming together quite nicely.

And when we nab the judge we'll have our key witness against you."

"You can't search this place without a warrant."

"Oh, we'll have a warrant. By the crack of dawn tomorrow morning. And just in case you get a hankering to travel anywhere, we have a roadblock set up. So don't even think of trying to slip them out that way. And leave the chopper grounded. Because we've got two of our own waiting to lift off the moment yours does."

Annabelle leaned down close into the man's sweating face. "By the way, we're well aware of your rep as being an asshole to every con that's ever walked through these doors. You like dishing out the pain, *little* man? Well, after your conviction, our strong recommendation to the correctional folks will be that wherever you go you're to be placed in the general prison population. Might save the Commonwealth the cost of an execution. Get my drift?"

"How dare you!" Tyree suddenly moved to strike Annabelle, but a massive hand was placed on his arm by Reuben.

"I would not advise that," the big man said. "Because then they'll have to shoot you."

Tyree looked around to see Harry and Alex pointing pistols at his head.

Annabelle said, "We'll see you bright and early tomorrow morning, Howie. Oh, and if I were you, I'd definitely get my affairs in order."

78

"They're coming," Stone said.

He and Knox stood and backed against the wall as the pounding of the approaching boots echoed down the hall.

"I hope you're right about what you saw," Knox said nervously.

"Cuff slot!" a voice barked.

Stone started forward but Knox stopped him.

"This one's mine. They tend to kick the crap out of the first guy. Guess they run out of energy."

"Joe, you don't have to do that."

"Why should *you* have all the fun?"

Knox backed to the door and put his hands through the slot. Someone grabbed them and pulled hard, causing Knox's head to slam back against the door.

As he shook the pain away, he said, "You'll have to do a lot better than that, jerk-offs."

That got him another slam, but he'd braced himself against the door so the damage was negligible. Knox smiled at this small victory even as his headache grew worse.

The two guards didn't bother to search them this time, and they weren't shackled. And it was George, the crotch-grabber. Manson was apparently still in the infirmary.

Or with any luck, dead, thought Stone.

"Where are your uniforms?" Stone asked George.

"Changing occupations?" Knox added. "I'm not sure that's the drug dealer look you want."

"Shut up!" roared the man.

They were hustled downstairs and through more corridors and then down a sloping, winding passageway until Stone could smell the pungent odor of wet dirt and slimy rock.

Up ahead they saw a light. When they approached the man came into view. Howard Tyree was dressed all in black and didn't look nearly so smug as usual.

Stone looked down at him. "I see the visit today triggered some things."

"How did you—" Tyree began, but Knox cut him off.

"Macklin Hayes has been under internal investigation for a year for basically being a deranged asshole. They were following him. He led them right to us. *And* you. You moron."

"Shit!" blurted out Tyree.

Stone said, "So you might just want to surrender, Warden. It's over."

Tyree smiled, a dangerous look on his face. "They might be the feds but they're not from around here.

Don't know our ways or our land." He gave Stone a hard shove in the back. "Now move!"

They walked, the ground sloping down more with each step. Mold clung to the walls, and the heavy smell of damp gripped just as fiercely to their lungs. They finally came to a heavy steel door. George unlocked it. They all stepped through, navigated another short passage and came to yet another massive door. This was unlocked and they stepped into what had to be a mineshaft. Stone and Knox were told to wait as the other man headed off down a side corridor.

Stone looked around at the long tunnel and brace posts in the dirt floor and beams and thick wire across the ceiling holding back the rock. It reminded him of the place with the snakes. And there were rattlers with him tonight too, just of the human variety. Low ceiling, dirt and rock, massive beams holding back the mountain along with the tonnage of the prison. It was claustrophobic, all of it. Stone didn't know which was worse, the cell or the mine.

Maybe, in a way, they are the same.

His philosophizing stopped when he saw the guard coming back and leading another person with him.

"Abby!" As she grew closer, Stone's rage swelled. In the beams of the flashlights carried by Tyree and her guard Abby's face clearly showed the beating she'd endured.

Stone lunged at Tyree, but with his hands behind his back, he was easily subdued.

"I will kill you," he said quietly to Tyree.

"I see it the other way around," the warden replied calmly.

They walked on, Abby next to him while Knox shot curious glances at them.

"Abby, what happened?" Stone whispered to her.

"They came to the house and got me. Maybe killed the man Tyree had guarding me, I don't know for sure."

"Why would they want you?"

"Something to do with Danny."

"So he *is* mixed up in this?"

A sob slipped from Abby's mouth. She just nodded mutely.

Stone was going to say something else, but a billy club hit him in the back.

"No more talking," the warden snapped.

Stone lost track of time. Minutes or hours, he couldn't tell down here in the black of a mountain's bowels. He couldn't imagine spending his life down here on his hands and knees digging out rock. Digging his own grave.

Knox, Stone and Abby were suddenly grabbed and told to stay still. The two guards ran ahead and Stone could hear scraping sounds, large things being moved and the grunts and curses of the men doing that heavy moving.

Up ahead the darkness suddenly turned a bit lighter.

Tyree pushed them forward. Stone and Knox exchanged a glance. Neither knew exactly what was going to happen in the next few seconds. Stone kept as close to Abby as he could. If need be he would shield her with his body. He strained against the cuffs, trying to free himself. They probably only had a few seconds left.

They ducked down and came out into a moonlit night. Freedom at last from Dead Rock. Except for the cuffs and the men with guns surrounding them. And except for the fact that their lives were about to end. Stone could hardly believe that what many men with special skills had tried to do and failed, a pudgy warden from a backwater hole-in-the-wall was going to succeed in doing. Kill him. And yet as he glanced over at Abby, he felt far worse for her. The truth was he should have been dead long ago. He had done things that he deserved to die for. But not Abby. It shouldn't end this way for her. And he told himself he would do everything in his power to prevent the woman's life from ending violently here on this high rock.

Stone glanced around. They appeared to be in the middle of mountainous forest, but as his eyesight adjusted he was able to make out a wide path that had been cut through the heavy brush.

Tyree took ahold of Stone's arm and propelled him forward. He tripped over a rock and fell awkwardly to the ground. He rose to his knees and looked at the warden.

"They have this place completely locked down."

"There are ways out of here that I know that nobody else does. You don't think I didn't plan for something like this?"

Knox looked at the guards. "Must've been more guys than this involved. You just going to leave the others for the feds?"

"What do you care? You'll be dead," Tyree sneered.

"Would it sound really stupid if I said you'll never get away with it?" said Stone.

"Yeah, it would."

"How about if I said it?"

Tyree and the others whirled around to see Alex Ford step from the shadows of the trees, his gun aimed at the warden's head. When the guards pulled their weapons, a bullet sailed over their heads and the men froze.

A wisp of smoke floating from his gun's muzzle, Harry Finn moved forward while Reuben leveled a shotgun at the men. Annabelle and Caleb stepped out of the woods and stood next to Reuben.

Tyree suddenly pulled Abby toward him and leveled his pistol at her head. He said, "You folks better back the hell off or this lady is dead."

"Put the gun down, Howard."

Tyree jerked at the sound of the voice and then looked for its source. His gaze stopped and held as Lincoln Tyree stepped from the tree line. "Put it down, Howard."

A smile eased across the warden's plump face. "You know you were never any good at telling your big brother what to do. Now why don't you stop playing detective and just go on back down to your little town and pretend you know what you're doing."

"I know what I'm doing, *big brother.* I'm arresting you for enough stuff that you're the one's who's gonna end up at Dead Rock."

Tyree jammed his pistol against Abby's neck, causing her to cry out in pain. "Maybe you didn't understand what I said. If you don't back off, this lady is going to die."

"Put the gun down," the sheriff said again. "Killing her gets you nothing. It's over."

"Gets me nothing? Nothing? I tell you what it gets me. Satisfaction."

Alex said, "Last chance. To all three of you. Weapons down, now!"

"Go to hell," screamed Tyree.

He started to pull the trigger. But his gun never fired because Stone slammed into him, knocking the pudgy man off his feet, his pistol flying away.

"Run, Abby," screamed Stone, as he struggled to get up.

Tyree stopped rolling and sat up. Unfortunately,

he'd stopped right next to his gun. He snatched it up and aimed for Stone's head.

The shot rang out and the round caught Tyree in the forehead. For a second or two the warden didn't seem to realize that he'd been killed. Then he fell on his back, his eyes staring up to the sky, the guard towers of Dead Rock visible in the distance, though he couldn't see them anymore.

Alex shouted, "Where did that shot come from?"

No one had time to answer that question because another man emerged from the tunnel and opened fire. And the weapon he carried was an MP-5 submachine gun that laid down a solid wall of fire all across the tree line. Stone had been in position to see this before anyone else. An instant before he fired he had gotten to his feet, lunged and tackled Abby as she was trying to run for cover.

Alex, Reuben and the others fell to the dirt as rounds zipped past overhead, shredding tree bark and anything else in their path. Ripped leaves rained down on them like snowflakes.

Sheriff Tyree yelled out as a round caught him in the leg. He fell heavily to the earth, grabbing at his thigh.

Stone glanced at the mineshaft opening. It was one-eyed Manson wearing a neck brace now along with the eye patch trying to kill them all.

God, I should have finished the son of a bitch when I had the chance.

Knox had thrown himself behind a large boulder, while George and his buddy had run off toward the woods. His buddy didn't make it very far because one of Manson's errant rounds caught him square in the back and he fell facedown in a wash of blood.

Stone got up and ran with every ounce of speed he had. He made a flying tackle on George and both men went down hard. Stone was still handcuffed so he couldn't hit him with his fists. He did the next best thing. He head-butted George flush in the face and the guard fell limp under him. Stone flipped over and, using his cuffed hands, tore at the leather pouch on George's belt. His fingers closed around the key. He felt for the opening and unlocked the restraints. He grabbed George's gun but looked down in dismay. The pistol had landed on a rock and the trigger had snapped off.

A moment later Stone ducked down as MP-5 rounds roared overhead and Abby screamed.

"Abby!" Stone slid like a snake through the dirt and rock, his clothes ripping and his skin tearing as he made his way frantically back to her. He'd done this exact same maneuver a thousand times through the jungles of Southeast Asia, yet never for a reason more important than now.

On his belly too, Knox had dragged himself over to the dead Tyree. He wrenched the gun from the dead man's hand and slid back toward where Stone was heading.

Manson was barely ten feet from Abby. He stopped again to slam in another clip. Alex, Harry and Reuben opened fire, but Manson had wisely taken up cover behind a large rock outcrop. When he came back out with fresh ammo his firepower would overwhelm them at the shortened distance. But clearly Abby would be the first to die.

"Oliver!"

Stone looked up at Knox's shout.

Still cuffed, Knox held up the gun between his feet and Stone nodded. Using his feet like a catapult Knox tossed and Stone caught. He had bare seconds.

"Stay down, Abby," he warned.

She frantically dug into the earth with bleeding fingers, trying to get as low as possible.

A second later Manson stepped out, the muzzle of the MP-5 searching for and finding her lying feet from him. Alex and the others had no line of fire because of the chunk of mountain lying between Manson and them.

Stone had no direct line of fire from where he was either. The first rule of the sniper was that any unintended movement of gun and shooter would spoil the shot. Steady hand, breath exhaled, heartbeat in the sixties and weapon locked in position against a stable surface—that's how one killed successfully. And Stone had mostly followed those rules in his career as the best assassin the U.S. ever had.

Mostly, but not always. Because sometimes what

looked good in planning went to shit in the field. When that happened the merely good and competent failed nine times out of ten.

The best cut those odds down to fifty-fifty.

The very best improvised and upped the percentage of success by twenty points.

And then there was John Carr.

John Carr, who had come back from the dead at least one more time, to save a good woman who did not deserve to die at the hands of a maniac wielding a weapon of mass destruction.

Stone leapt, his pistol arrayed out at the sharpest angle he could hold it and still get a shot off. Manson's finger closed on the trigger.

Stone fired. Joe Knox would later claim that he had seen the damn bullet actually bend around the chunk of rock. No one argued with him.

Manson pulled the trigger and the MP-5 roared. But all the rounds went straight up into the air because there was a massive hole in the side of Manson's neck. The shredded arteries released their rich blood supply high into the air and for several horrifying moments a red rain poured down on the dying Manson. Then he hit the dirt, his one eye open but now as unseeing as the other.

79

Stone raced to Abby and helped her up. She was scared, but okay.

Alex and Harry Finn were putting a tourniquet on Tyree's leg using a stick and a piece of Finn's jacket. The tall sheriff was sitting up now, grimacing with pain.

Stone and Abby came over to him and she knelt down next to him, took his hand.

"Tyree, are you okay?"

He tried hard not to show the pain. "Hell, take more than this to get me all worked up."

The shout made them all turn toward the woods.

Caleb was running back to them. "Hurry. Hurry."

They raced after him, Stone and Reuben in the lead. They plowed through the brush and vines.

When Stone saw what Caleb was pointing to, he felt like he had just died. He rushed to the fallen man's side.

"Danny? Danny?"

Danny Riker was lying on his back, a scoped deer rifle in the brush next to him. Stone wasn't focusing on the weapon, but rather on the large splotch of red on Danny's chest.

Danny's eyes focused on him. He managed a smile. "Don't think I ducked in time," he said weakly.

Stone looked back over his shoulder toward where Manson lay. That first blast from the MP-5 had hit right here. He turned back and counted no less than three bullet holes in Danny's shirt. And they were placed at locations that Stone knew did not allow for survival, even if they could get him to a hospital in the next few minutes, which they couldn't. He had brought Willie Coombs back from the dead using the juice from a spark plug wire. There would be no such miracle for Danny Riker.

Reuben squatted next to his friend and picked up the rifle. "He was the one who took out the warden."

"Damn right," Danny said, his voice growing stronger for an instant. "He killed Willie. Told the little son of a bitch what I'd do if he did that." His hardened features softened. "Get my ma, will-ya, Ben?"

Stone felt rather than heard the presence behind him. He rose and stared at Abby, whose gaze was only on her son.

"I'm sorry, Abby," Stone said. "I'm sorry."

Blood was spilling out of Danny's mouth. "Ma?"

She dropped to her knees next to him, taking his hand in hers. The sob burst from her with such force that all the others, who'd clustered somberly around mother and son, felt tears rise to their own eyes. Her features looked like those of a child fleeing a monster in a nightmare. Yet then Abby almost instantly calmed, perhaps sensing that her son needed her to be strong; that her boy's last moments on earth would not be taken up with the sight of a hysterical mother.

"I'm sorry, Ma. For all the stuff."

Stone knelt and held the young man's other hand. He felt it growing cold.

She said, "I love you, Danny. I've always loved you more than I loved anything."

"Shouldn't got mixed up in all this drug stuff. But didn't want to work the mines. And didn't want to take the death money either. You know?"

"I know. I know, baby." Tears were spilling from them both.

"Didn't have nothing to do with any killing. 'Cept the bastard warden." Danny's pupils were losing their focus, receding into the white pools of the eyes, as Stone had seen on many a dying man.

"I love you, Danny."

He looked over at Stone. When he spoke his voice was so weak Stone had to bend close to hear. "Me and Willie. State champs . . . Boy caught everything I threw at him. Shoulda played at Tech together. You know?"

"You two were the best, Danny," Stone said, gripping the cold hand. "The best."

"California dreaming, man."

He turned back to his mother. "California dreaming . . ."

Danny's eyes grew hard and flat, and the fingers that had gripped his mother's now fell away. Abby bent down and kissed her son and then wrapped her arms around him. And just held him.

Just held him.

80

The Camel Club sat at Rita's Restaurant. The place was not open for business today, but Abby had insisted that they use it and her home for as long as necessary. Sheriff Tyree was expected to make a full recovery. He had summoned the Virginia State Police, who were currently sorting out the mess in Divine. Since transport of drugs across interstate lines had occurred, the feds had also been called in. Knox and Alex had run interference with their government colleagues and Stone, Annabelle, Caleb, Reuben and Harry were not part of that questioning. Prison guards had been rounded up, bodies collected and other evidence secured. Judge Mosley had been stopped at a small airport in West Virginia trying to board a regional jet for Dulles International Airport with a travel itinerary that included several countries that had no extradition agreement with the United States.

Stone and the others watched the street through the front windows of Rita's. Along with the cop cars and black sedans swooping up and down the road, they observed several citizens of Divine walking around as though in shock, some holding dividend checks that they now knew were nothing more than drug money.

Danny's body had been taken to the morgue in Roanoke along with Howard Tyree's. Only when the police had zipped him up in a black body bag did Abby relinquish her grip on her son's hand. And even then she walked down the road after the slowly departing medical examiner's wagon.

When everyone had had some food and coffee, Stone stood in the middle of the small circle of the best and perhaps only friends he had in the world.

"I would like to thank you for what you did," he began, looking at each of them in turn.

Reuben immediately piped in, "Oliver, don't go sappy on us. You would have done the same for any one of us."

"You *have* done the same for every one of us," said Annabelle.

Stone shook his head. "I know how much you risked. I know what you sacrificed to come here and do what you did." His gaze settled on Alex Ford. "I especially know what you did, Alex. Even though it went against all your instincts as a Secret Service agent. And I appreciate it more than I can ever express."

Alex could only meet Stone's heartfelt gaze for a few moments before he looked down at his shoes.

When the door opened, they all turned to see who it was.

Abby had changed her clothes and washed her face, though the imprint of the tears she had bled with Danny's death seemed to linger. Apparently, no soap could reach that. When Stone rose and went to her, the others silently made their way out of the restaurant and out onto the street.

Abby and Stone sat at a back table. When Stone handed her some napkins she shook her head. "I've got no more left. No more tears."

"Just in case then," he said. "What will you do now?"

"You mean after I bury my son? Haven't thought that far ahead."

"He saved us, Abby. But for what he did, you and I would be dead. He was a brave man who tried to do the right thing. That's how you have to remember him."

"I told you I lost my husband. Danny was all I had left. Now he's gone too."

"I know it's hard, Abby. It's harder than anything else you'll ever have to do."

"You lost your wife, but you still have your daughter."

"What?" Stone said, startled.

"That woman out there said she was your daughter."

"Oh." Stone looked embarrassed. "That was a cover story, I'm afraid. My daughter." He stumbled over what he was about to say. "My daughter died, like I said."

"How?"

"Abby, you don't—"

"Please tell me. I want to know."

Stone slowly looked up to see her gazing at him pleadingly. "She was shot right in front of me when she was an adult. And the thing was she didn't even know I was her dad. The last time I'd seen her she was only two years old. I found her again after all those years and then I lost her. Forever."

Abby reached out and took his hand. "I'm sorry . . . Oliver."

"But you do survive it, Abby. You never get over it, but you can keep on living. Because you really don't have a choice."

"I'm scared. I'm alone and I'm scared."

"You're not alone."

She laughed halfheartedly. "What? Tyree? The wonderful town of Divine?"

"Me."

She sat back and looked at him. "You? How?"

"I'm here. Now."

"But for how long?"

Stone hesitated. He could not lie to the woman. "I have to go away."

"Sure, of course you do. I understand," she said offhandedly.

"I have some things that I have to take care of. Some wrongs finally need to be righted."

"Okay, whatever you have to do."

"Abby, I mean it. I will be there for you. Even if I'm not physically here."

He caught her gaze and held it with a pleading one of his own.

"I want to believe that."

"You can believe it."

"When do you have to go?"

"Soon. Sooner than later."

"Are you sure things will work out for you?"

"I won't lie to you, there are no guarantees."

"The trouble you might be in?"

"Yes."

"Will they put you in prison?"

"It's certainly possible," Stone admitted.

A quiet sob escaped her lips and she rested her face on the back of his hand.

"Will you promise me one thing?"

"I'll try my best."

"If you can't come back here, will you never forget me?"

"Abby—"

She sat up and put a hand against his lips. "Will you never forget me?"

"I will never forget you," he said truthfully.

She leaned across the table and kissed him on the cheek. "Because I'll never forget you."

A few minutes later Joe Knox came in. Stone looked over at him.

"You ready?" he asked Stone. "We need to get this done."

Stone gave Abby's hand one final squeeze and rose.

"I'm ready."

81

The front door to Macklin Hayes' stately brownstone in Georgetown was thrown open so hard it smacked the wall hard enough to make a dent in the plaster.

"What the hell?" began the man as he half rose from his chair, the book he'd been holding falling to the floor. When he saw who it was he sat back down, stunned.

"Hey, *sir*, how goes it?" Knox said as he strode in.

"Knox?" Hayes began nervously. "How did you get past the guards outside?"

"Oh, that. One of them is a buddy. I said I'd only be a few minutes. So they went down the street for a cup of coffee."

A panicked look came to the general's face. "Knox, let me explain—"

When Hayes saw Stone walk into the room, he could only gape in astonishment. When he observed that Stone's hands were manacled together, he started to breathe again.

"Mack," Stone said. "Nice place you have here. A

lot nicer than the one Joe and I were in. But then you know that, don't you?"

Hayes finally wrenched his gaze from Stone.

"Knox, this will earn you that retirement you've been after, plus anything else in my power. Anything! I swear it."

"Thank you, sir."

Obviously encouraged by this, Hayes rose and put a bony arm around Knox's burly shoulders, drawing him aside.

"You really shouldn't have brought him here, though. Particularly since you sent my guards off. He is a dangerous man, handcuffed or not."

"There was really no other place to take him. And after you left my ass in that hellhole, well, there weren't a whole lot of options once we broke out."

"So you . . . broke out? The police are looking for you?" he said nervously.

"I would think they are. I mean, we killed five or six guards along the way." He turned to Stone. "Was it six?"

Stone said with an impassive expression, "Eight. I got two more while you were strangling the warden."

Knox turned back to a stunned Hayes. "Okay, so it was eight. I gotta tell you, we weren't in there all that long, but that place just drives you insane. Frigging out of your mind. I would've killed my own mother."

Hayes took his arm away, his hands visibly shaking.

When he spoke, his voice shook as much as his hands. "Listen, Knox, I know what happened was unfortunate. But it was necessary until I could get a handle on what to do with Carr. As you can imagine, it was a highly delicate situation. In fact, I was about to send my men up there to do an extraction. Rest assured, I was not going to let one of my best men rot in that place one second longer than necessary. I swear to God."

Knox shook his head sadly. "I appreciate that, sir. I really do. But it would have helped to know that *before* I killed all those people to get out of the place."

Hayes' face was paper white now. "I'll talk to someone for you. We'll figure something out. This is a national security issue."

"I doubt that's possible now. In fact, that's why I brought Carr along with me."

Hayes glanced sharply over at Stone. "I don't quite understand."

"Well, *I* might forgive you. But he sure as hell isn't about to. So since we're both wanted for murder, I mean . . ."

"What the hell are you saying, Knox?"

Stone answered. "What he's saying is we've already done eight. Who the hell cares about one more, especially if it's you?"

Hayes staggered back against the wall, his hand to his chest. "Knox, you can't allow this. I am your superior."

"You *were* my superior. At least in rank. In reality, I've always considered you quite inferior."

"How dare you—"

Knox uncuffed Stone and then slipped a knife from his pocket and handed it to him. Stone automatically gripped it in his favored killing position.

"Knox!" Hayes screamed.

Stone advanced. "Do you know how many times I've done this on behalf of the United States government?"

"Knox, for godsakes."

"You should have given the man his medal," Knox said.

Hayes screamed, "I'll give you your damn medal, Carr. It's yours."

Knox sat in a chair and said, "You were a piece of crap for pulling the plug on it just because he wouldn't follow your order to slaughter an innocent village in Nam."

"I know that now. I'm sorry. I should never have given that order."

Stone stopped next to the quaking Hayes and looked him up and down, apparently deciding on the best place to deliver the lethal blow.

Knox added, "And you shouldn't have come up to that prison and made a deal with that warden to keep me there because I'd found out the truth."

Stone was now holding the knife against Hayes' throat.

"I've dreamed about this for nearly forty years, Mack," said Stone.

"Knox," wailed Hayes. "I'm begging you. I'm sorry for what I did at the prison. I never should have left you there. I'm sorry. For God's sake make him stop."

"Okay," Knox said. "Oliver, go ahead and stop."

Stone stepped back and flipped the knife to Knox, who pulled out a walkie-talkie and said into it, "Okay, come on in."

Five men came rushing through the door seconds later and strode up to the still cowering but confused-looking Hayes.

One of the men said, "Macklin Hayes, you're under arrest for obstruction of justice, false imprisonment, war crimes, covering up a drug ring, conspiracy to commit same and for using government property to blow up a civilian car in a public place resulting in reckless endangerment." The man then gave him his Miranda warning.

Knox pulled out a DVD from his pocket and tossed it to Hayes. "You can share that with your lawyers."

Hayes looked down at it. "What the hell is it?"

"The place where you met with us at the prison and told us everything because you figured we'd never get out? It was an *interrogation* room, you dumbshit. Warden up there was real keen on surveillance. There was a hidden camera and it recorded every syllable you said." He looked at the men. "Take his ass away. I'm sick of looking at him."

As they pulled Hayes from the room in cuffs, he screamed, "That man is John Carr. He killed Carter Gray and Roger Simpson. Arrest him, arrest him right now."

One of the men said, "Shut up!" and then pushed Hayes out the door.

After they were gone, Knox and Stone left the house and walked down the dark, quiet, lamplit streets of Georgetown as a chill wind blew in off the nearby Potomac.

"You know," Knox said, "Hayes was the only one who was after you. I reported only to him. He was doing this on his own authority, it wasn't an Agency thing."

"He's a man who holds his grudges," agreed Stone.

"My point is, as far as you're concerned, it's over." He put out his hand and Stone shook it. Knox continued, "Now, I'm going to walk that way." He pointed to his right. "And I suggest you go the other way."

"I can't do that, Joe."

"Oliver, get out of this place and go start over somewhere. I'll even get you some money and a new ID. But you have to go. Now."

Stone sat down on a weathered stone step and gazed up at the man.

"I've been *going* for thirty years and I'm just tired."

"But the FBI is still investigating the murders. And with Hayes out of the way any impediment to them turning in your direction is gone. Sooner or later, they're going to knock on your door. Particularly with Hayes screaming his head off about you."

"I know that."

"And, what, you're going to just wait until they come get you?"

Stone stood. "No. I'm not going to wait. I'm going right to the top on this. But first I need to go get something."

"Get something? Where?"

"At a graveyard."

82

The Secret Service examined the contents of the box that Stone had brought with him. It was the same one he'd hidden at Milton's burial plot before leaving Washington. Knox had driven him over to the graveyard where he'd gotten the box, called Alex Ford and made the arrangements to be where the three men were now.

The White House looked particularly impressive in the crisp morning sunlight. Alex knew the agents on duty today at the northeast gate entrance and he talked to them as Knox and Stone went through the metal detector and security process.

After that Alex led them up the driveway and into the White House. They passed the guards stationed at that entrance. As they walked toward the West Lobby, the security badges issued to the three men bounced against their chests. They arrived at the small West Lobby and were cleared. Stone and Alex sat while Knox nervously paced.

In a calming voice Alex said, "Down that hall is the Roosevelt Room. It's got a painting of FDR over the fireplace mantel and one of Teddy Roosevelt on the south wall. Straight ahead of that is the reception room, and to the immediate right of that is the Oval Office. The president doesn't actually work there. He's got another office nearby where he can get some real work done."

"Interesting," said Knox as he continued to pace the room, shooting glances here and there. All three men were dressed in suits. Alex and Knox had chipped in to buy Stone some appropriate clothes and he looked distinguished, if uncomfortable in his jacket and tie.

"You sure he's going to see us?" Knox asked Alex.

"We're on the schedule. So unless war is declared or a hurricane hits somewhere, we're going to see the man."

Knox let out a deep breath and slumped in a chair. "Jesus, Joseph, Mary."

As soon as he said the last name, a woman appeared and said, "The president will see you now, gentlemen."

In the Oval Office, President Brennan rose from behind the Resolute Desk and shook hands with all three, lingering over Alex, who'd taken a bullet while trying to prevent the president from being kidnapped in Brennan's hometown.

"Great to see you, Alex. You all recovered, I trust?"

"Yes, sir, thank you, sir."

"I can never express how grateful I am for what you did for me back then."

"Well, Mr. President, that's partly why we're here."

Brennan looked confused. "The schedule said you wanted me to meet some friends of yours?" He looked at Knox and Stone. "These gentlemen, I'm assuming?"

"It's a bit more complicated than that, sir, if you could spare us a few minutes."

The president motioned them to sit down in chairs set in front of the fireplace.

Alex started speaking and didn't stop for over twenty minutes. Nor did Brennan, known for being an inveterate questioner, ever interrupt him. He just sat in his chair absorbing what Alex was telling him about the events in Pennsylvania and up to what had happened at Murder Mountain and then on to the confrontation at the Visitor Center underneath the U.S. Capitol where Milton Farb had been killed and Harry Finn's son rescued. Knox took up the tale from there, and though clearly nervous in the presence of the commander in chief, his voice was strong and his details meticulous as he took Brennan through his part of the story, including Stone being denied the Medal of Honor, their time in prison and ending with Macklin Hayes' arrest.

Brennan sat back. "My God, this is incredible. Truly incredible. I can't believe this about Carter

Gray. He was one of my most trusted advisors." He glanced over at Stone. "And you are John Carr?"

Stone nodded. "I am."

"With this entity called the Triple Six?"

"Yes, sir."

"It's amazing to me that we engaged in that sort of thing."

"It wasn't amazing to me. I was just following orders. It was only later that my conscience got the better of me."

"But to kill your family. To come after you like that. I'm sorry, Alex, it just doesn't sound like the people I knew."

Stone held up the box. "Do you mind, Mr. President? I have something here that might convince you."

Brennan hesitated but then nodded.

Stone opened the box and took out the small recorder. He hit the play button and a voice came on loud and clear. It was Carter Gray. At Murder Mountain.

"I thought you had to give that recording back to Gray," said Alex as he hit the stop button. "And Finn said they had a device there that could tell if it had been duplicated, and it hadn't."

"Before I gave the phone with the recording on it to Gray I just held this recorder up to it and copied it. Sometimes people forget all about the low-tech ways."

He hit the play button and as they listened they

came to the part that Stone had particularly wanted the president to hear. When it was over, Brennan stared at them, his face flushed.

"He was going to kill me. Carter Gray was going to kill me so he could start an all-out war with the Muslims!"

"Yes, sir," said Stone. "He was."

"And you were the one who saved me," he said to Stone. "That was your voice on there convincing him not to do it. After the woman was killed. Who was she?"

"She was my daughter, Beth."

Alex quickly explained to the president how Roger Simpson and his wife had come to adopt Stone's daughter.

Brennan sat back in his chair, his mind obviously whirling. "They killed your wife and took your daughter. The man who had your wife murdered and tried to have you killed took your daughter and raised her as his own? And Gray, what he did to you. What he almost did to me. It's . . . it's beyond horrible, John. I'm rarely at a loss for words but I don't know what to say."

"There's something else I need to tell you, sir."

Knox and Alex both took deep breaths and then held them, their bodies tense as boards.

"What's that?"

"Carter Gray and Roger Simpson were both murdered, Mr. President."

"Yes, I know that—" He broke off and locked gazes with Stone.

"I see," he said. "I see." He sat back and looked over at the fireplace.

Nearly a minute went by and no one broke the silence.

Finally, Stone said, "Thank you for your time, sir. I plan to turn myself in to the authorities. But I wanted you to hear the story from me first. After thirty years of lies I thought it was finally time for the truth."

As Stone and the other two rose to leave, Brennan looked up at him.

"Listen to me, Carr. You've put me in a difficult position. Probably the most agonizingly difficult spot I've ever been in, and that's saying something for a two-term president. And yet with all that, I don't think it approaches the pain that you've suffered at the hands of a country that should have known better." He paused and stood. "I tell you what I'm going to do, since I wouldn't even be alive now and this country would be in the middle of a disastrous war but for your efforts, I'm going to take this under advisement. I don't want you mentioning this to anyone, much less turning yourself in. Do you understand me?"

Stone looked at Alex and then Knox and then back at the president. "Are you sure, sir?"

"No, I'm not sure," he snapped. "But that's the

way it's going to be. I don't condone vigilantism. Never have and never will. But I also have a heart and a soul, and a sense of honor and decency despite what some of my political opponents claim. So until you hear from me you are to do *nothing* except carry on with your life. Understood? I know you're no longer technically in the military, but I am still the leader of this country. And you will obey that order."

"Yes, sir," said an obviously surprised Stone.

As they turned to leave Brennan added, "Oh, and it'll be a long term of taking it under advisement. So long in fact and with all the other issues I'm confronted with as president, it is highly likely that I may completely forget all about it. Good-bye, Carr. And good luck."

As they closed the door behind them, both Knox and Alex exhaled in relief.

"Holy shit, do I need a drink," said Knox. "Come on, I'm buying."

83

Oliver Stone opened the gates to Mt. Zion Cemetery and walked up to his cottage. The front door was unlocked, and when he went in he saw that the changes Annabelle had made were no longer there. Everything was just as he had left it.

He sat down behind his desk and ran his hand over the old wood, squeaked back in the chair and gazed over at his wall of beloved books. He made a cup of coffee and carried a mug with him as he explored the grounds of the cemetery, noting where work needed to be done that he would get to the next day. He was once more the official caretaker of hallowed ground. It was where he belonged.

That evening, the others came by to see him. He hugged Reuben, Caleb and Annabelle, thanking each in turn again for what they had done for him. Reuben brought a few six-packs while Caleb had a nice bottle of red wine. Later, Alex, Finn and Knox joined them.

As Knox and Stone sat in front of the fireplace, Alex and Annabelle were engaged in animated conversation in one corner of the room. She held a glass of wine and he had a beer.

"Why did you really come to help us?" she said suddenly.

"Friends don't let friends die by stupidity."

"Gee, thanks."

He drew closer to her. "Well, actually, I did it because it occurred to me that we had left things on the wrong foot. And I wanted to tell you that despite all the mean, nasty things you said about me, I'd still like to hang out with you on occasion."

"Oh, is that right?"

"That's pretty right, yeah."

"Is that the best 'please come back to me' line Secret Service agents are taught?"

"We're more the strong and silent types."

Annabelle hooked her arm through his. "What you did was pretty wonderful," she said into his ear. "And I am sorry for the things I said." She glanced over at Reuben. "He really set me right on things."

"Let's just start over and see where it goes."

Reuben, who was watching all this from the other side of the room along with Caleb, said, "Oh, man, I'm going to puke."

Caleb replied, "Don't be jealous, Reuben. He's younger and much better-looking than you are. And besides, I don't have anyone either. I'm as big a loser in the female department as you are. I hope that makes you feel better."

Reuben drank down his entire beer and stalked off muttering.

Everyone looked over when Alex's cell phone began to ring. He answered it.

"Hello? What?" He suddenly snapped to attention and almost dropped his beer. "Yes, sir. Absolutely, sir. I'll make sure he's there. You can count on it, sir."

He clicked off and looked at the others in complete astonishment.

Knox said, "Who was that? Not the president?"

Alex slowly shook his head and walked over to Stone and put a hand on his shoulder. "That was the chairman of the Joint Chiefs of Staff."

"What?" Reuben exclaimed, his features growing pale. "What the hell did he want? You know, technically, I'm not AWOL. It was a misunderstanding."

"He called about you, Oliver," said Alex.

Stone looked up at him. "What *about* me?"

"We're taking another trip to the White House. Tomorrow."

"What? Why?"

Alex smiled. "Something about a medal, my friend. A long-overdue one. The top brass reviewed your war record, made the recommendation and the president immediately accepted it."

Reuben roared, "That's fantastic." He slapped Stone on the back as the others crowded around him, offering their congratulations.

When things quieted Stone said, "Alex, will you please call them back and tell them I appreciate the gesture but I can't accept it."

"What!" exclaimed a stricken Reuben.

Alex added, "Oliver, no one turns down the Medal of Honor. No one. Hell, a lot of soldiers who get it are dead."

"I'm not turning it down. That would be a dishonor to everyone who earned it. But I just want them to withdraw the offer. They made a mistake."

"Mistake, hell. You earned it," Finn said. "I read your record, Oliver."

"Maybe I did deserve it. Back then. And back then I would have accepted it. But I don't deserve it now. And for me to take it would dishonor the memory of every soldier who was awarded it."

Annabelle said, "Oliver, please, don't do this. Think about it. You'll be a part of American history. How many people get a shot at that?"

"I already *am* a part of American history, Annabelle. I know what I did on that battlefield. And I did it because I couldn't let my men die. But I also know very clearly what I did *after* I left the army. Very clearly. And that's the difference."

"But you were just following orders," said Alex.

"Sheep follow blindly. We're not supposed to be sheep."

Caleb went over to Stone and put a hand on his shoulder. "I never served in the military, so I can't really speak to any of that. But I do want to say one thing. I was very proud of you when they offered you the medal. But I think I'm even prouder of you for not accepting it."

After they all left, saying they would be back soon, Stone took the box out that he had kept the recording in. It also contained two other items.

He looked first at the photo of his baby daughter, Beth, who had grown up and then died never knowing that he was her father. Then he turned to the other faded picture.

In this image his wife Claire was suspended forever as a young wife and mother. In his mind every day it was Claire Carr who kept him going. In that prison while Tyree and his men were brutalizing him it had been her memory to which he'd clung.

He could never part with that image because in a visceral way it was the only shred of identity he had left. It was the one memory that kept alive the spirit of a young soldier, husband and father named John Carr. Not the assassin, not the killer. Just him, or who he used to be.

With his fingers he touched her hair, her face, skated along the line of her mouth. She and his daughter had been the only good things in a life that otherwise had been filled with scars and hurt and violence.

And yet memories of them were enough to take away all of it. Gone, like the cleansing force of the purest water.

He sat in the chair holding his wife and daughter.

And at least for a few moments everything again was all right.

After he put the box away he pulled out the new cell phone Annabelle had given him and punched in the number from memory. With each smack of his finger against the pad, Stone was growing more and more confident of what he was about to do.

After all, how much time could a man like him really expect to have left? He told himself he could not afford to waste another minute of it.

When the voice answered, he said quietly, "Abby, it's me."